OBLIVION SONG

CREATED BY
ROBERT KIRKMAN
AND
LORENZO DE FELICI

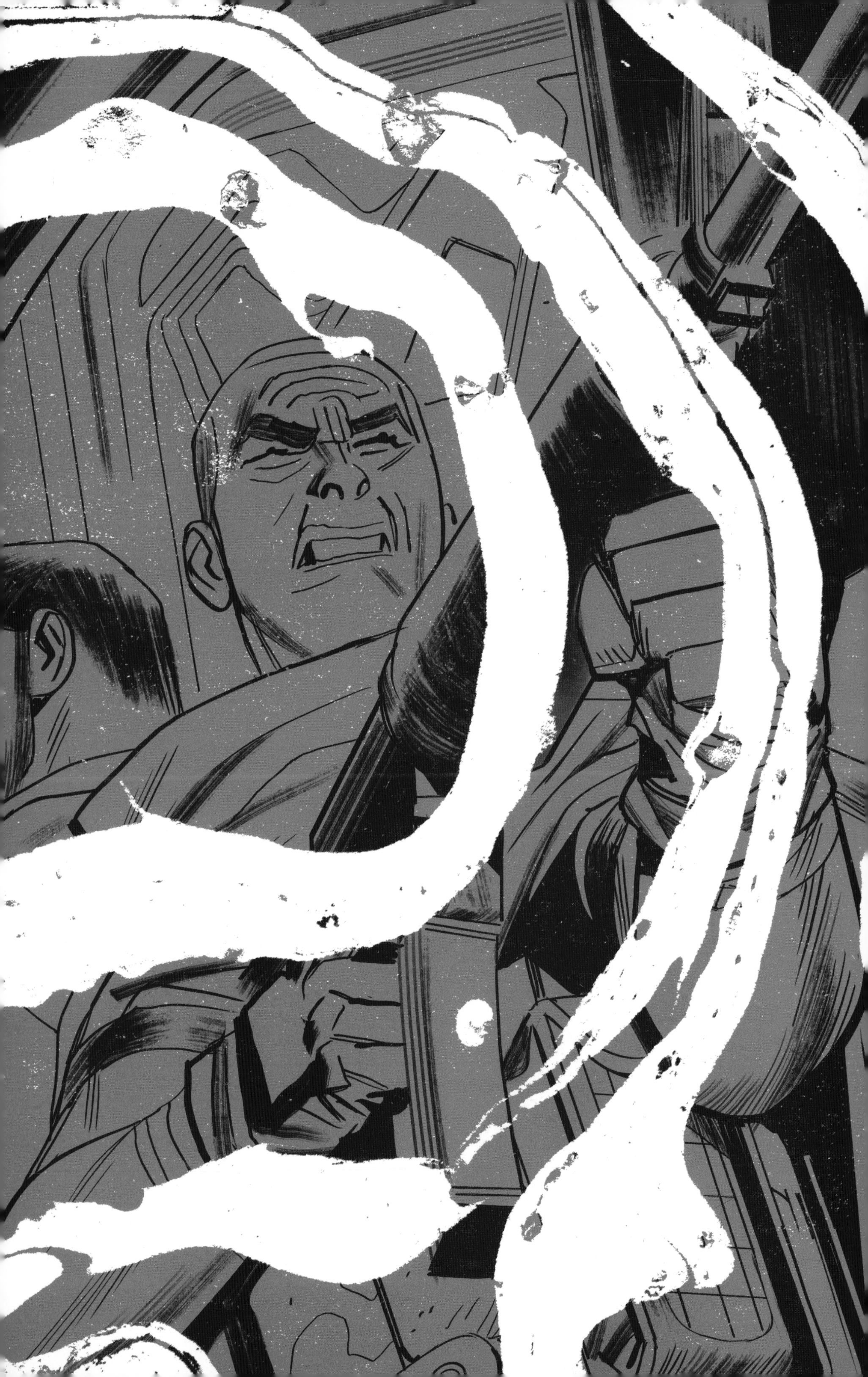

ROBERT KIRKMAN
WRITER/CREATOR

LORENZO DE FELICI
ARTIST/CREATOR

ANNALISA LEONI
COLORIST

RUS WOOTON
LETTERER

SEAN MACKIEWICZ
EDITOR

ANDRES JUAREZ
LOGO & COLLECTION DESIGN

CARINA TAYLOR
PRODUCTION

FOR SKYBOUND ENTERTAINMENT

ROBERT KIRKMAN *Chairman* ▪ DAVID ALPERT *CEO* ▪ SEAN MACKIEWICZ *SVP, Editor-in-Chief*
SHAWN KIRKHAM *SVP, Business Development* ▪ BRIAN HUNTINGTON *VP of Online Content*
SHAUNA WYNNE *Sn. Director, Corporate Communications* ▪ ANDRES JUAREZ *Art Director*
ARUNE SINGH *Director of Brand, Editorial* ▪ ALEX ANTONE *Senior Editor* ▪ AMANDA LaFRANCO *Editor*
JON MOISAN *Editor* ▪ CARINA TAYLOR *Graphic Designer* ▪ JOHNNY O'DELL *Social Media Manager*
DAN PETERSEN *Sn. Director of Operations & Events*
Foreign Rights & Licensing Inquiries: contact@skybound.com
SKYBOUND.COM

IMAGE COMICS, INC.

TODD McFARLANE *President* ▪ JIM VALENTINO *Vice President* ▪ MARC SILVESTRI *Chief Executive
Officer* ▪ ERIK LARSEN *Chief Financial Officer* ▪ ROBERT KIRKMAN *Chief Operating Officer*
ERIC STEPHENSON *Publisher / Chief Creative Officer* ▪ NICOLE LAPALME *Controller* ▪ LEANNA
CAUNTER *Accounting Analyst* ▪ SUE KORPELA *Accounting & HR Manager* ▪ MARLA EIZIK *Talent
Liaison* ▪ JEFF BOISON *Director of Sales & Publishing Planning* ▪ DIRK WOOD *Director of International
Sales & Licensing* ▪ ALEX COX *Director of Direct Market Sales* ▪ CHLOE RAMOS *Book Market & Library Sales
Manager* ▪ EMILIO BAUTISTA *Digital Sales Coordinator* ▪ JON SCHLAFFMAN *Specialty Sales Coordinator* ▪ KAT
SALAZAR *Director of PR & Marketing* ▪ DREW FITZGERALD *Marketing Content Associate* ▪ HEATHER DOORNINK
Production Director ▪ DREW GILL *Art Director* ▪ HILARY DILORETO *Print Manager* TRICIA RAMOS *Traffic
Manager* ▪ MELISSA GIFFORD *Content Manager* ▪ ERIKA SCHNATZ *Senior Production Artist* ▪ RYAN BREWER
Production Artist ▪ DEANNA PHELPS *Production Artist* ▪ IMAGECOMICS.COM

OBLIVION SONG BOOK TWO.
First Printing. ISBN: 978-1-5343-1950-9

CHAPTER

THREE

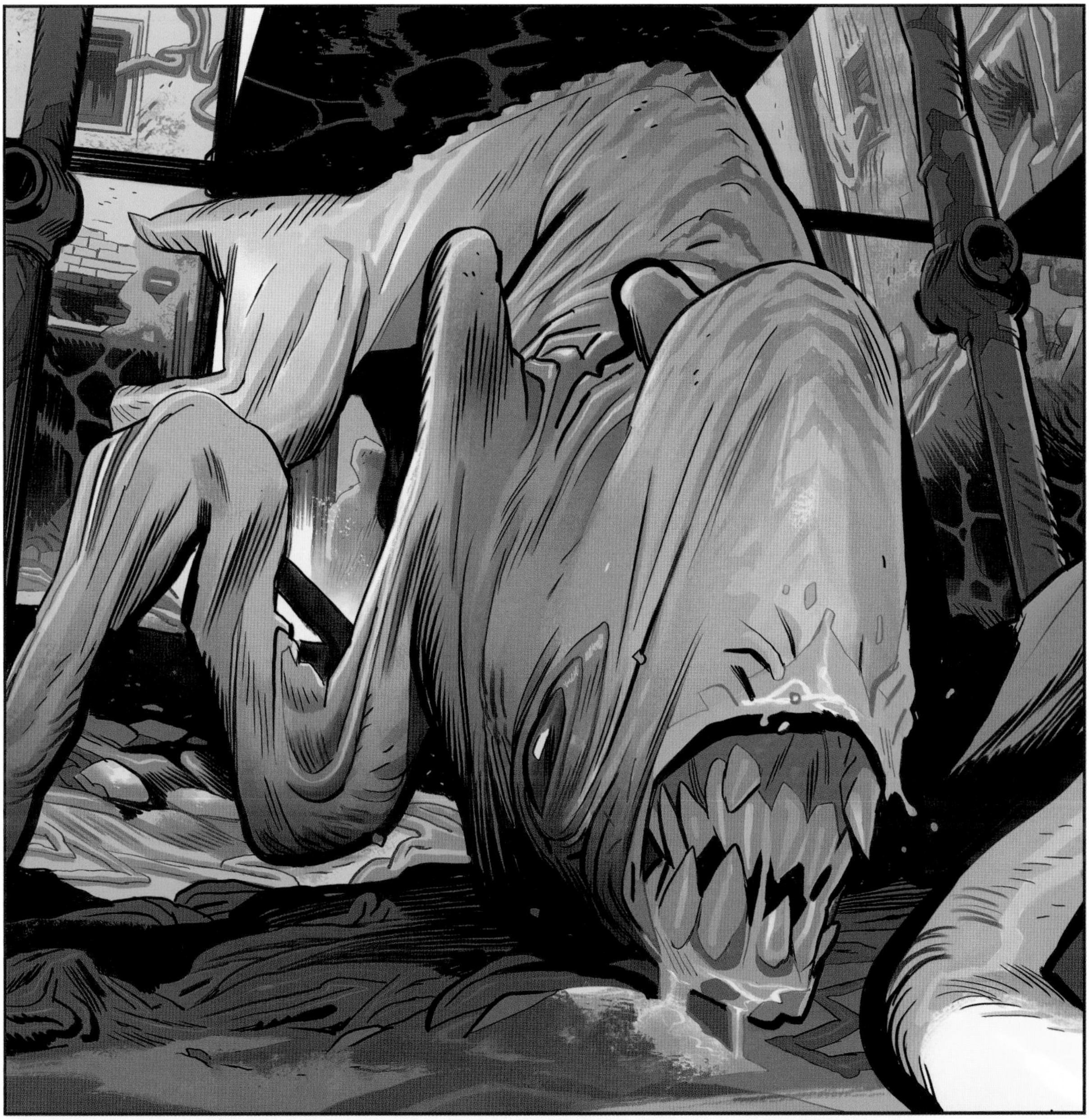

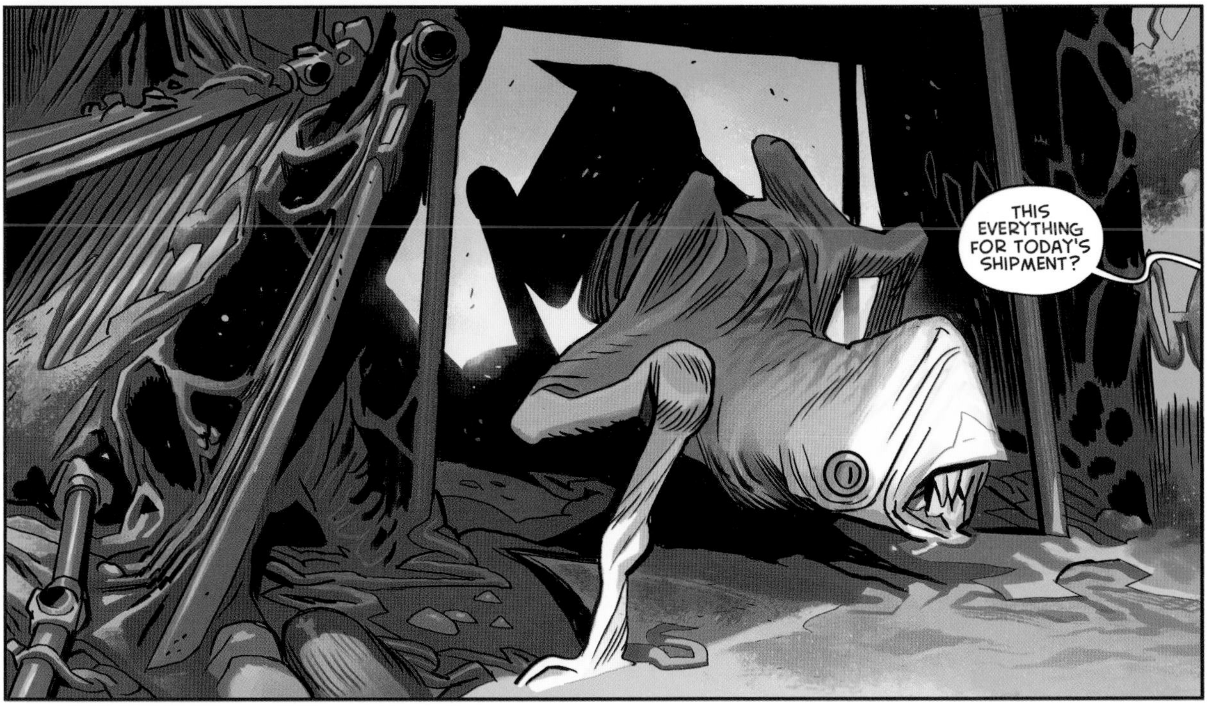
THIS EVERYTHING FOR TODAY'S SHIPMENT?

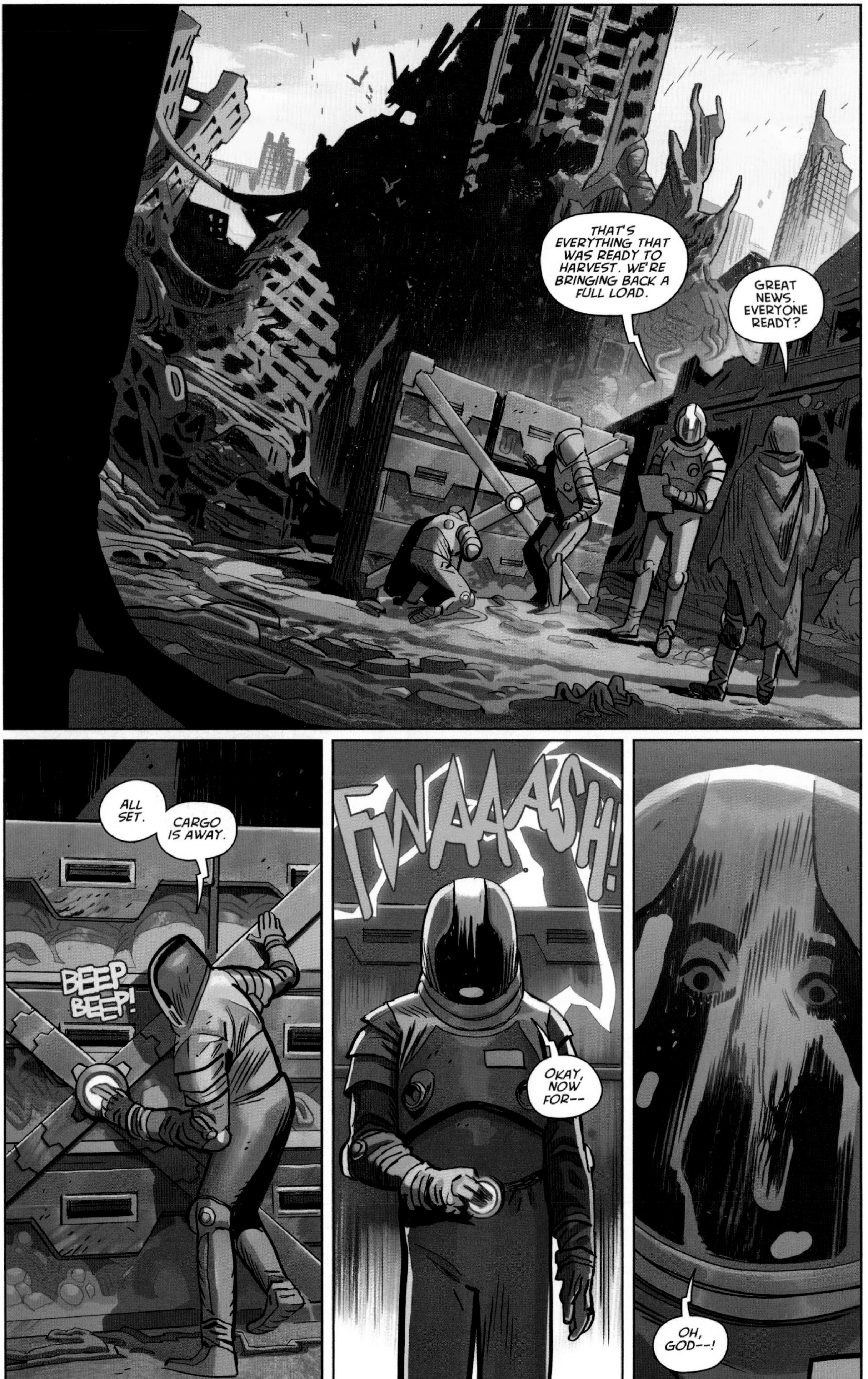
THAT'S EVERYTHING THAT WAS READY TO HARVEST. WE'RE BRINGING BACK A FULL LOAD.
GREAT NEWS. EVERYONE READY?
ALL SET.
CARGO IS AWAY.
BEEP BEEP!
FWAAASH!
OKAY, NOW FOR--
OH, GOD--!

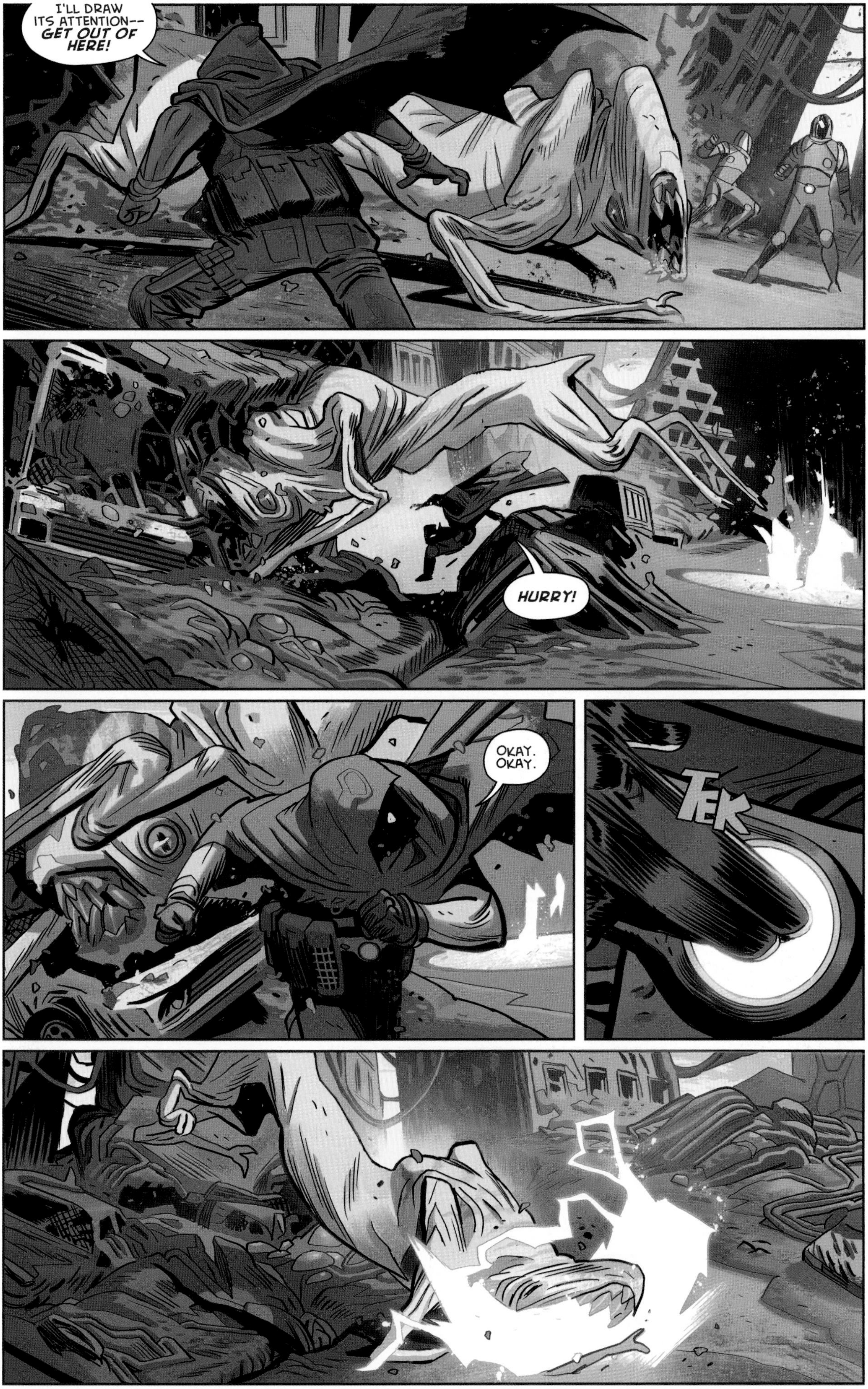
I'LL DRAW ITS ATTENTION-- GET OUT OF HERE!
HURRY!
OKAY. OKAY.
TEK

T H R E E   Y E A

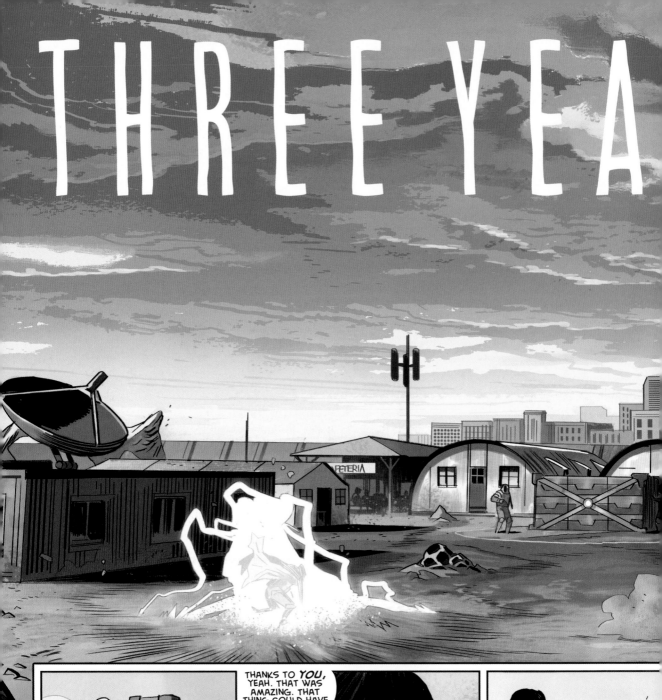

EVERYONE BACK OKAY?

THANKS TO *YOU*, YEAH. THAT WAS AMAZING. THAT THING COULD HAVE KILLED YOU.

JUST DOING MY JOB, CYNTHIA.

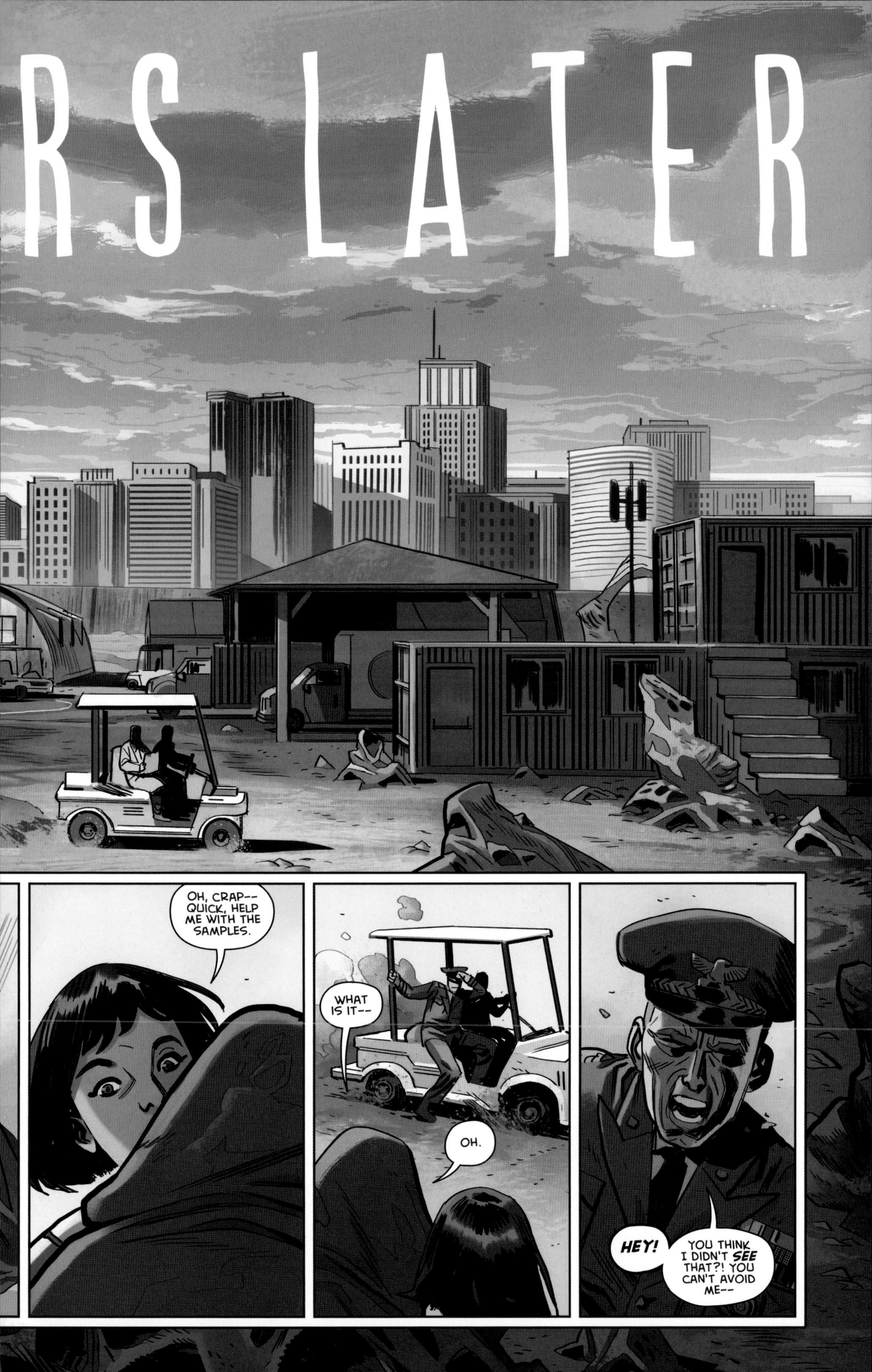
RS LATER
OH, CRAP--QUICK, HELP ME WITH THE SAMPLES.
WHAT IS IT--
OH.
HEY!
YOU THINK I DIDN'T SEE THAT?! YOU CAN'T AVOID ME--

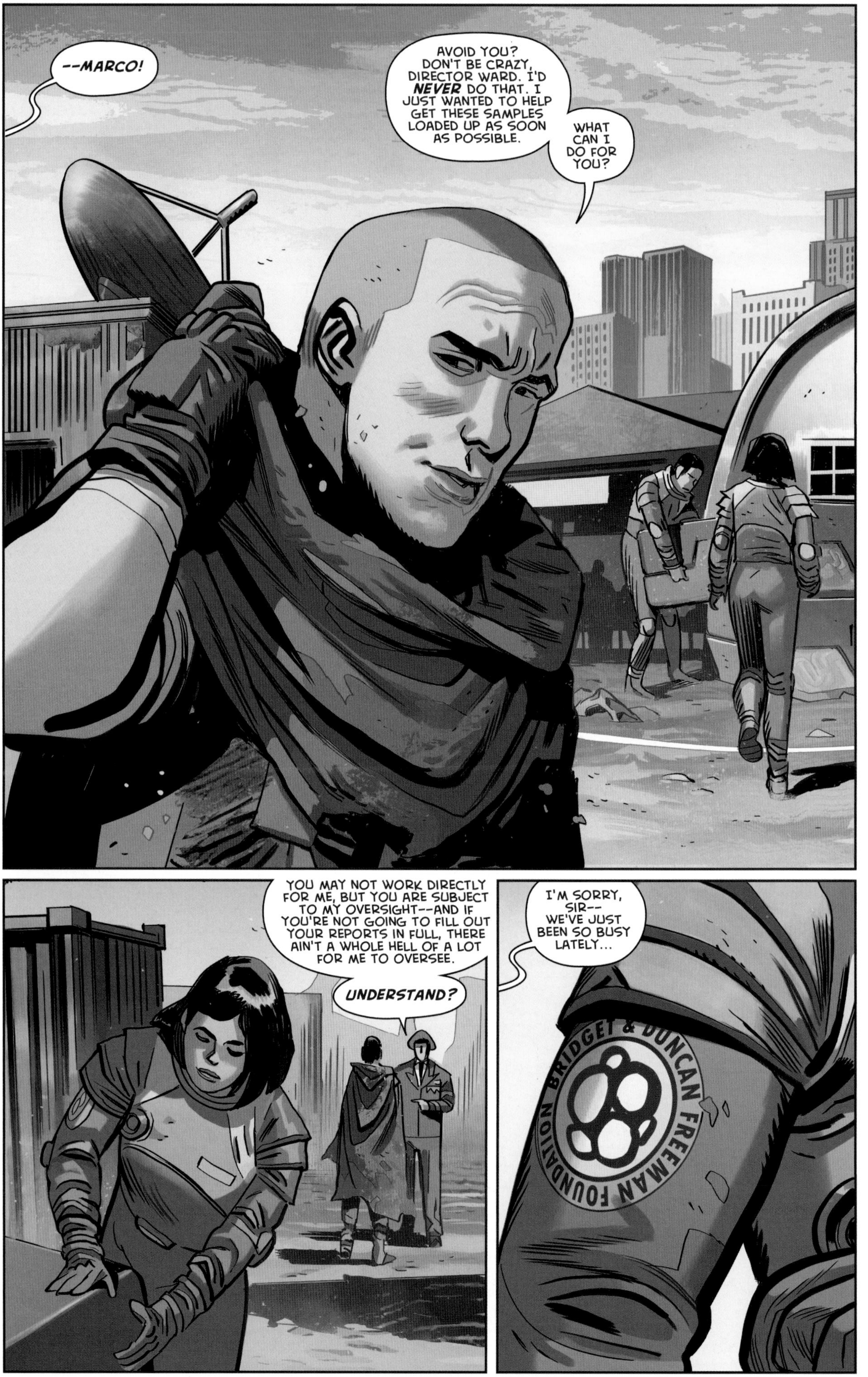
--MARCO!
AVOID YOU? DON'T BE CRAZY, DIRECTOR WARD. I'D NEVER DO THAT. I JUST WANTED TO HELP GET THESE SAMPLES LOADED UP AS SOON AS POSSIBLE.
WHAT CAN I DO FOR YOU?
YOU MAY NOT WORK DIRECTLY FOR ME, BUT YOU ARE SUBJECT TO MY OVERSIGHT--AND IF YOU'RE NOT GOING TO FILL OUT YOUR REPORTS IN FULL, THERE AIN'T A WHOLE HELL OF A LOT FOR ME TO OVERSEE.
UNDERSTAND?
I'M SORRY, SIR-- WE'VE JUST BEEN SO BUSY LATELY...
BRIDGET & DUNCAN FREEMAN FOUNDATION

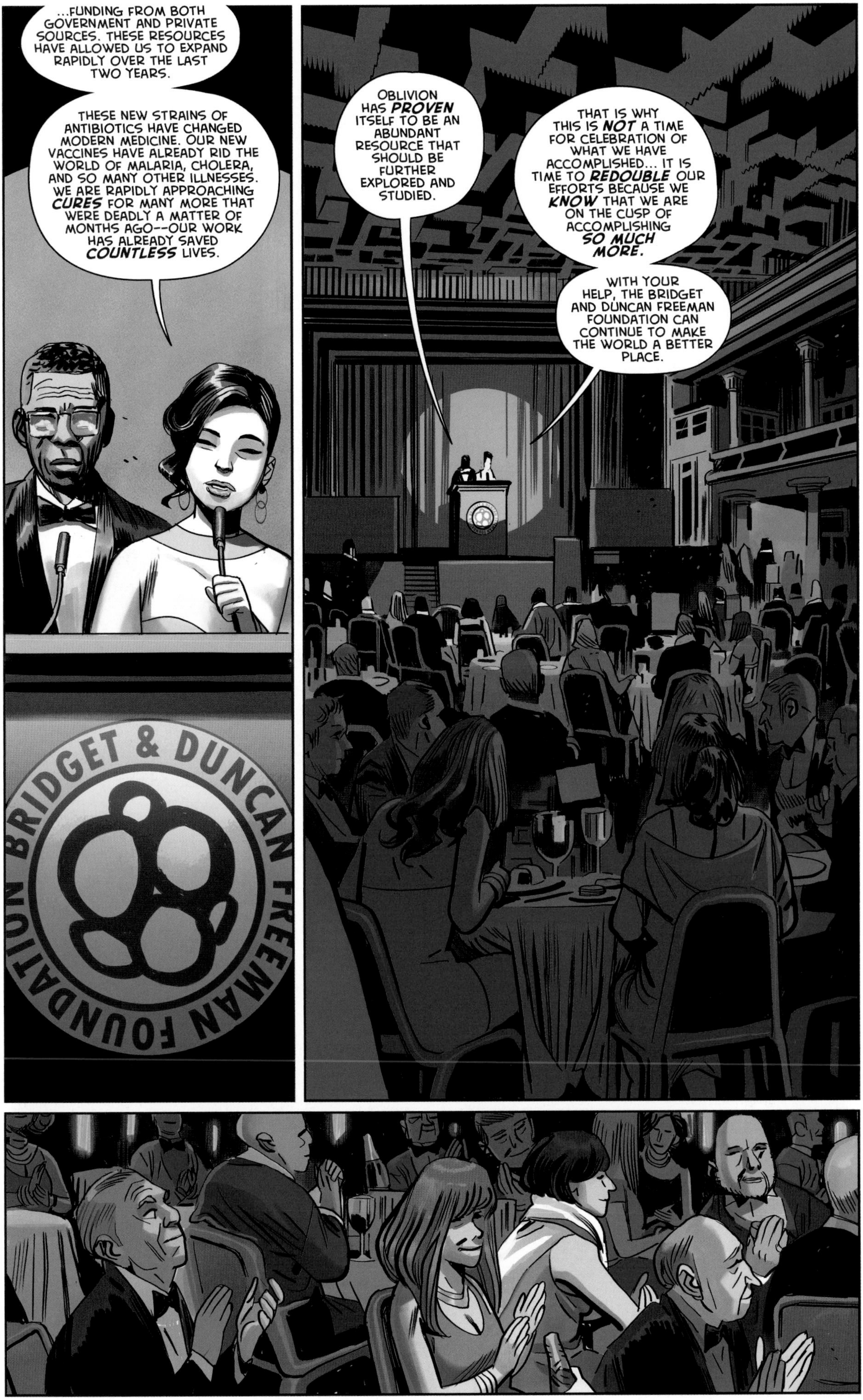
...FUNDING FROM BOTH GOVERNMENT AND PRIVATE SOURCES. THESE RESOURCES HAVE ALLOWED US TO EXPAND RAPIDLY OVER THE LAST TWO YEARS.
THESE NEW STRAINS OF ANTIBIOTICS HAVE CHANGED MODERN MEDICINE. OUR NEW VACCINES HAVE ALREADY RID THE WORLD OF MALARIA, CHOLERA, AND SO MANY OTHER ILLNESSES. WE ARE RAPIDLY APPROACHING *CURES* FOR MANY MORE THAT WERE DEADLY A MATTER OF MONTHS AGO--OUR WORK HAS ALREADY SAVED *COUNTLESS* LIVES.
BRIDGET & DUNCAN FREEMAN FOUNDATION
OBLIVION HAS *PROVEN* ITSELF TO BE AN ABUNDANT RESOURCE THAT SHOULD BE FURTHER EXPLORED AND STUDIED.
THAT IS WHY THIS IS *NOT* A TIME FOR CELEBRATION OF WHAT WE HAVE ACCOMPLISHED... IT IS TIME TO *REDOUBLE* OUR EFFORTS BECAUSE WE *KNOW* THAT WE ARE ON THE CUSP OF ACCOMPLISHING *SO MUCH MORE.*
WITH YOUR HELP, THE BRIDGET AND DUNCAN FREEMAN FOUNDATION CAN CONTINUE TO MAKE THE WORLD A BETTER PLACE.

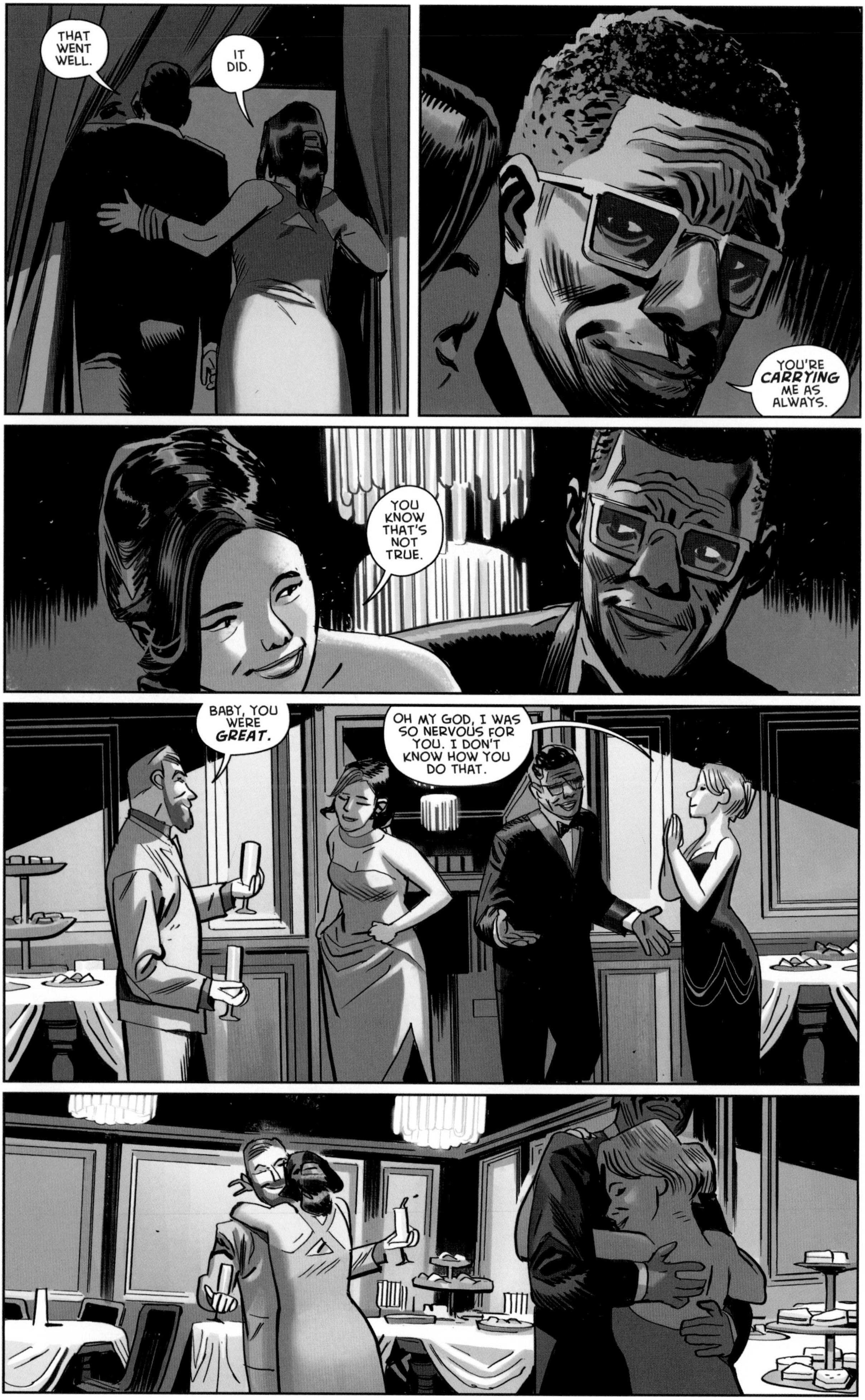
THAT WENT WELL.
IT DID.
YOU'RE **CARRYING** ME AS ALWAYS.
YOU KNOW THAT'S NOT TRUE.
BABY, YOU WERE **GREAT.**
OH MY GOD, I WAS SO NERVOUS FOR YOU. I DON'T KNOW HOW YOU DO THAT.

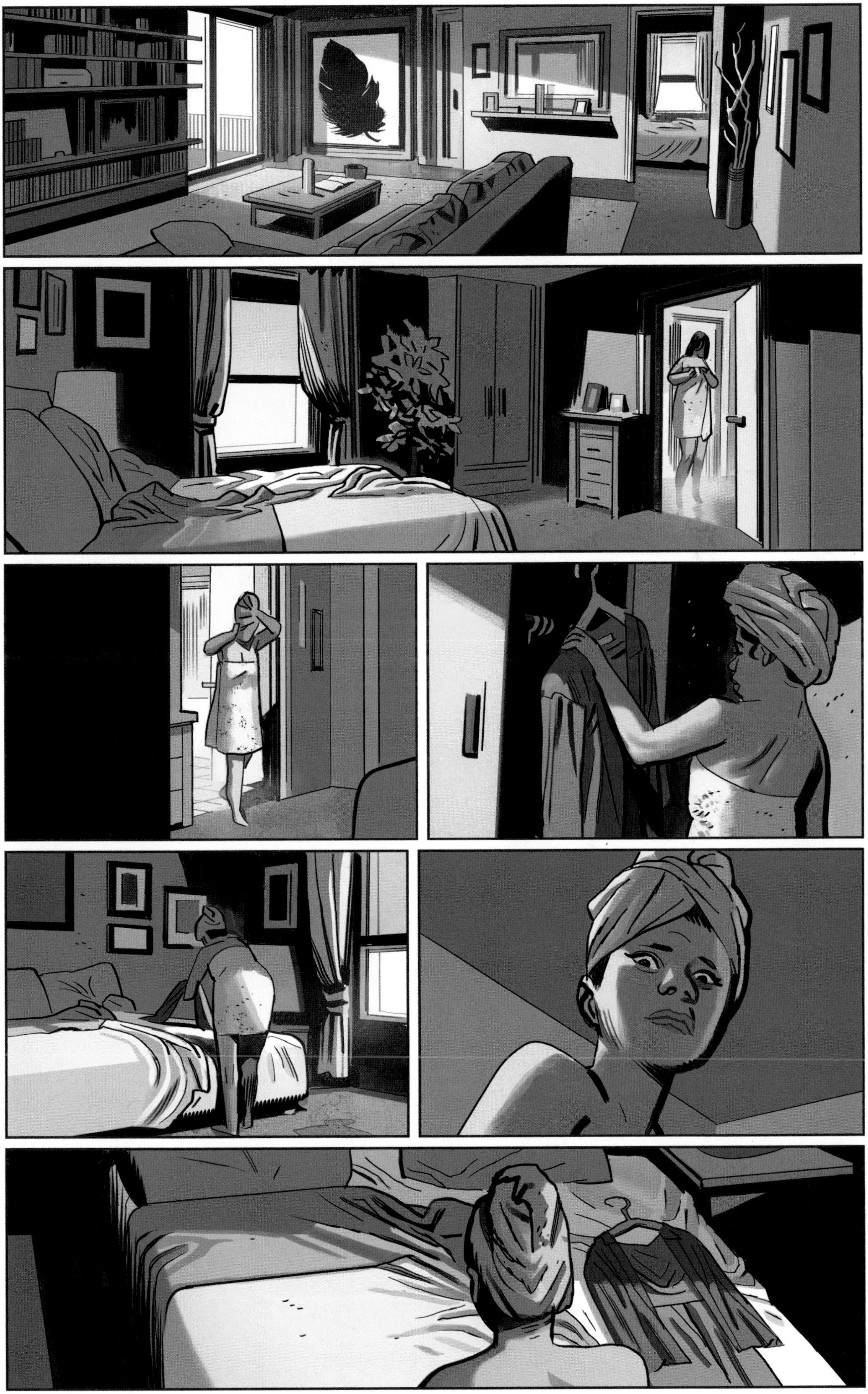

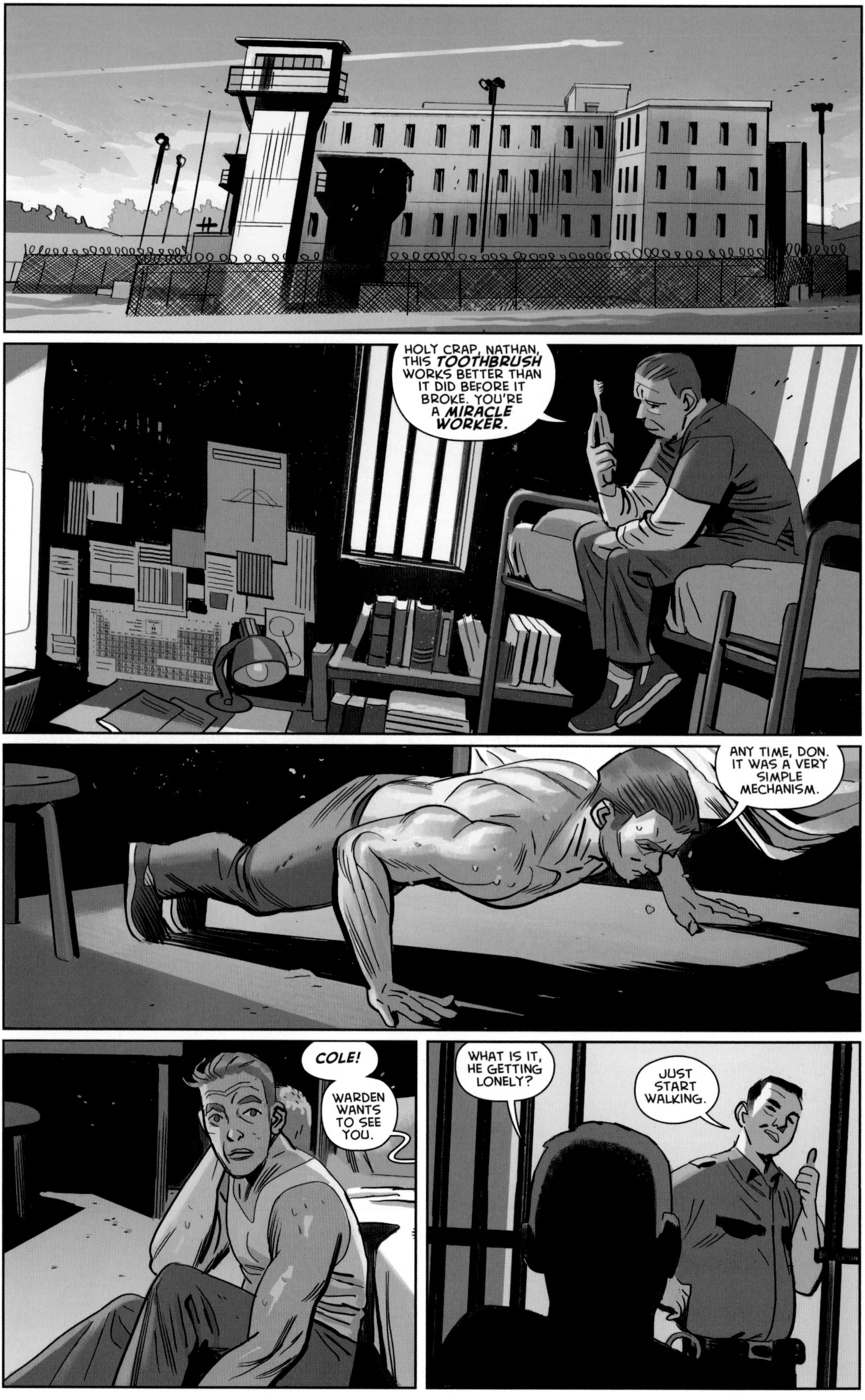
HOLY CRAP, NATHAN, THIS TOOTHBRUSH WORKS BETTER THAN IT DID BEFORE IT BROKE. YOU'RE A MIRACLE WORKER.
ANY TIME, DON. IT WAS A VERY SIMPLE MECHANISM.
COLE!
WARDEN WANTS TO SEE YOU.
WHAT IS IT, HE GETTING LONELY?
JUST START WALKING.

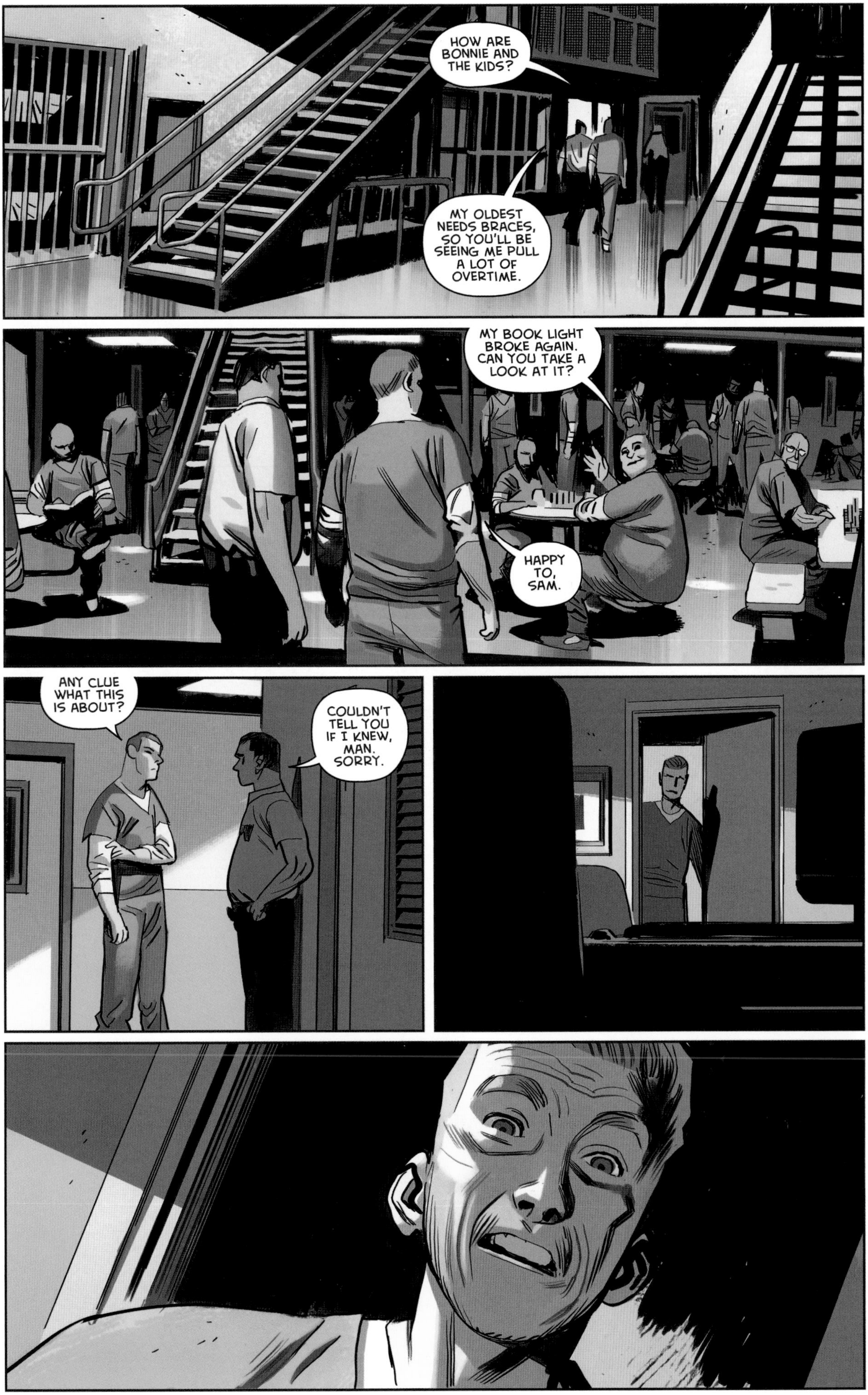
HOW ARE BONNIE AND THE KIDS?
MY OLDEST NEEDS BRACES, SO YOU'LL BE SEEING ME PULL A LOT OF OVERTIME.
MY BOOK LIGHT BROKE AGAIN. CAN YOU TAKE A LOOK AT IT?
HAPPY TO, SAM.
ANY CLUE WHAT THIS IS ABOUT?
COULDN'T TELL YOU IF I KNEW, MAN. SORRY.

DIRECTOR WARD? THIS CAN'T BE GOOD.

TAKE A SEAT, NATHAN. WE'RE GOING TO HAVE US A LITTLE CHAT.

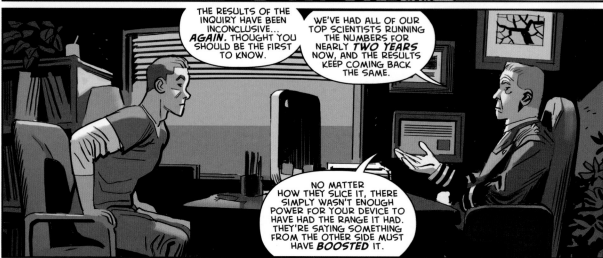

THE RESULTS OF THE INQUIRY HAVE BEEN INCONCLUSIVE... *AGAIN.* THOUGHT YOU SHOULD BE THE FIRST TO KNOW.

WE'VE HAD ALL OF OUR TOP SCIENTISTS RUNNING THE NUMBERS FOR NEARLY *TWO YEARS* NOW, AND THE RESULTS KEEP COMING BACK THE SAME.

NO MATTER HOW THEY SLICE IT, THERE SIMPLY WASN'T ENOUGH POWER FOR YOUR DEVICE TO HAVE HAD THE RANGE IT HAD. THEY'RE SAYING SOMETHING FROM THE OTHER SIDE MUST HAVE *BOOSTED* IT.

FROM EVERYTHING I'VE ALWAYS SEEN IN OBLIVION, IT'S A PRIMITIVE WORLD...

...BUT MAYBE.

BOTTOM LINE, IT'S CALLING INTO QUESTION JUST HOW *RESPONSIBLE* YOU WERE FOR THE TRANSFERENCE...

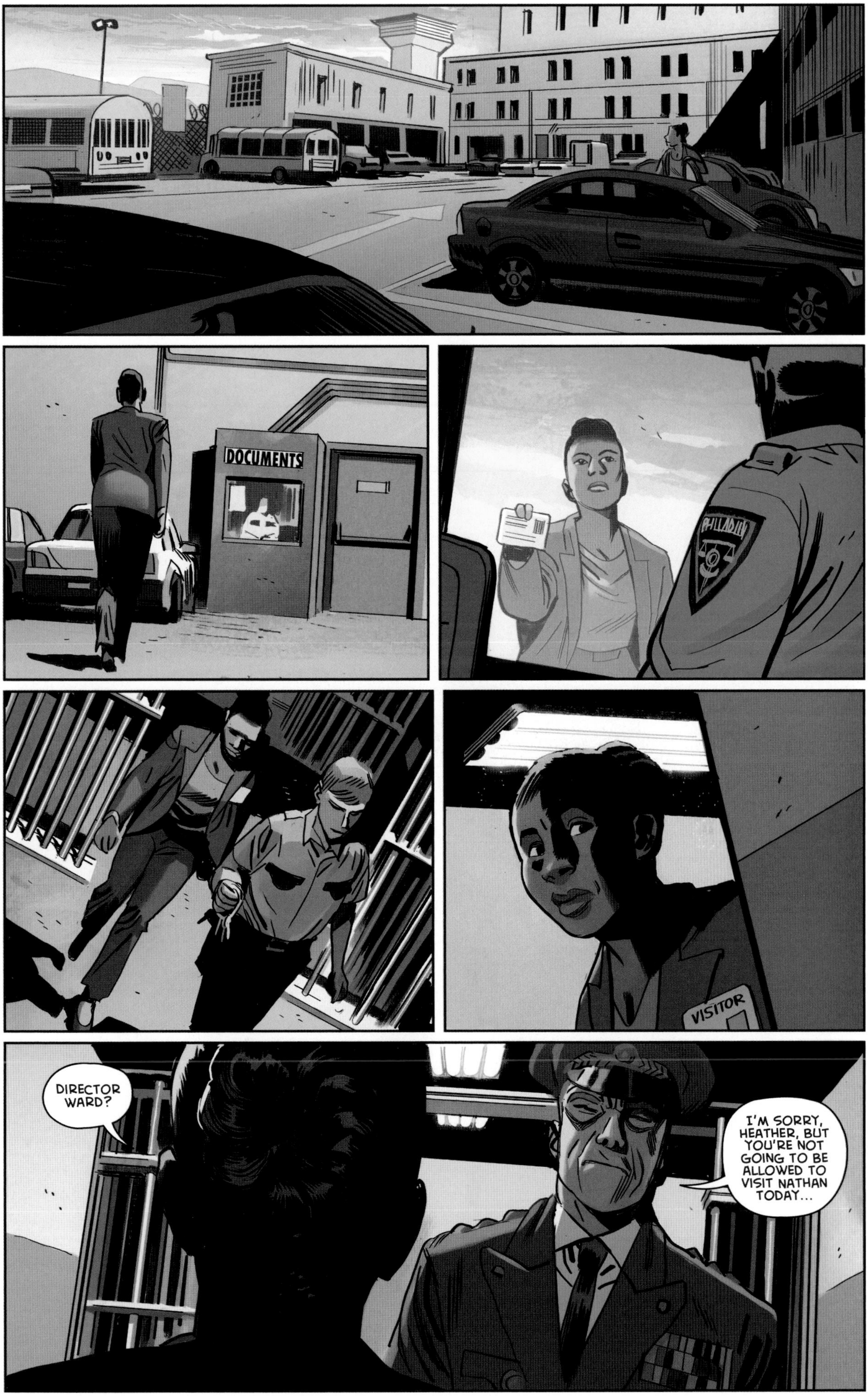
DOCUMENTS
VISITOR
DIRECTOR WARD?
I'M SORRY, HEATHER, BUT YOU'RE NOT GOING TO BE ALLOWED TO VISIT NATHAN TODAY...

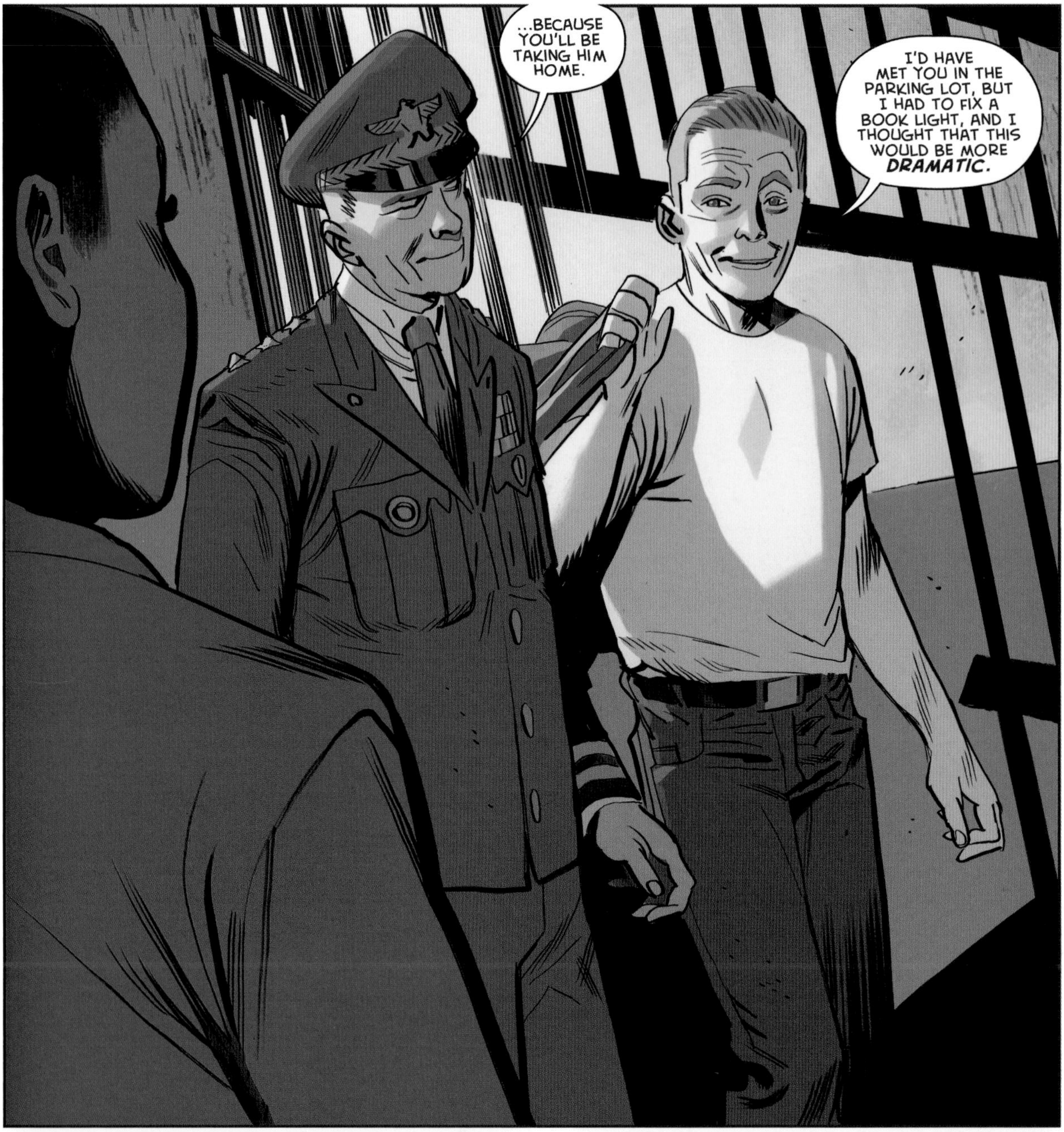
...BECAUSE YOU'LL BE TAKING HIM HOME.
I'D HAVE MET YOU IN THE PARKING LOT, BUT I HAD TO FIX A BOOK LIGHT, AND I THOUGHT THAT THIS WOULD BE MORE *DRAMATIC.*

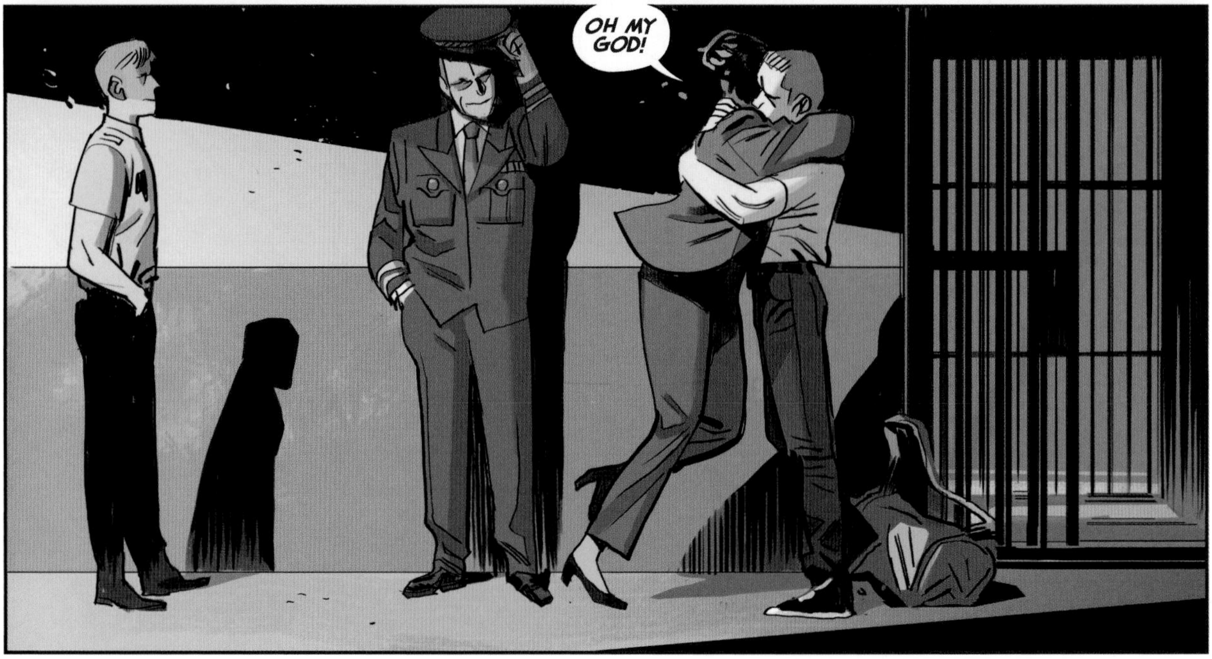
OH MY GOD!

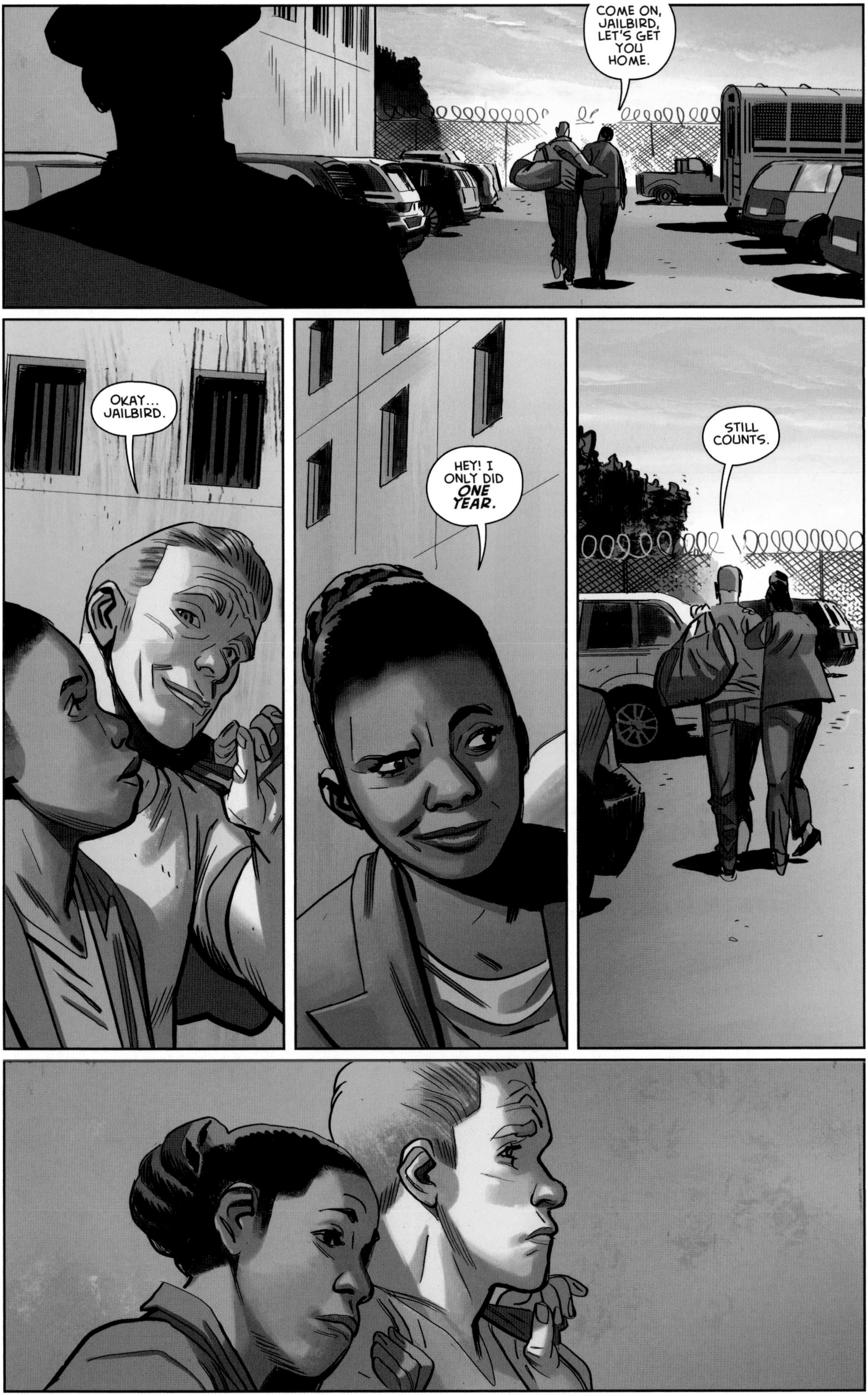
COME ON, JAILBIRD, LET'S GET YOU HOME.
OKAY... JAILBIRD.
HEY! I ONLY DID ONE YEAR.
STILL COUNTS.

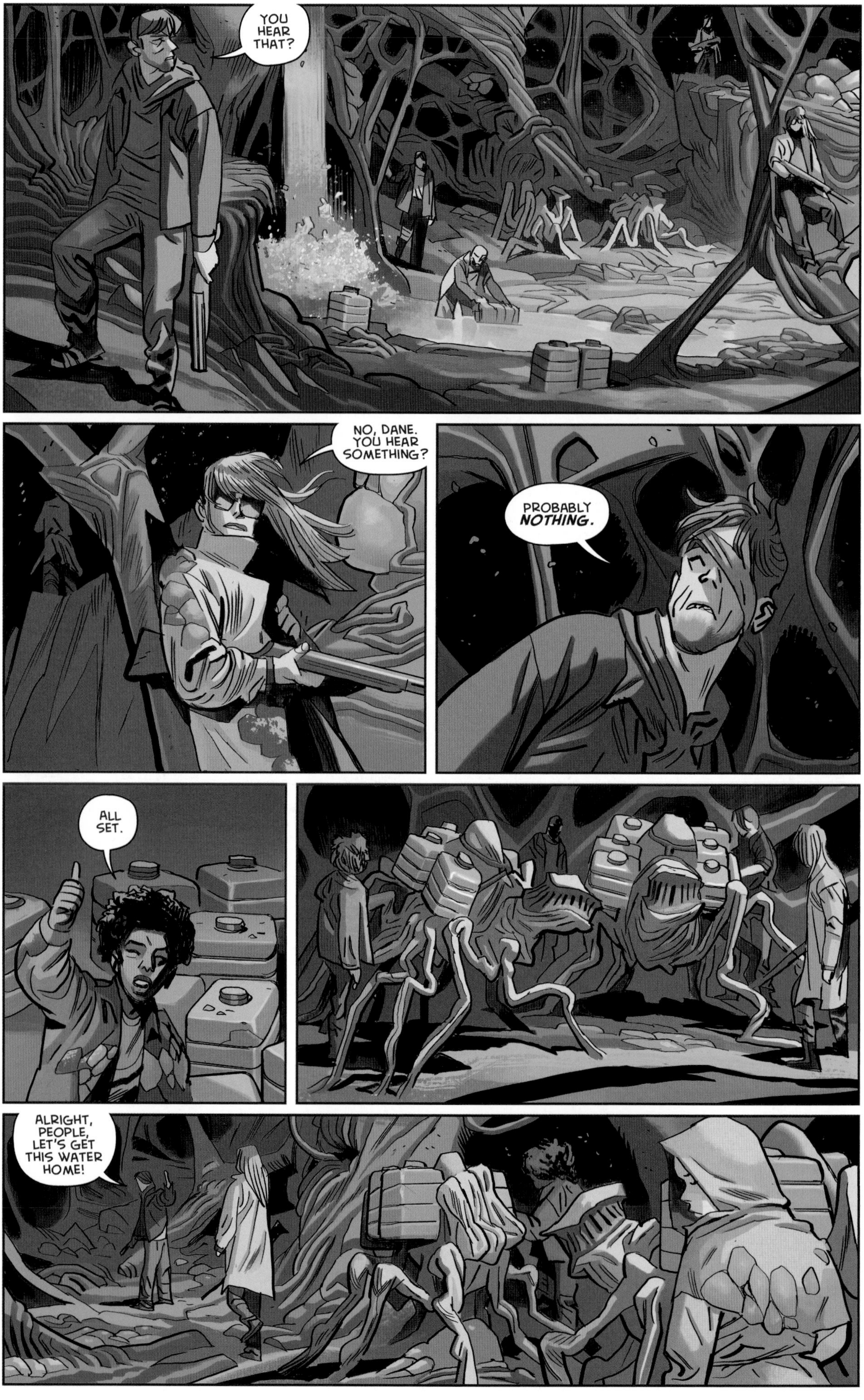
YOU HEAR THAT?
NO, DANE. YOU HEAR SOMETHING?
PROBABLY NOTHING.
ALL SET.
ALRIGHT, PEOPLE, LET'S GET THIS WATER HOME!

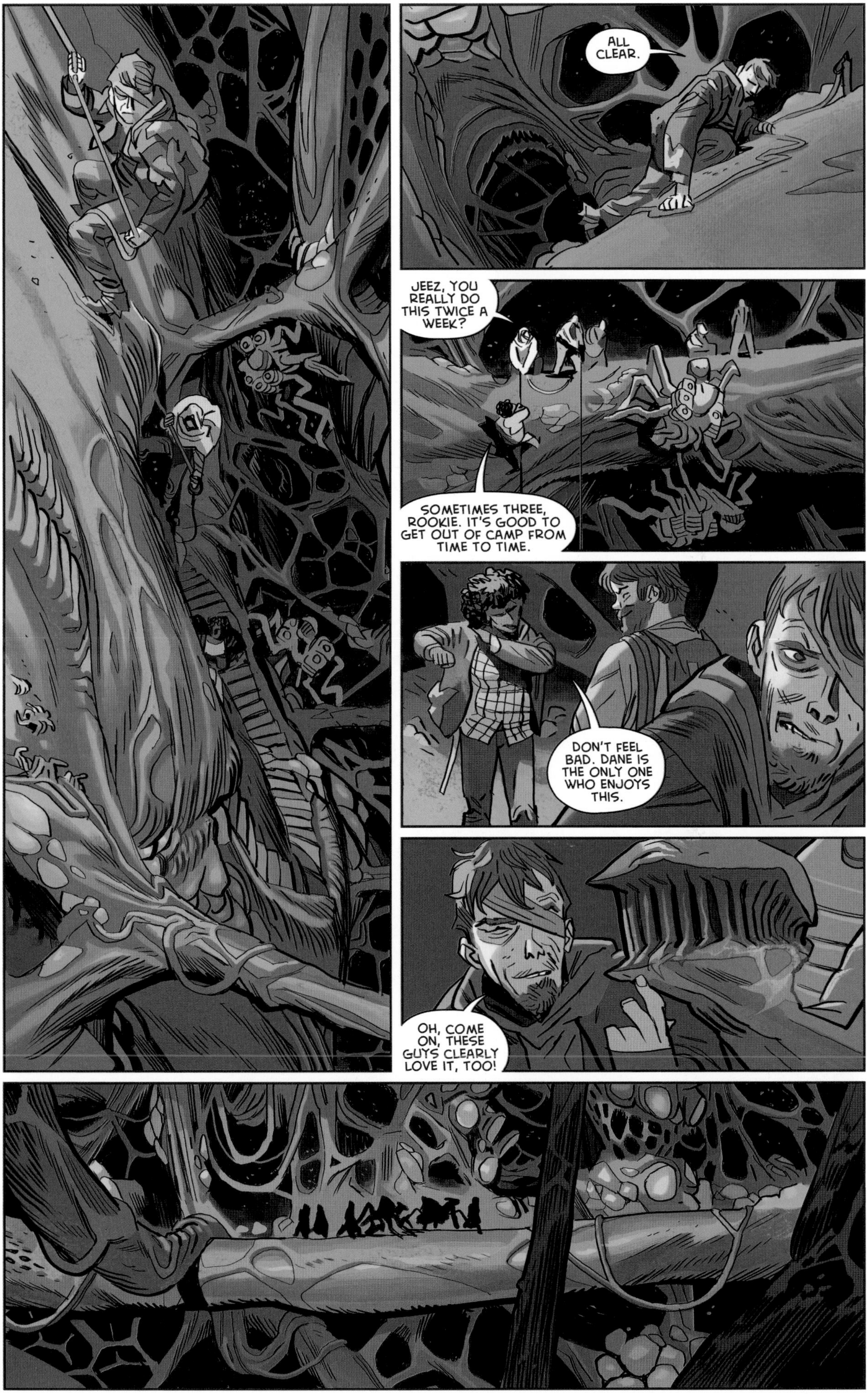
ALL CLEAR.
JEEZ, YOU REALLY DO THIS TWICE A WEEK?
SOMETIMES THREE, ROOKIE. IT'S GOOD TO GET OUT OF CAMP FROM TIME TO TIME.
DON'T FEEL BAD. DANE IS THE ONLY ONE WHO ENJOYS THIS.
OH, COME ON, THESE GUYS CLEARLY LOVE IT, TOO!

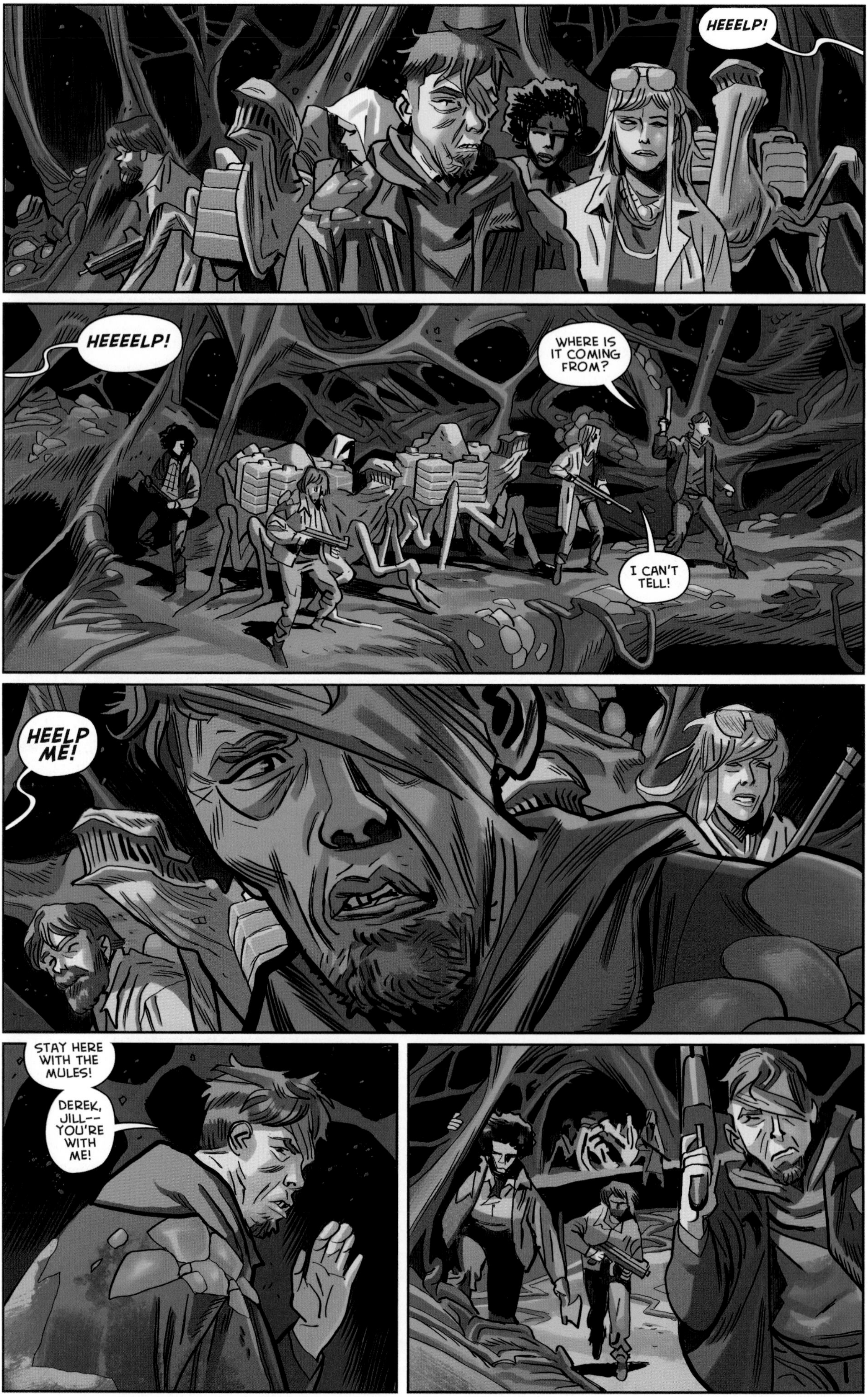
HEEELP!
HEEEELP!
WHERE IS IT COMING FROM?
I CAN'T TELL!
HEELP ME!
STAY HERE WITH THE MULES!
DEREK, JILL-- YOU'RE WITH ME!

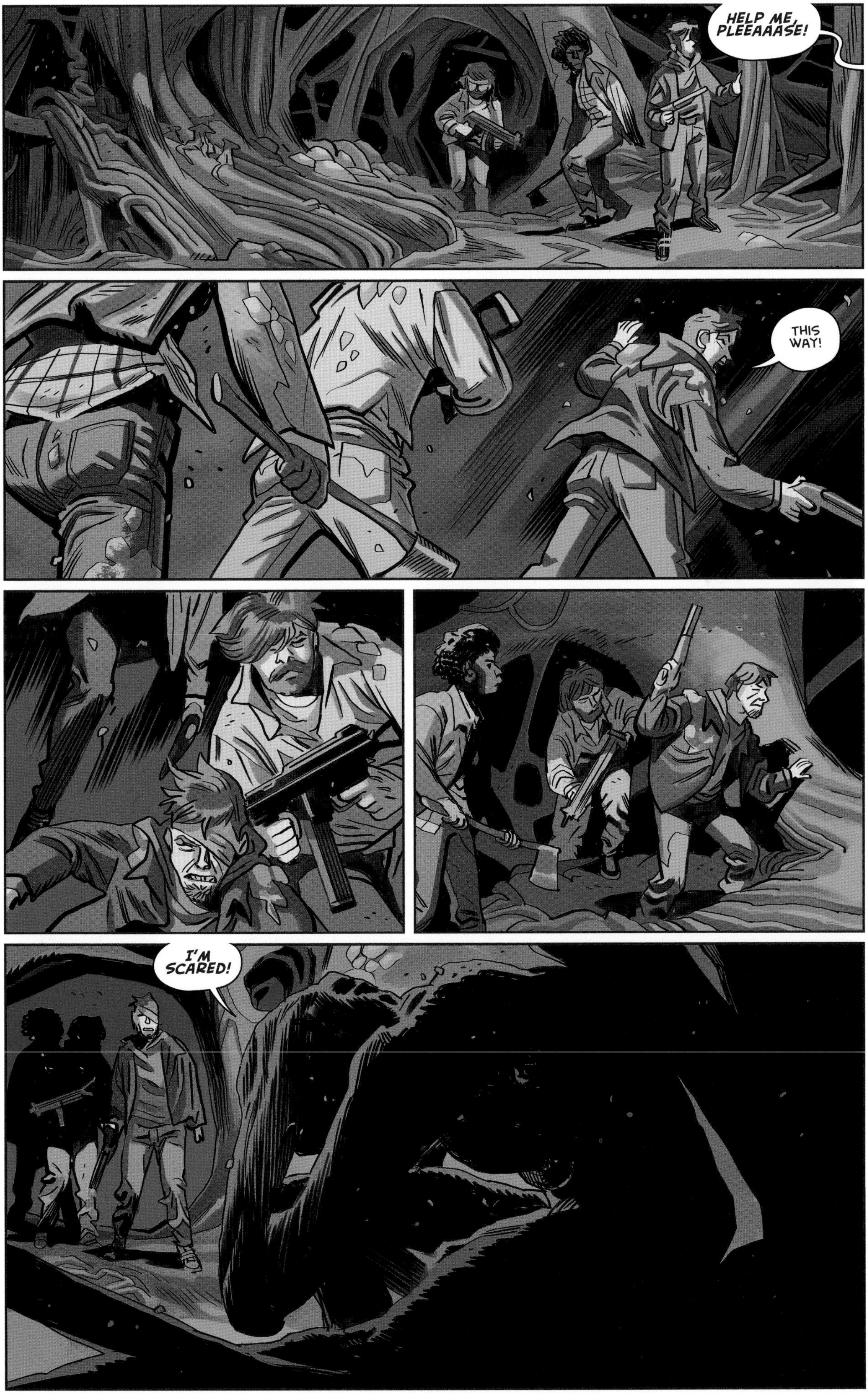
HELP ME, PLEEAAAASE!
THIS WAY!
I'M SCARED!

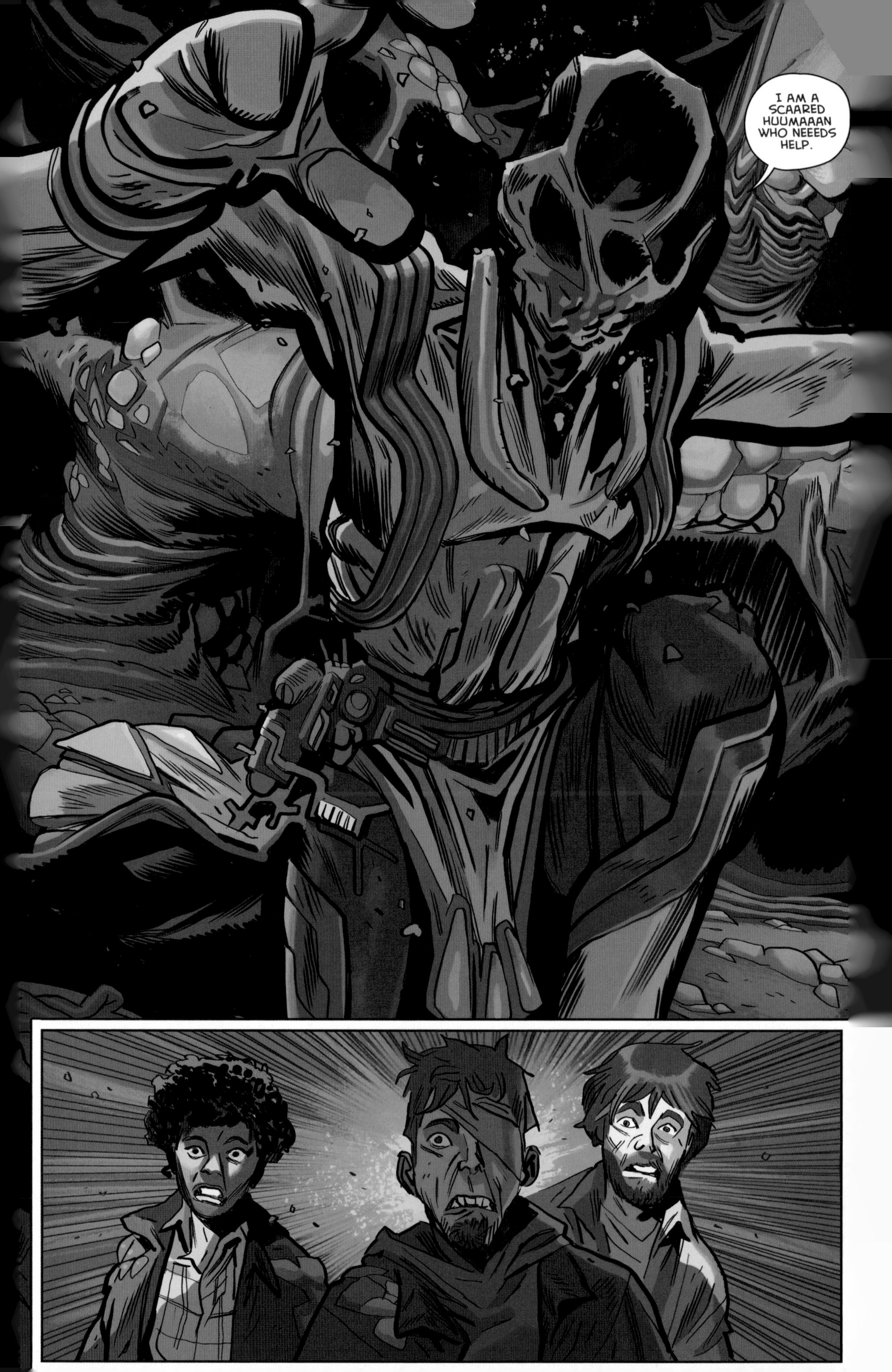
I AM A SCAARED HUUMAAAN WHO NEEEDS HELP.

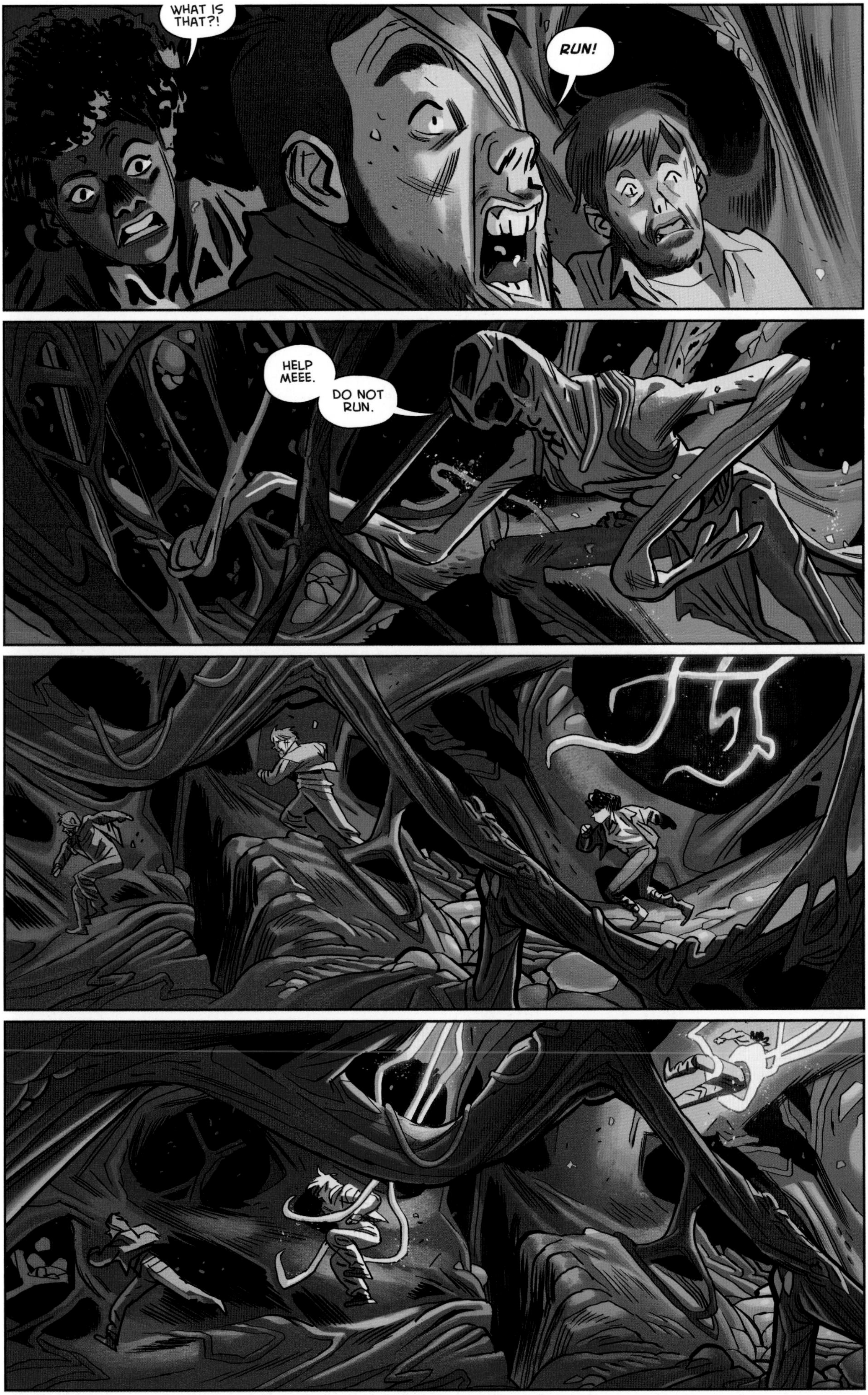
WHAT IS THAT?!
RUN!
HELP MEEE.
DO NOT RUN.

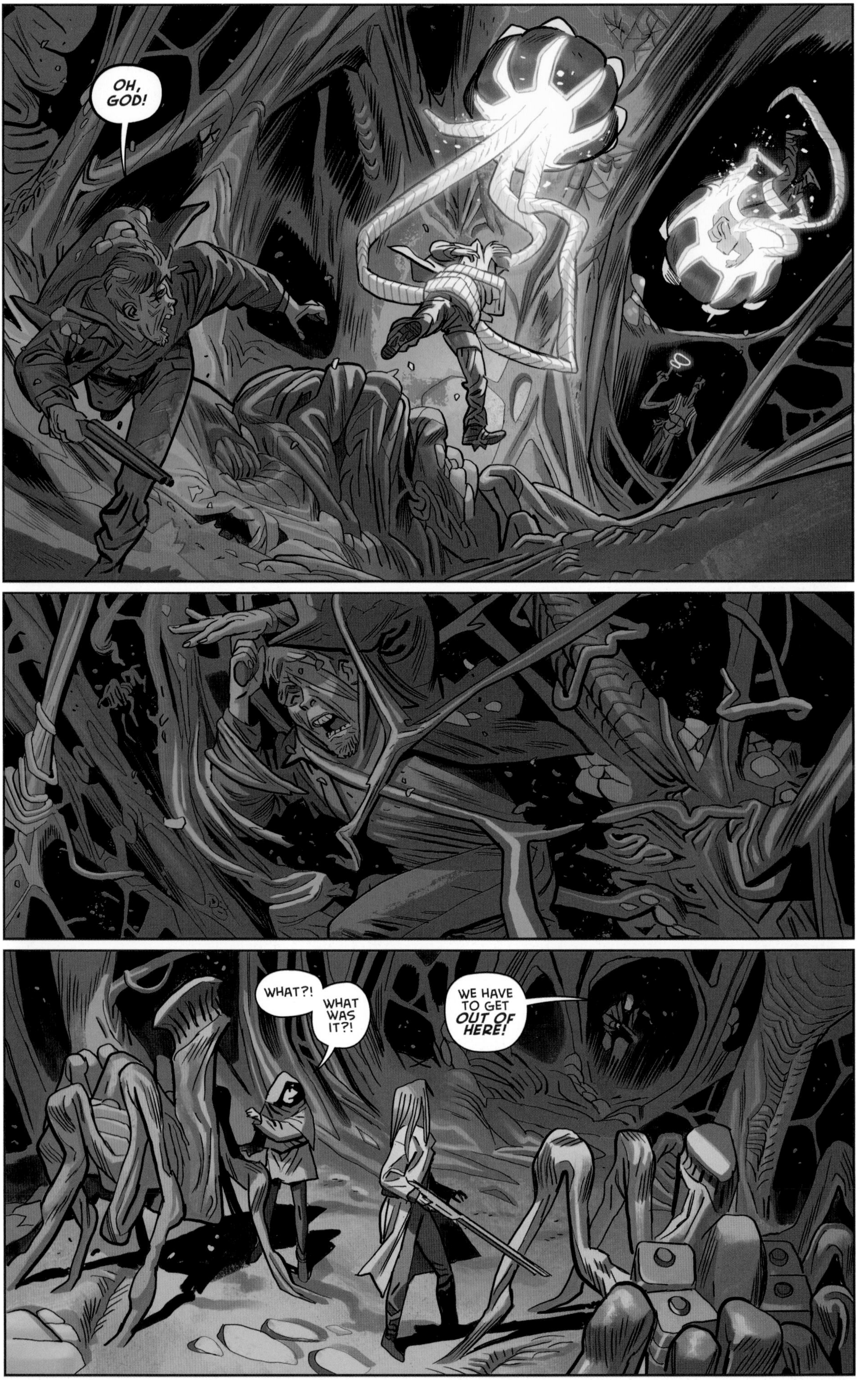
OH, GOD!
WHAT?!
WHAT WAS IT?!
WE HAVE TO GET OUT OF HERE!

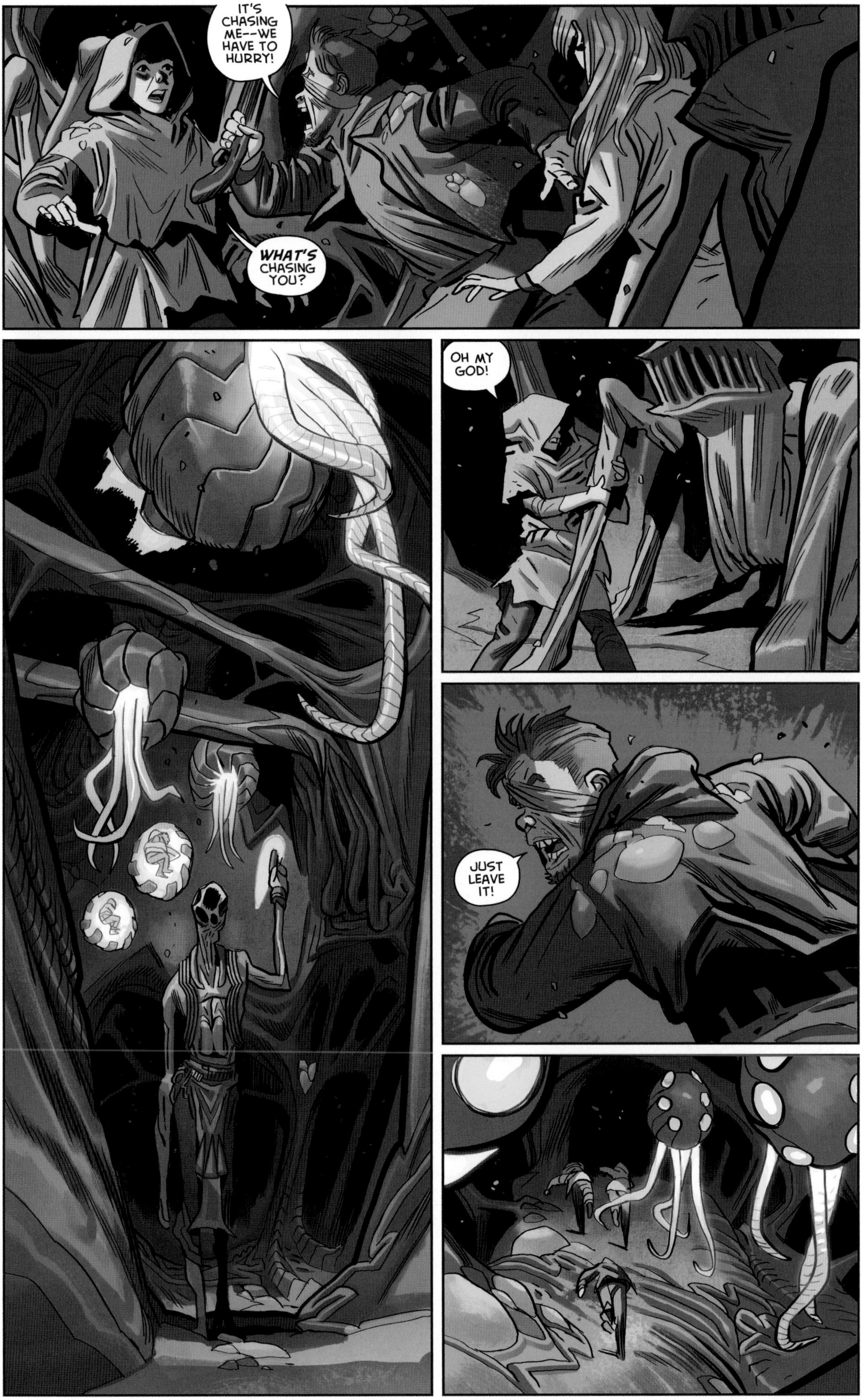
IT'S CHASING ME--WE HAVE TO HURRY!
WHAT'S CHASING YOU?
OH MY GOD!
JUST LEAVE IT!

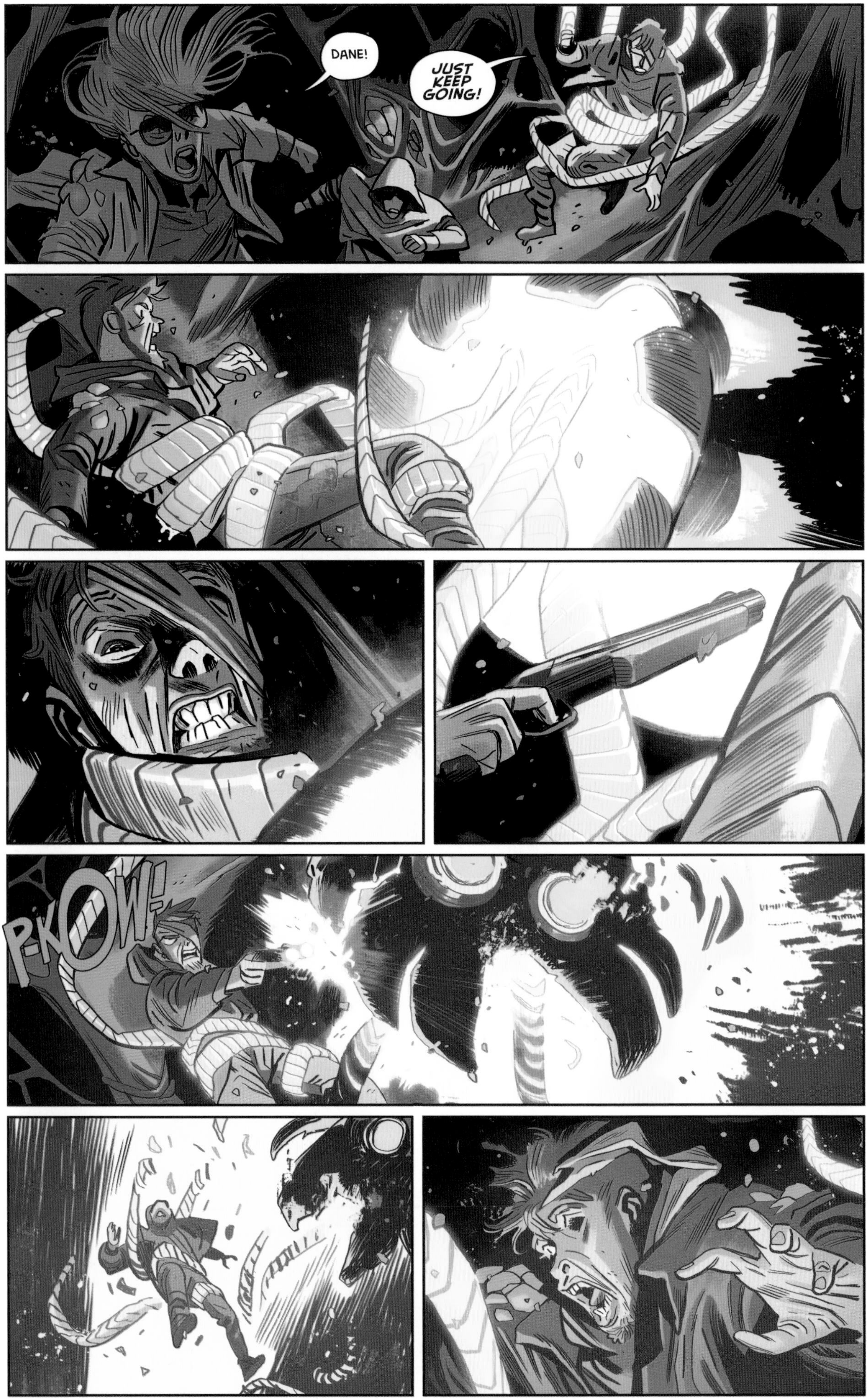
DANE!
JUST KEEP GOING!
P-KOW!

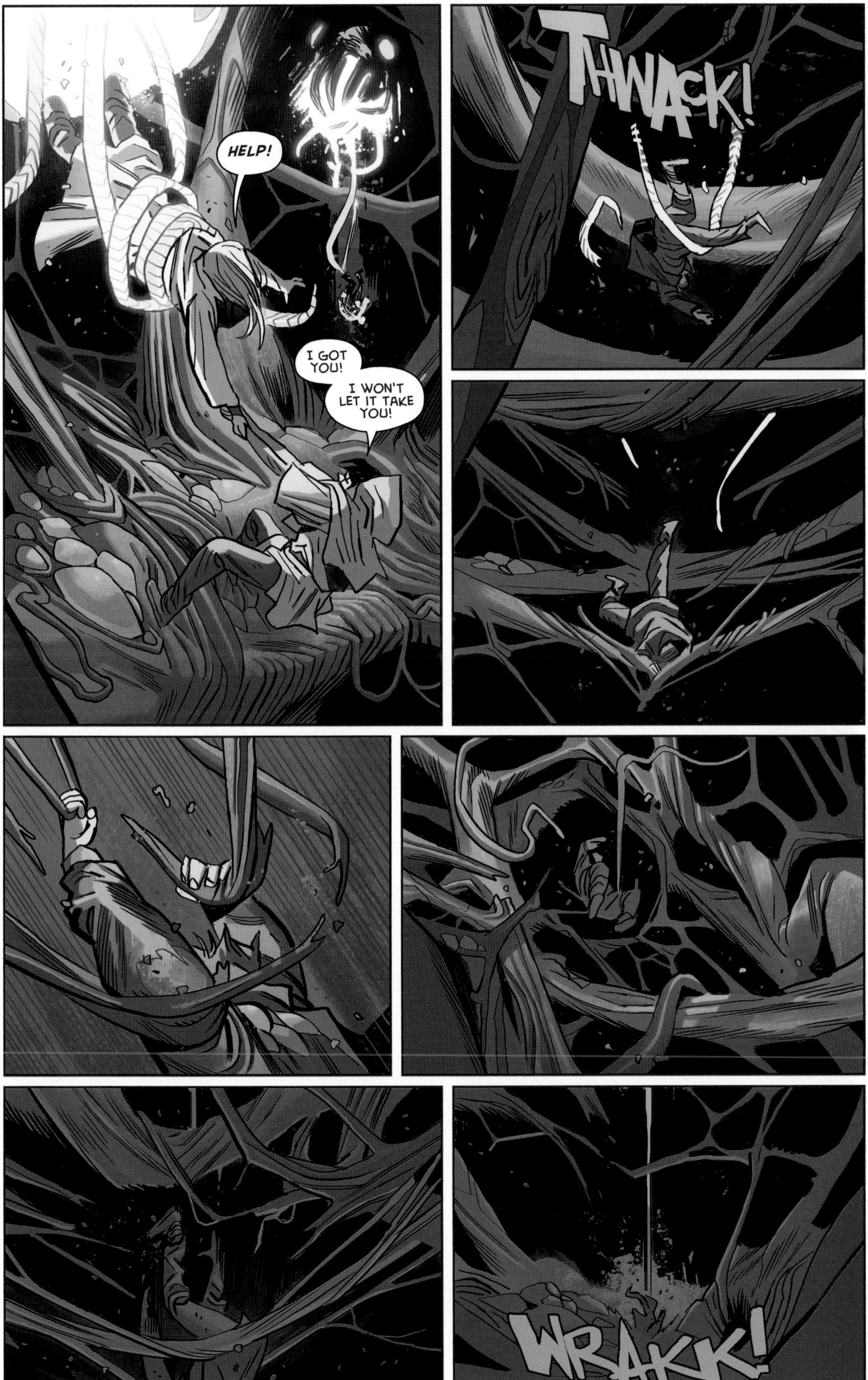

HELP!
I GOT YOU!
I WON'T LET IT TAKE YOU!
THWACK!
WRAKK!

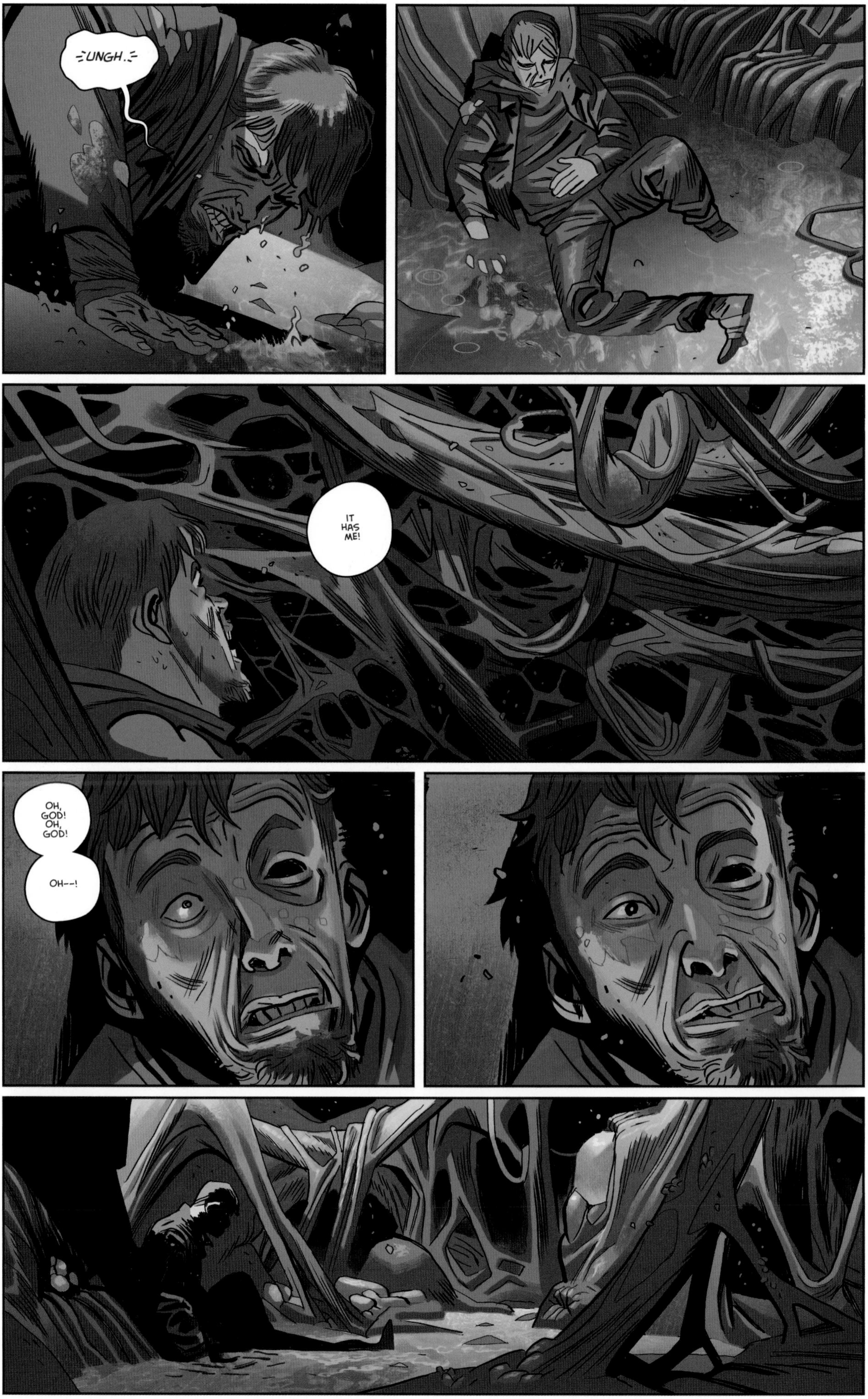
UNGH.
IT HAS ME!
OH, GOD! OH, GOD!
OH--!

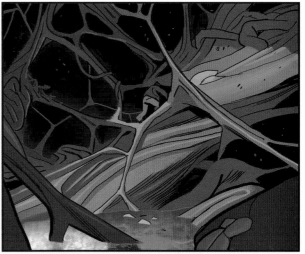

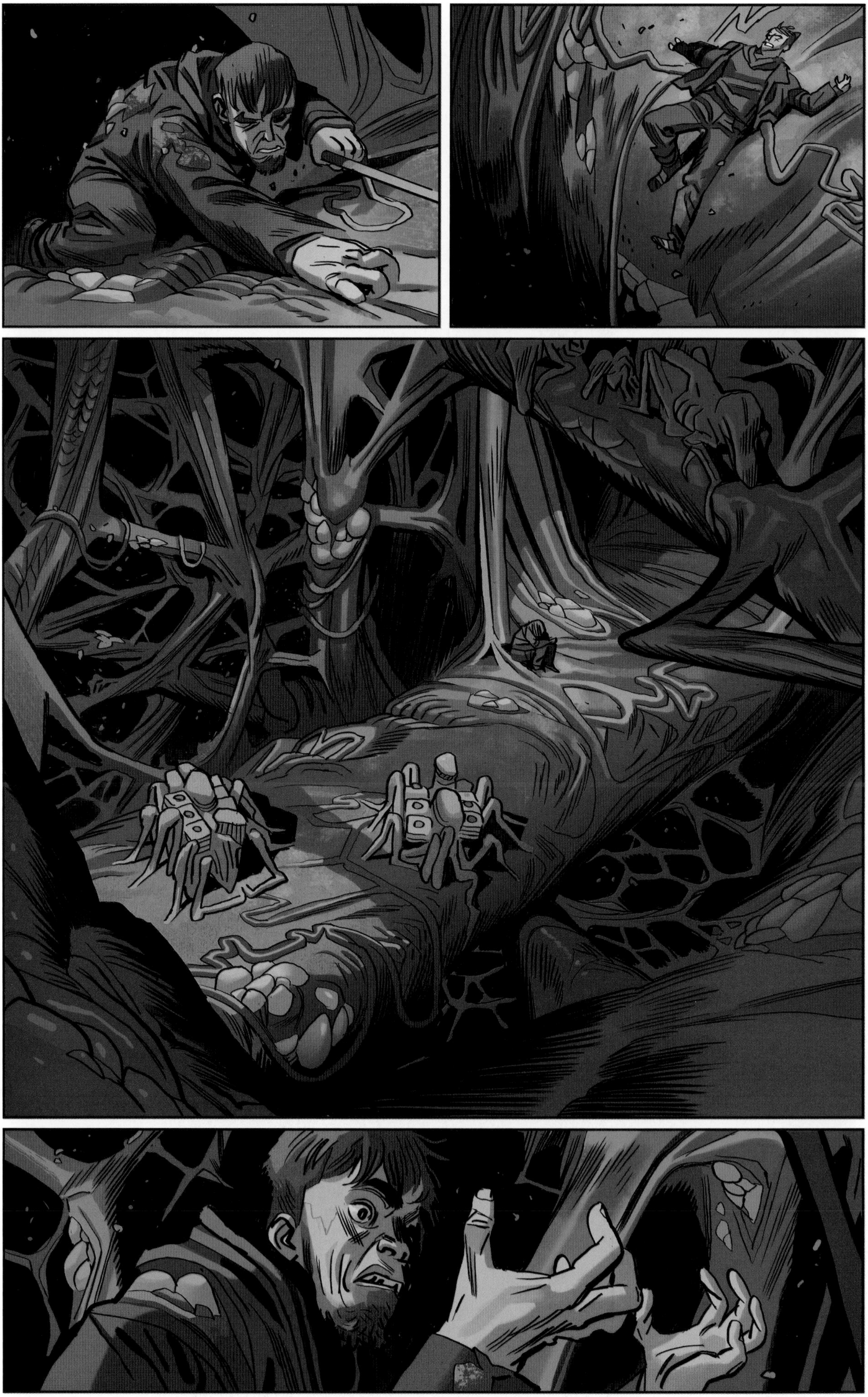

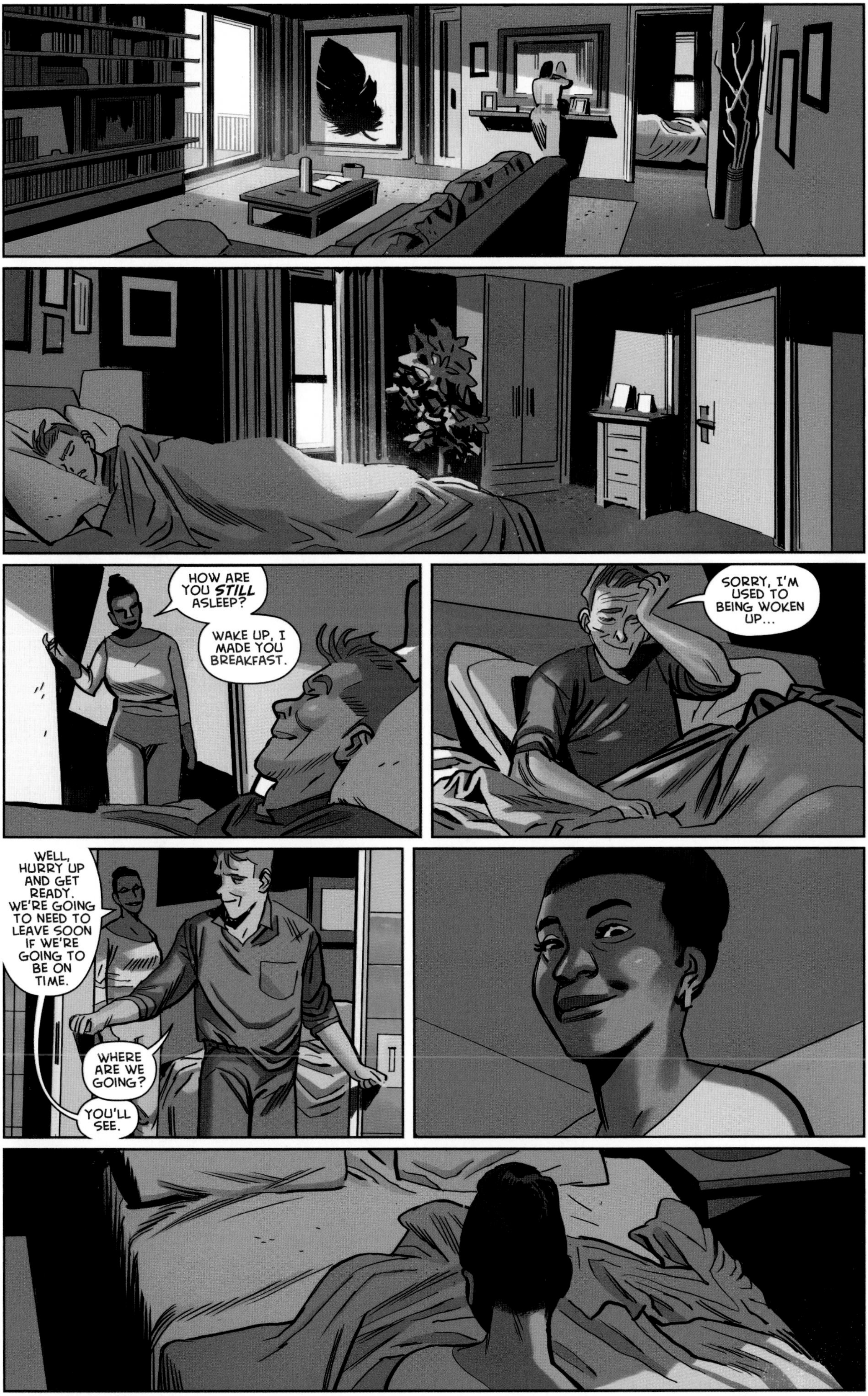
HOW ARE YOU STILL ASLEEP?
WAKE UP, I MADE YOU BREAKFAST.
SORRY, I'M USED TO BEING WOKEN UP...
WELL, HURRY UP AND GET READY. WE'RE GOING TO NEED TO LEAVE SOON IF WE'RE GOING TO BE ON TIME.
WHERE ARE WE GOING?
YOU'LL SEE.

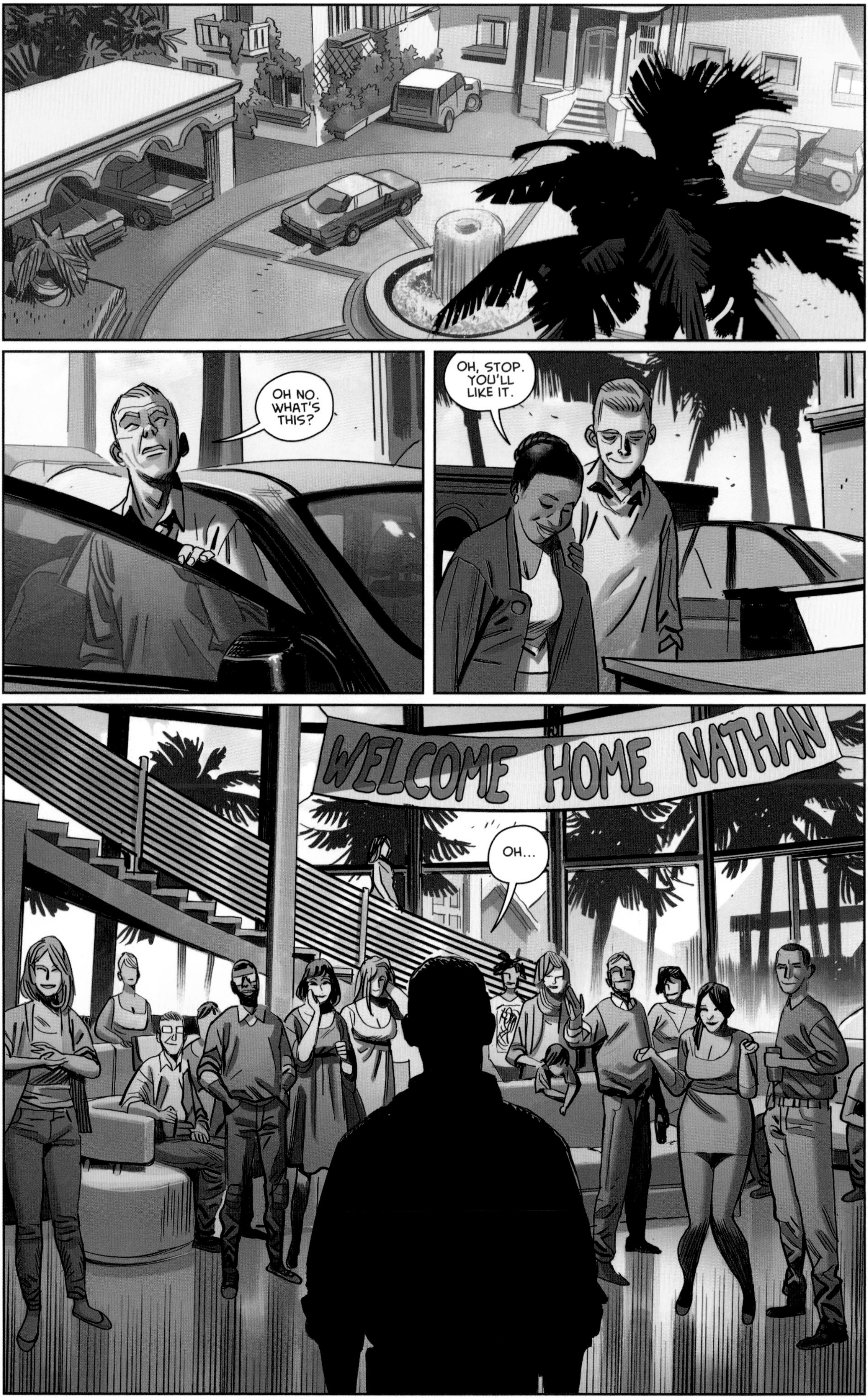
OH NO. WHAT'S THIS?
OH, STOP. YOU'LL LIKE IT.
WELCOME HOME NATHAN
OH...

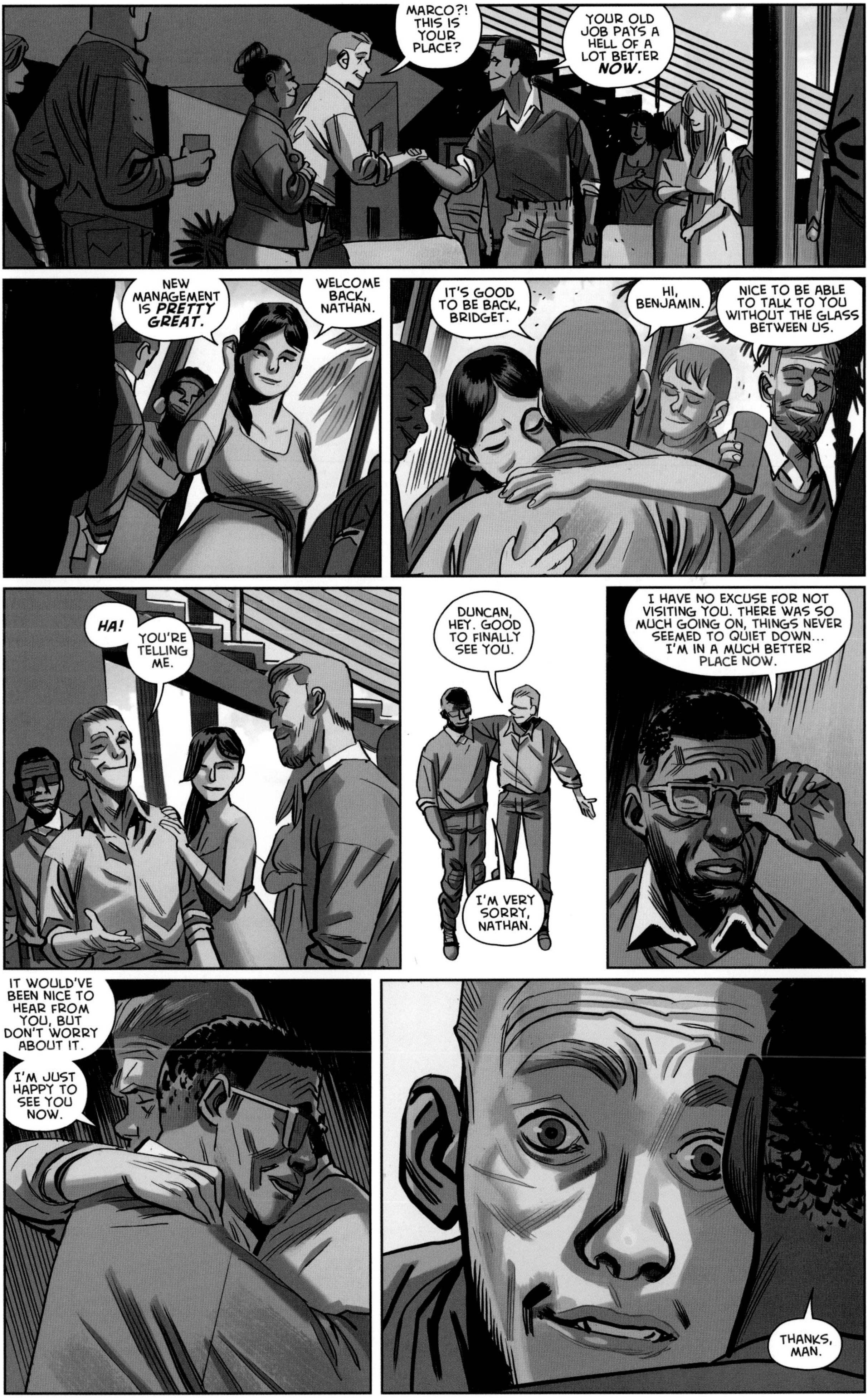
MARCO?! THIS IS YOUR PLACE?
YOUR OLD JOB PAYS A HELL OF A LOT BETTER *NOW.*
NEW MANAGEMENT IS *PRETTY GREAT.*
WELCOME BACK, NATHAN.
IT'S GOOD TO BE BACK, BRIDGET.
HI, BENJAMIN.
NICE TO BE ABLE TO TALK TO YOU WITHOUT THE GLASS BETWEEN US.
HA!
YOU'RE TELLING ME.
DUNCAN, HEY. GOOD TO FINALLY SEE YOU.
I'M VERY SORRY, NATHAN.
I HAVE NO EXCUSE FOR NOT VISITING YOU. THERE WAS SO MUCH GOING ON, THINGS NEVER SEEMED TO QUIET DOWN... I'M IN A MUCH BETTER PLACE NOW.
IT WOULD'VE BEEN NICE TO HEAR FROM YOU, BUT DON'T WORRY ABOUT IT.
I'M JUST HAPPY TO SEE YOU NOW.
THANKS, MAN.

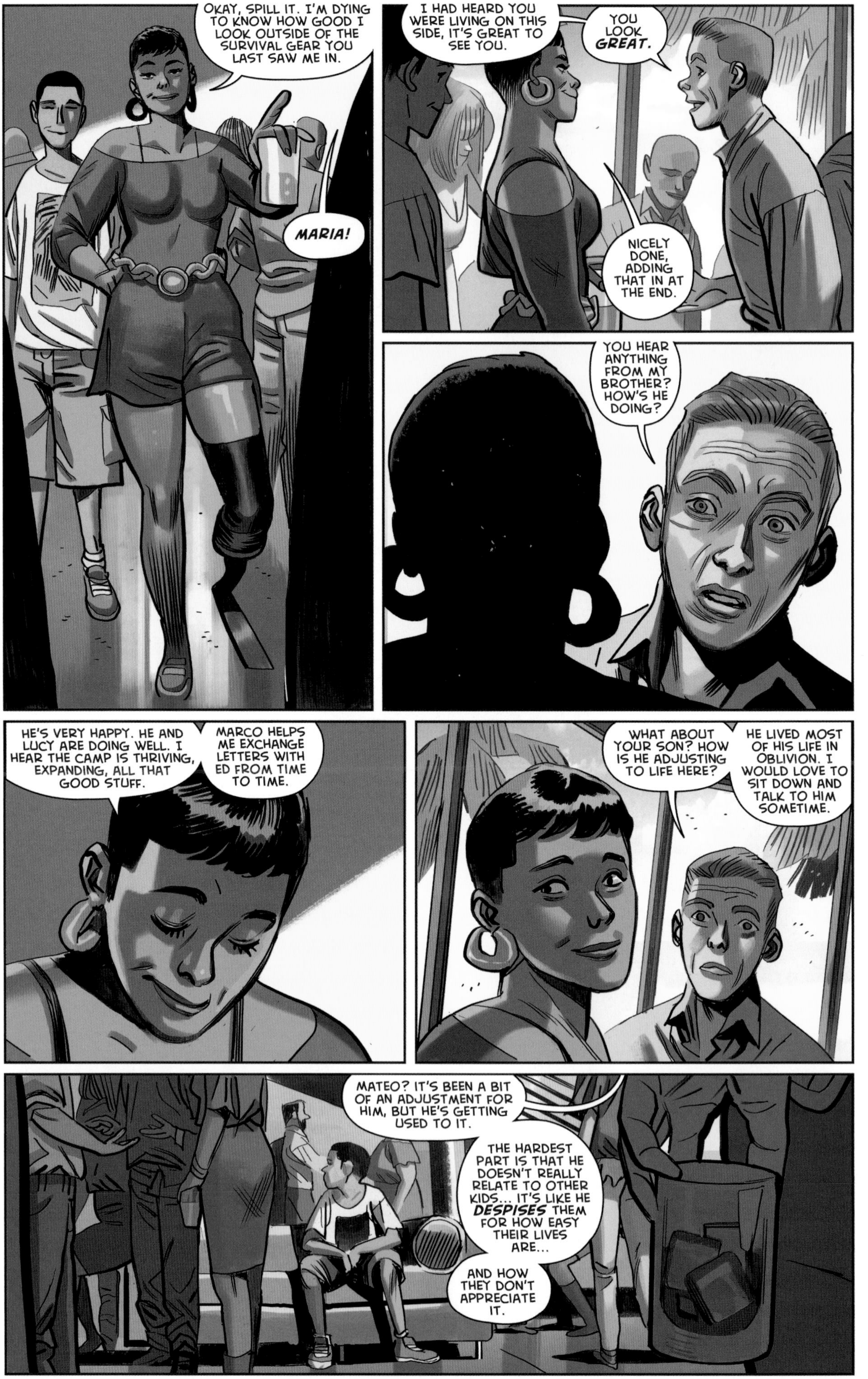
OKAY, SPILL IT. I'M DYING TO KNOW HOW GOOD I LOOK OUTSIDE OF THE SURVIVAL GEAR YOU LAST SAW ME IN.
MARIA!
I HAD HEARD YOU WERE LIVING ON THIS SIDE, IT'S GREAT TO SEE YOU.
YOU LOOK GREAT.
NICELY DONE, ADDING THAT IN AT THE END.
YOU HEAR ANYTHING FROM MY BROTHER? HOW'S HE DOING?
HE'S VERY HAPPY. HE AND LUCY ARE DOING WELL. I HEAR THE CAMP IS THRIVING, EXPANDING, ALL THAT GOOD STUFF.
MARCO HELPS ME EXCHANGE LETTERS WITH ED FROM TIME TO TIME.
WHAT ABOUT YOUR SON? HOW IS HE ADJUSTING TO LIFE HERE?
HE LIVED MOST OF HIS LIFE IN OBLIVION. I WOULD LOVE TO SIT DOWN AND TALK TO HIM SOMETIME.
MATEO? IT'S BEEN A BIT OF AN ADJUSTMENT FOR HIM, BUT HE'S GETTING USED TO IT.
THE HARDEST PART IS THAT HE DOESN'T REALLY RELATE TO OTHER KIDS... IT'S LIKE HE DESPISES THEM FOR HOW EASY THEIR LIVES ARE...
AND HOW THEY DON'T APPRECIATE IT.

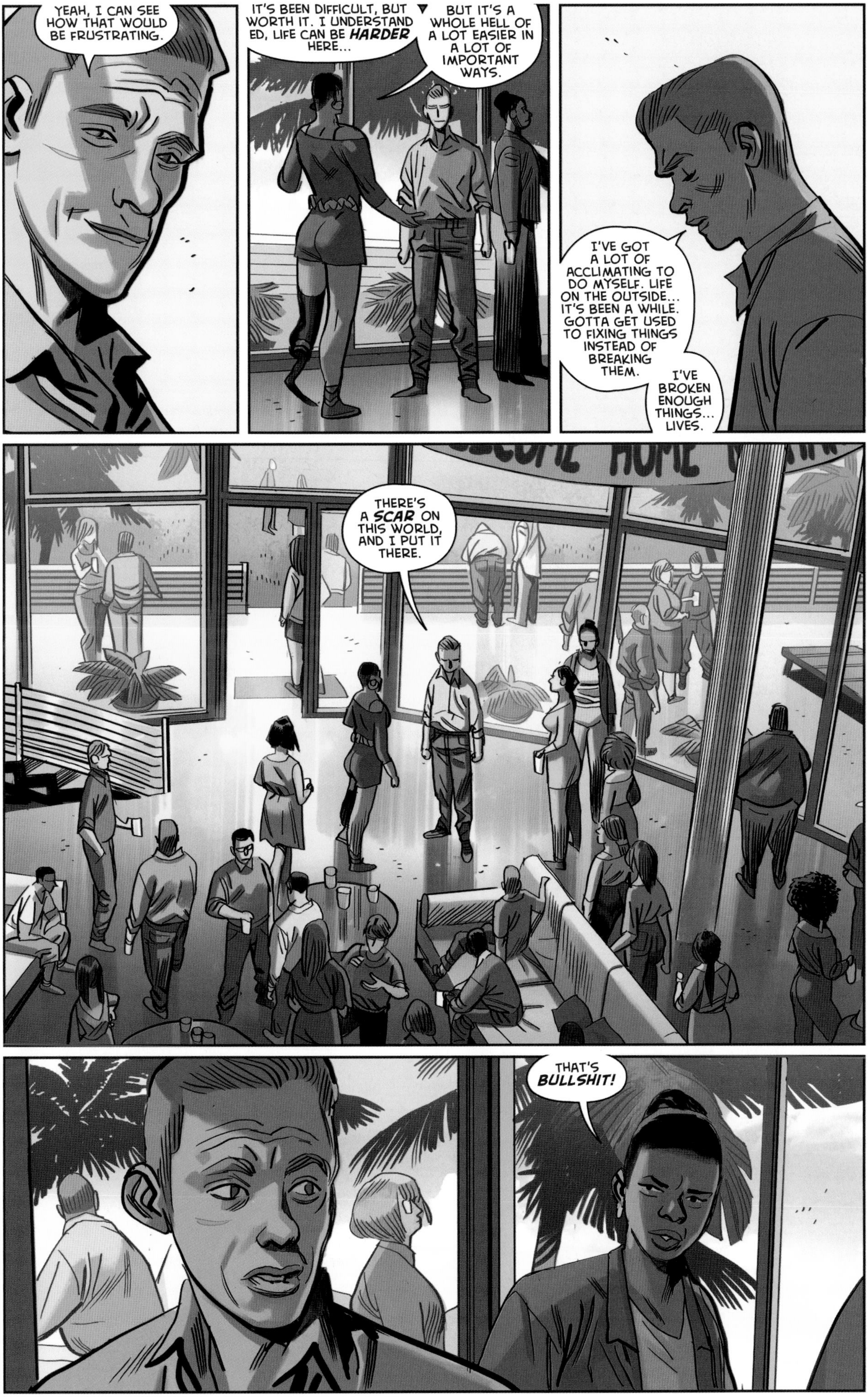
YEAH, I CAN SEE HOW THAT WOULD BE FRUSTRATING.
IT'S BEEN DIFFICULT, BUT WORTH IT. I UNDERSTAND ED, LIFE CAN BE *HARDER* HERE...
BUT IT'S A WHOLE HELL OF A LOT EASIER IN A LOT OF IMPORTANT WAYS.
I'VE GOT A LOT OF ACCLIMATING TO DO MYSELF. LIFE ON THE OUTSIDE... IT'S BEEN A WHILE. GOTTA GET USED TO FIXING THINGS INSTEAD OF BREAKING THEM.
I'VE BROKEN ENOUGH THINGS... LIVES.
THERE'S A *SCAR* ON THIS WORLD, AND I PUT IT THERE.
THAT'S *BULLSHIT!*

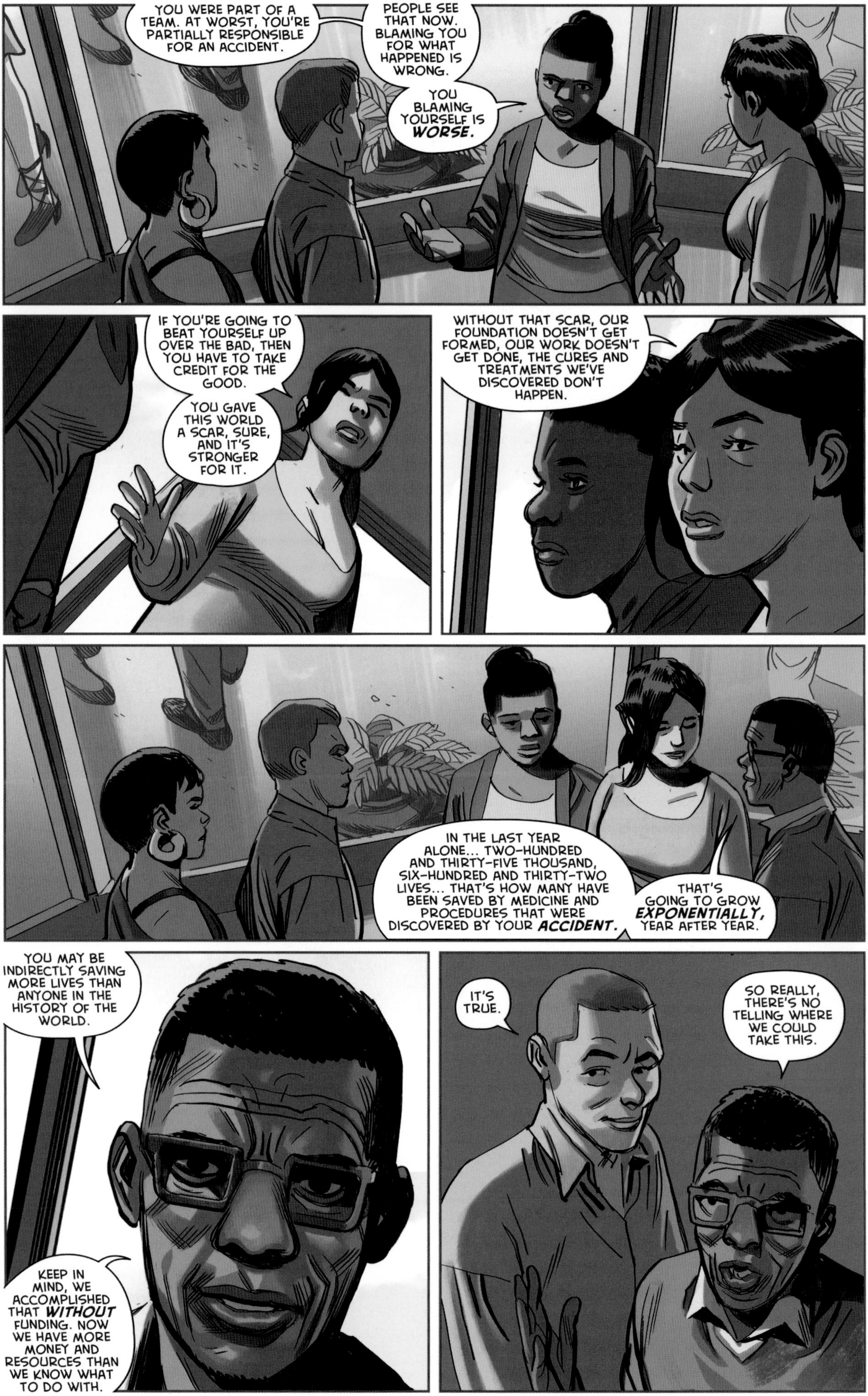
YOU WERE PART OF A TEAM. AT WORST, YOU'RE PARTIALLY RESPONSIBLE FOR AN ACCIDENT.
PEOPLE SEE THAT NOW. BLAMING YOU FOR WHAT HAPPENED IS WRONG.
YOU BLAMING YOURSELF IS WORSE.
IF YOU'RE GOING TO BEAT YOURSELF UP OVER THE BAD, THEN YOU HAVE TO TAKE CREDIT FOR THE GOOD.
YOU GAVE THIS WORLD A SCAR, SURE, AND IT'S STRONGER FOR IT.
WITHOUT THAT SCAR, OUR FOUNDATION DOESN'T GET FORMED, OUR WORK DOESN'T GET DONE, THE CURES AND TREATMENTS WE'VE DISCOVERED DON'T HAPPEN.
IN THE LAST YEAR ALONE... TWO-HUNDRED AND THIRTY-FIVE THOUSAND, SIX-HUNDRED AND THIRTY-TWO LIVES... THAT'S HOW MANY HAVE BEEN SAVED BY MEDICINE AND PROCEDURES THAT WERE DISCOVERED BY YOUR ACCIDENT.
THAT'S GOING TO GROW EXPONENTIALLY, YEAR AFTER YEAR.
YOU MAY BE INDIRECTLY SAVING MORE LIVES THAN ANYONE IN THE HISTORY OF THE WORLD.
KEEP IN MIND, WE ACCOMPLISHED THAT WITHOUT FUNDING. NOW WE HAVE MORE MONEY AND RESOURCES THAN WE KNOW WHAT TO DO WITH.
IT'S TRUE.
SO REALLY, THERE'S NO TELLING WHERE WE COULD TAKE THIS.

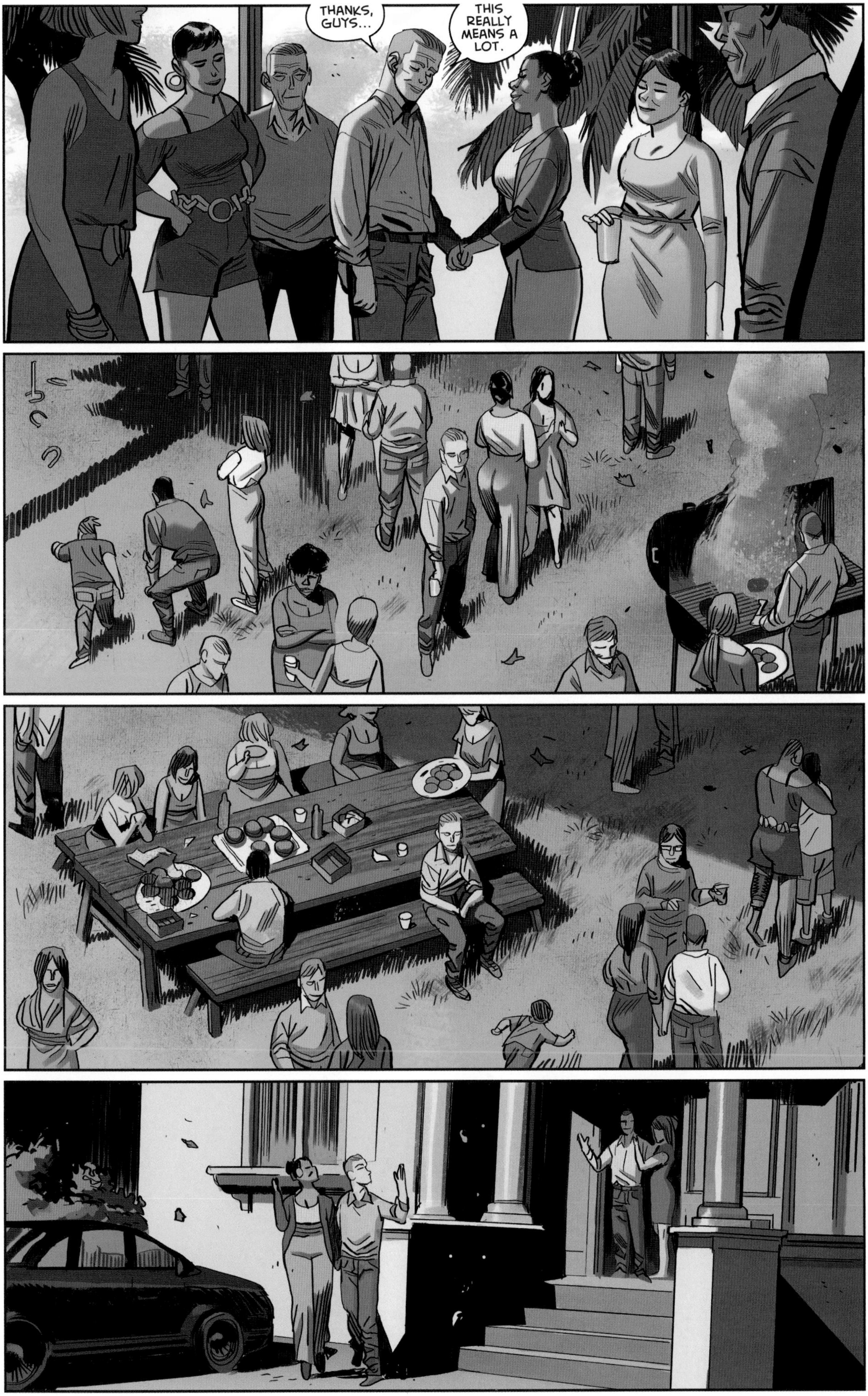
THANKS, GUYS...
THIS REALLY MEANS A LOT.

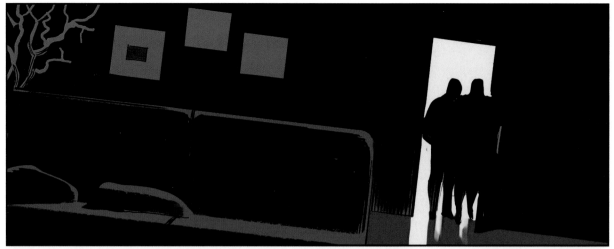

HAVE A GOOD TIME?

YEAH.

YOU HARDLY SAID A WORD AFTER EVERYONE'S BIG PEP TALK.

YEAH... THAT...

THAT *HELPED.*

BEING OUT... ALL THE EYES ON ME... I CAN'T HELP BUT WONDER WHAT PEOPLE THINK ABOUT ME. I CAN ONLY IMAGINE WHAT THEY THINK ABOUT WHAT I DID AND HOW IT MAY HAVE HURT THEM OR SOMEONE THEY LOVED.

NOW THAT EVERYONE KNOWS THE TRUTH ABOUT WHAT HAPPENED... IT REALLY WEARS ON ME.

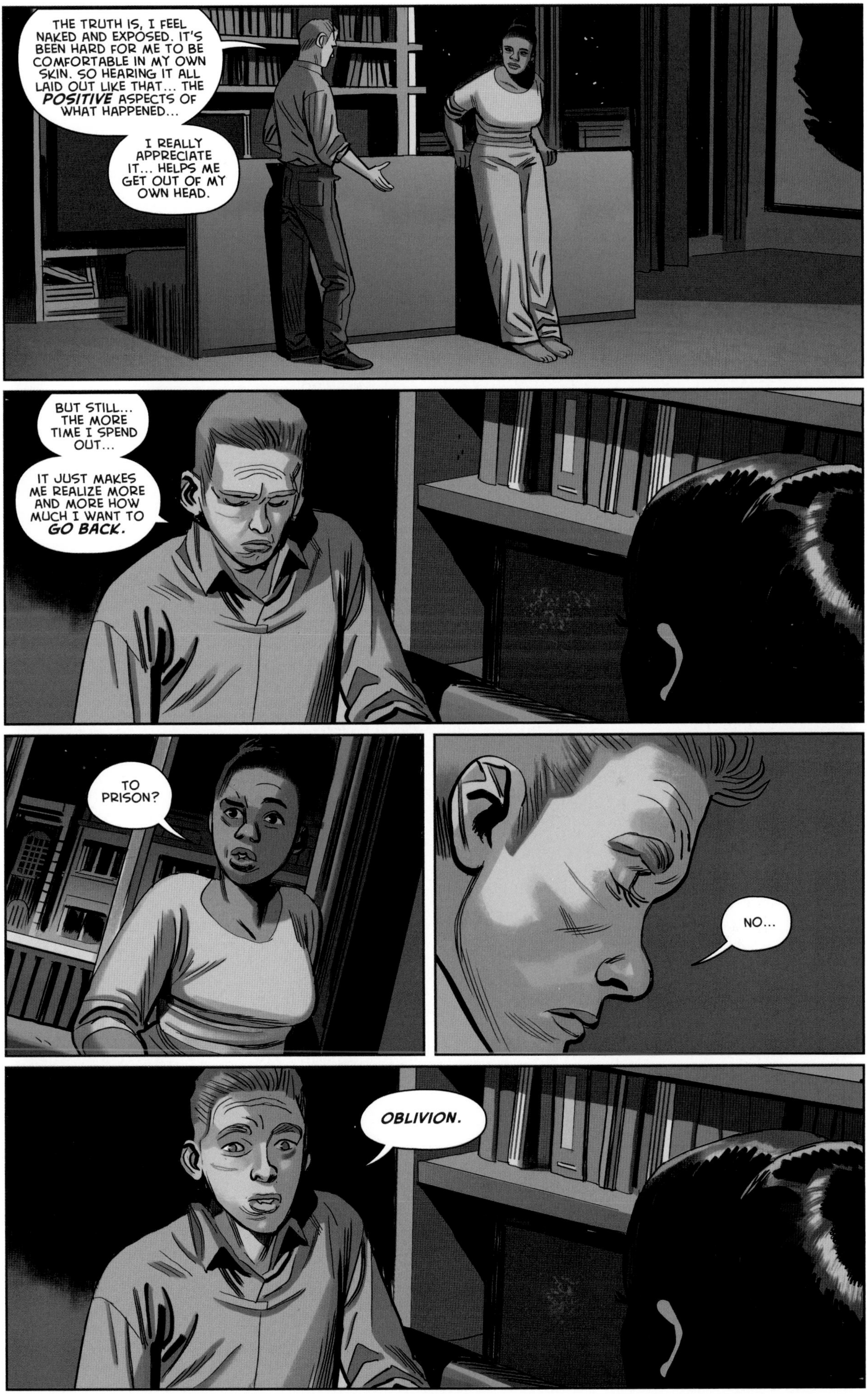
THE TRUTH IS, I FEEL NAKED AND EXPOSED. IT'S BEEN HARD FOR ME TO BE COMFORTABLE IN MY OWN SKIN. SO HEARING IT ALL LAID OUT LIKE THAT... THE POSITIVE ASPECTS OF WHAT HAPPENED...
I REALLY APPRECIATE IT... HELPS ME GET OUT OF MY OWN HEAD.
BUT STILL... THE MORE TIME I SPEND OUT...
IT JUST MAKES ME REALIZE MORE AND MORE HOW MUCH I WANT TO GO BACK.
TO PRISON?
NO...
OBLIVION.

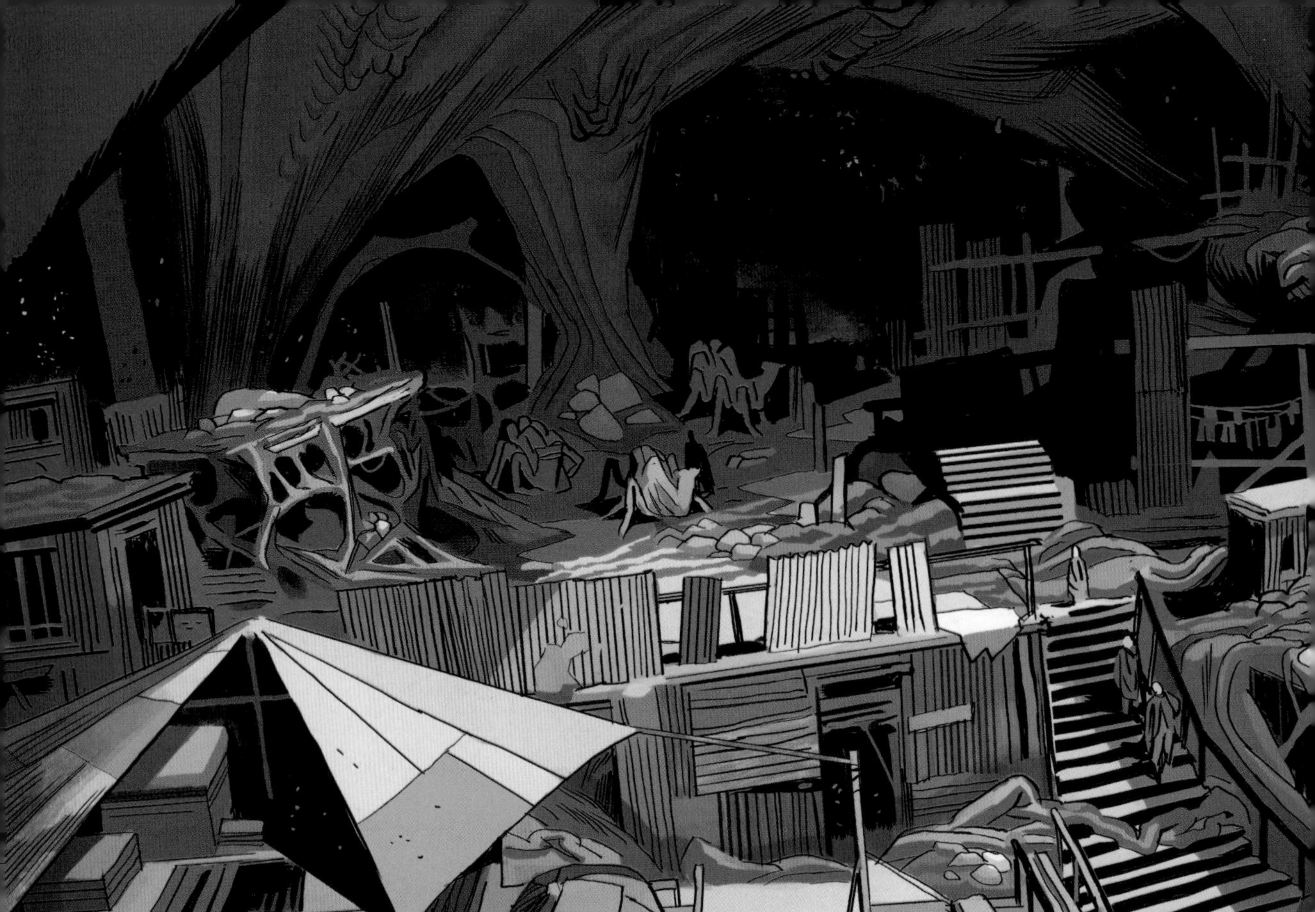

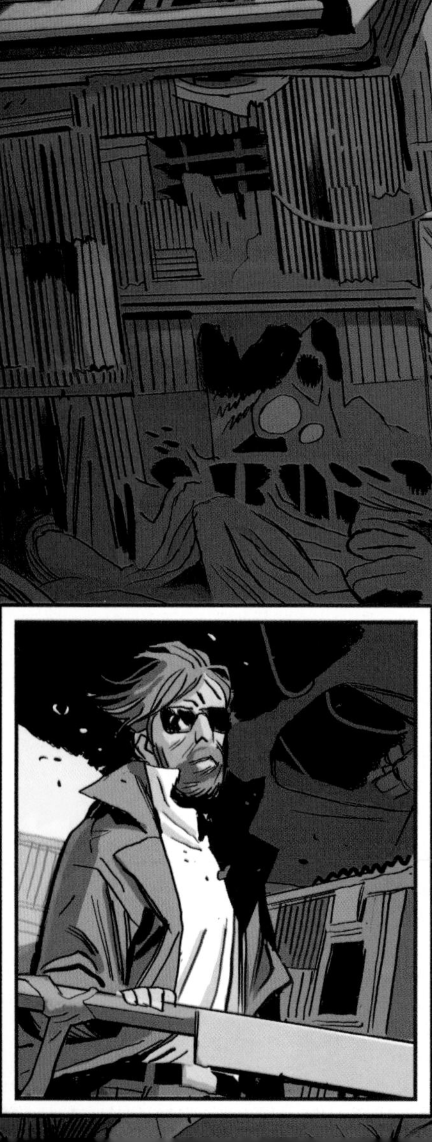

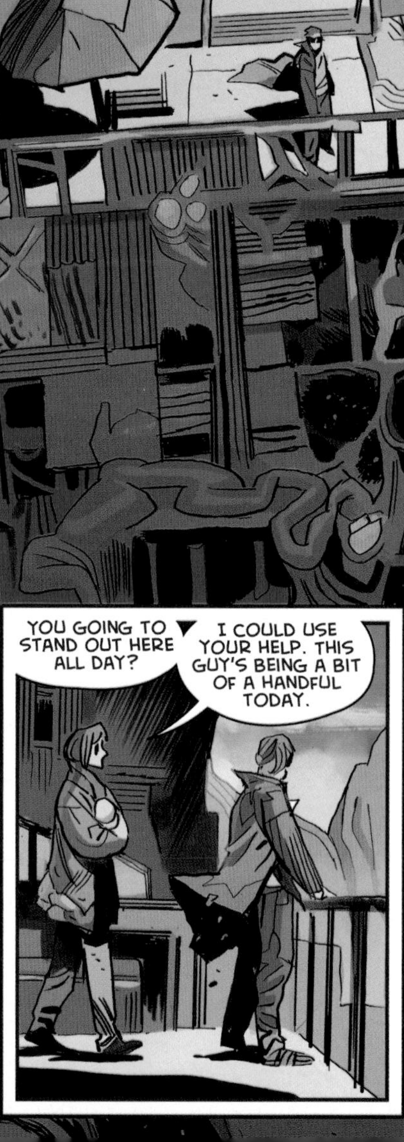
YOU GOING TO STAND OUT HERE ALL DAY?
I COULD USE YOUR HELP. THIS GUY'S BEING A BIT OF A HANDFUL TODAY.

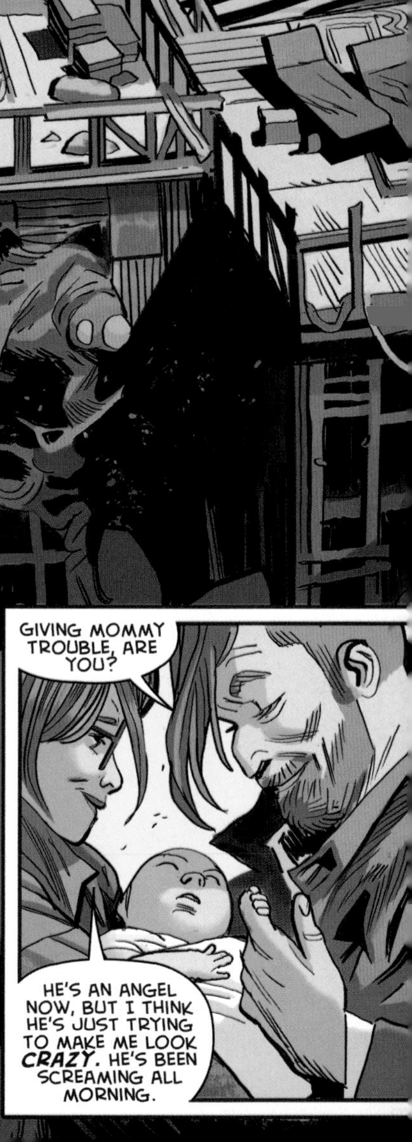
GIVING MOMMY TROUBLE, ARE YOU?
HE'S AN ANGEL NOW, BUT I THINK HE'S JUST TRYING TO MAKE ME LOOK ***CRAZY***. HE'S BEEN SCREAMING ALL MORNING.

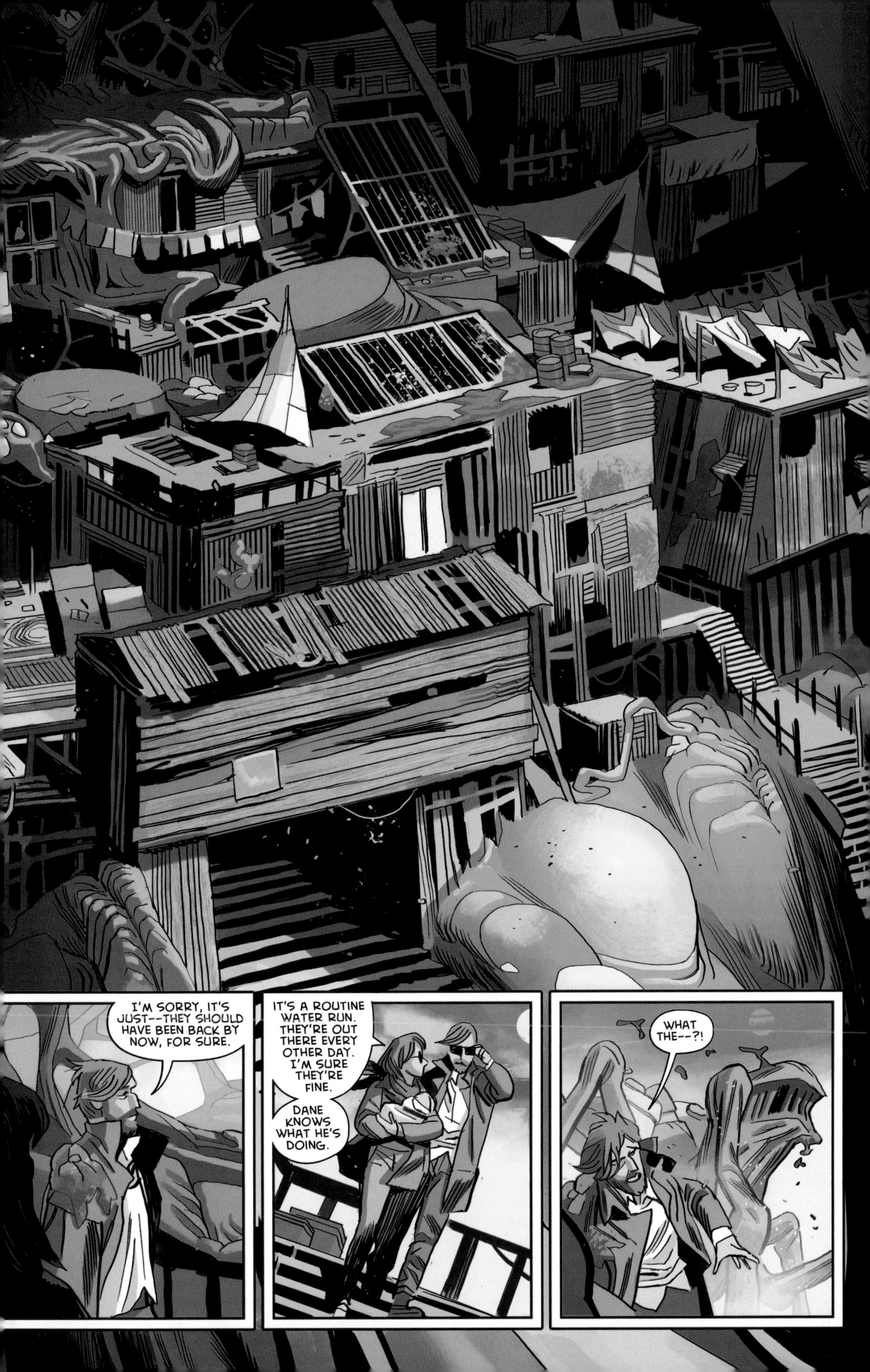
I'M SORRY, IT'S JUST--THEY SHOULD HAVE BEEN BACK BY NOW, FOR SURE.
IT'S A ROUTINE WATER RUN. THEY'RE OUT THERE EVERY OTHER DAY. I'M SURE THEY'RE FINE.
DANE KNOWS WHAT HE'S DOING.
WHAT THE--?!

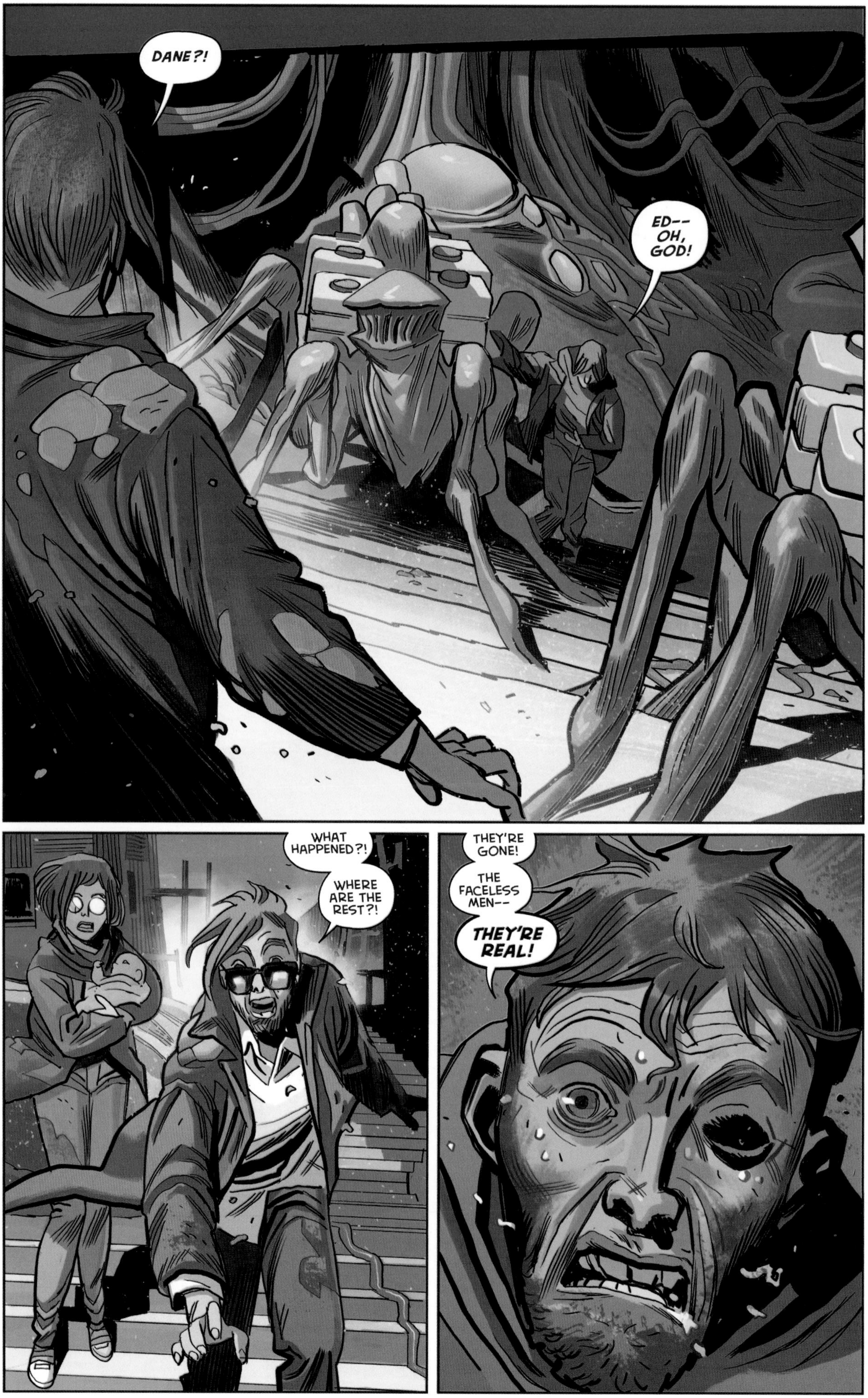
DANE?!
ED-- OH, GOD!
WHAT HAPPENED?!
WHERE ARE THE REST?!
THEY'RE GONE!
THE FACELESS MEN--
THEY'RE REAL!

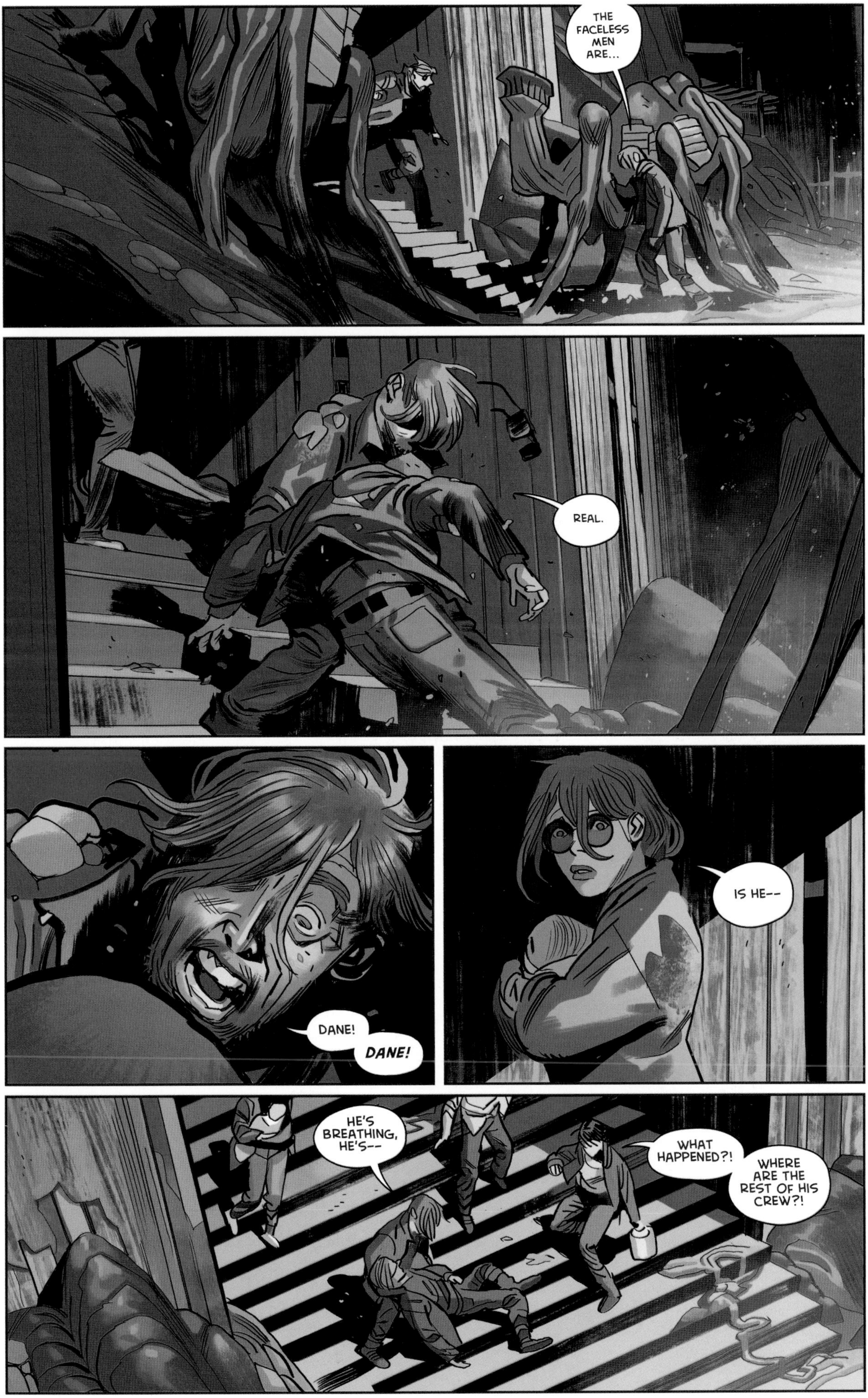

THE FACELESS MEN ARE...
REAL.
DANE! DANE!
IS HE--
HE'S BREATHING, HE'S--
WHAT HAPPENED?!
WHERE ARE THE REST OF HIS CREW?!

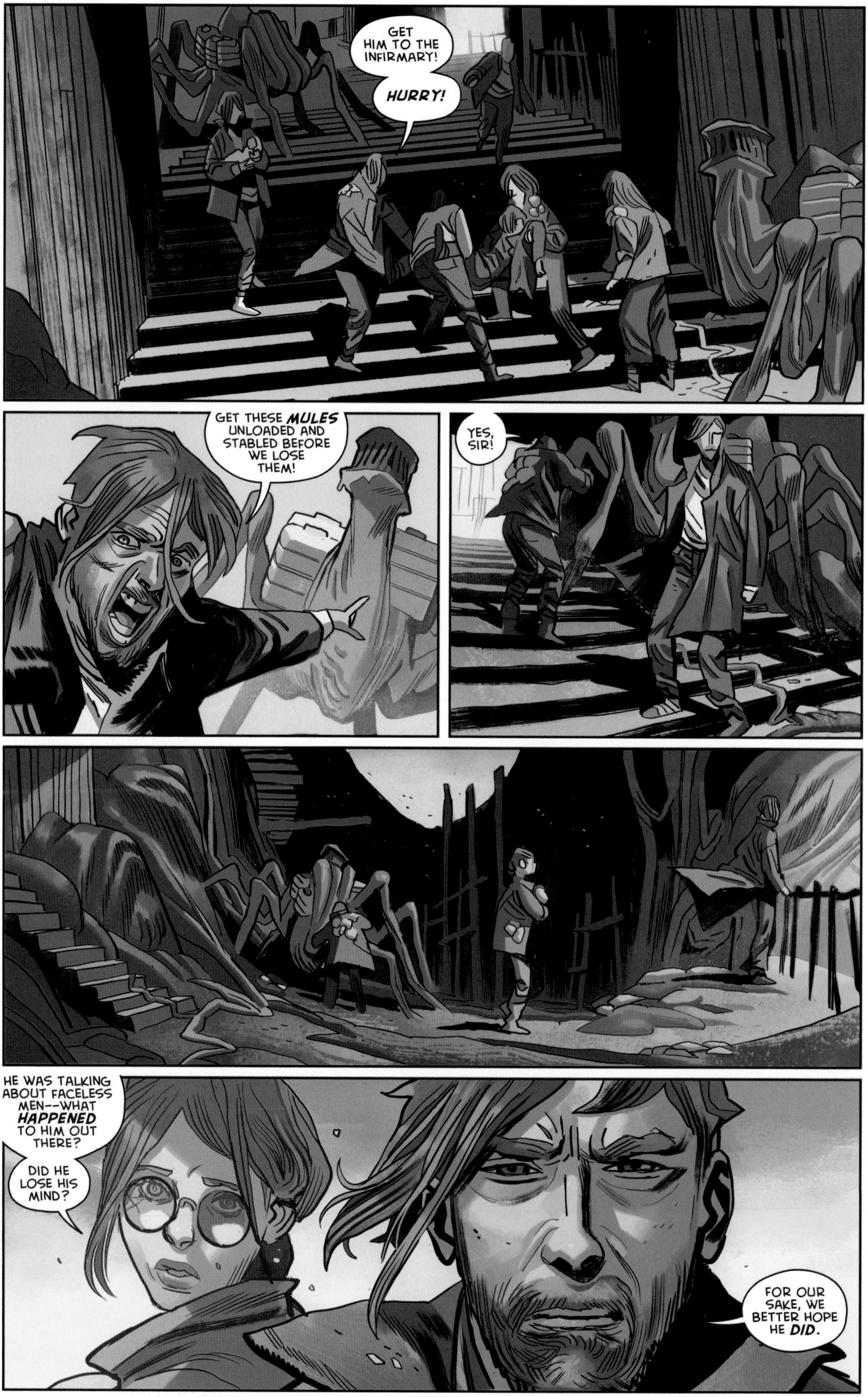
GET HIM TO THE INFIRMARY!
HURRY!
GET THESE MULES UNLOADED AND STABLED BEFORE WE LOSE THEM!
YES, SIR!
HE WAS TALKING ABOUT FACELESS MEN--WHAT HAPPENED TO HIM OUT THERE?
DID HE LOSE HIS MIND?
FOR OUR SAKE, WE BETTER HOPE HE DID.

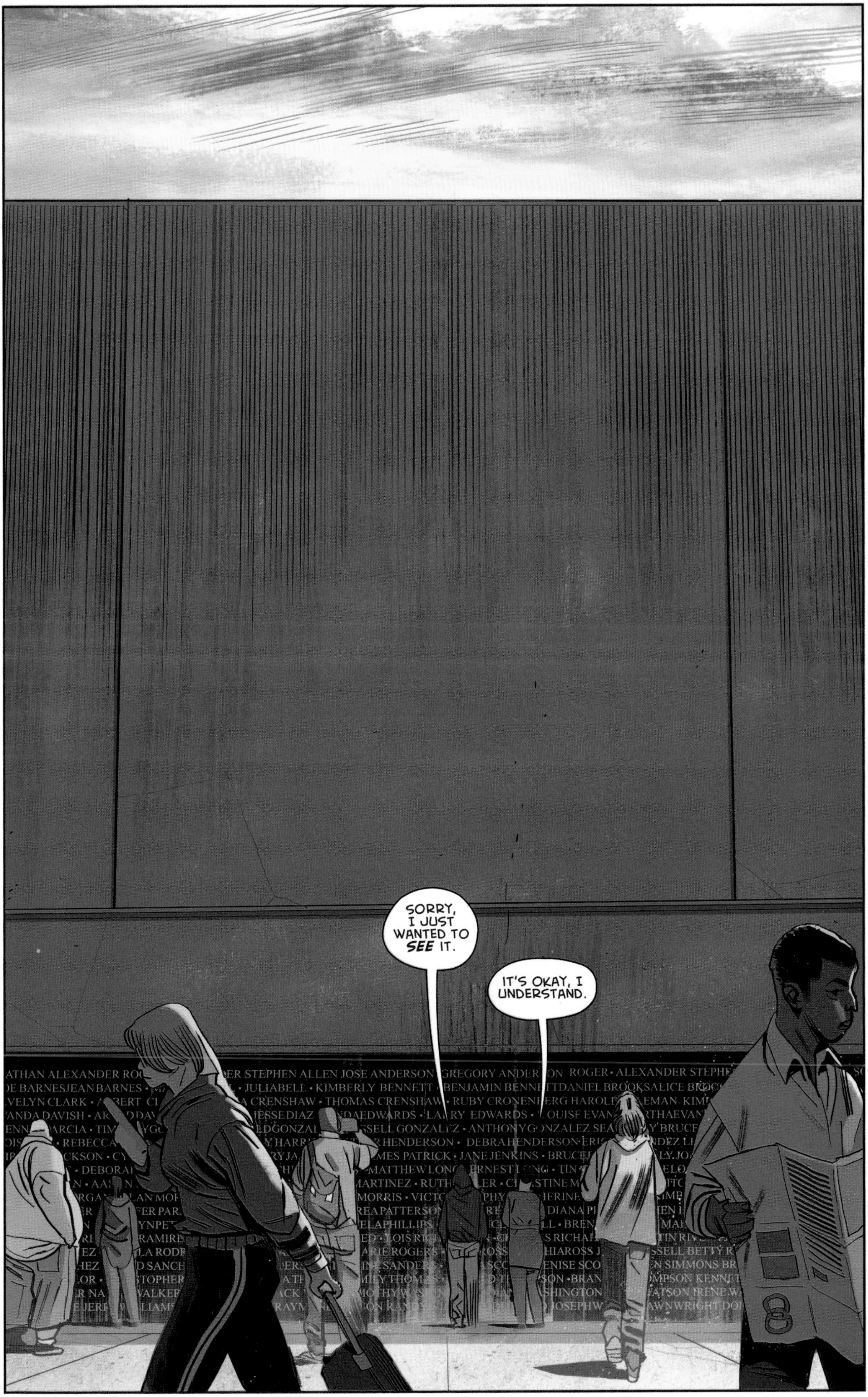
SORRY, I JUST WANTED TO SEE IT.
IT'S OKAY, I UNDERSTAND.

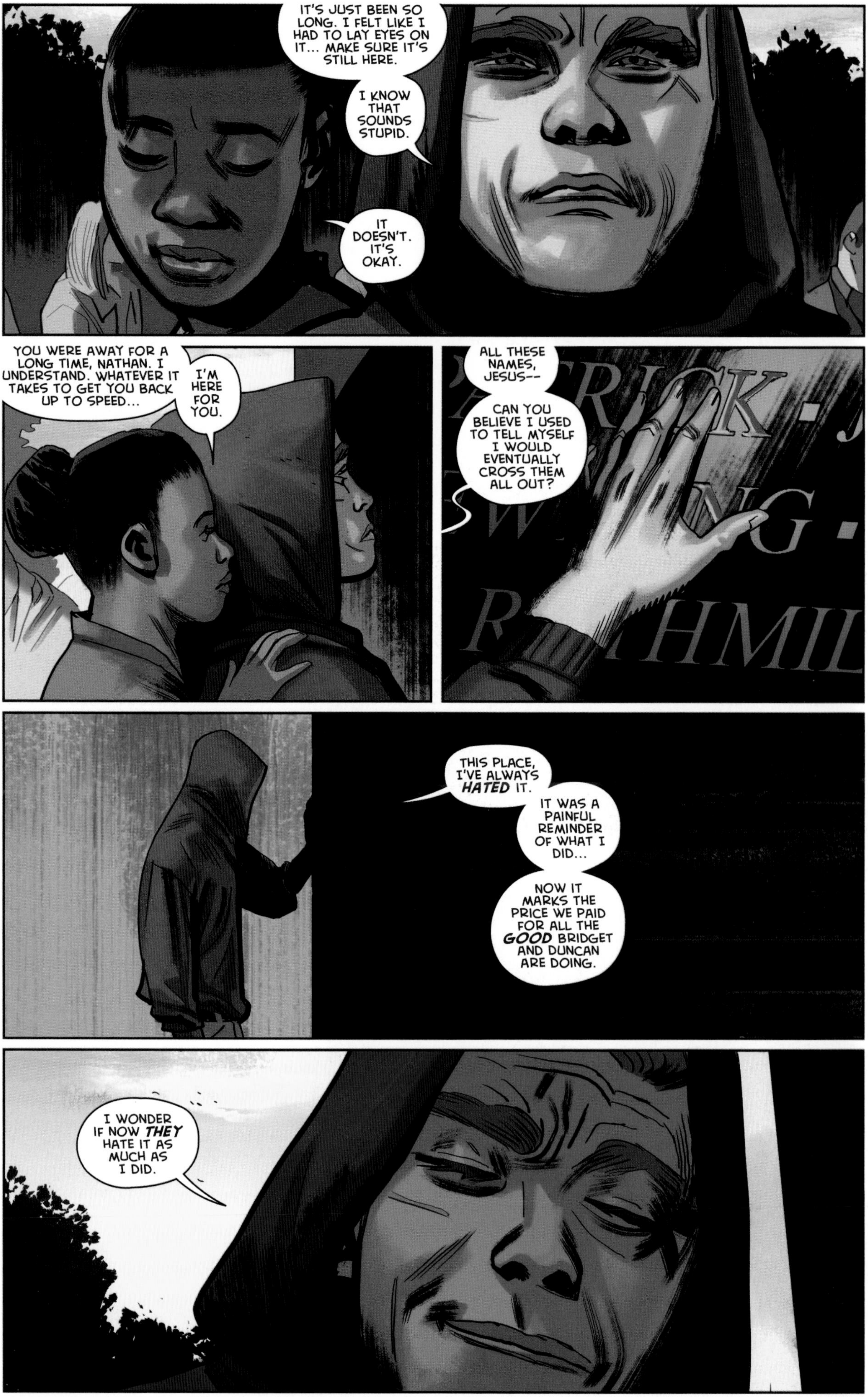
IT'S JUST BEEN SO LONG. I FELT LIKE I HAD TO LAY EYES ON IT... MAKE SURE IT'S STILL HERE.
I KNOW THAT SOUNDS STUPID.
IT DOESN'T. IT'S OKAY.
YOU WERE AWAY FOR A LONG TIME, NATHAN. I UNDERSTAND. WHATEVER IT TAKES TO GET YOU BACK UP TO SPEED...
I'M HERE FOR YOU.
ALL THESE NAMES, JESUS--
CAN YOU BELIEVE I USED TO TELL MYSELF I WOULD EVENTUALLY CROSS THEM ALL OUT?
THIS PLACE, I'VE ALWAYS HATED IT.
IT WAS A PAINFUL REMINDER OF WHAT I DID...
NOW IT MARKS THE PRICE WE PAID FOR ALL THE GOOD BRIDGET AND DUNCAN ARE DOING.
I WONDER IF NOW THEY HATE IT AS MUCH AS I DID.

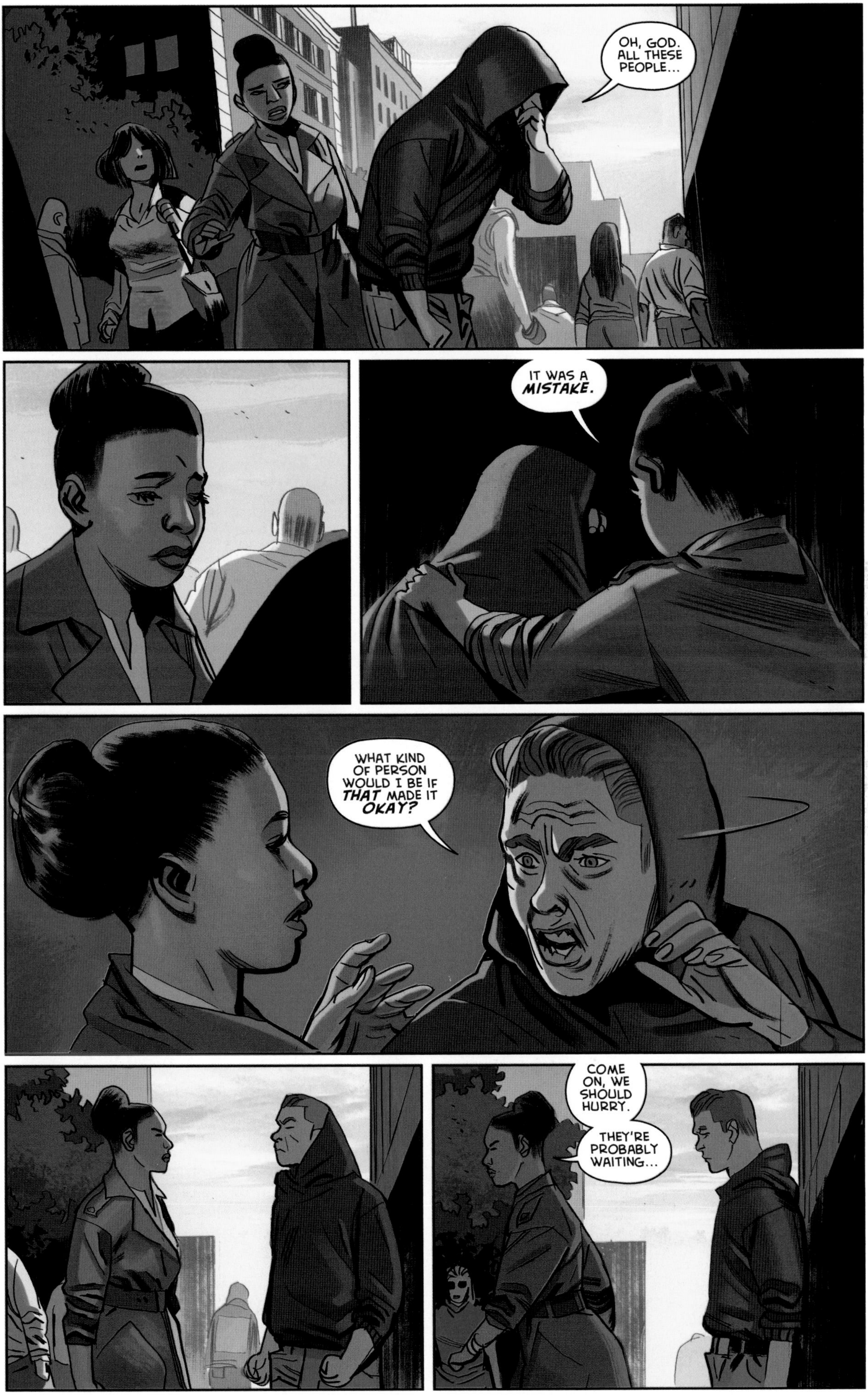
OH, GOD. ALL THESE PEOPLE...
IT WAS A MISTAKE.
WHAT KIND OF PERSON WOULD I BE IF THAT MADE IT OKAY?
COME ON, WE SHOULD HURRY.
THEY'RE PROBABLY WAITING...

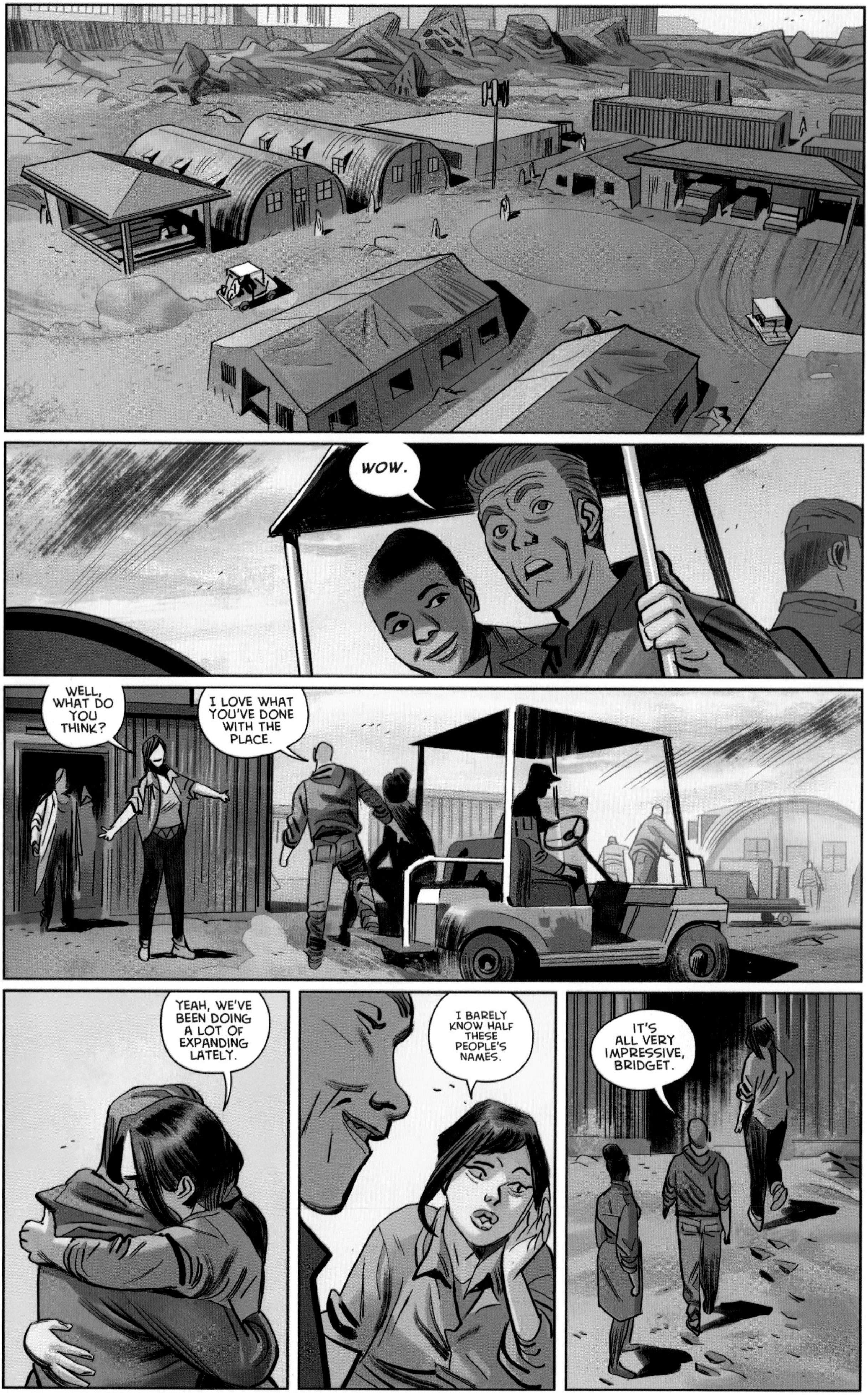
WOW.
WELL, WHAT DO YOU THINK?
I LOVE WHAT YOU'VE DONE WITH THE PLACE.
YEAH, WE'VE BEEN DOING A LOT OF EXPANDING LATELY.
I BARELY KNOW HALF THESE PEOPLE'S NAMES.
IT'S ALL VERY IMPRESSIVE, BRIDGET.

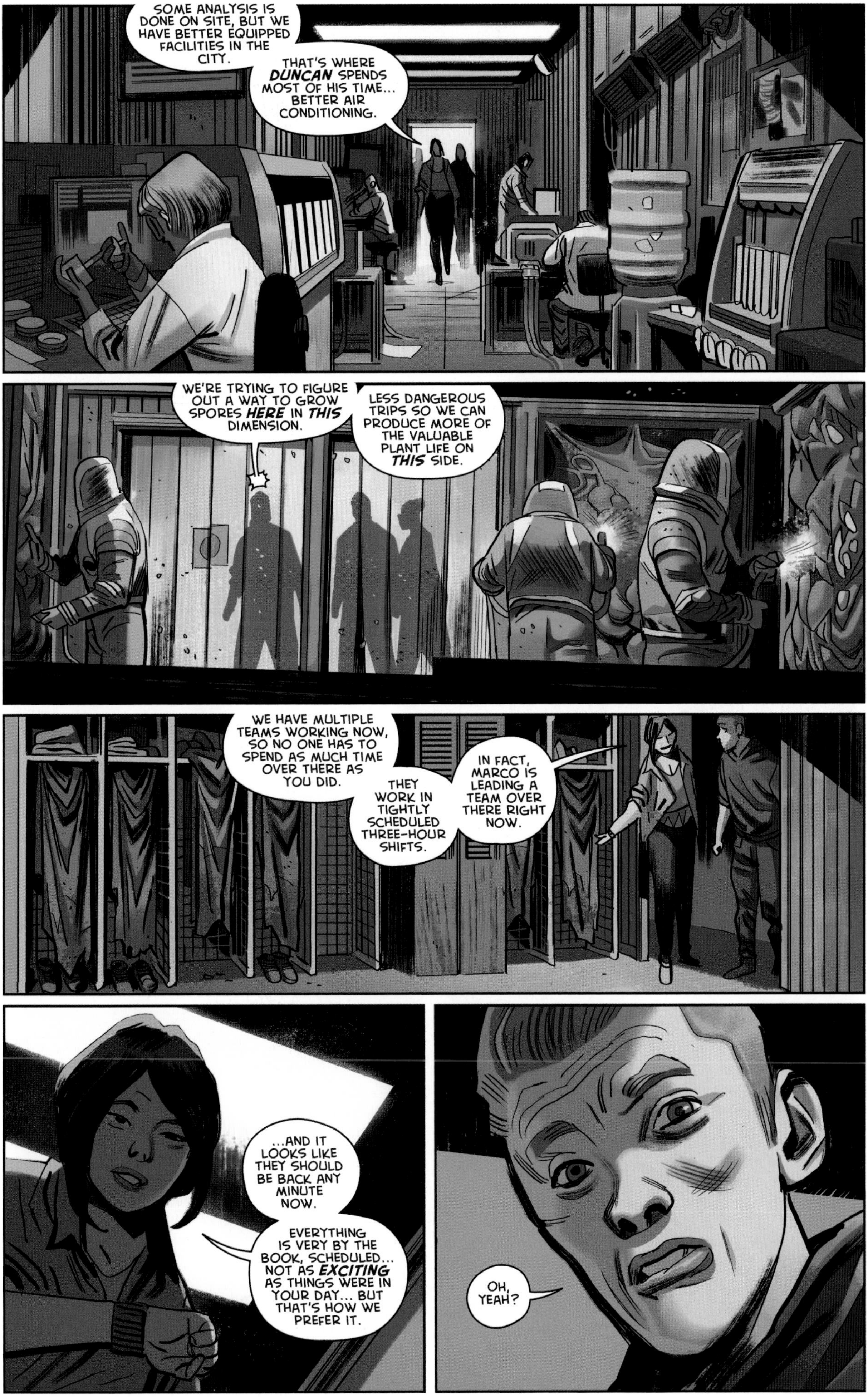
SOME ANALYSIS IS DONE ON SITE, BUT WE HAVE BETTER EQUIPPED FACILITIES IN THE CITY.
THAT'S WHERE **DUNCAN** SPENDS MOST OF HIS TIME... BETTER AIR CONDITIONING.
WE'RE TRYING TO FIGURE OUT A WAY TO GROW SPORES **HERE** IN **THIS** DIMENSION.
LESS DANGEROUS TRIPS SO WE CAN PRODUCE MORE OF THE VALUABLE PLANT LIFE ON **THIS** SIDE.
WE HAVE MULTIPLE TEAMS WORKING NOW, SO NO ONE HAS TO SPEND AS MUCH TIME OVER THERE AS YOU DID.
THEY WORK IN TIGHTLY SCHEDULED THREE-HOUR SHIFTS.
IN FACT, MARCO IS LEADING A TEAM OVER THERE RIGHT NOW.
...AND IT LOOKS LIKE THEY SHOULD BE BACK ANY MINUTE NOW.
EVERYTHING IS VERY BY THE BOOK, SCHEDULED... NOT AS **EXCITING** AS THINGS WERE IN YOUR DAY... BUT THAT'S HOW WE PREFER IT.
OH, YEAH?

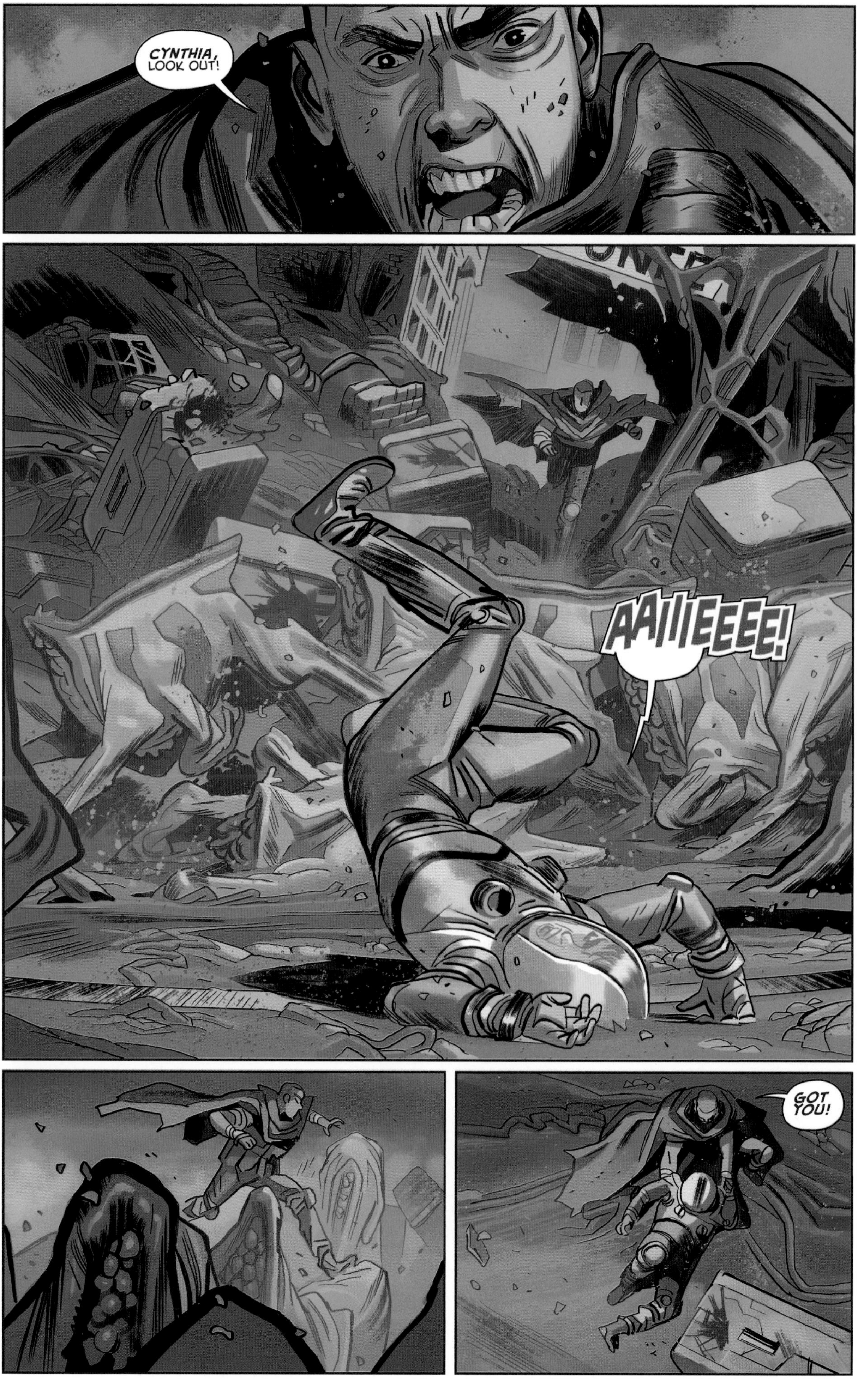
CYNTHIA, LOOK OUT!
AAIIIEEEE!
GOT YOU!

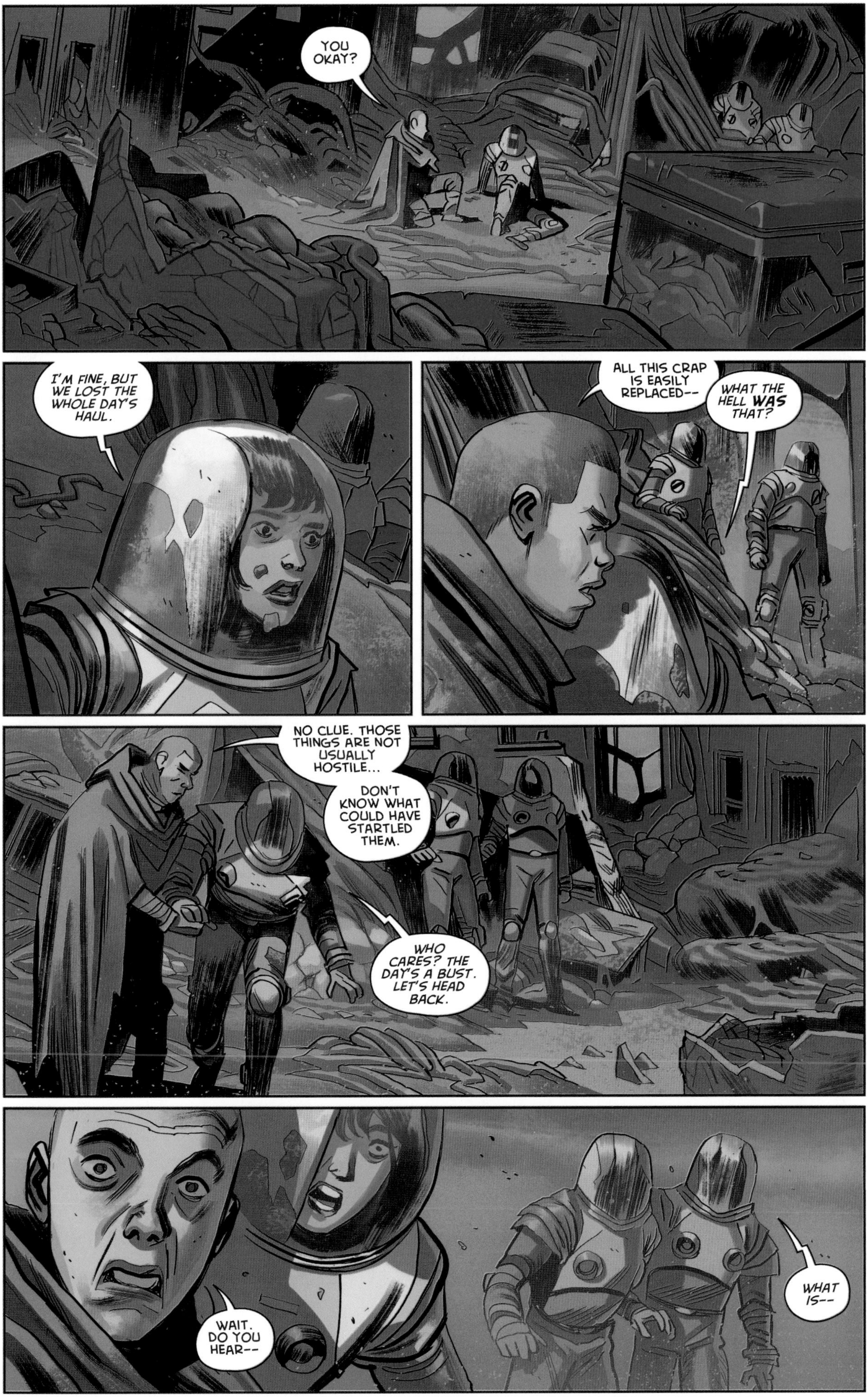
YOU OKAY?
I'M FINE, BUT WE LOST THE WHOLE DAY'S HAUL.
ALL THIS CRAP IS EASILY REPLACED--
WHAT THE HELL **WAS** THAT?
NO CLUE. THOSE THINGS ARE NOT USUALLY HOSTILE...
DON'T KNOW WHAT COULD HAVE STARTLED THEM.
WHO CARES? THE DAY'S A BUST. LET'S HEAD BACK.
WAIT. DO YOU HEAR--
WHAT IS--

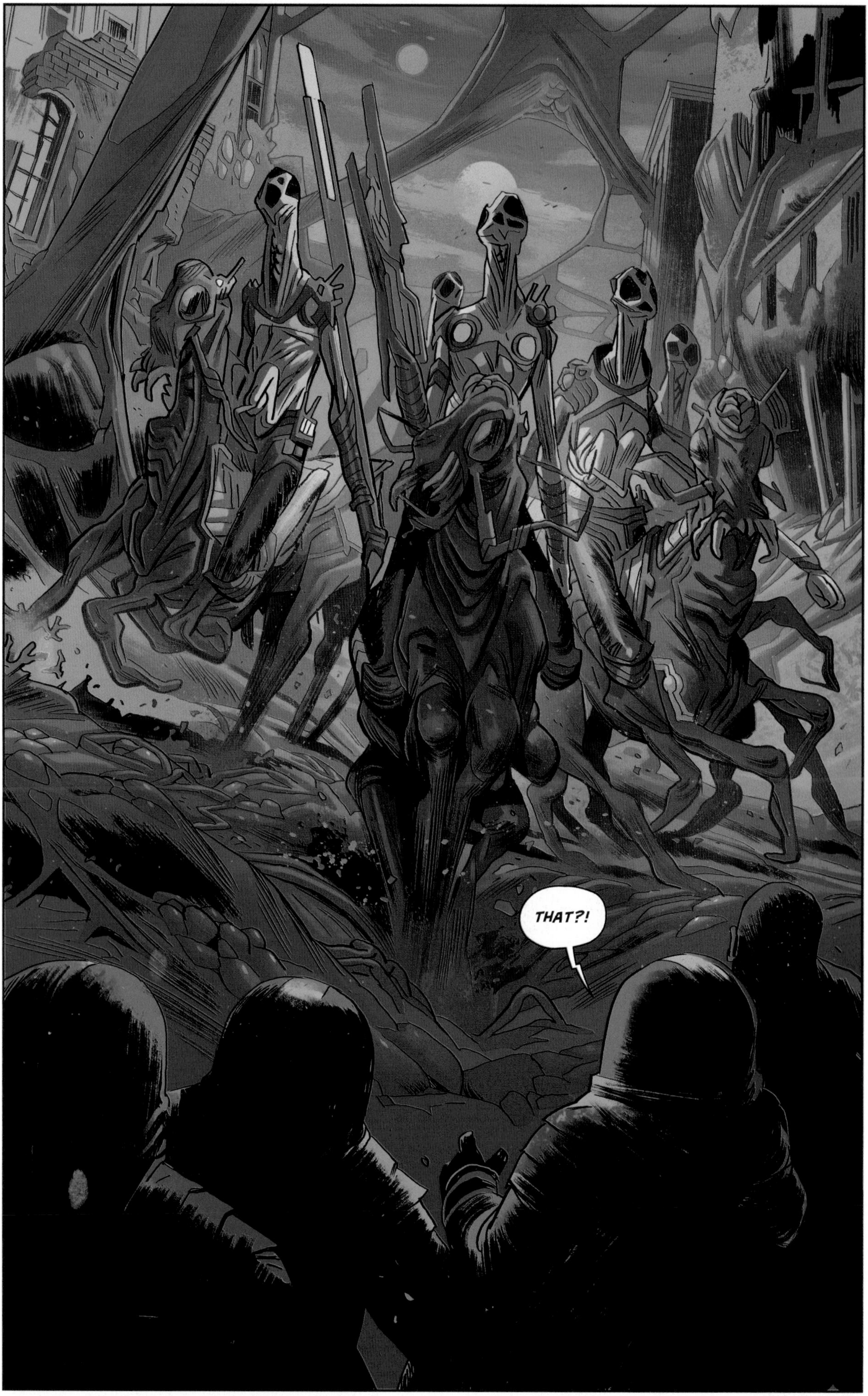
THAT?!

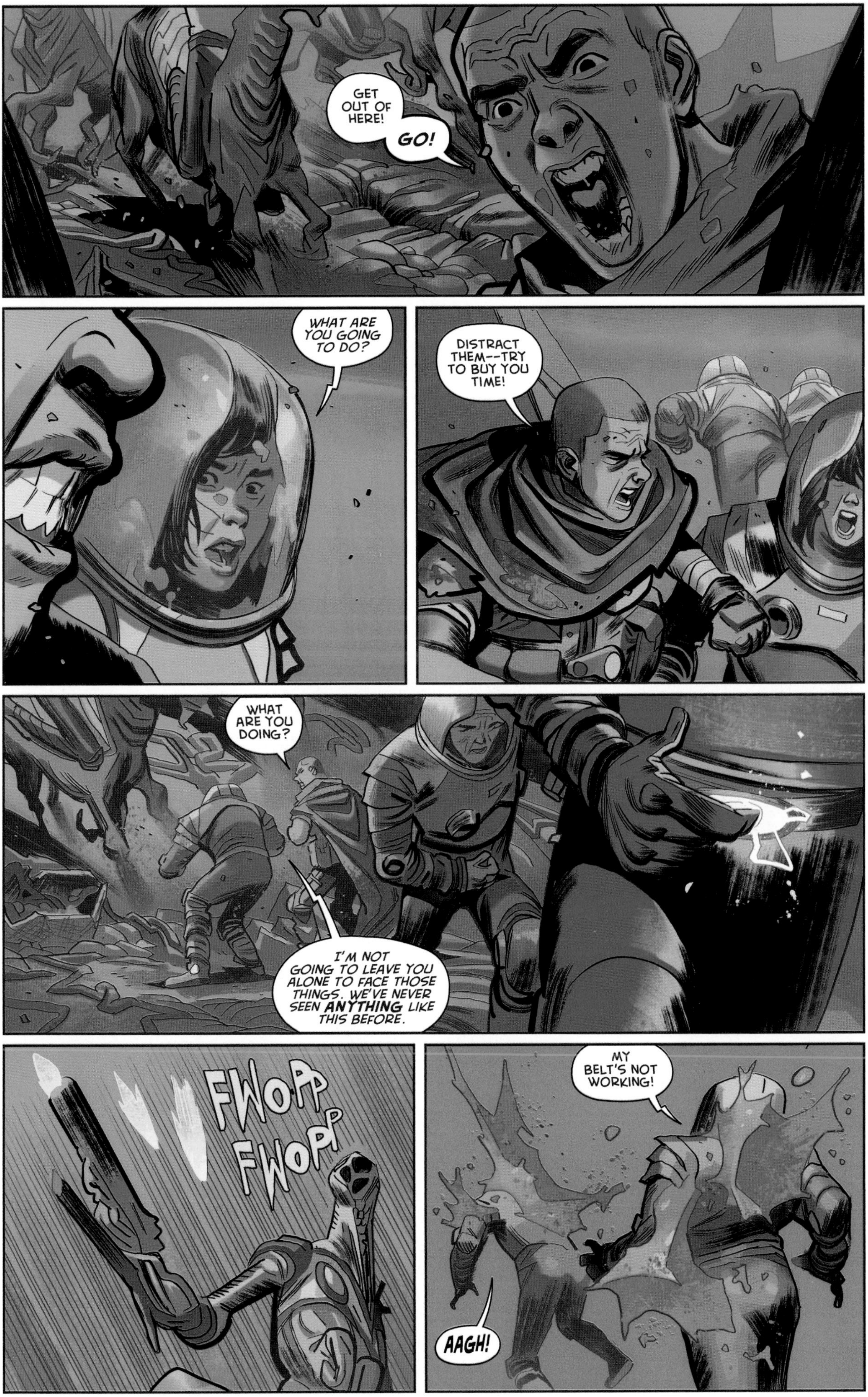
GET OUT OF HERE!
GO!
WHAT ARE YOU GOING TO DO?
DISTRACT THEM--TRY TO BUY YOU TIME!
WHAT ARE YOU DOING?
I'M NOT GOING TO LEAVE YOU ALONE TO FACE THOSE THINGS. WE'VE NEVER SEEN ANYTHING LIKE THIS BEFORE.
FWOPP
FWOPP
MY BELT'S NOT WORKING!
AAGH!

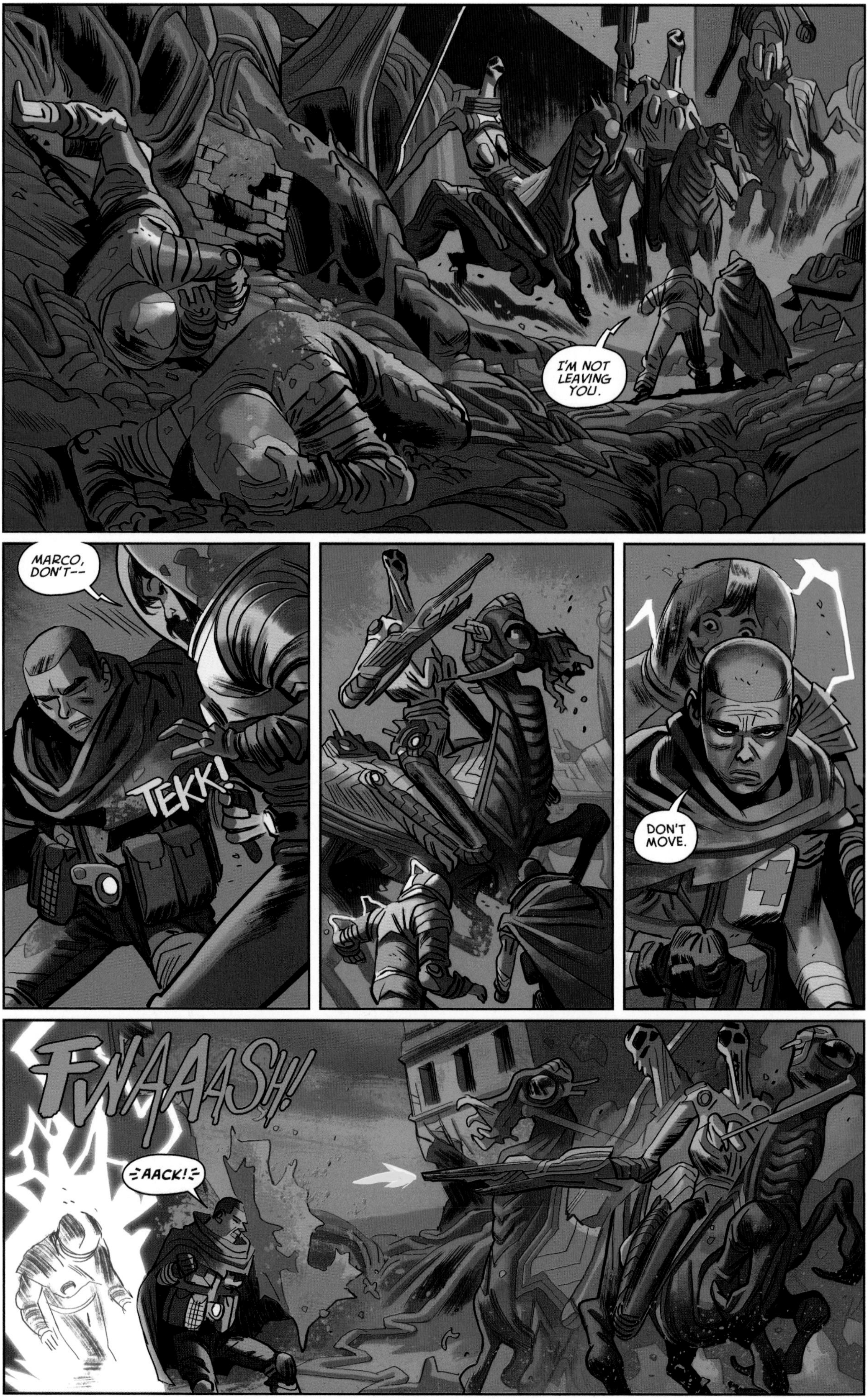
I'M NOT LEAVING YOU.
MARCO, DON'T--
TEKK!
DON'T MOVE.
FWAAAASH!
AACK!

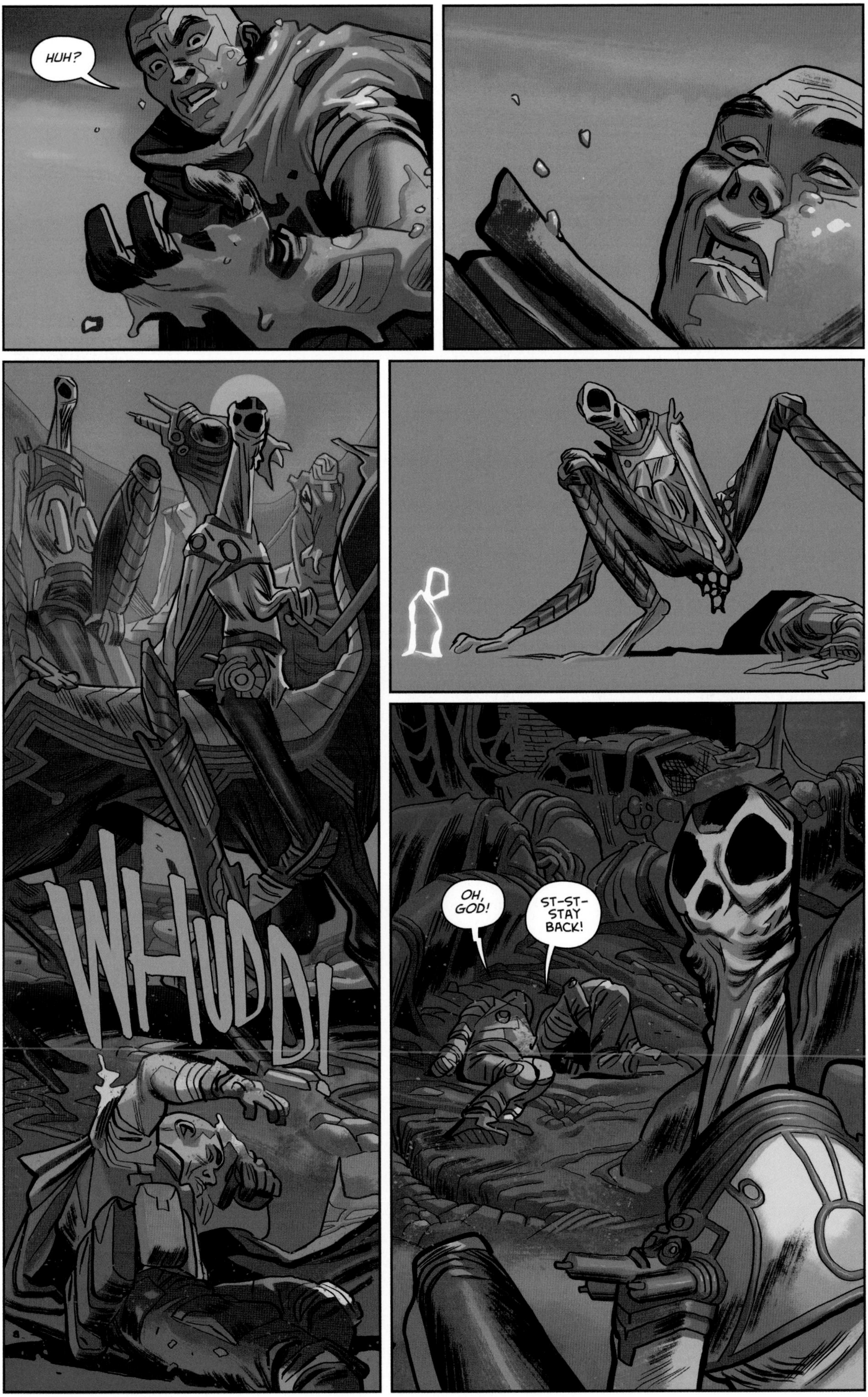
HUH?
WHUDD!
OH, GOD!
ST-ST-STAY BACK!

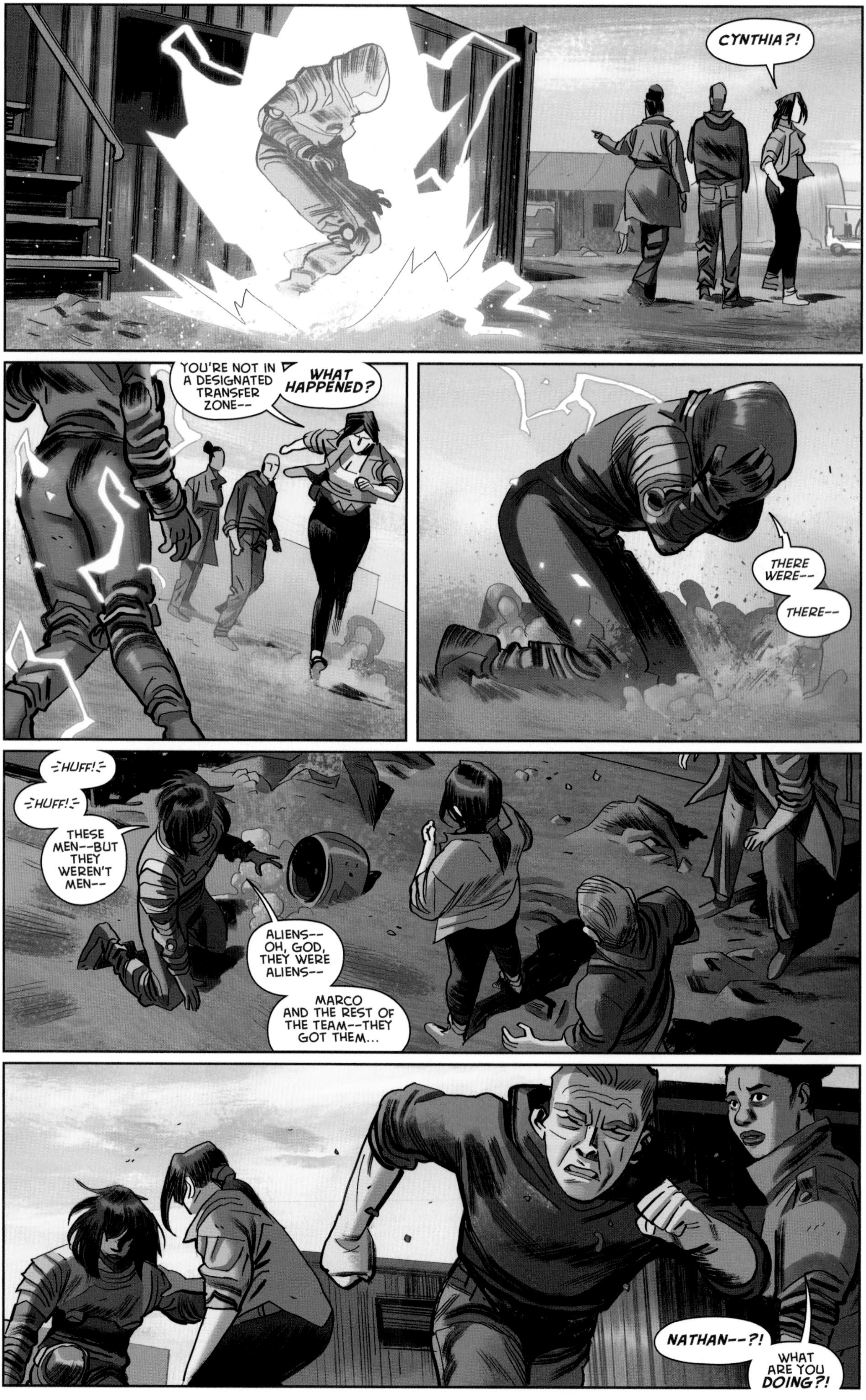
CYNTHIA?!
YOU'RE NOT IN A DESIGNATED TRANSFER ZONE--
WHAT HAPPENED?
THERE WERE--
THERE--
HUFF!
HUFF!
THESE MEN--BUT THEY WEREN'T MEN--
ALIENS-- OH, GOD, THEY WERE ALIENS--
MARCO AND THE REST OF THE TEAM--THEY GOT THEM...
NATHAN--?!
WHAT ARE YOU DOING?!

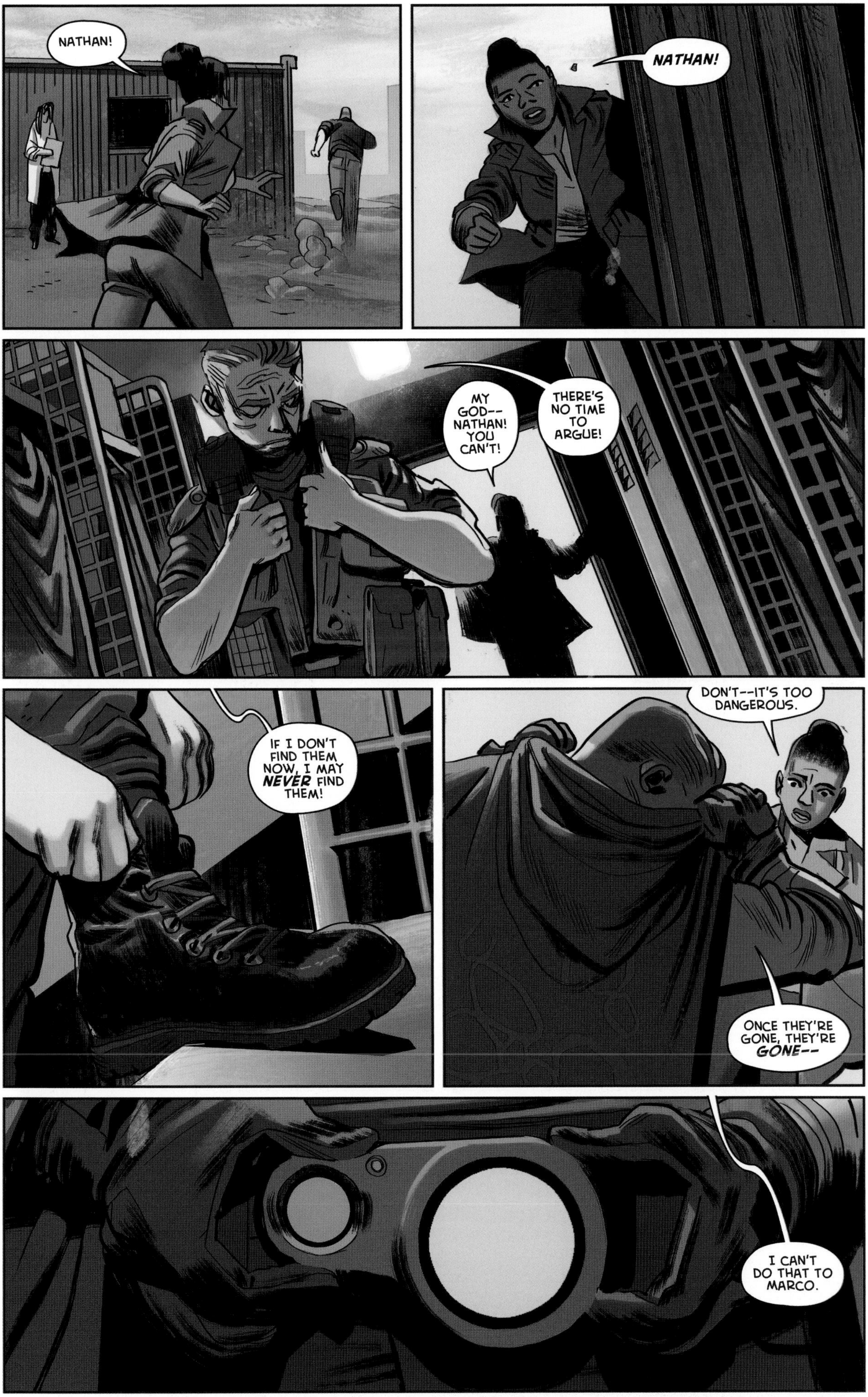
NATHAN!
NATHAN!
MY GOD--NATHAN! YOU CAN'T!
THERE'S NO TIME TO ARGUE!
IF I DON'T FIND THEM NOW, I MAY NEVER FIND THEM!
DON'T--IT'S TOO DANGEROUS.
ONCE THEY'RE GONE, THEY'RE GONE--
I CAN'T DO THAT TO MARCO.

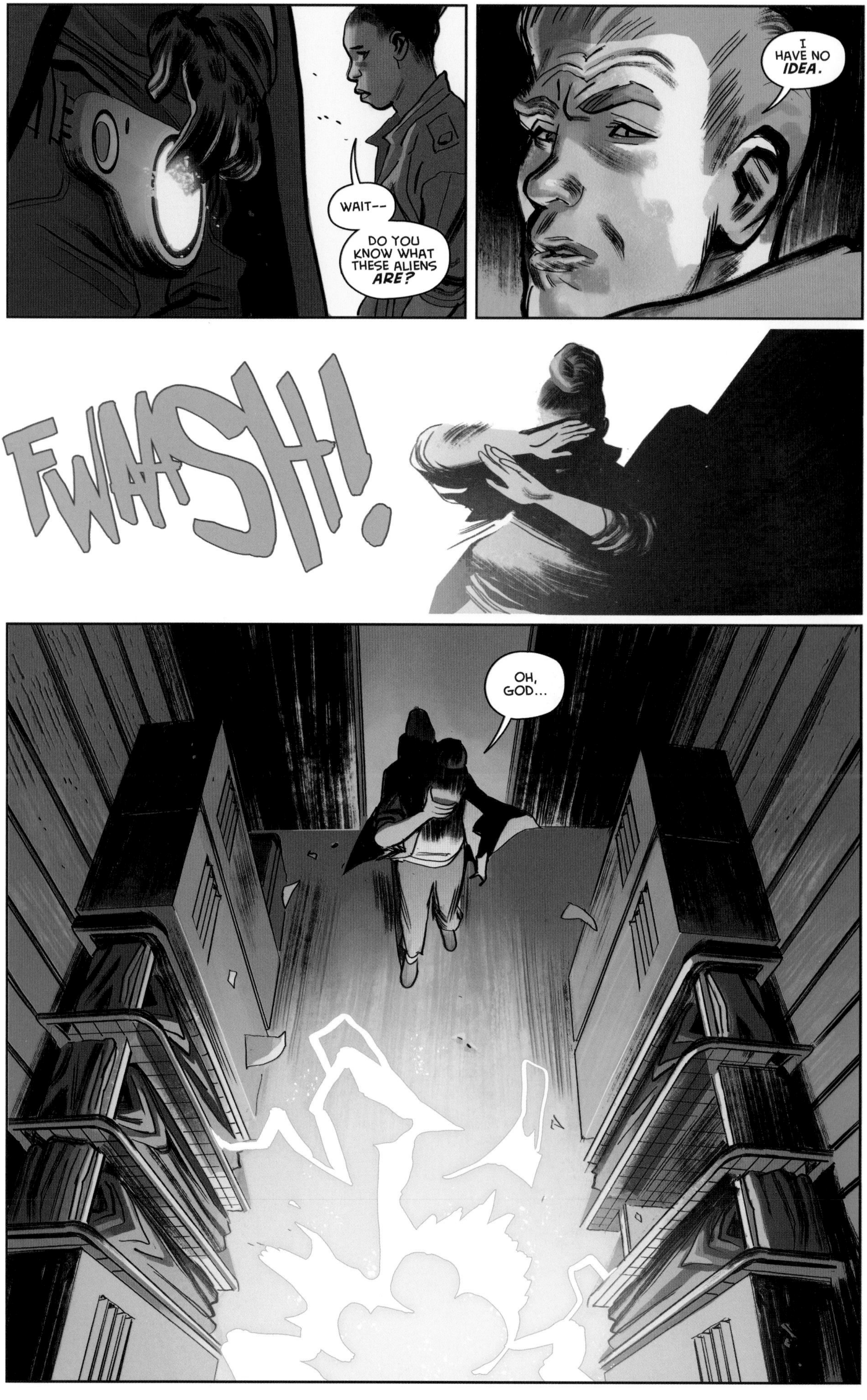
...
WAIT--
DO YOU KNOW WHAT THESE ALIENS ARE?
I HAVE NO IDEA.
FWASH!
OH, GOD...

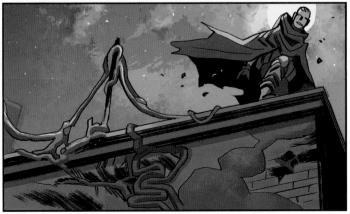

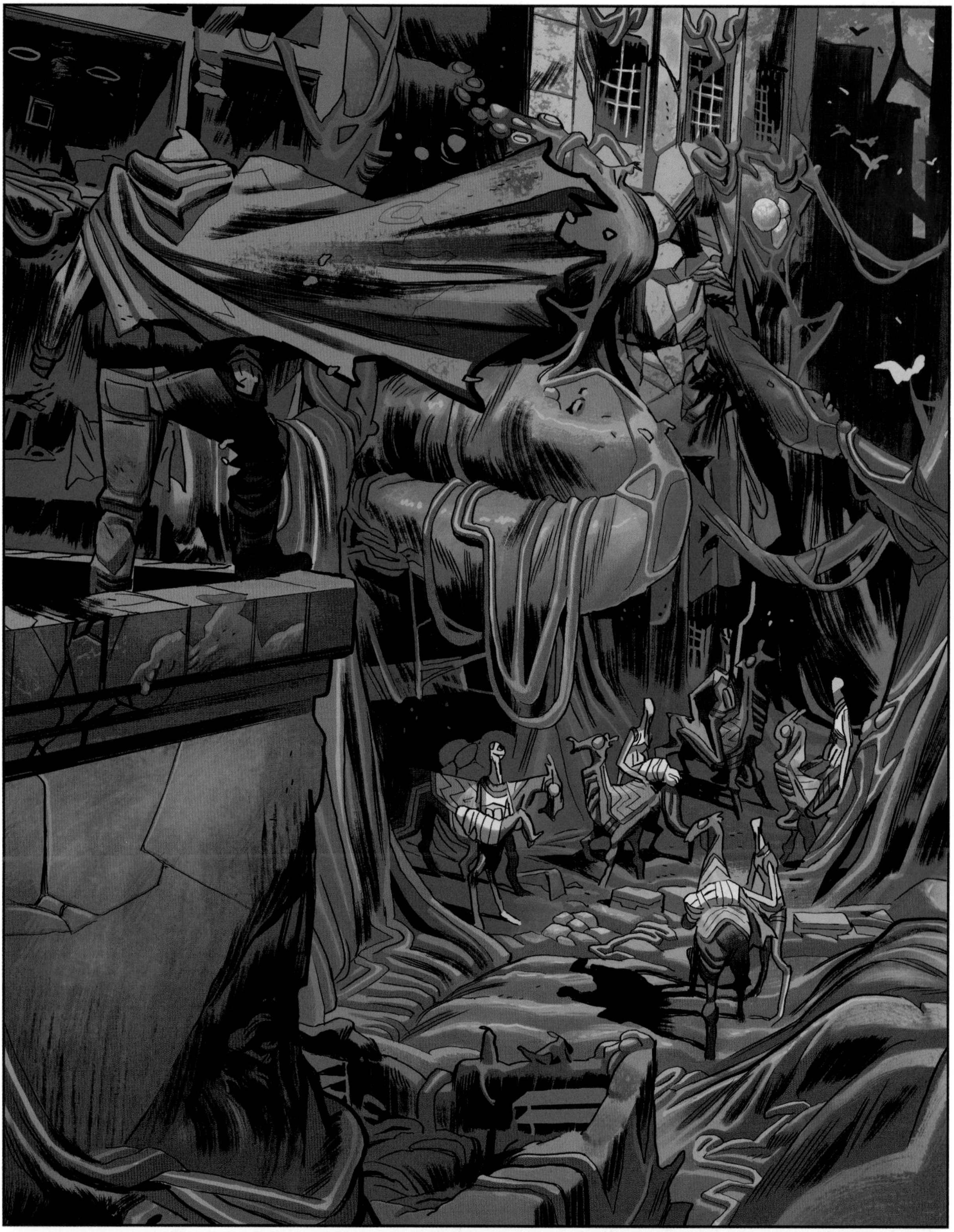
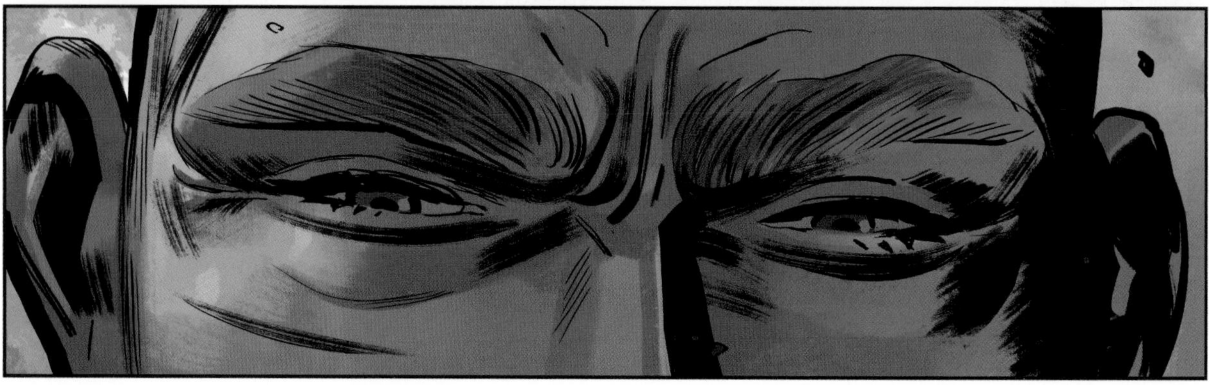

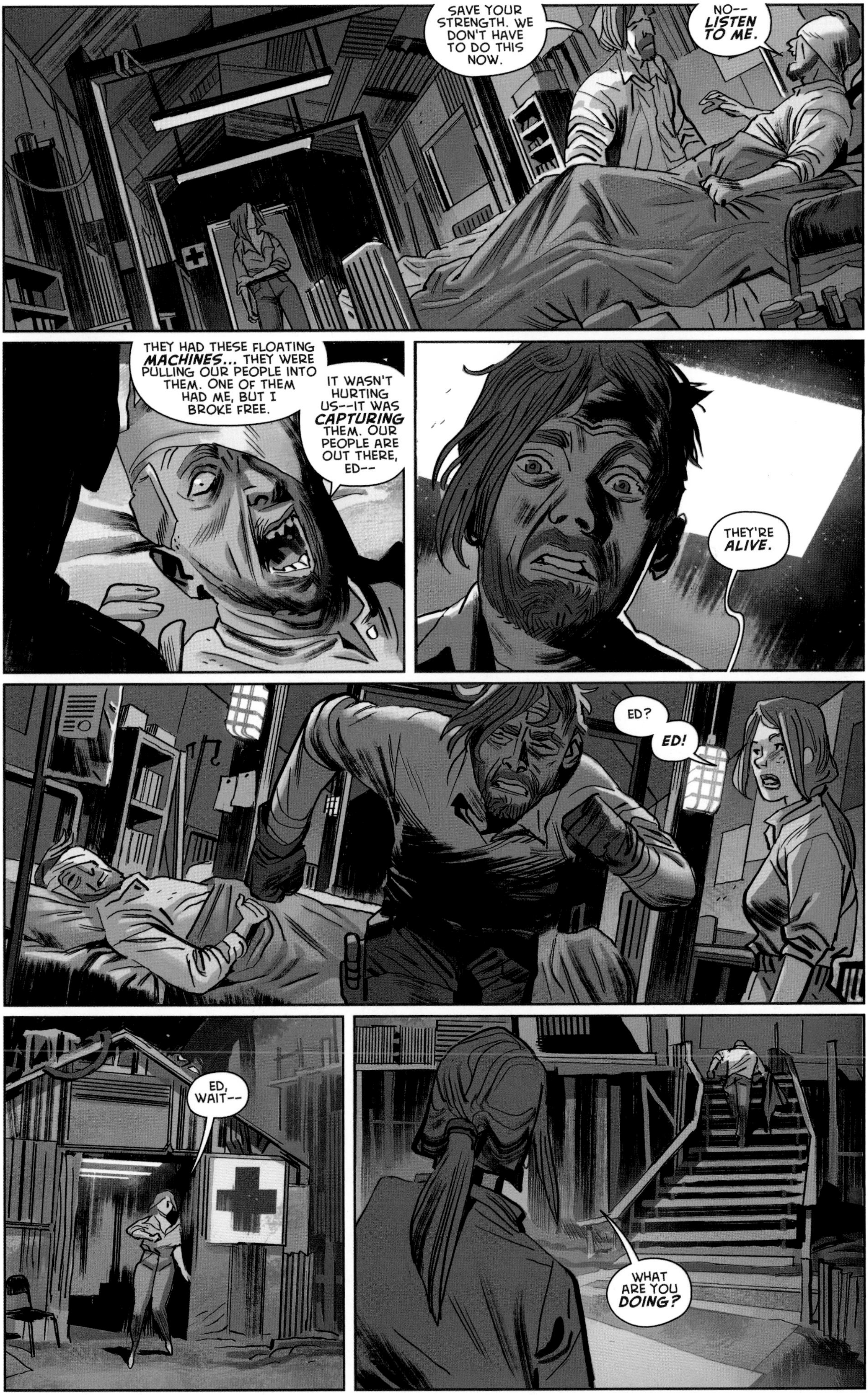
SAVE YOUR STRENGTH. WE DON'T HAVE TO DO THIS NOW.
NO-- LISTEN TO ME.
THEY HAD THESE FLOATING MACHINES... THEY WERE PULLING OUR PEOPLE INTO THEM. ONE OF THEM HAD ME, BUT I BROKE FREE.
IT WASN'T HURTING US--IT WAS CAPTURING THEM. OUR PEOPLE ARE OUT THERE, ED--
THEY'RE ALIVE.
ED?
ED!
ED, WAIT--
WHAT ARE YOU DOING?

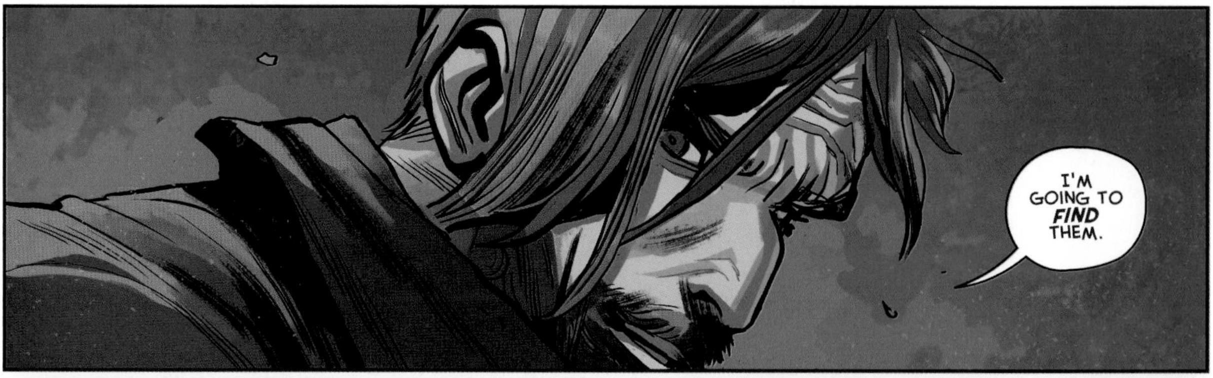
I'M GOING TO FIND THEM.

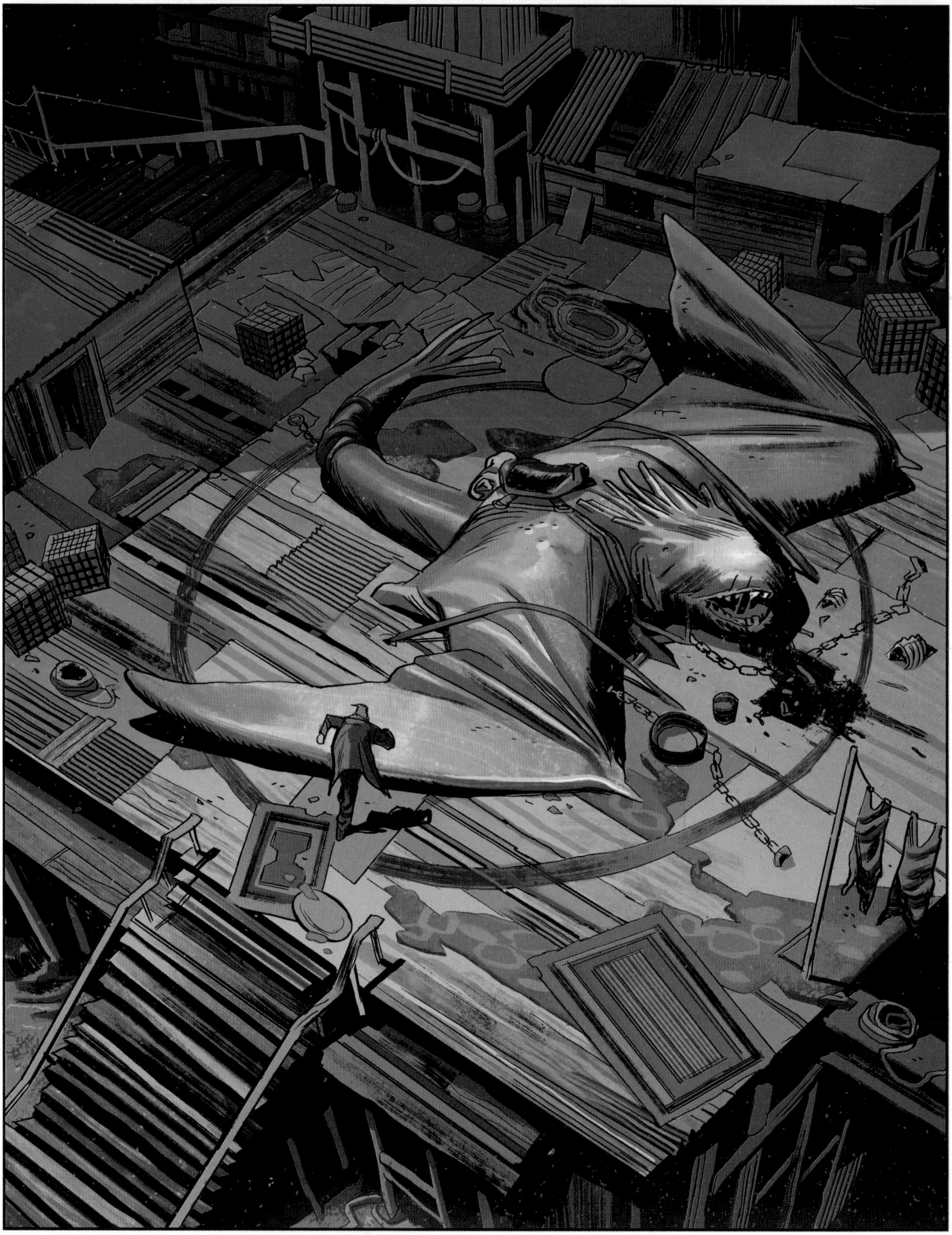

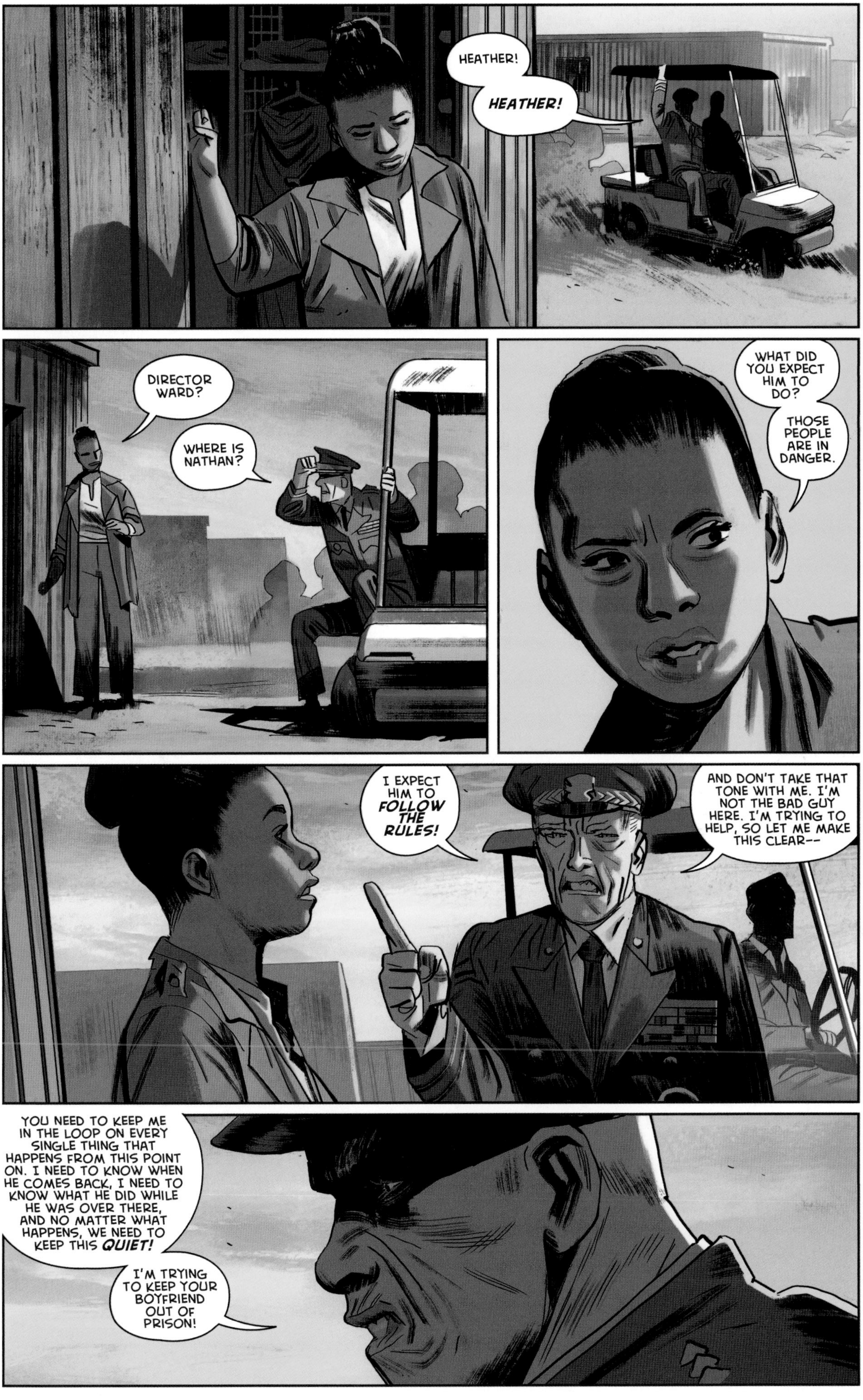
HEATHER!
HEATHER!
DIRECTOR WARD?
WHERE IS NATHAN?
WHAT DID YOU EXPECT HIM TO DO?
THOSE PEOPLE ARE IN DANGER.
I EXPECT HIM TO FOLLOW THE RULES!
AND DON'T TAKE THAT TONE WITH ME. I'M NOT THE BAD GUY HERE. I'M TRYING TO HELP, SO LET ME MAKE THIS CLEAR--
YOU NEED TO KEEP ME IN THE LOOP ON EVERY SINGLE THING THAT HAPPENS FROM THIS POINT ON. I NEED TO KNOW WHEN HE COMES BACK, I NEED TO KNOW WHAT HE DID WHILE HE WAS OVER THERE, AND NO MATTER WHAT HAPPENS, WE NEED TO KEEP THIS QUIET!
I'M TRYING TO KEEP YOUR BOYFRIEND OUT OF PRISON!

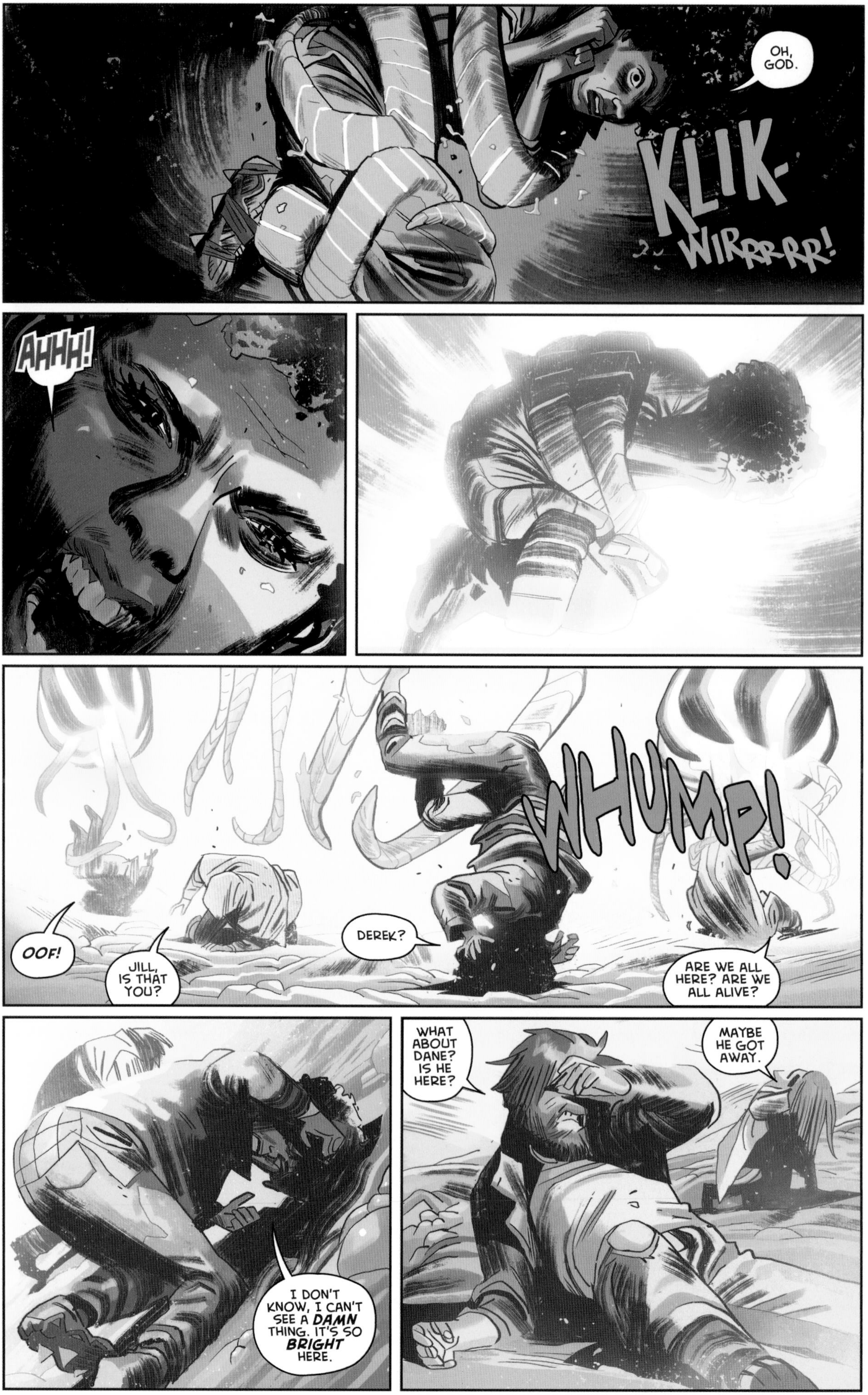
OH, GOD.
KLIK-WIRRRRR!
AHHH!
WHUMP!
OOF!
JILL, IS THAT YOU?
DEREK?
ARE WE ALL HERE? ARE WE ALL ALIVE?
I DON'T KNOW, I CAN'T SEE A DAMN THING. IT'S SO BRIGHT HERE.
WHAT ABOUT DANE? IS HE HERE?
MAYBE HE GOT AWAY.

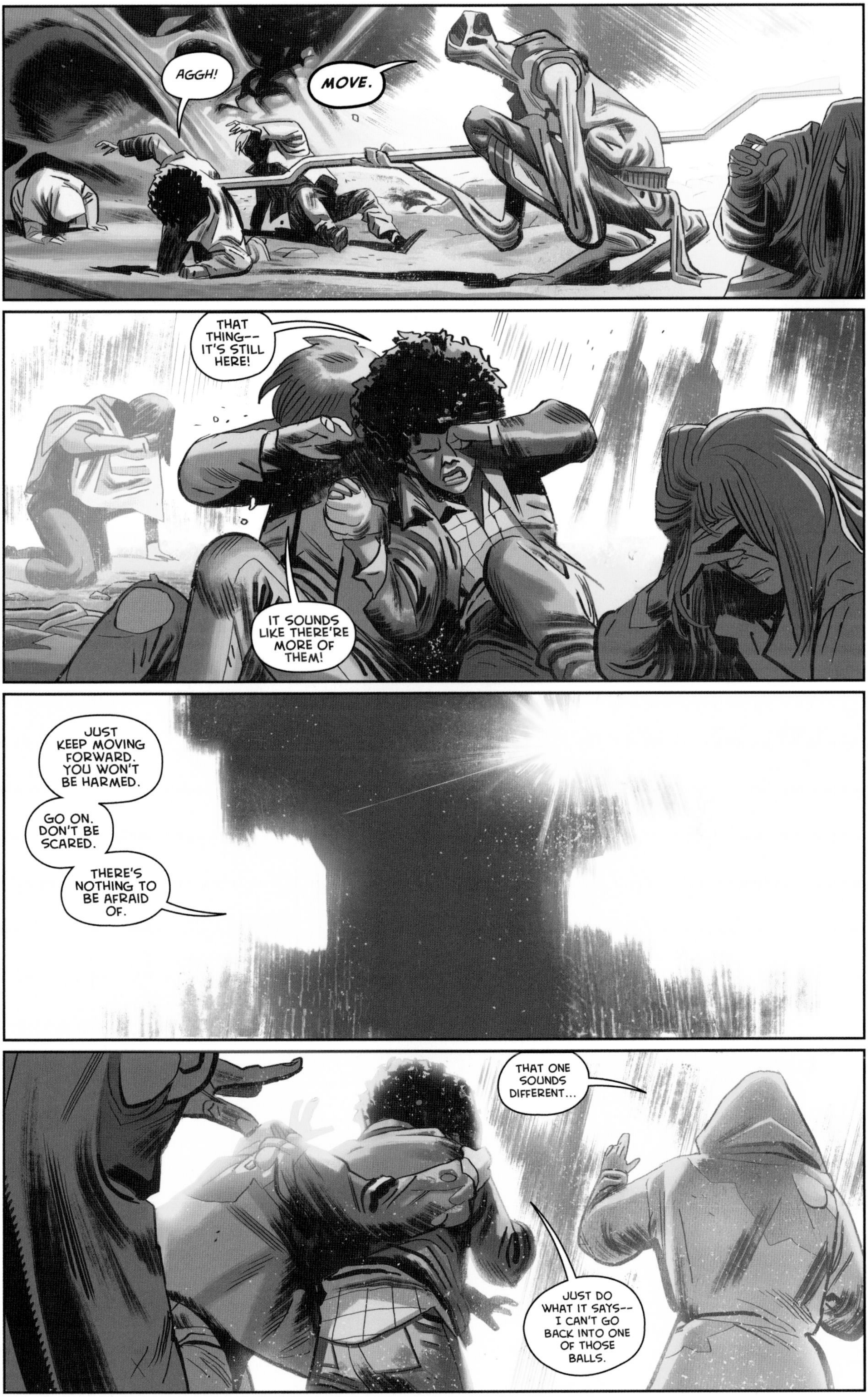
AGGH!
MOVE.
THAT THING-- IT'S STILL HERE!
IT SOUNDS LIKE THERE'RE MORE OF THEM!
JUST KEEP MOVING FORWARD. YOU WON'T BE HARMED.
GO ON. DON'T BE SCARED.
THERE'S NOTHING TO BE AFRAID OF.
THAT ONE SOUNDS DIFFERENT...
JUST DO WHAT IT SAYS-- I CAN'T GO BACK INTO ONE OF THOSE BALLS.

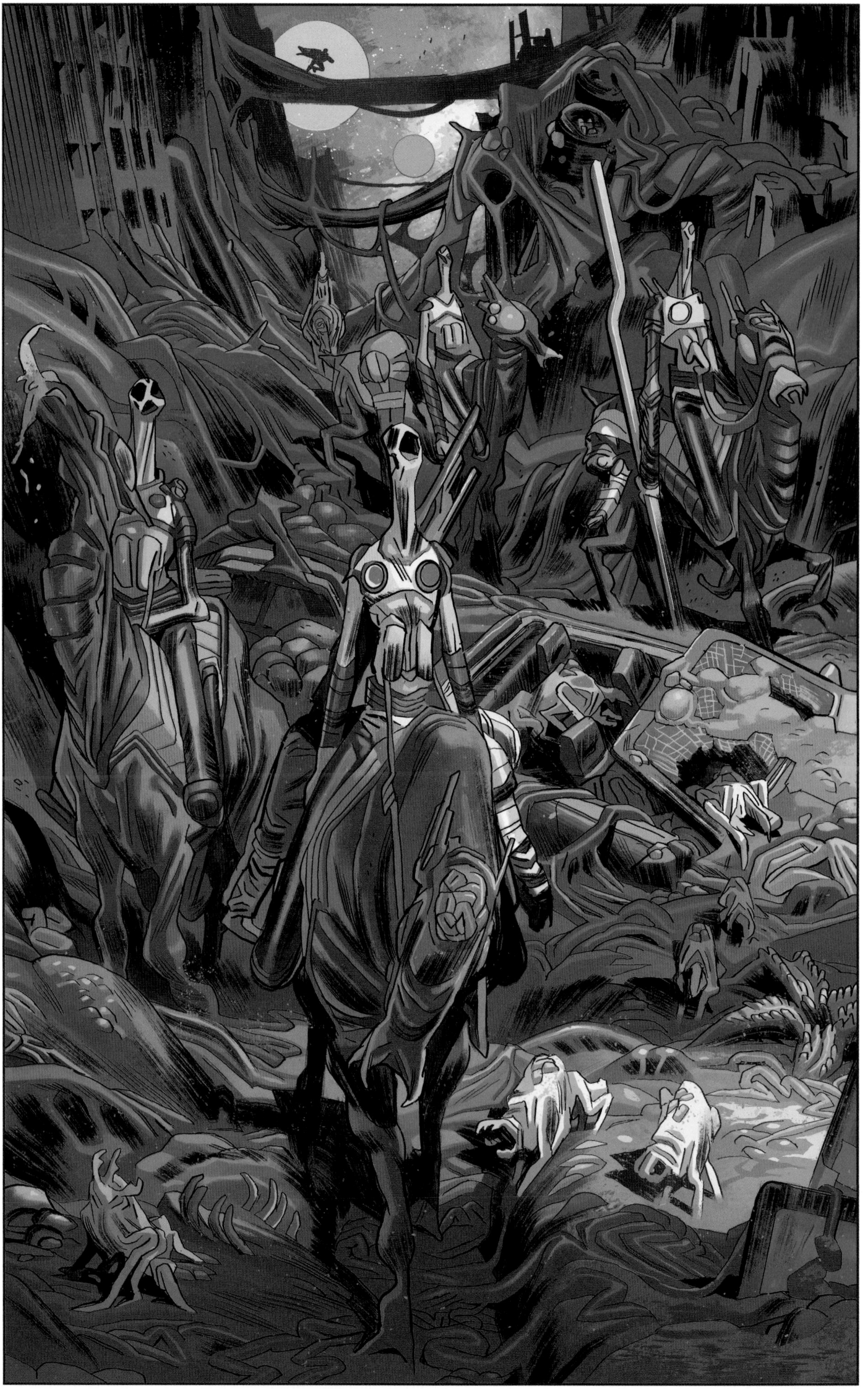

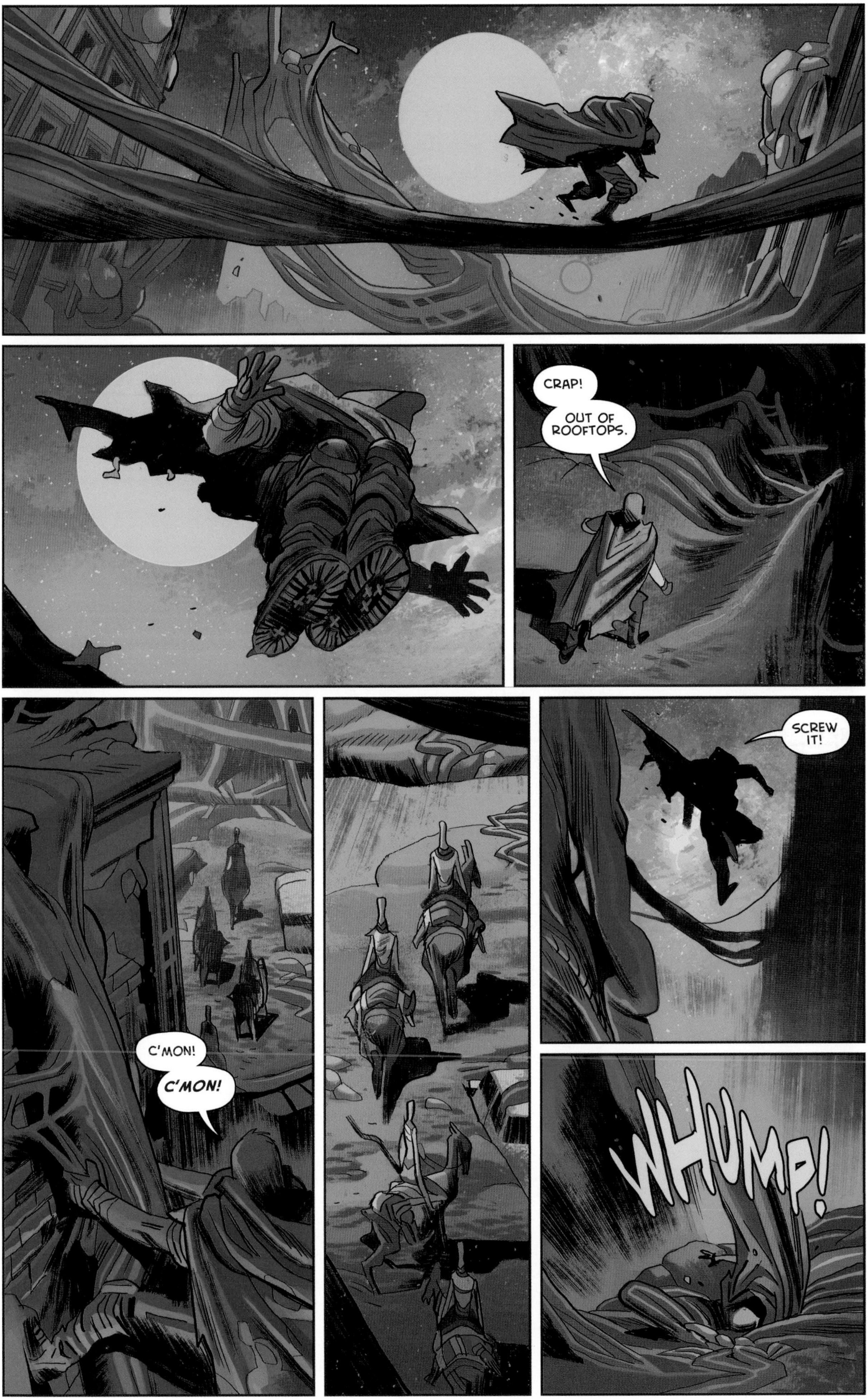
CRAP!
OUT OF ROOFTOPS.
C'MON!
C'MON!
SCREW IT!
WHUMP!

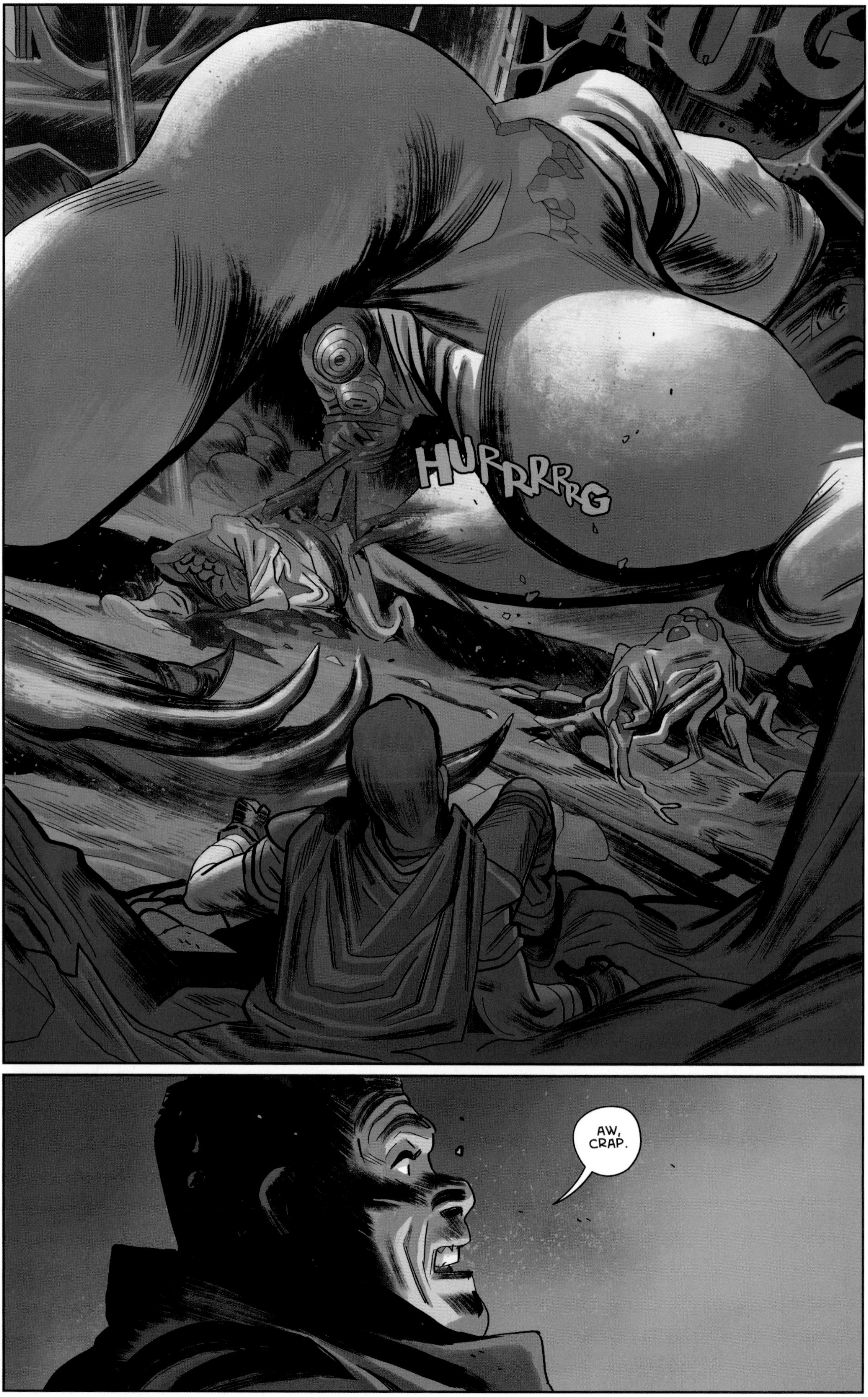
HURRRRG
AW, CRAP.

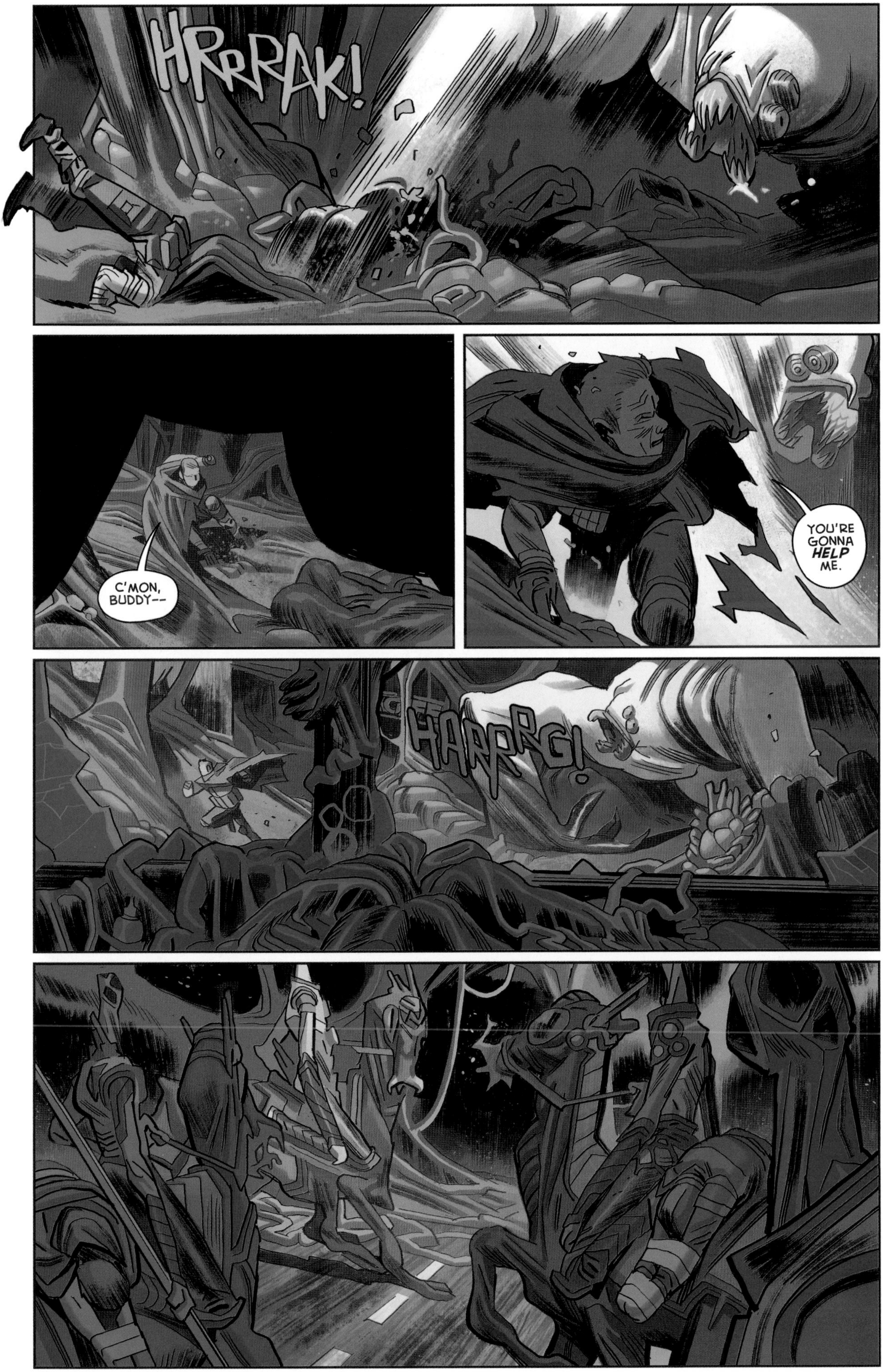

HRRRAK!
C'MON, BUDDY--
YOU'RE GONNA HELP ME.
HARRRG!

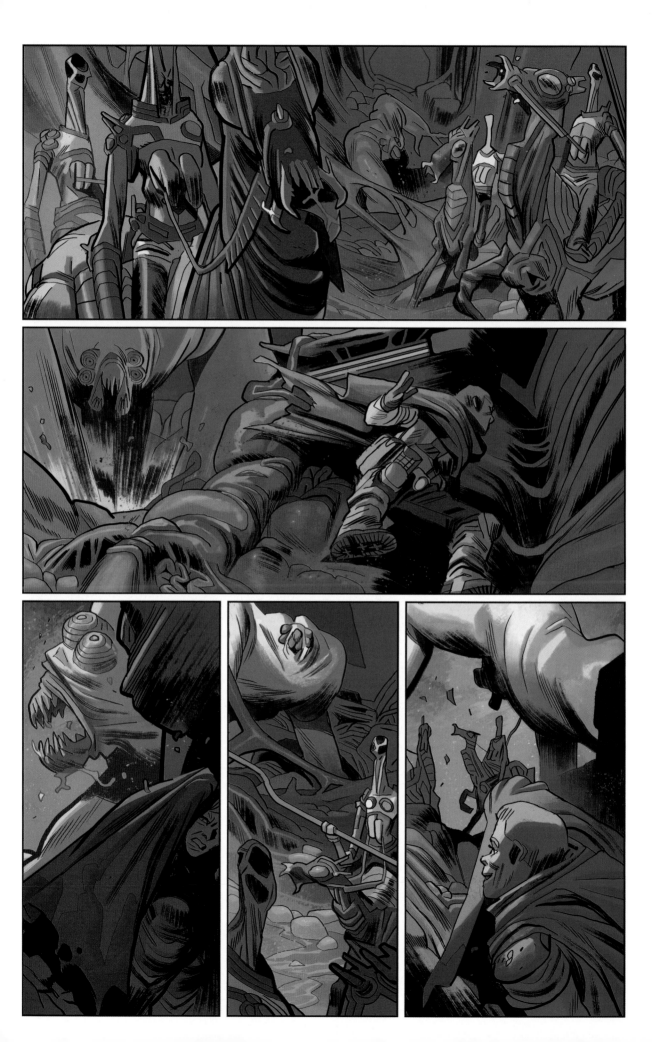

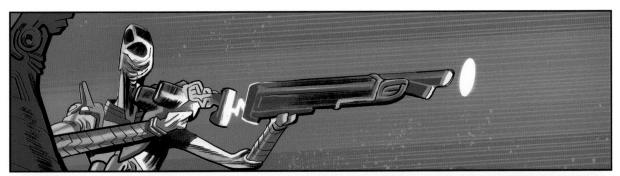

GOTTA EVEN THE ODDS.

FUNT

FUNT

THREE... TWO...

BEEP BEEP

BEEP

FA-FAASH!

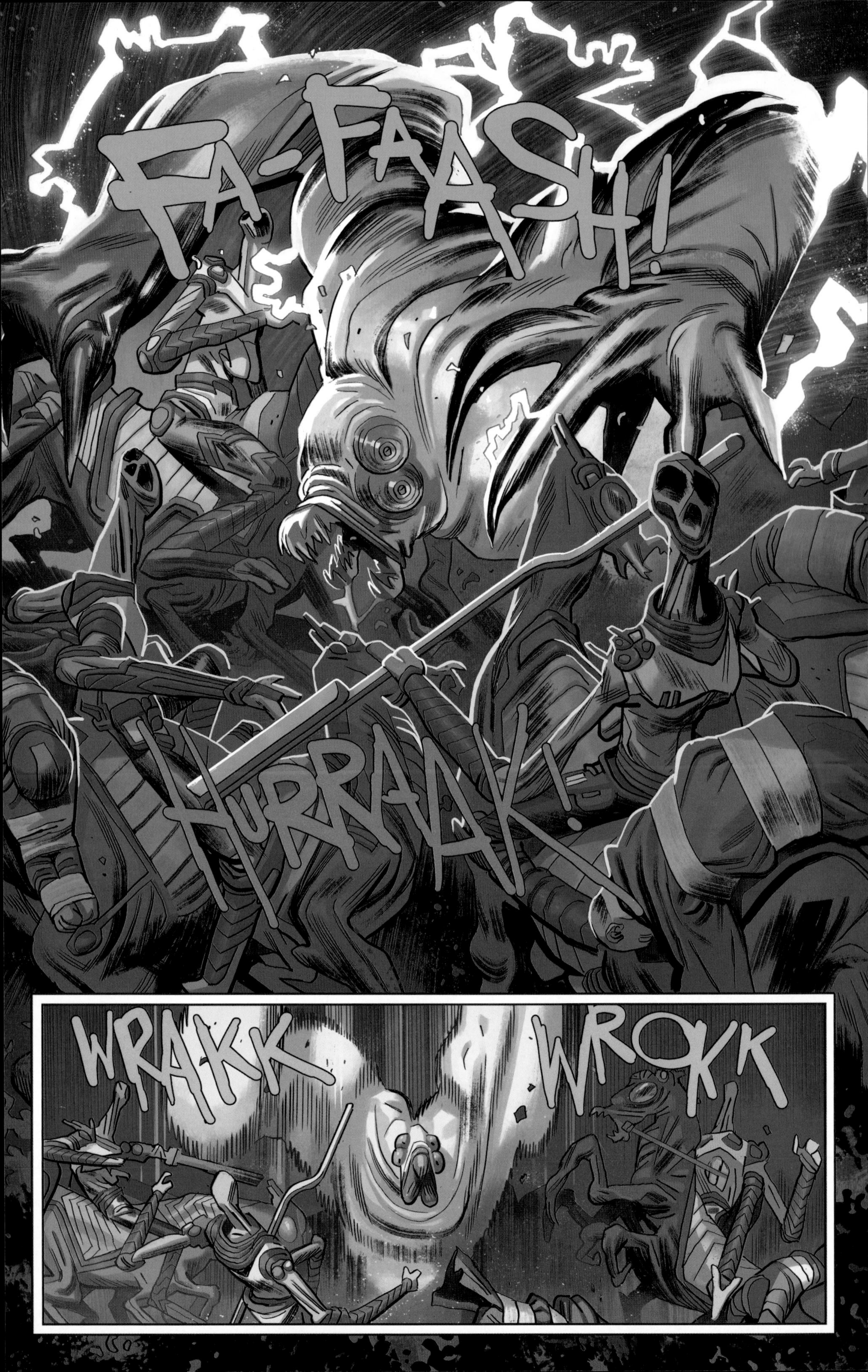
FA-FAASH!
HURRAAK!
WRAKK
WROKK

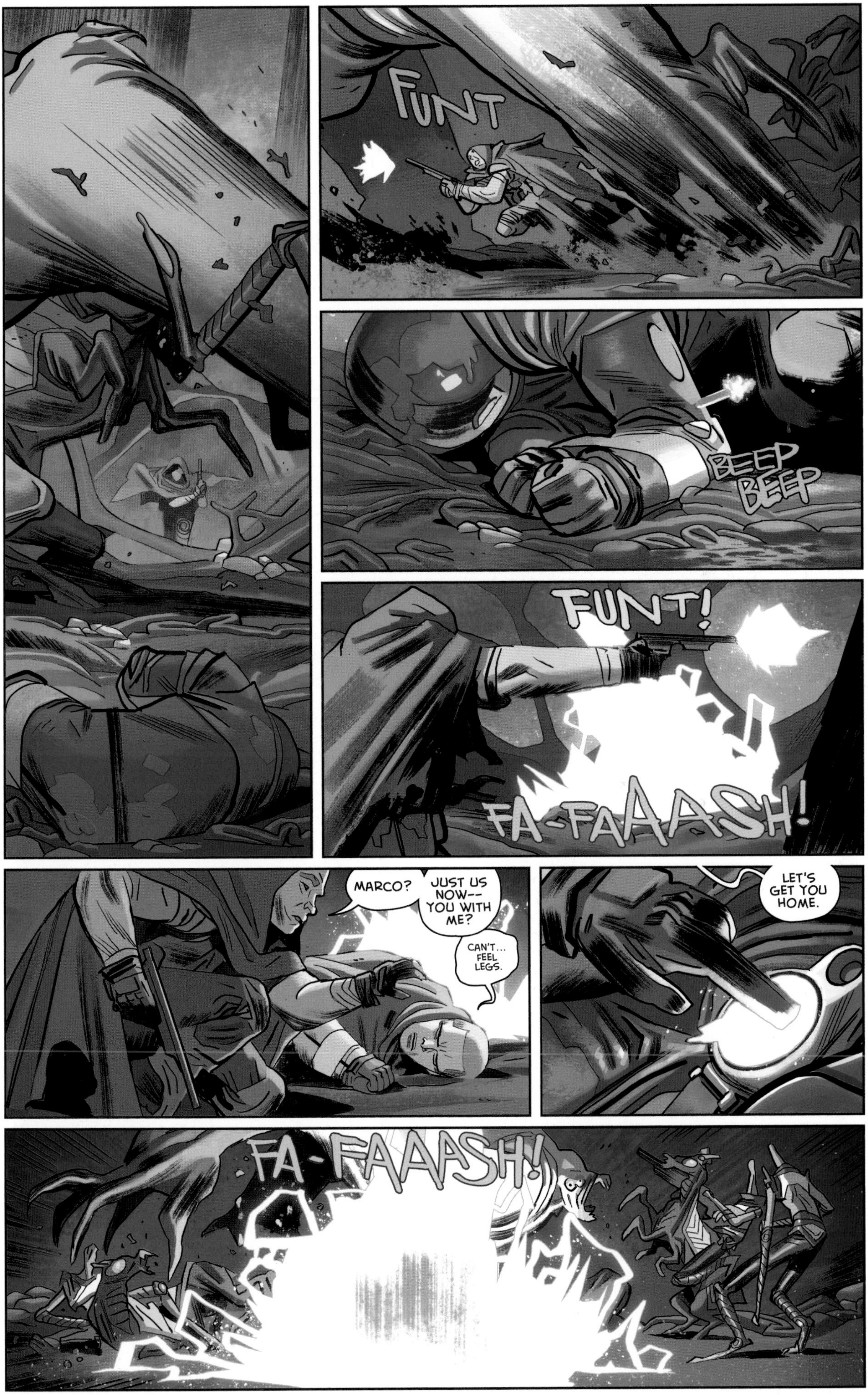
FUNT
BEEP BEEP
FUNT!
FA-FAAAASH!
MARCO?
JUST US NOW-- YOU WITH ME?
CAN'T... FEEL LEGS.
LET'S GET YOU HOME.
FA-FAAASH!

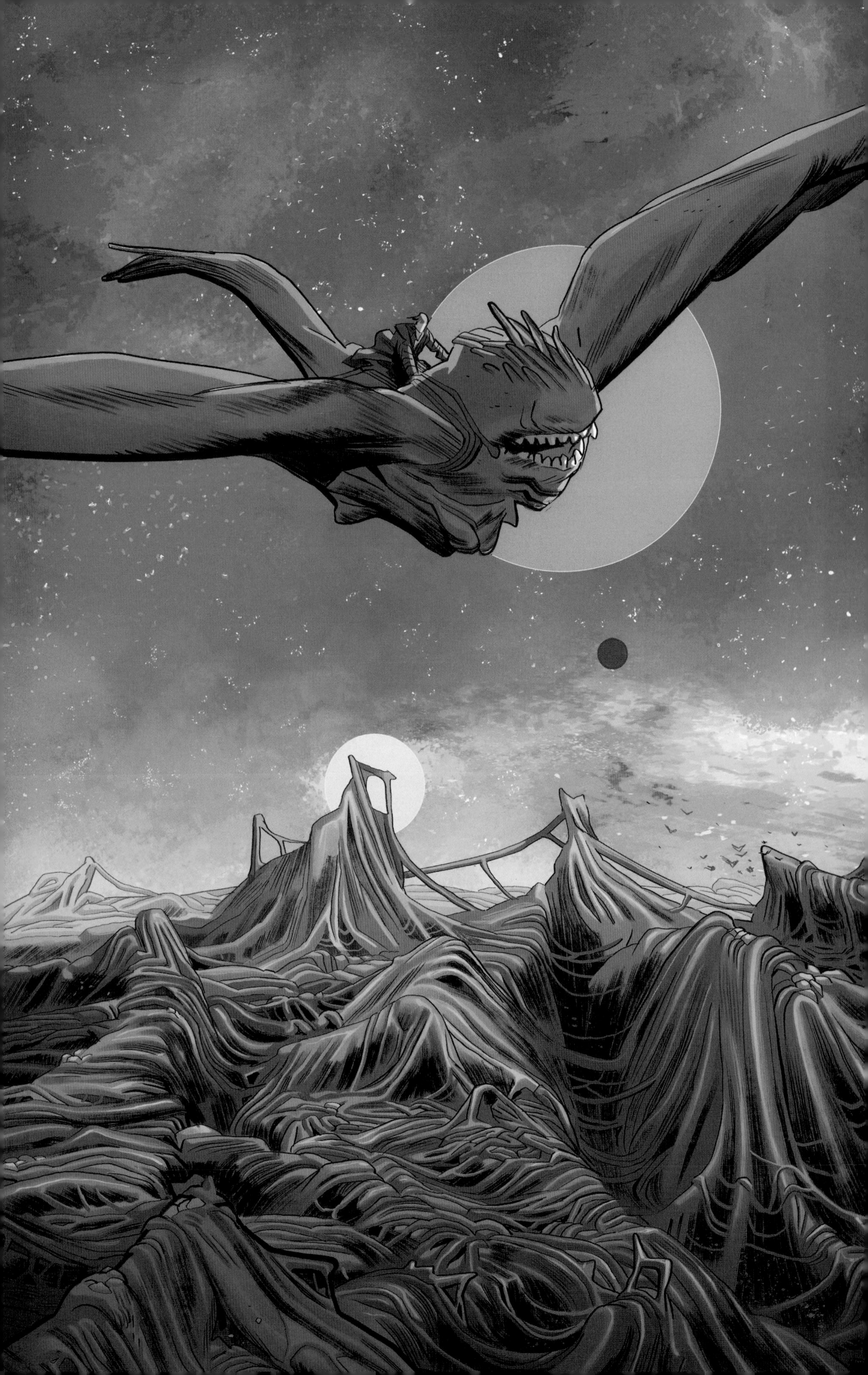

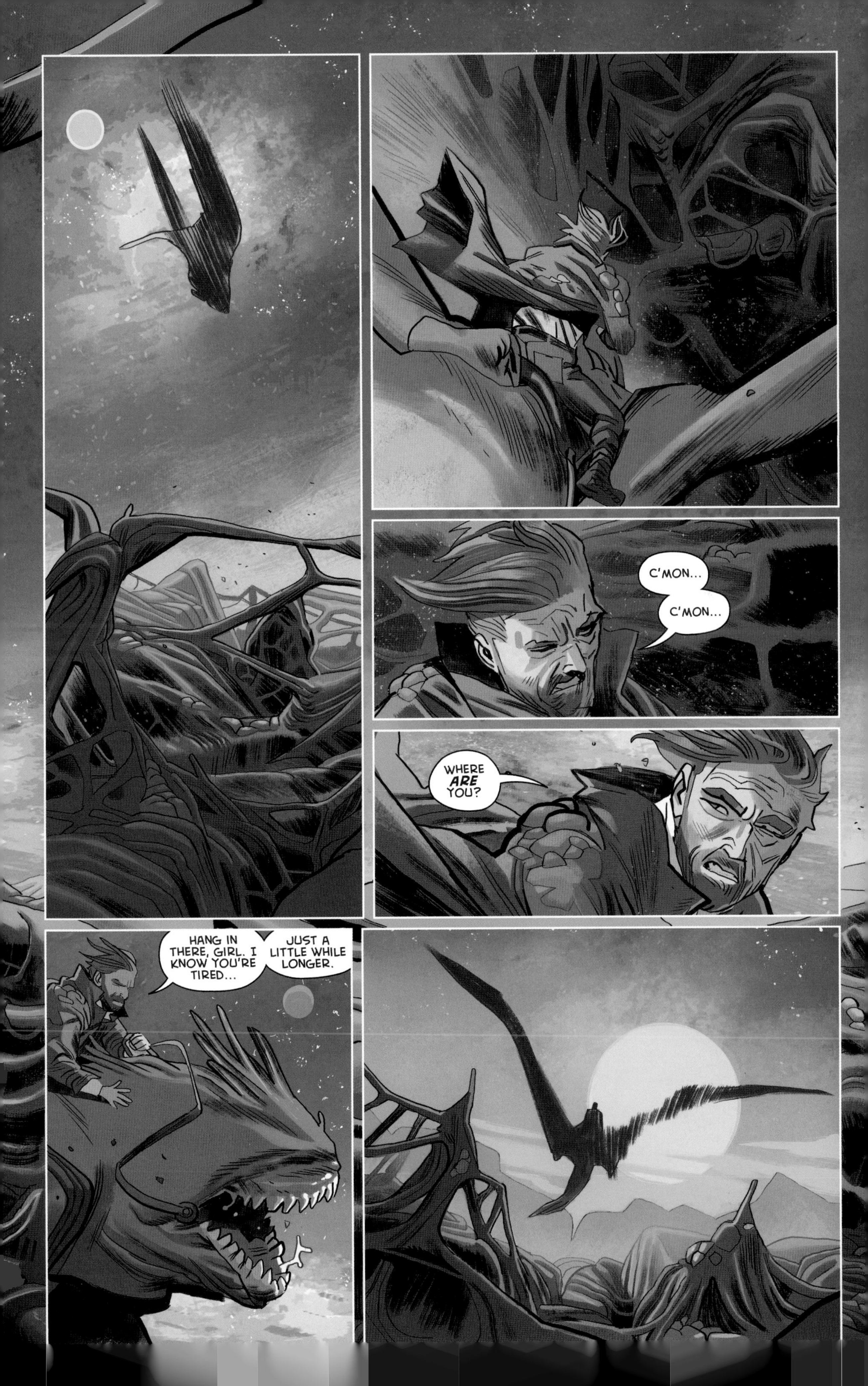
C'MON...
C'MON...
WHERE ARE YOU?
HANG IN THERE, GIRL. I KNOW YOU'RE TIRED...
JUST A LITTLE WHILE LONGER.

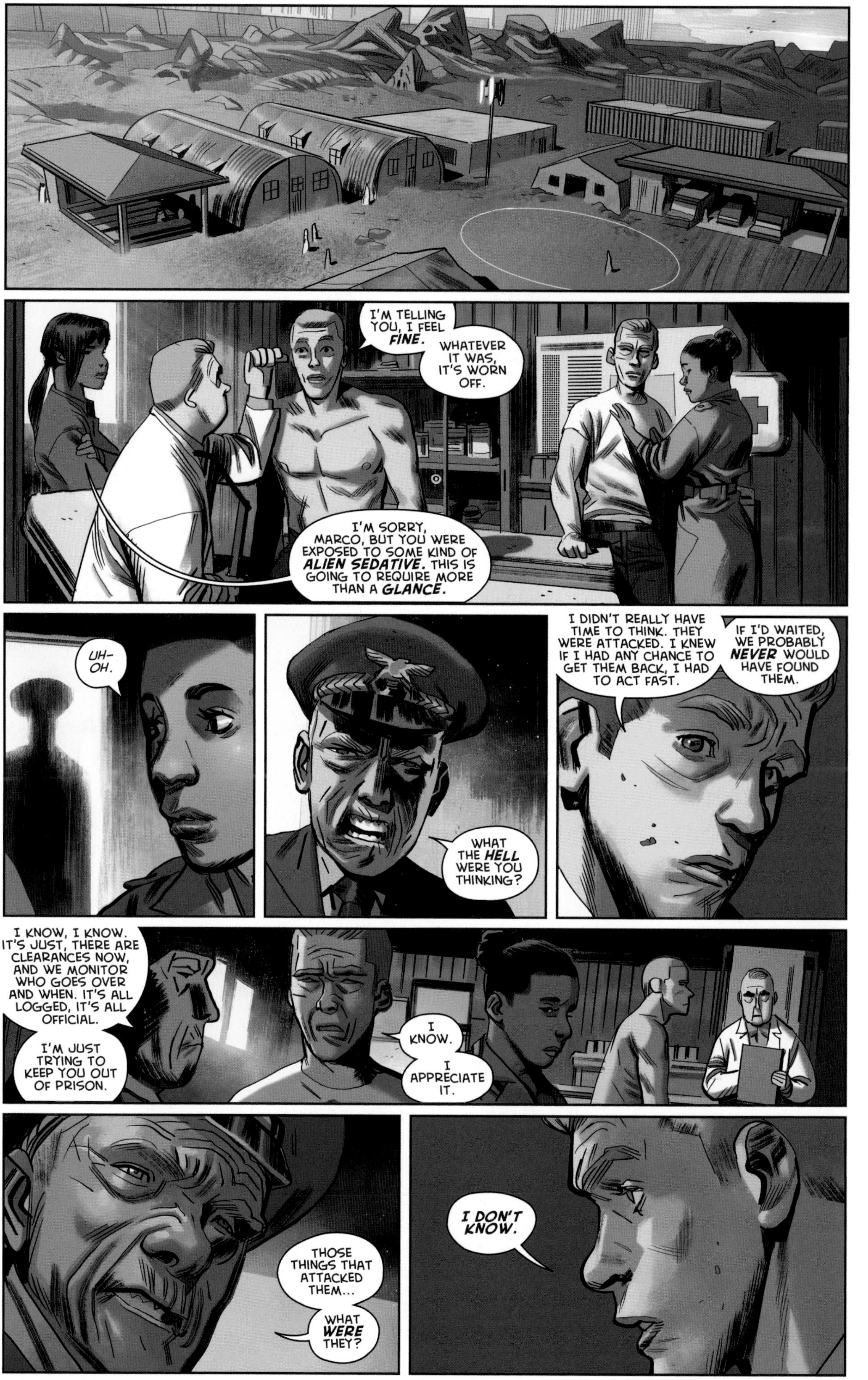
I'M TELLING YOU, I FEEL FINE.
WHATEVER IT WAS, IT'S WORN OFF.
I'M SORRY, MARCO, BUT YOU WERE EXPOSED TO SOME KIND OF ALIEN SEDATIVE. THIS IS GOING TO REQUIRE MORE THAN A GLANCE.
UH-OH.
WHAT THE HELL WERE YOU THINKING?
I DIDN'T REALLY HAVE TIME TO THINK. THEY WERE ATTACKED. I KNEW IF I HAD ANY CHANCE TO GET THEM BACK, I HAD TO ACT FAST.
IF I'D WAITED, WE PROBABLY NEVER WOULD HAVE FOUND THEM.
I KNOW, I KNOW. IT'S JUST, THERE ARE CLEARANCES NOW, AND WE MONITOR WHO GOES OVER AND WHEN. IT'S ALL LOGGED, IT'S ALL OFFICIAL.
I'M JUST TRYING TO KEEP YOU OUT OF PRISON.
I KNOW.
I APPRECIATE IT.
THOSE THINGS THAT ATTACKED THEM...
WHAT WERE THEY?
I DON'T KNOW.

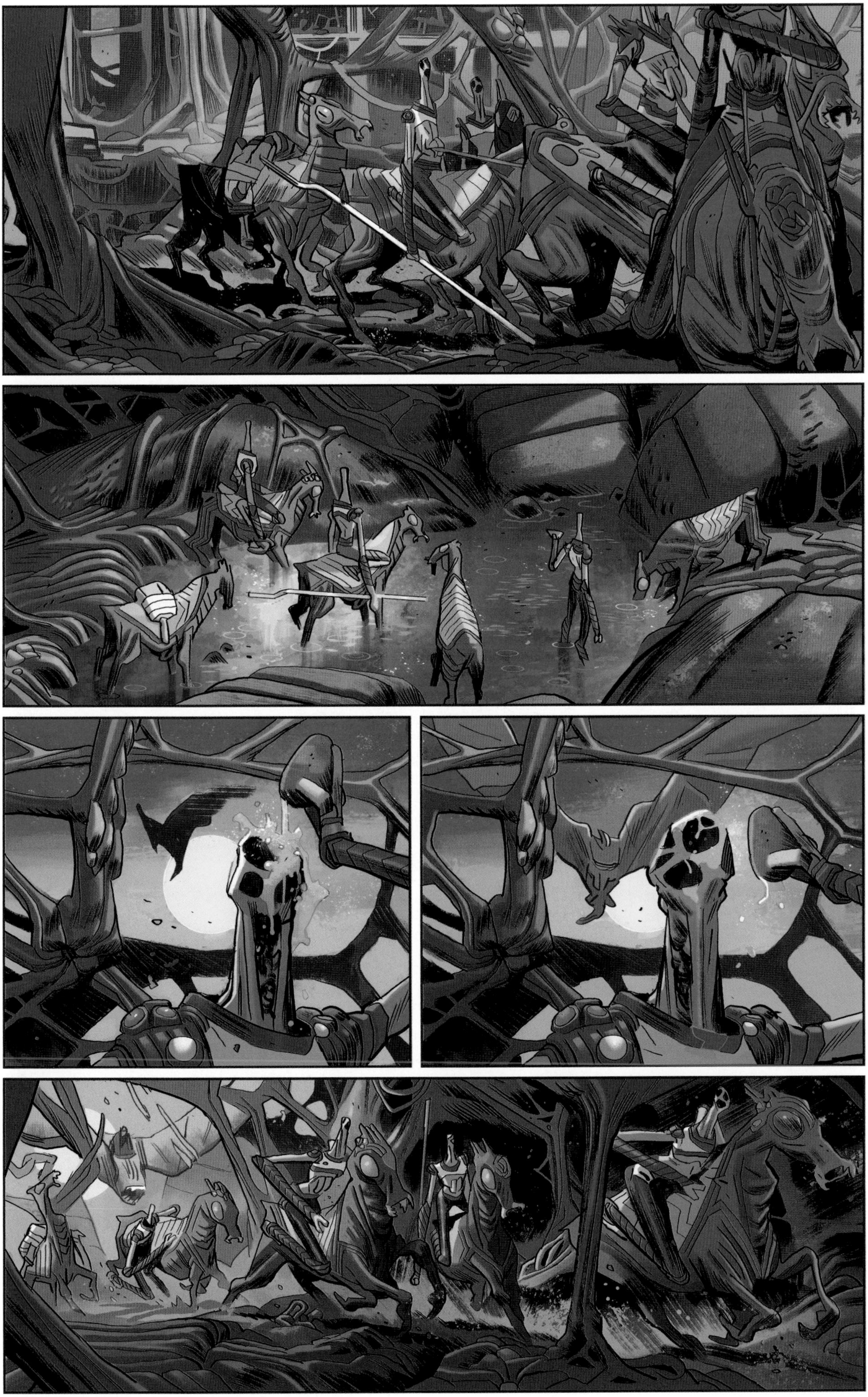

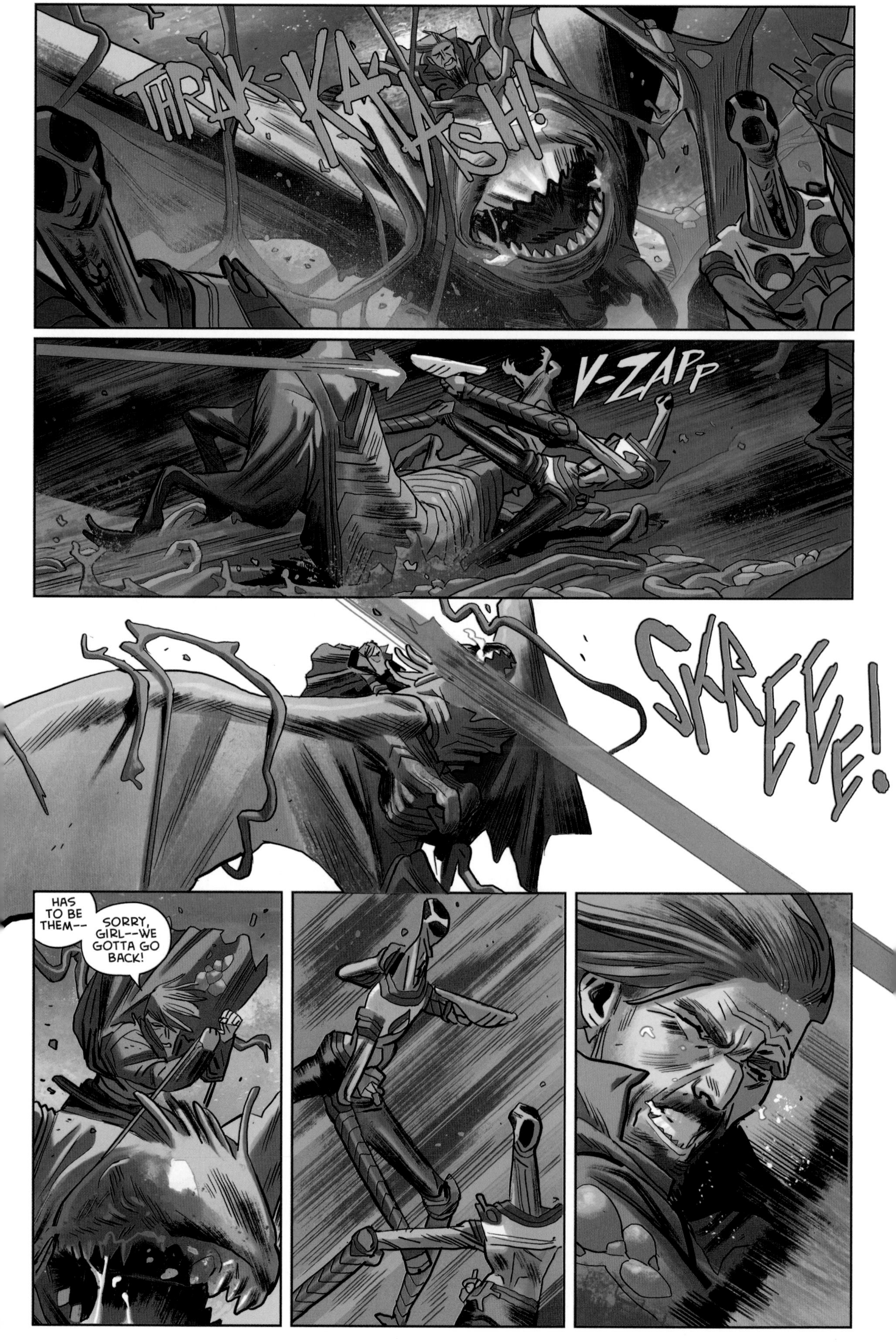
THRAK-KAKASH!
V-ZAPP
SKREEEE!
HAS TO BE THEM--
SORRY, GIRL--WE GOTTA GO BACK!

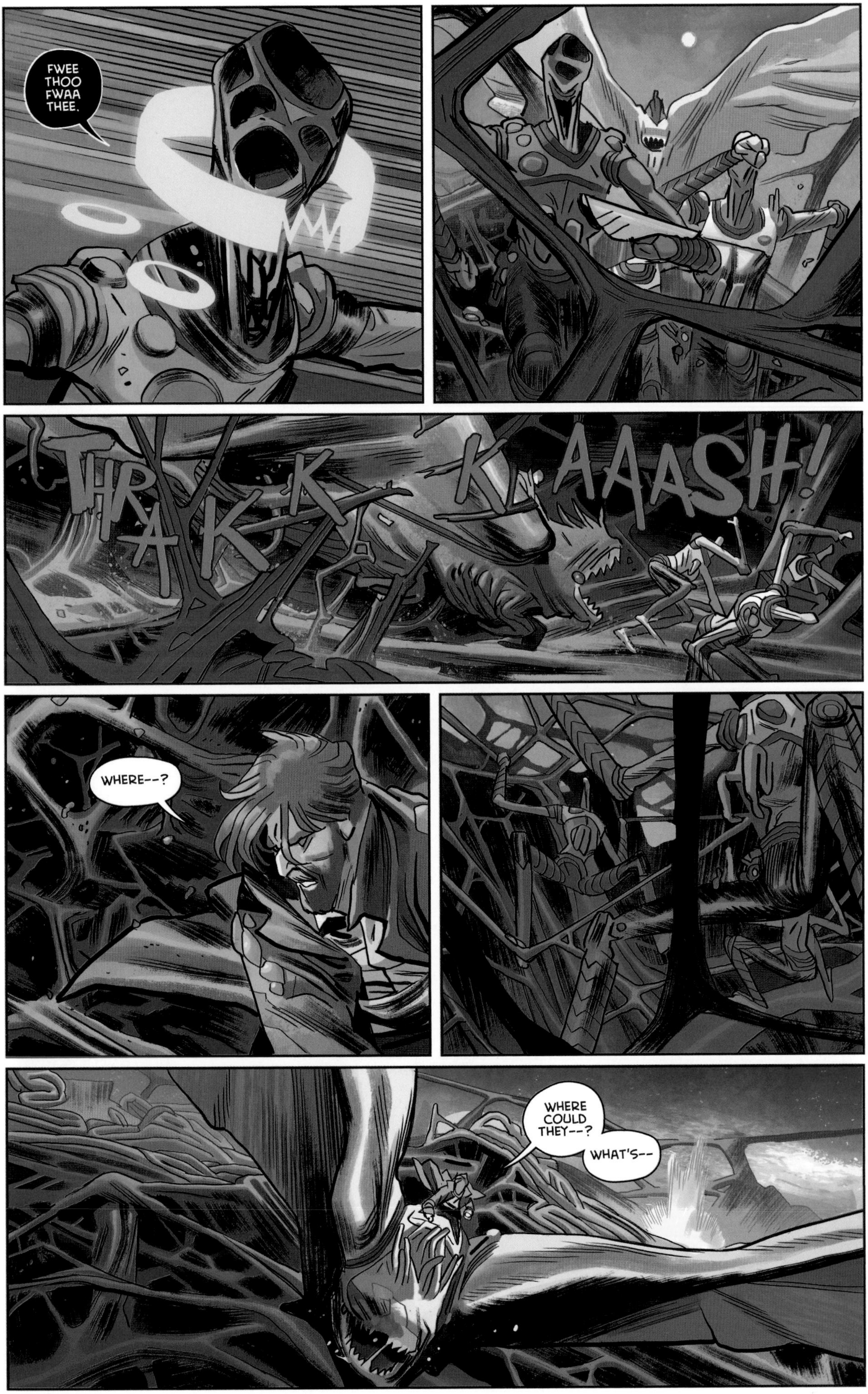
FWEE THOO FWAA THEE.
THRAKK
KAAASH!
WHERE--?
WHERE COULD THEY--?
WHAT'S--

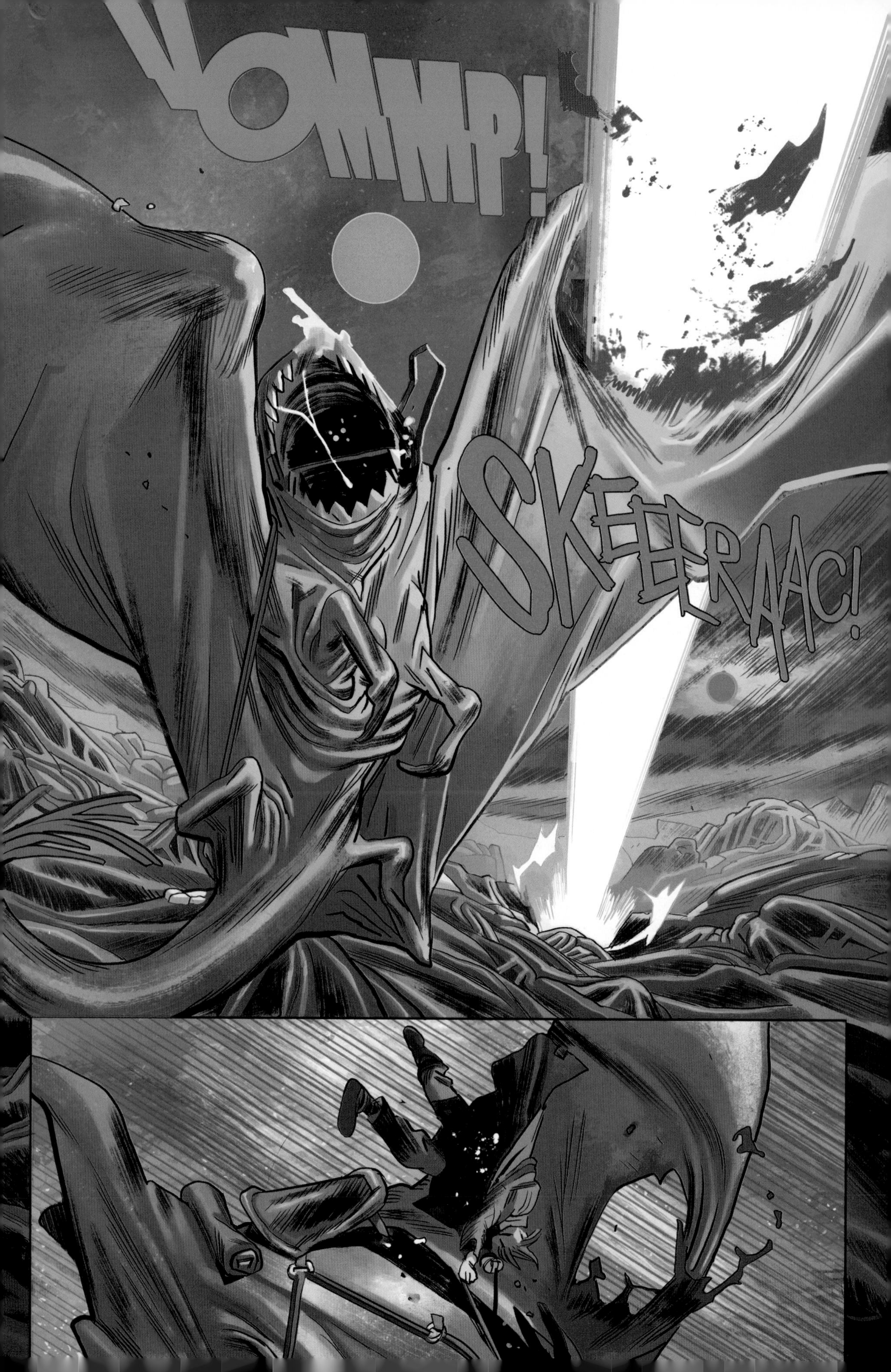
VOMMP!
SKEEERAAC!

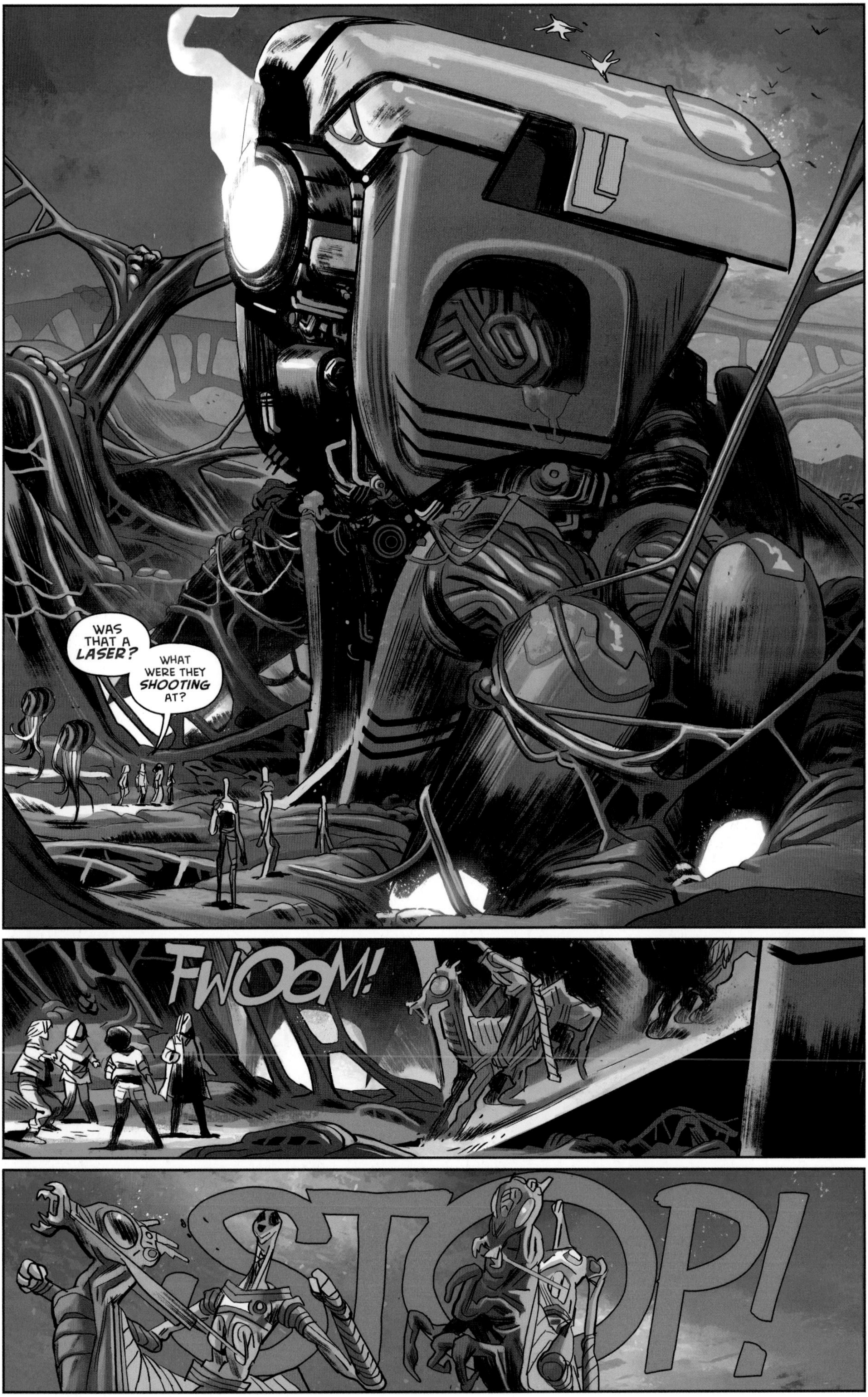
WAS THAT A LASER?
WHAT WERE THEY SHOOTING AT?
FWOOM!
STOP!

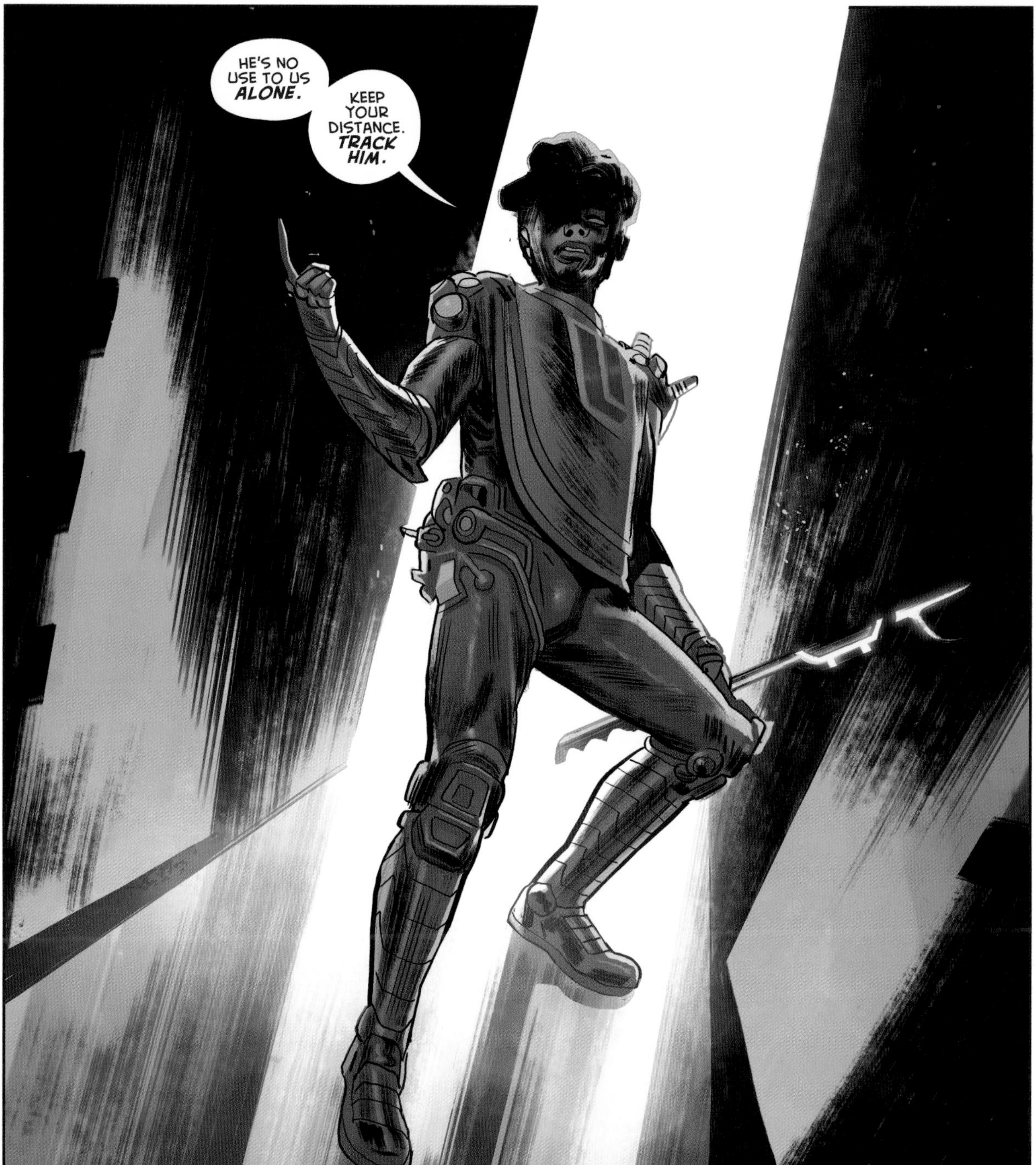
HE'S NO USE TO US ALONE.
KEEP YOUR DISTANCE. TRACK HIM.

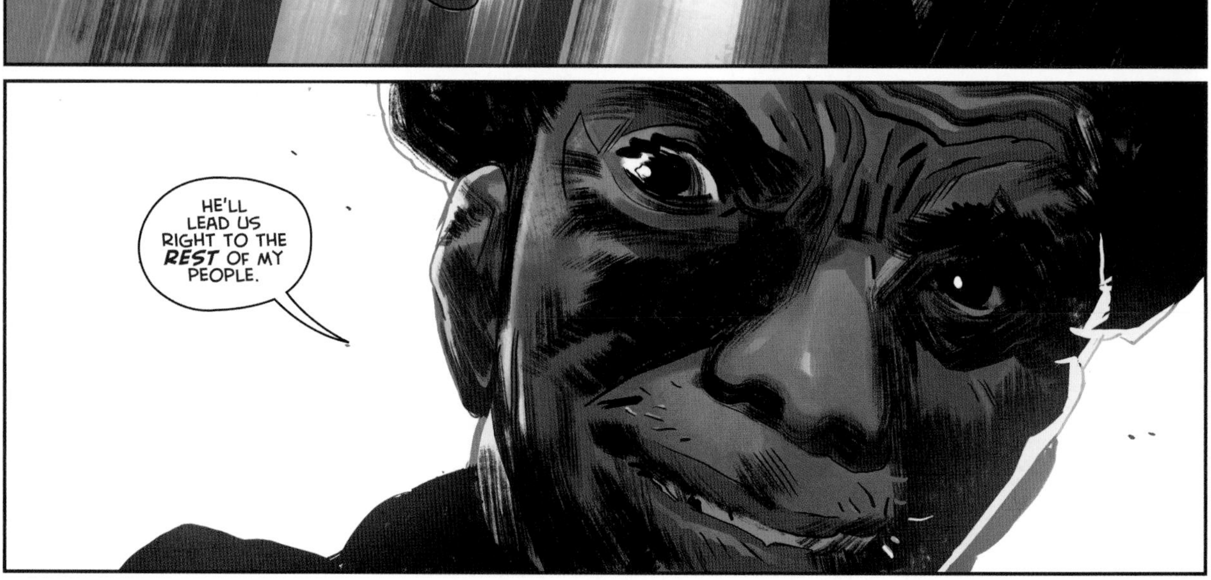
HE'LL LEAD US RIGHT TO THE REST OF MY PEOPLE.

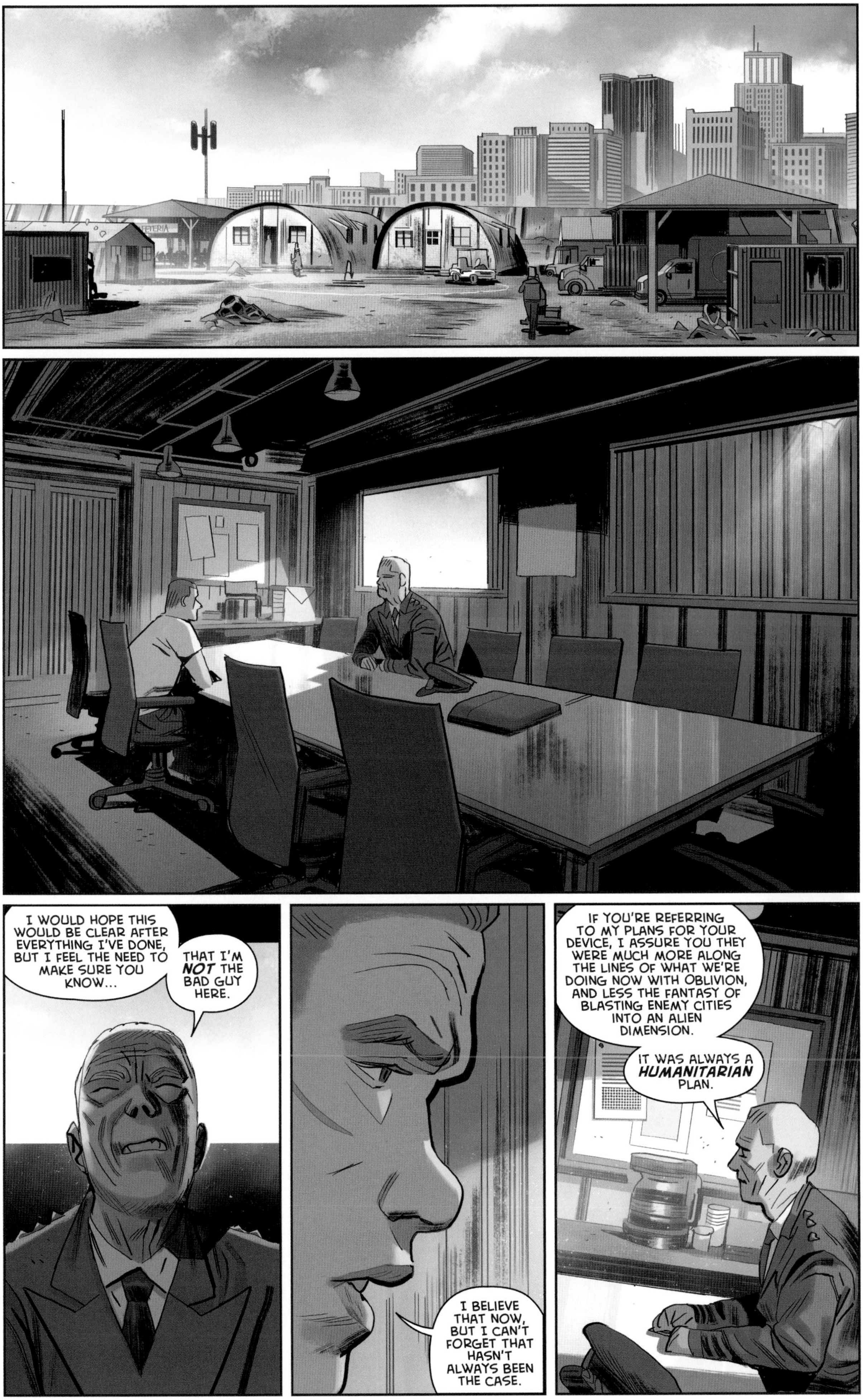
I WOULD HOPE THIS WOULD BE CLEAR AFTER EVERYTHING I'VE DONE, BUT I FEEL THE NEED TO MAKE SURE YOU KNOW...
THAT I'M ***NOT*** THE BAD GUY HERE.
I BELIEVE THAT NOW, BUT I CAN'T FORGET THAT HASN'T ALWAYS BEEN THE CASE.
IF YOU'RE REFERRING TO MY PLANS FOR YOUR DEVICE, I ASSURE YOU THEY WERE MUCH MORE ALONG THE LINES OF WHAT WE'RE DOING NOW WITH OBLIVION, AND LESS THE FANTASY OF BLASTING ENEMY CITIES INTO AN ALIEN DIMENSION.
IT WAS ALWAYS A ***HUMANITARIAN*** PLAN.

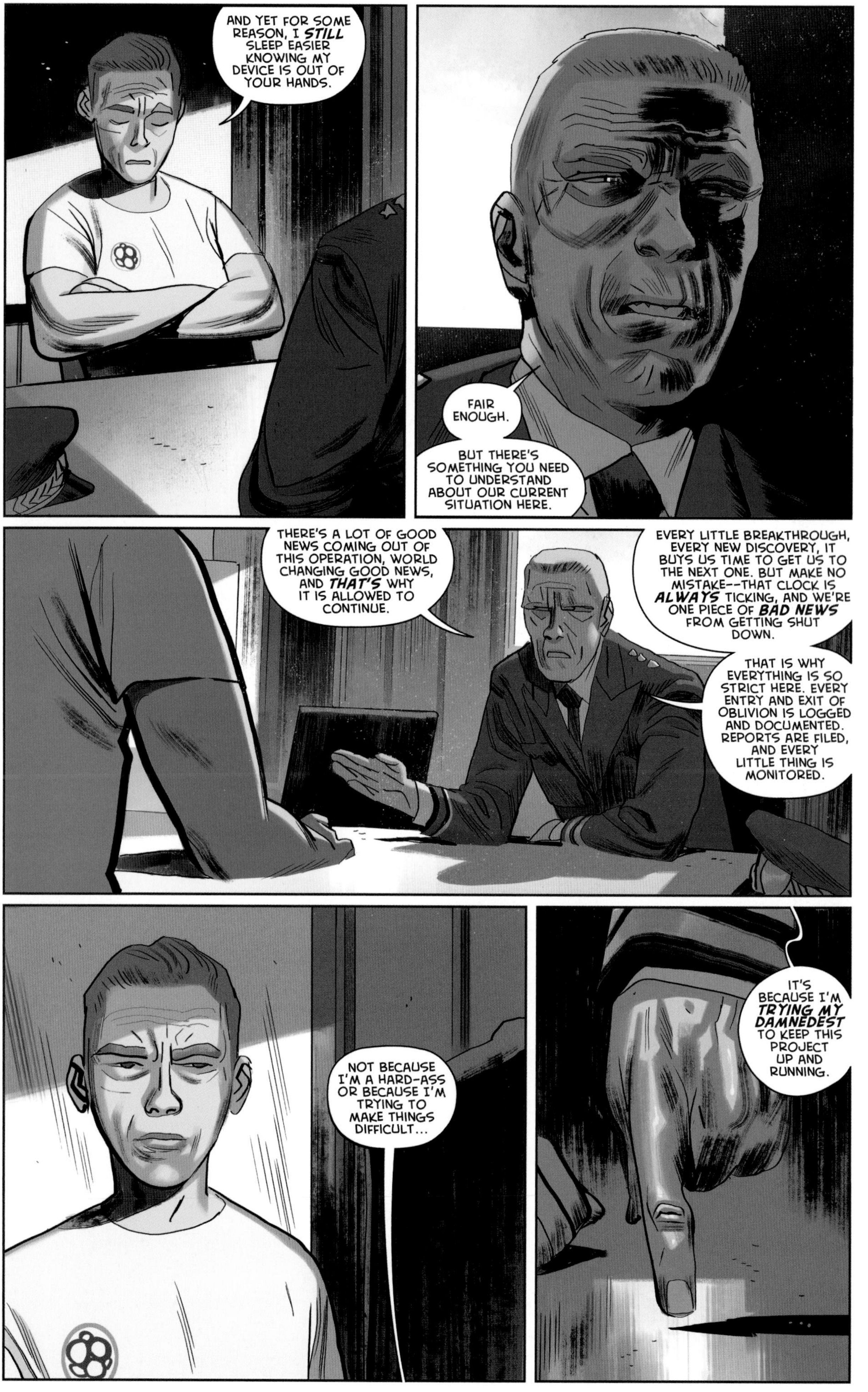
AND YET FOR SOME REASON, I STILL SLEEP EASIER KNOWING MY DEVICE IS OUT OF YOUR HANDS.
FAIR ENOUGH.
BUT THERE'S SOMETHING YOU NEED TO UNDERSTAND ABOUT OUR CURRENT SITUATION HERE.
THERE'S A LOT OF GOOD NEWS COMING OUT OF THIS OPERATION, WORLD CHANGING GOOD NEWS, AND THAT'S WHY IT IS ALLOWED TO CONTINUE.
EVERY LITTLE BREAKTHROUGH, EVERY NEW DISCOVERY, IT BUYS US TIME TO GET US TO THE NEXT ONE. BUT MAKE NO MISTAKE--THAT CLOCK IS ALWAYS TICKING, AND WE'RE ONE PIECE OF BAD NEWS FROM GETTING SHUT DOWN.
THAT IS WHY EVERYTHING IS SO STRICT HERE. EVERY ENTRY AND EXIT OF OBLIVION IS LOGGED AND DOCUMENTED. REPORTS ARE FILED, AND EVERY LITTLE THING IS MONITORED.
NOT BECAUSE I'M A HARD-ASS OR BECAUSE I'M TRYING TO MAKE THINGS DIFFICULT...
IT'S BECAUSE I'M TRYING MY DAMNEDEST TO KEEP THIS PROJECT UP AND RUNNING.

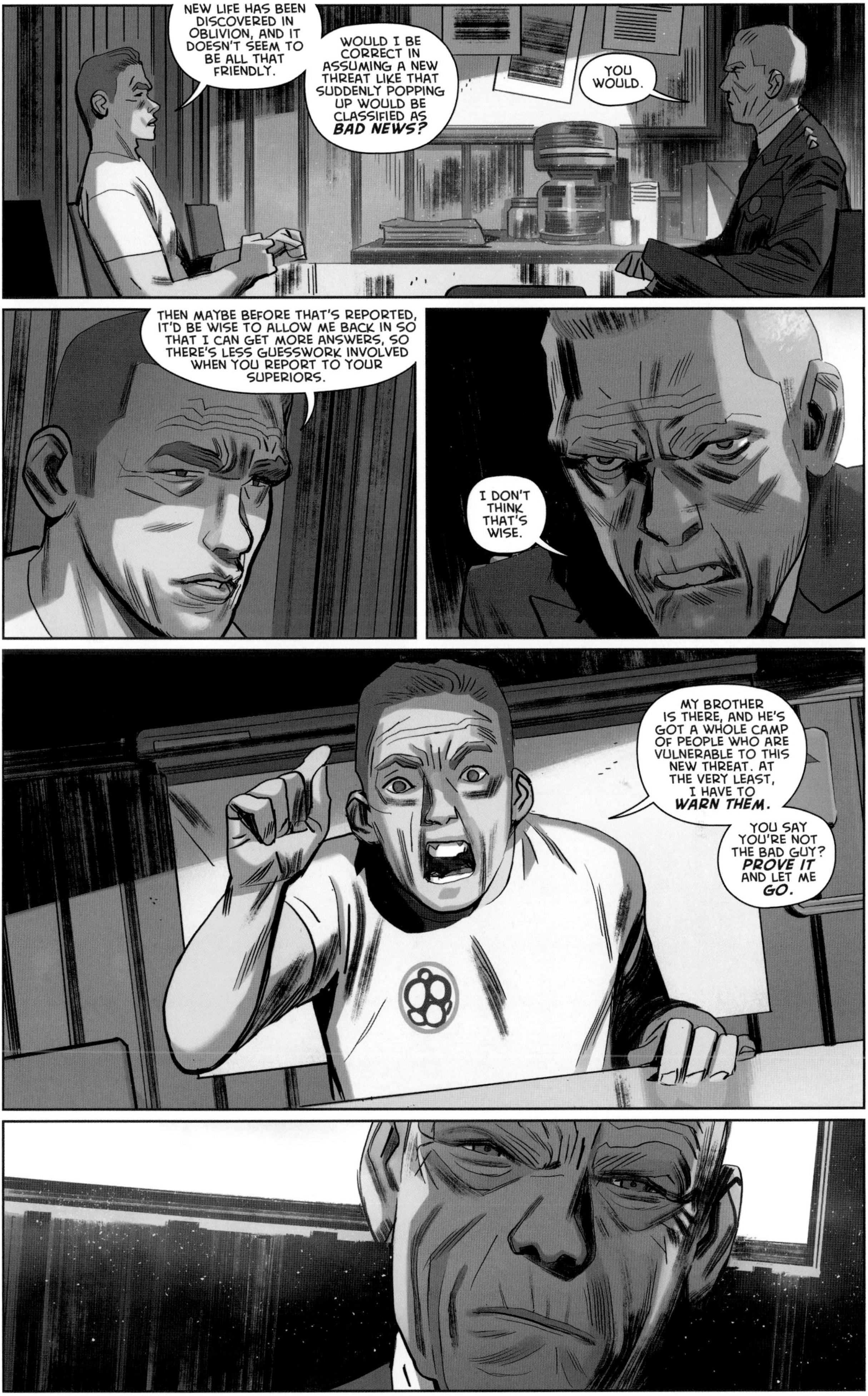
NEW LIFE HAS BEEN DISCOVERED IN OBLIVION, AND IT DOESN'T SEEM TO BE ALL THAT FRIENDLY.
WOULD I BE CORRECT IN ASSUMING A NEW THREAT LIKE THAT SUDDENLY POPPING UP WOULD BE CLASSIFIED AS ***BAD NEWS?***
YOU WOULD.
THEN MAYBE BEFORE THAT'S REPORTED, IT'D BE WISE TO ALLOW ME BACK IN SO SO THAT I CAN GET MORE ANSWERS, SO THERE'S LESS GUESSWORK INVOLVED WHEN YOU REPORT TO YOUR SUPERIORS.
I DON'T THINK THAT'S WISE.
MY BROTHER IS THERE, AND HE'S GOT A WHOLE CAMP OF PEOPLE WHO ARE VULNERABLE TO THIS NEW THREAT. AT THE VERY LEAST, I HAVE TO ***WARN THEM.***
YOU SAY YOU'RE NOT THE BAD GUY? ***PROVE IT*** AND LET ME ***GO.***

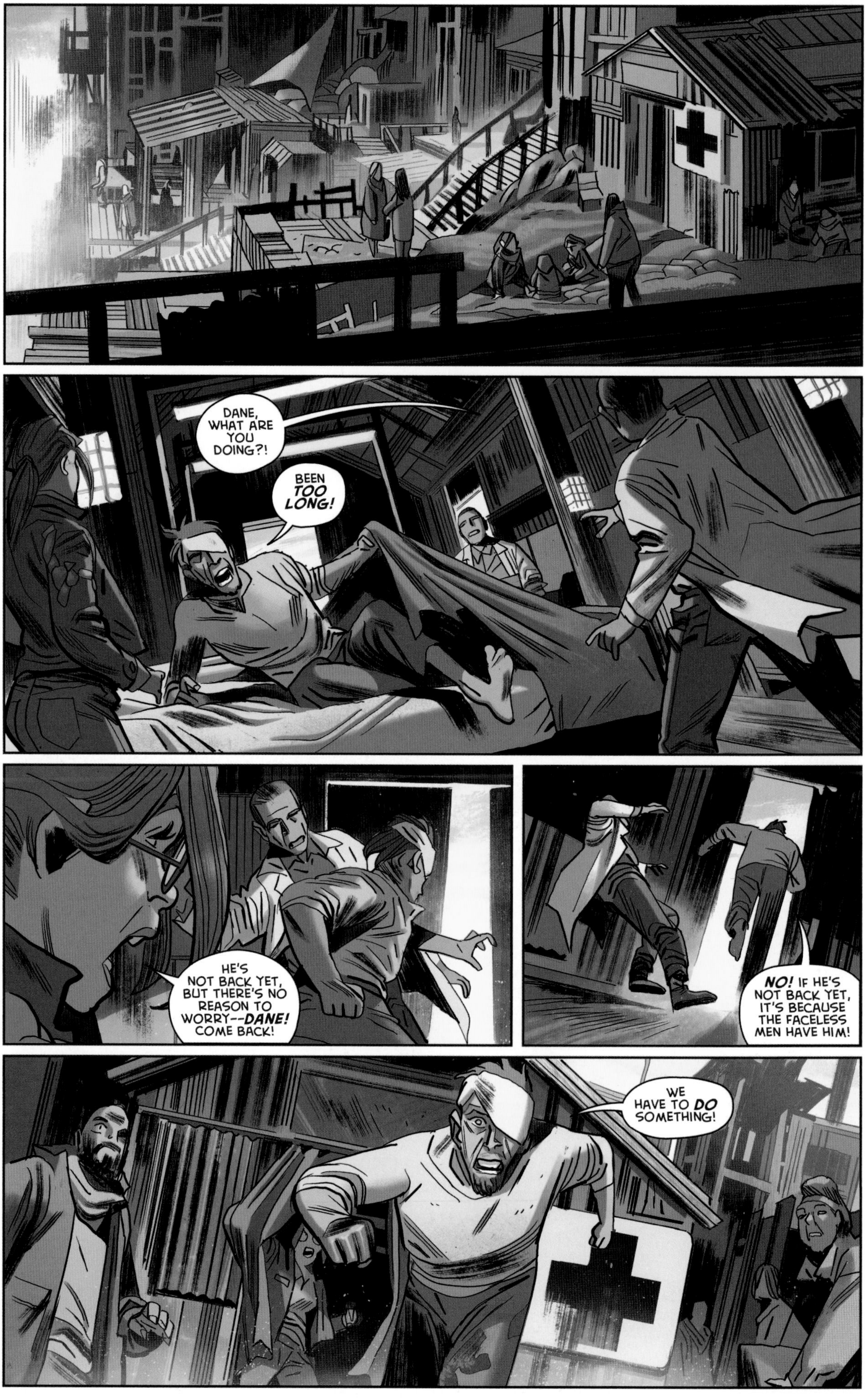
DANE, WHAT ARE YOU DOING?!
BEEN TOO LONG!
HE'S NOT BACK YET, BUT THERE'S NO REASON TO WORRY--DANE! COME BACK!
NO! IF HE'S NOT BACK YET, IT'S BECAUSE THE FACELESS MEN HAVE HIM!
WE HAVE TO DO SOMETHING!

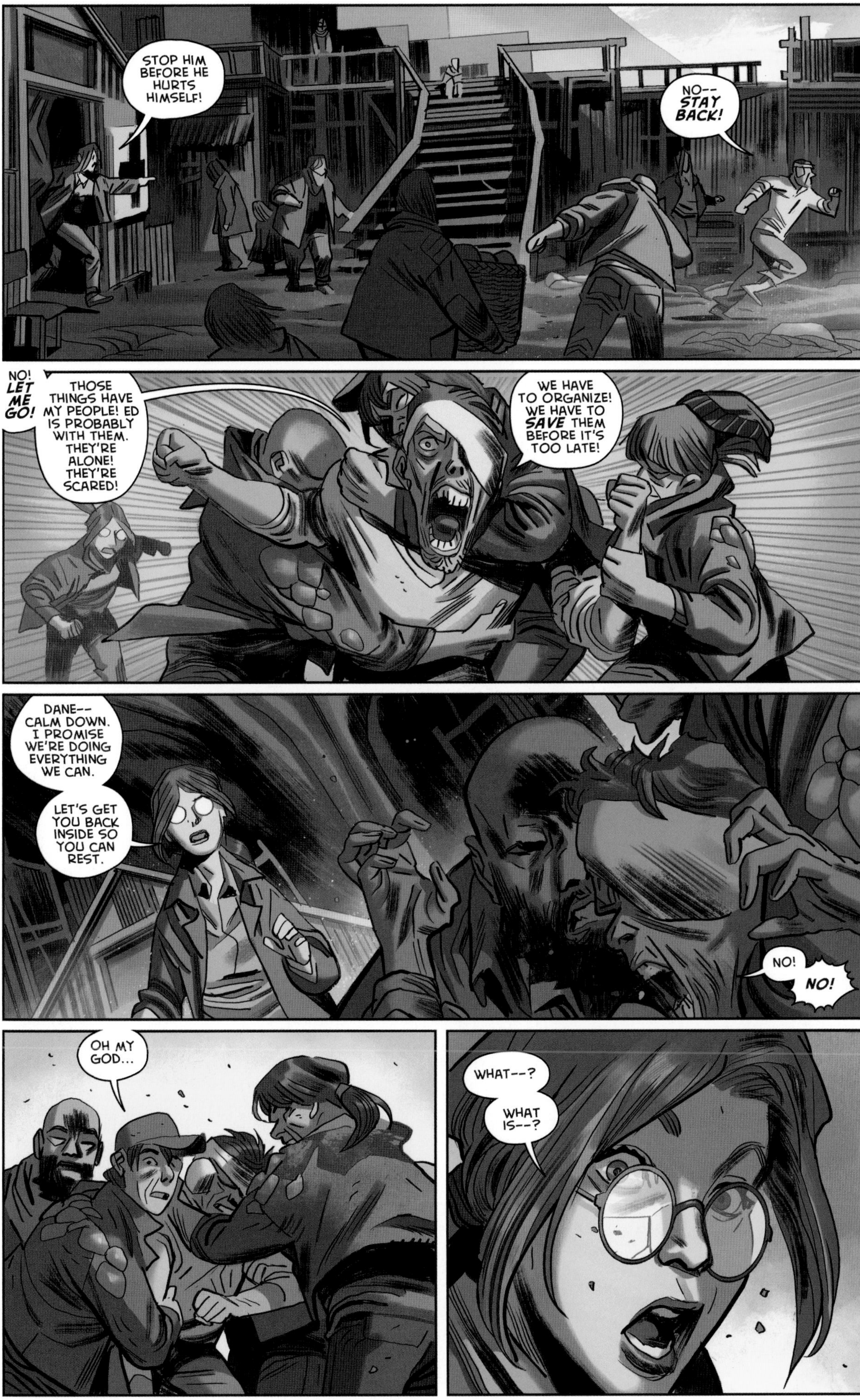
STOP HIM BEFORE HE HURTS HIMSELF!
NO-- STAY BACK!
NO! LET ME GO!
THOSE THINGS HAVE MY PEOPLE! ED IS PROBABLY WITH THEM. THEY'RE ALONE! THEY'RE SCARED!
WE HAVE TO ORGANIZE! WE HAVE TO SAVE THEM BEFORE IT'S TOO LATE!
DANE-- CALM DOWN. I PROMISE WE'RE DOING EVERYTHING WE CAN.
LET'S GET YOU BACK INSIDE SO YOU CAN REST.
NO!
NO!
OH MY GOD...
WHAT--?
WHAT IS--?

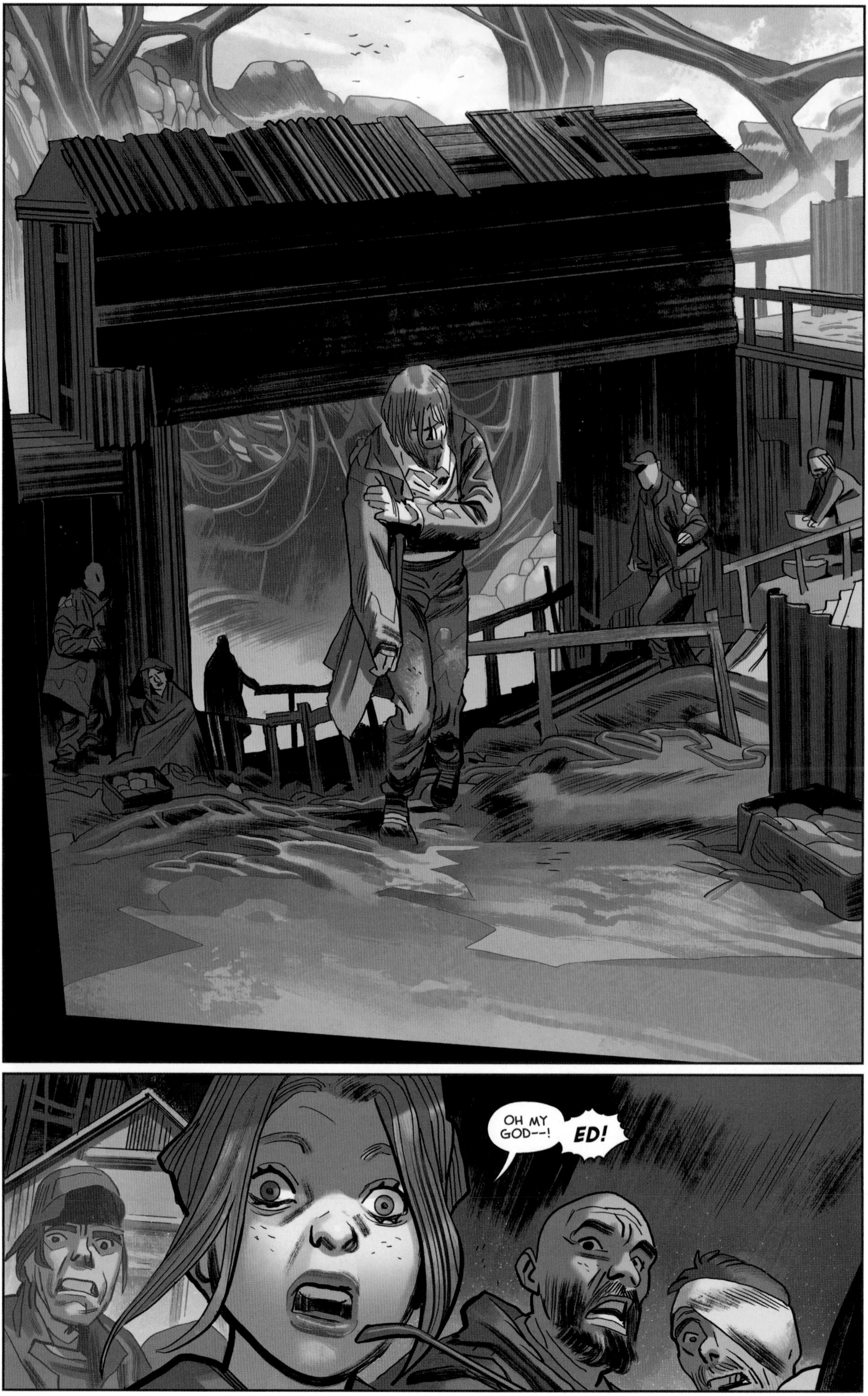
OH MY GOD--!
ED!

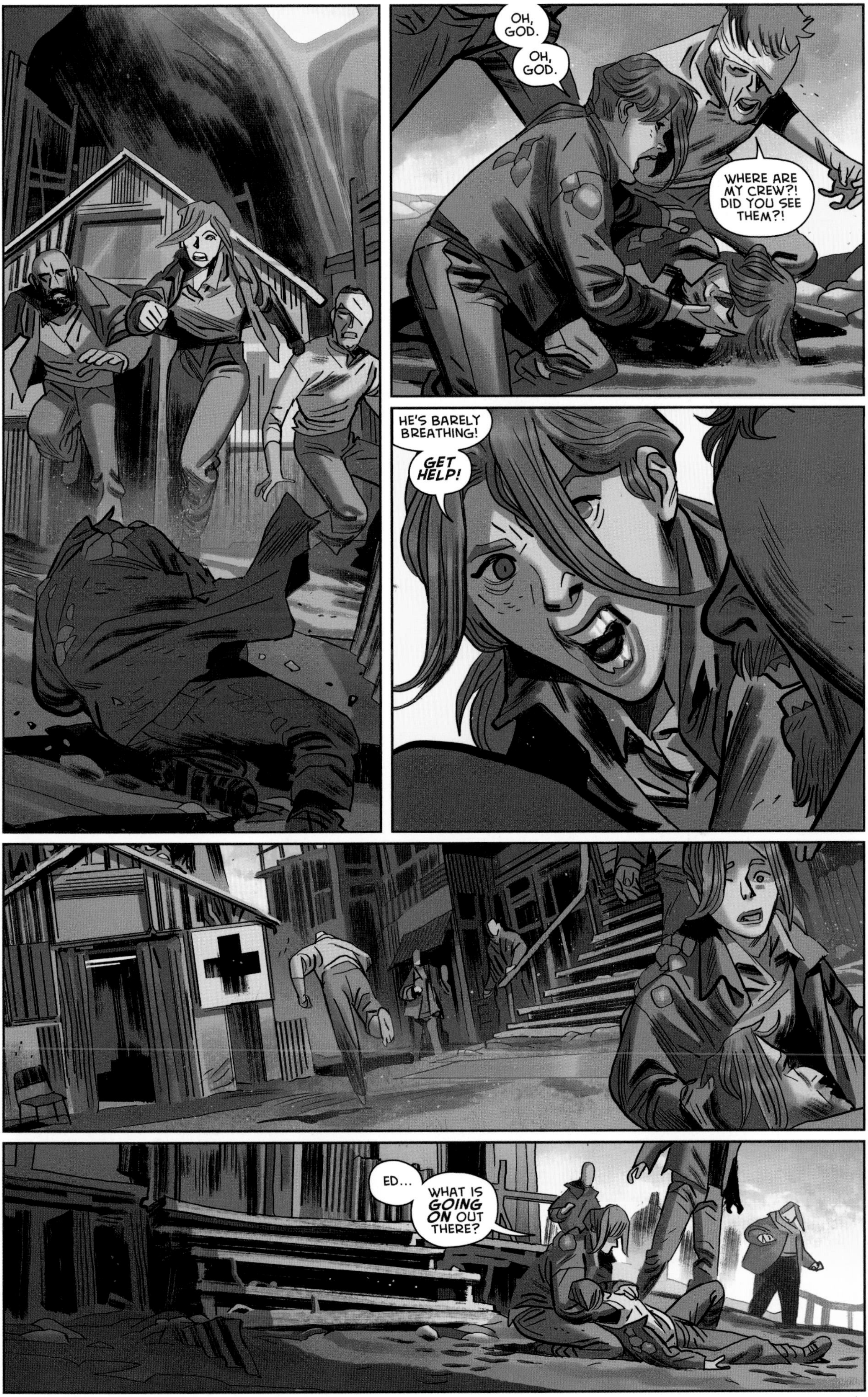
OH, GOD.
OH, GOD.
WHERE ARE MY CREW?! DID YOU SEE THEM?!
HE'S BARELY BREATHING!
GET HELP!
ED...
WHAT IS GOING ON OUT THERE?

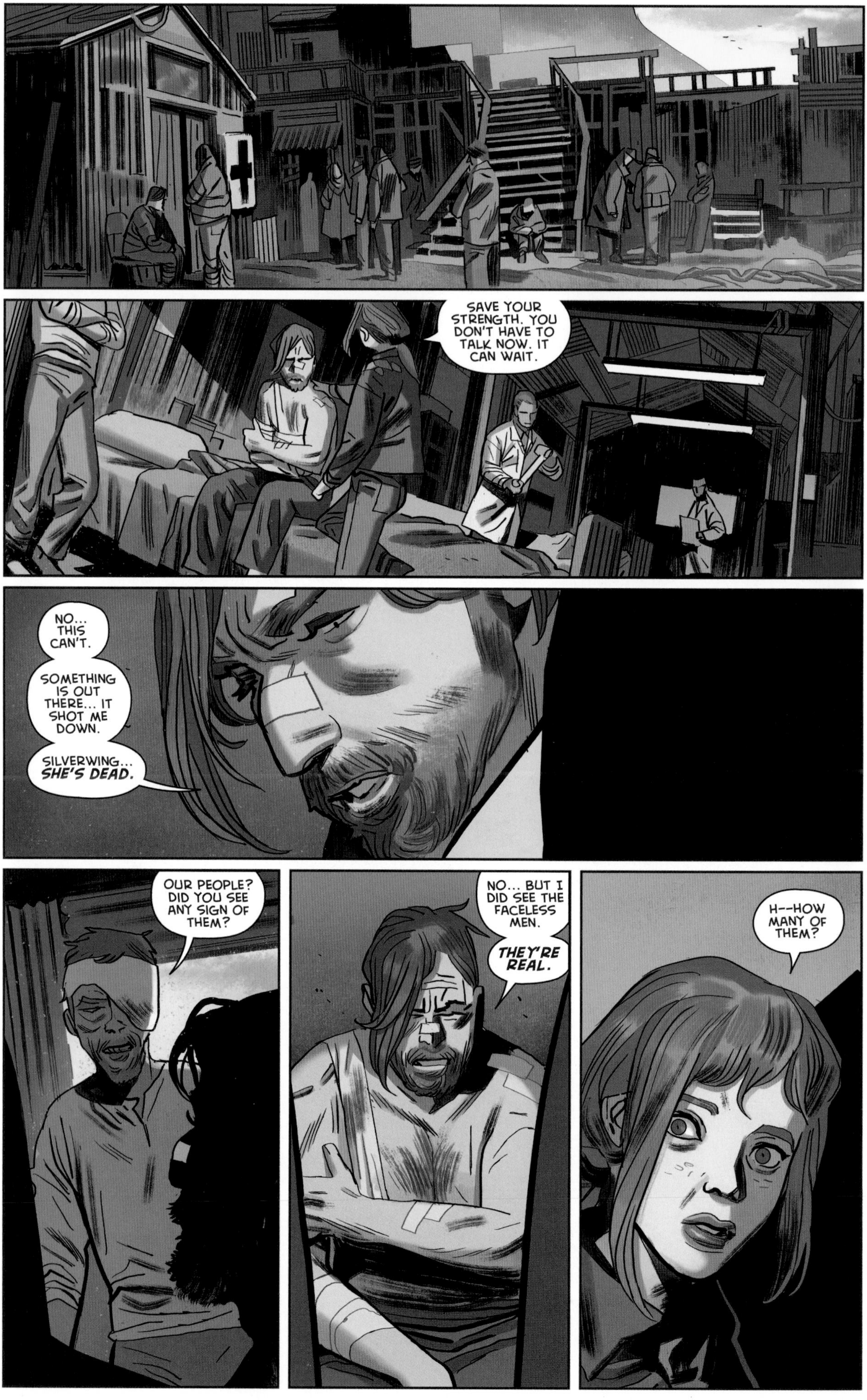
SAVE YOUR STRENGTH. YOU DON'T HAVE TO TALK NOW. IT CAN WAIT.
NO... THIS CAN'T.
SOMETHING IS OUT THERE... IT SHOT ME DOWN.
SILVERWING... **SHE'S DEAD.**
OUR PEOPLE? DID YOU SEE ANY SIGN OF THEM?
NO... BUT I DID SEE THE FACELESS MEN.
THEY'RE REAL.
H--HOW MANY OF THEM?

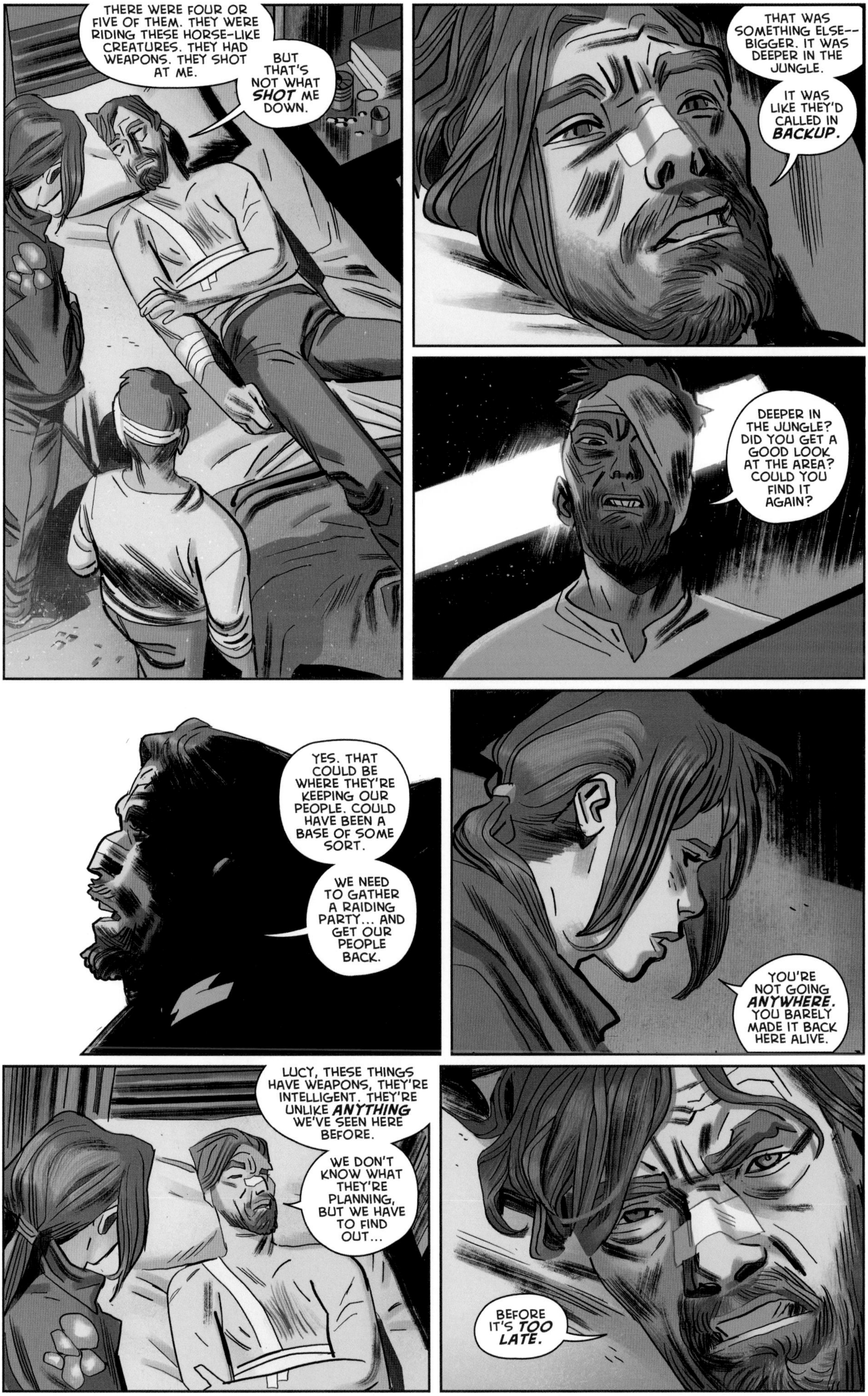

THERE WERE FOUR OR FIVE OF THEM. THEY WERE RIDING THESE HORSE-LIKE CREATURES. THEY HAD WEAPONS. THEY SHOT AT ME.
BUT THAT'S NOT WHAT SHOT ME DOWN.
THAT WAS SOMETHING ELSE-- BIGGER. IT WAS DEEPER IN THE JUNGLE.
IT WAS LIKE THEY'D CALLED IN BACKUP.
DEEPER IN THE JUNGLE? DID YOU GET A GOOD LOOK AT THE AREA? COULD YOU FIND IT AGAIN?
YES. THAT COULD BE WHERE THEY'RE KEEPING OUR PEOPLE. COULD HAVE BEEN A BASE OF SOME SORT.
WE NEED TO GATHER A RAIDING PARTY... AND GET OUR PEOPLE BACK.
YOU'RE NOT GOING ANYWHERE. YOU BARELY MADE IT BACK HERE ALIVE.
LUCY, THESE THINGS HAVE WEAPONS, THEY'RE INTELLIGENT. THEY'RE UNLIKE ANYTHING WE'VE SEEN HERE BEFORE.
WE DON'T KNOW WHAT THEY'RE PLANNING, BUT WE HAVE TO FIND OUT...
BEFORE IT'S TOO LATE.

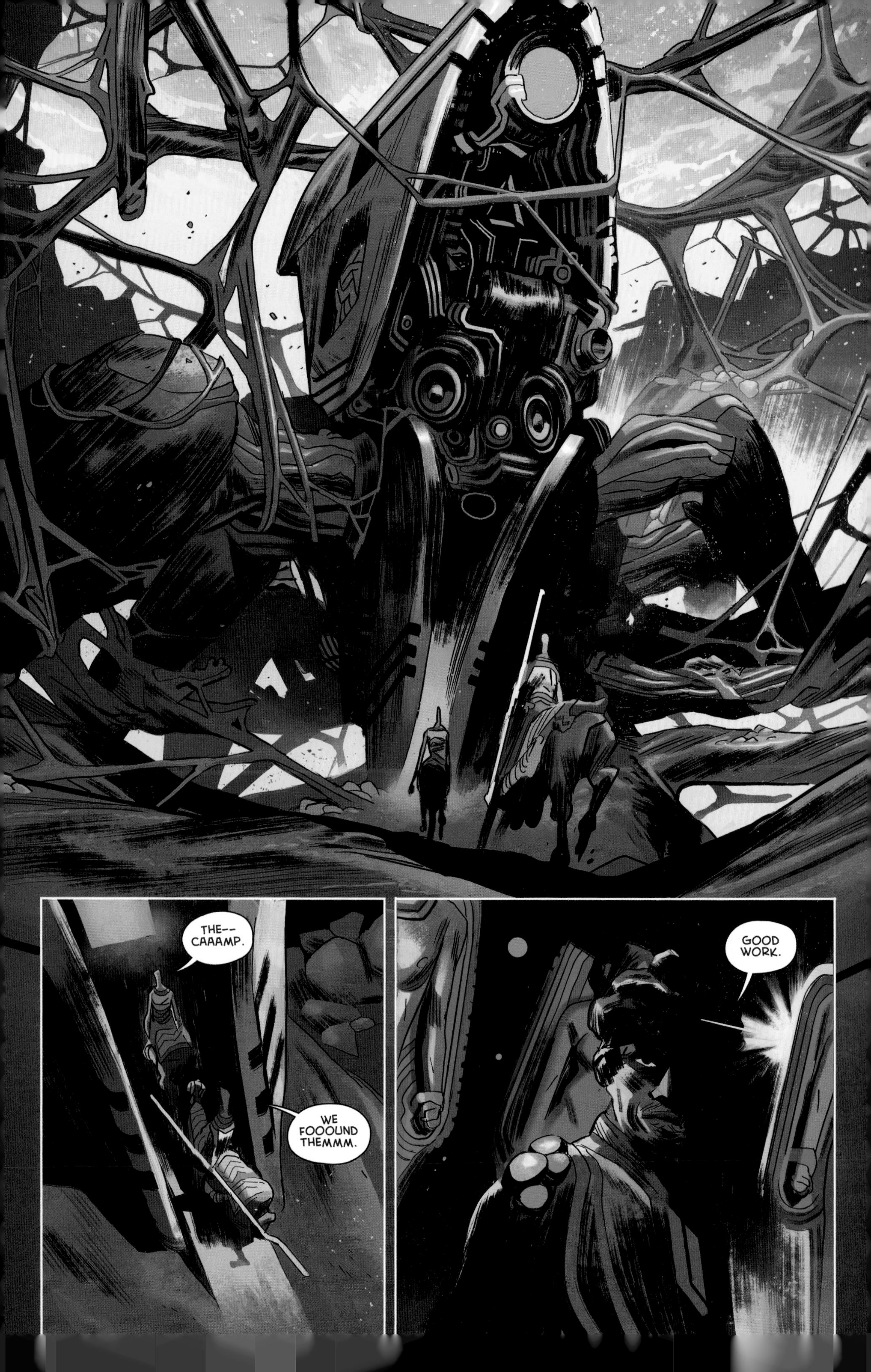
THE--
CAAAMP.
WE FOOOUND THEMMM.
GOOD WORK.

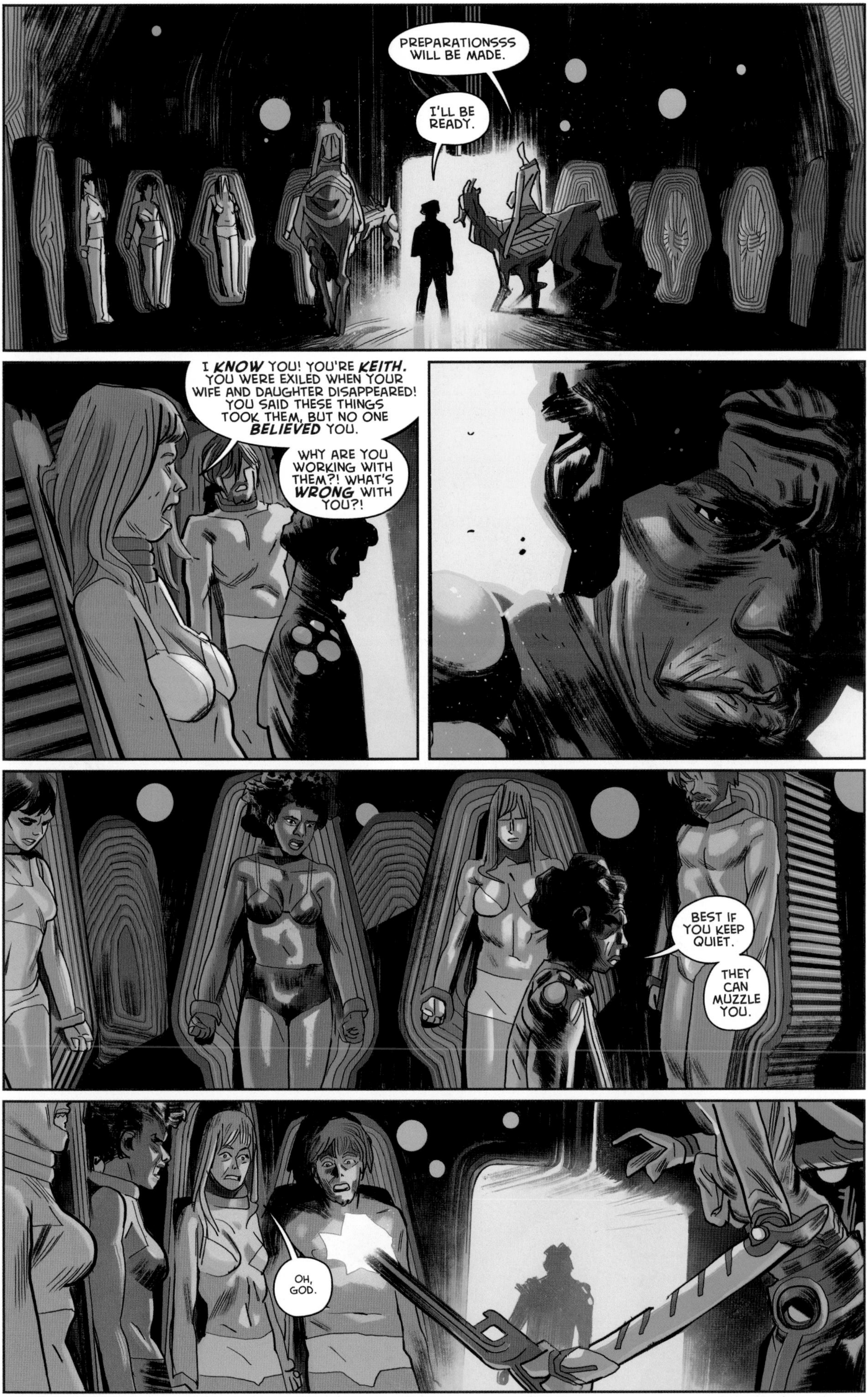
PREPARATIONSSS WILL BE MADE.
I'LL BE READY.
I KNOW YOU! YOU'RE KEITH. YOU WERE EXILED WHEN YOUR WIFE AND DAUGHTER DISAPPEARED! YOU SAID THESE THINGS TOOK THEM, BUT NO ONE BELIEVED YOU.
WHY ARE YOU WORKING WITH THEM?! WHAT'S WRONG WITH YOU?!
BEST IF YOU KEEP QUIET.
THEY CAN MUZZLE YOU.
OH, GOD.

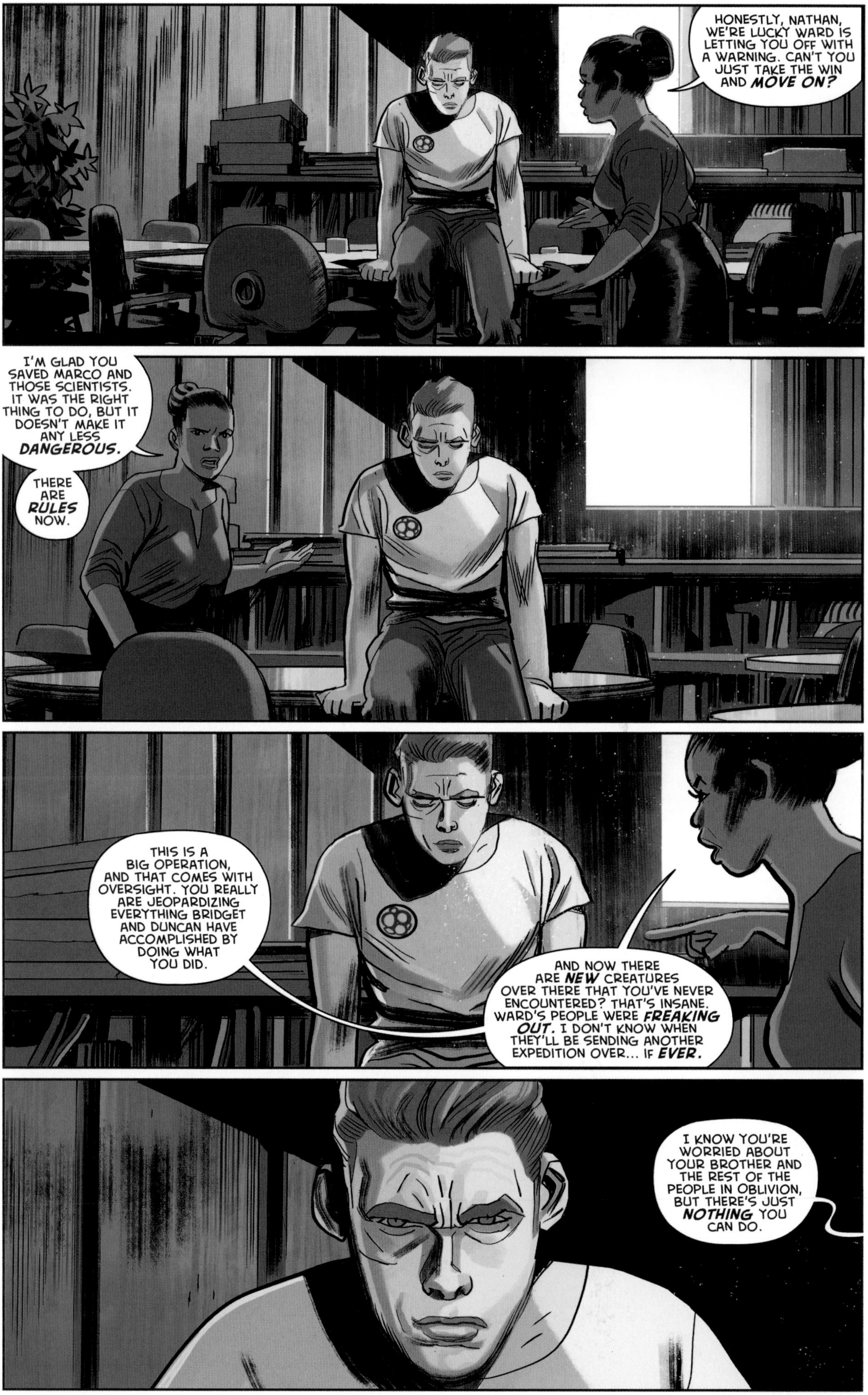
HONESTLY, NATHAN, WE'RE LUCKY WARD IS LETTING YOU OFF WITH A WARNING. CAN'T YOU JUST TAKE THE WIN AND **MOVE ON?**
I'M GLAD YOU SAVED MARCO AND THOSE SCIENTISTS. IT WAS THE RIGHT THING TO DO, BUT IT DOESN'T MAKE IT ANY LESS **DANGEROUS.**
THERE ARE **RULES** NOW.
THIS IS A BIG OPERATION, AND THAT COMES WITH OVERSIGHT. YOU REALLY ARE JEOPARDIZING EVERYTHING BRIDGET AND DUNCAN HAVE ACCOMPLISHED BY DOING WHAT YOU DID.
AND NOW THERE ARE **NEW** CREATURES OVER THERE THAT YOU'VE NEVER ENCOUNTERED? THAT'S INSANE. WARD'S PEOPLE WERE **FREAKING OUT.** I DON'T KNOW WHEN THEY'LL BE SENDING ANOTHER EXPEDITION OVER... IF **EVER.**
I KNOW YOU'RE WORRIED ABOUT YOUR BROTHER AND THE REST OF THE PEOPLE IN OBLIVION, BUT THERE'S JUST **NOTHING** YOU CAN DO.

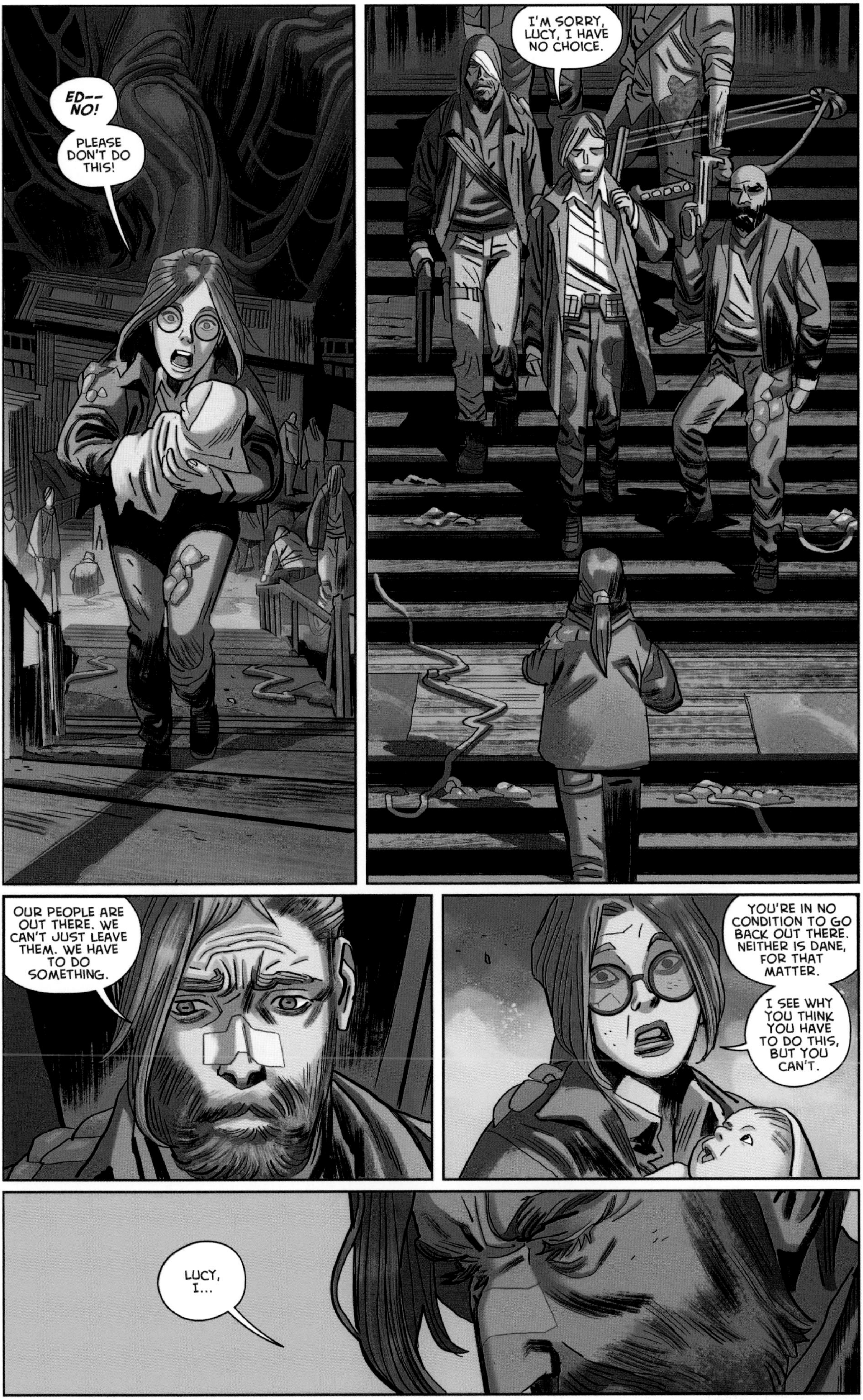
ED-- NO!
PLEASE DON'T DO THIS!
I'M SORRY, LUCY, I HAVE NO CHOICE.
OUR PEOPLE ARE OUT THERE. WE CAN'T JUST LEAVE THEM. WE HAVE TO DO SOMETHING.
YOU'RE IN NO CONDITION TO GO BACK OUT THERE. NEITHER IS DANE, FOR THAT MATTER.
I SEE WHY YOU THINK YOU HAVE TO DO THIS, BUT YOU CAN'T.
LUCY, I...

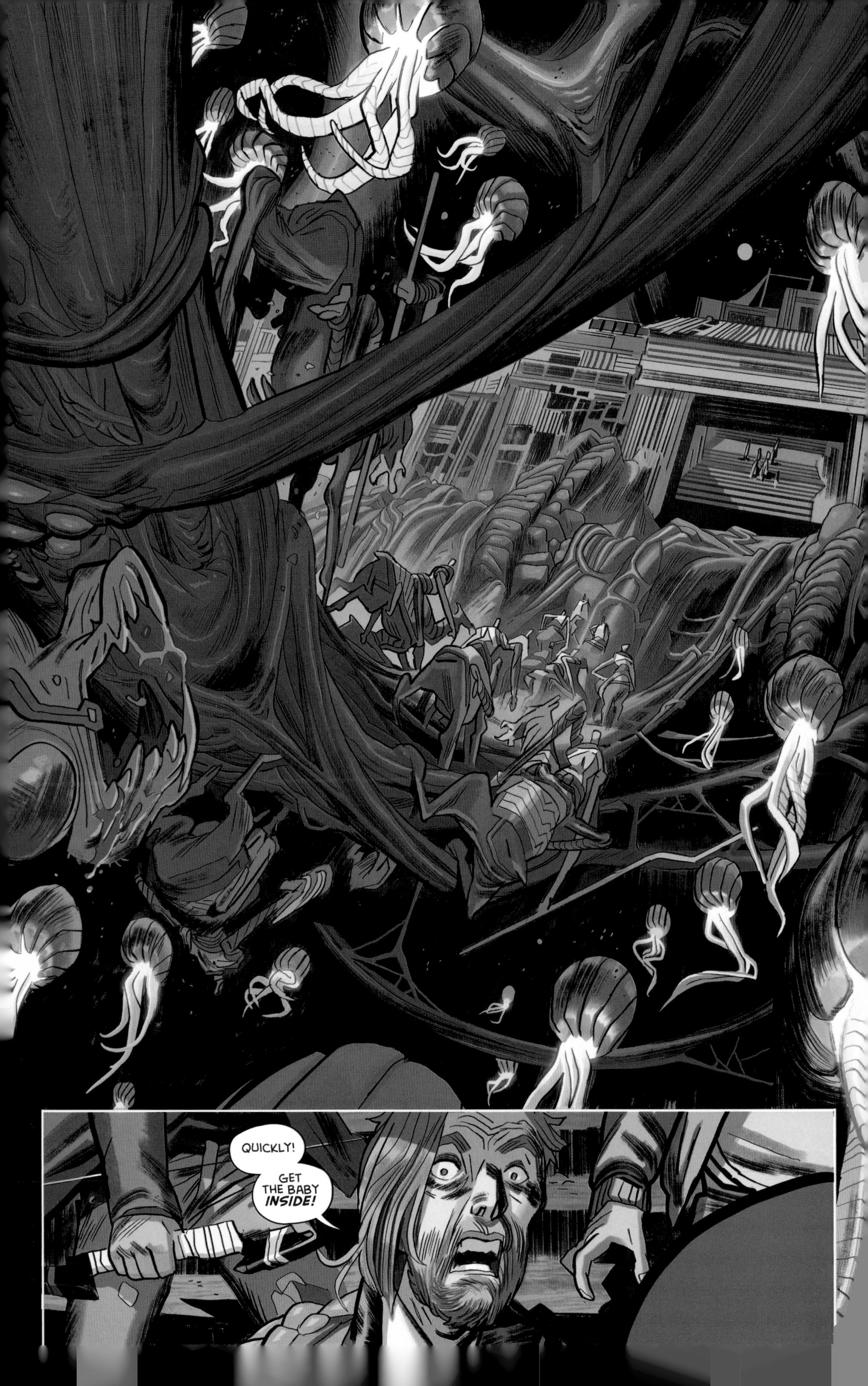
QUICKLY!
GET THE BABY **INSIDE!**

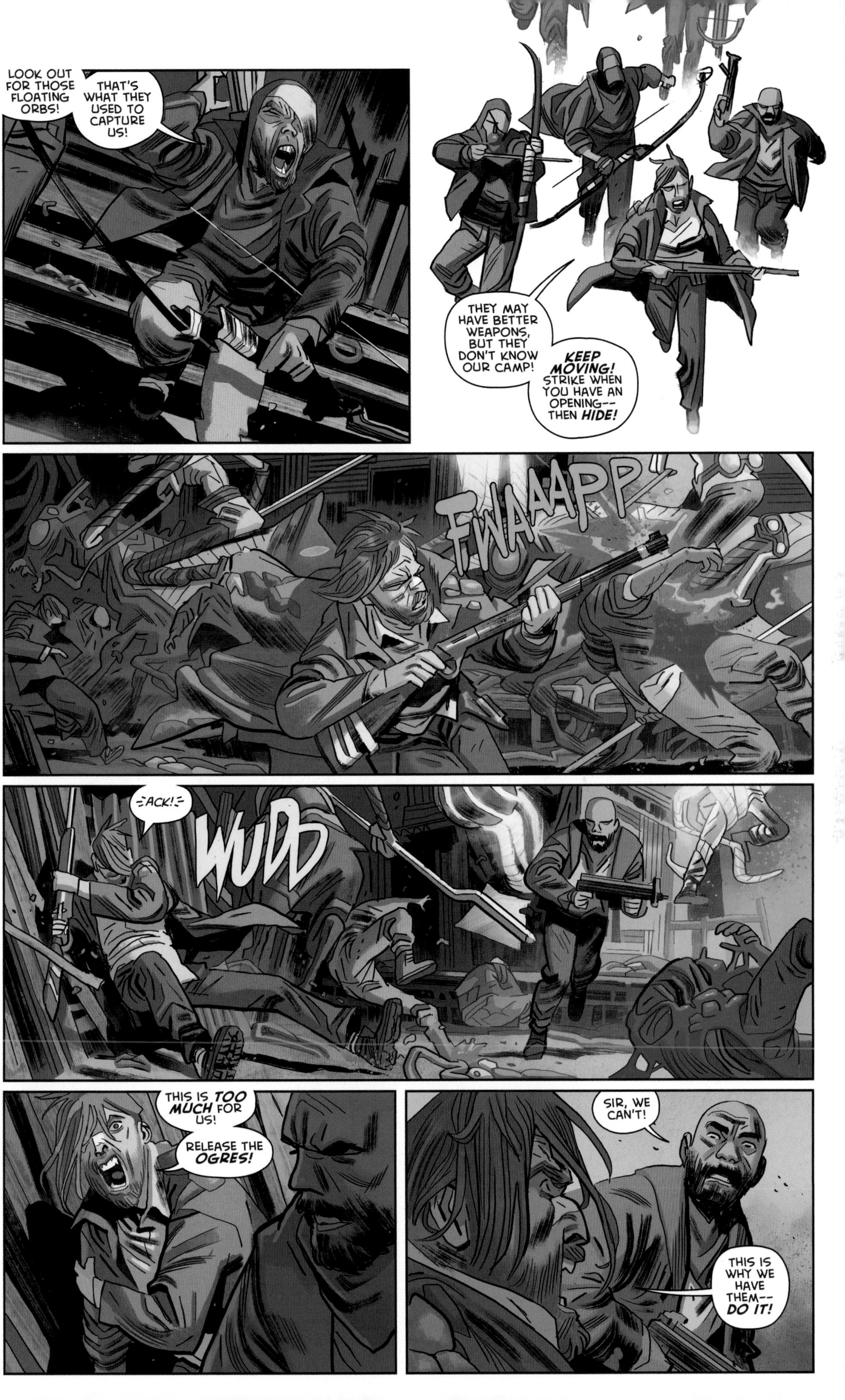
LOOK OUT FOR THOSE FLOATING ORBS!
THAT'S WHAT THEY USED TO CAPTURE US!
THEY MAY HAVE BETTER WEAPONS, BUT THEY DON'T KNOW OUR CAMP!
KEEP MOVING! STRIKE WHEN YOU HAVE AN OPENING-- THEN HIDE!
FWAAAPP
ACK!
WUDD
THIS IS TOO MUCH FOR US!
RELEASE THE OGRES!
SIR, WE CAN'T!
THIS IS WHY WE HAVE THEM-- DO IT!

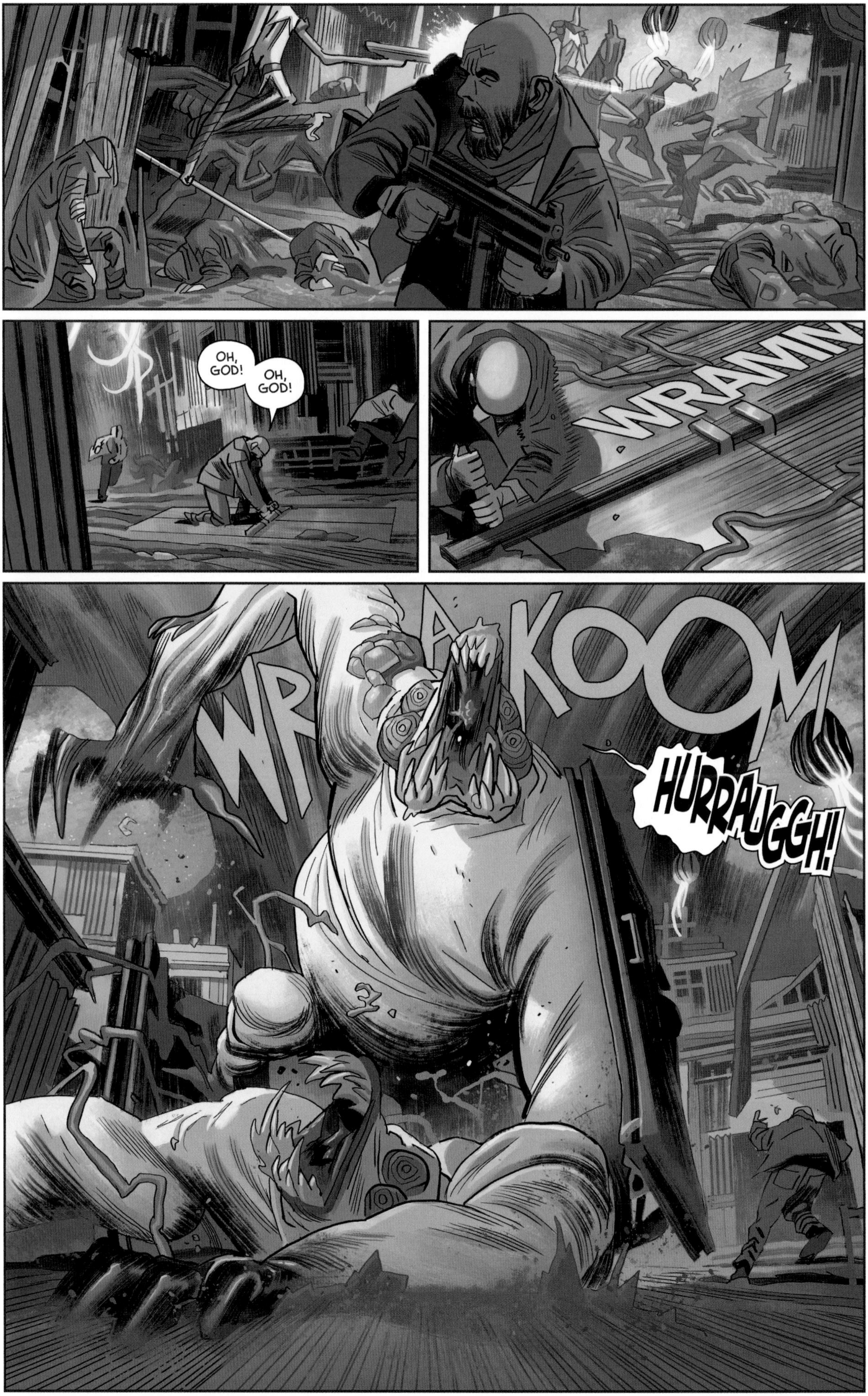
OH, GOD!
OH, GOD!
WRAMM
WRAKOOM
HURRAUGGH!

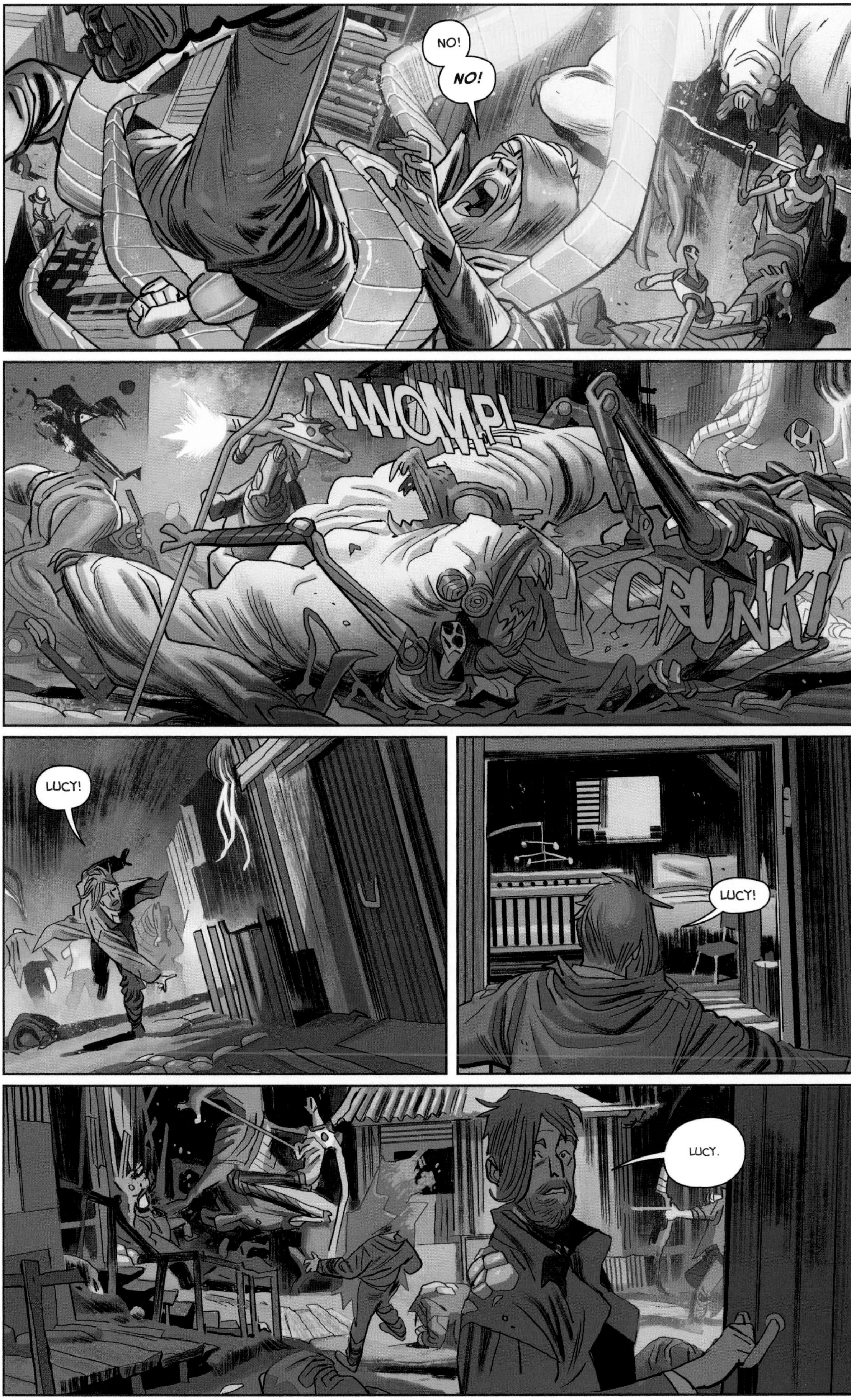
NO!
NO!
WOMP!
CRUNK!
LUCY!
LUCY!
LUCY.

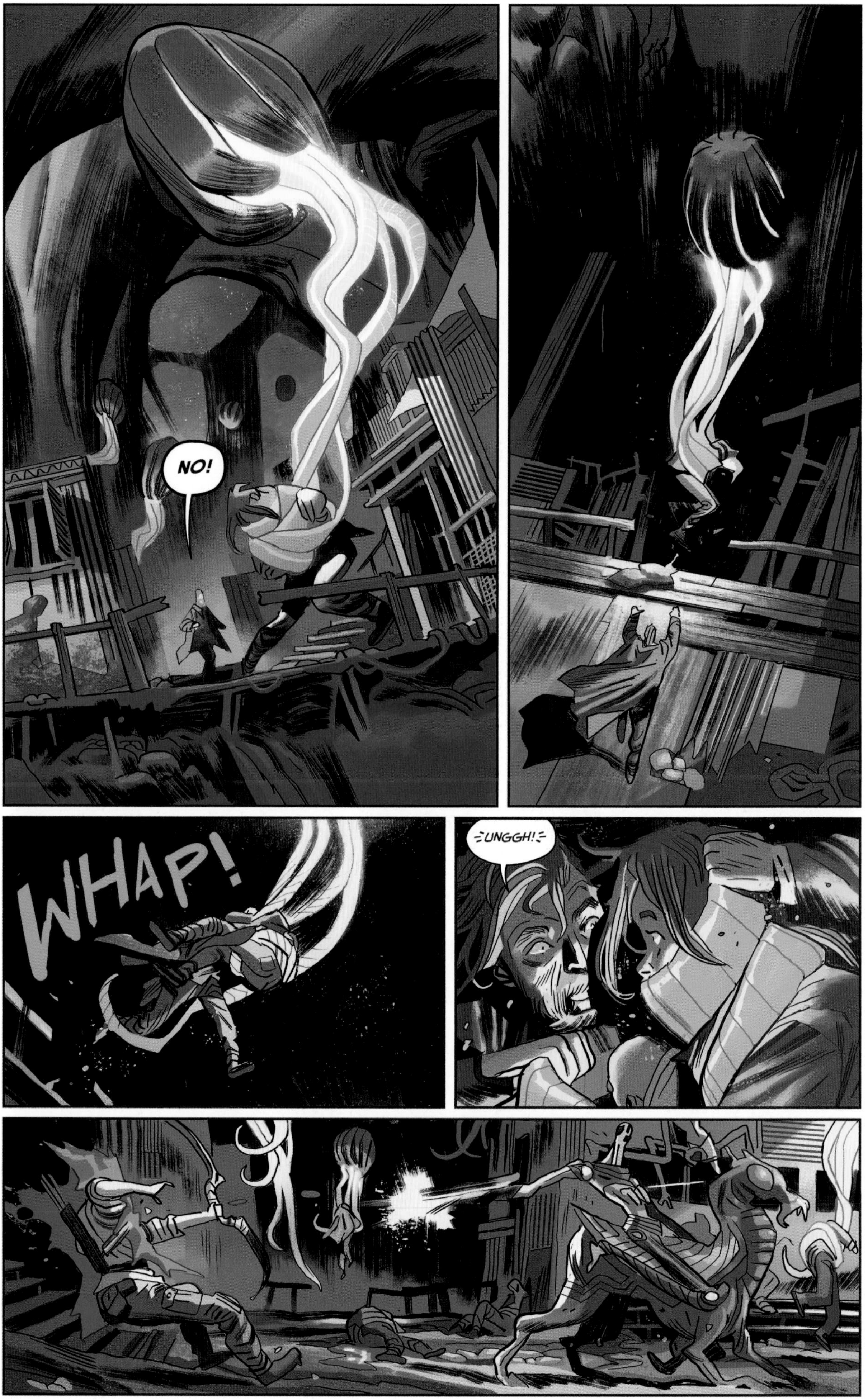
NO!
WHAP!
UNGGH!

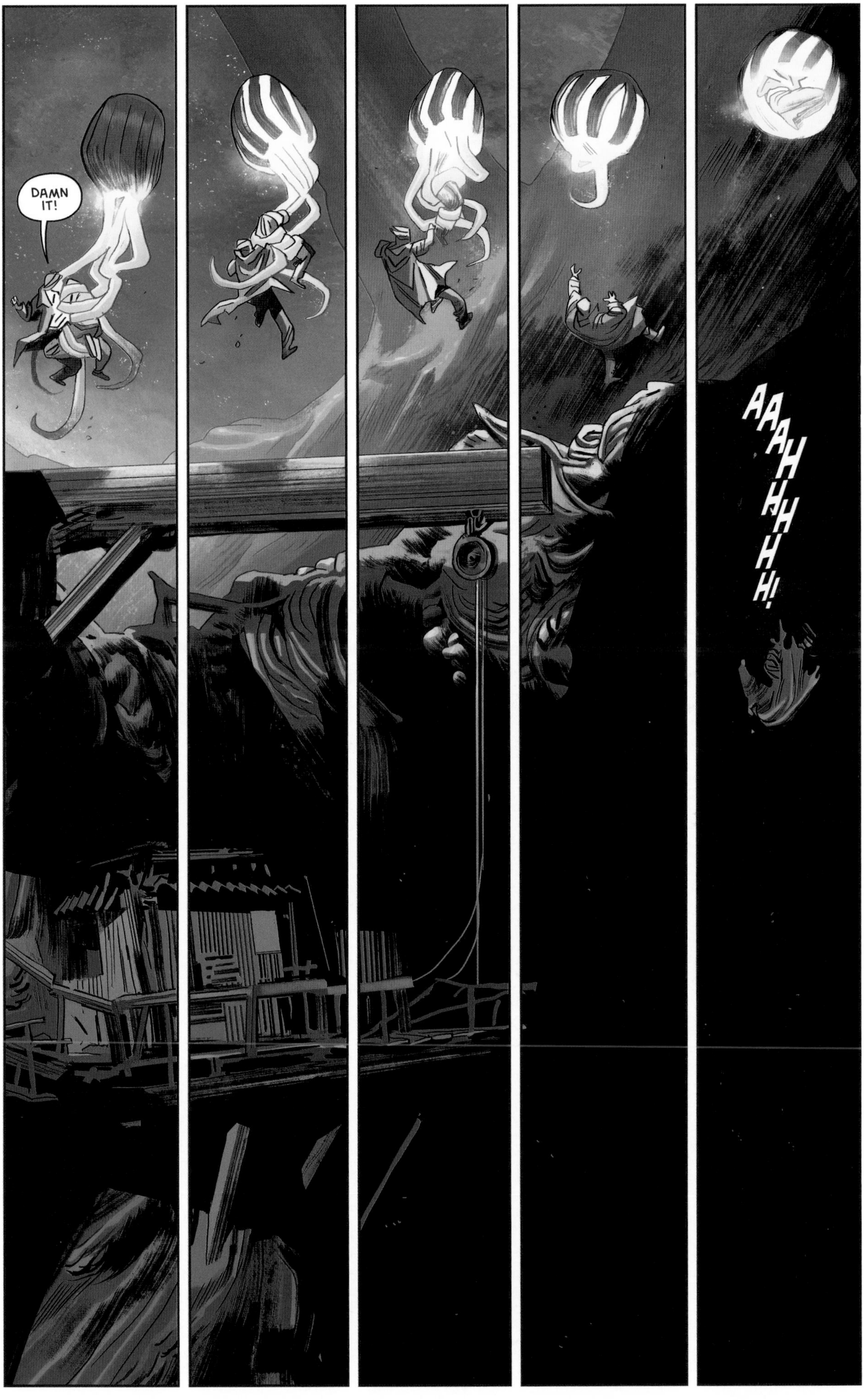
DAMN IT!
AAAHHHHHH!

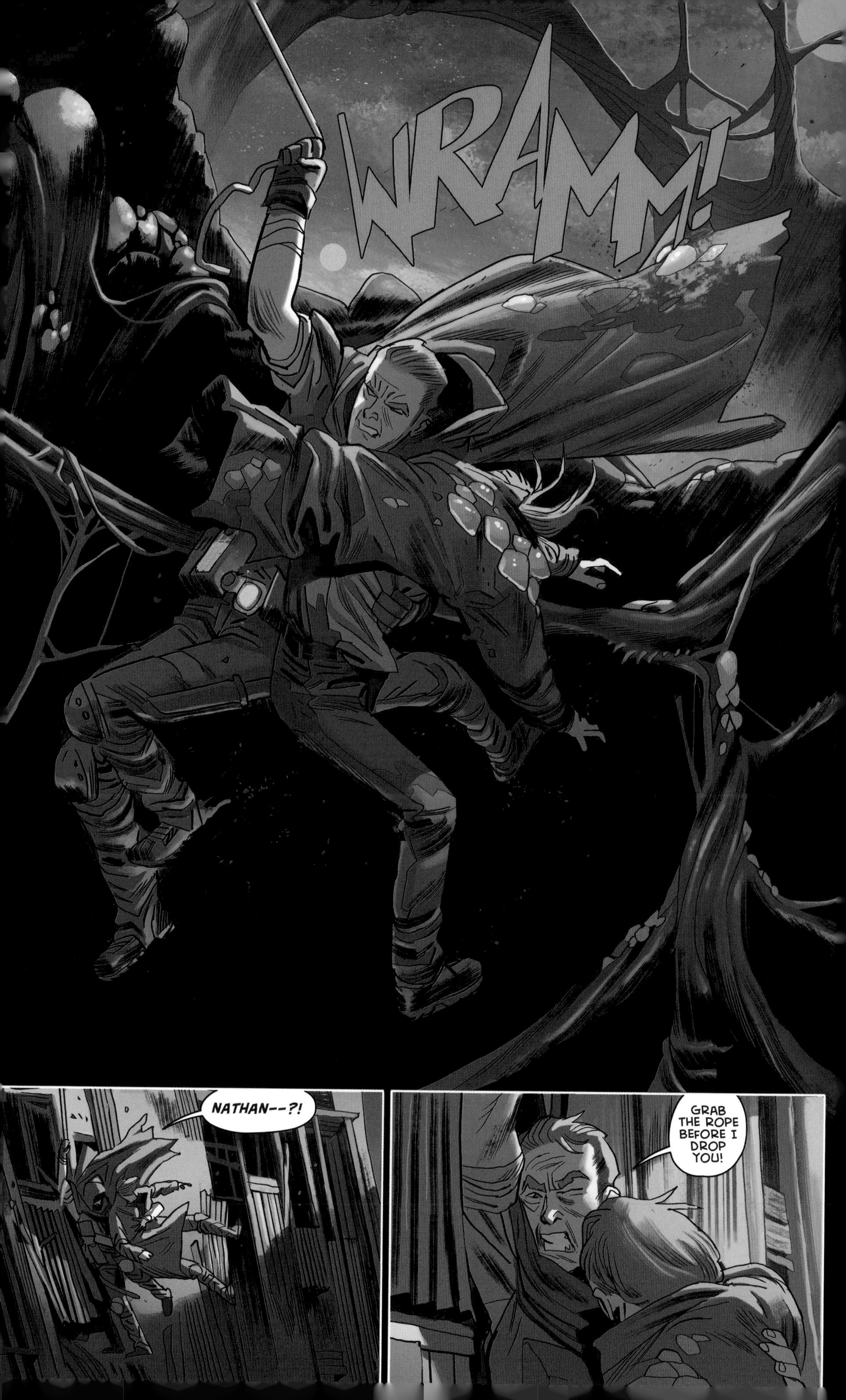
WRAMM!
NATHAN--?!
GRAB THE ROPE BEFORE I DROP YOU!

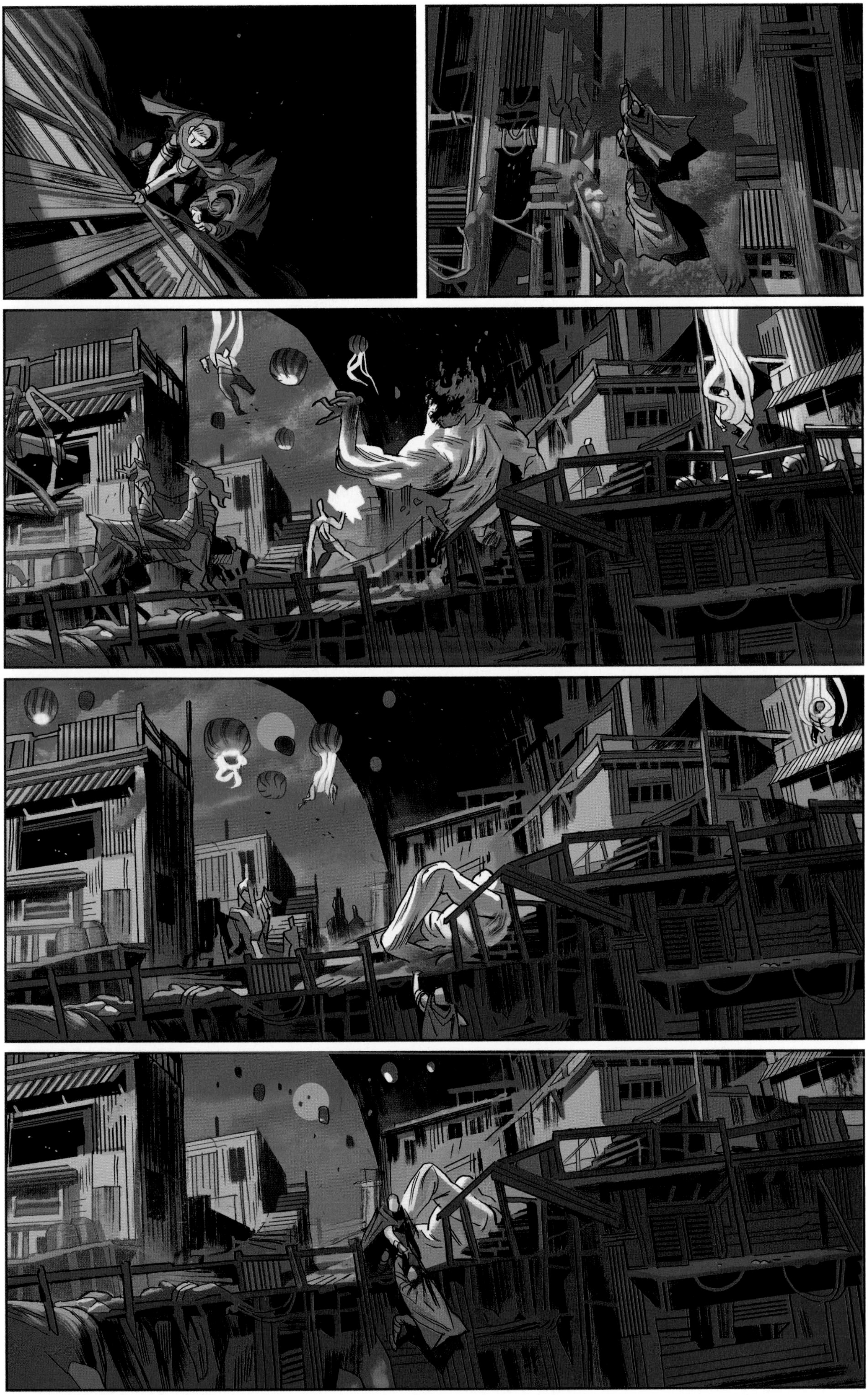

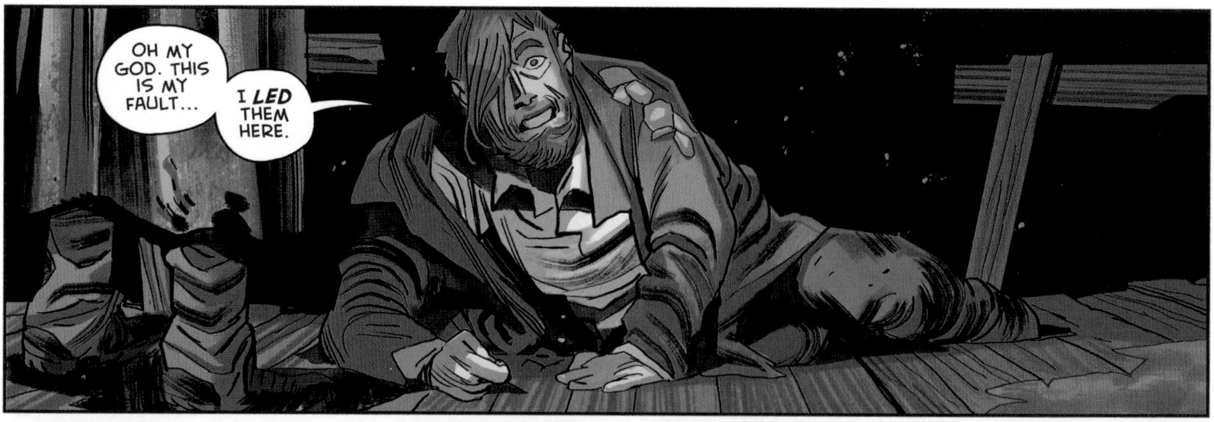
OH MY GOD. THIS IS MY FAULT...
I LED THEM HERE.

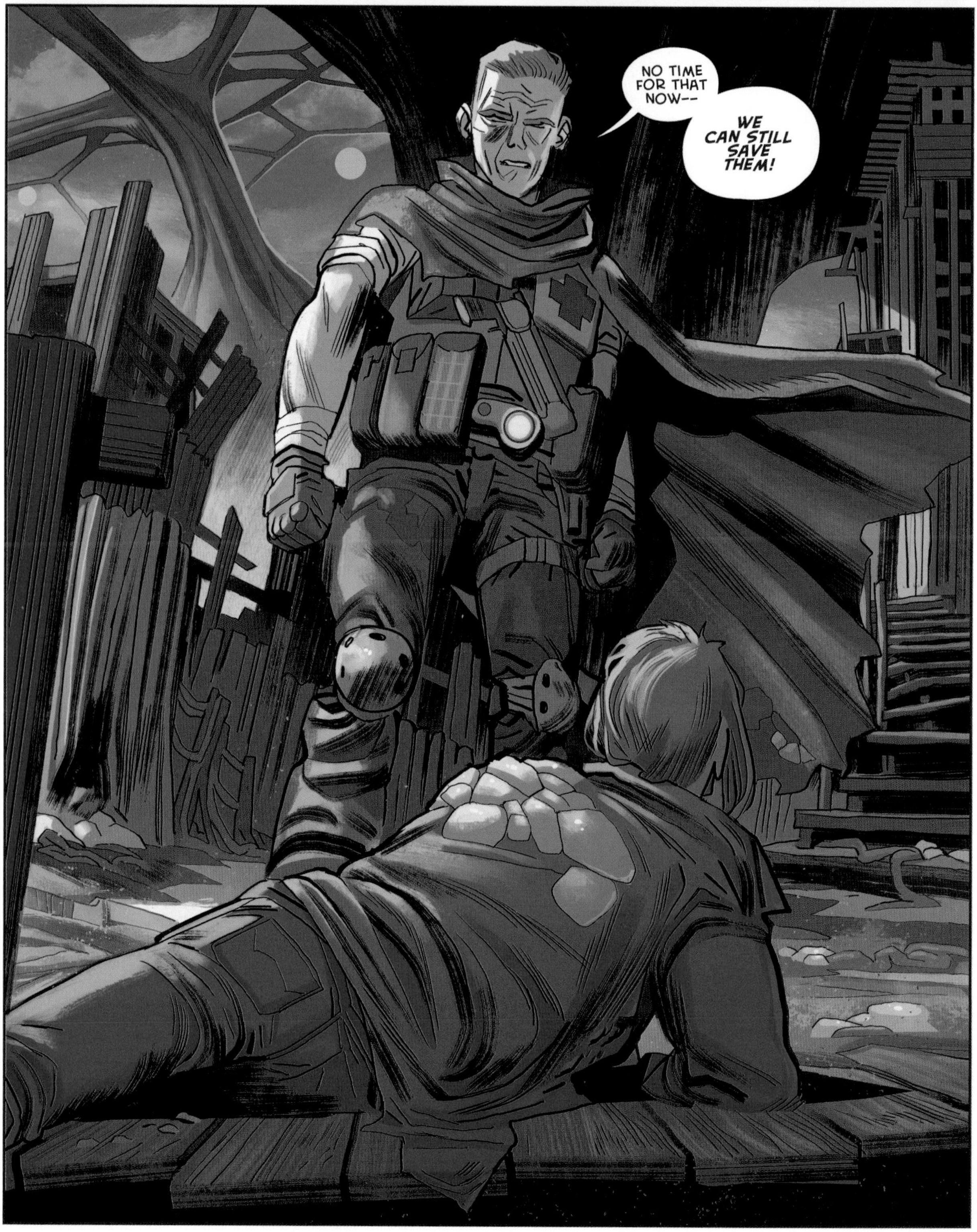
NO TIME FOR THAT NOW--
WE CAN STILL SAVE THEM!

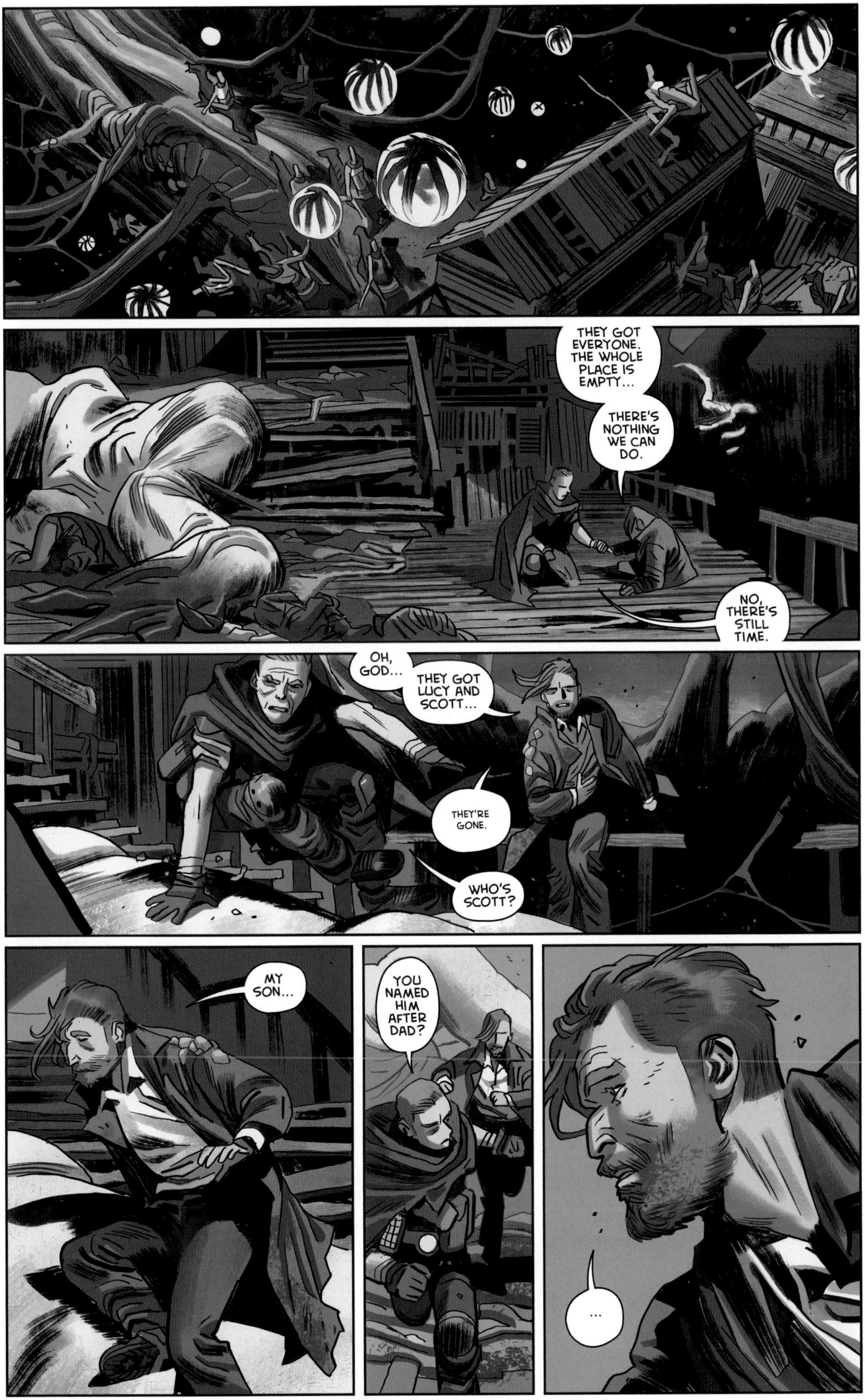
THEY GOT EVERYONE. THE WHOLE PLACE IS EMPTY...
THERE'S NOTHING WE CAN DO.
NO, THERE'S STILL TIME.
OH, GOD...
THEY GOT LUCY AND SCOTT...
THEY'RE GONE.
WHO'S SCOTT?
MY SON...
YOU NAMED HIM AFTER DAD?
...

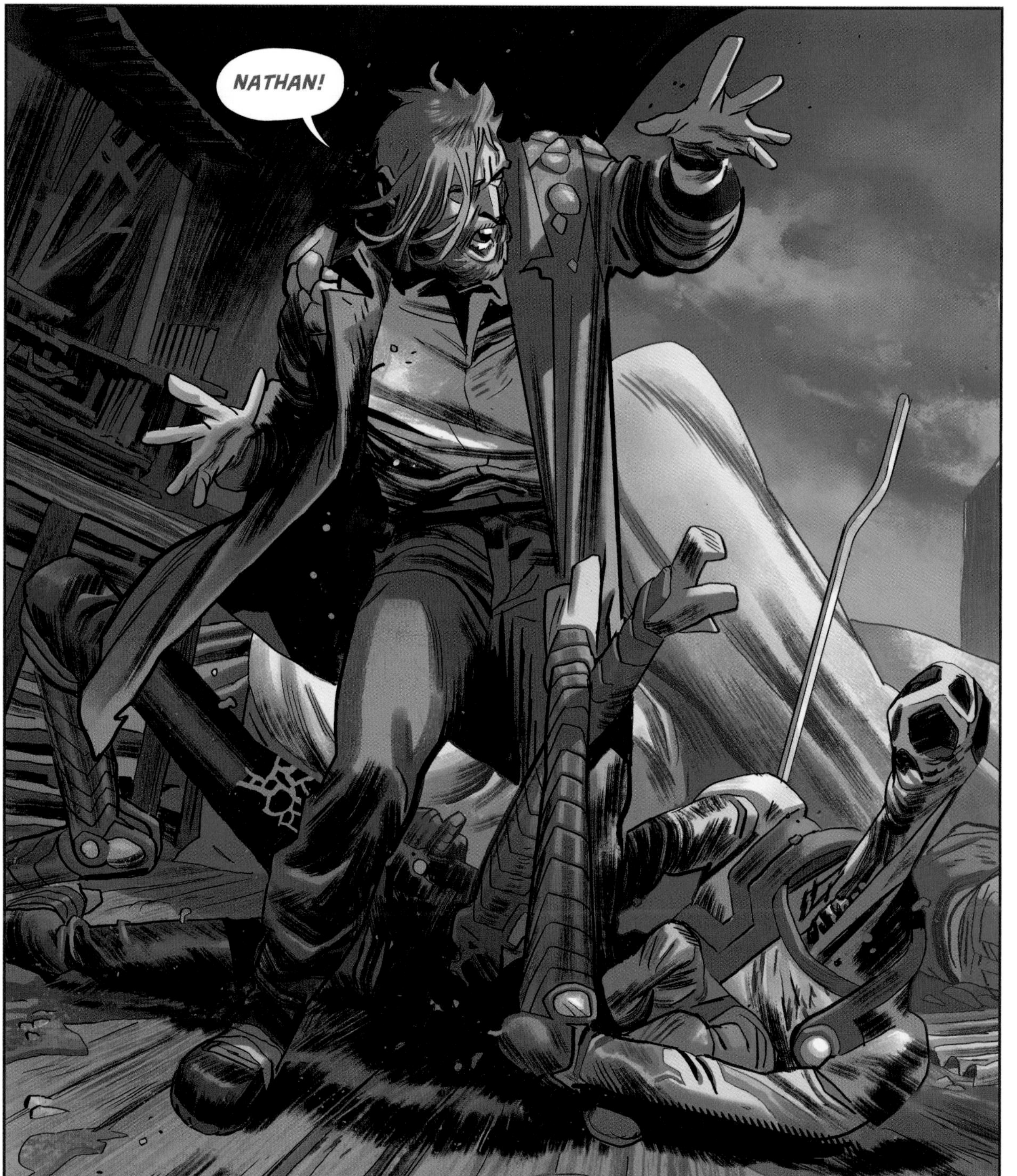
NATHAN!

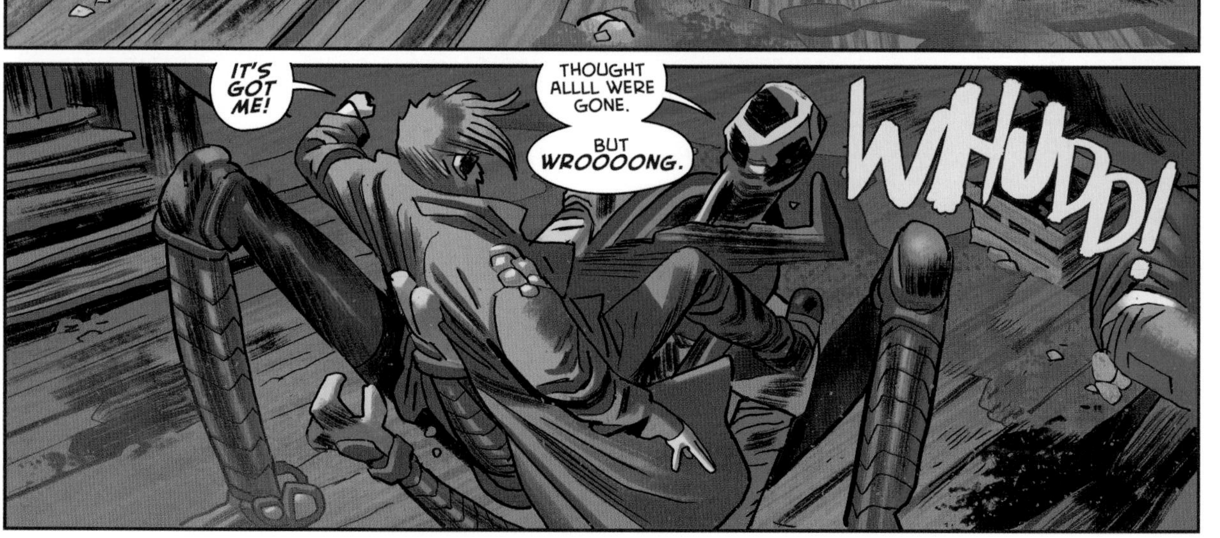
IT'S GOT ME!
THOUGHT ALLLL WERE GONE.
BUT WROOOONG.
WHUDD!

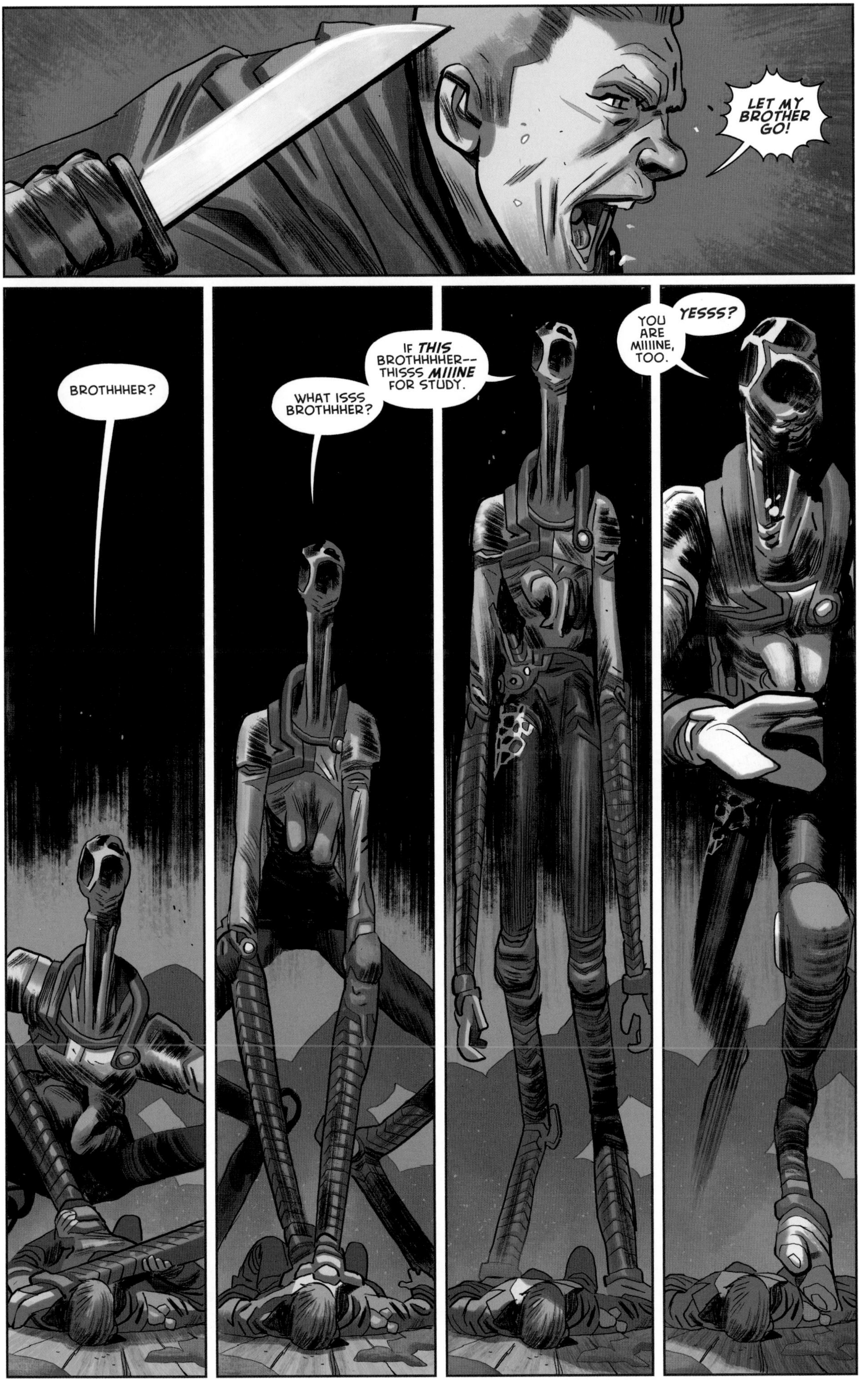
LET MY BROTHER GO!
BROTHHHER?
WHAT ISSS BROTHHHER?
IF THIS BROTHHHHER-- THISSS MIIINE FOR STUDY.
YESSS?
YOU ARE MIIIINE, TOO.

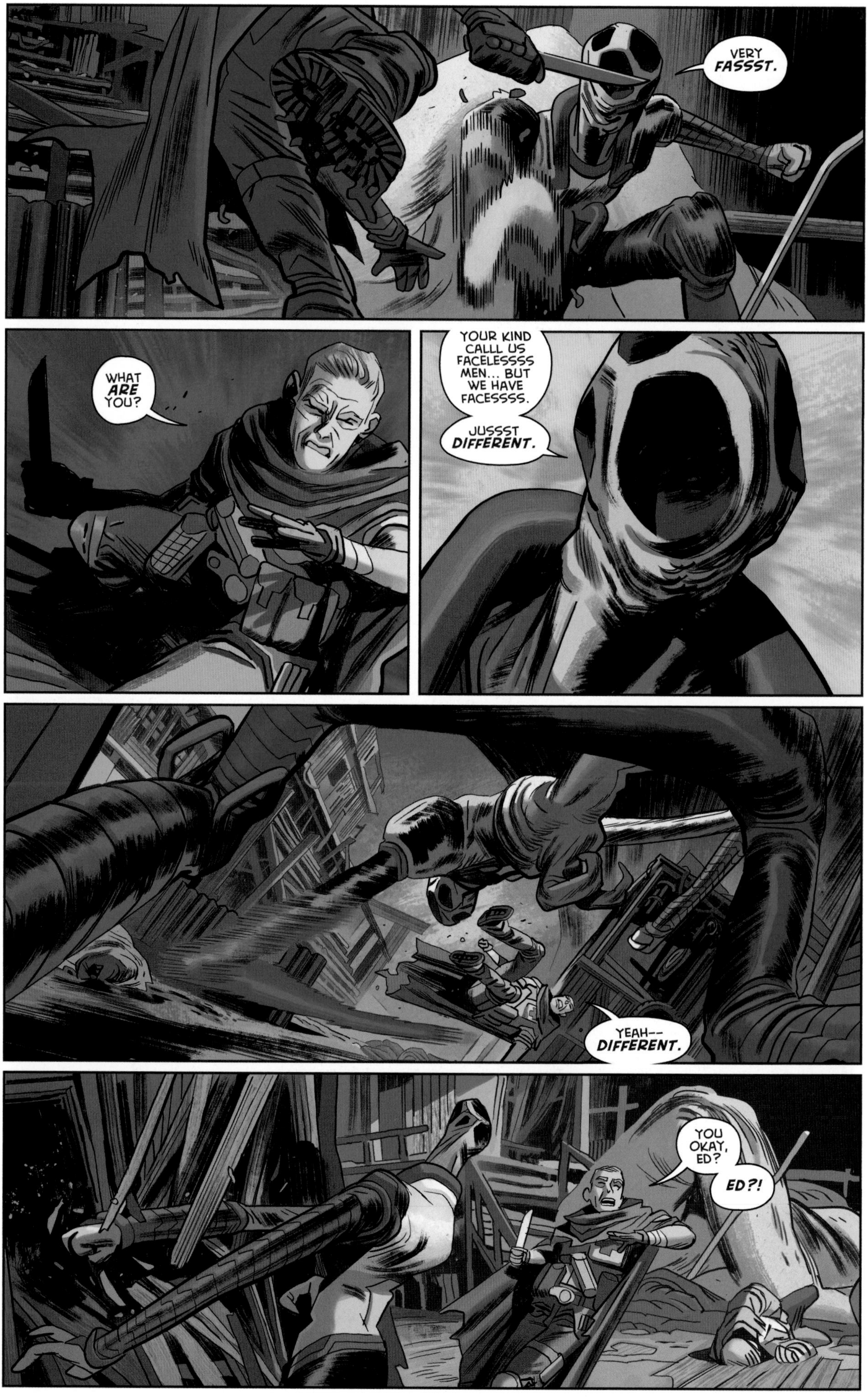
VERY FASSST.
WHAT ARE YOU?
YOUR KIND CALLL US FACELESSSS MEN... BUT WE HAVE FACESSSS.
JUSSST DIFFERENT.
YEAH-- DIFFERENT.
YOU OKAY, ED?
ED?!

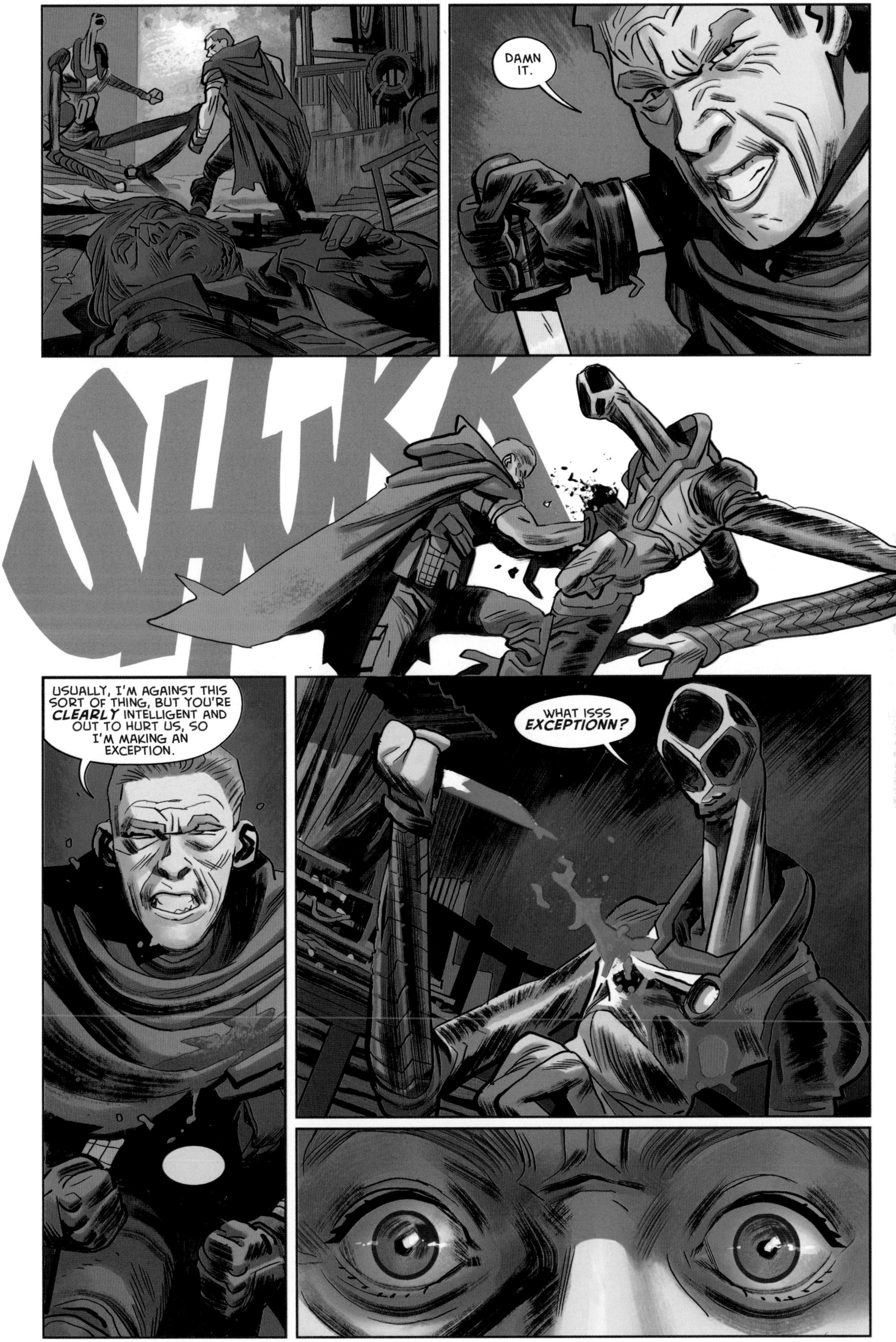
DAMN IT.
SHUKK
USUALLY, I'M AGAINST THIS SORT OF THING, BUT YOU'RE *CLEARLY* INTELLIGENT AND OUT TO HURT US, SO I'M MAKING AN EXCEPTION.
WHAT ISSS *EXCEPTIONN?*

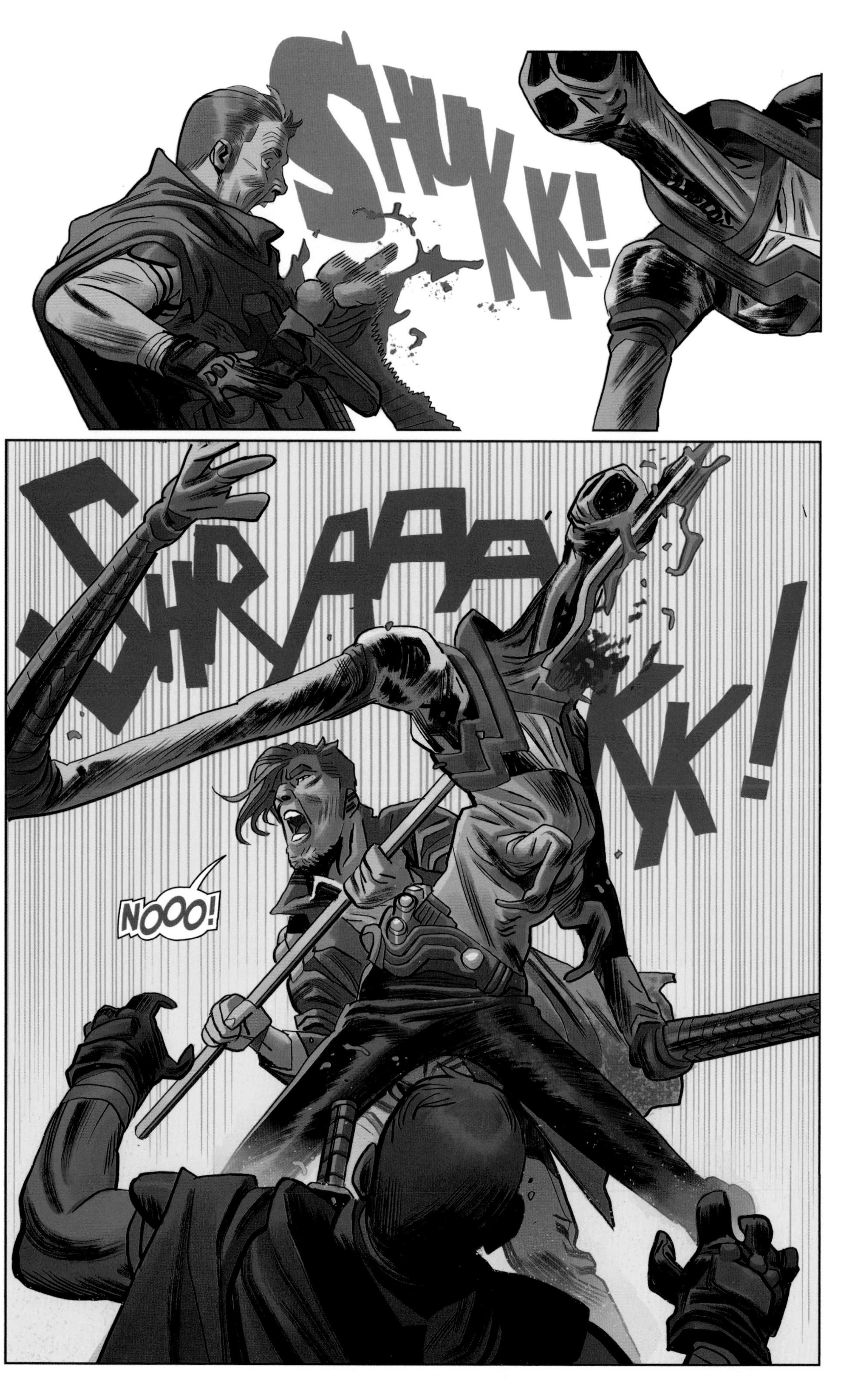
SHUKK!
SHRAAAKK!
NOOO!

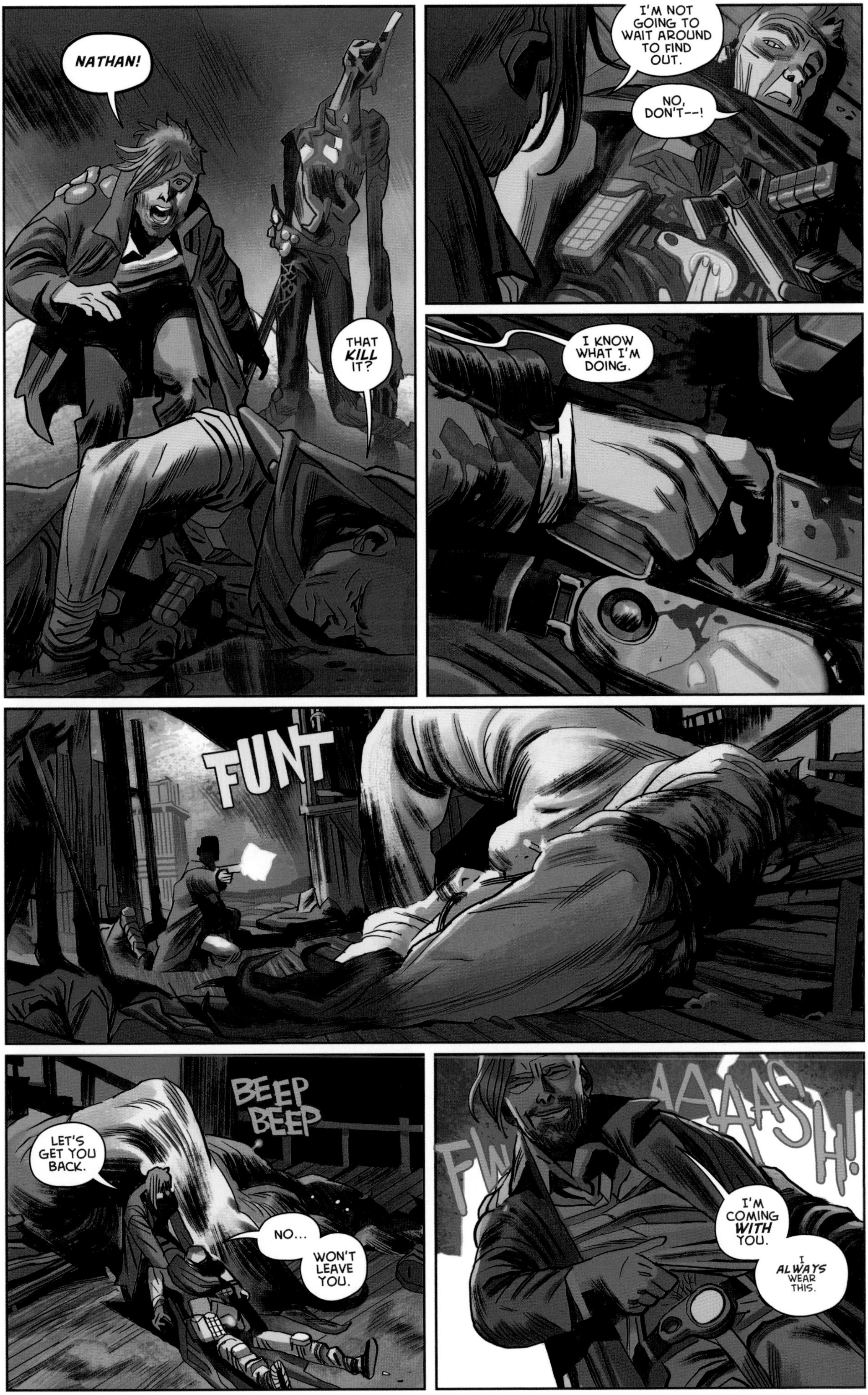
NATHAN!
THAT KILL IT?
I'M NOT GOING TO WAIT AROUND TO FIND OUT.
NO, DON'T--!
I KNOW WHAT I'M DOING.
FUNT
BEEP BEEP
LET'S GET YOU BACK.
NO...
WON'T LEAVE YOU.
FWAAAASH!
I'M COMING WITH YOU.
I ALWAYS WEAR THIS.

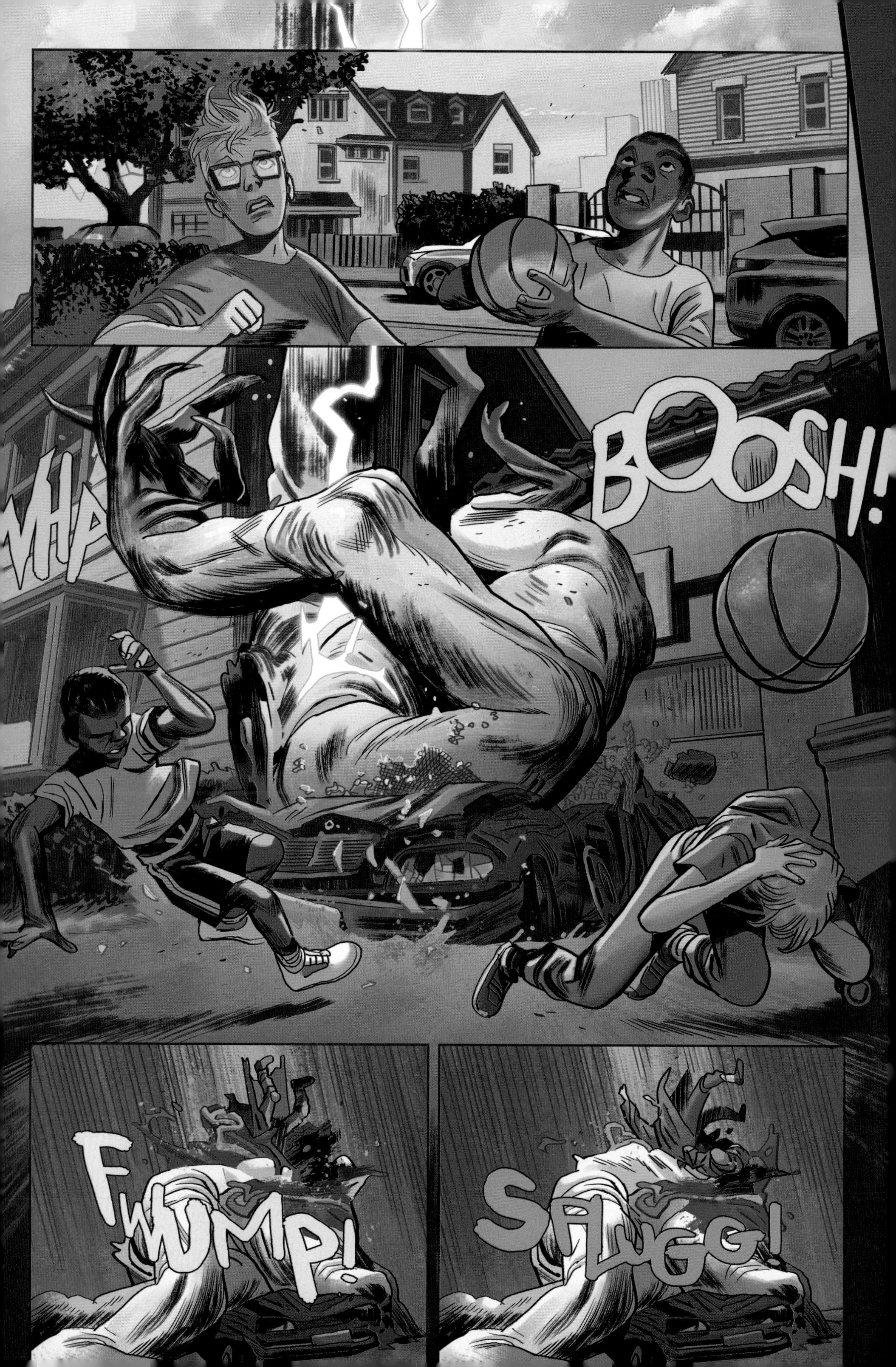
BOOSH!
FWUMP!
SPLUGG!

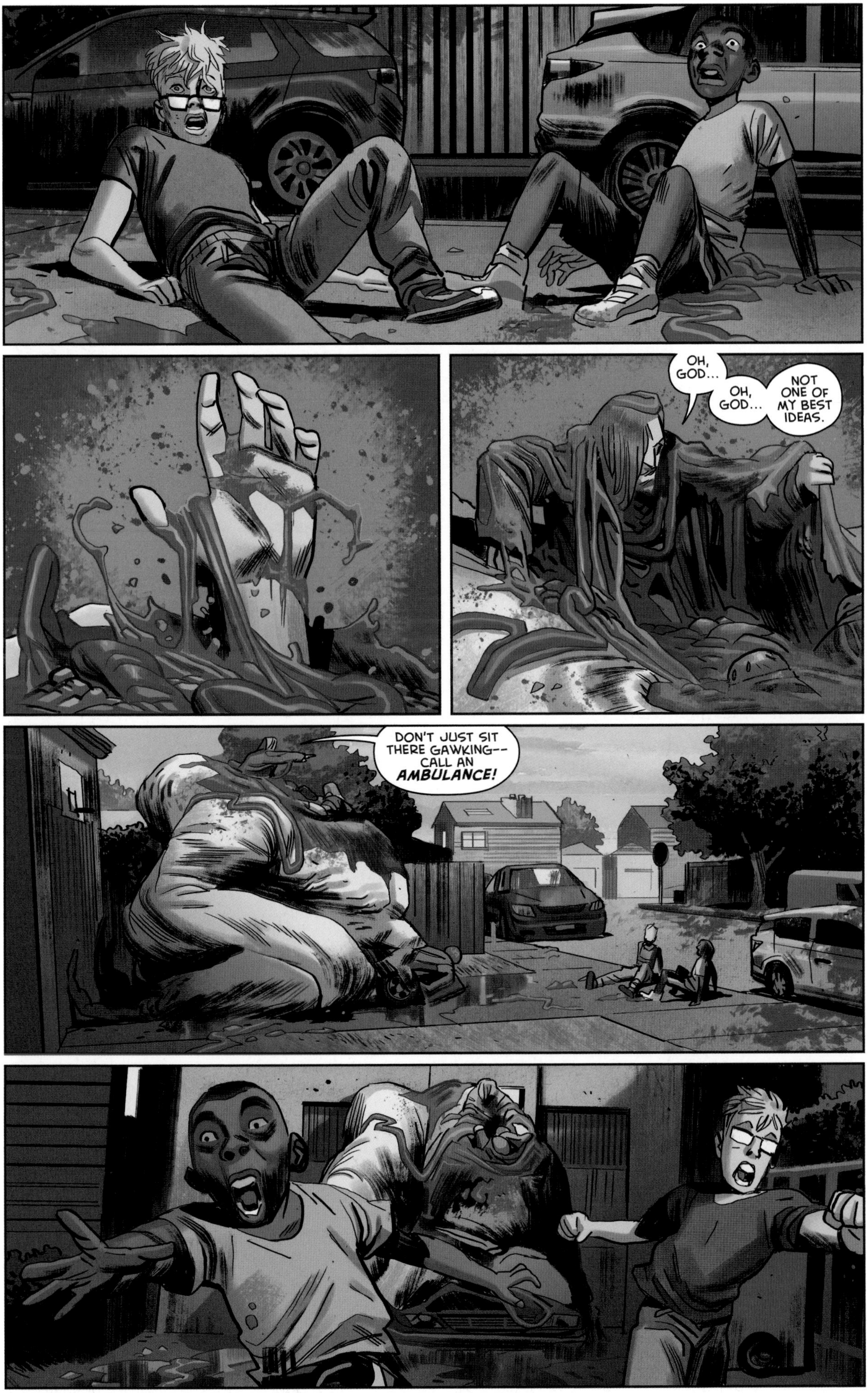
OH, GOD...
OH, GOD...
NOT ONE OF MY BEST IDEAS.
DON'T JUST SIT THERE GAWKING-- CALL AN *AMBULANCE!*

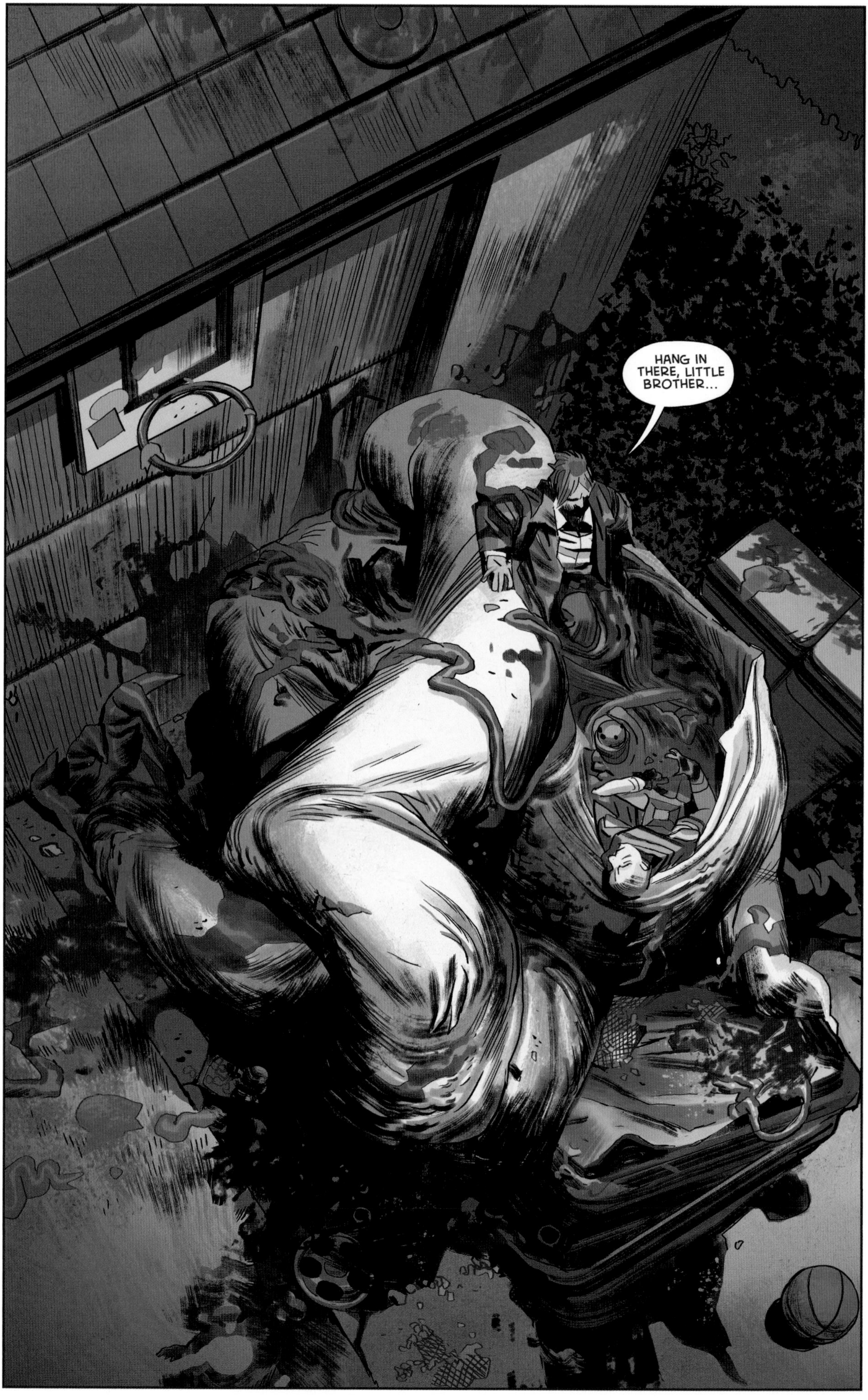
HANG IN THERE, LITTLE BROTHER...

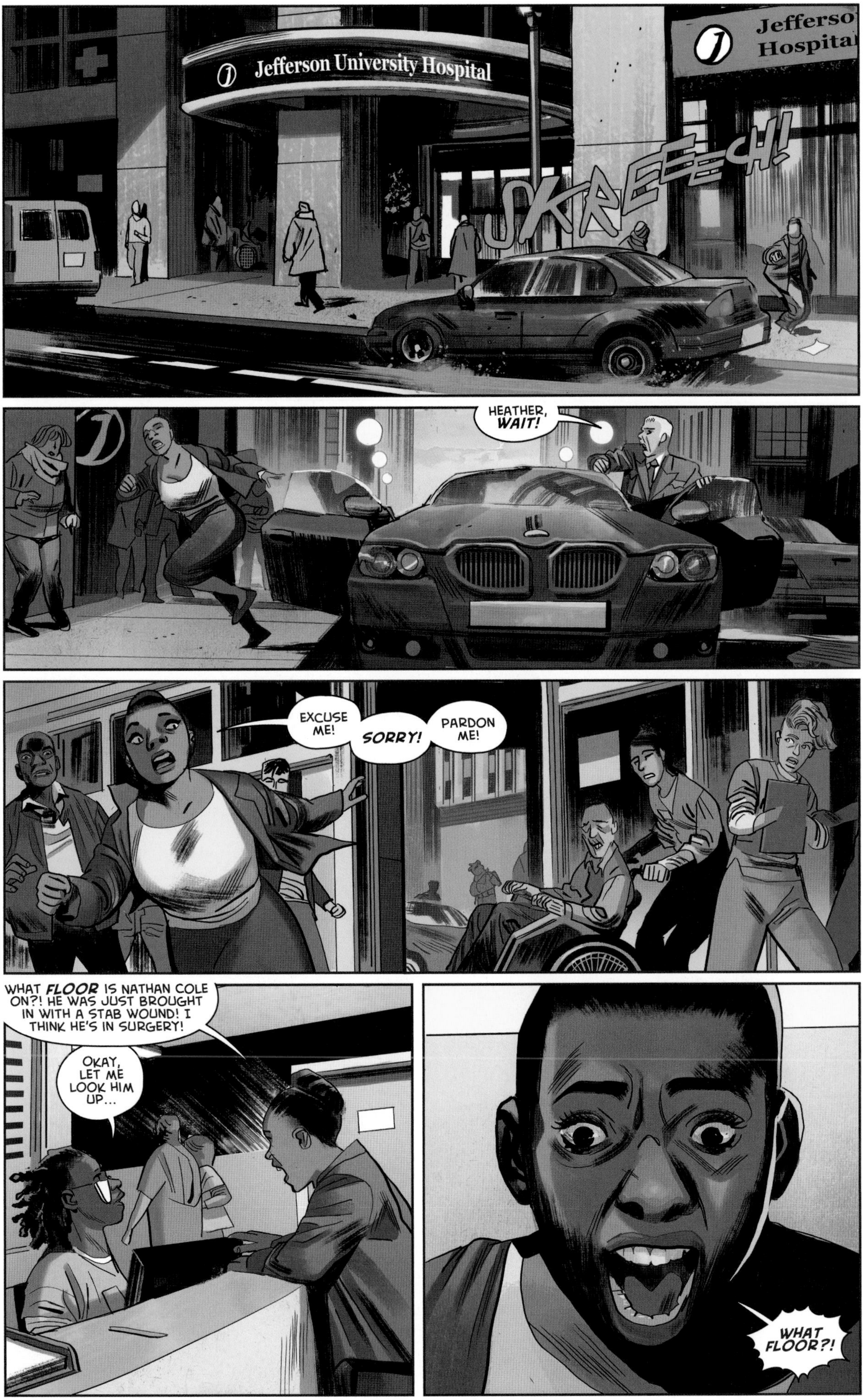
Jefferson University Hospital
SKREEEECH!
HEATHER, WAIT!
EXCUSE ME!
SORRY!
PARDON ME!
WHAT FLOOR IS NATHAN COLE ON?! HE WAS JUST BROUGHT IN WITH A STAB WOUND! I THINK HE'S IN SURGERY!
OKAY, LET ME LOOK HIM UP...
WHAT FLOOR?!

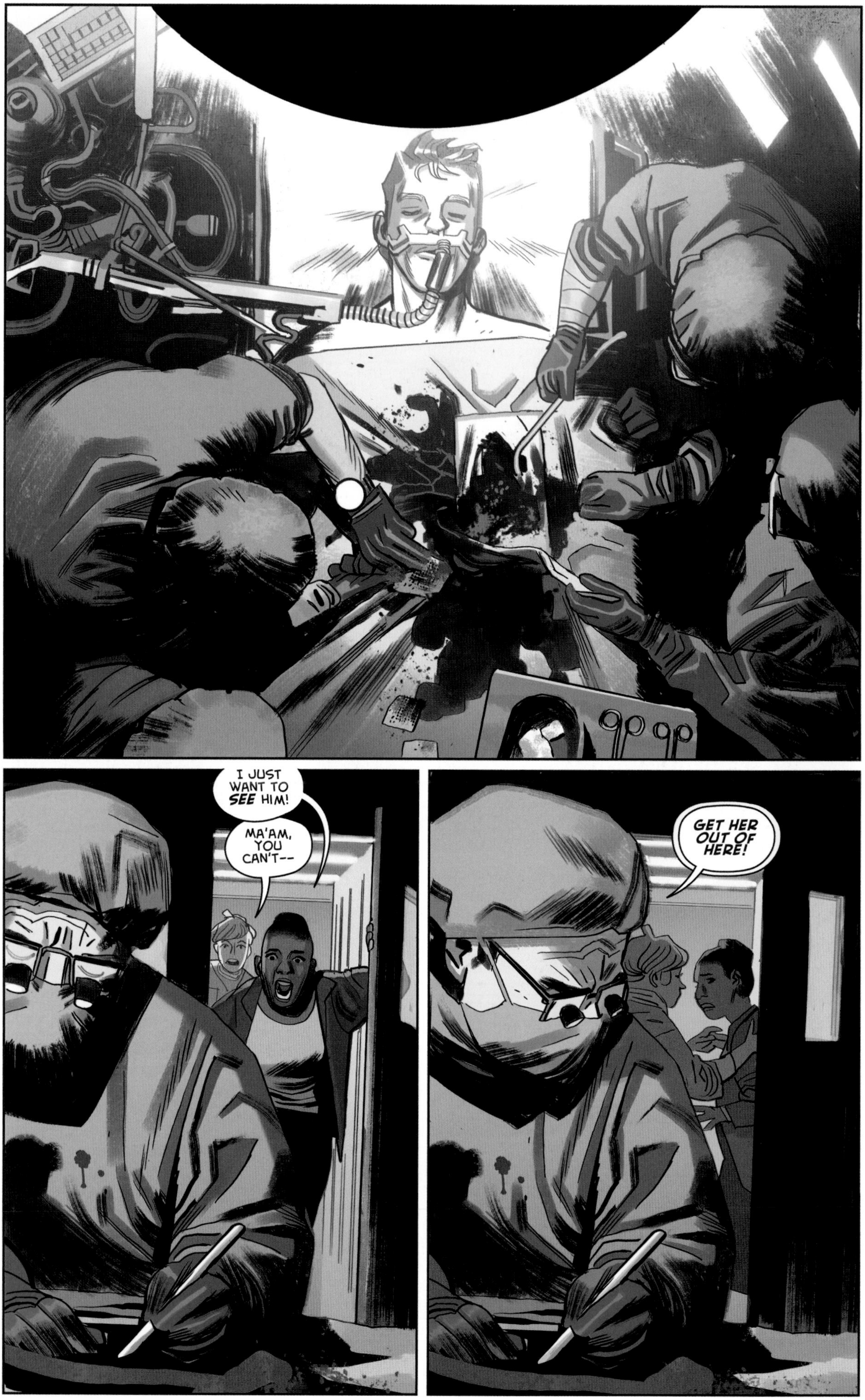
I JUST WANT TO SEE HIM!
MA'AM, YOU CAN'T--
GET HER OUT OF HERE!

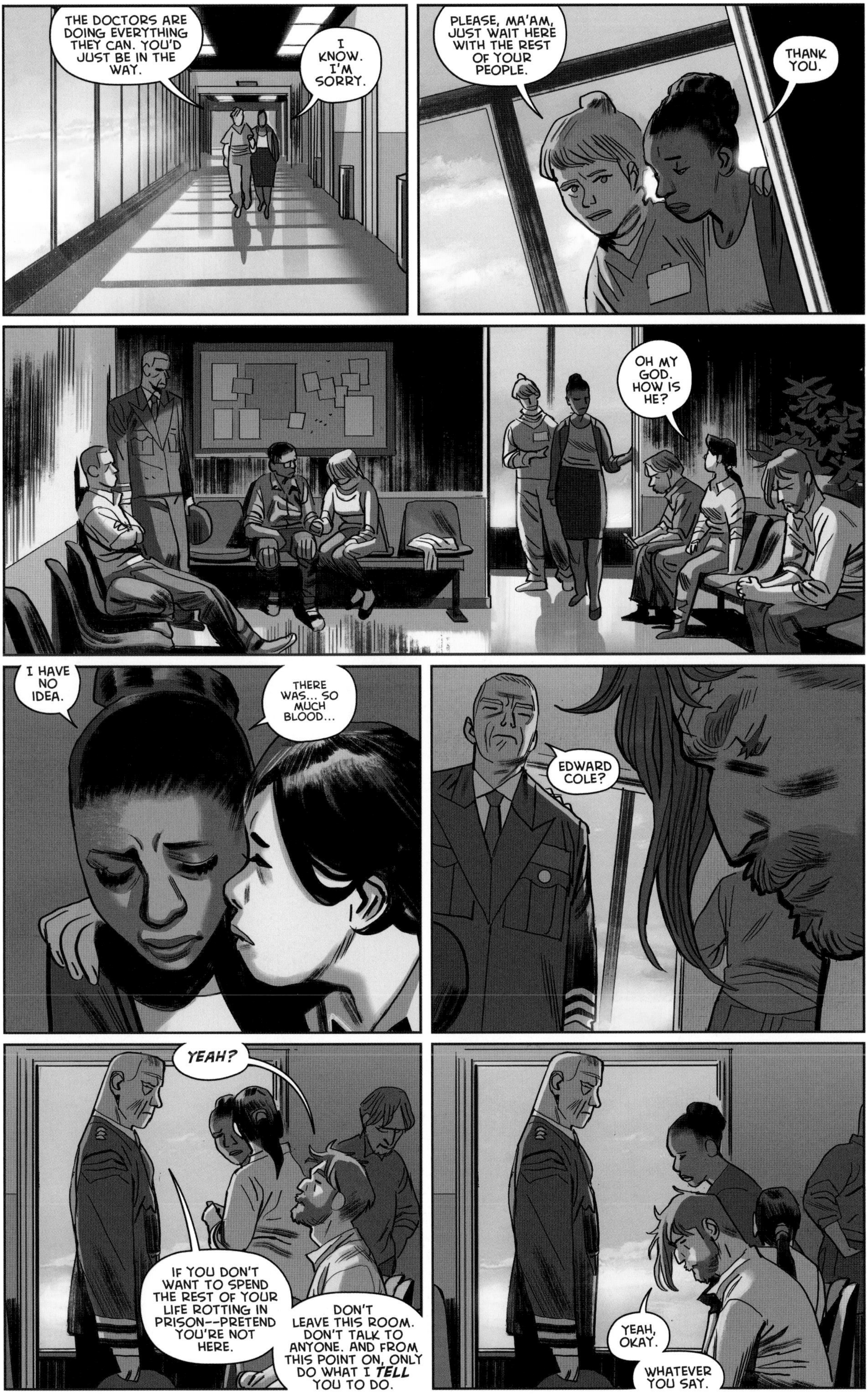
THE DOCTORS ARE DOING EVERYTHING THEY CAN. YOU'D JUST BE IN THE WAY.
I KNOW. I'M SORRY.
PLEASE, MA'AM, JUST WAIT HERE WITH THE REST OF YOUR PEOPLE.
THANK YOU.
OH MY GOD. HOW IS HE?
I HAVE NO IDEA.
THERE WAS... SO MUCH BLOOD...
EDWARD COLE?
YEAH?
IF YOU DON'T WANT TO SPEND THE REST OF YOUR LIFE ROTTING IN PRISON--PRETEND YOU'RE NOT HERE.
DON'T LEAVE THIS ROOM. DON'T TALK TO ANYONE. AND FROM THIS POINT ON, ONLY DO WHAT I TELL YOU TO DO.
YEAH, OKAY.
WHATEVER YOU SAY.

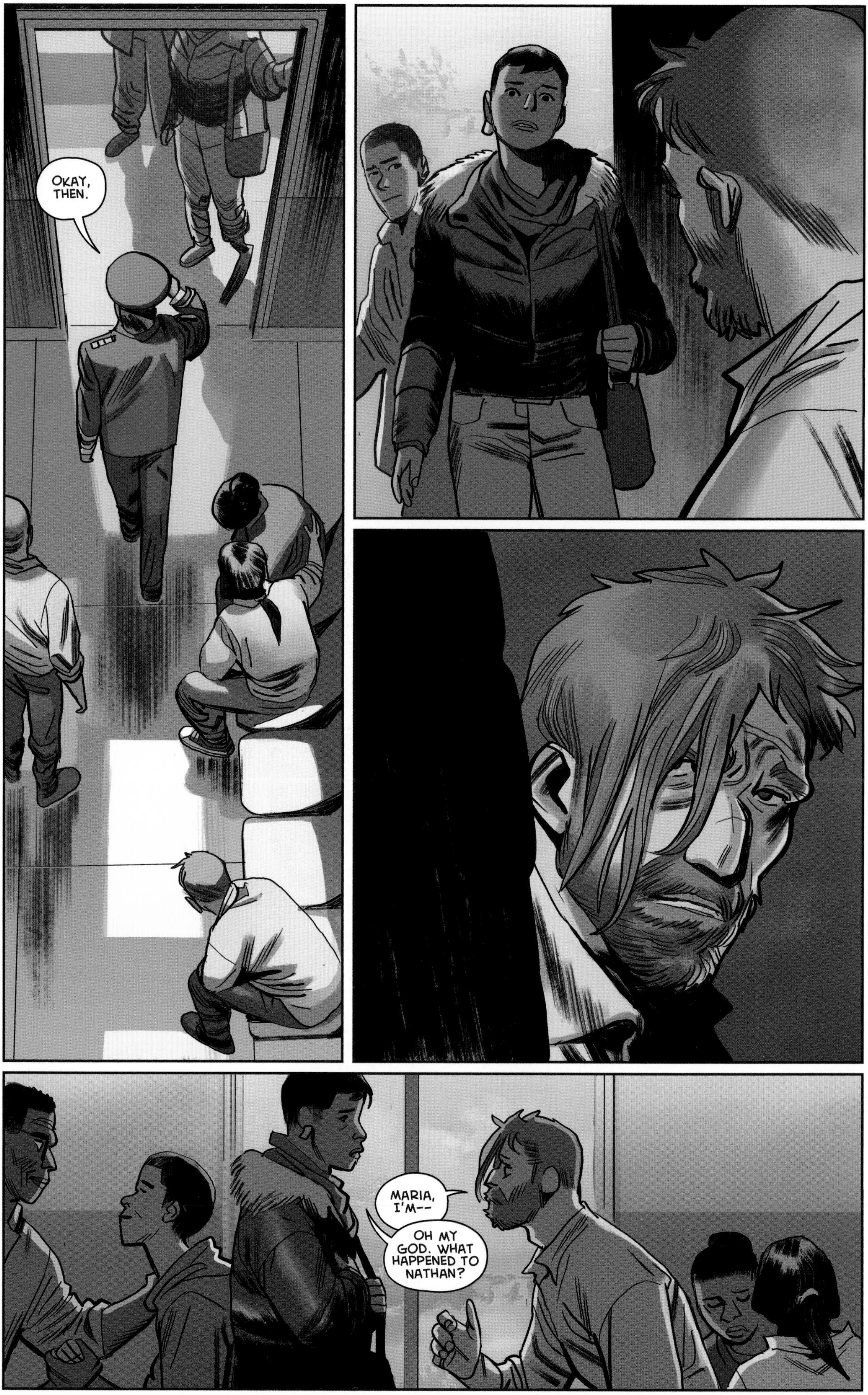
OKAY, THEN.
MARIA, I'M--
OH MY GOD. WHAT HAPPENED TO NATHAN?

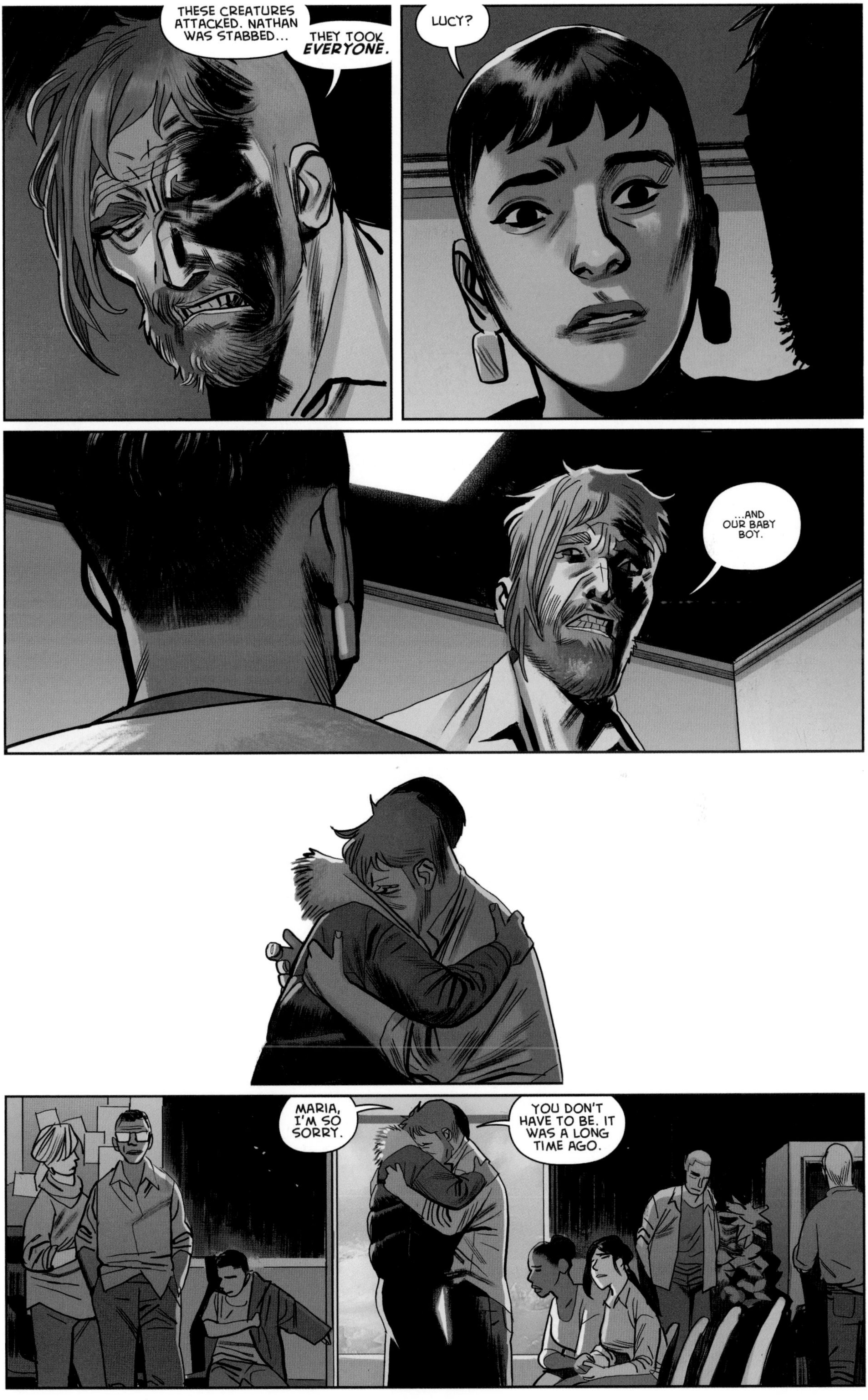

THESE CREATURES ATTACKED. NATHAN WAS STABBED...
THEY TOOK EVERYONE.
LUCY?
...AND OUR BABY BOY.
MARIA, I'M SO SORRY.
YOU DON'T HAVE TO BE. IT WAS A LONG TIME AGO.

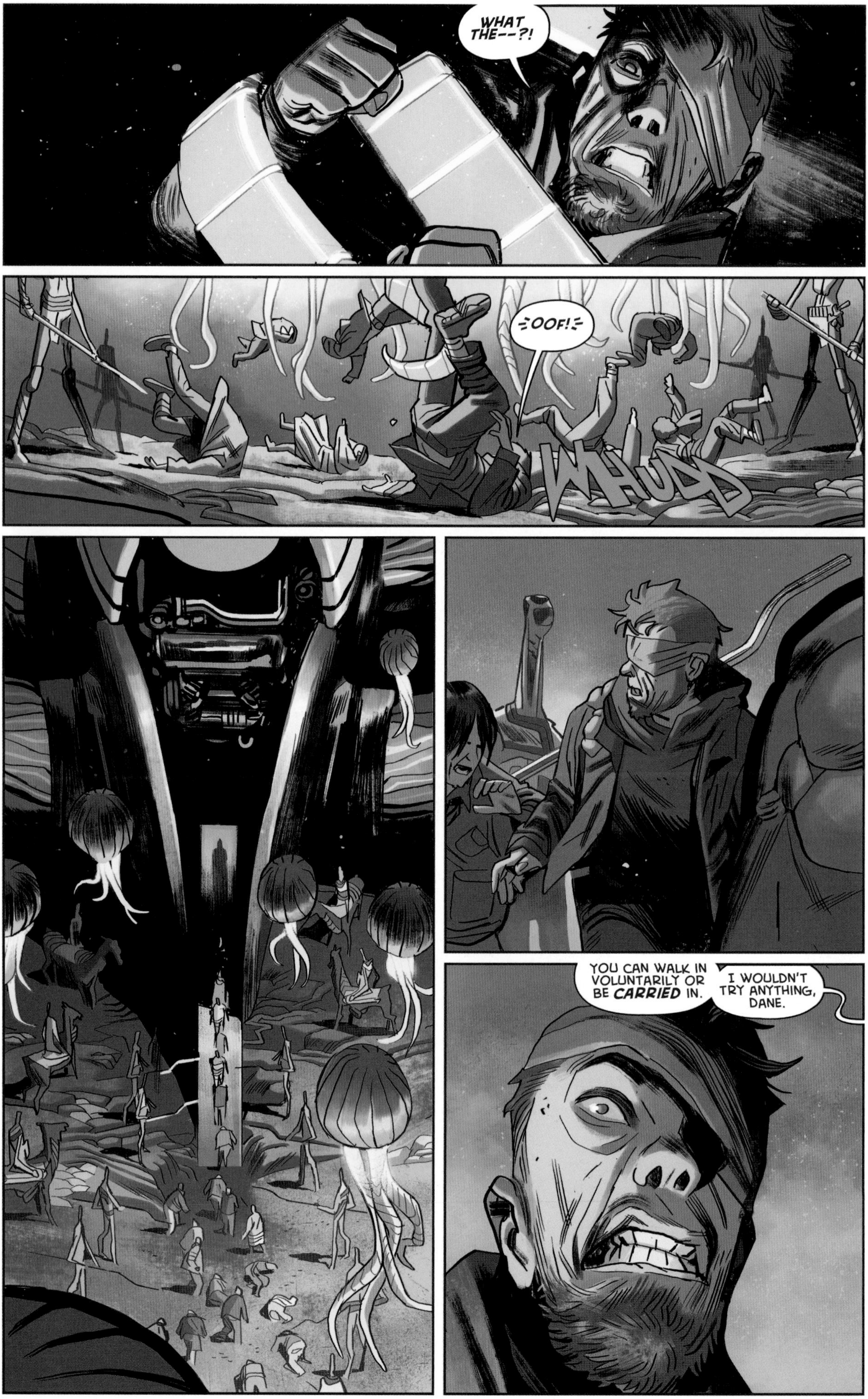
WHAT THE--?!
OOF!
WHUDD
YOU CAN WALK IN VOLUNTARILY OR BE CARRIED IN.
I WOULDN'T TRY ANYTHING, DANE.

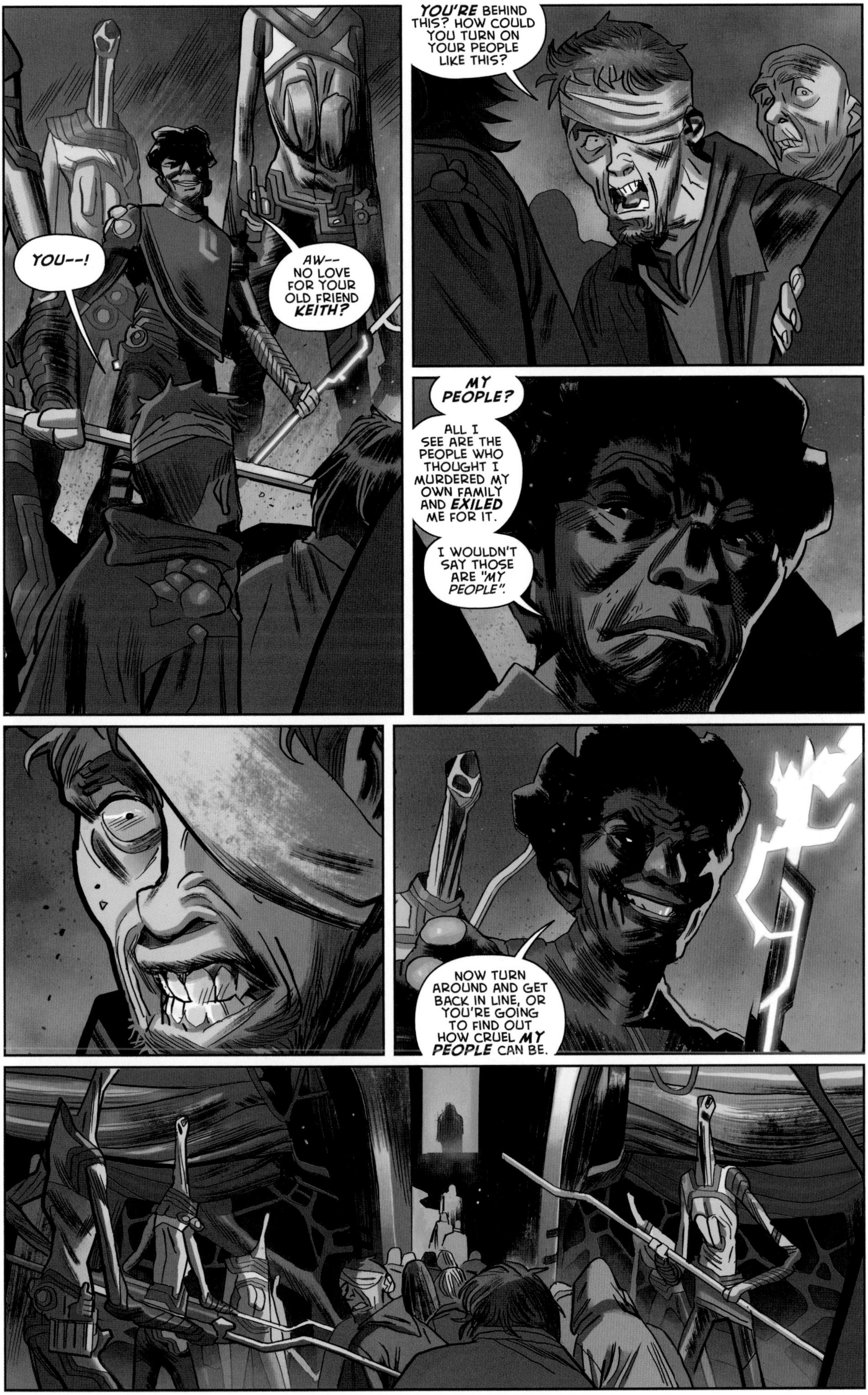
YOU--!
AW-- NO LOVE FOR YOUR OLD FRIEND KEITH?
YOU'RE BEHIND THIS? HOW COULD YOU TURN ON YOUR PEOPLE LIKE THIS?
MY PEOPLE?
ALL I SEE ARE THE PEOPLE WHO THOUGHT I MURDERED MY OWN FAMILY AND EXILED ME FOR IT.
I WOULDN'T SAY THOSE ARE "MY PEOPLE".
NOW TURN AROUND AND GET BACK IN LINE, OR YOU'RE GOING TO FIND OUT HOW CRUEL MY PEOPLE CAN BE.

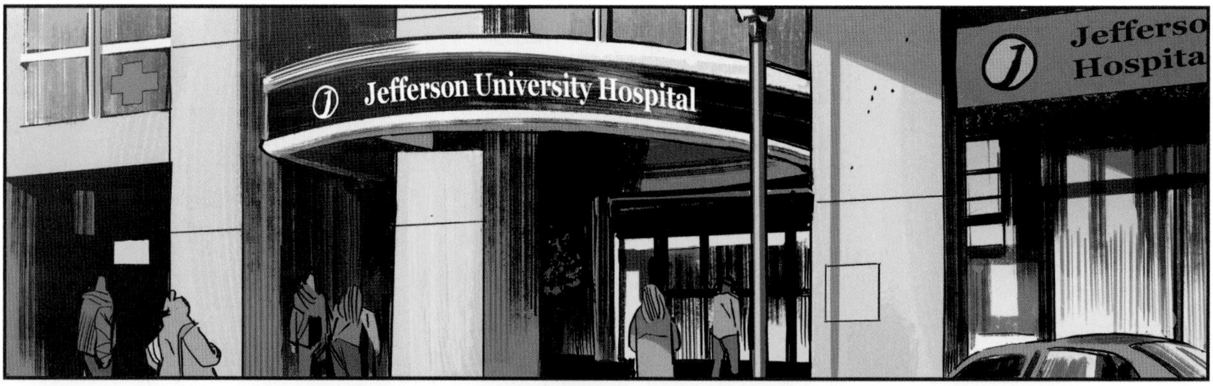
Jefferson University Hospital

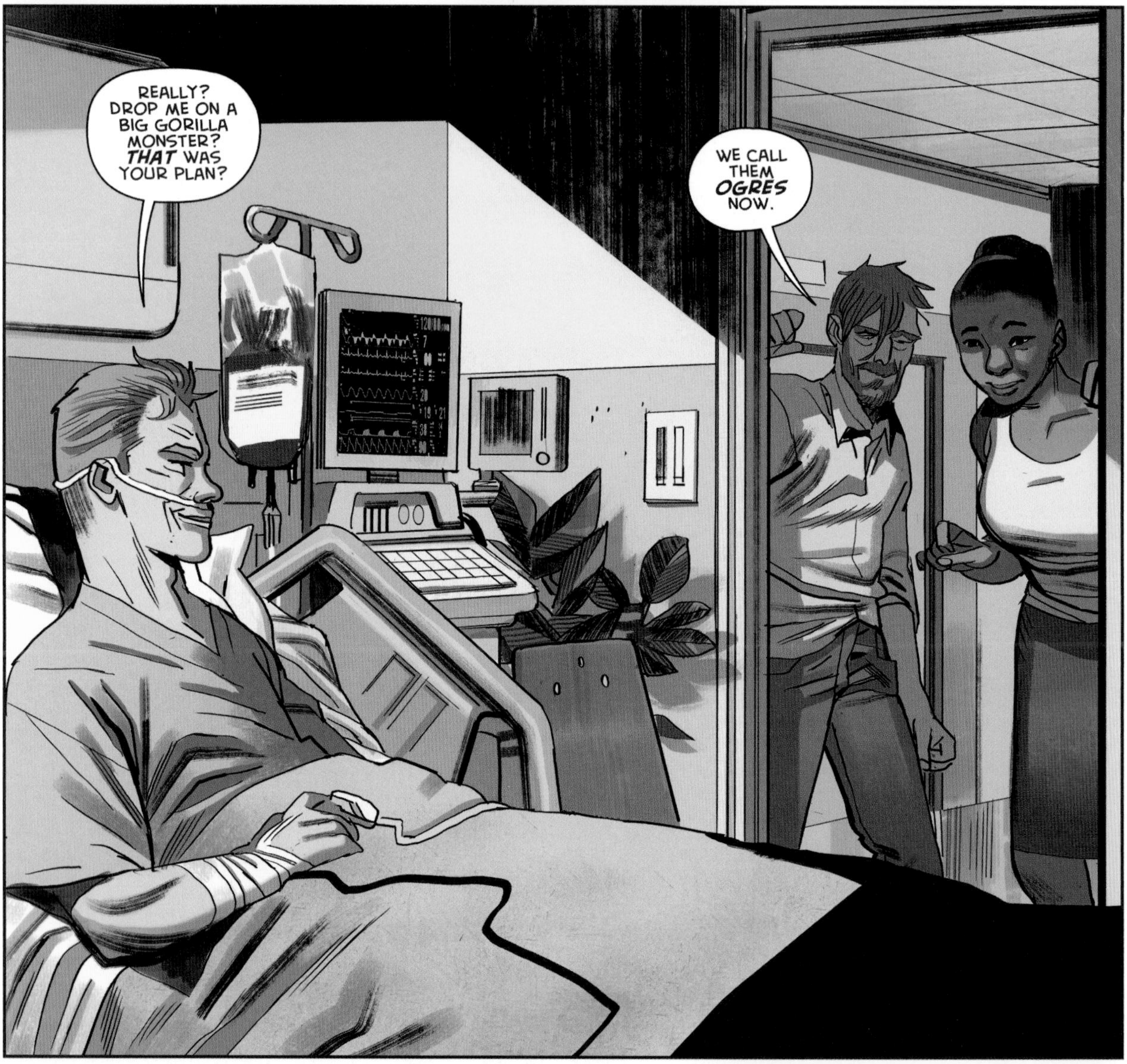
REALLY? DROP ME ON A BIG GORILLA MONSTER? THAT WAS YOUR PLAN?
WE CALL THEM OGRES NOW.

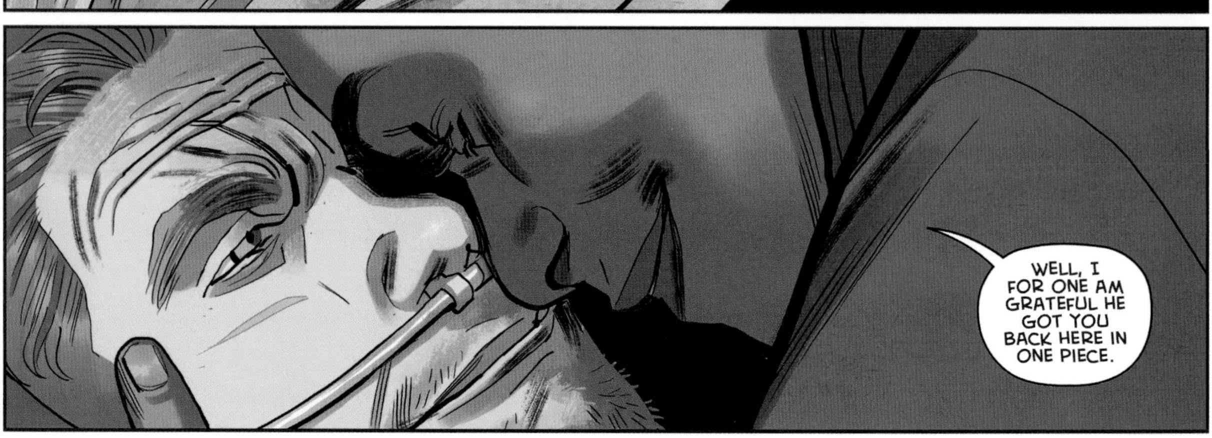
WELL, I FOR ONE AM GRATEFUL HE GOT YOU BACK HERE IN ONE PIECE.

I'M SORRY.

IT'S OKAY. THAT MANY PEOPLE TAKEN--HAD TO LEAVE A TRAIL.

WE'LL FIND THEM. I *KNOW* WE WILL.

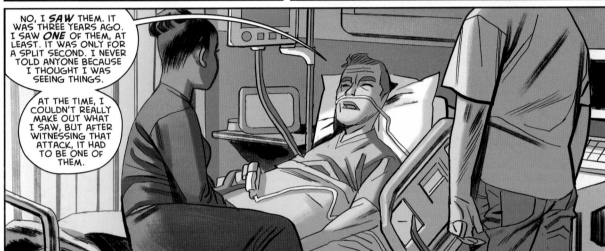

NO, I *SAW* THEM. IT WAS THREE YEARS AGO. I SAW *ONE* OF THEM, AT LEAST. IT WAS ONLY FOR A SPLIT SECOND. I NEVER TOLD ANYONE BECAUSE I THOUGHT I WAS SEEING THINGS.

AT THE TIME, I COULDN'T REALLY MAKE OUT WHAT I SAW, BUT AFTER WITNESSING THAT ATTACK, IT HAD TO BE ONE OF THEM.

NOT FEELING *GUILTY* ABOUT NOT SAYING SOMETHING. THIS ISN'T THAT. I DON'T FEEL RESPONSIBLE FOR THE ATTACK ON YOUR COMMUNITY.

I KNOW I COULDN'T HAVE KNOWN THIS WOULD HAPPEN.

WHAT I SAW LOOKED LIKE A *BASE*. I THINK I *KNOW* HOW TO FIND THEM.

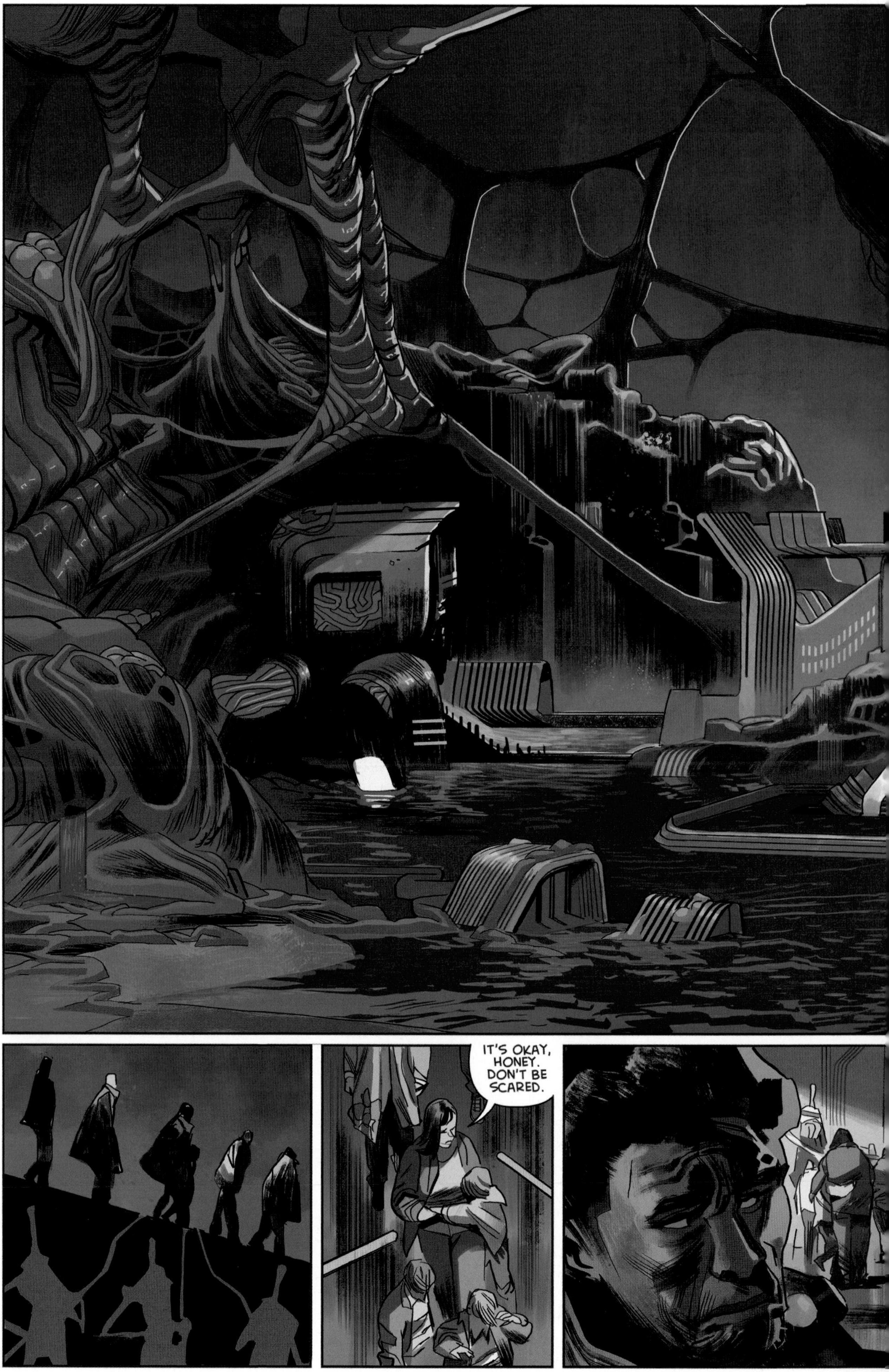
IT'S OKAY, HONEY. DON'T BE SCARED.

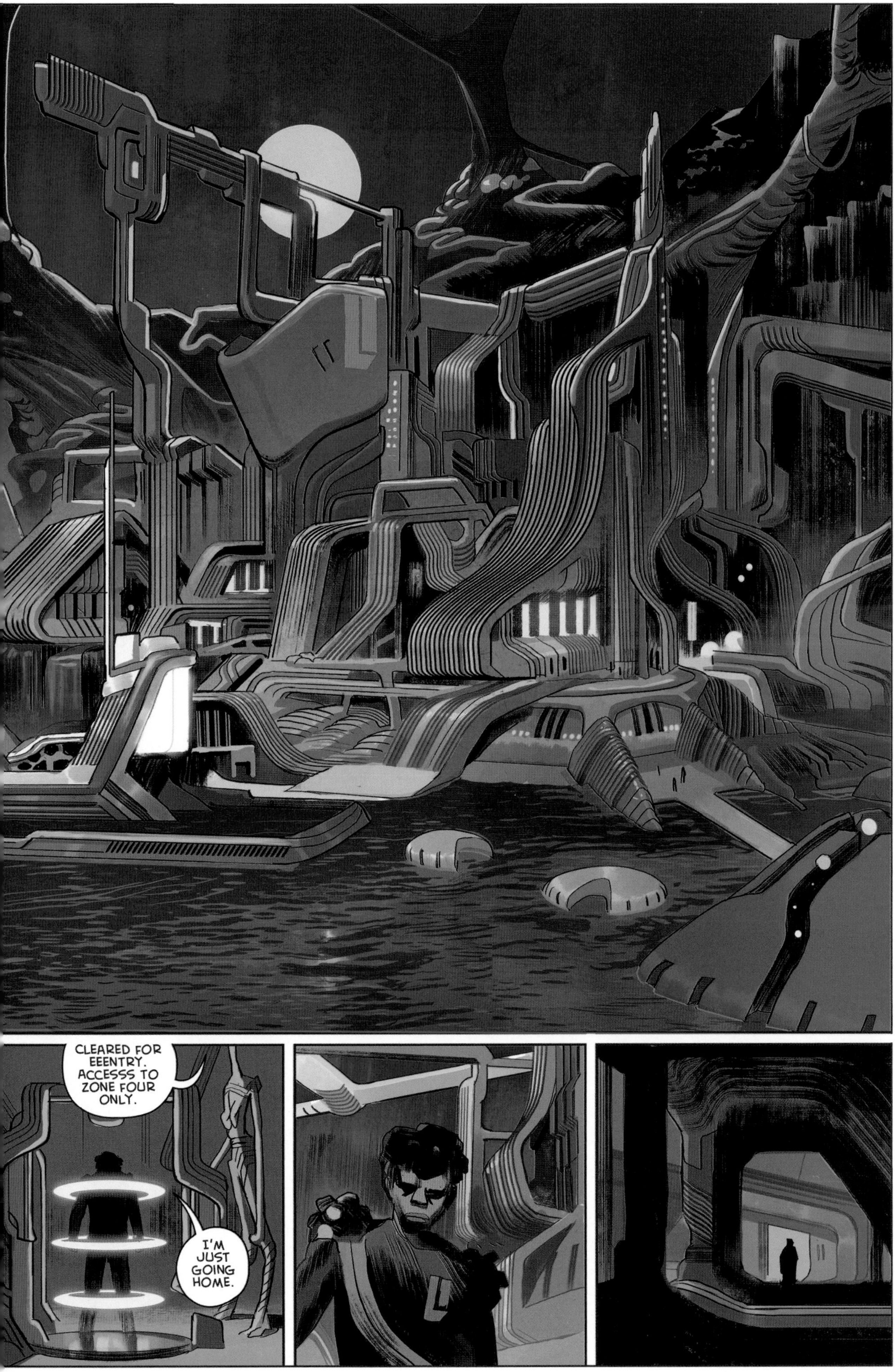
CLEARED FOR EEENTRY. ACCESSS TO ZONE FOUR ONLY.
I'M JUST GOING HOME.

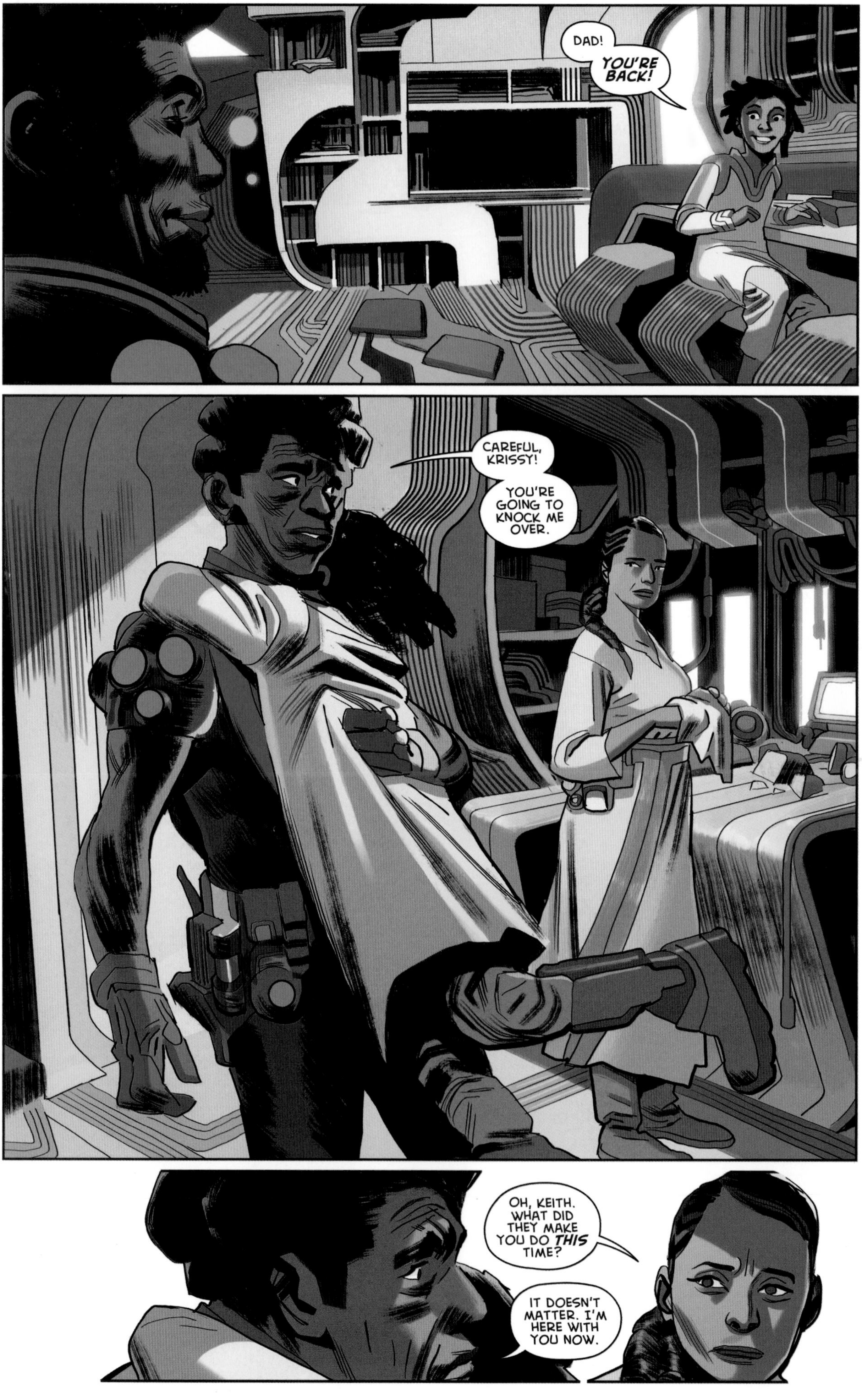
DAD!
YOU'RE BACK!
CAREFUL, KRISSY!
YOU'RE GOING TO KNOCK ME OVER.
OH, KEITH. WHAT DID THEY MAKE YOU DO THIS TIME?
IT DOESN'T MATTER. I'M HERE WITH YOU NOW.

CHAPTER

FOUR

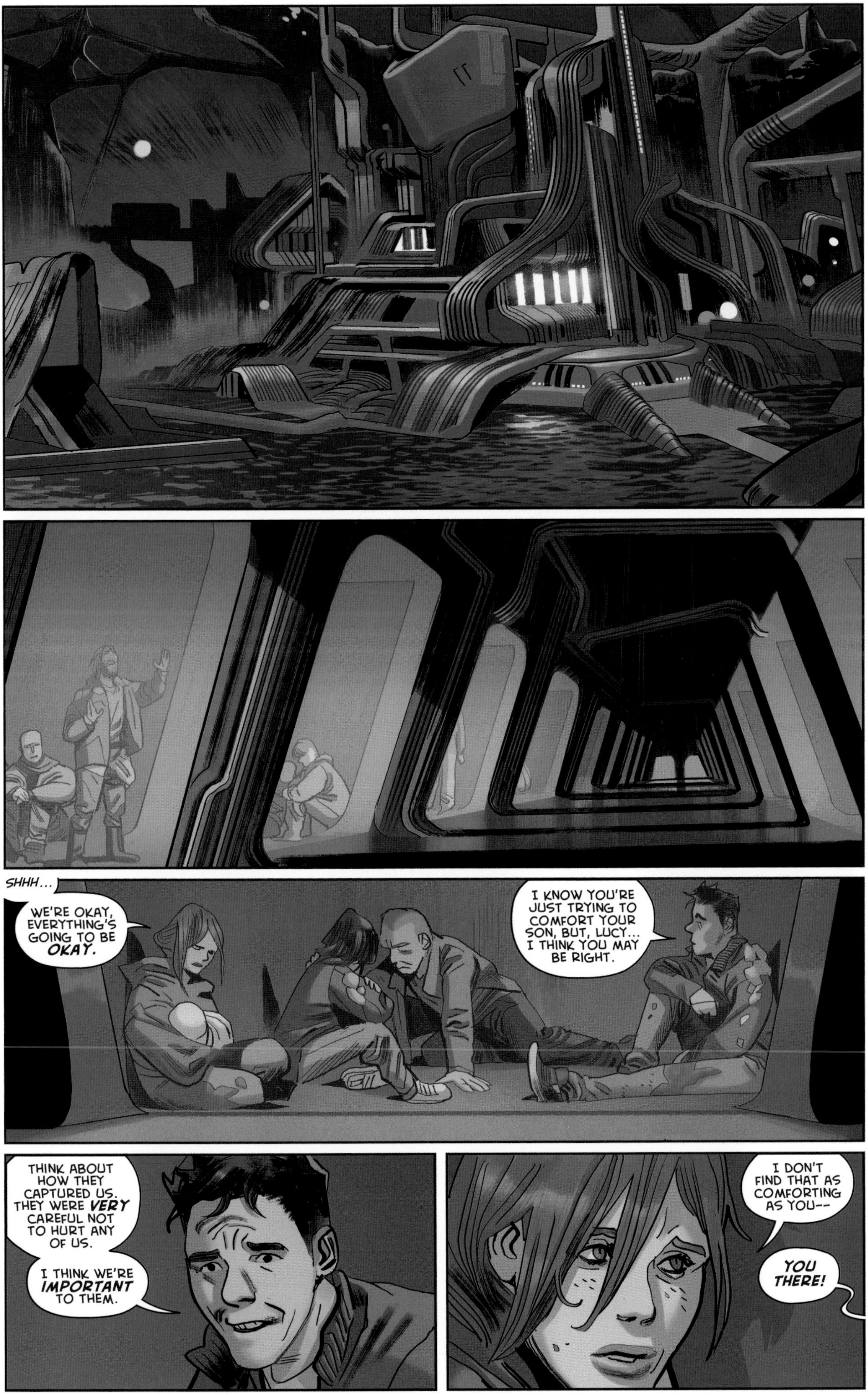
SHHH...
WE'RE OKAY, EVERYTHING'S GOING TO BE OKAY.
I KNOW YOU'RE JUST TRYING TO COMFORT YOUR SON, BUT, LUCY... I THINK YOU MAY BE RIGHT.
THINK ABOUT HOW THEY CAPTURED US. THEY WERE VERY CAREFUL NOT TO HURT ANY OF US.
I THINK WE'RE IMPORTANT TO THEM.
I DON'T FIND THAT AS COMFORTING AS YOU--
YOU THERE!

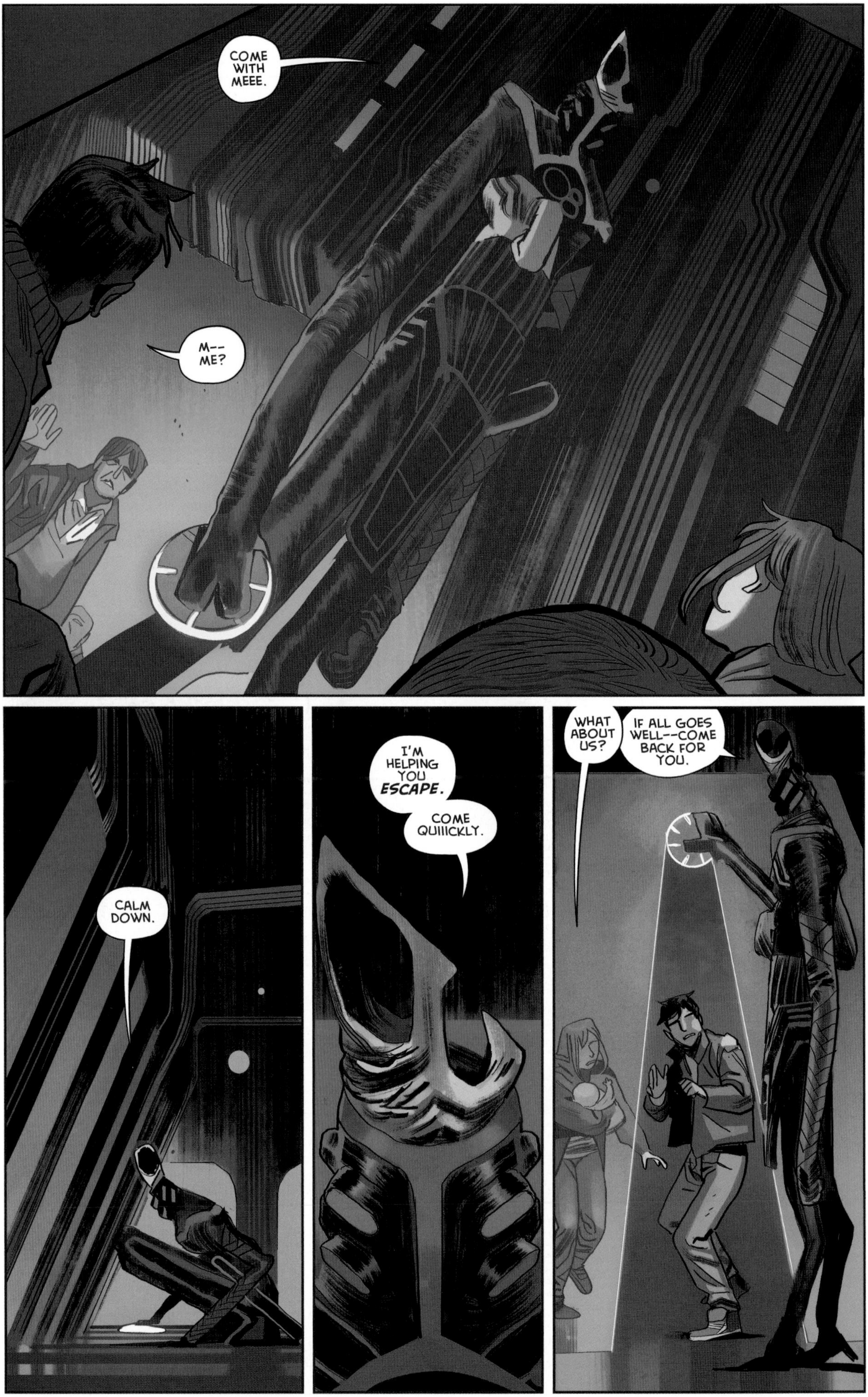
COME WITH MEEE.
M--ME?
CALM DOWN.
I'M HELPING YOU ESCAPE.
COME QUIIICKLY.
WHAT ABOUT US?
IF ALL GOES WELL--COME BACK FOR YOU.

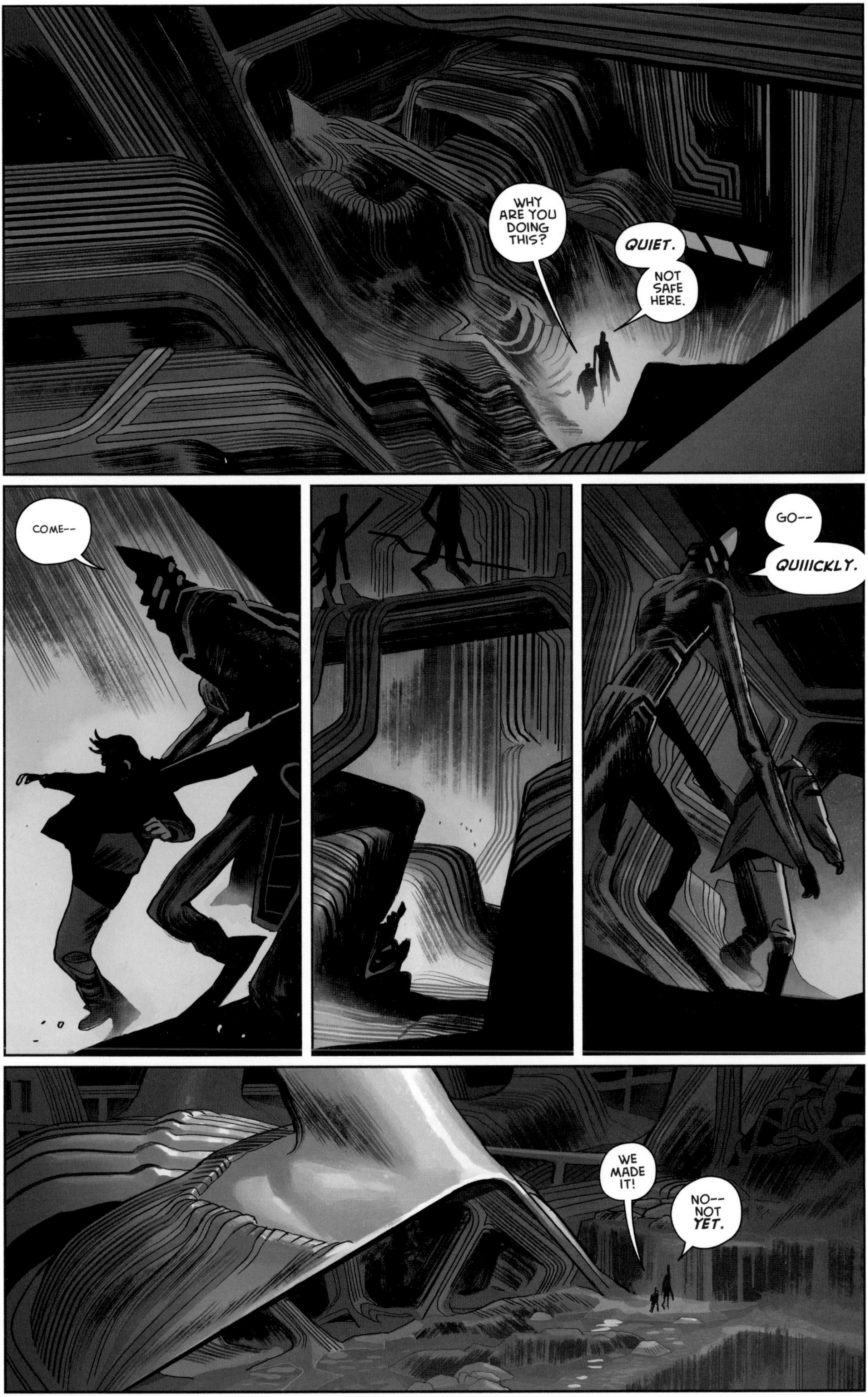
WHY ARE YOU DOING THIS?
QUIET.
NOT SAFE HERE.
COME--
GO--
QUIIICKLY.
WE MADE IT!
NO--NOT YET.

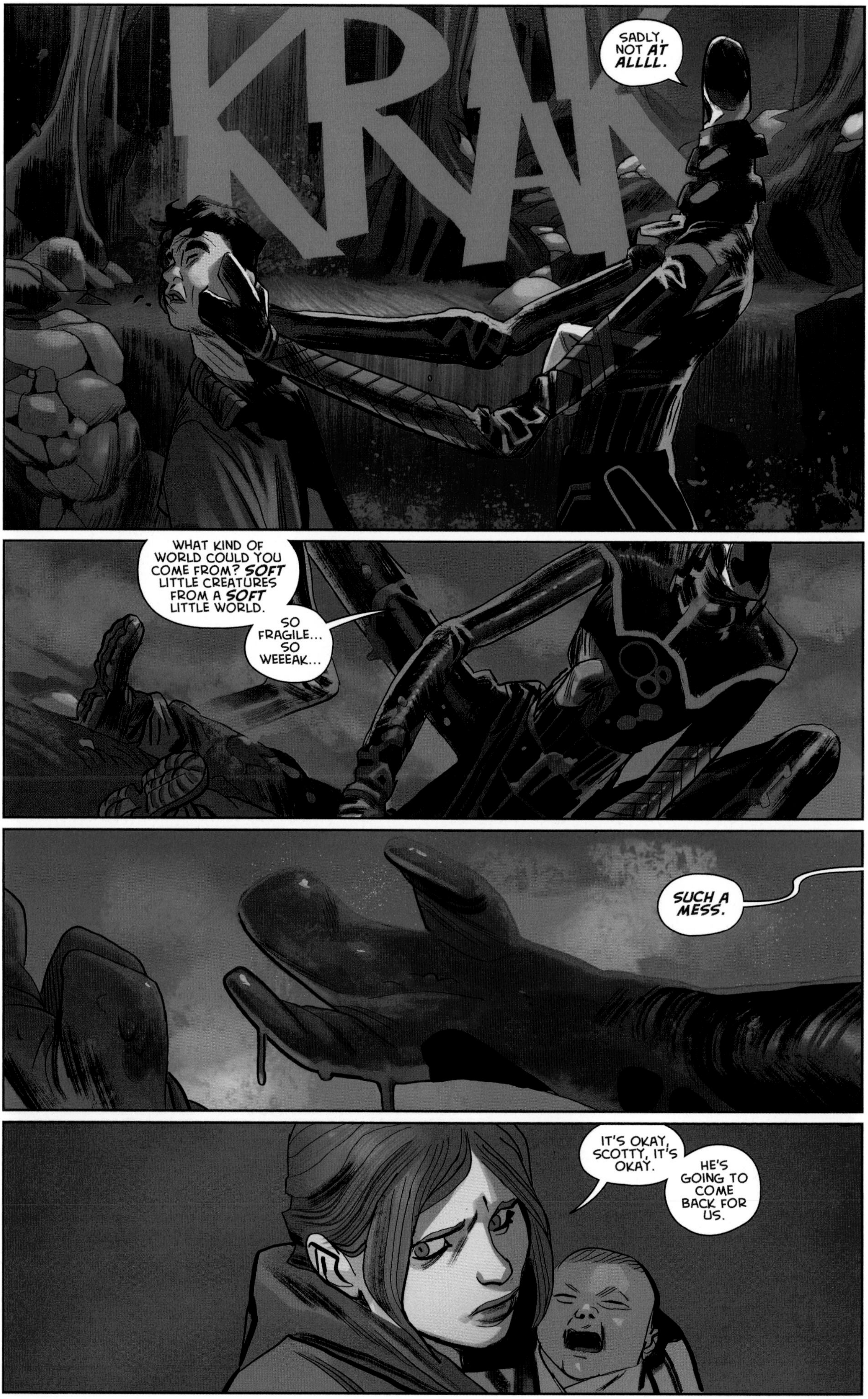
KRAK
SADLY, NOT AT ALLLL.
WHAT KIND OF WORLD COULD YOU COME FROM? SOFT LITTLE CREATURES FROM A SOFT LITTLE WORLD.
SO FRAGILE... SO WEEEAK...
SUCH A MESS.
IT'S OKAY, SCOTTY, IT'S OKAY.
HE'S GOING TO COME BACK FOR US.

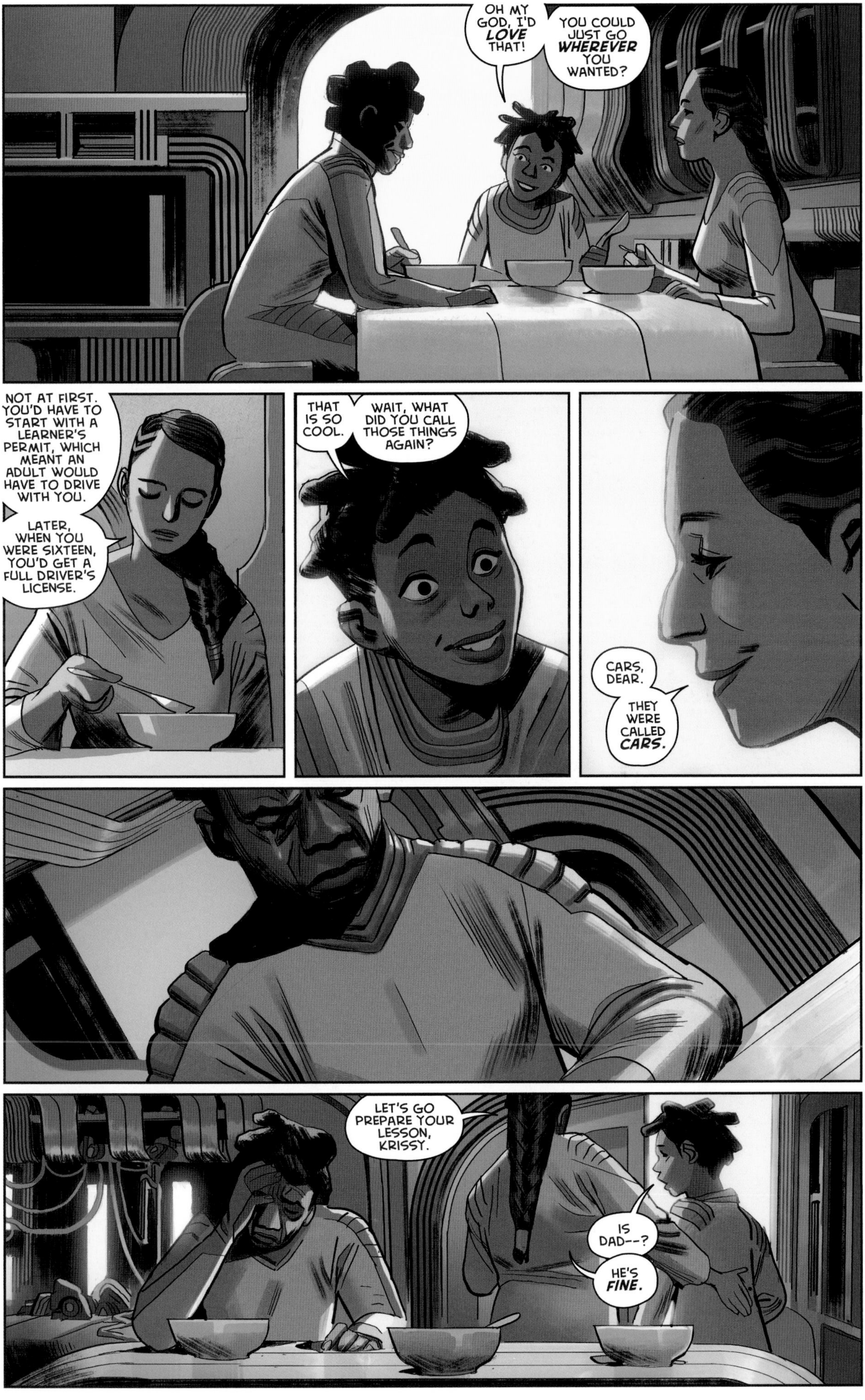
OH MY GOD, I'D **LOVE** THAT!
YOU COULD JUST GO **WHEREVER** YOU WANTED?
NOT AT FIRST. YOU'D HAVE TO START WITH A LEARNER'S PERMIT, WHICH MEANT AN ADULT WOULD HAVE TO DRIVE WITH YOU.
LATER, WHEN YOU WERE SIXTEEN, YOU'D GET A FULL DRIVER'S LICENSE.
THAT IS SO COOL.
WAIT, WHAT DID YOU CALL THOSE THINGS AGAIN?
CARS, DEAR.
THEY WERE CALLED **CARS.**
LET'S GO PREPARE YOUR LESSON, KRISSY.
IS DAD--?
HE'S **FINE.**

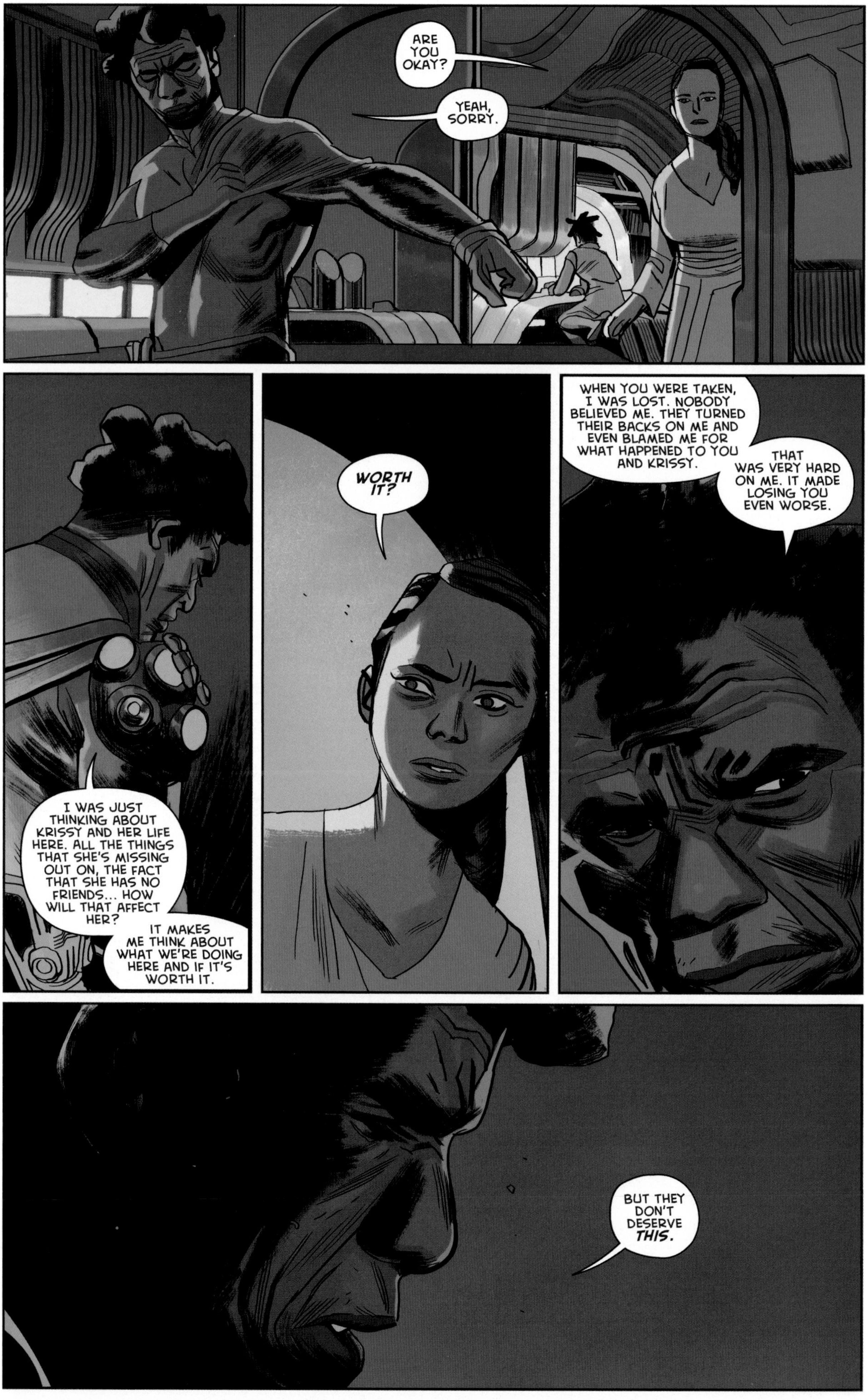
ARE YOU OKAY?
YEAH, SORRY.
I WAS JUST THINKING ABOUT KRISSY AND HER LIFE HERE. ALL THE THINGS THAT SHE'S MISSING OUT ON, THE FACT THAT SHE HAS NO FRIENDS... HOW WILL THAT AFFECT HER?
IT MAKES ME THINK ABOUT WHAT WE'RE DOING HERE AND IF IT'S WORTH IT.
WORTH IT?
WHEN YOU WERE TAKEN, I WAS LOST. NOBODY BELIEVED ME. THEY TURNED THEIR BACKS ON ME AND EVEN BLAMED ME FOR WHAT HAPPENED TO YOU AND KRISSY.
THAT WAS VERY HARD ON ME. IT MADE LOSING YOU EVEN WORSE.
BUT THEY DON'T DESERVE THIS.

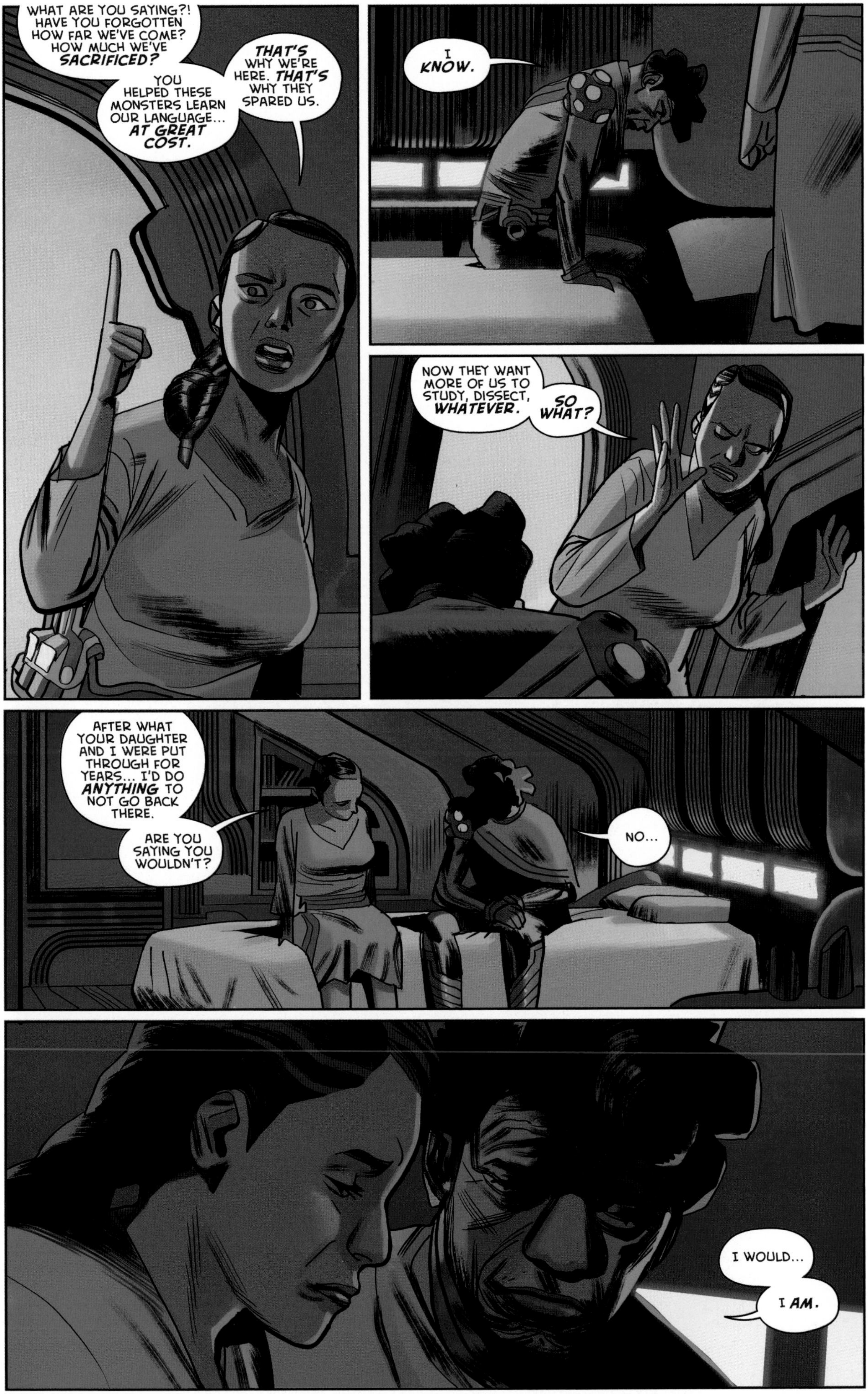
WHAT ARE YOU SAYING?! HAVE YOU FORGOTTEN HOW FAR WE'VE COME? HOW MUCH WE'VE SACRIFICED?
YOU HELPED THESE MONSTERS LEARN OUR LANGUAGE... AT GREAT COST.
THAT'S WHY WE'RE HERE. THAT'S WHY THEY SPARED US.
I KNOW.
NOW THEY WANT MORE OF US TO STUDY, DISSECT, WHATEVER.
SO WHAT?
AFTER WHAT YOUR DAUGHTER AND I WERE PUT THROUGH FOR YEARS... I'D DO ANYTHING TO NOT GO BACK THERE.
ARE YOU SAYING YOU WOULDN'T?
NO...
I WOULD...
I AM.

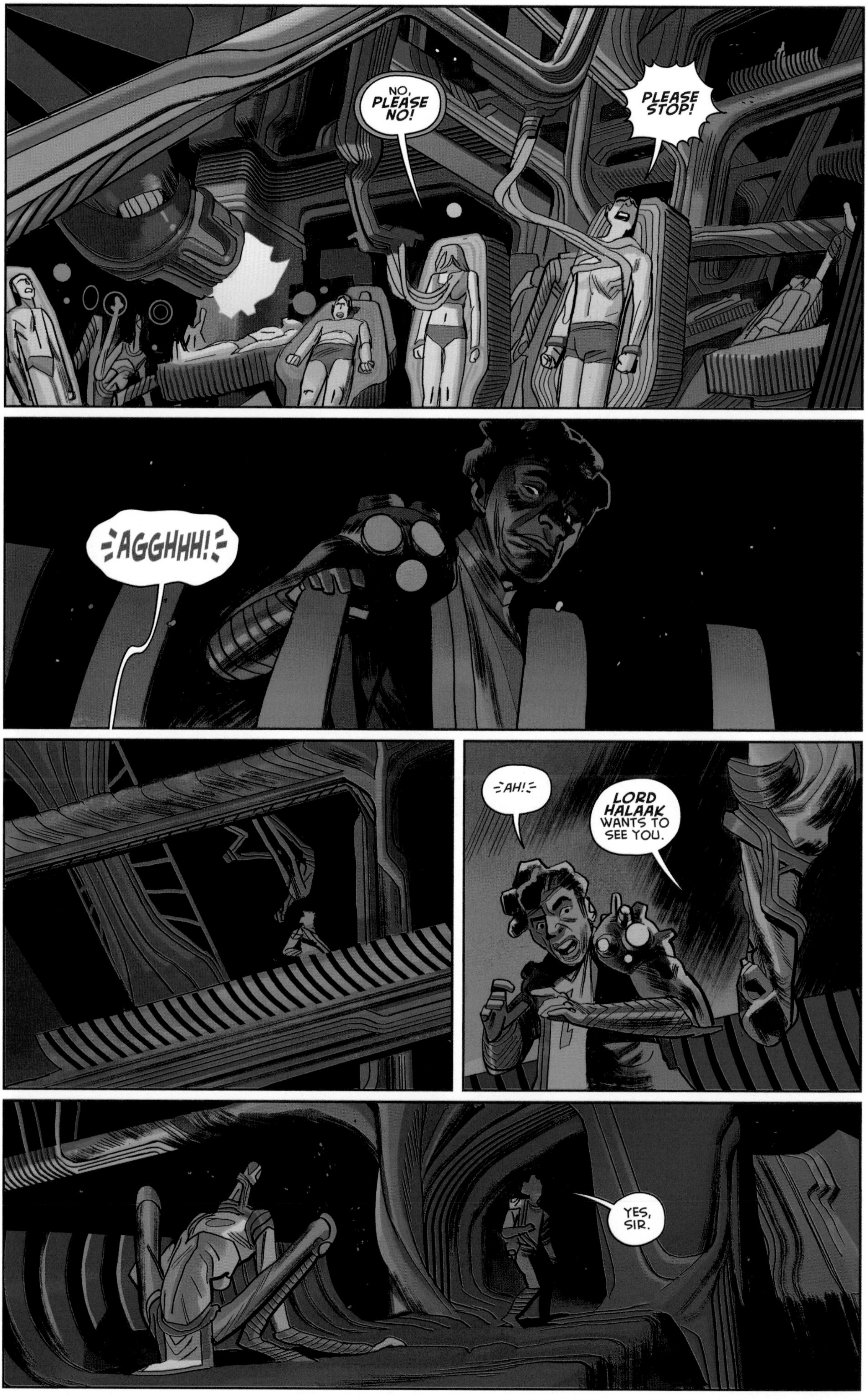
NO, PLEASE NO!
PLEASE STOP!
AGGHHH!
AH!
LORD HALAAK WANTS TO SEE YOU.
YES, SIR.

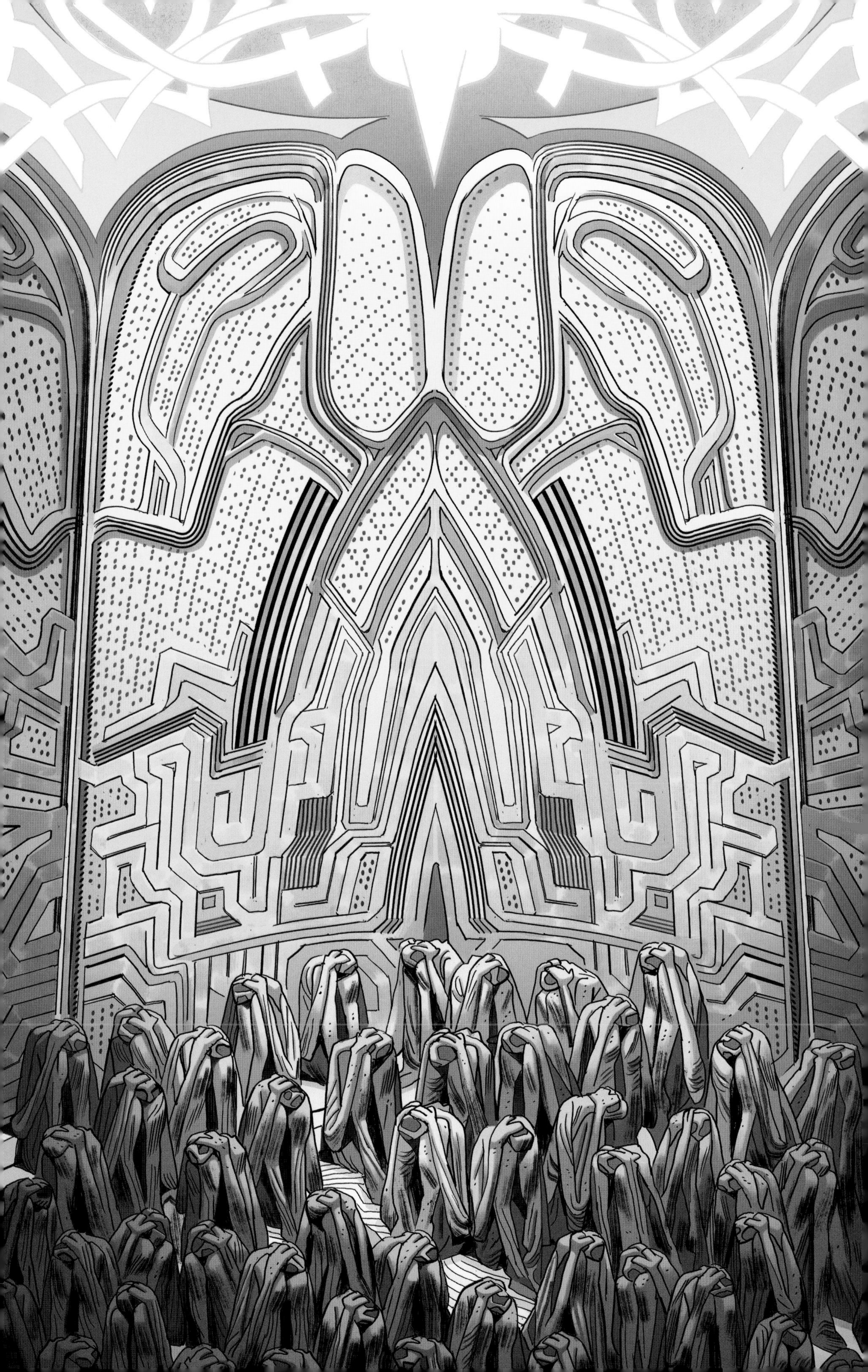

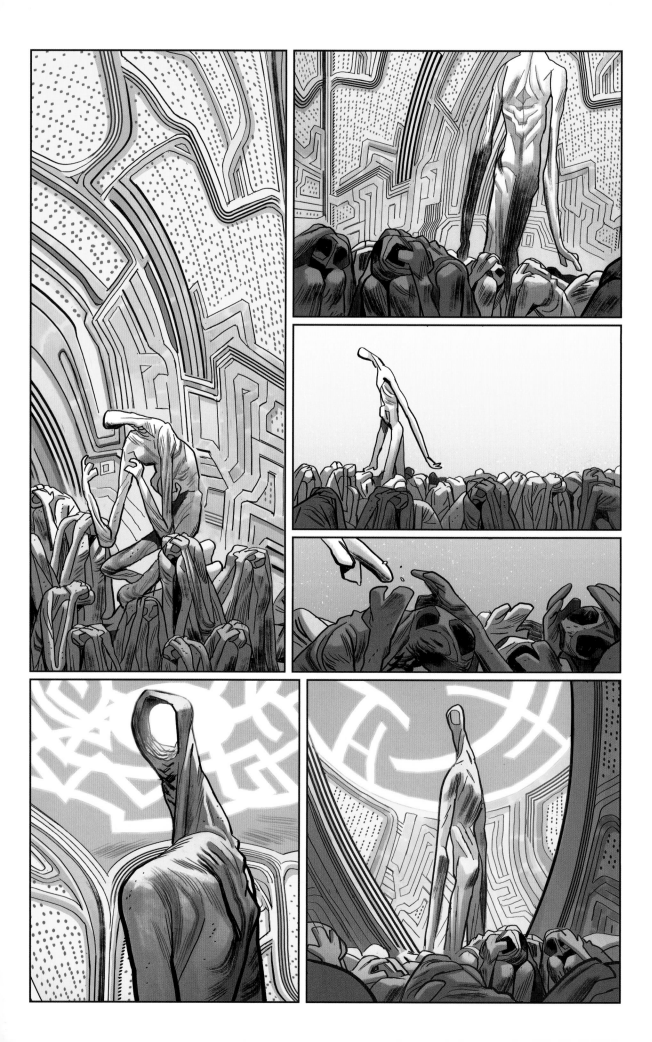

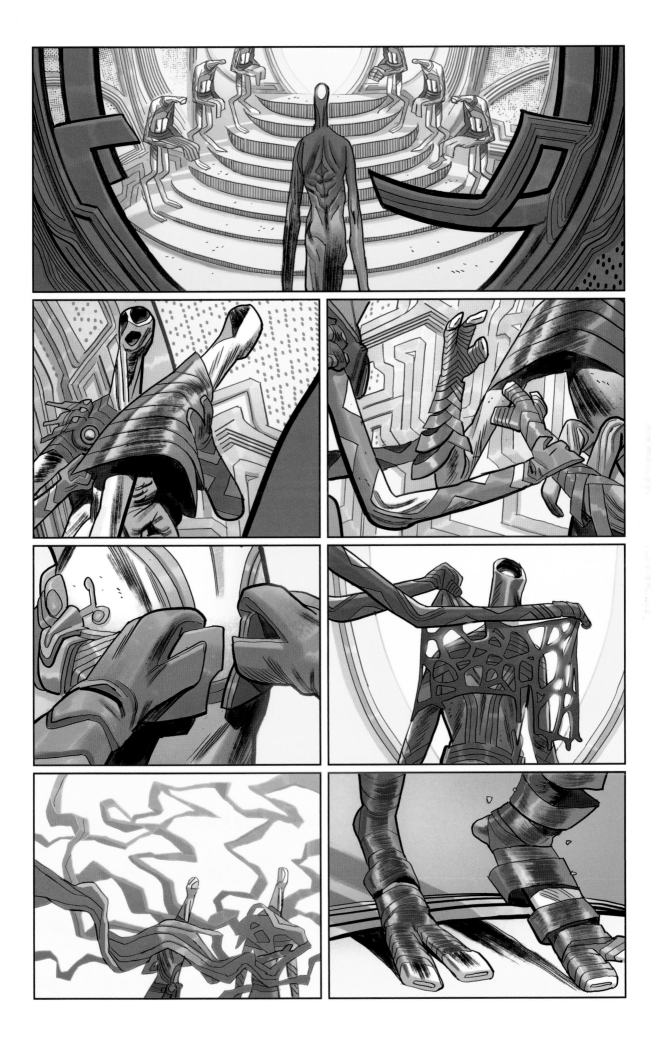

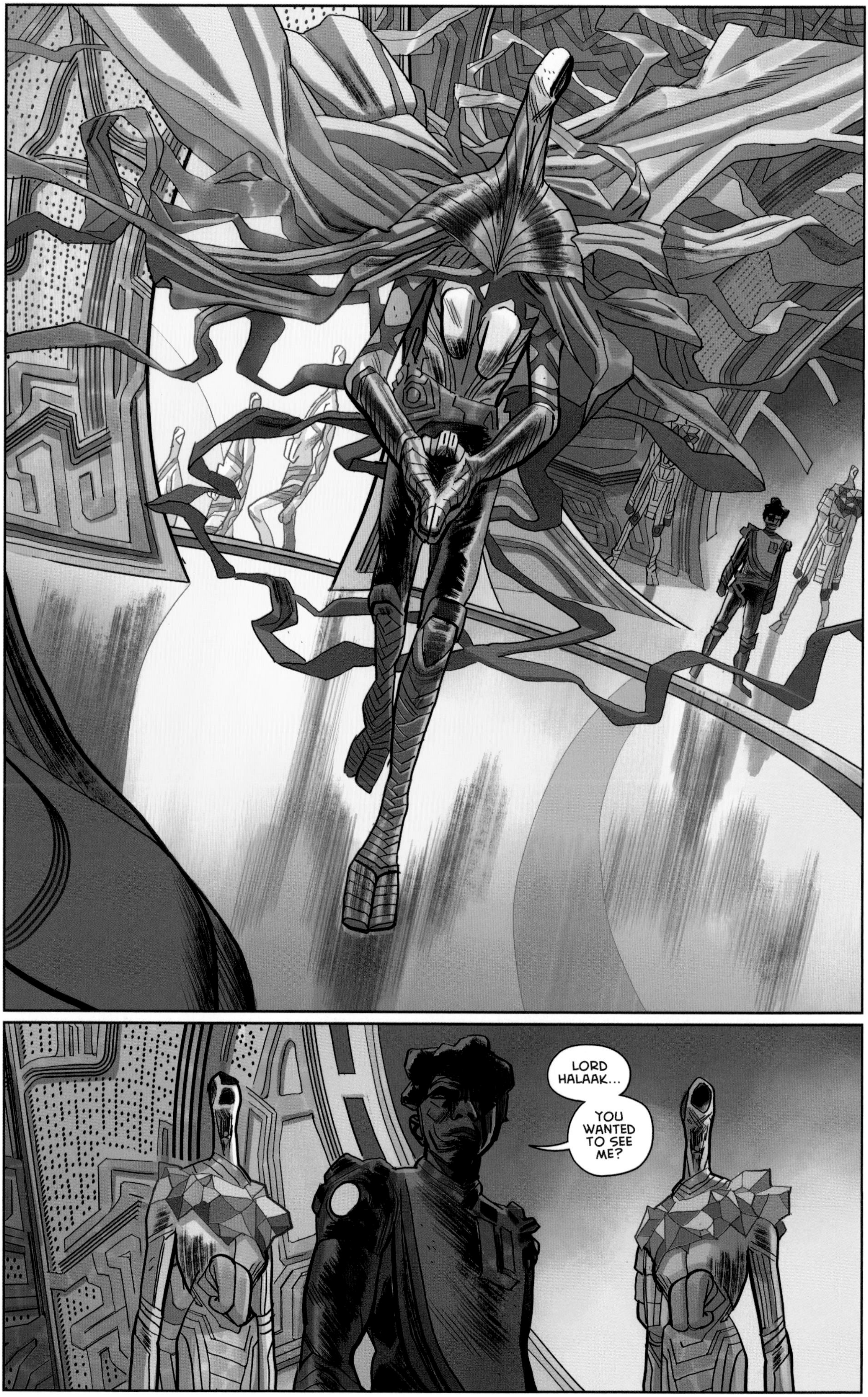
LORD HALAAK...
YOU WANTED TO SEE ME?

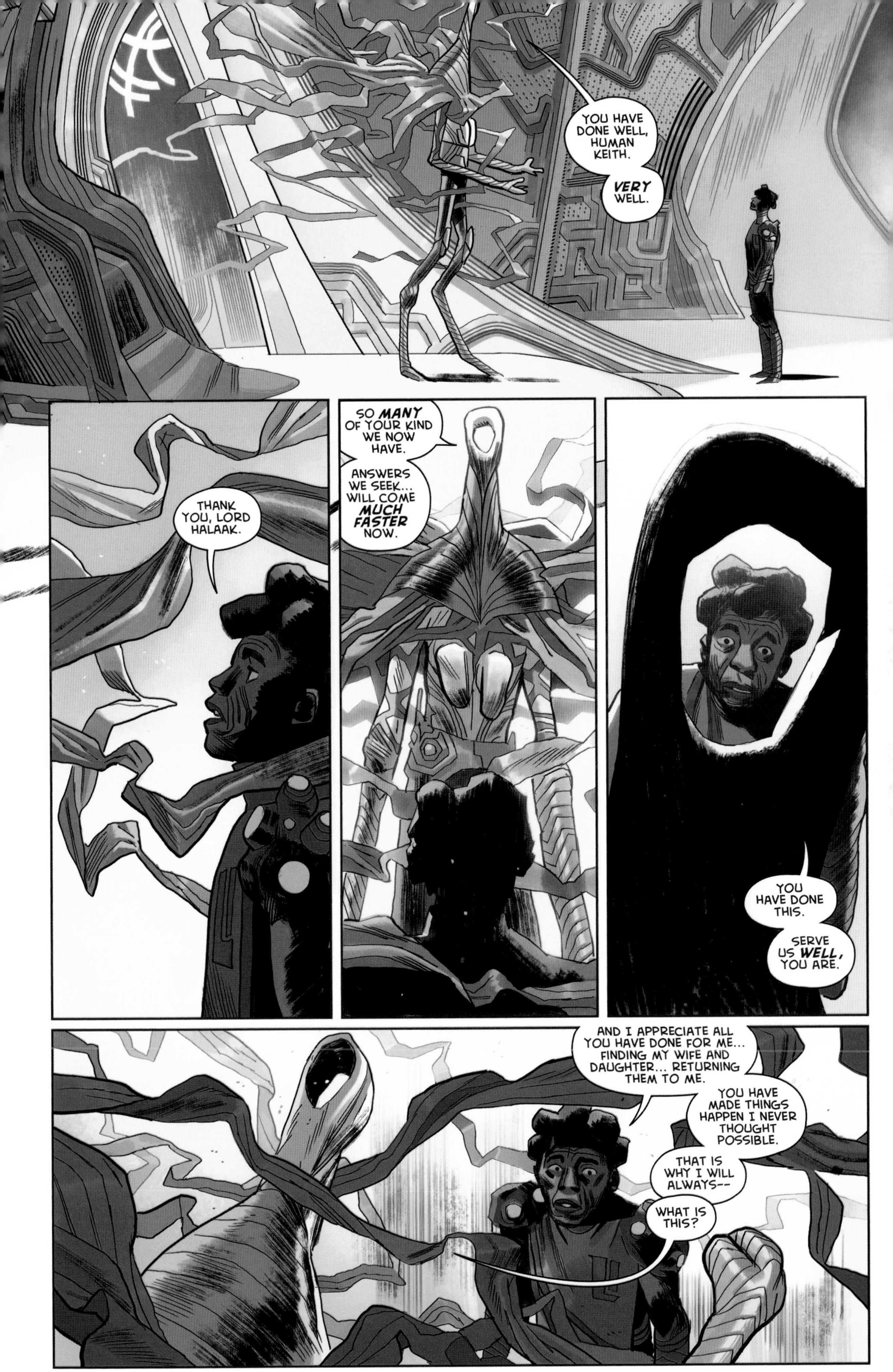
YOU HAVE DONE WELL, HUMAN KEITH.
VERY WELL.
THANK YOU, LORD HALAAK.
SO MANY OF YOUR KIND WE NOW HAVE.
ANSWERS WE SEEK... WILL COME MUCH FASTER NOW.
YOU HAVE DONE THIS.
SERVE US WELL, YOU ARE.
AND I APPRECIATE ALL YOU HAVE DONE FOR ME... FINDING MY WIFE AND DAUGHTER... RETURNING THEM TO ME.
YOU HAVE MADE THINGS HAPPEN I NEVER THOUGHT POSSIBLE.
THAT IS WHY I WILL ALWAYS--
WHAT IS THIS?

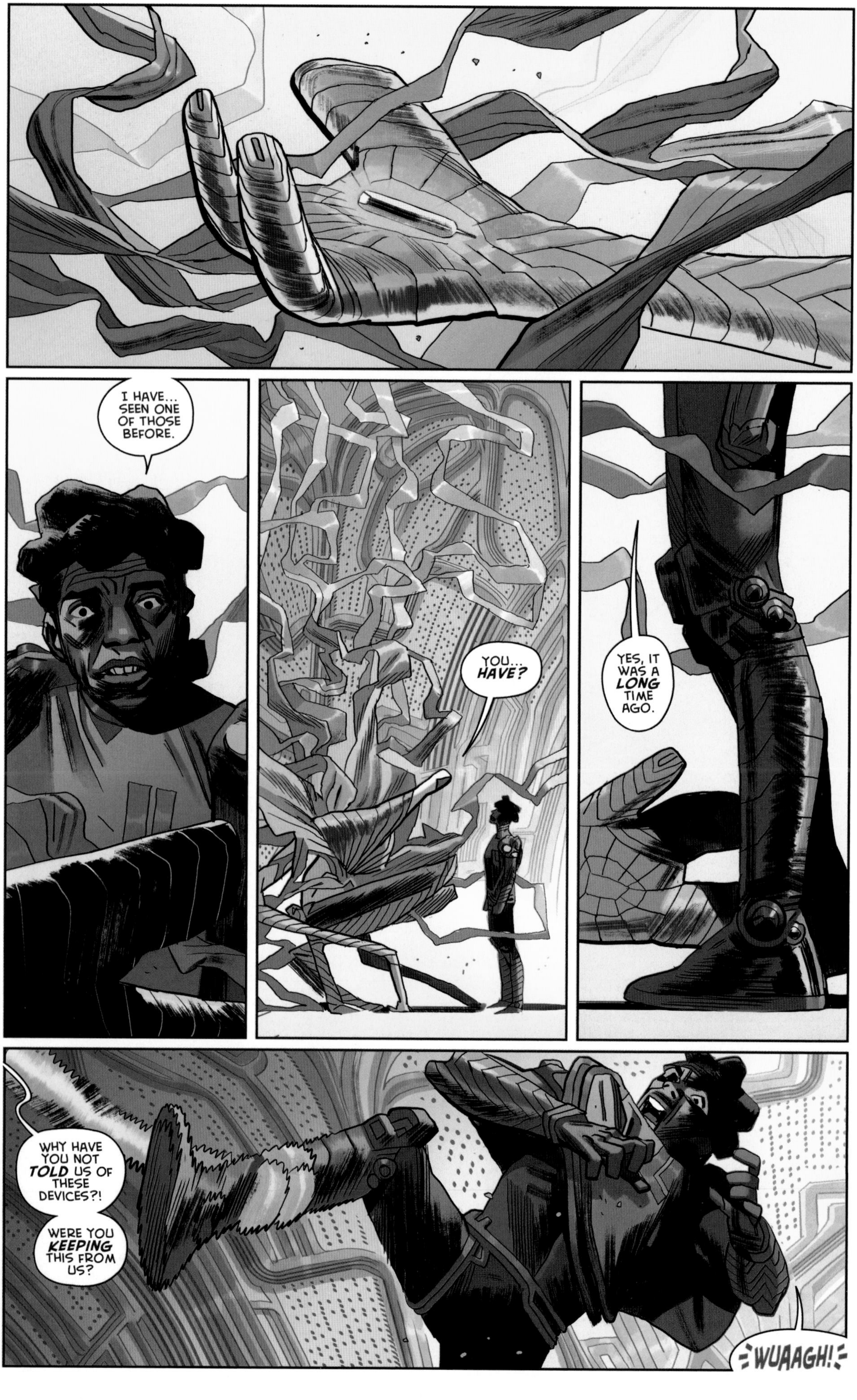
I HAVE... SEEN ONE OF THOSE BEFORE.
YOU... HAVE?
YES, IT WAS A LONG TIME AGO.
WHY HAVE YOU NOT TOLD US OF THESE DEVICES?!
WERE YOU KEEPING THIS FROM US?
WUAAGH!

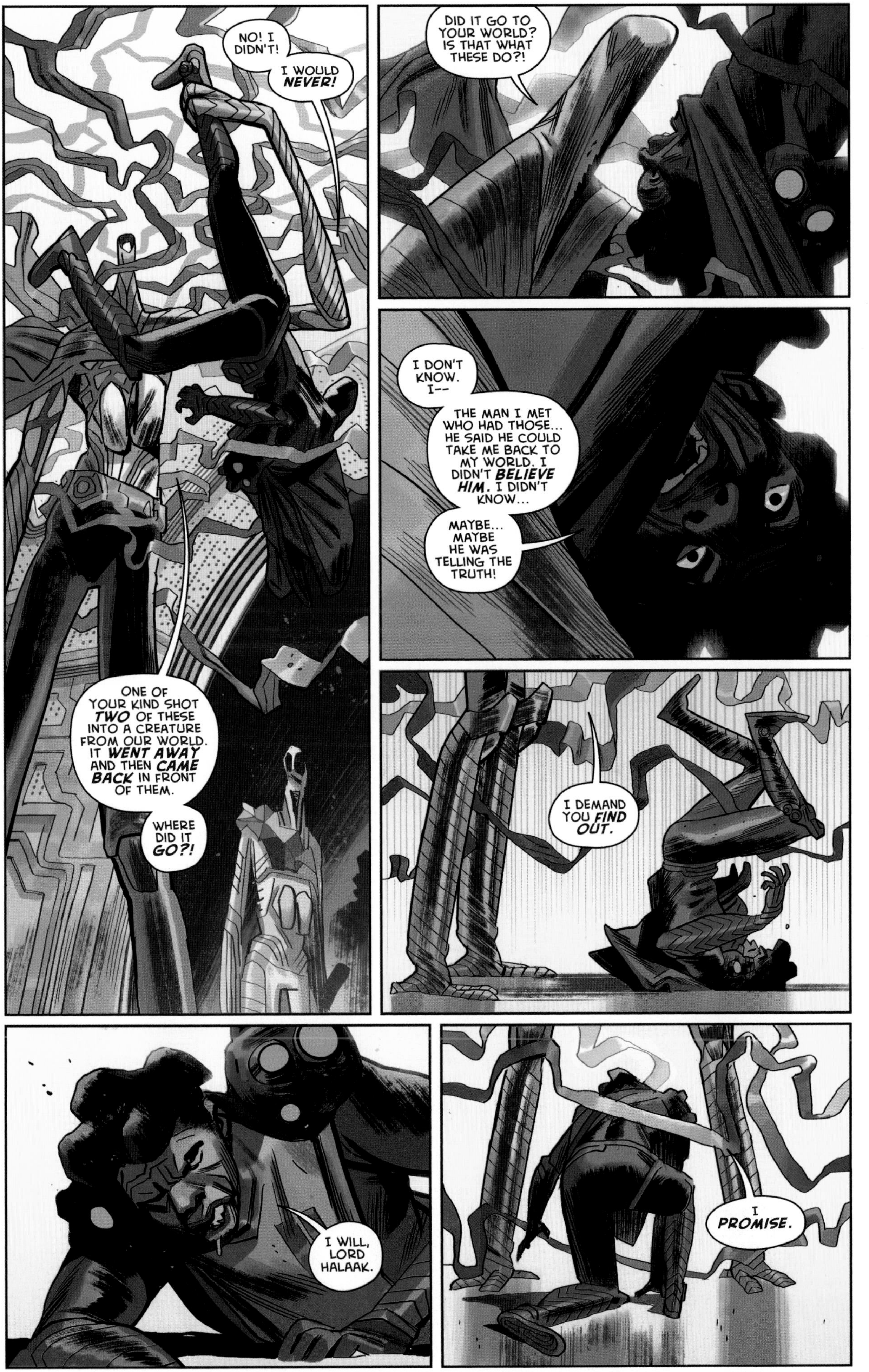

NO! I DIDN'T!
I WOULD NEVER!
ONE OF YOUR KIND SHOT TWO OF THESE INTO A CREATURE FROM OUR WORLD. IT WENT AWAY AND THEN CAME BACK IN FRONT OF THEM.
WHERE DID IT GO?!
DID IT GO TO YOUR WORLD? IS THAT WHAT THESE DO?!
I DON'T KNOW. I--
THE MAN I MET WHO HAD THOSE... HE SAID HE COULD TAKE ME BACK TO MY WORLD. I DIDN'T BELIEVE HIM. I DIDN'T KNOW...
MAYBE... MAYBE HE WAS TELLING THE TRUTH!
I DEMAND YOU FIND OUT.
I WILL, LORD HALAAK.
I PROMISE.

GHOZAN DAKUUL-- *ENTER.*

WHY HAVE YOU SUMMONED ME, HALAAK?

YOU WILL REFER TO ME BY THE EARTH TITLE, *LORD.* IT APPLIES TO MY STATION. I *PREFER* IT.

SHOW ME RESPECT.

YOU ARE NOT *MY* LORD, SO I WILL NOT ANSWER TO YOU AS SUCH.

IT IS BAD ENOUGH YOU INSIST ON USING THEIR LANGUAGE.

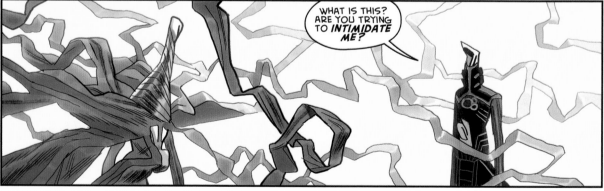

WHAT IS THIS? ARE YOU TRYING TO *INTIMIDATE* ME?

WE FOUND ANOTHER ONE, DAKUUL.

ANOTHER *WHAT?*

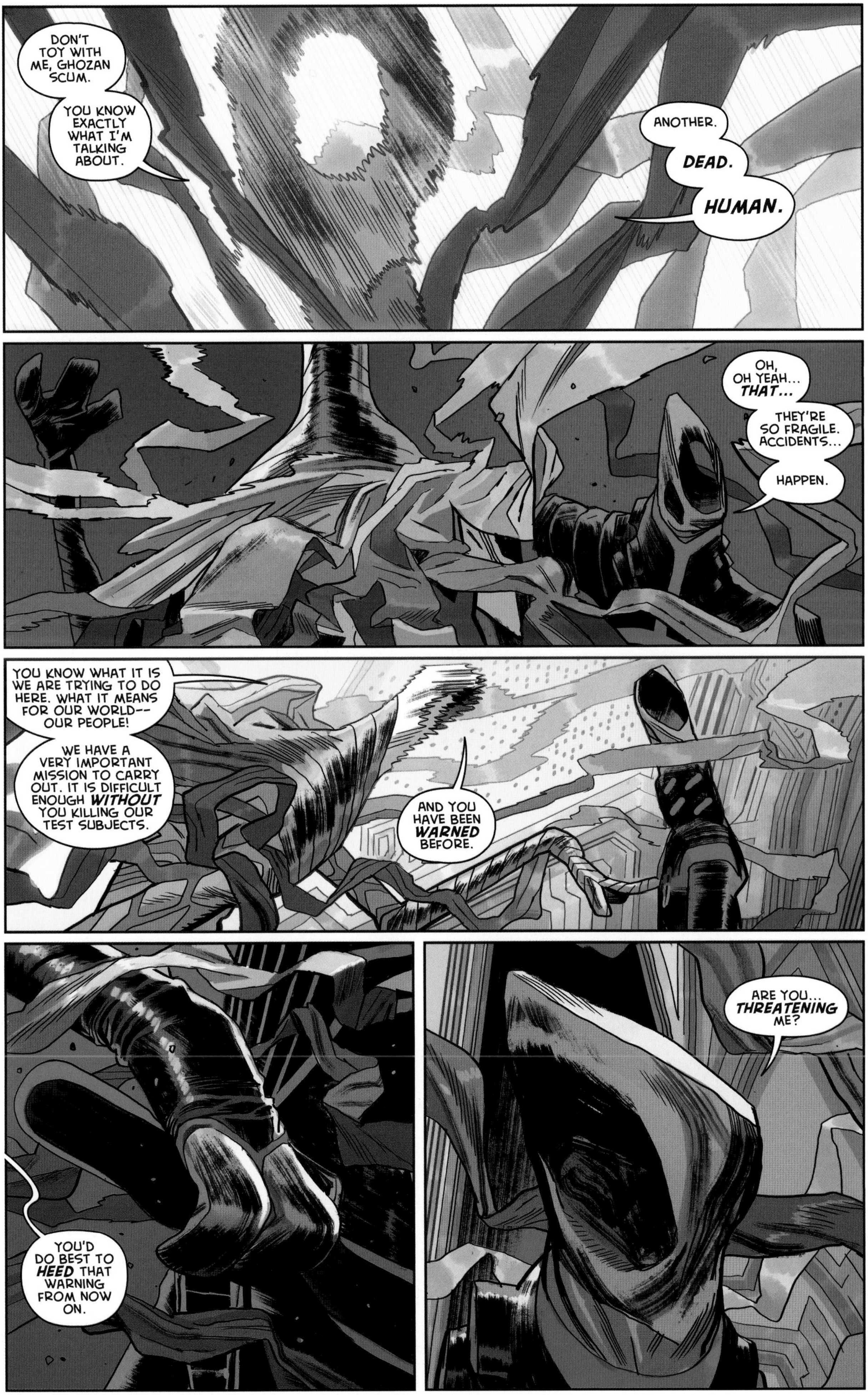
DON'T TOY WITH ME, GHOZAN SCUM.
YOU KNOW EXACTLY WHAT I'M TALKING ABOUT.
ANOTHER.
DEAD.
HUMAN.
OH, OH YEAH... **THAT...**
THEY'RE SO FRAGILE. ACCIDENTS...
HAPPEN.
YOU KNOW WHAT IT IS WE ARE TRYING TO DO HERE. WHAT IT MEANS FOR OUR WORLD-- OUR PEOPLE!
WE HAVE A VERY IMPORTANT MISSION TO CARRY OUT. IT IS DIFFICULT ENOUGH **WITHOUT** YOU KILLING OUR TEST SUBJECTS.
AND YOU HAVE BEEN **WARNED** BEFORE.
YOU'D DO BEST TO **HEED** THAT WARNING FROM NOW ON.
ARE YOU... **THREATENING** ME?

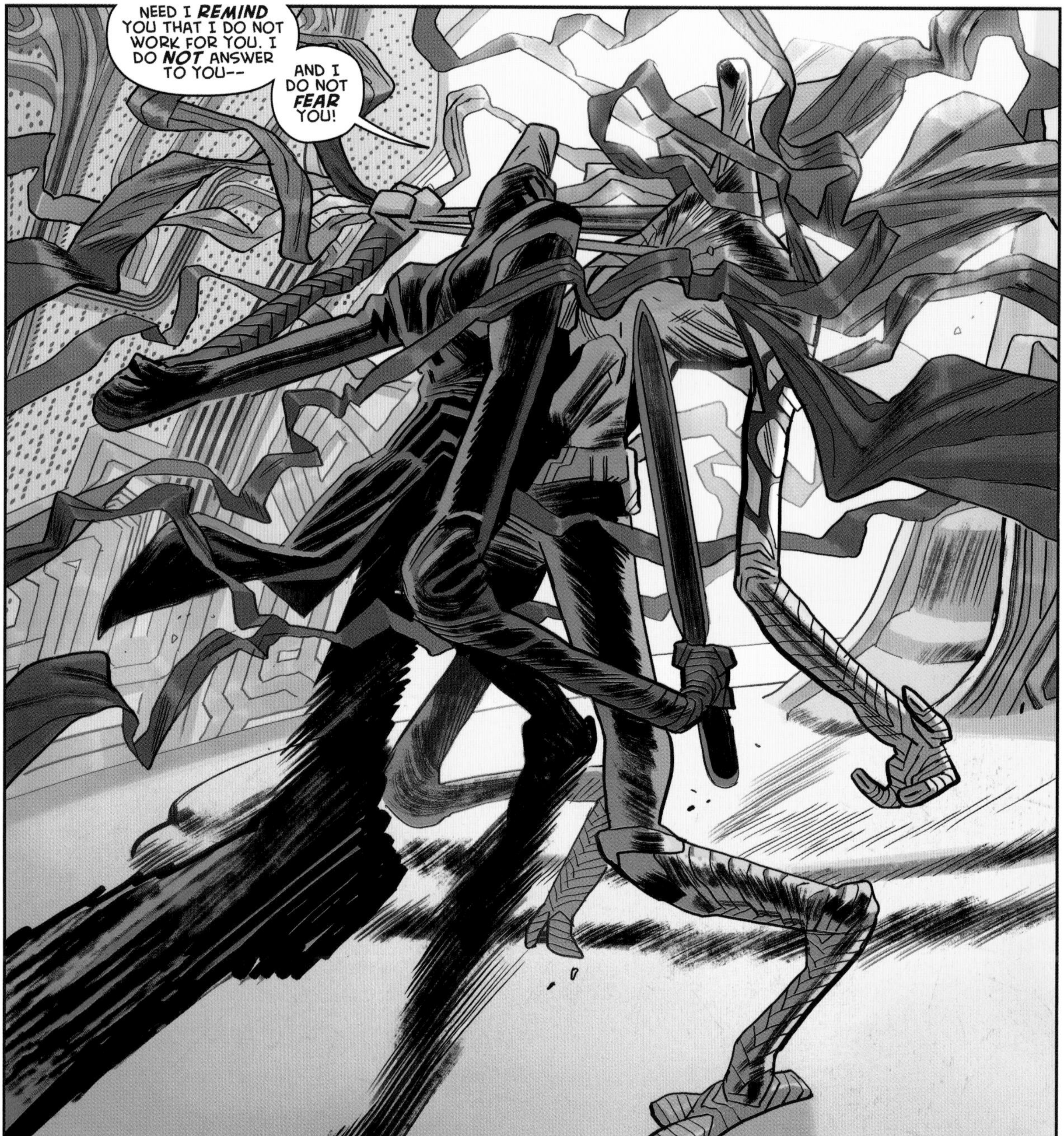
NEED I REMIND YOU THAT I DO NOT WORK FOR YOU. I DO NOT ANSWER TO YOU--
AND I DO NOT FEAR YOU!

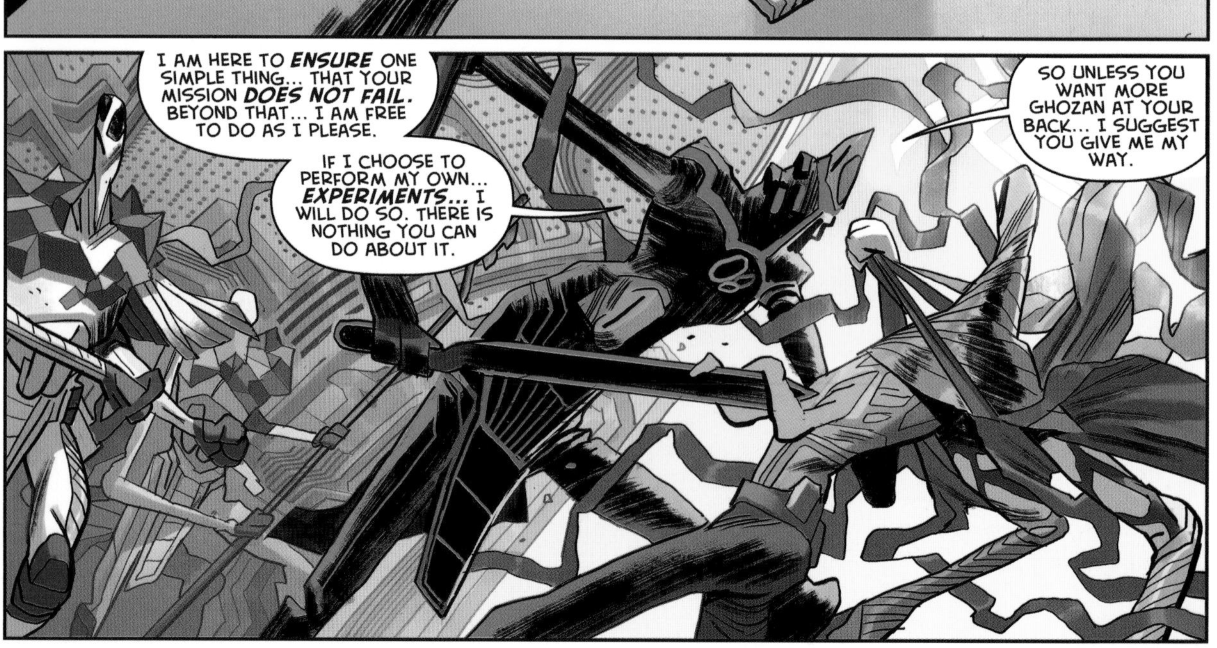
I AM HERE TO ENSURE ONE SIMPLE THING... THAT YOUR MISSION DOES NOT FAIL. BEYOND THAT... I AM FREE TO DO AS I PLEASE.
IF I CHOOSE TO PERFORM MY OWN... EXPERIMENTS... I WILL DO SO. THERE IS NOTHING YOU CAN DO ABOUT IT.
SO UNLESS YOU WANT MORE GHOZAN AT YOUR BACK... I SUGGEST YOU GIVE ME MY WAY.

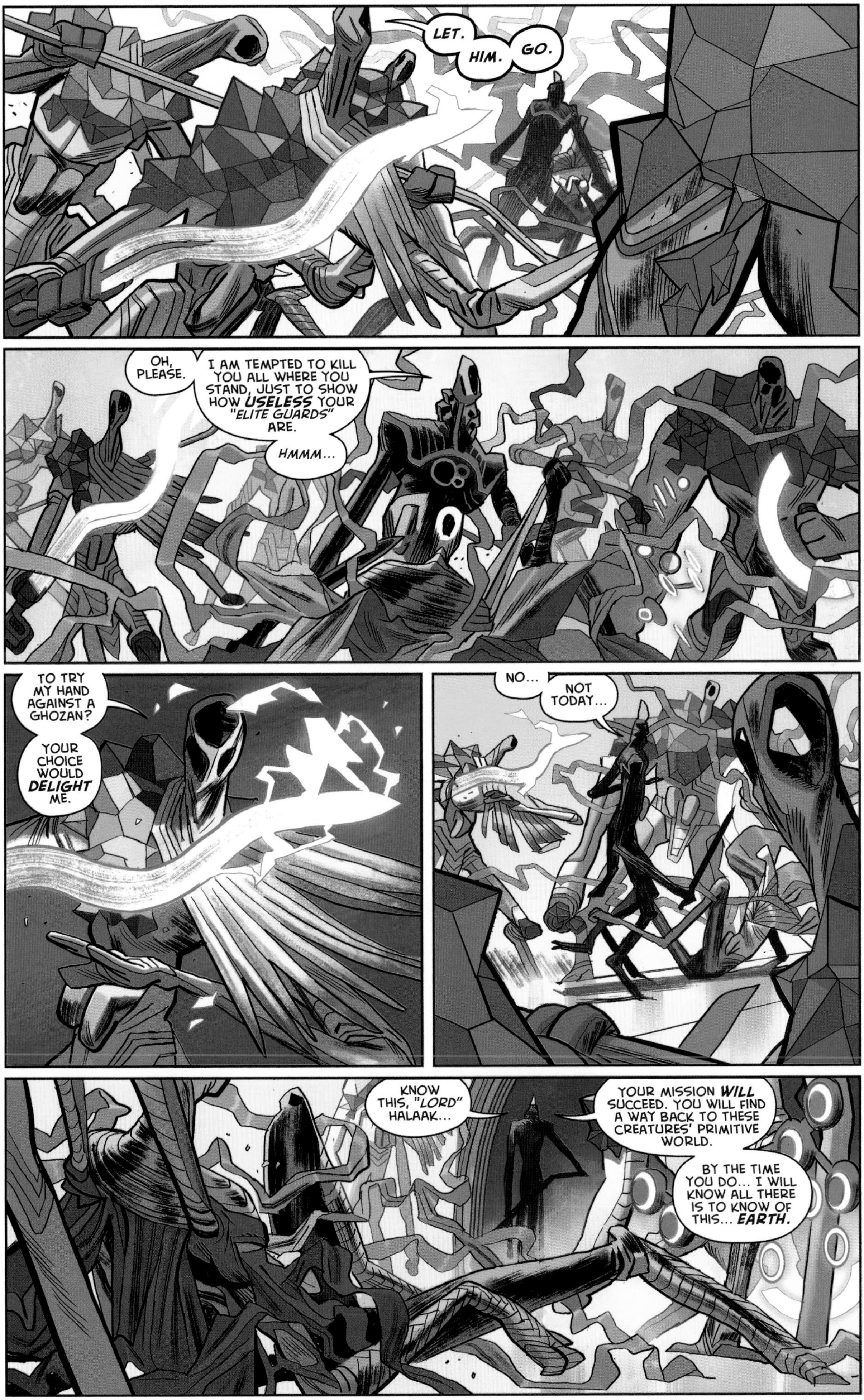
LET. HIM. GO.
OH, PLEASE.
I AM TEMPTED TO KILL YOU ALL WHERE YOU STAND, JUST TO SHOW HOW USELESS YOUR "ELITE GUARDS" ARE.
HMMM...
TO TRY MY HAND AGAINST A GHOZAN?
YOUR CHOICE WOULD DELIGHT ME.
NO...
NOT TODAY...
KNOW THIS, "LORD" HALAAK...
YOUR MISSION WILL SUCCEED. YOU WILL FIND A WAY BACK TO THESE CREATURES' PRIMITIVE WORLD.
BY THE TIME YOU DO... I WILL KNOW ALL THERE IS TO KNOW OF THIS... EARTH.

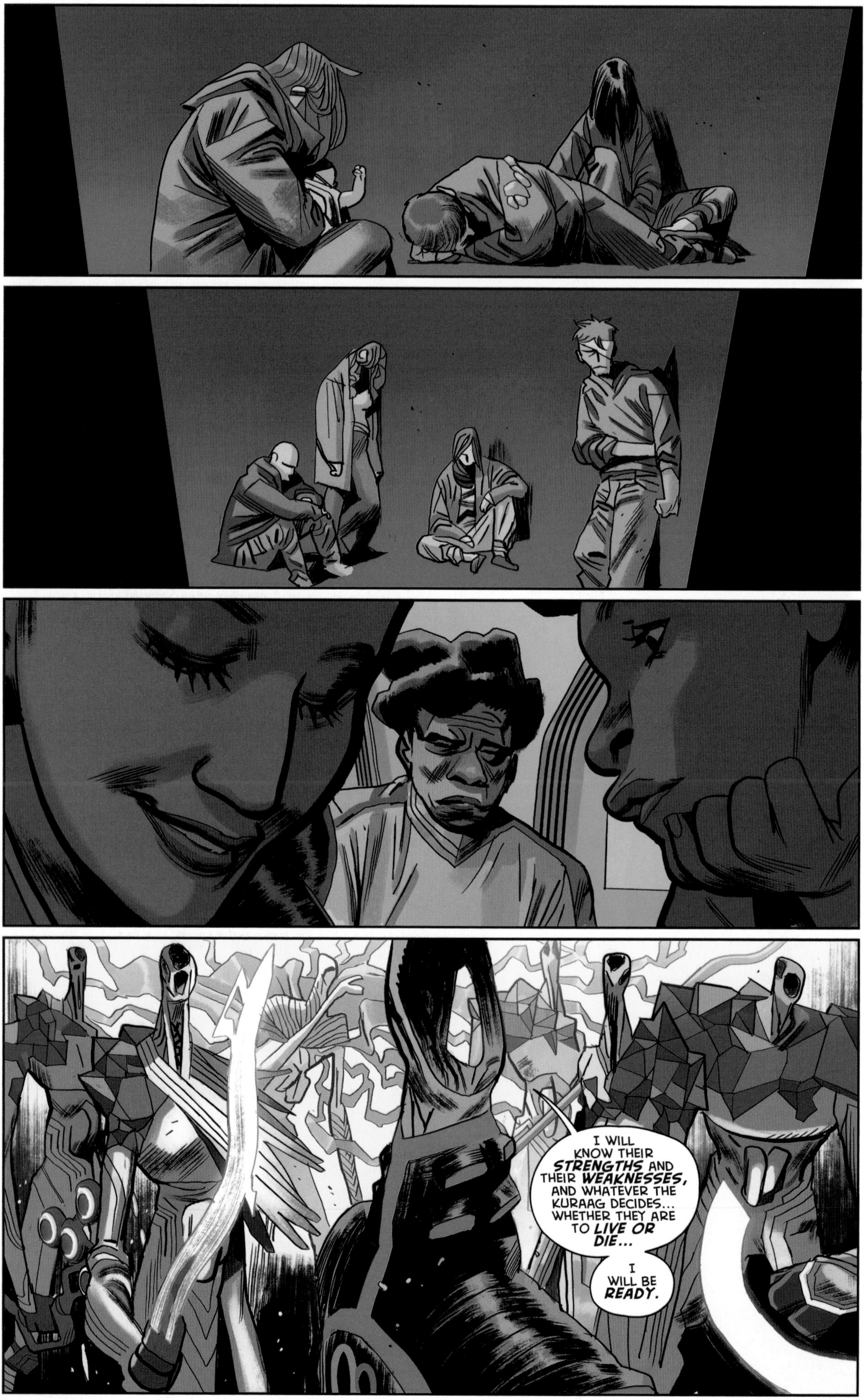
I WILL KNOW THEIR STRENGTHS AND THEIR WEAKNESSES, AND WHATEVER THE KURAAG DECIDES... WHETHER THEY ARE TO LIVE OR DIE...
I WILL BE READY.

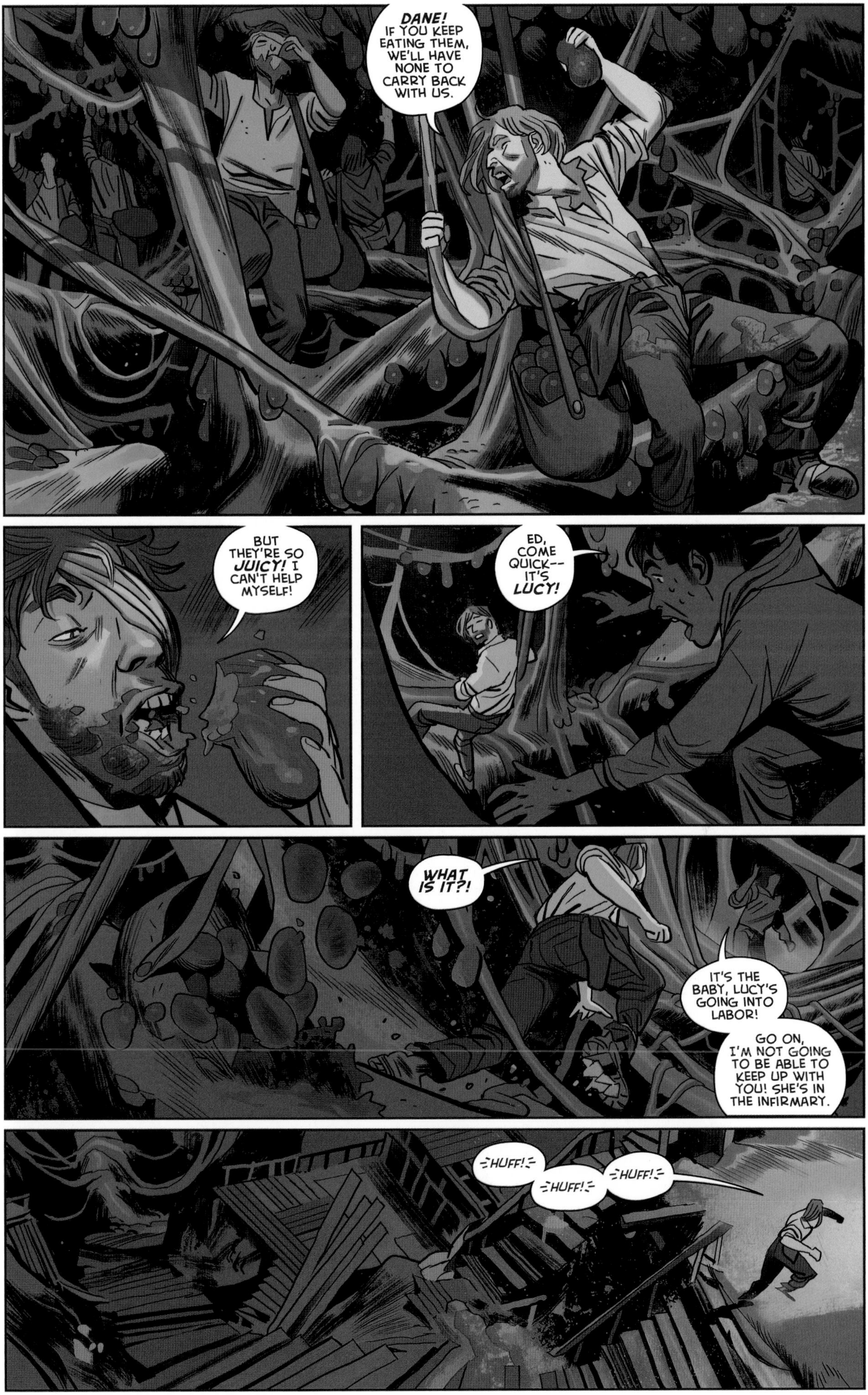
DANE! IF YOU KEEP EATING THEM, WE'LL HAVE NONE TO CARRY BACK WITH US.
BUT THEY'RE SO JUICY! I CAN'T HELP MYSELF!
ED, COME QUICK-- IT'S LUCY!
WHAT IS IT?!
IT'S THE BABY, LUCY'S GOING INTO LABOR!
GO ON, I'M NOT GOING TO BE ABLE TO KEEP UP WITH YOU! SHE'S IN THE INFIRMARY.
HUFF!
HUFF!
HUFF!

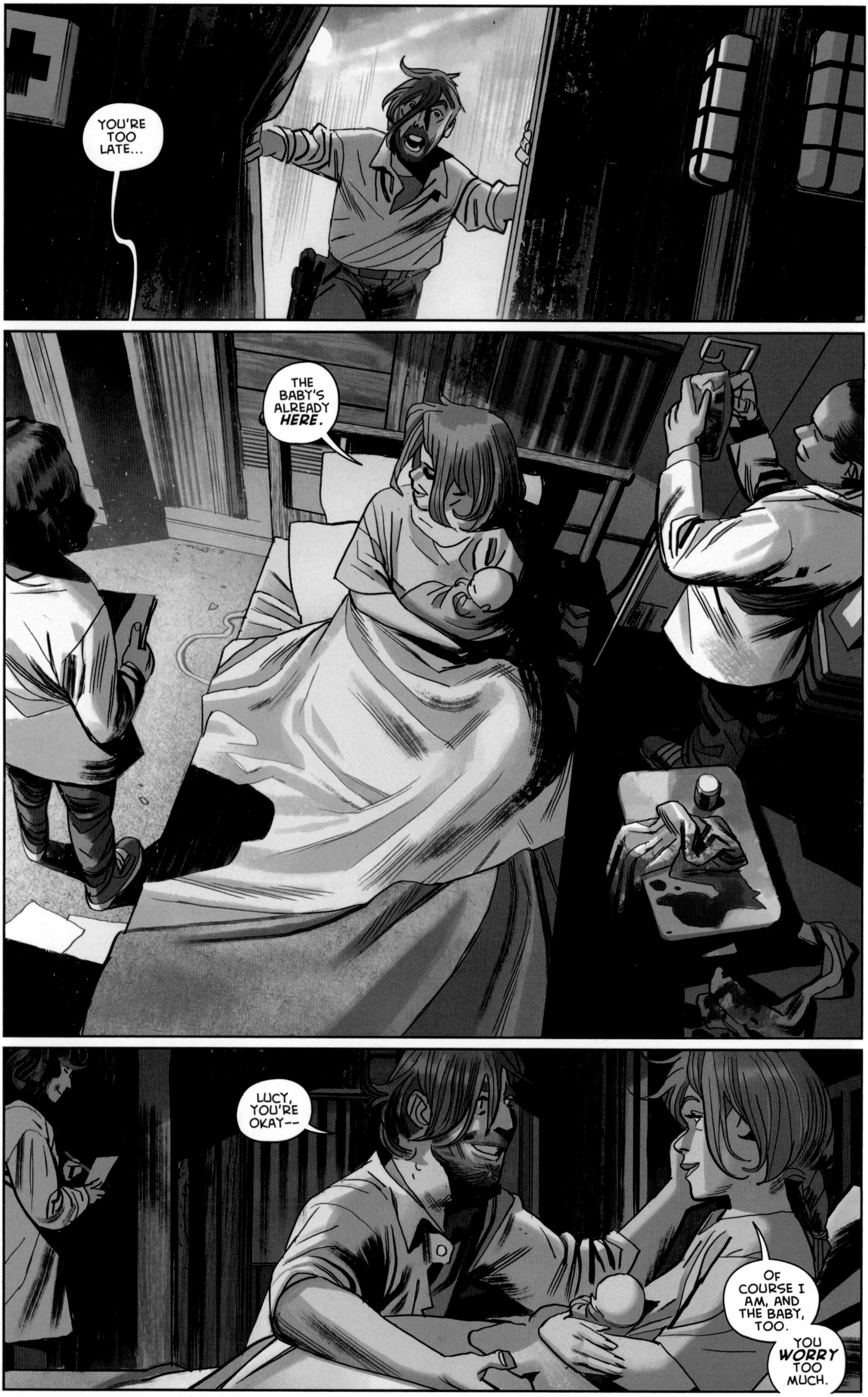
YOU'RE TOO LATE...
THE BABY'S ALREADY *HERE*.
LUCY, YOU'RE OKAY--
OF COURSE I AM, AND THE BABY, TOO.
YOU *WORRY* TOO MUCH.

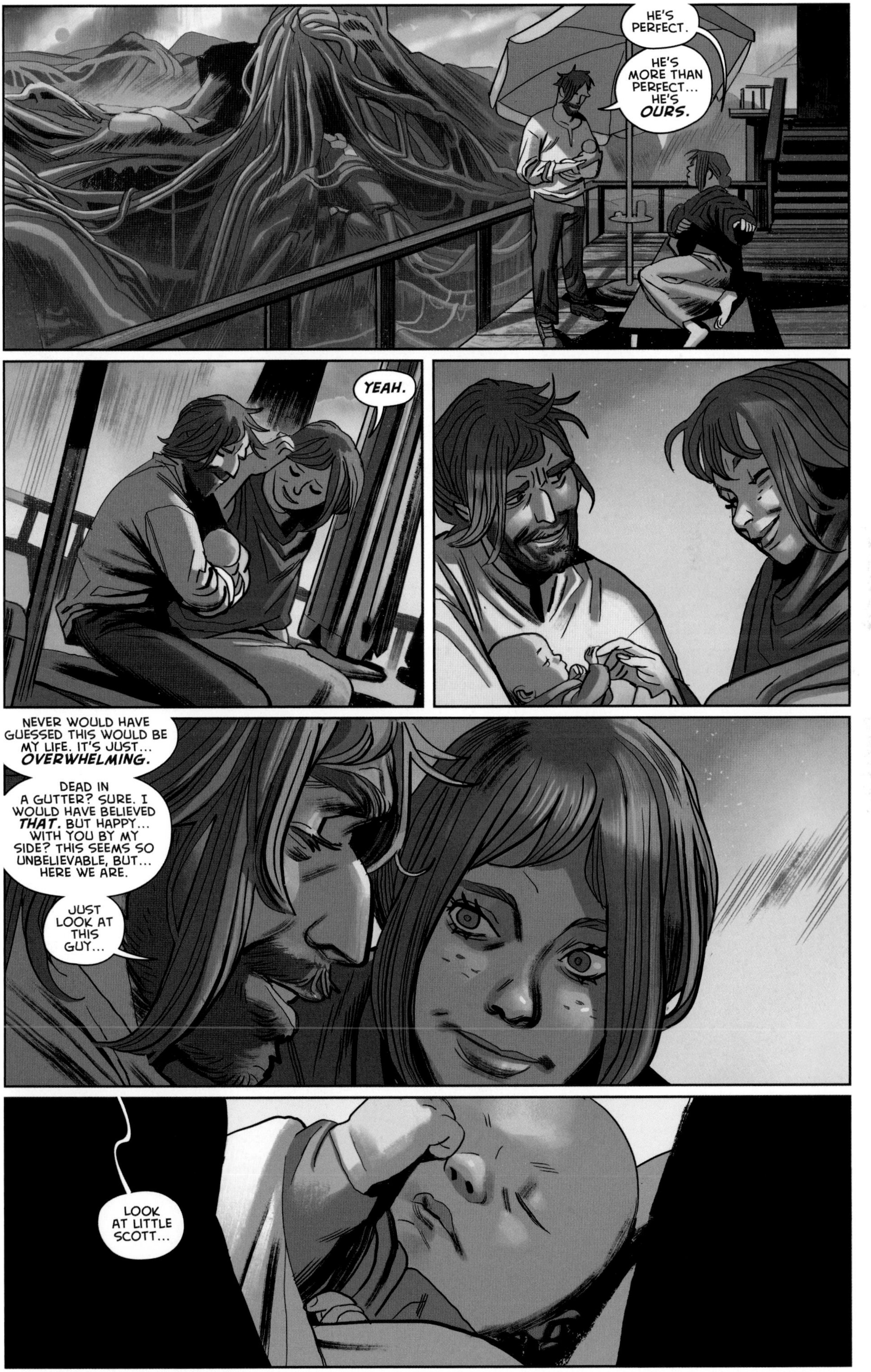
HE'S PERFECT.
HE'S MORE THAN PERFECT... HE'S OURS.
YEAH.
NEVER WOULD HAVE GUESSED THIS WOULD BE MY LIFE. IT'S JUST... OVERWHELMING.
DEAD IN A GUTTER? SURE. I WOULD HAVE BELIEVED THAT. BUT HAPPY... WITH YOU BY MY SIDE? THIS SEEMS SO UNBELIEVABLE, BUT... HERE WE ARE.
JUST LOOK AT THIS GUY...
LOOK AT LITTLE SCOTT...

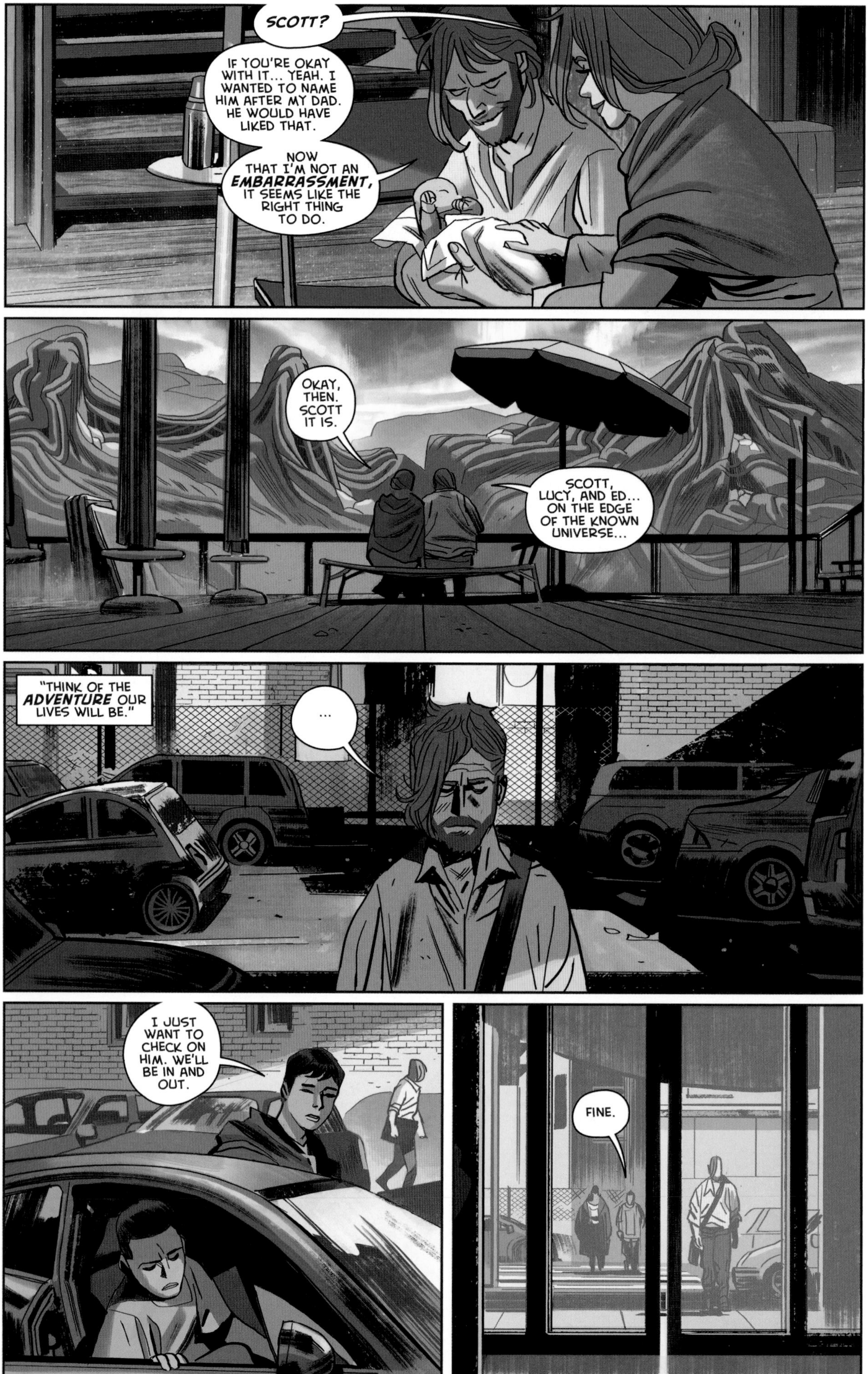
SCOTT?
IF YOU'RE OKAY WITH IT... YEAH. I WANTED TO NAME HIM AFTER MY DAD. HE WOULD HAVE LIKED THAT.
NOW THAT I'M NOT AN EMBARRASSMENT, IT SEEMS LIKE THE RIGHT THING TO DO.
OKAY, THEN. SCOTT IT IS.
SCOTT, LUCY, AND ED... ON THE EDGE OF THE KNOWN UNIVERSE...
"THINK OF THE ADVENTURE OUR LIVES WILL BE."
...
I JUST WANT TO CHECK ON HIM. WE'LL BE IN AND OUT.
FINE.

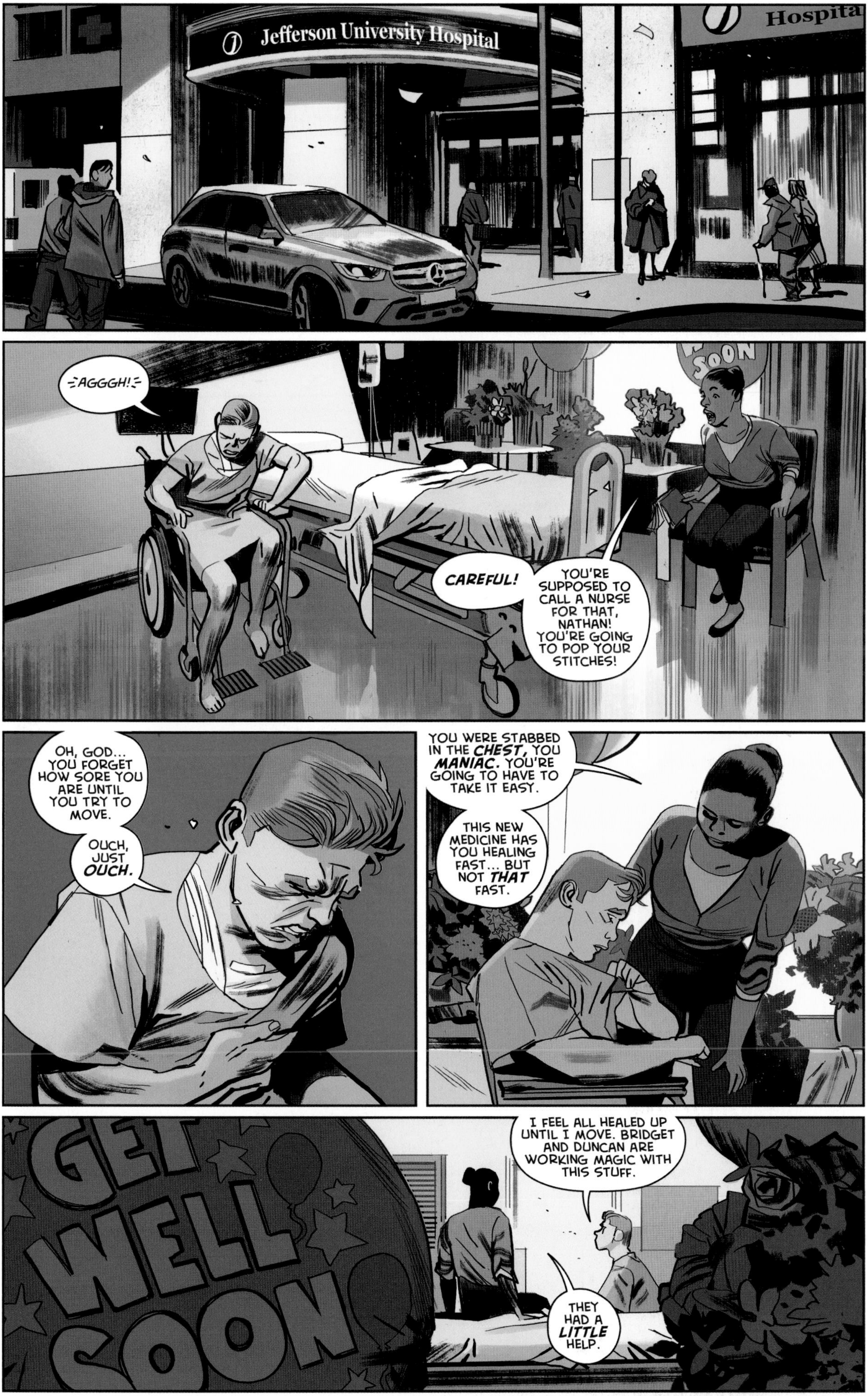
Jefferson University Hospital
Hospita
AGGGH!
CAREFUL!
YOU'RE SUPPOSED TO CALL A NURSE FOR THAT, NATHAN! YOU'RE GOING TO POP YOUR STITCHES!
OH, GOD... YOU FORGET HOW SORE YOU ARE UNTIL YOU TRY TO MOVE.
OUCH, JUST OUCH.
YOU WERE STABBED IN THE CHEST, YOU MANIAC. YOU'RE GOING TO HAVE TO TAKE IT EASY.
THIS NEW MEDICINE HAS YOU HEALING FAST... BUT NOT THAT FAST.
GET WELL SOON
I FEEL ALL HEALED UP UNTIL I MOVE. BRIDGET AND DUNCAN ARE WORKING MAGIC WITH THIS STUFF.
THEY HAD A LITTLE HELP.

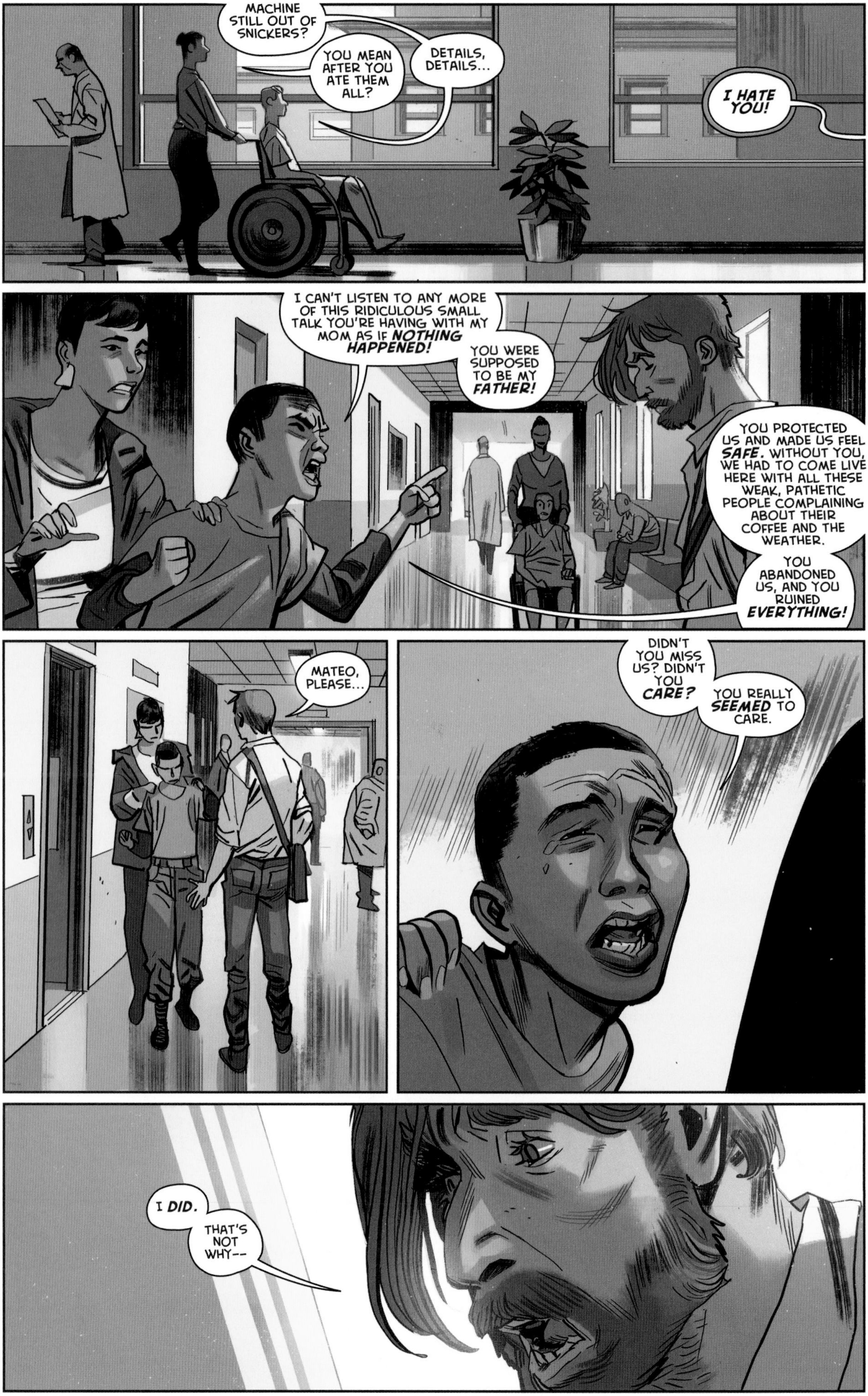

MACHINE STILL OUT OF SNICKERS?
YOU MEAN AFTER YOU ATE THEM ALL?
DETAILS, DETAILS...
I HATE YOU!
I CAN'T LISTEN TO ANY MORE OF THIS RIDICULOUS SMALL TALK YOU'RE HAVING WITH MY MOM AS IF NOTHING HAPPENED!
YOU WERE SUPPOSED TO BE MY FATHER!
YOU PROTECTED US AND MADE US FEEL SAFE. WITHOUT YOU, WE HAD TO COME LIVE HERE WITH ALL THESE WEAK, PATHETIC PEOPLE COMPLAINING ABOUT THEIR COFFEE AND THE WEATHER.
YOU ABANDONED US, AND YOU RUINED EVERYTHING!
MATEO, PLEASE...
DIDN'T YOU MISS US? DIDN'T YOU CARE?
YOU REALLY SEEMED TO CARE.
I DID.
THAT'S NOT WHY--

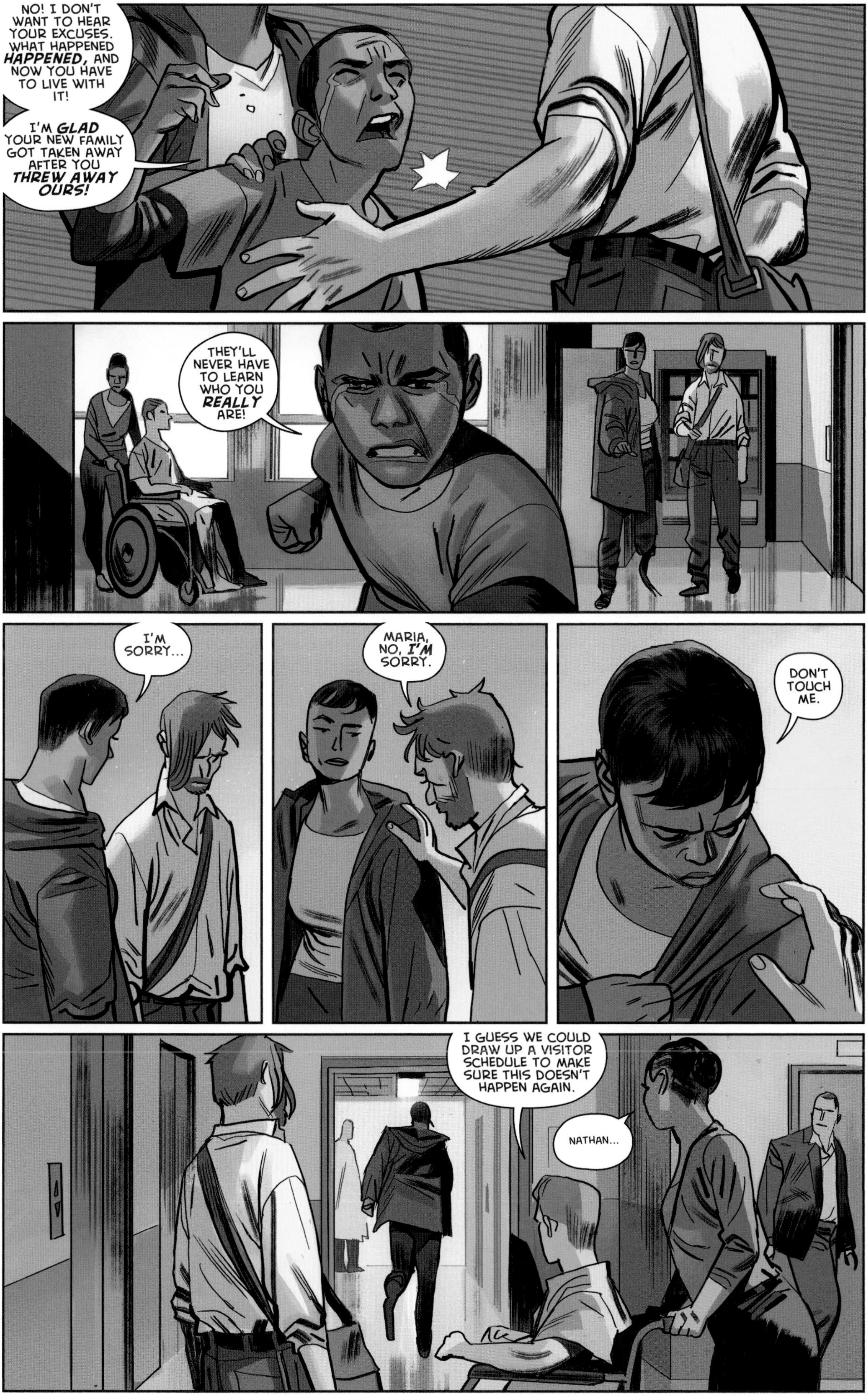
NO! I DON'T WANT TO HEAR YOUR EXCUSES. WHAT HAPPENED HAPPENED, AND NOW YOU HAVE TO LIVE WITH IT!
I'M GLAD YOUR NEW FAMILY GOT TAKEN AWAY AFTER YOU THREW AWAY OURS!
THEY'LL NEVER HAVE TO LEARN WHO YOU REALLY ARE!
I'M SORRY...
MARIA, NO, I'M SORRY.
DON'T TOUCH ME.
I GUESS WE COULD DRAW UP A VISITOR SCHEDULE TO MAKE SURE THIS DOESN'T HAPPEN AGAIN.
NATHAN...

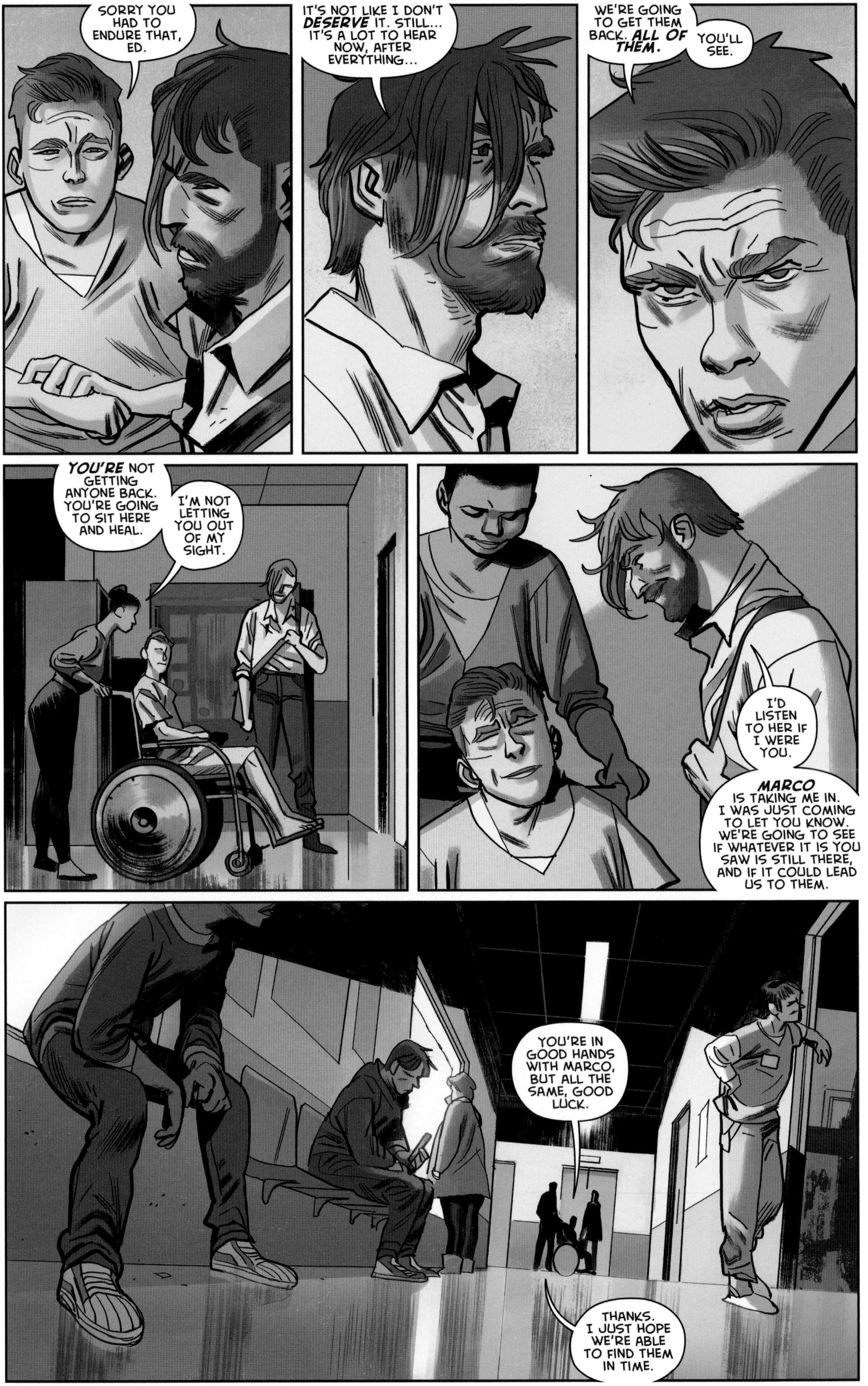
SORRY YOU HAD TO ENDURE THAT, ED.
IT'S NOT LIKE I DON'T DESERVE IT. STILL... IT'S A LOT TO HEAR NOW, AFTER EVERYTHING...
WE'RE GOING TO GET THEM BACK. ALL OF THEM.
YOU'LL SEE.
YOU'RE NOT GETTING ANYONE BACK. YOU'RE GOING TO SIT HERE AND HEAL.
I'M NOT LETTING YOU OUT OF MY SIGHT.
I'D LISTEN TO HER IF I WERE YOU.
MARCO IS TAKING ME IN. I WAS JUST COMING TO LET YOU KNOW. WE'RE GOING TO SEE IF WHATEVER IT IS YOU SAW IS STILL THERE, AND IF IT COULD LEAD US TO THEM.
YOU'RE IN GOOD HANDS WITH MARCO, BUT ALL THE SAME, GOOD LUCK.
THANKS. I JUST HOPE WE'RE ABLE TO FIND THEM IN TIME.

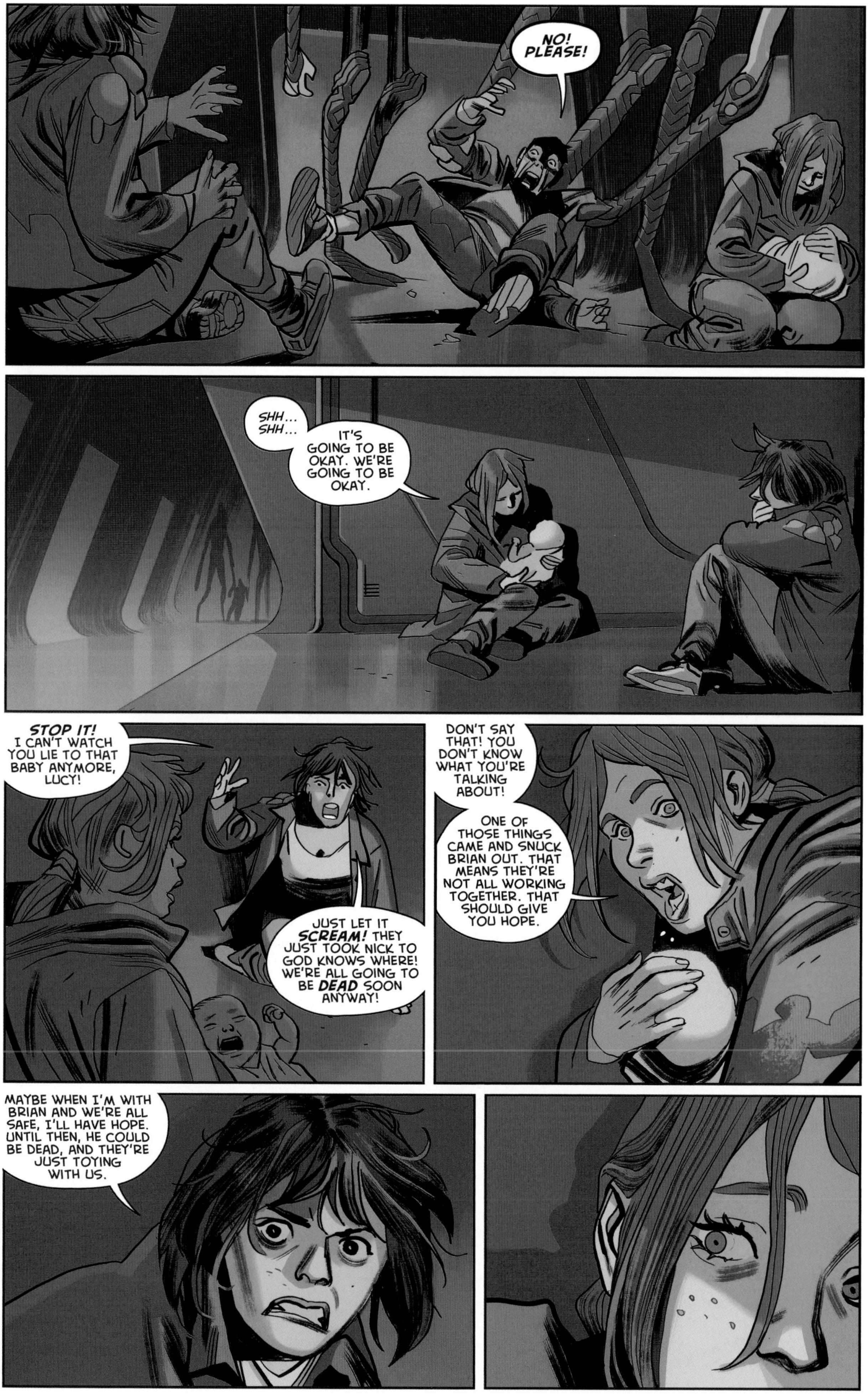
NO! PLEASE!
SHH... SHH...
IT'S GOING TO BE OKAY. WE'RE GOING TO BE OKAY.
STOP IT! I CAN'T WATCH YOU LIE TO THAT BABY ANYMORE, LUCY!
JUST LET IT SCREAM! THEY JUST TOOK NICK TO GOD KNOWS WHERE! WE'RE ALL GOING TO BE DEAD SOON ANYWAY!
DON'T SAY THAT! YOU DON'T KNOW WHAT YOU'RE TALKING ABOUT!
ONE OF THOSE THINGS CAME AND SNUCK BRIAN OUT. THAT MEANS THEY'RE NOT ALL WORKING TOGETHER. THAT SHOULD GIVE YOU HOPE.
MAYBE WHEN I'M WITH BRIAN AND WE'RE ALL SAFE, I'LL HAVE HOPE. UNTIL THEN, HE COULD BE DEAD, AND THEY'RE JUST TOYING WITH US.

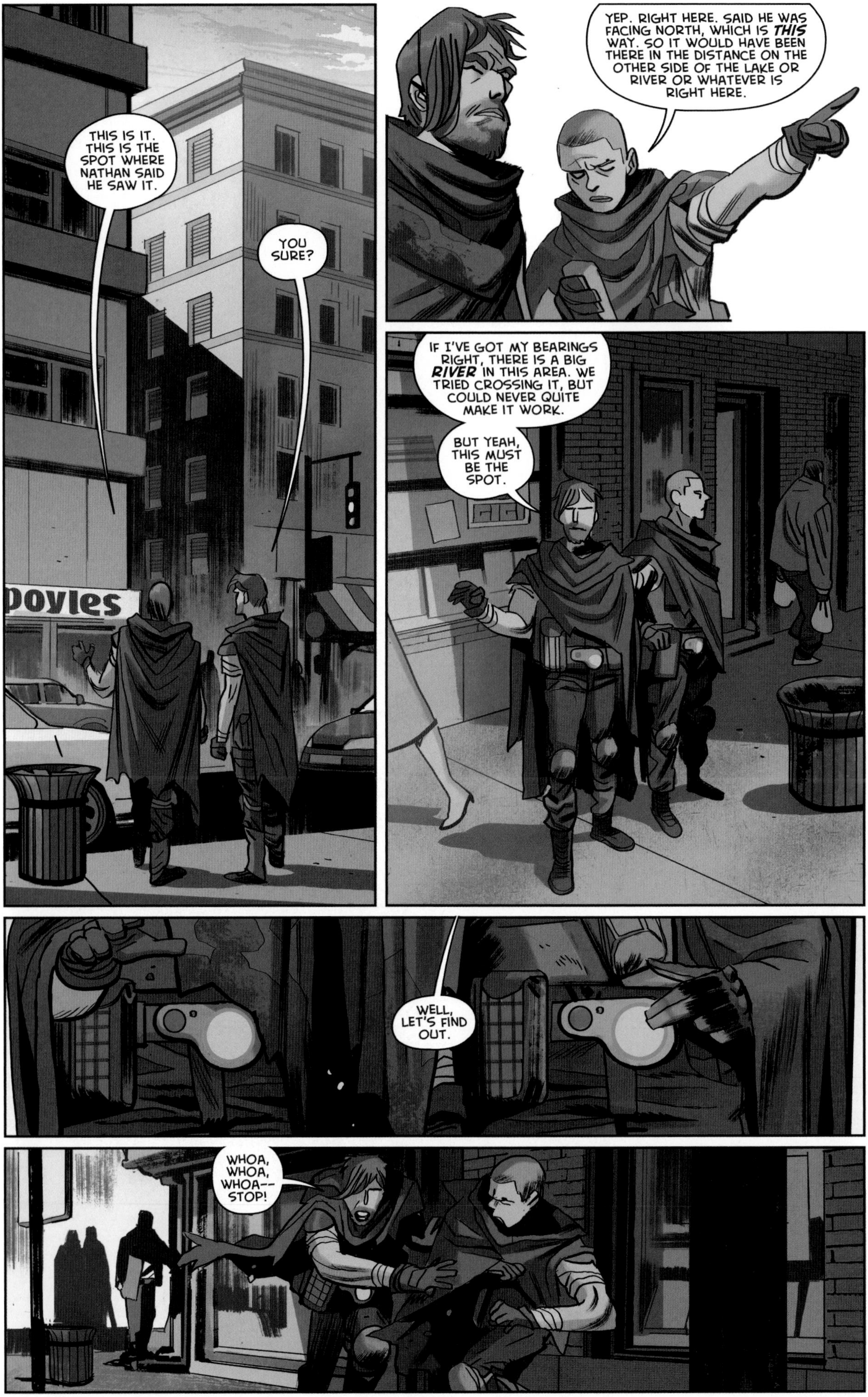
THIS IS IT. THIS IS THE SPOT WHERE NATHAN SAID HE SAW IT.
YOU SURE?
YEP. RIGHT HERE. SAID HE WAS FACING NORTH, WHICH IS ***THIS*** WAY. SO IT WOULD HAVE BEEN THERE IN THE DISTANCE ON THE OTHER SIDE OF THE LAKE OR RIVER OR WHATEVER IS RIGHT HERE.
IF I'VE GOT MY BEARINGS RIGHT, THERE IS A BIG ***RIVER*** IN THIS AREA. WE TRIED CROSSING IT, BUT COULD NEVER QUITE MAKE IT WORK.
BUT YEAH, THIS MUST BE THE SPOT.
WELL, LET'S FIND OUT.
WHOA, WHOA, WHOA-- STOP!
Doyles

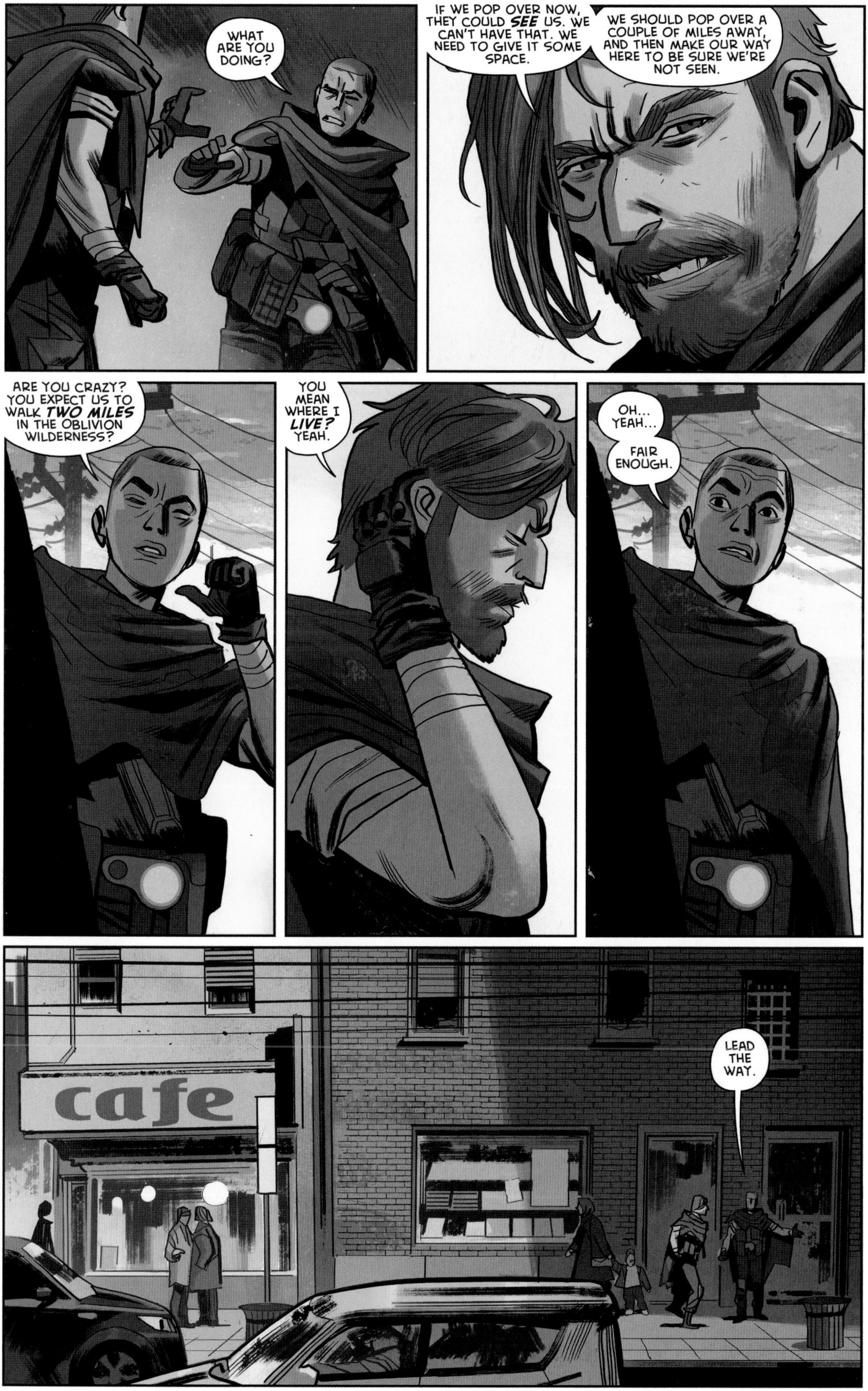
WHAT ARE YOU DOING?
IF WE POP OVER NOW, THEY COULD SEE US. WE CAN'T HAVE THAT. WE NEED TO GIVE IT SOME SPACE.
WE SHOULD POP OVER A COUPLE OF MILES AWAY, AND THEN MAKE OUR WAY HERE TO BE SURE WE'RE NOT SEEN.
ARE YOU CRAZY? YOU EXPECT US TO WALK TWO MILES IN THE OBLIVION WILDERNESS?
YOU MEAN WHERE I LIVE? YEAH.
OH... YEAH...
FAIR ENOUGH.
cafe
LEAD THE WAY.

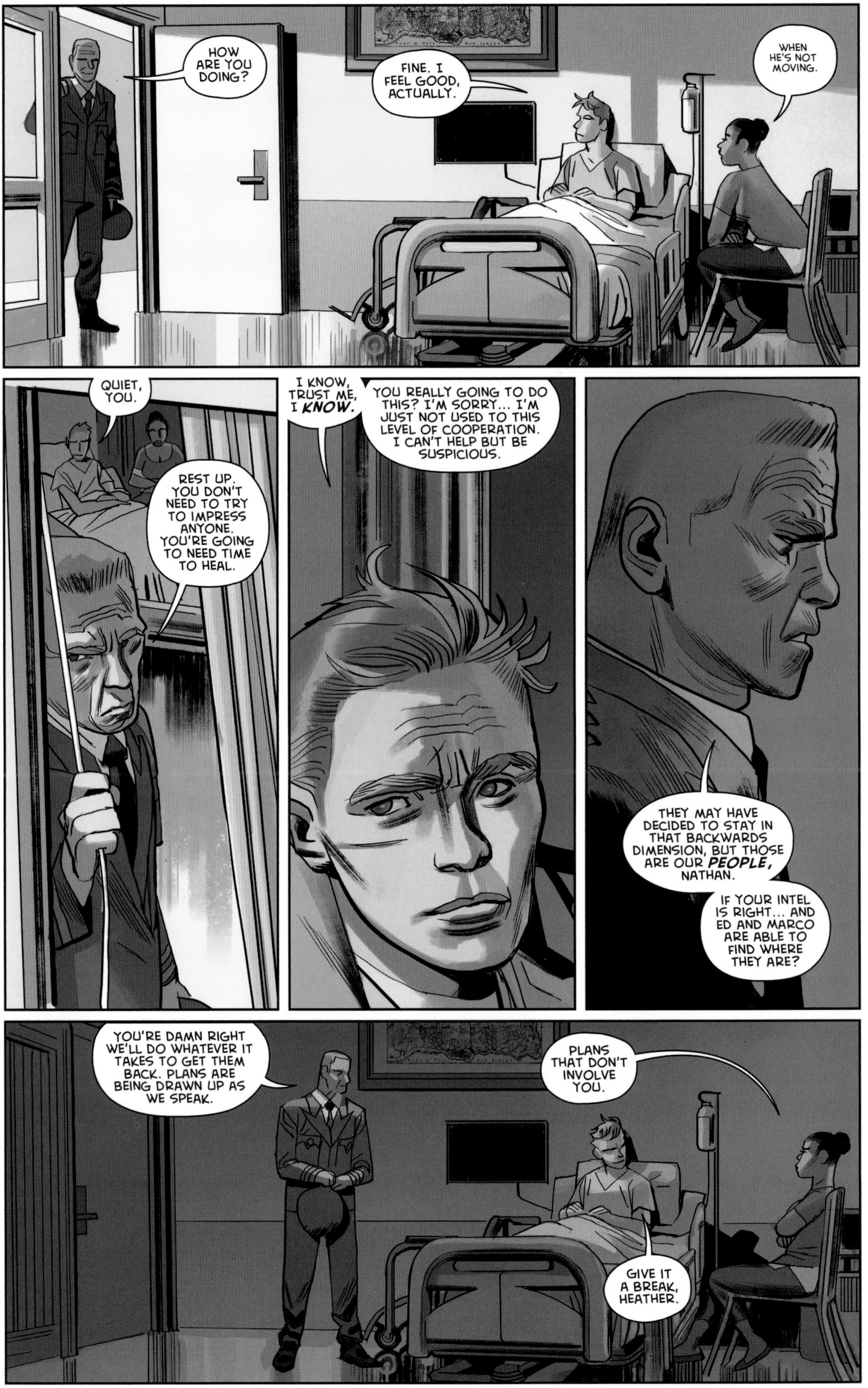
HOW ARE YOU DOING?
FINE. I FEEL GOOD, ACTUALLY.
WHEN HE'S NOT MOVING.
QUIET, YOU.
REST UP. YOU DON'T NEED TO TRY TO IMPRESS ANYONE. YOU'RE GOING TO NEED TIME TO HEAL.
I KNOW, TRUST ME, I *KNOW.*
YOU REALLY GOING TO DO THIS? I'M SORRY... I'M JUST NOT USED TO THIS LEVEL OF COOPERATION. I CAN'T HELP BUT BE SUSPICIOUS.
THEY MAY HAVE DECIDED TO STAY IN THAT BACKWARDS DIMENSION, BUT THOSE ARE OUR ***PEOPLE,*** NATHAN.
IF YOUR INTEL IS RIGHT... AND ED AND MARCO ARE ABLE TO FIND WHERE THEY ARE?
YOU'RE DAMN RIGHT WE'LL DO WHATEVER IT TAKES TO GET THEM BACK. PLANS ARE BEING DRAWN UP AS WE SPEAK.
PLANS THAT DON'T INVOLVE YOU.
GIVE IT A BREAK, HEATHER.

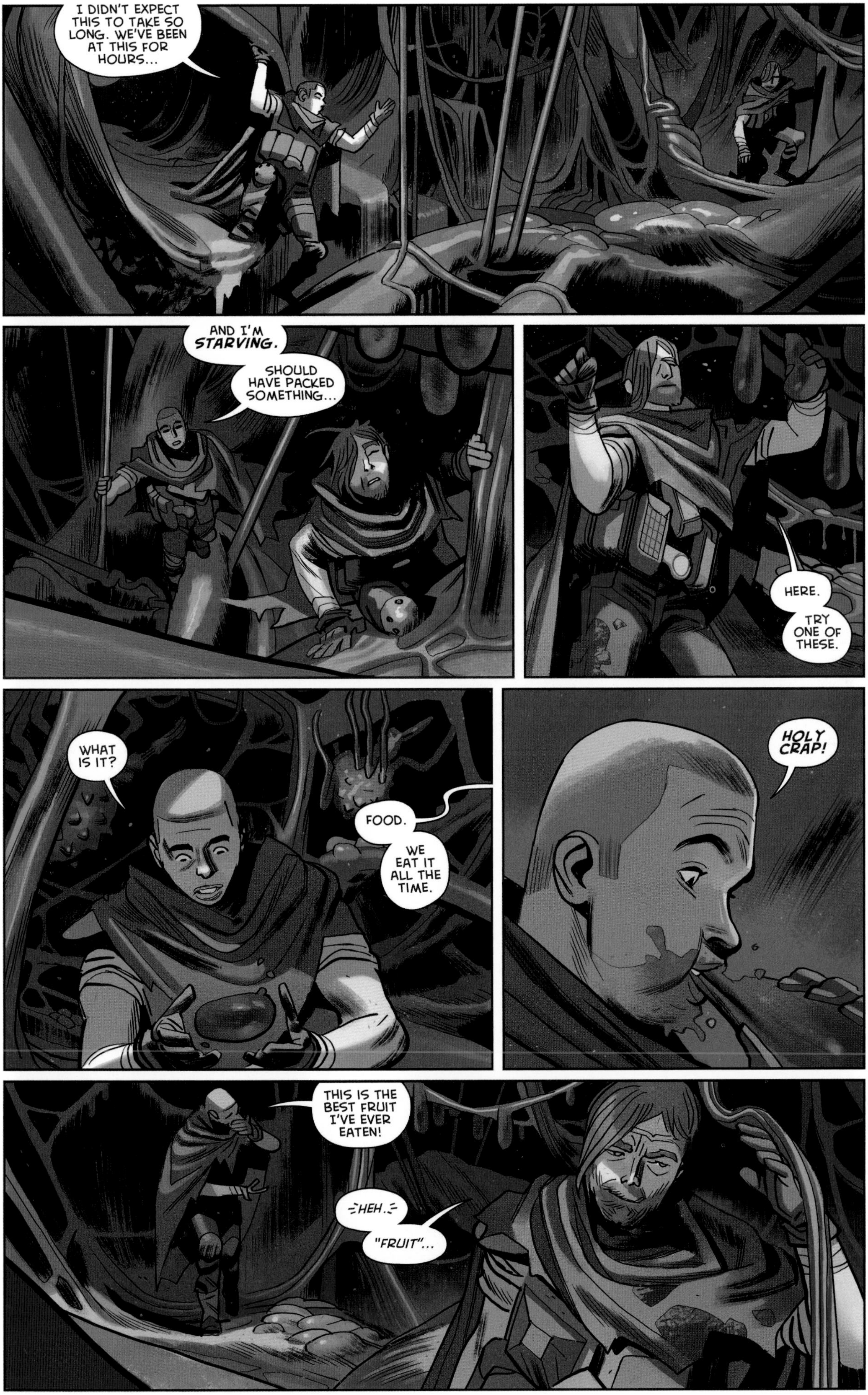
I DIDN'T EXPECT THIS TO TAKE SO LONG. WE'VE BEEN AT THIS FOR HOURS...
AND I'M STARVING.
SHOULD HAVE PACKED SOMETHING...
HERE.
TRY ONE OF THESE.
WHAT IS IT?
FOOD.
WE EAT IT ALL THE TIME.
HOLY CRAP!
THIS IS THE BEST FRUIT I'VE EVER EATEN!
HEH.
"FRUIT"...

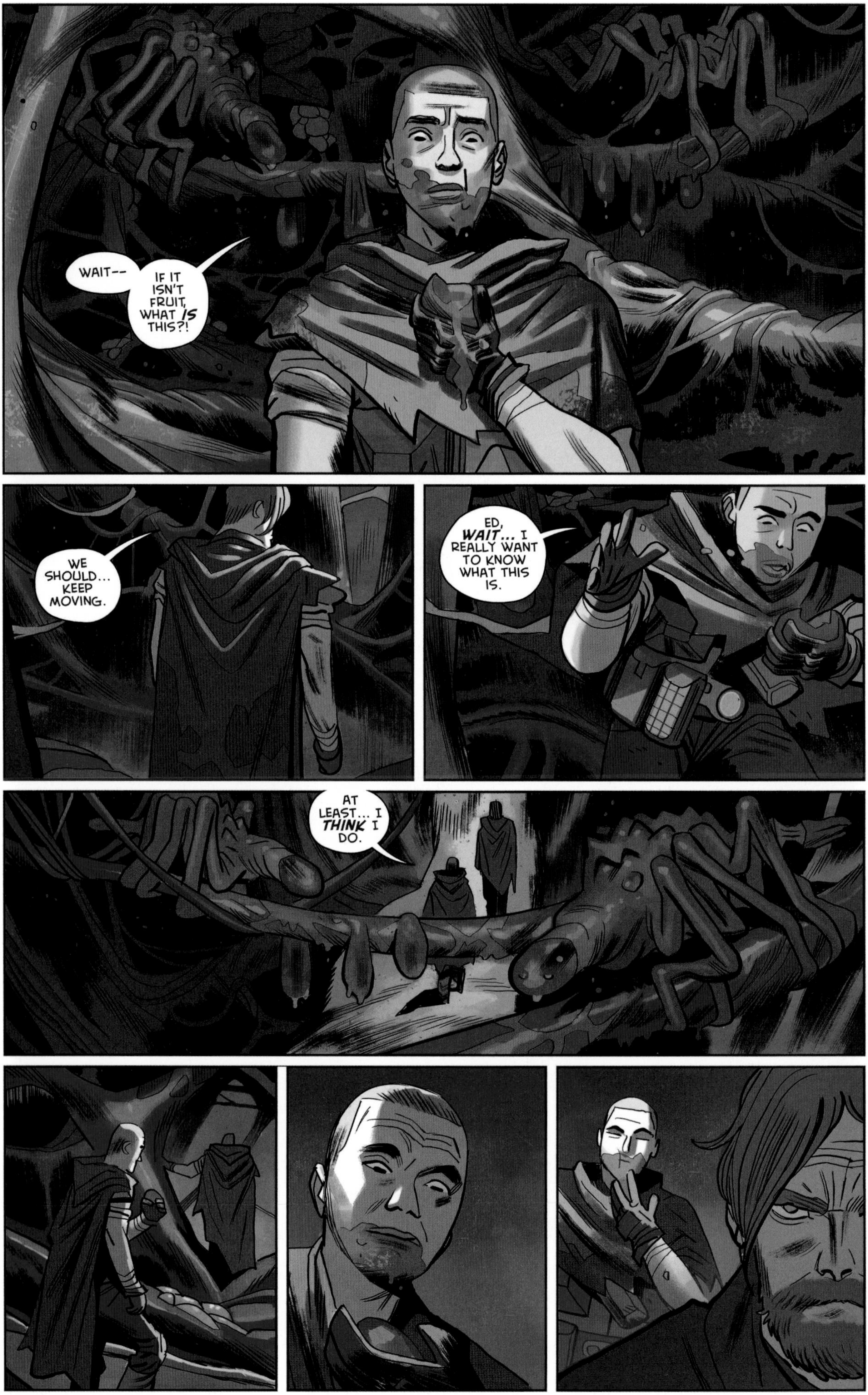
WAIT--
IF IT ISN'T FRUIT, WHAT *IS* THIS?!
WE SHOULD... KEEP MOVING.
ED, *WAIT...* I REALLY WANT TO KNOW WHAT THIS IS.
AT LEAST... I *THINK* I DO.

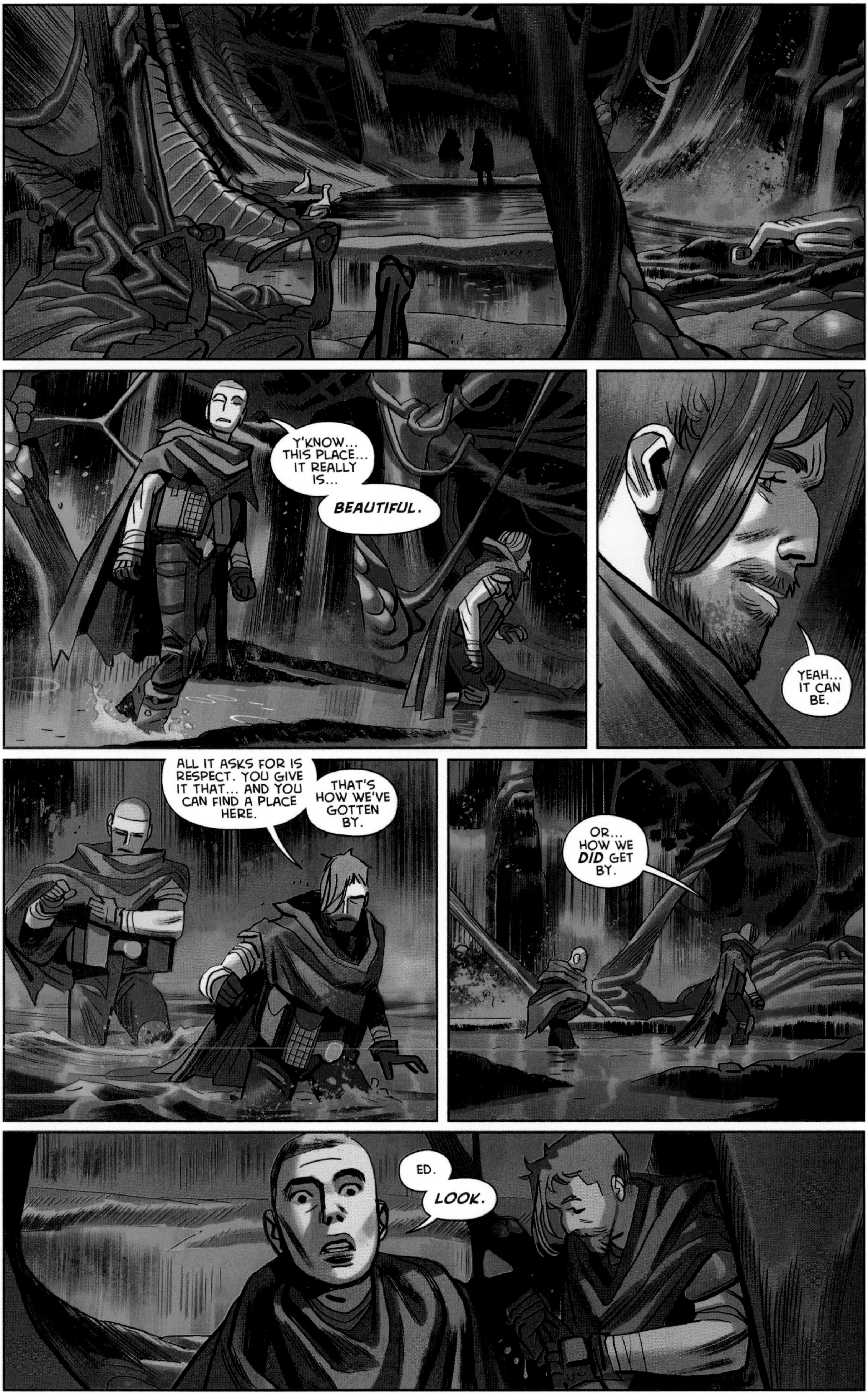
Y'KNOW... THIS PLACE... IT REALLY IS...
BEAUTIFUL.
YEAH... IT CAN BE.
ALL IT ASKS FOR IS RESPECT. YOU GIVE IT THAT... AND YOU CAN FIND A PLACE HERE.
THAT'S HOW WE'VE GOTTEN BY.
OR... HOW WE DID GET BY.
ED.
LOOK.

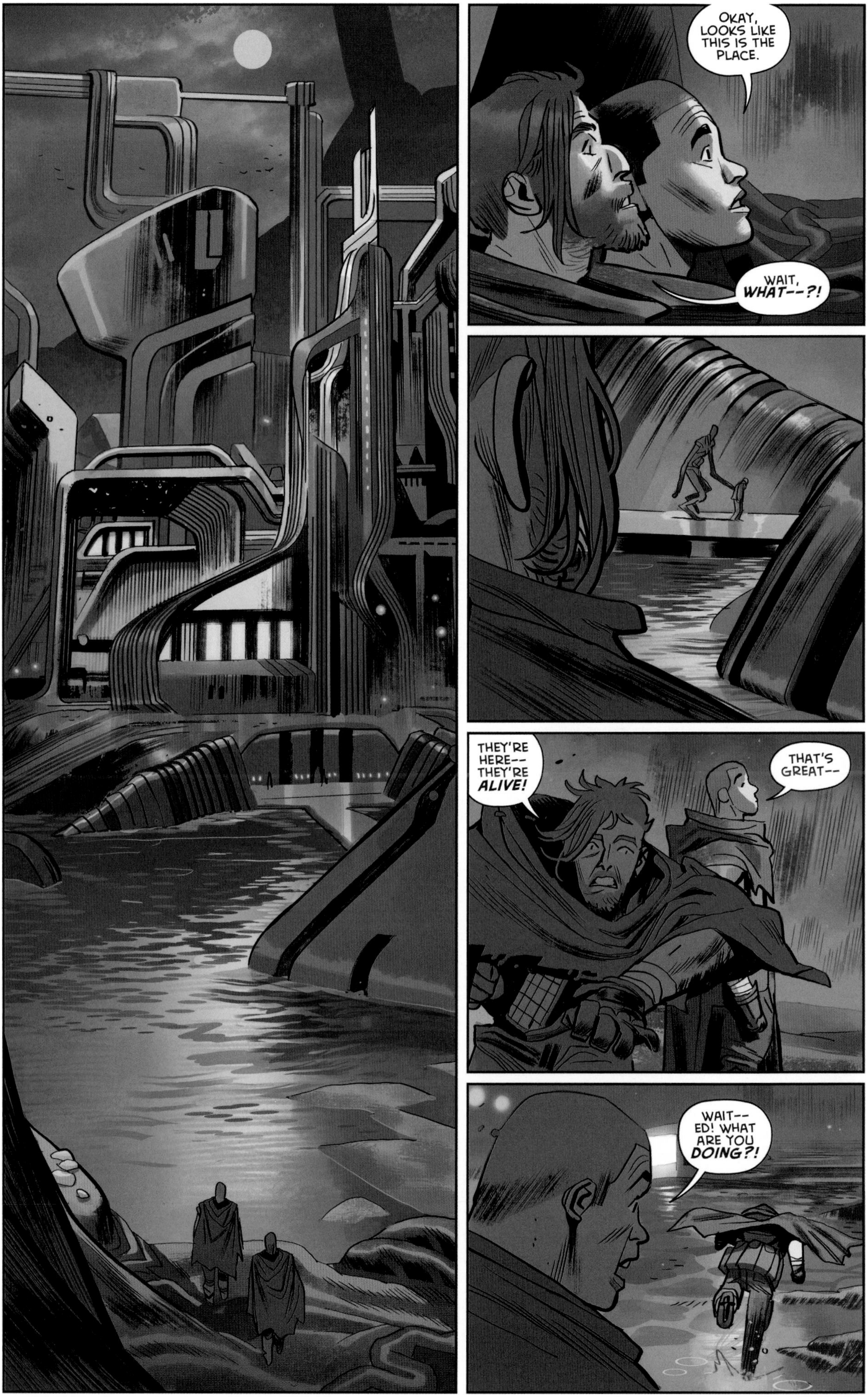
OKAY, LOOKS LIKE THIS IS THE PLACE.
WAIT, WHAT--?!
THEY'RE HERE-- THEY'RE ALIVE!
THAT'S GREAT--
WAIT-- ED! WHAT ARE YOU DOING?!

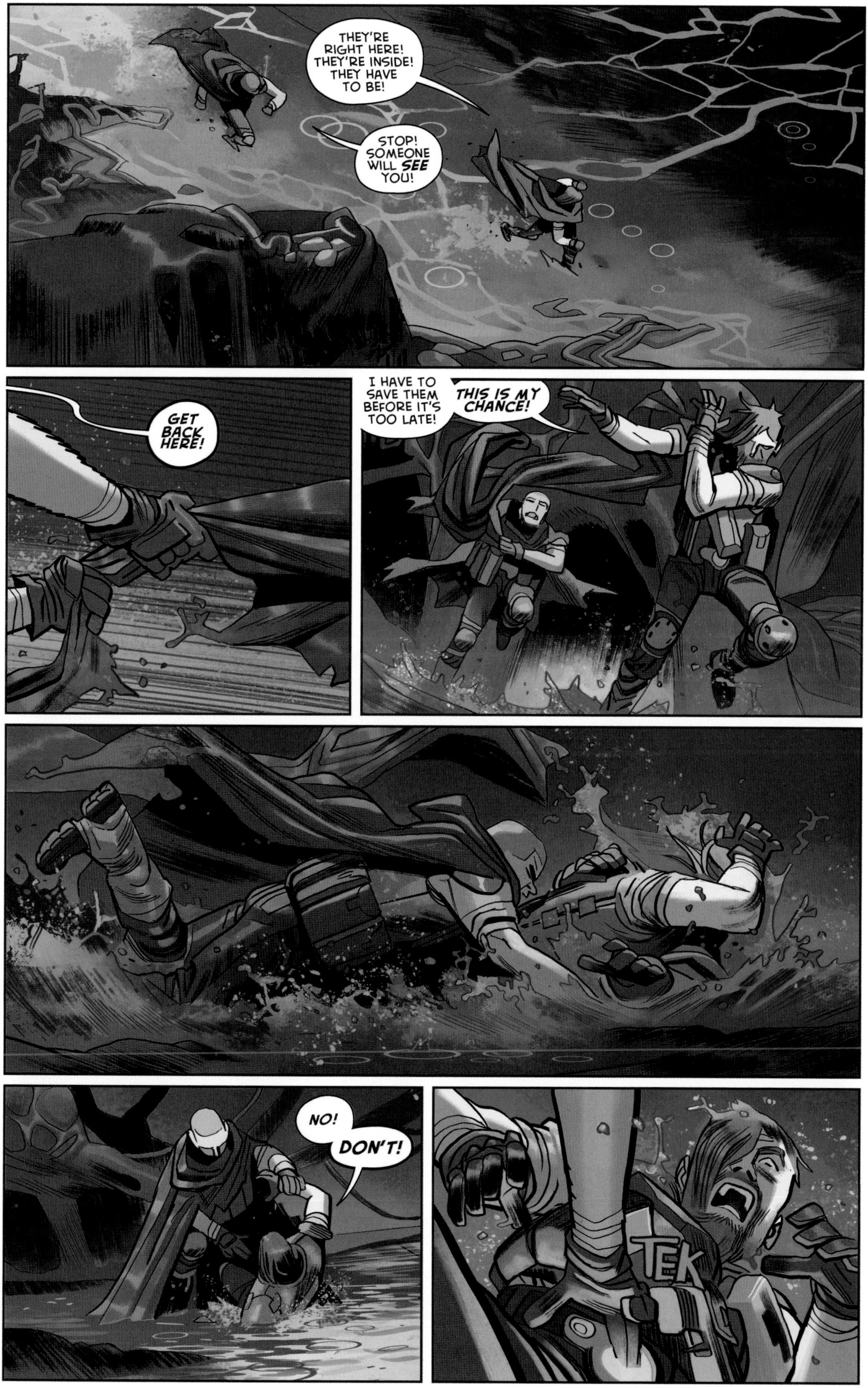
THEY'RE RIGHT HERE! THEY'RE INSIDE! THEY HAVE TO BE!
STOP! SOMEONE WILL SEE YOU!
GET BACK HERE!
I HAVE TO SAVE THEM BEFORE IT'S TOO LATE!
THIS IS MY CHANCE!
NO!
DON'T!
TEK

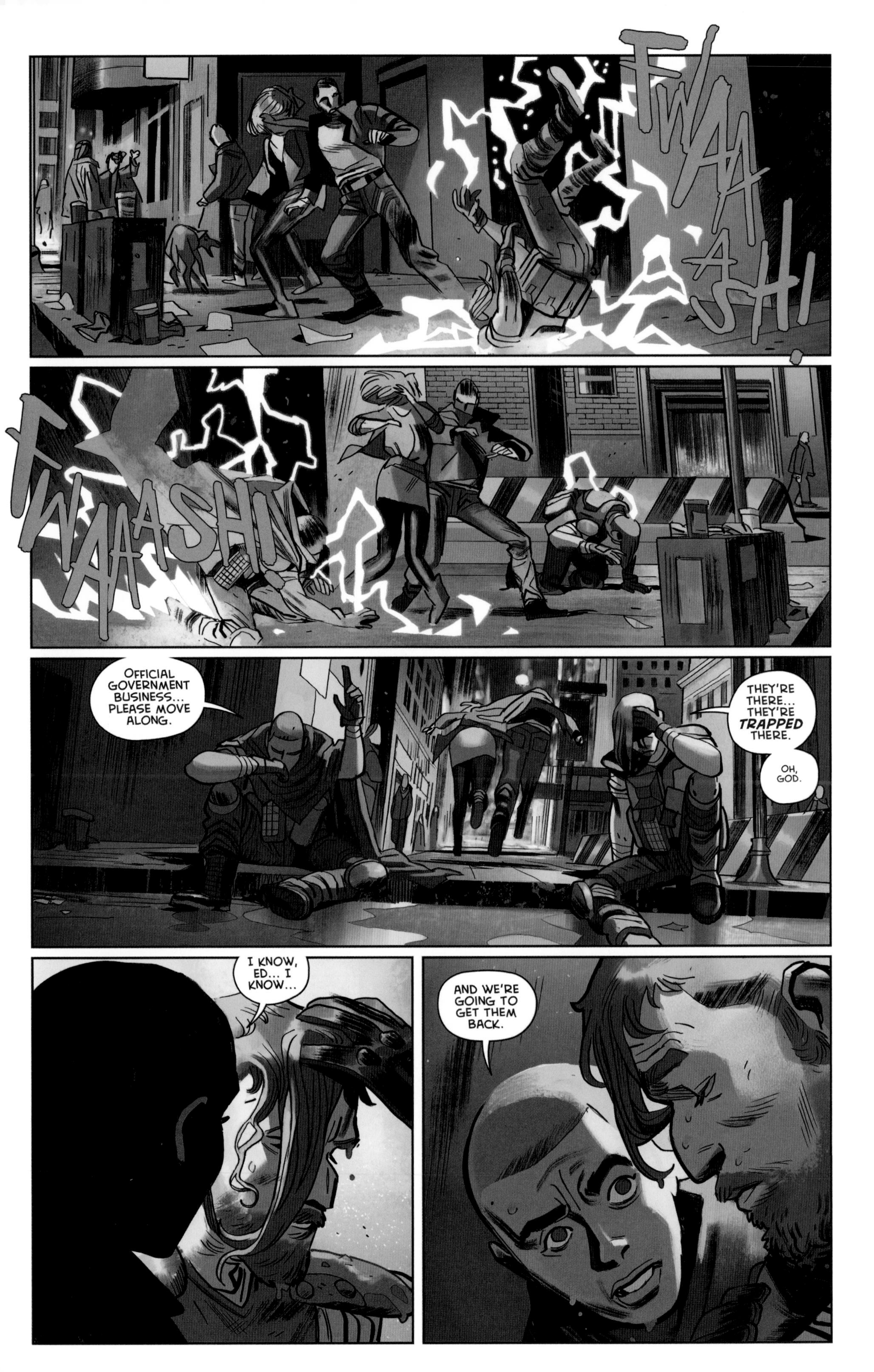
FWAAASH!
FWAAASH!
OFFICIAL GOVERNMENT BUSINESS... PLEASE MOVE ALONG.
THEY'RE THERE... THEY'RE ***TRAPPED*** THERE.
OH, GOD.
I KNOW, ED... I KNOW...
AND WE'RE GOING TO GET THEM BACK.

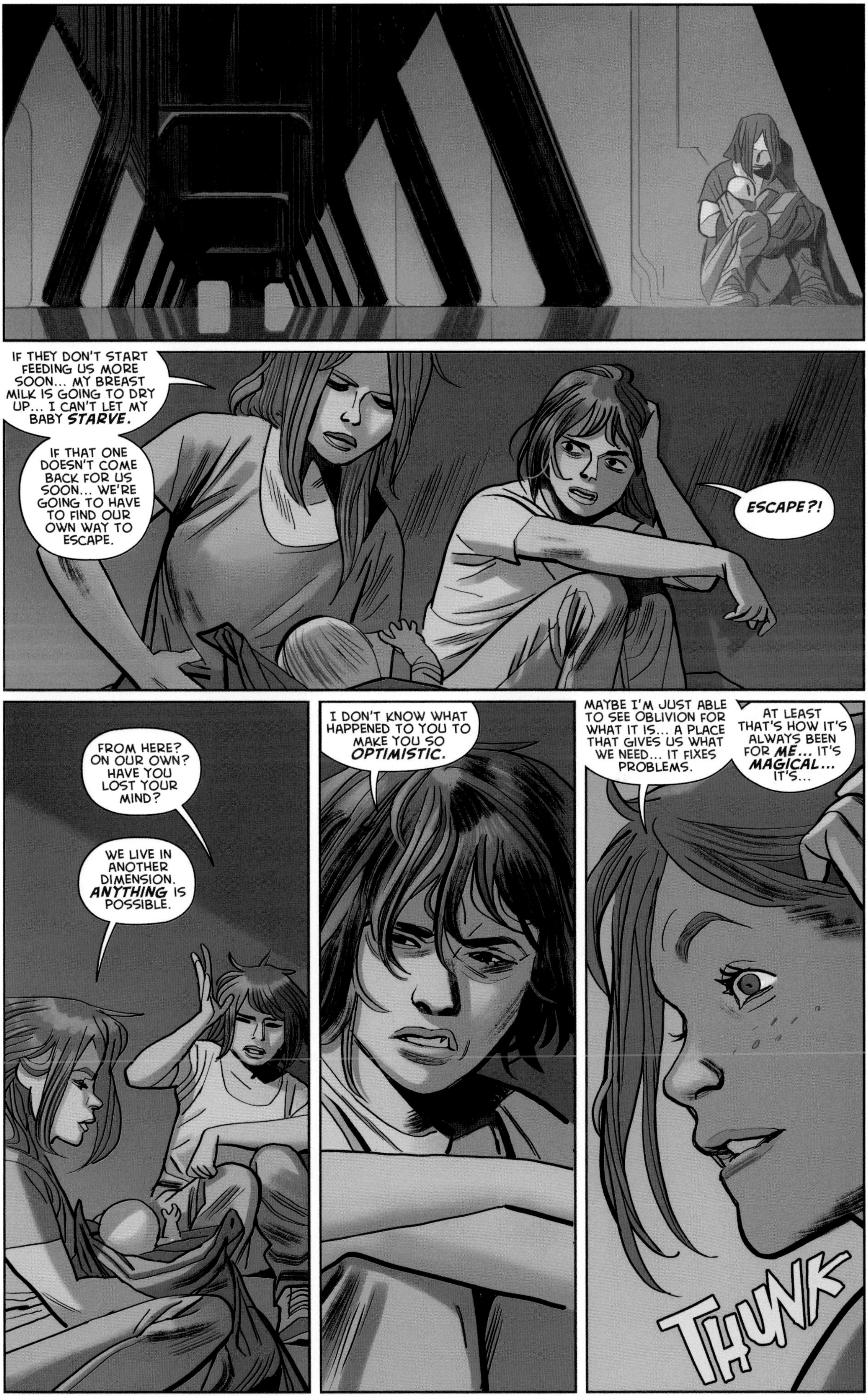
IF THEY DON'T START FEEDING US MORE SOON... MY BREAST MILK IS GOING TO DRY UP... I CAN'T LET MY BABY STARVE.
IF THAT ONE DOESN'T COME BACK FOR US SOON... WE'RE GOING TO HAVE TO FIND OUR OWN WAY TO ESCAPE.
ESCAPE?!
FROM HERE? ON OUR OWN? HAVE YOU LOST YOUR MIND?
WE LIVE IN ANOTHER DIMENSION. ANYTHING IS POSSIBLE.
I DON'T KNOW WHAT HAPPENED TO YOU TO MAKE YOU SO OPTIMISTIC.
MAYBE I'M JUST ABLE TO SEE OBLIVION FOR WHAT IT IS... A PLACE THAT GIVES US WHAT WE NEED... IT FIXES PROBLEMS.
AT LEAST THAT'S HOW IT'S ALWAYS BEEN FOR ME... IT'S MAGICAL... IT'S...
THUNK

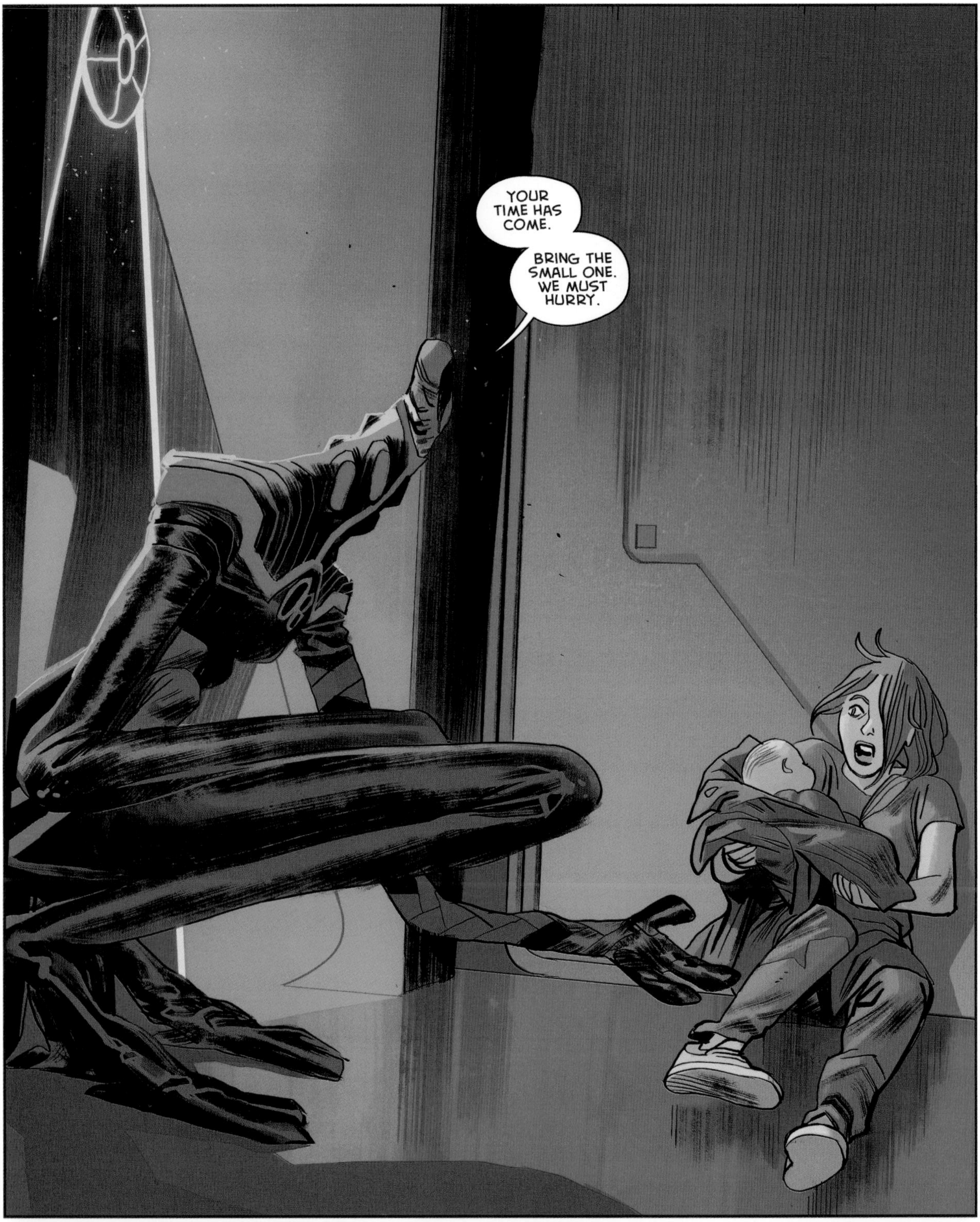
YOUR TIME HAS COME.
BRING THE SMALL ONE. WE MUST HURRY.

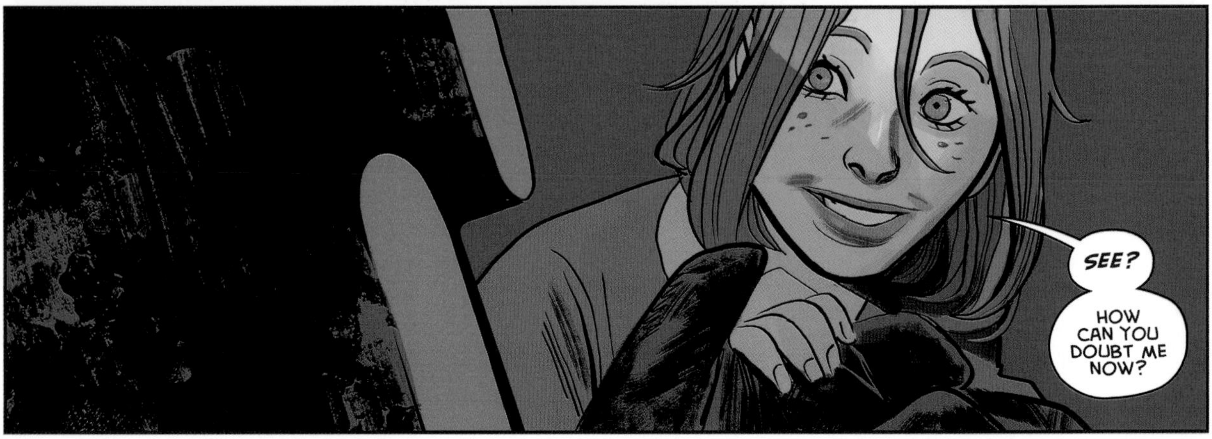
SEE?
HOW CAN YOU DOUBT ME NOW?

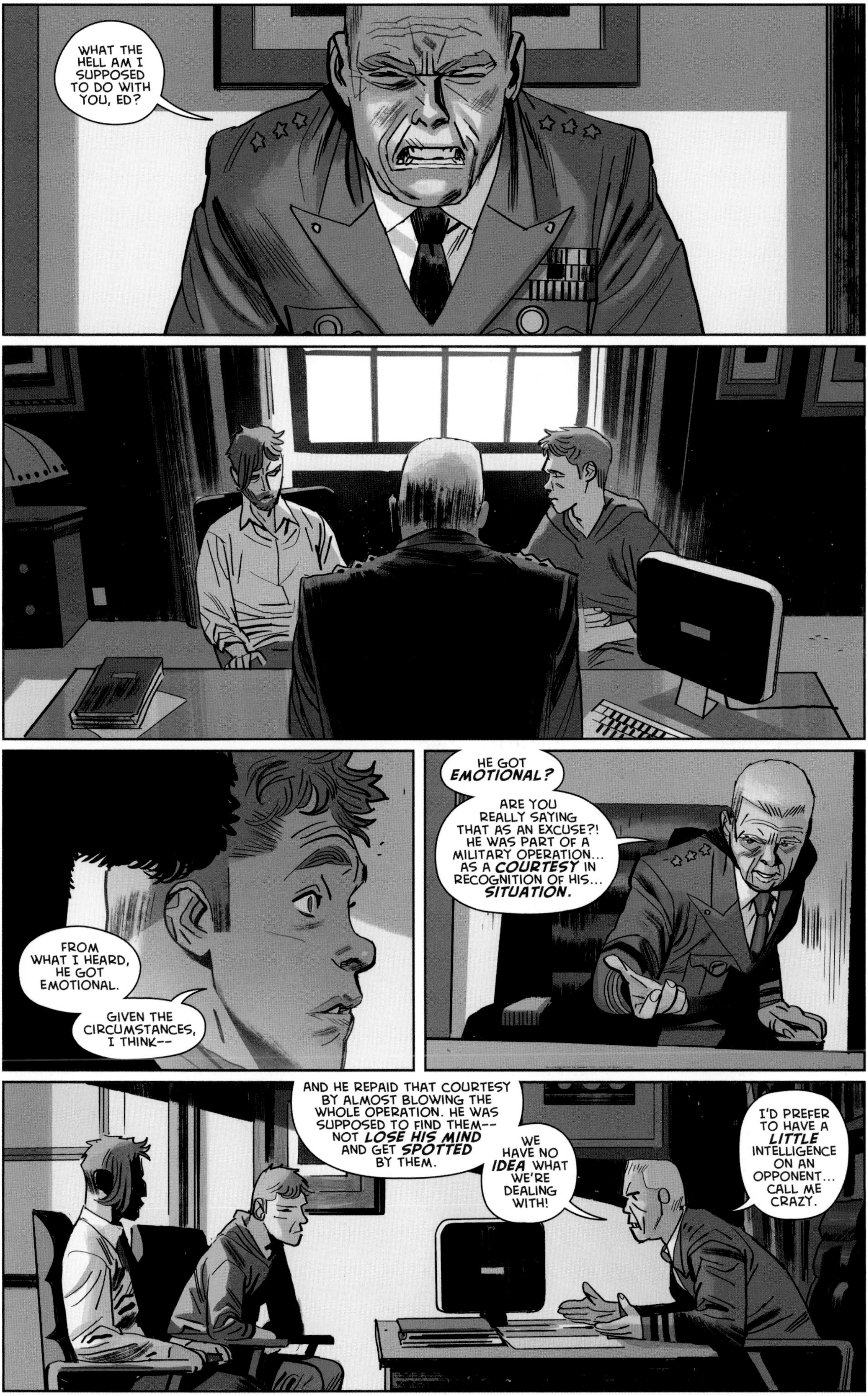

WHAT THE HELL AM I SUPPOSED TO DO WITH YOU, ED?
FROM WHAT I HEARD, HE GOT EMOTIONAL.
GIVEN THE CIRCUMSTANCES, I THINK--
HE GOT EMOTIONAL?
ARE YOU REALLY SAYING THAT AS AN EXCUSE?! HE WAS PART OF A MILITARY OPERATION... AS A COURTESY IN RECOGNITION OF HIS... SITUATION.
AND HE REPAID THAT COURTESY BY ALMOST BLOWING THE WHOLE OPERATION. HE WAS SUPPOSED TO FIND THEM-- NOT LOSE HIS MIND AND GET SPOTTED BY THEM.
WE HAVE NO IDEA WHAT WE'RE DEALING WITH!
I'D PREFER TO HAVE A LITTLE INTELLIGENCE ON AN OPPONENT... CALL ME CRAZY.

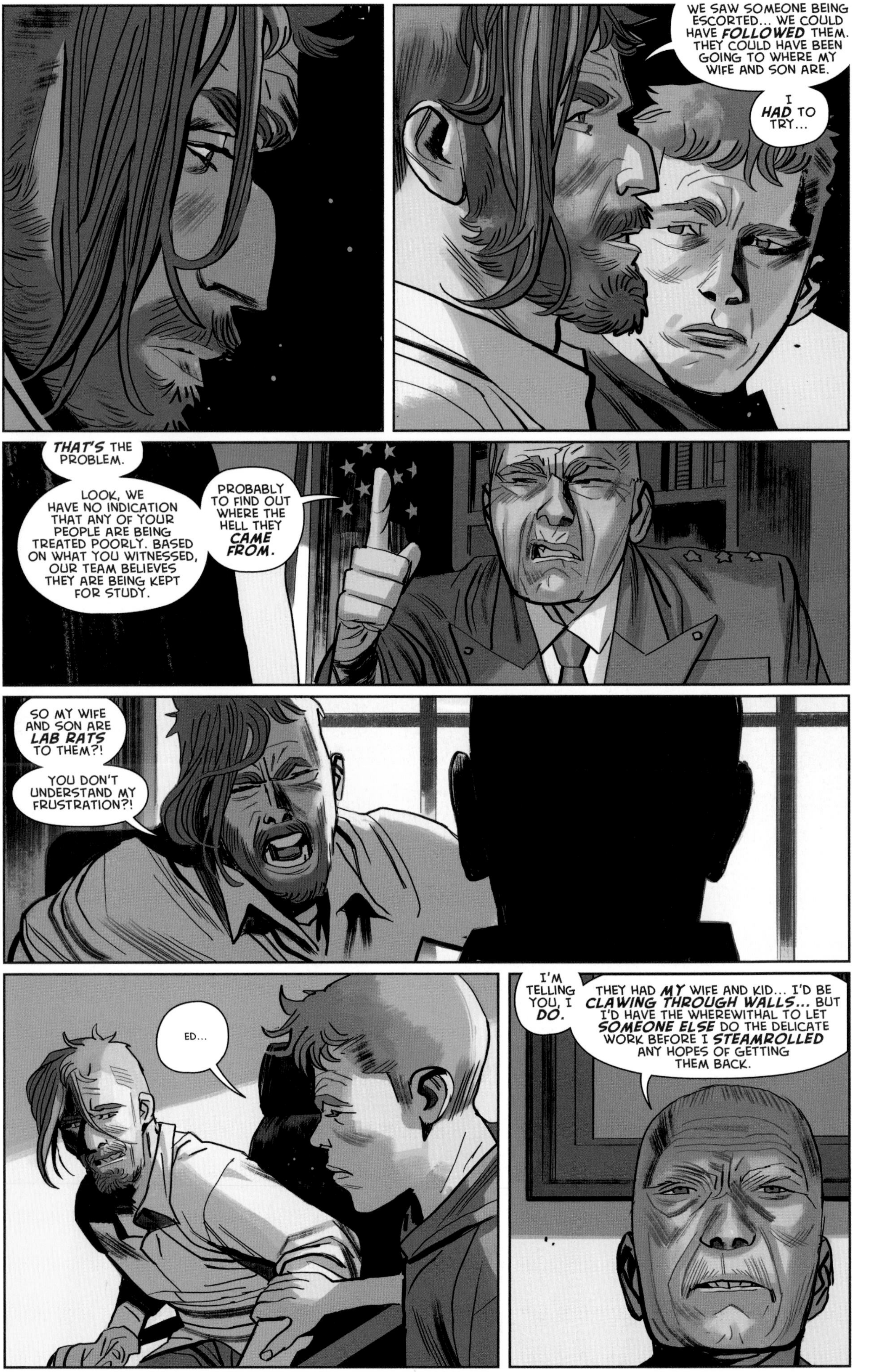
WE SAW SOMEONE BEING ESCORTED... WE COULD HAVE FOLLOWED THEM. THEY COULD HAVE BEEN GOING TO WHERE MY WIFE AND SON ARE.
I HAD TO TRY...
THAT'S THE PROBLEM.
LOOK, WE HAVE NO INDICATION THAT ANY OF YOUR PEOPLE ARE BEING TREATED POORLY. BASED ON WHAT YOU WITNESSED, OUR TEAM BELIEVES THEY ARE BEING KEPT FOR STUDY.
PROBABLY TO FIND OUT WHERE THE HELL THEY CAME FROM.
SO MY WIFE AND SON ARE LAB RATS TO THEM?!
YOU DON'T UNDERSTAND MY FRUSTRATION?!
ED...
I'M TELLING YOU, I DO.
THEY HAD MY WIFE AND KID... I'D BE CLAWING THROUGH WALLS... BUT I'D HAVE THE WHEREWITHAL TO LET SOMEONE ELSE DO THE DELICATE WORK BEFORE I STEAMROLLED ANY HOPES OF GETTING THEM BACK.

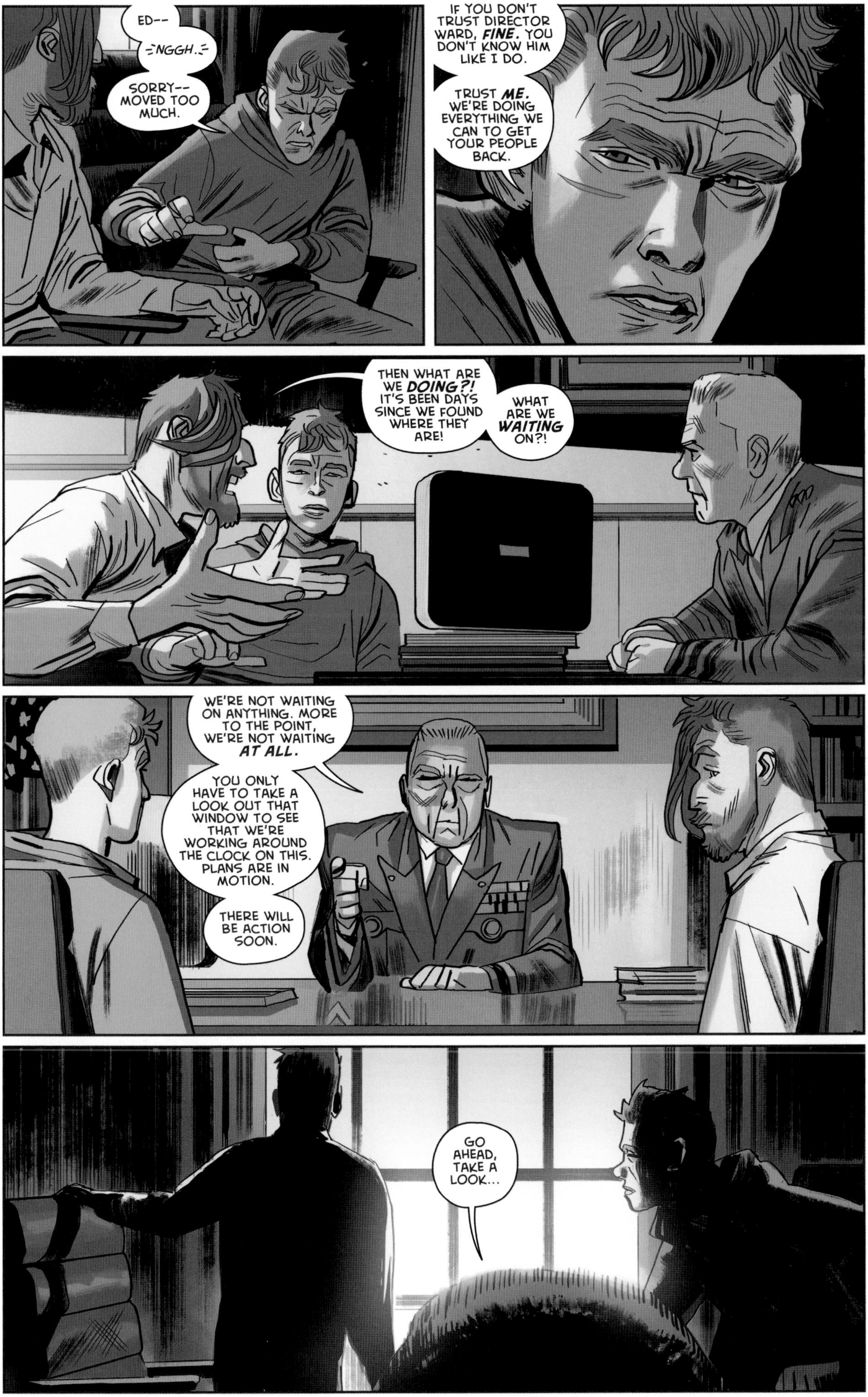
ED--
NGGH.
SORRY-- MOVED TOO MUCH.
IF YOU DON'T TRUST DIRECTOR WARD, FINE. YOU DON'T KNOW HIM LIKE I DO.
TRUST ME. WE'RE DOING EVERYTHING WE CAN TO GET YOUR PEOPLE BACK.
THEN WHAT ARE WE DOING?! IT'S BEEN DAYS SINCE WE FOUND WHERE THEY ARE!
WHAT ARE WE WAITING ON?!
WE'RE NOT WAITING ON ANYTHING. MORE TO THE POINT, WE'RE NOT WAITING AT ALL.
YOU ONLY HAVE TO TAKE A LOOK OUT THAT WINDOW TO SEE THAT WE'RE WORKING AROUND THE CLOCK ON THIS. PLANS ARE IN MOTION.
THERE WILL BE ACTION SOON.
GO AHEAD, TAKE A LOOK...

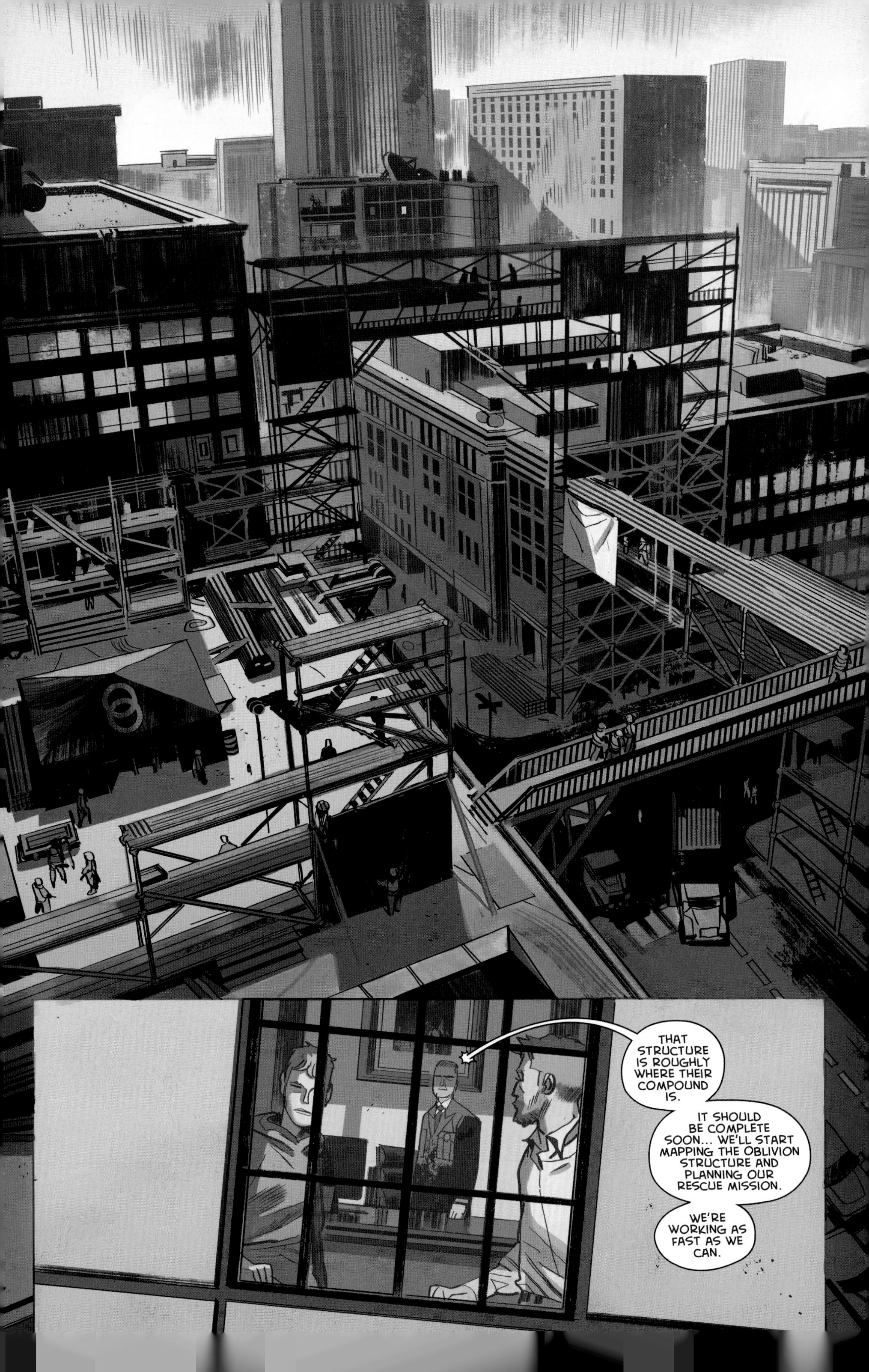
THAT STRUCTURE IS ROUGHLY WHERE THEIR COMPOUND IS.
IT SHOULD BE COMPLETE SOON... WE'LL START MAPPING THE OBLIVION STRUCTURE AND PLANNING OUR RESCUE MISSION.
WE'RE WORKING AS FAST AS WE CAN.

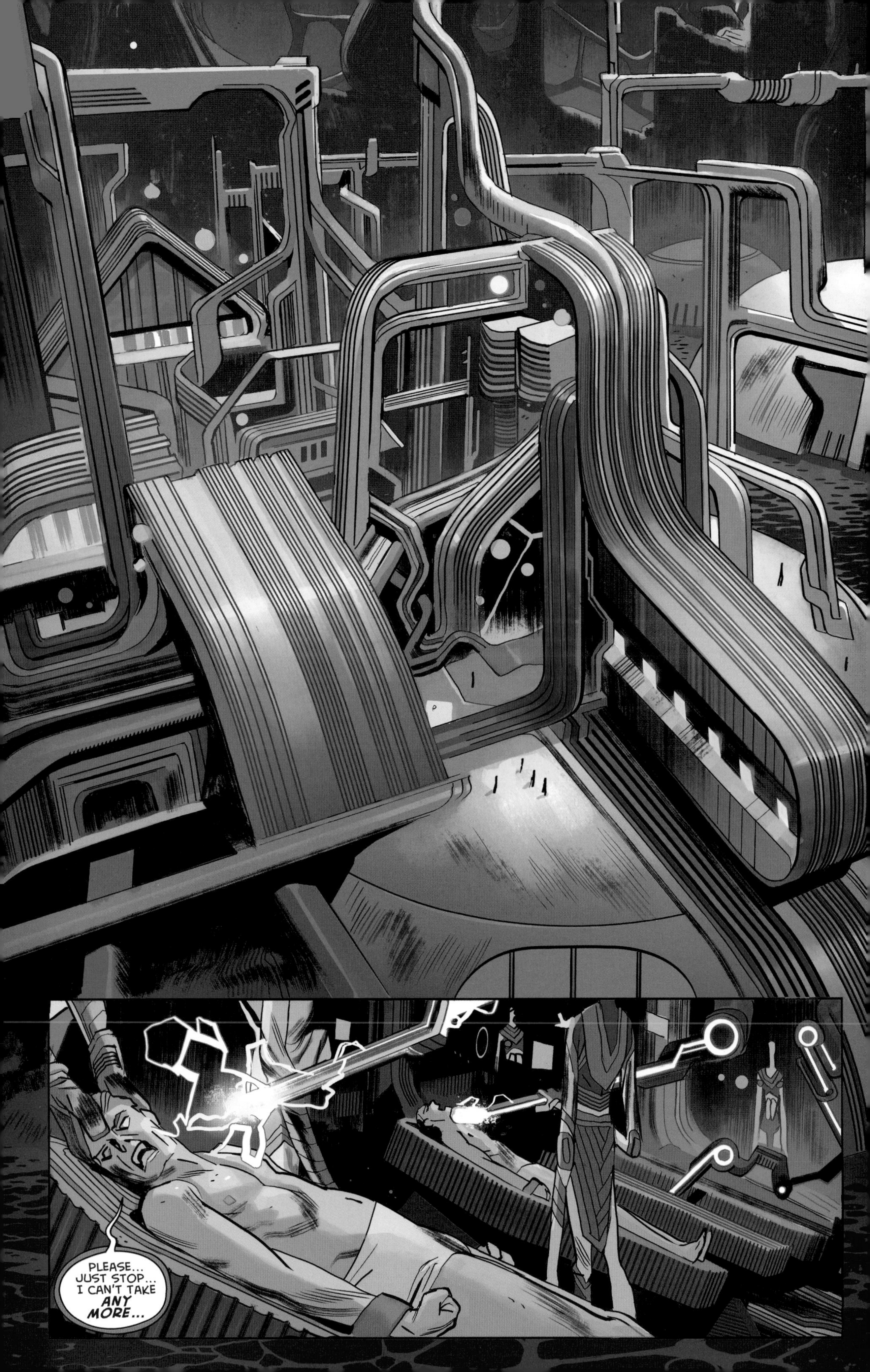
PLEASE... JUST STOP... I CAN'T TAKE ANY MORE...

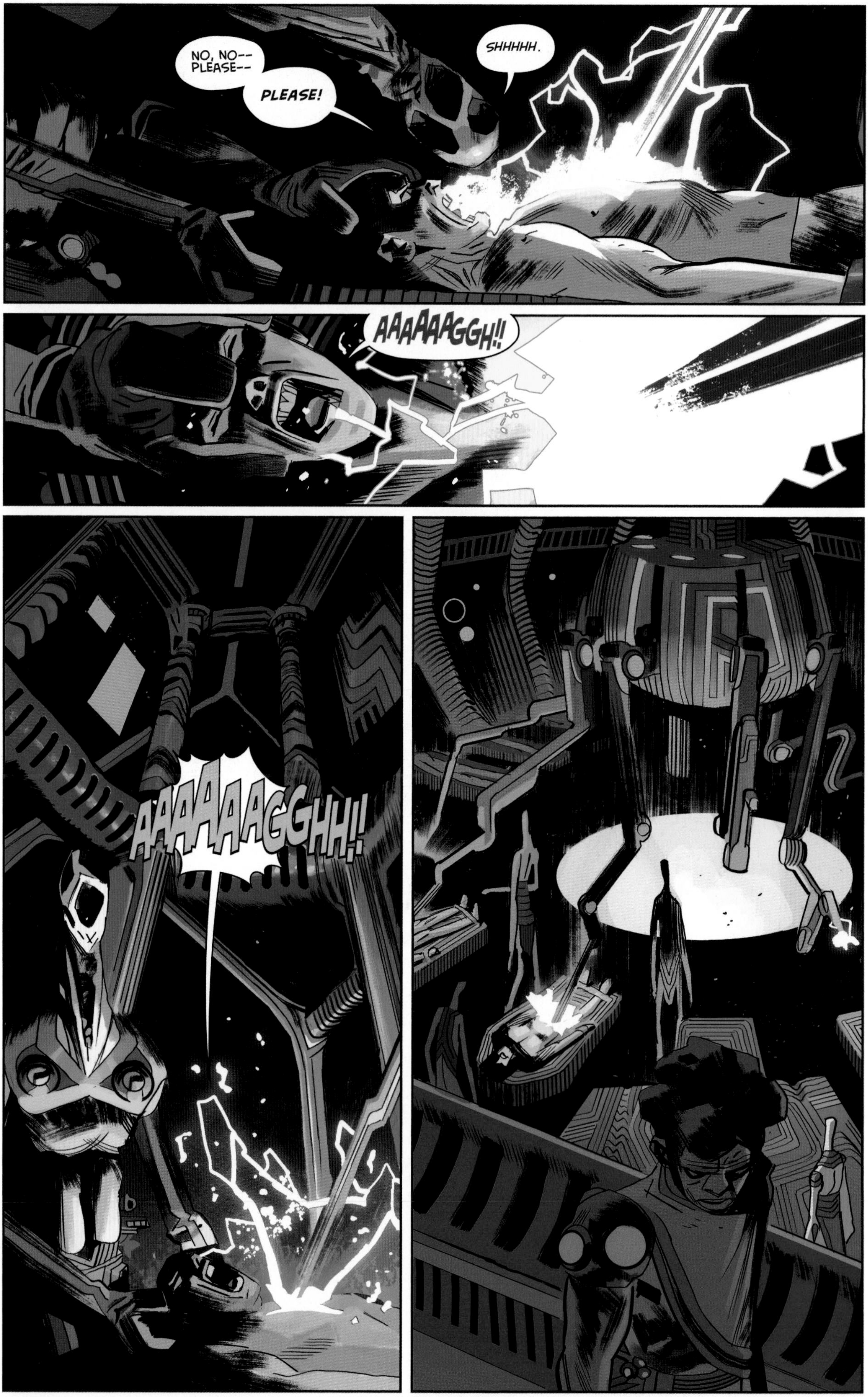
NO, NO--
PLEASE--
PLEASE!
SHHHHH.
AAAAAAGGH!!
AAAAAAGGHH!!

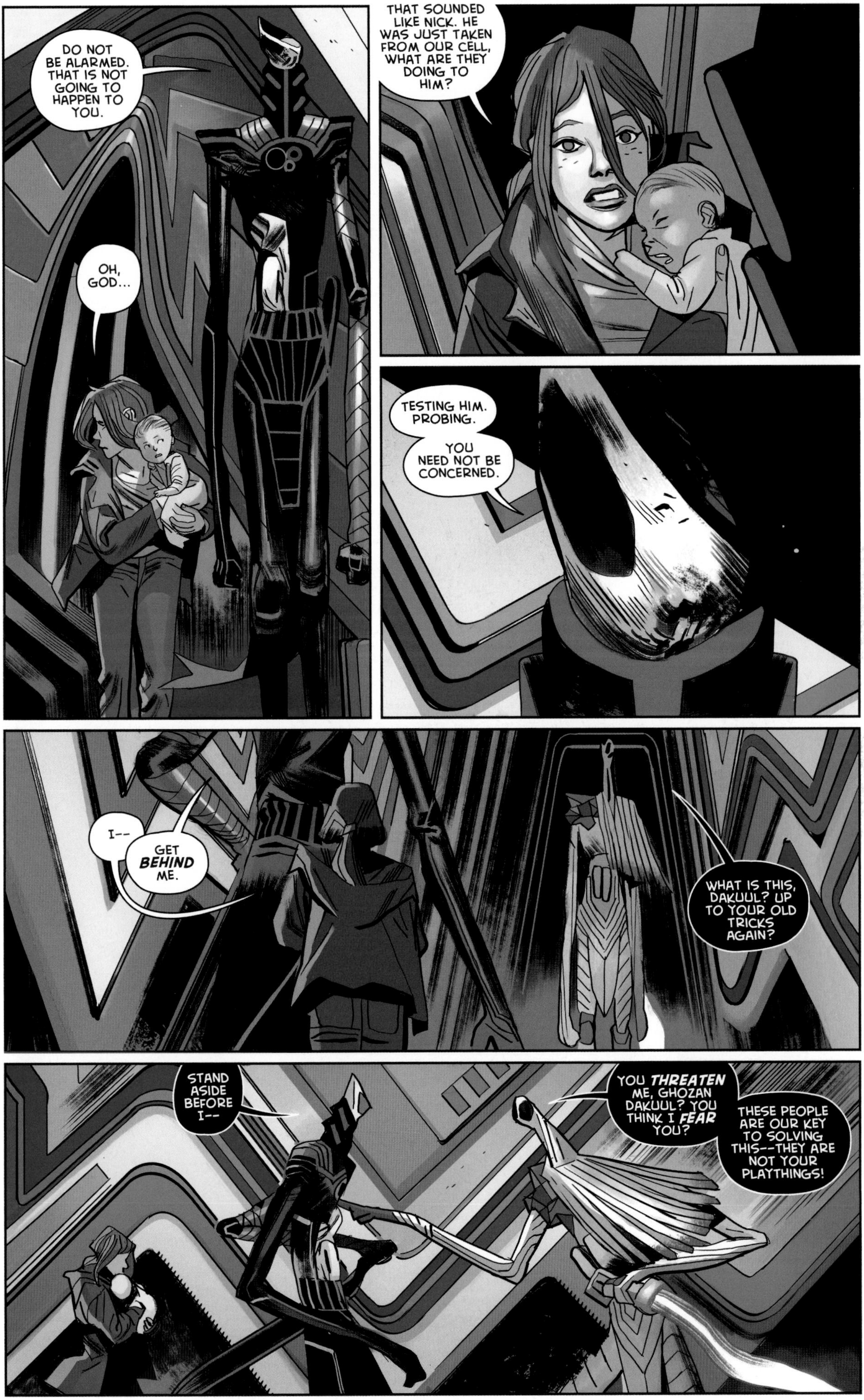
DO NOT BE ALARMED. THAT IS NOT GOING TO HAPPEN TO YOU.
OH, GOD...
THAT SOUNDED LIKE NICK. HE WAS JUST TAKEN FROM OUR CELL, WHAT ARE THEY DOING TO HIM?
TESTING HIM. PROBING.
YOU NEED NOT BE CONCERNED.
I--
GET BEHIND ME.
WHAT IS THIS, DAKUUL? UP TO YOUR OLD TRICKS AGAIN?
STAND ASIDE BEFORE I--
YOU THREATEN ME, GHOZAN DAKUUL? YOU THINK I FEAR YOU?
THESE PEOPLE ARE OUR KEY TO SOLVING THIS--THEY ARE NOT YOUR PLAYTHINGS!

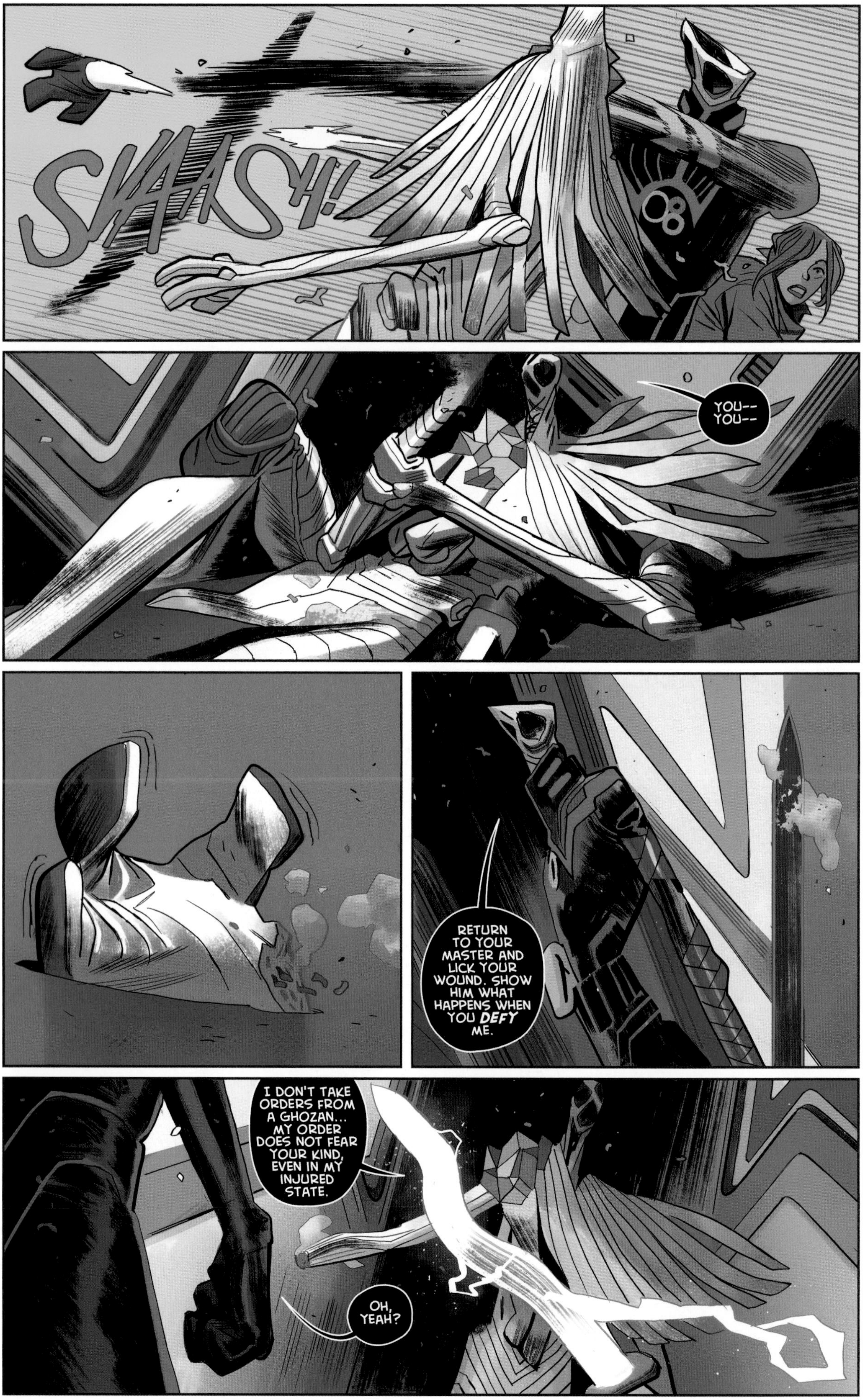
SHAASH!
YOU-- YOU--
RETURN TO YOUR MASTER AND LICK YOUR WOUND. SHOW HIM WHAT HAPPENS WHEN YOU DEFY ME.
I DON'T TAKE ORDERS FROM A GHOZAN... MY ORDER DOES NOT FEAR YOUR KIND, EVEN IN MY INJURED STATE.
OH, YEAH?

KLASSH!

≒AHHH!≒

SHRAKK!

YOUR ORDER IS *PATHETIC*. THE GHOZAN LEGION HAS STOOD STRONG FOR A THOUSAND YEARS!

YOU CAN'T--

KLANK

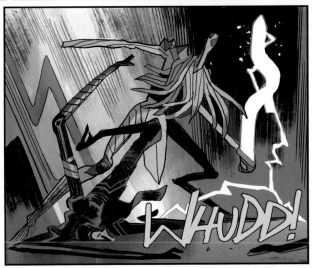

WHUDD!

YOUR RECKLESS WAYS ARE AT AN END, DAKUUL. OUR WORK HERE IS TOO IMPORTANT FOR YOUR DISTRACTION.

YOU MAY BE GHOZAN, BUT THEIR *BEST* ARE NOT SENT TO THE FORGOTTEN LANDS TO *OBSERVE.*

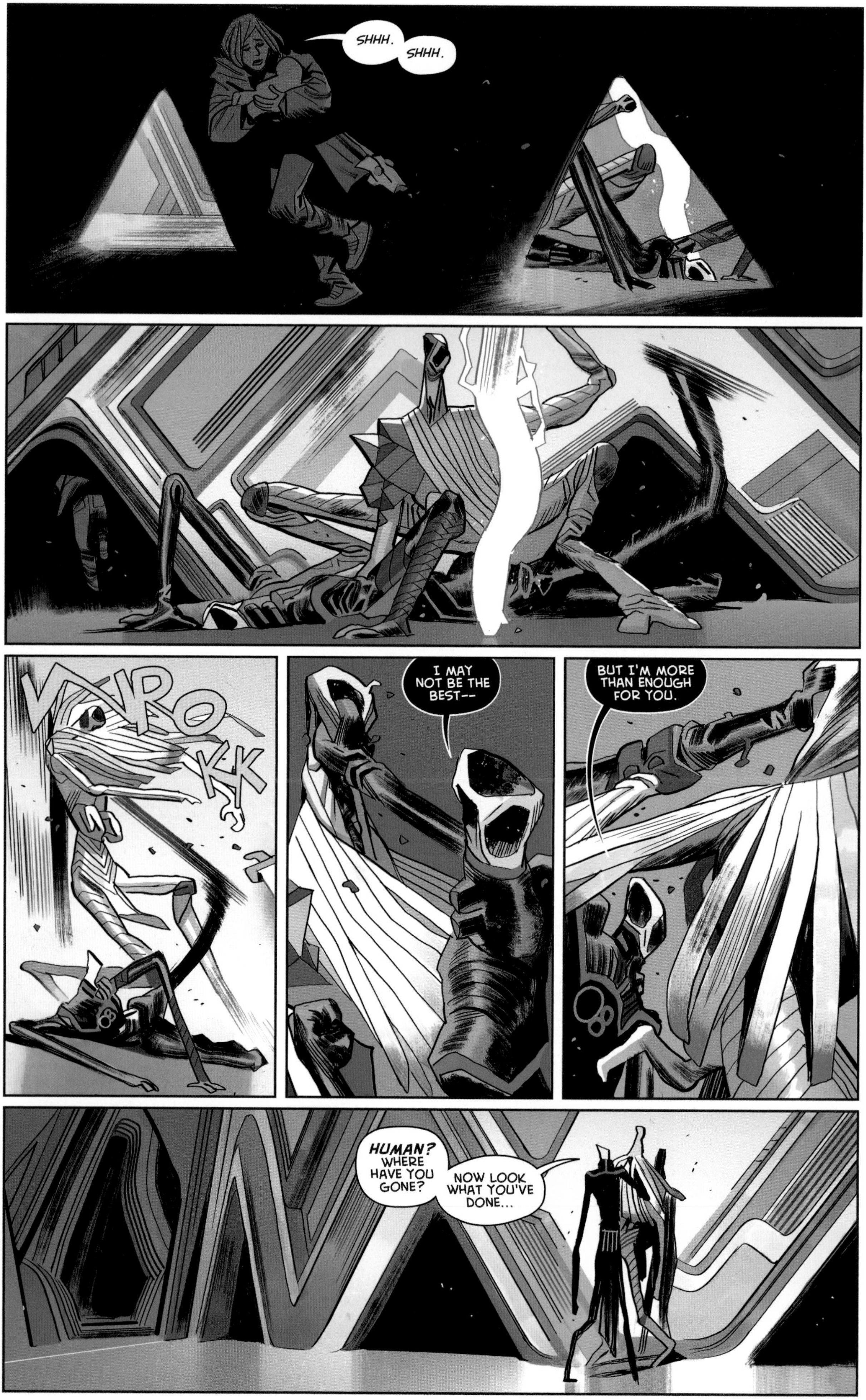

SHHH.
SHHH.
VRRO KK
I MAY NOT BE THE BEST--
BUT I'M MORE THAN ENOUGH FOR YOU.
HUMAN? WHERE HAVE YOU GONE?
NOW LOOK WHAT YOU'VE DONE...

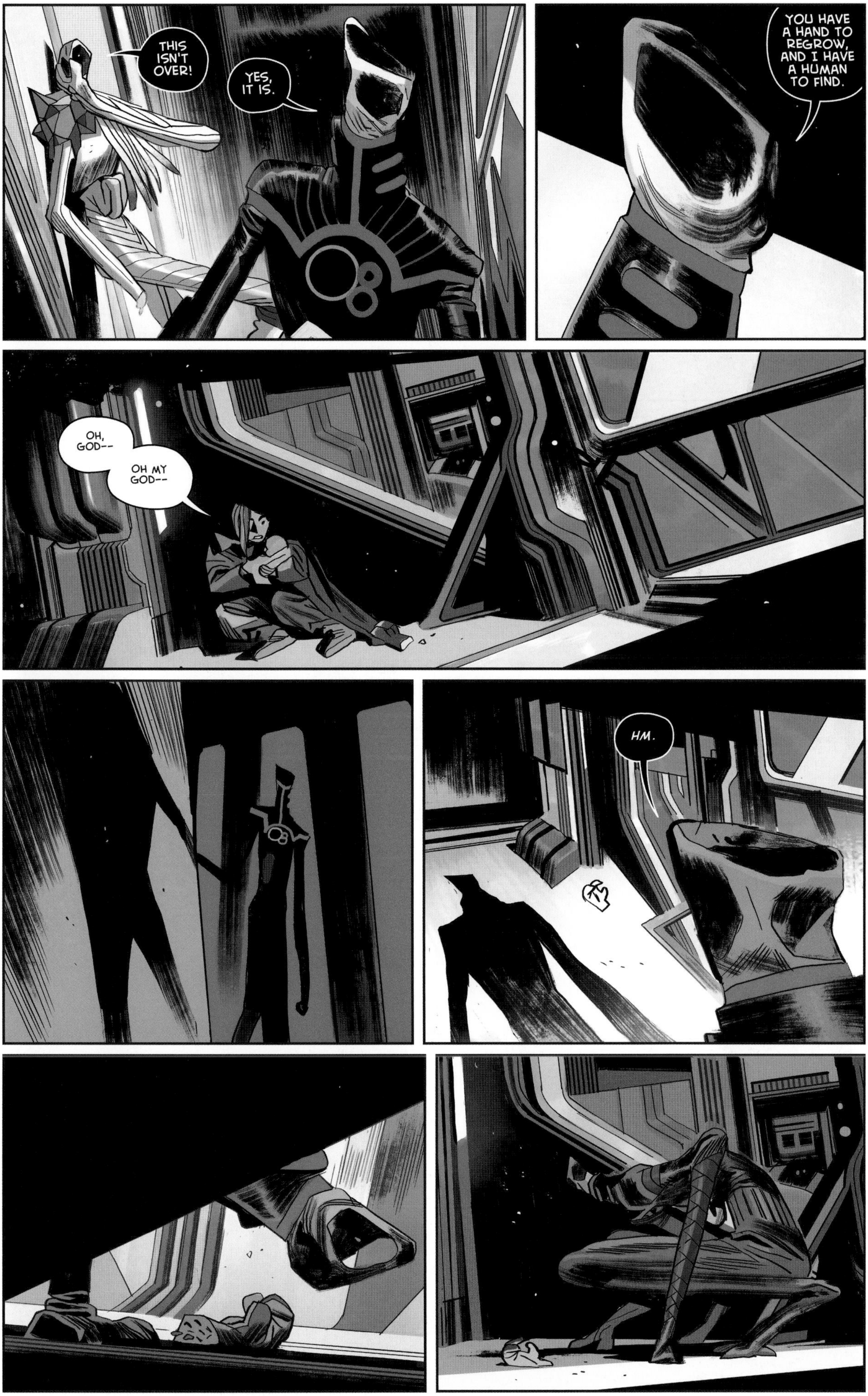
THIS ISN'T OVER!
YES, IT IS.
YOU HAVE A HAND TO REGROW, AND I HAVE A HUMAN TO FIND.
OH, GOD--
OH MY GOD--
HM.

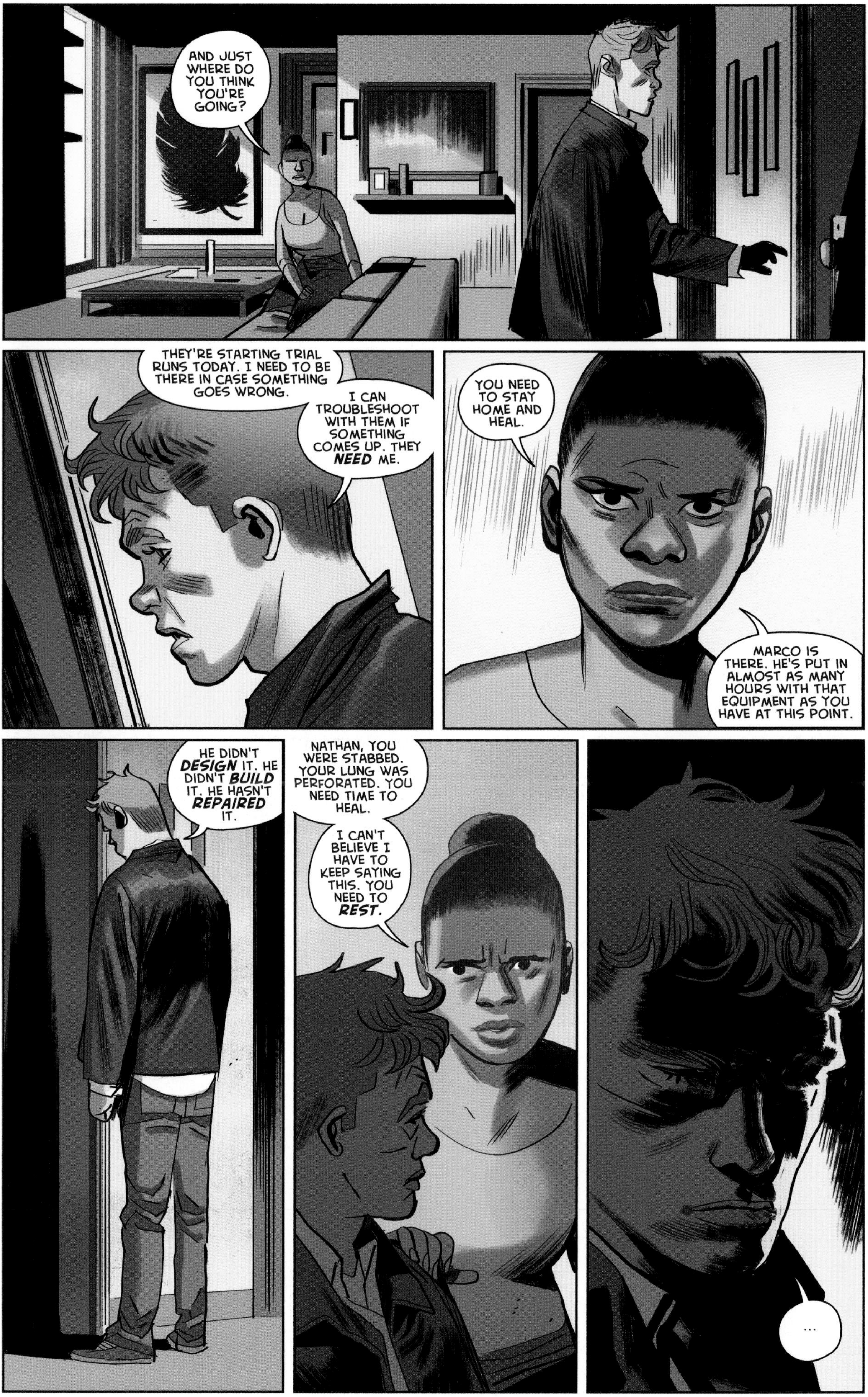
AND JUST WHERE DO YOU THINK YOU'RE GOING?
THEY'RE STARTING TRIAL RUNS TODAY. I NEED TO BE THERE IN CASE SOMETHING GOES WRONG.
I CAN TROUBLESHOOT WITH THEM IF SOMETHING COMES UP. THEY *NEED* ME.
YOU NEED TO STAY HOME AND HEAL.
MARCO IS THERE. HE'S PUT IN ALMOST AS MANY HOURS WITH THAT EQUIPMENT AS YOU HAVE AT THIS POINT.
HE DIDN'T *DESIGN* IT. HE DIDN'T *BUILD* IT. HE HASN'T *REPAIRED* IT.
NATHAN, YOU WERE STABBED. YOUR LUNG WAS PERFORATED. YOU NEED TIME TO HEAL.
I CAN'T BELIEVE I HAVE TO KEEP SAYING THIS. YOU NEED TO *REST.*
...

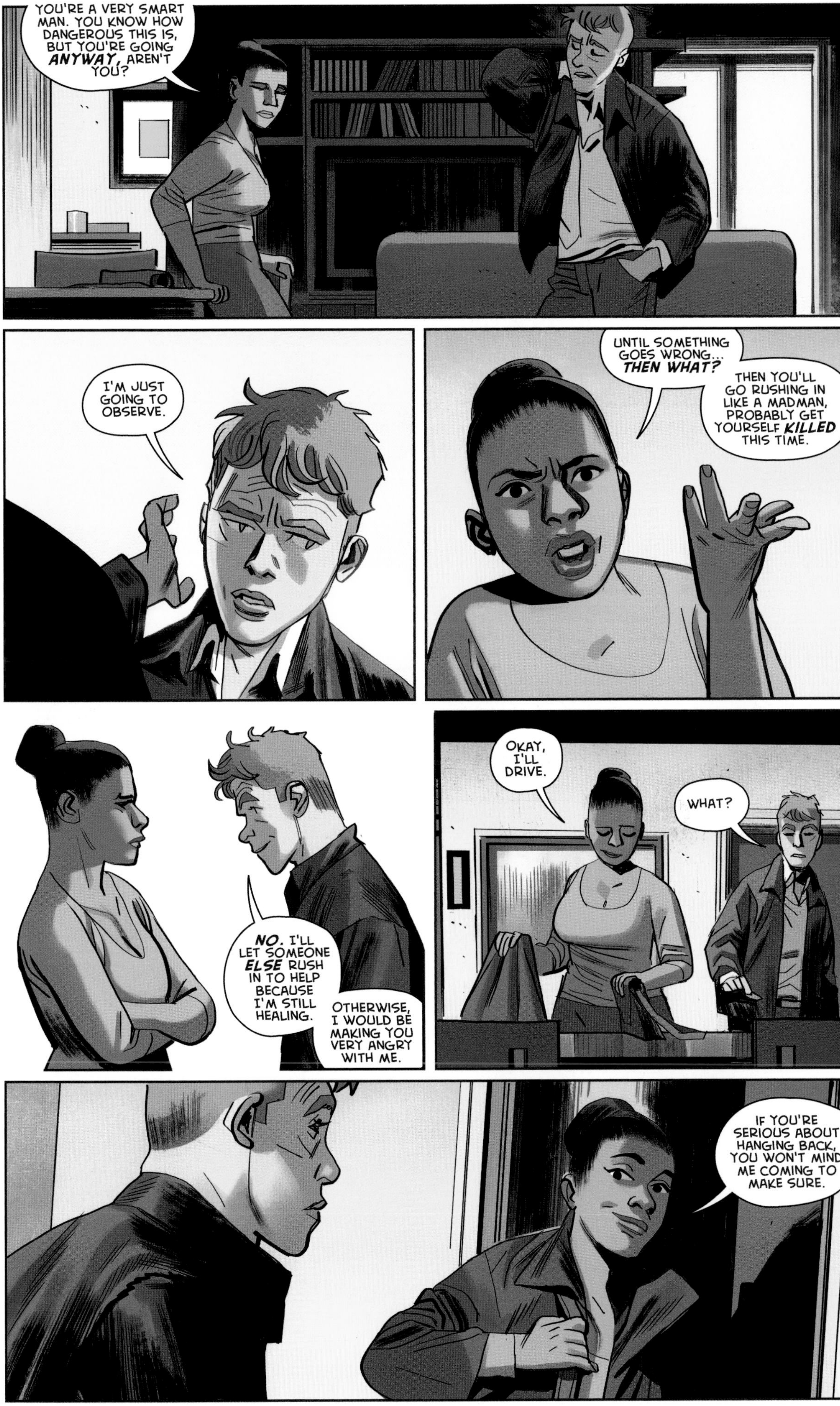
YOU'RE A VERY SMART MAN. YOU KNOW HOW DANGEROUS THIS IS, BUT YOU'RE GOING **ANYWAY**, AREN'T YOU?
I'M JUST GOING TO OBSERVE.
UNTIL SOMETHING GOES WRONG... **THEN WHAT?**
THEN YOU'LL GO RUSHING IN LIKE A MADMAN, PROBABLY GET YOURSELF **KILLED** THIS TIME.
NO. I'LL LET SOMEONE **ELSE** RUSH IN TO HELP BECAUSE I'M STILL HEALING.
OTHERWISE, I WOULD BE MAKING YOU VERY ANGRY WITH ME.
OKAY, I'LL DRIVE.
WHAT?
IF YOU'RE SERIOUS ABOUT HANGING BACK, YOU WON'T MIND ME COMING TO MAKE SURE.

ALL SET, MARCO?

I'M IN POSITION AND READY TO GO.

WISH ME LUCK.

TEK

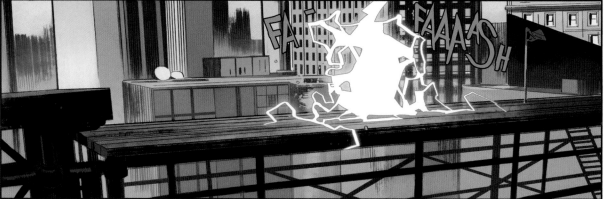

FA... FAAAASH

HOW LONG BEFORE WE SHOULD GET WORRIED?

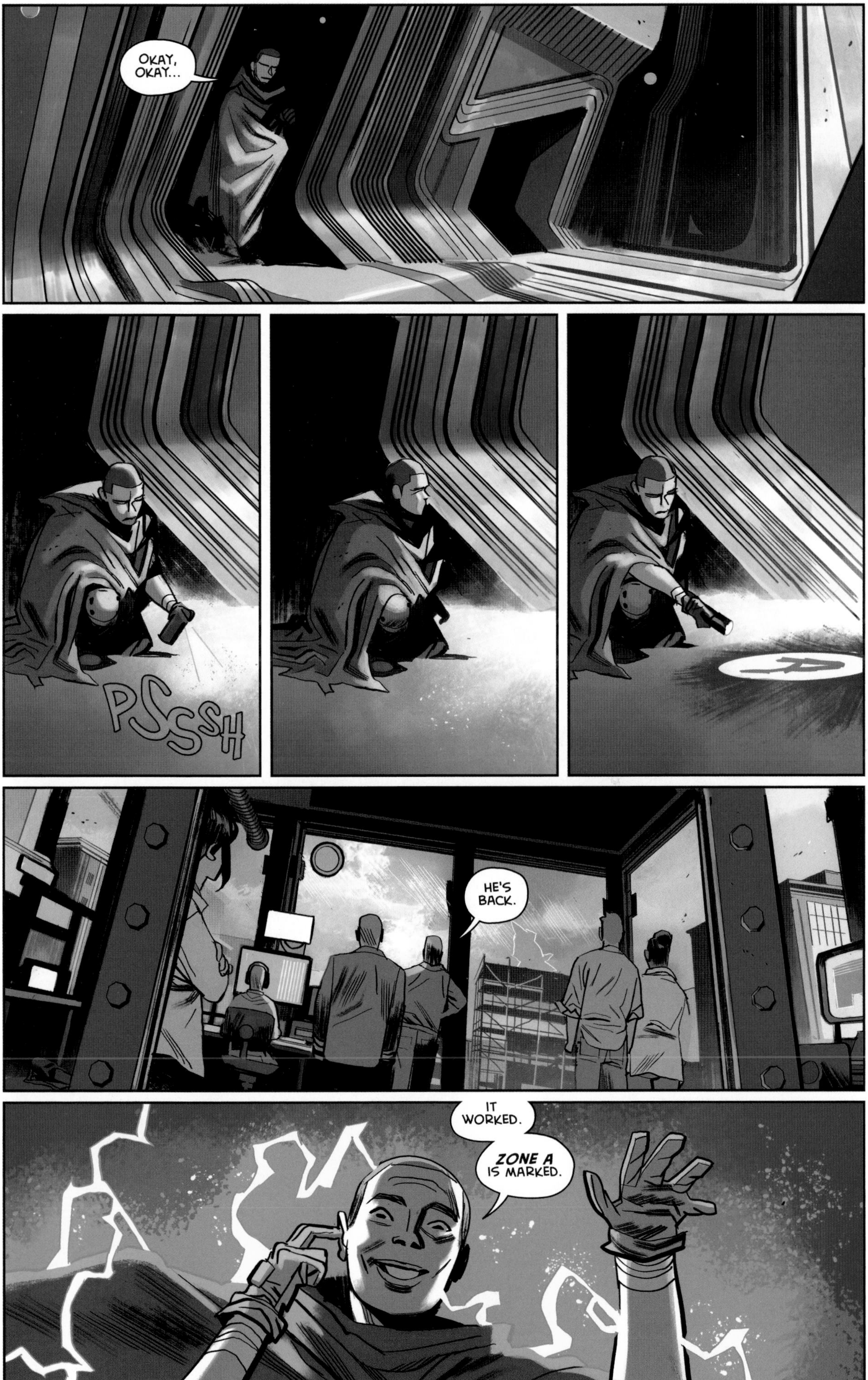
OKAY, OKAY...
PSSSH
HE'S BACK.
IT WORKED.
ZONE A IS MARKED.

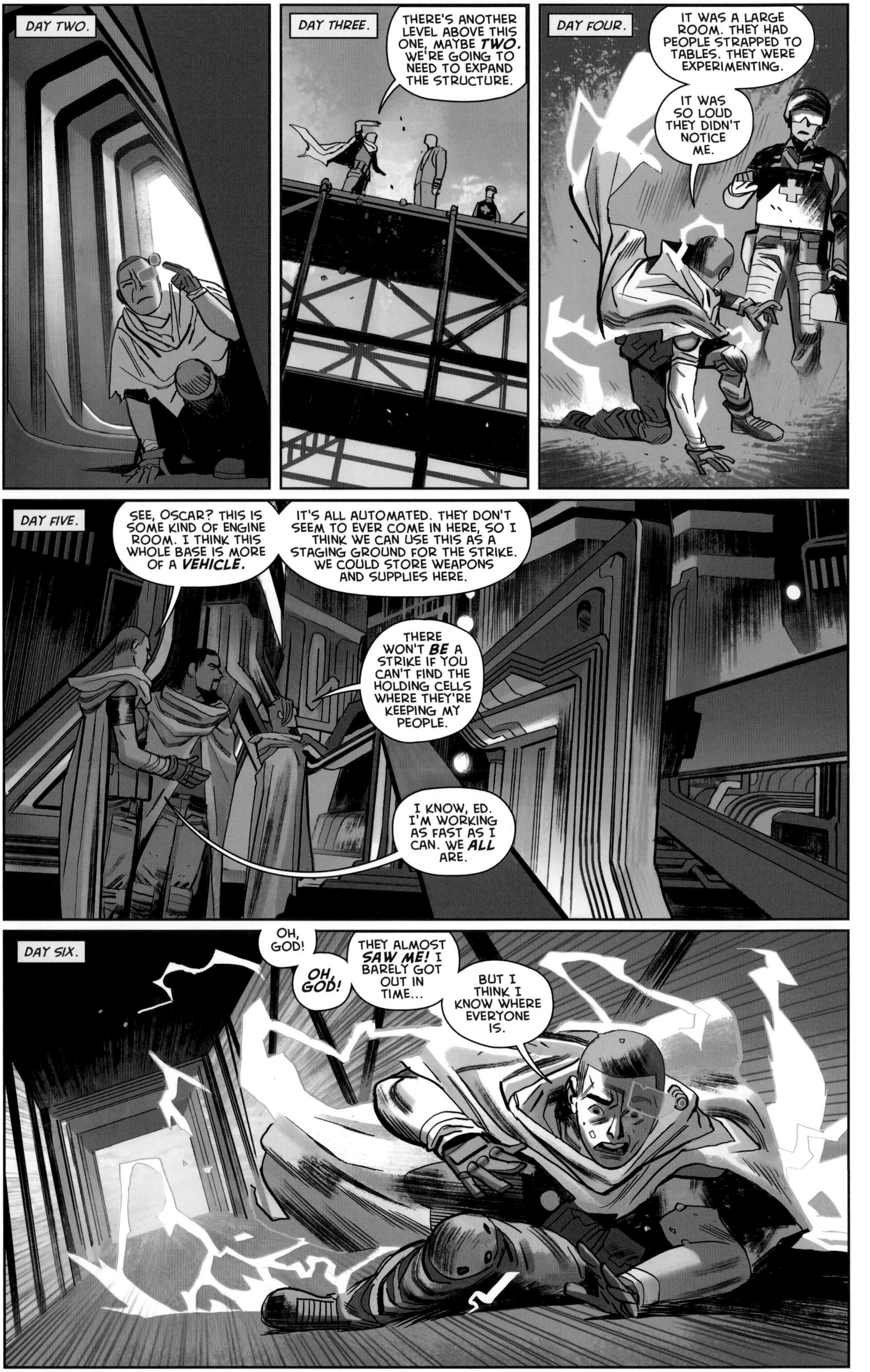
DAY TWO.
DAY THREE.
THERE'S ANOTHER LEVEL ABOVE THIS ONE, MAYBE TWO. WE'RE GOING TO NEED TO EXPAND THE STRUCTURE.
DAY FOUR.
IT WAS A LARGE ROOM. THEY HAD PEOPLE STRAPPED TO TABLES. THEY WERE EXPERIMENTING.
IT WAS SO LOUD THEY DIDN'T NOTICE ME.
DAY FIVE.
SEE, OSCAR? THIS IS SOME KIND OF ENGINE ROOM. I THINK THIS WHOLE BASE IS MORE OF A VEHICLE.
IT'S ALL AUTOMATED. THEY DON'T SEEM TO EVER COME IN HERE, SO I THINK WE CAN USE THIS AS A STAGING GROUND FOR THE STRIKE. WE COULD STORE WEAPONS AND SUPPLIES HERE.
THERE WON'T BE A STRIKE IF YOU CAN'T FIND THE HOLDING CELLS WHERE THEY'RE KEEPING MY PEOPLE.
I KNOW, ED. I'M WORKING AS FAST AS I CAN. WE ALL ARE.
DAY SIX.
OH, GOD!
OH, GOD!
THEY ALMOST SAW ME! I BARELY GOT OUT IN TIME...
BUT I THINK I KNOW WHERE EVERYONE IS.

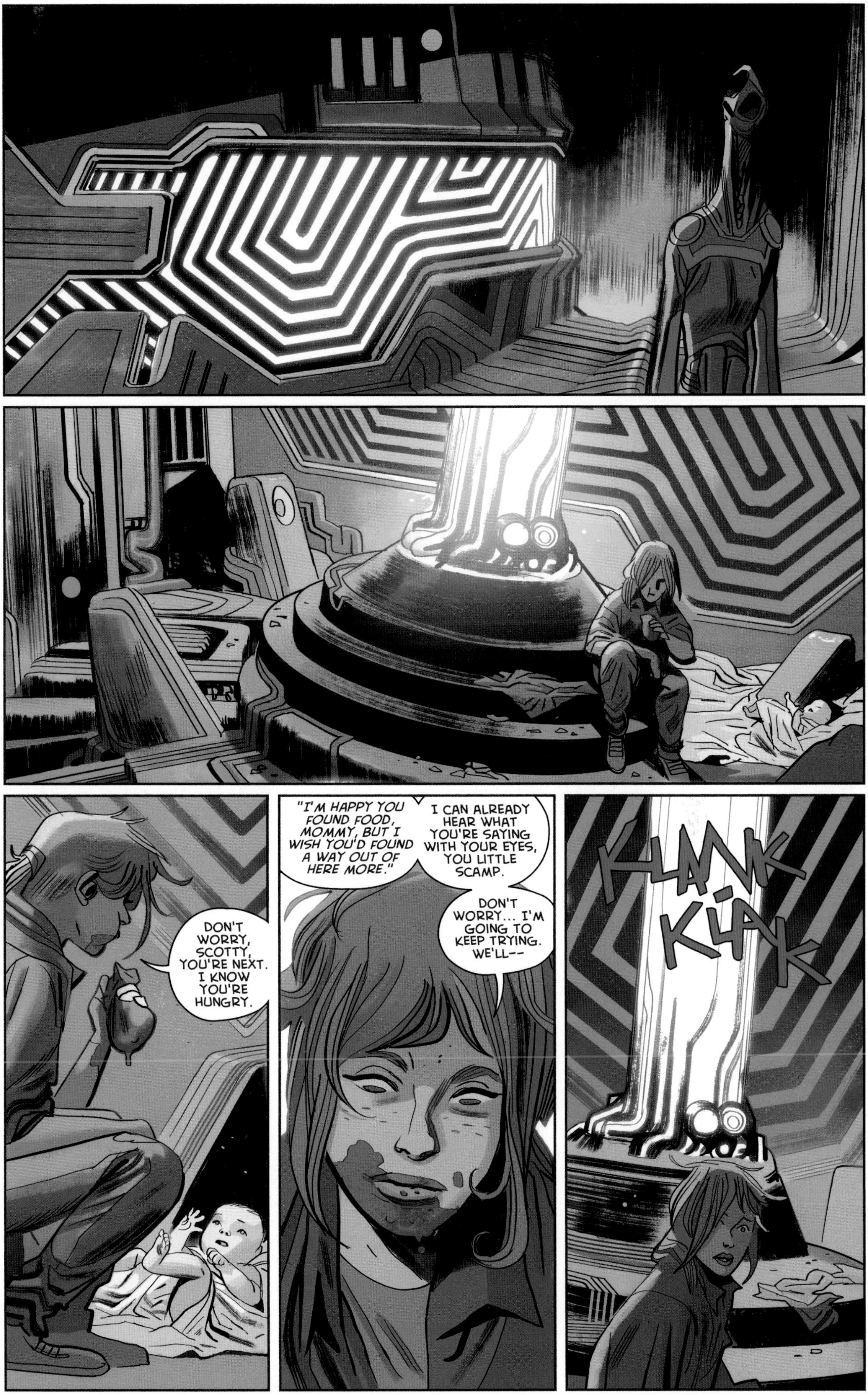

DON'T WORRY, SCOTTY, YOU'RE NEXT. I KNOW YOU'RE HUNGRY.
"I'M HAPPY YOU FOUND FOOD, MOMMY, BUT I WISH YOU'D FOUND A WAY OUT OF HERE MORE."
I CAN ALREADY HEAR WHAT YOU'RE SAYING WITH YOUR EYES, YOU LITTLE SCAMP.
DON'T WORRY... I'M GOING TO KEEP TRYING. WE'LL--
KLANK KLANK

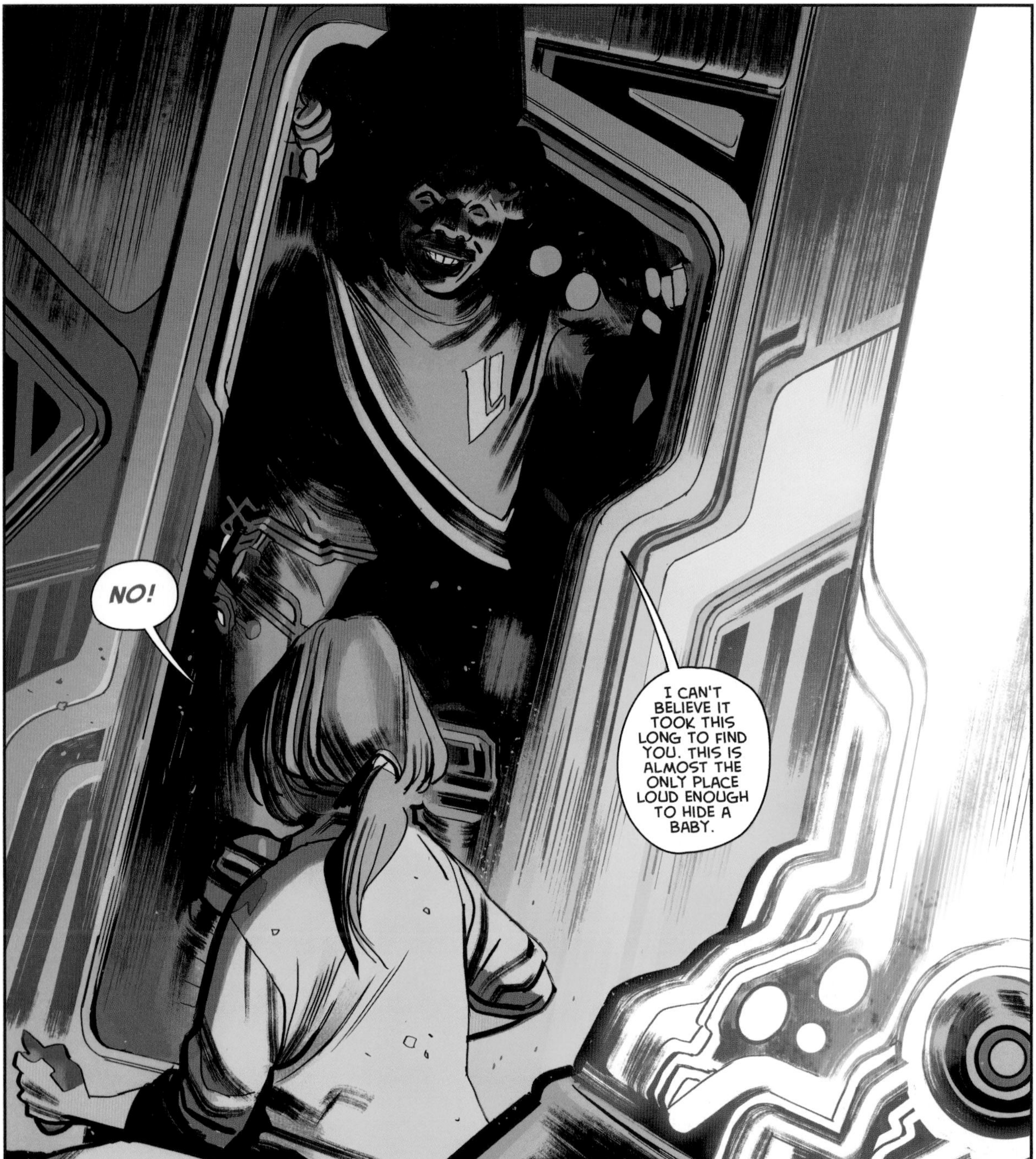
NO!
I CAN'T BELIEVE IT TOOK THIS LONG TO FIND YOU. THIS IS ALMOST THE ONLY PLACE LOUD ENOUGH TO HIDE A BABY.

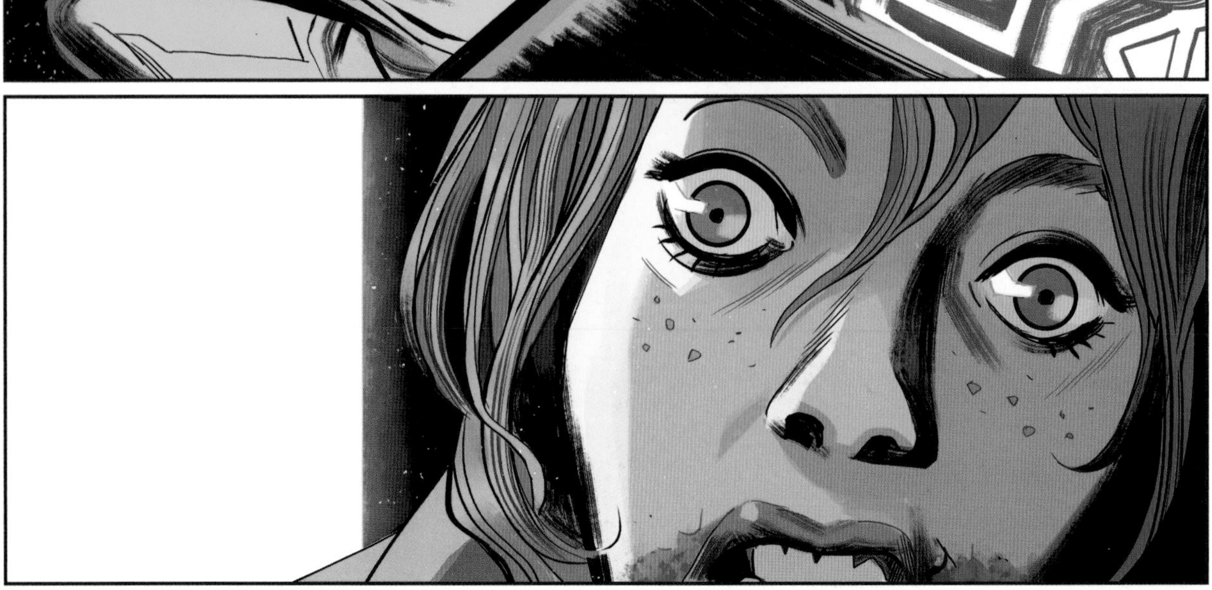

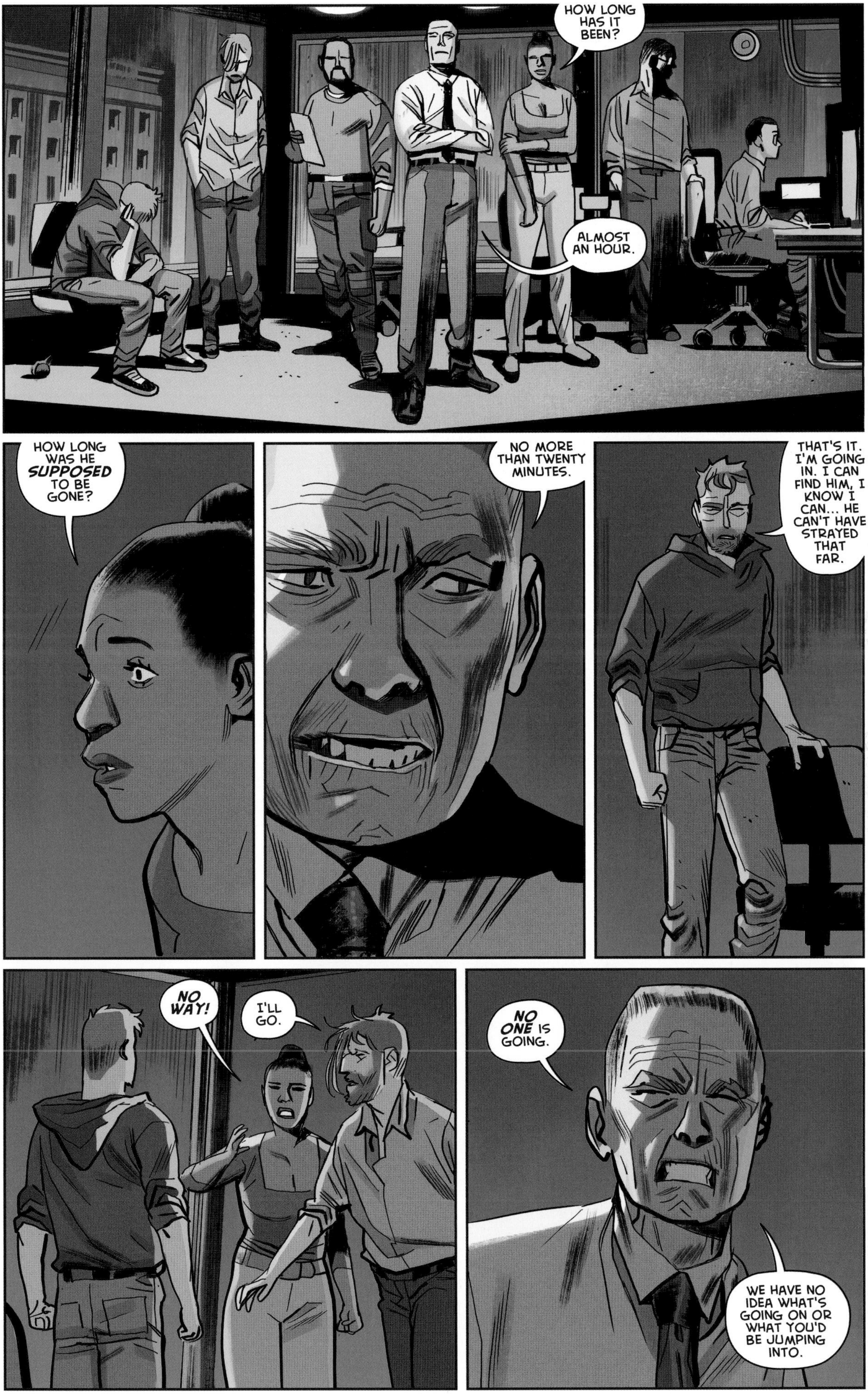
HOW LONG HAS IT BEEN?
ALMOST AN HOUR.
HOW LONG WAS HE *SUPPOSED* TO BE GONE?
NO MORE THAN TWENTY MINUTES.
THAT'S IT. I'M GOING IN. I CAN FIND HIM, I KNOW I CAN... HE CAN'T HAVE STRAYED THAT FAR.
NO WAY!
I'LL GO.
NO ONE IS GOING.
WE HAVE NO IDEA WHAT'S GOING ON OR WHAT YOU'D BE JUMPING INTO.

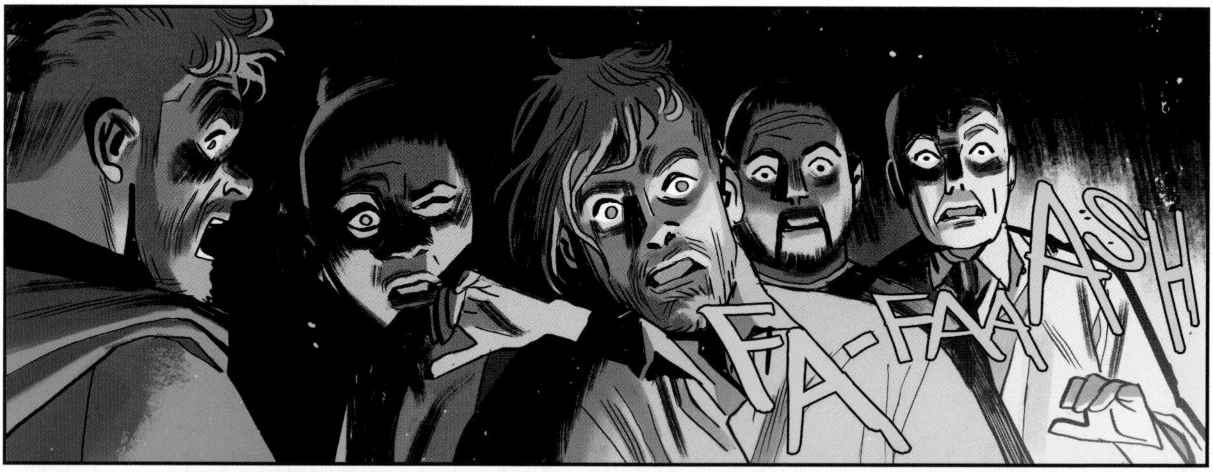
FA-FAA-AASH

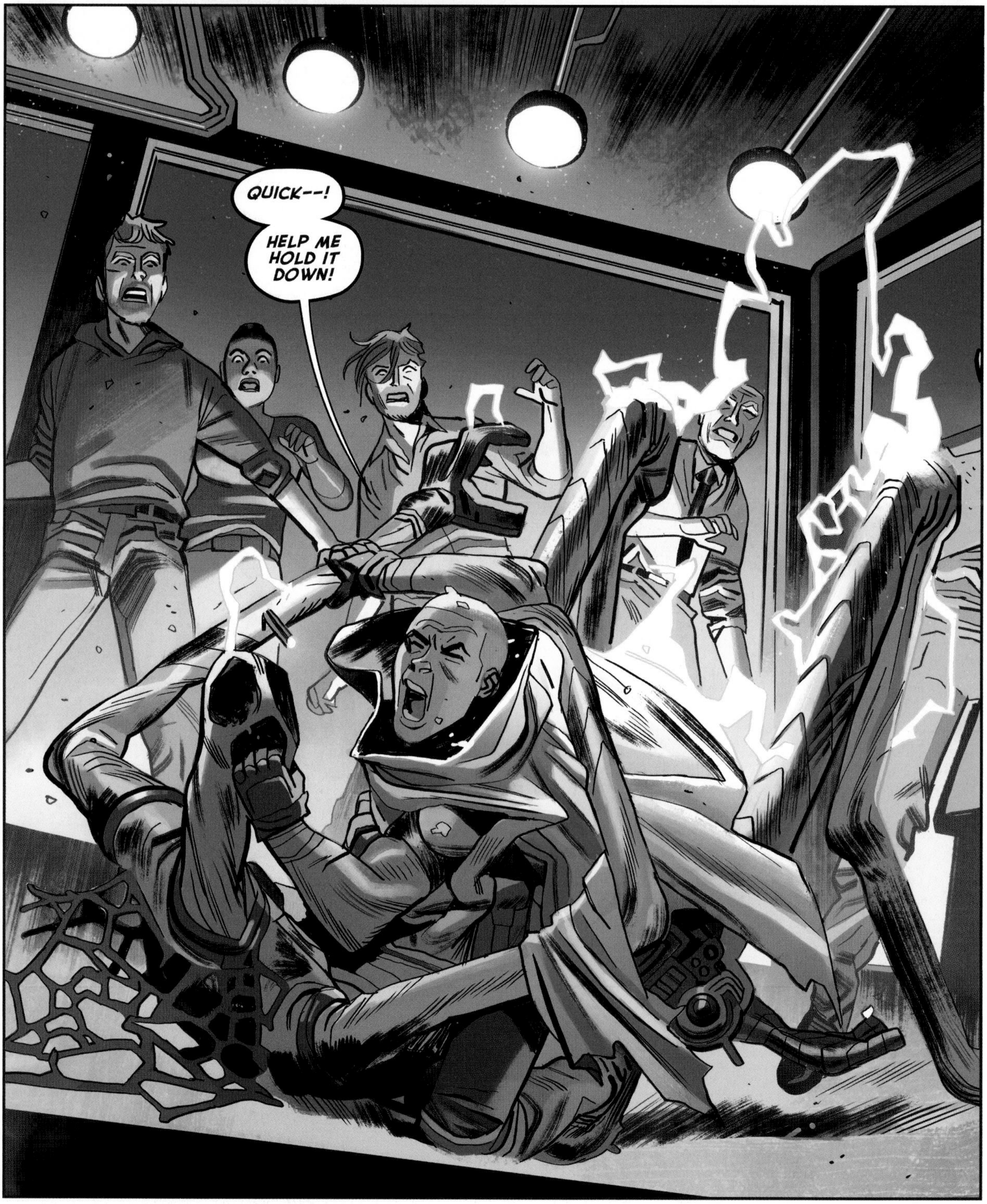
QUICK--!
HELP ME HOLD IT DOWN!

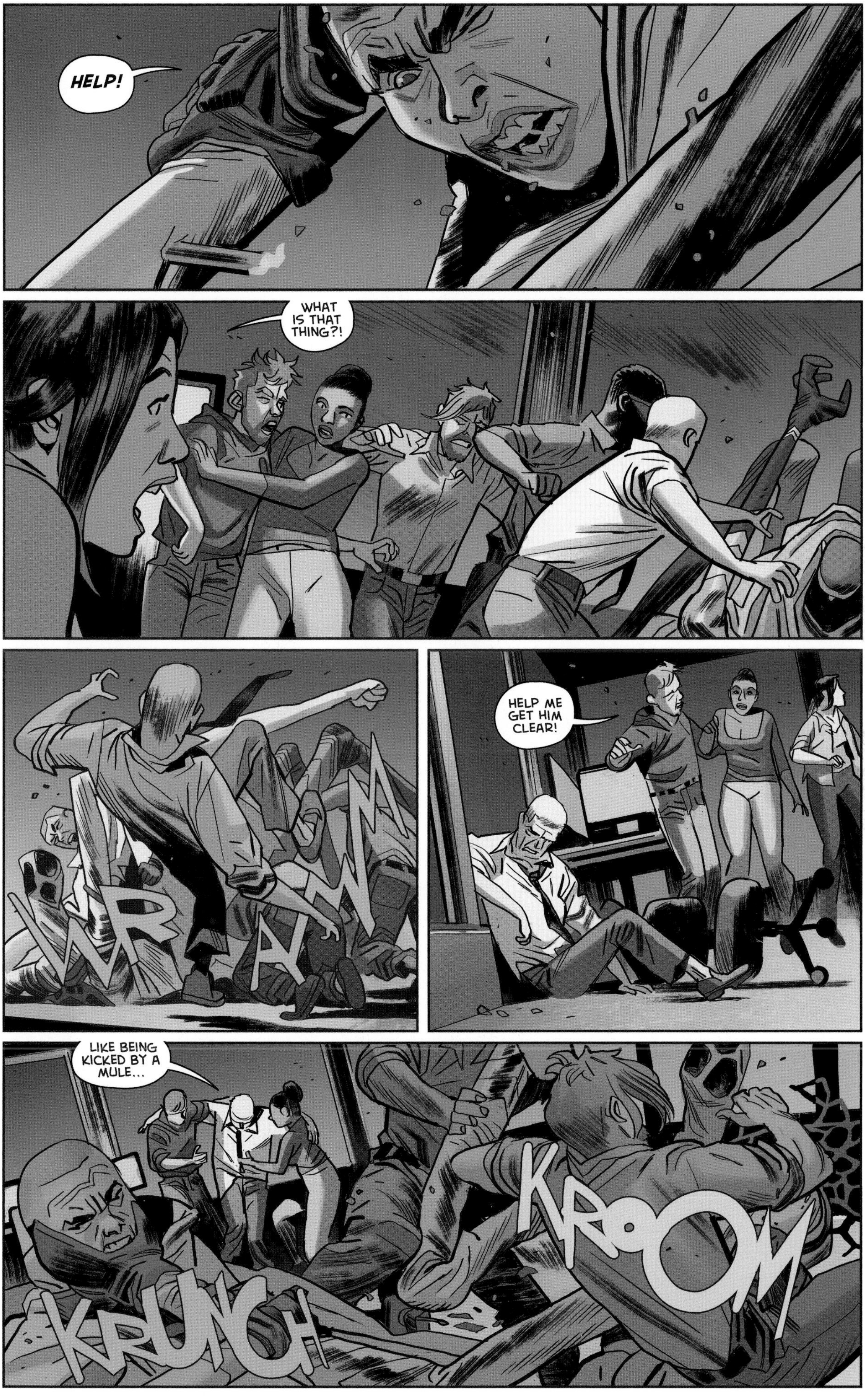
HELP!
WHAT IS THAT THING?!
WRAM
HELP ME GET HIM CLEAR!
LIKE BEING KICKED BY A MULE...
KROOM
KRUNCH

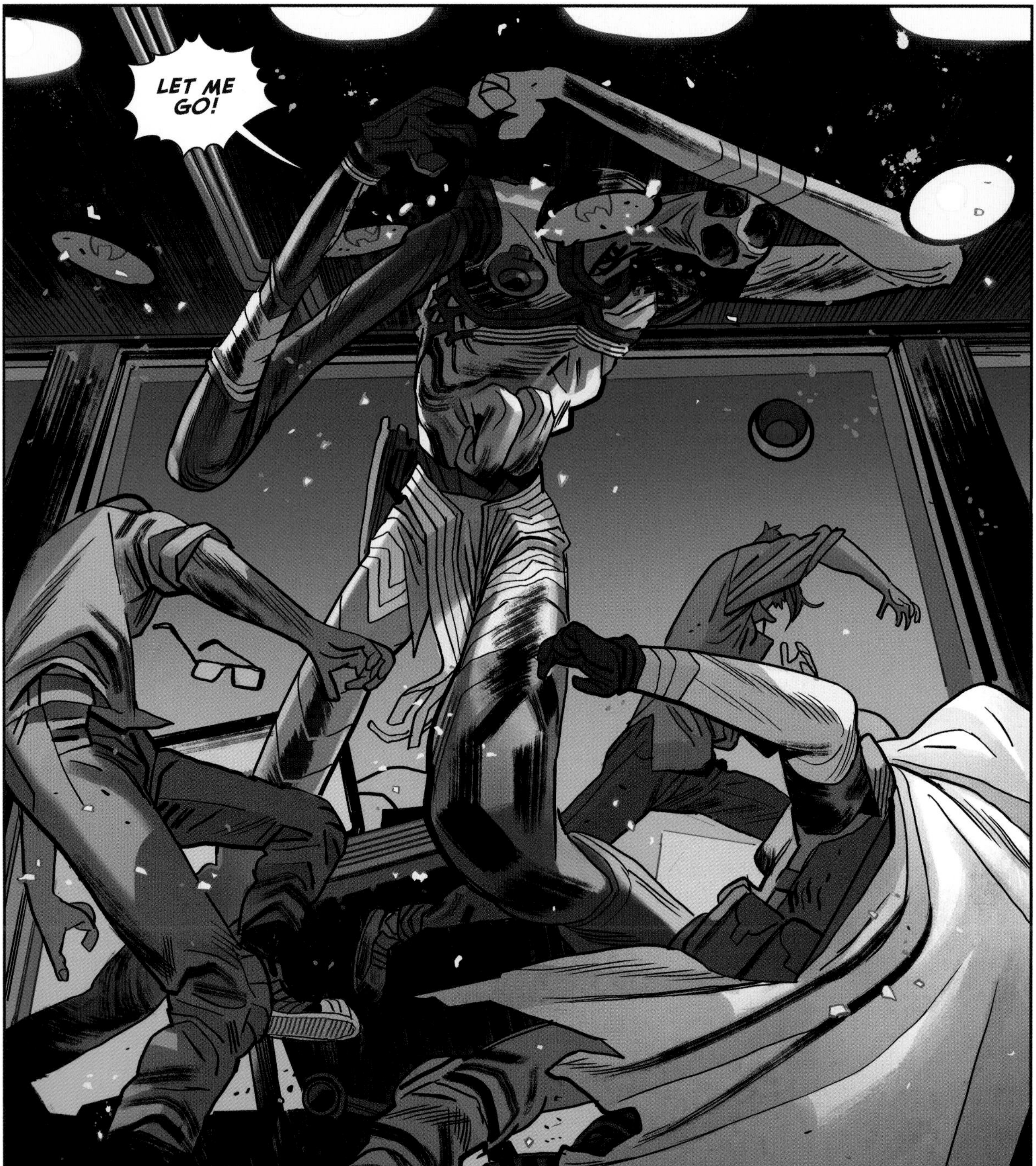
LET ME GO!

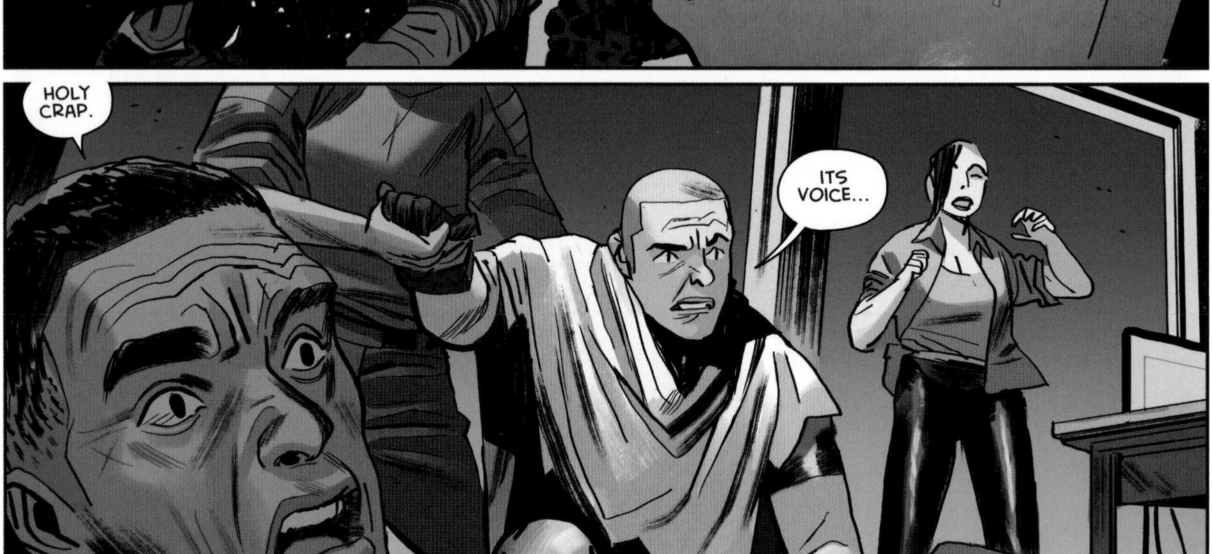
HOLY CRAP.
ITS VOICE...

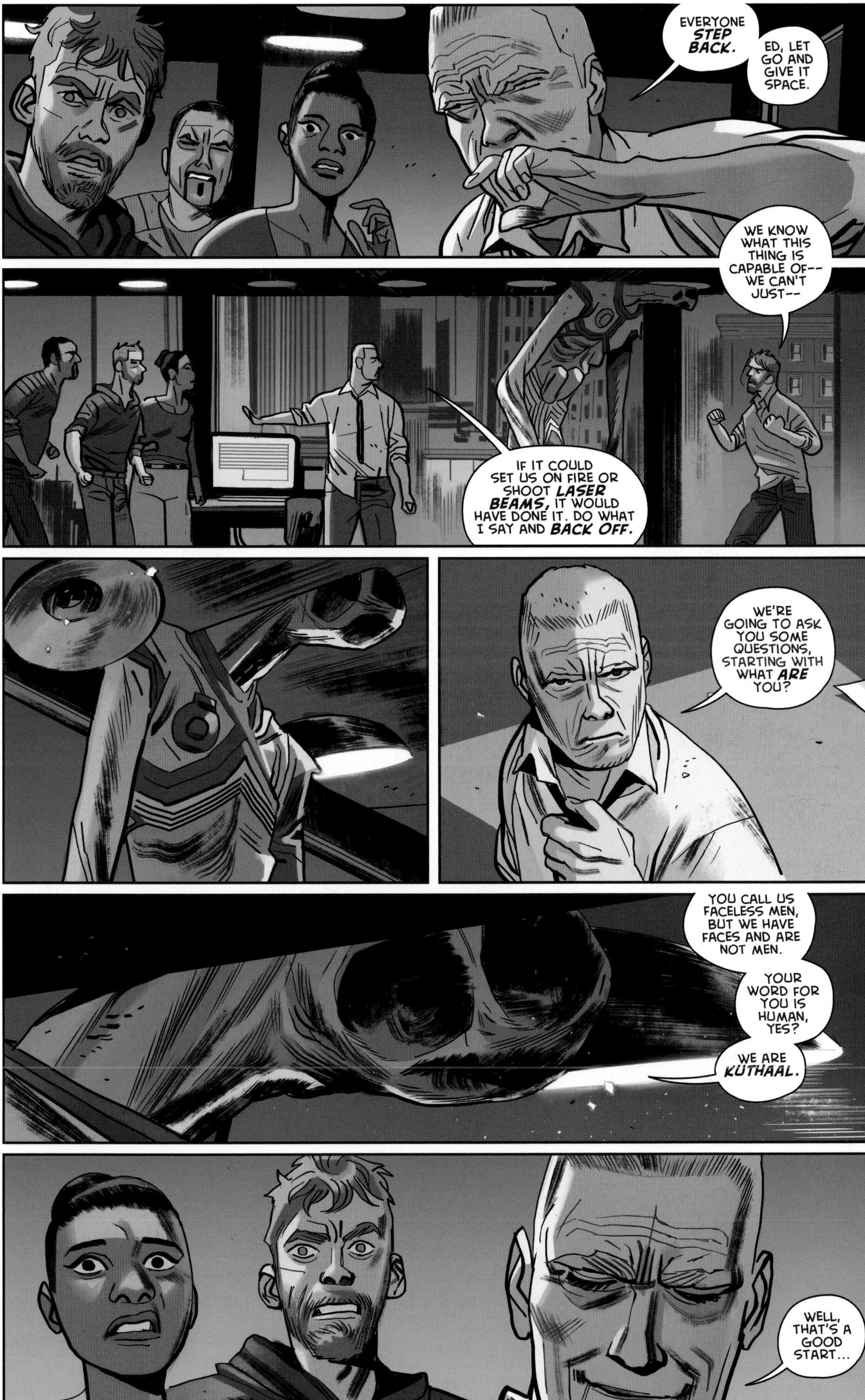
EVERYONE STEP BACK.
ED, LET GO AND GIVE IT SPACE.
WE KNOW WHAT THIS THING IS CAPABLE OF-- WE CAN'T JUST--
IF IT COULD SET US ON FIRE OR SHOOT LASER BEAMS, IT WOULD HAVE DONE IT. DO WHAT I SAY AND BACK OFF.
WE'RE GOING TO ASK YOU SOME QUESTIONS, STARTING WITH WHAT ARE YOU?
YOU CALL US FACELESS MEN, BUT WE HAVE FACES AND ARE NOT MEN.
YOUR WORD FOR YOU IS HUMAN, YES?
WE ARE KUTHAAL.
WELL, THAT'S A GOOD START...

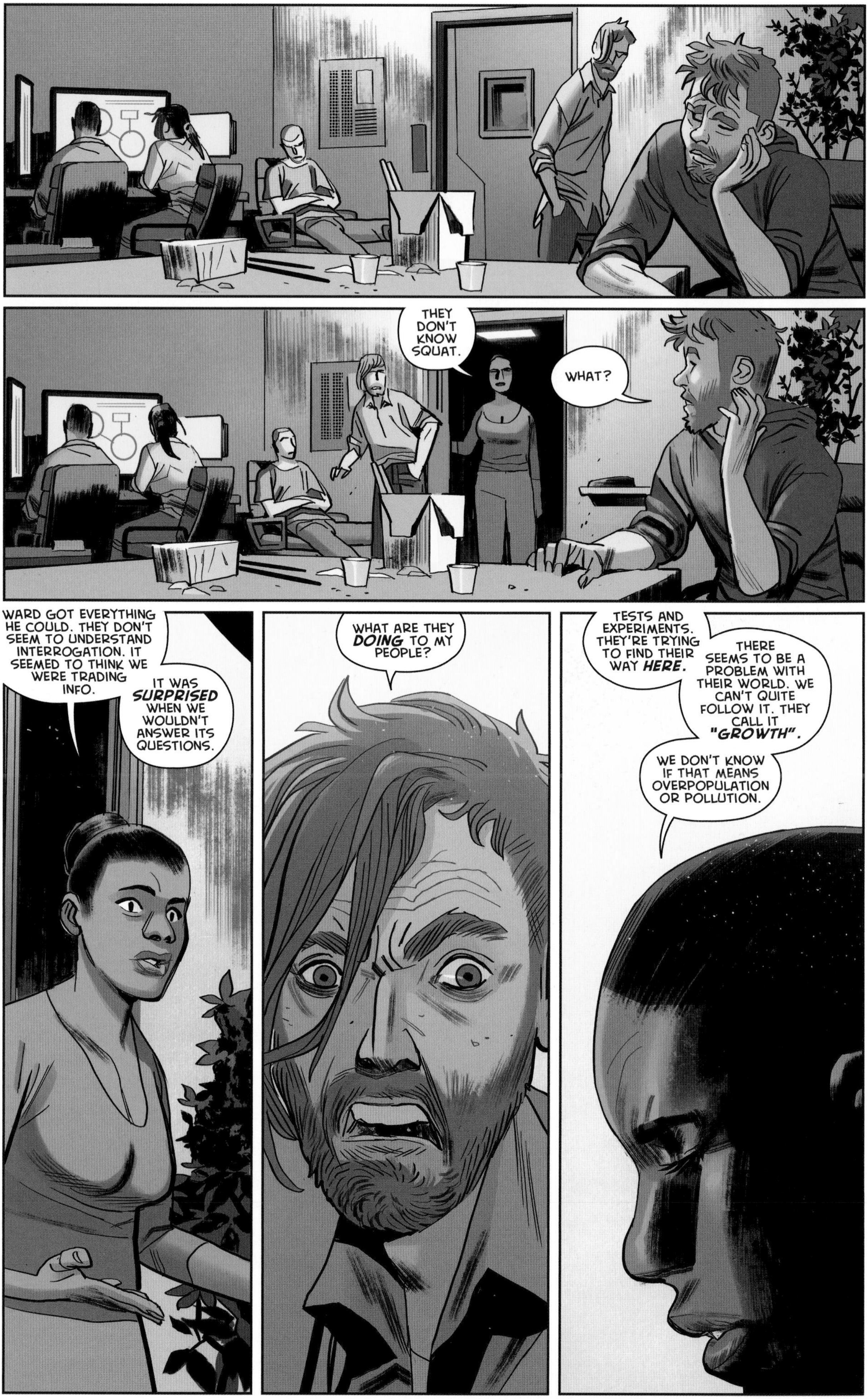
THEY DON'T KNOW SQUAT.
WHAT?
WARD GOT EVERYTHING HE COULD. THEY DON'T SEEM TO UNDERSTAND INTERROGATION. IT SEEMED TO THINK WE WERE TRADING INFO.
IT WAS SURPRISED WHEN WE WOULDN'T ANSWER ITS QUESTIONS.
WHAT ARE THEY DOING TO MY PEOPLE?
TESTS AND EXPERIMENTS. THEY'RE TRYING TO FIND THEIR WAY HERE.
THERE SEEMS TO BE A PROBLEM WITH THEIR WORLD. WE CAN'T QUITE FOLLOW IT. THEY CALL IT "GROWTH".
WE DON'T KNOW IF THAT MEANS OVERPOPULATION OR POLLUTION.

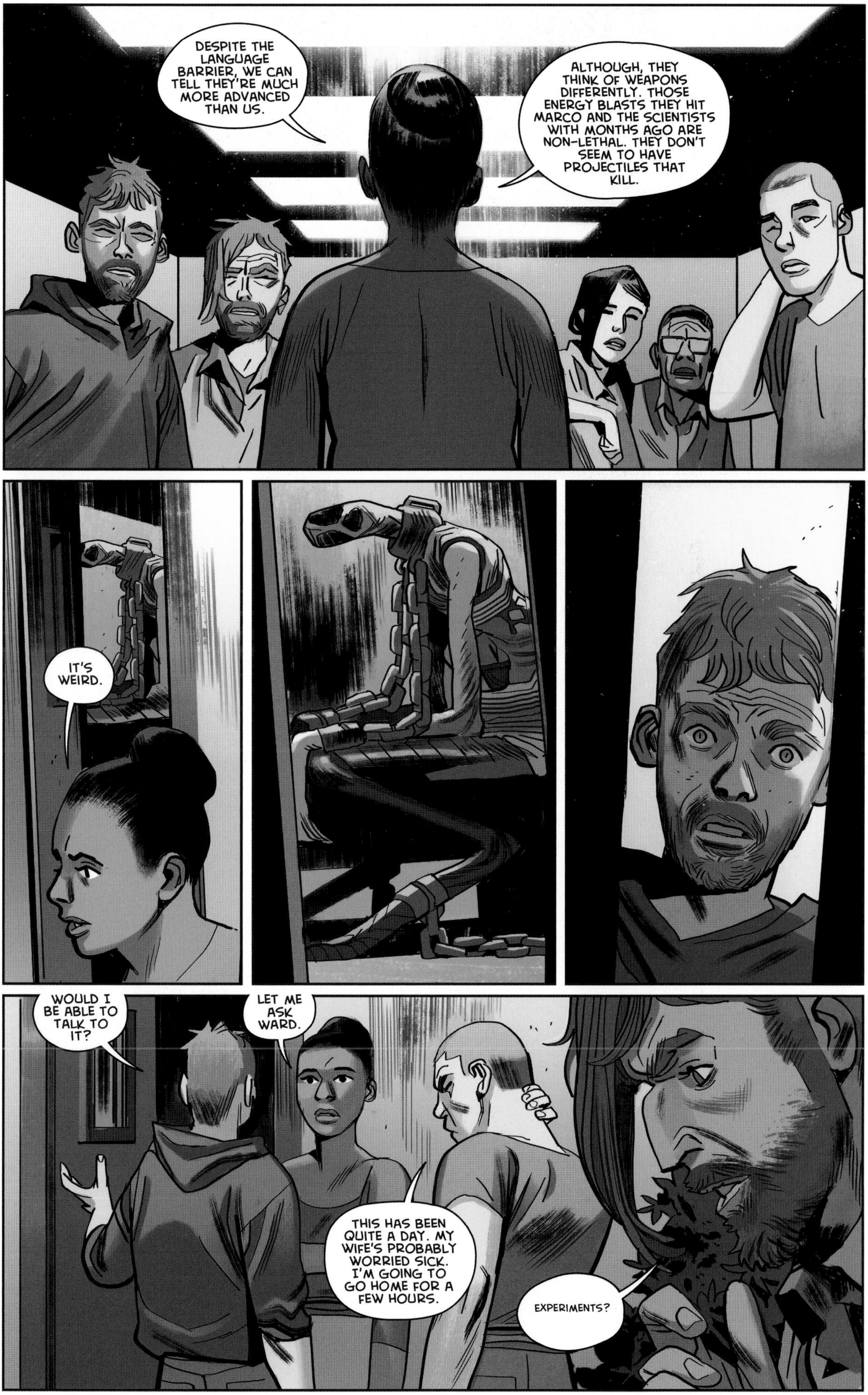
DESPITE THE LANGUAGE BARRIER, WE CAN TELL THEY'RE MUCH MORE ADVANCED THAN US.
ALTHOUGH, THEY THINK OF WEAPONS DIFFERENTLY. THOSE ENERGY BLASTS THEY HIT MARCO AND THE SCIENTISTS WITH MONTHS AGO ARE NON-LETHAL. THEY DON'T SEEM TO HAVE PROJECTILES THAT KILL.
IT'S WEIRD.
WOULD I BE ABLE TO TALK TO IT?
LET ME ASK WARD.
THIS HAS BEEN QUITE A DAY. MY WIFE'S PROBABLY WORRIED SICK. I'M GOING TO GO HOME FOR A FEW HOURS.
EXPERIMENTS?

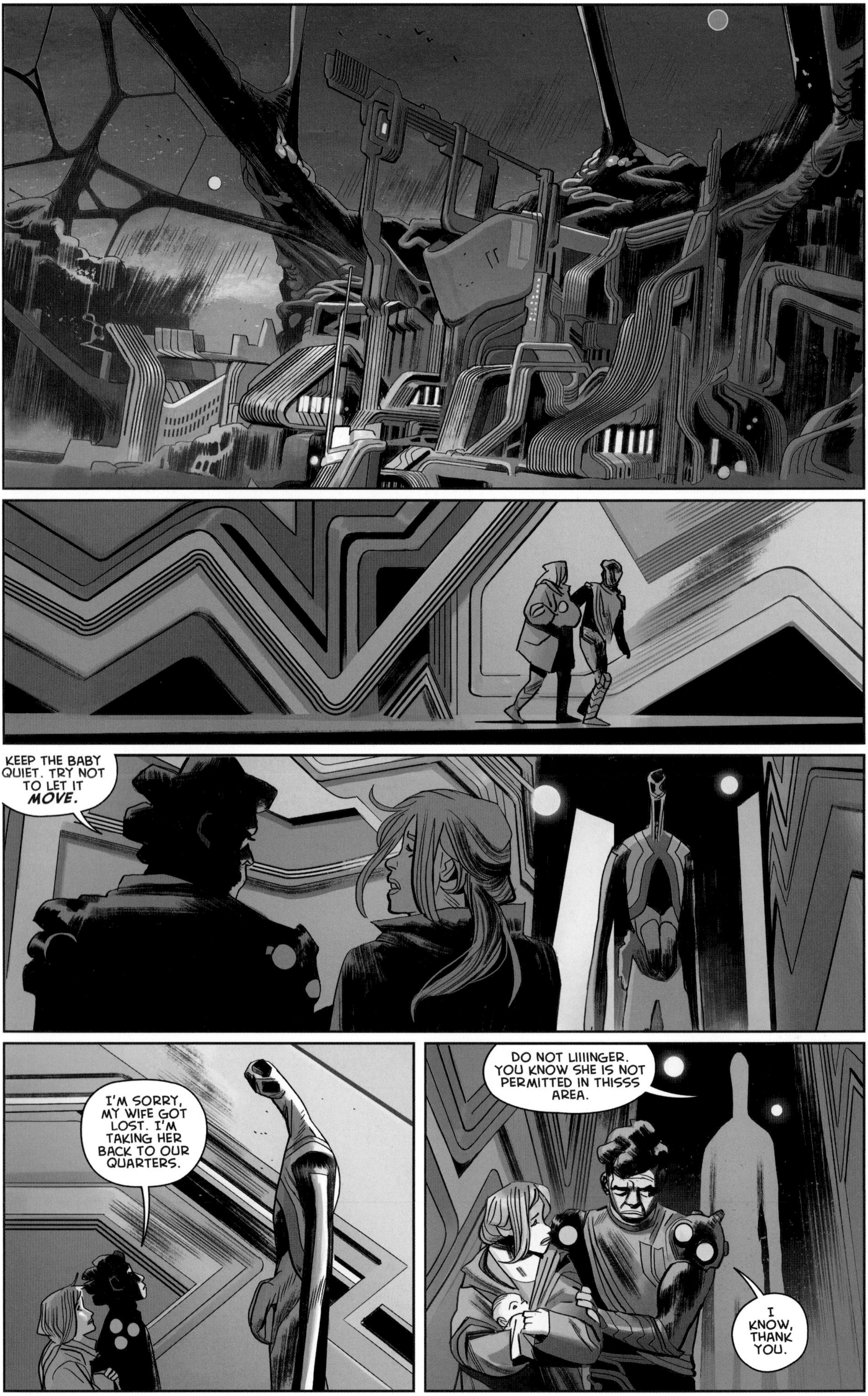
KEEP THE BABY QUIET. TRY NOT TO LET IT *MOVE.*
I'M SORRY, MY WIFE GOT LOST. I'M TAKING HER BACK TO OUR QUARTERS.
DO NOT LIIIINGER. YOU KNOW SHE IS NOT PERMITTED IN THISSS AREA.
I KNOW, THANK YOU.

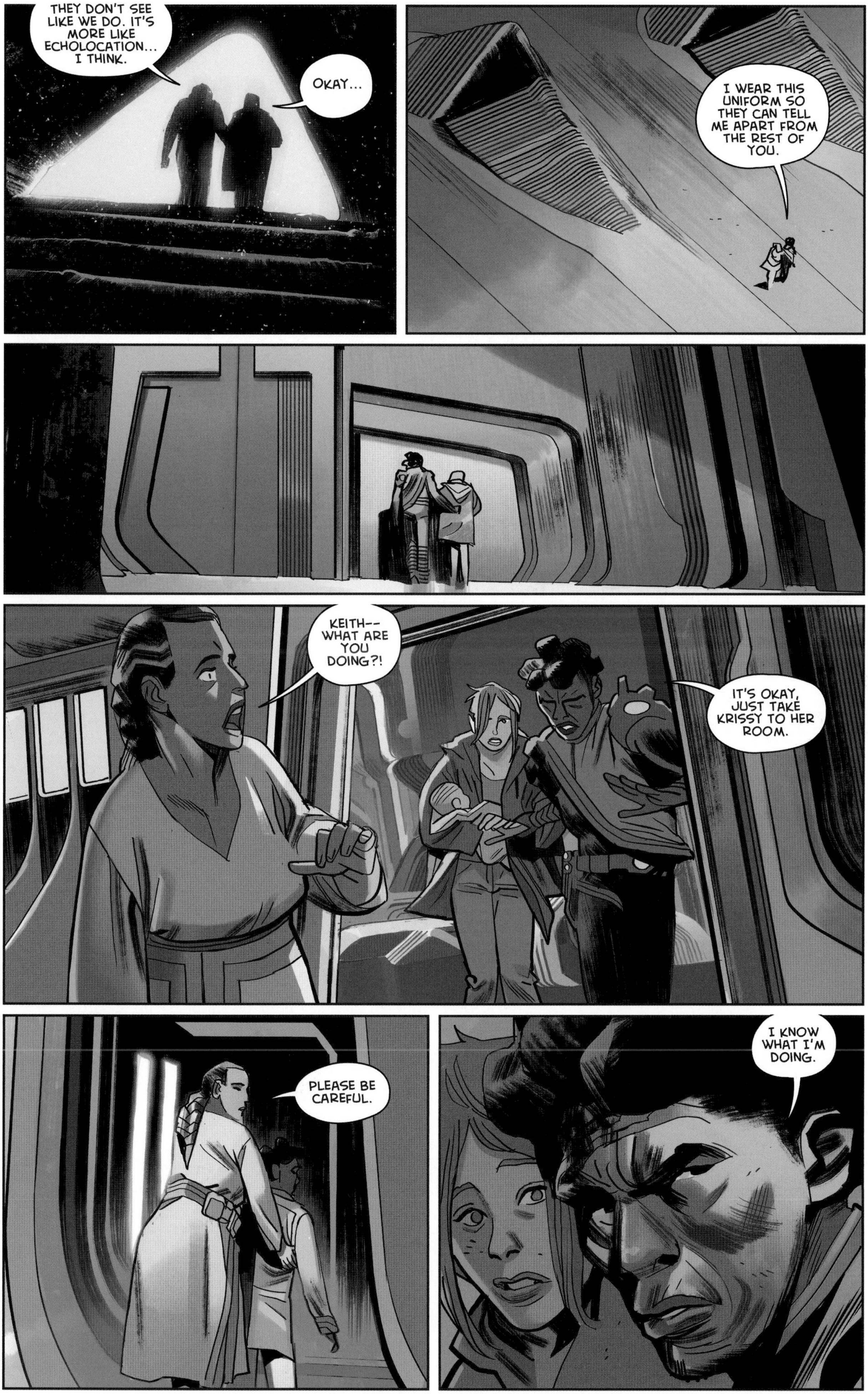
THEY DON'T SEE LIKE WE DO. IT'S MORE LIKE ECHOLOCATION... I THINK.
OKAY...
I WEAR THIS UNIFORM SO THEY CAN TELL ME APART FROM THE REST OF YOU.
KEITH-- WHAT ARE YOU DOING?!
IT'S OKAY, JUST TAKE KRISSY TO HER ROOM.
PLEASE BE CAREFUL.
I KNOW WHAT I'M DOING.

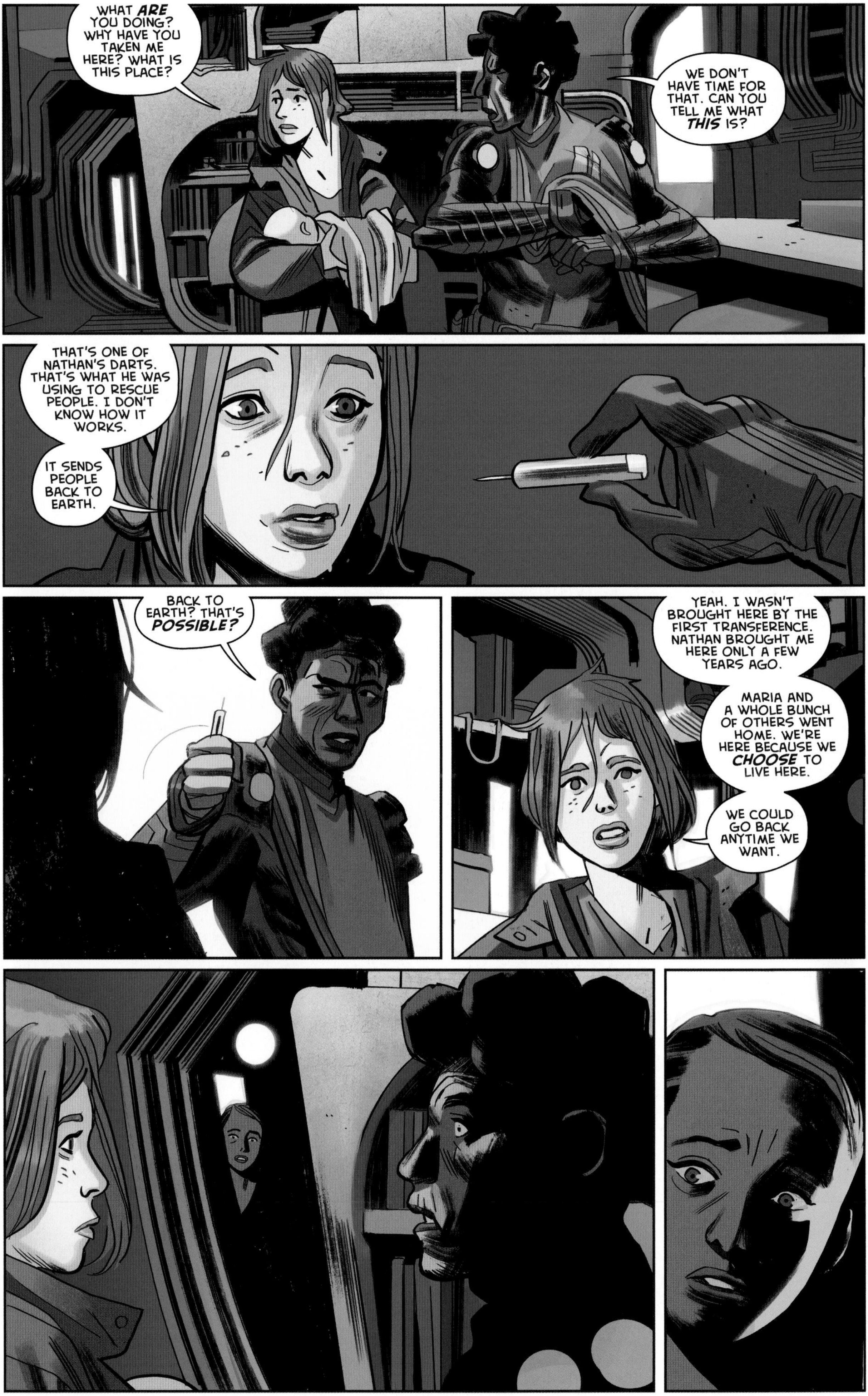
WHAT ARE YOU DOING? WHY HAVE YOU TAKEN ME HERE? WHAT IS THIS PLACE?
WE DON'T HAVE TIME FOR THAT. CAN YOU TELL ME WHAT THIS IS?
THAT'S ONE OF NATHAN'S DARTS. THAT'S WHAT HE WAS USING TO RESCUE PEOPLE. I DON'T KNOW HOW IT WORKS.
IT SENDS PEOPLE BACK TO EARTH.
BACK TO EARTH? THAT'S POSSIBLE?
YEAH. I WASN'T BROUGHT HERE BY THE FIRST TRANSFERENCE. NATHAN BROUGHT ME HERE ONLY A FEW YEARS AGO.
MARIA AND A WHOLE BUNCH OF OTHERS WENT HOME. WE'RE HERE BECAUSE WE CHOOSE TO LIVE HERE.
WE COULD GO BACK ANYTIME WE WANT.

ARE YOU HURT?

HURTTT?

NO. NOT HURRRT.

I WANT YOU TO KNOW, WE'RE GOING TO FIGURE THIS OUT AND GET YOU HOME.

WE DON'T WANT TO HURT YOU OR YOUR KIND. WE JUST WANT TO GET OUR PEOPLE BACK.

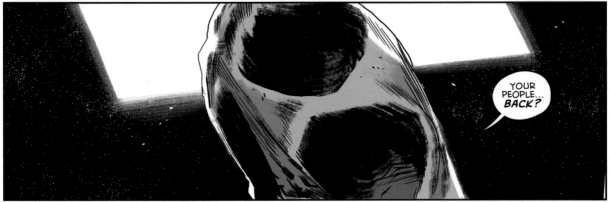

YOUR PEOPLE... *BACK?*

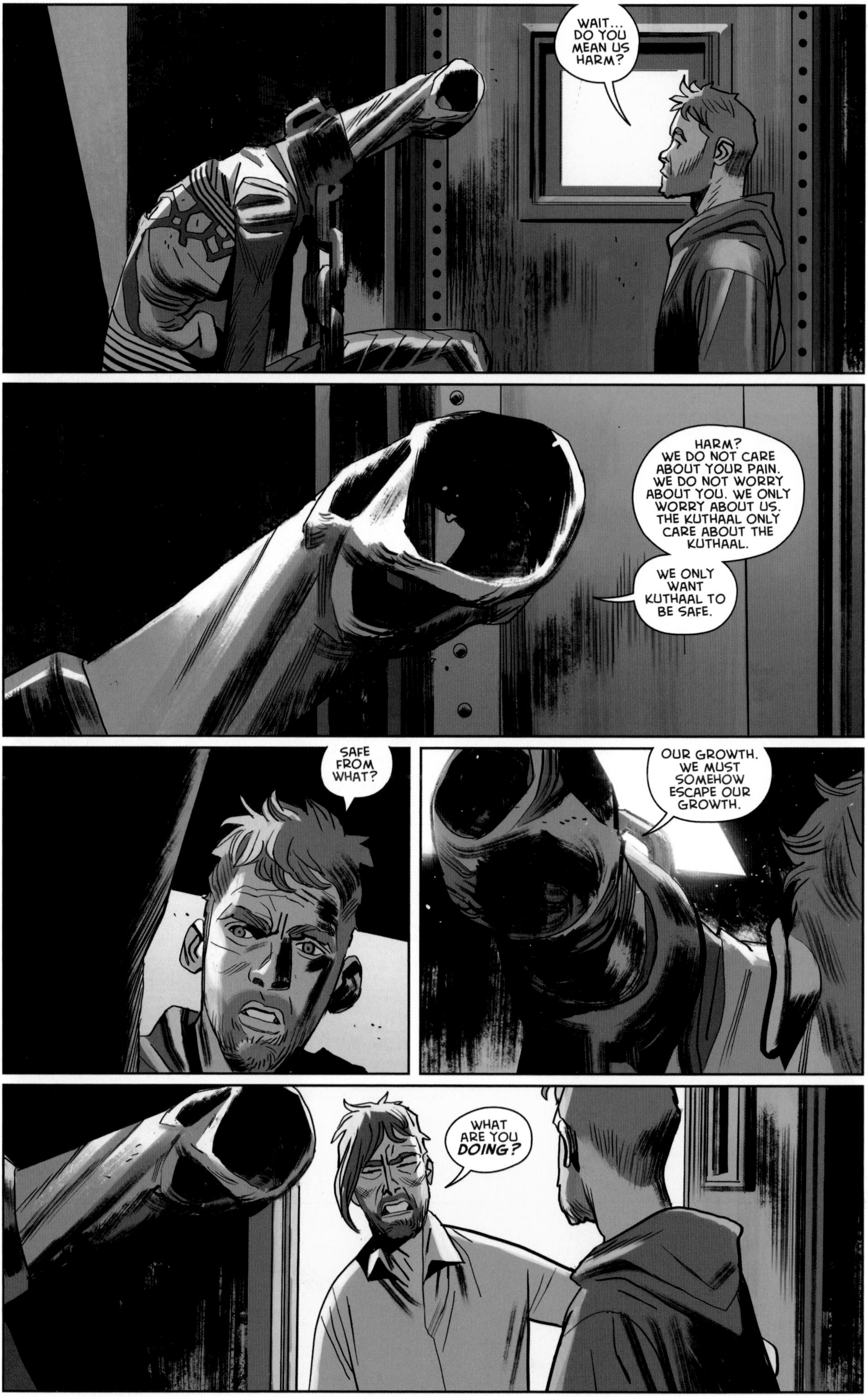
WAIT... DO YOU MEAN US HARM?
HARM? WE DO NOT CARE ABOUT YOUR PAIN. WE DO NOT WORRY ABOUT YOU. WE ONLY WORRY ABOUT US. THE KUTHAAL ONLY CARE ABOUT THE KUTHAAL.
WE ONLY WANT KUTHAAL TO BE SAFE.
SAFE FROM WHAT?
OUR GROWTH. WE MUST SOMEHOW ESCAPE OUR GROWTH.
WHAT ARE YOU *DOING?*

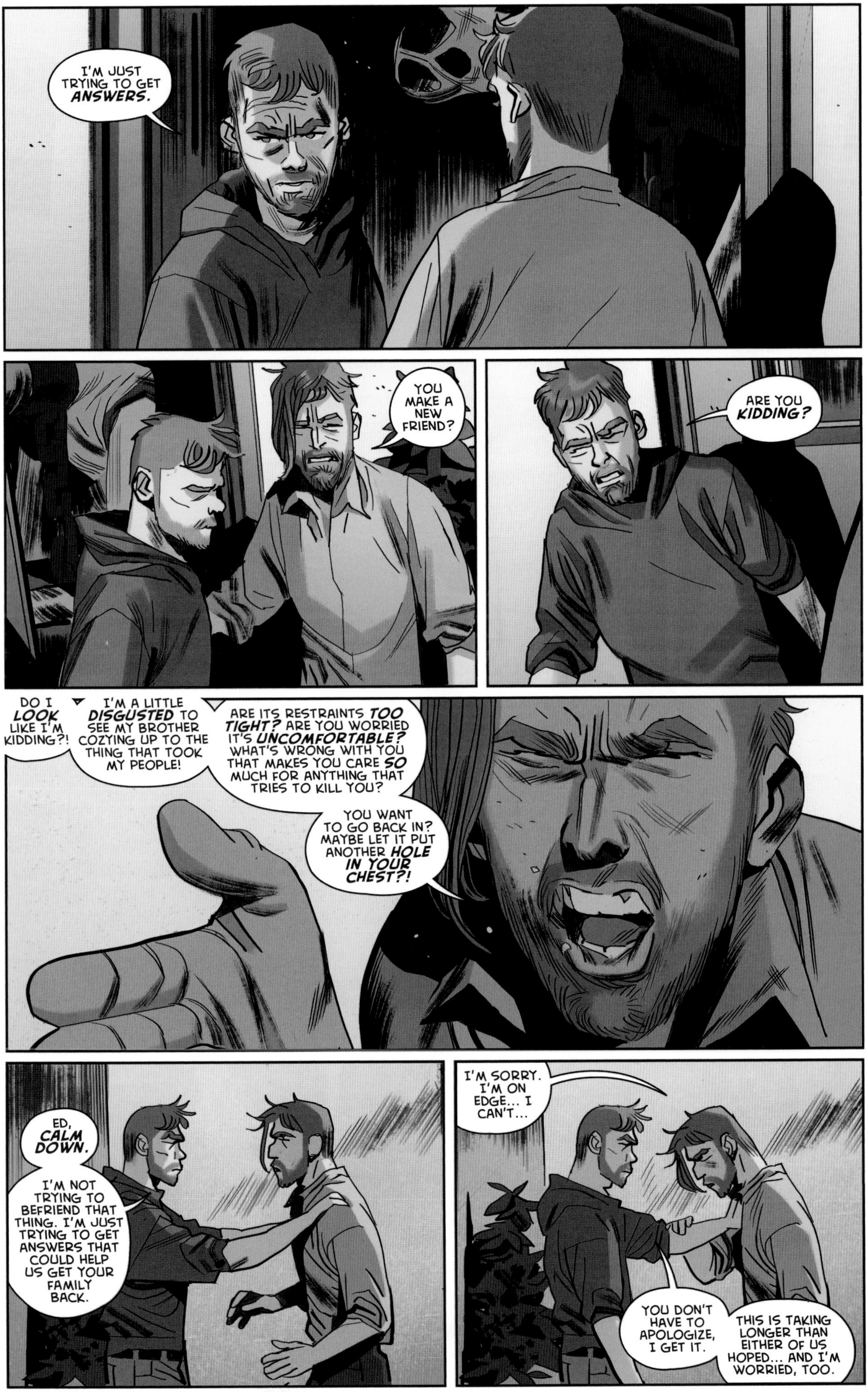
I'M JUST TRYING TO GET ANSWERS.
YOU MAKE A NEW FRIEND?
ARE YOU KIDDING?
DO I LOOK LIKE I'M KIDDING?!
I'M A LITTLE DISGUSTED TO SEE MY BROTHER COZYING UP TO THE THING THAT TOOK MY PEOPLE!
ARE ITS RESTRAINTS TOO TIGHT? ARE YOU WORRIED IT'S UNCOMFORTABLE? WHAT'S WRONG WITH YOU THAT MAKES YOU CARE SO MUCH FOR ANYTHING THAT TRIES TO KILL YOU?
YOU WANT TO GO BACK IN? MAYBE LET IT PUT ANOTHER HOLE IN YOUR CHEST?!
ED, CALM DOWN.
I'M NOT TRYING TO BEFRIEND THAT THING. I'M JUST TRYING TO GET ANSWERS THAT COULD HELP US GET YOUR FAMILY BACK.
I'M SORRY. I'M ON EDGE... I CAN'T...
YOU DON'T HAVE TO APOLOGIZE, I GET IT.
THIS IS TAKING LONGER THAN EITHER OF US HOPED... AND I'M WORRIED, TOO.

DAMN IT!

GOING WELL, IS IT?

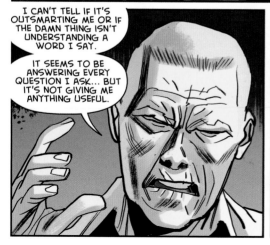

I CAN'T TELL IF IT'S OUTSMARTING ME OR IF THE DAMN THING ISN'T UNDERSTANDING A WORD I SAY.

IT SEEMS TO BE ANSWERING EVERY QUESTION I ASK... BUT IT'S NOT GIVING ME ANYTHING USEFUL.

THEN WHAT THE HELL ARE WE WAITING FOR?

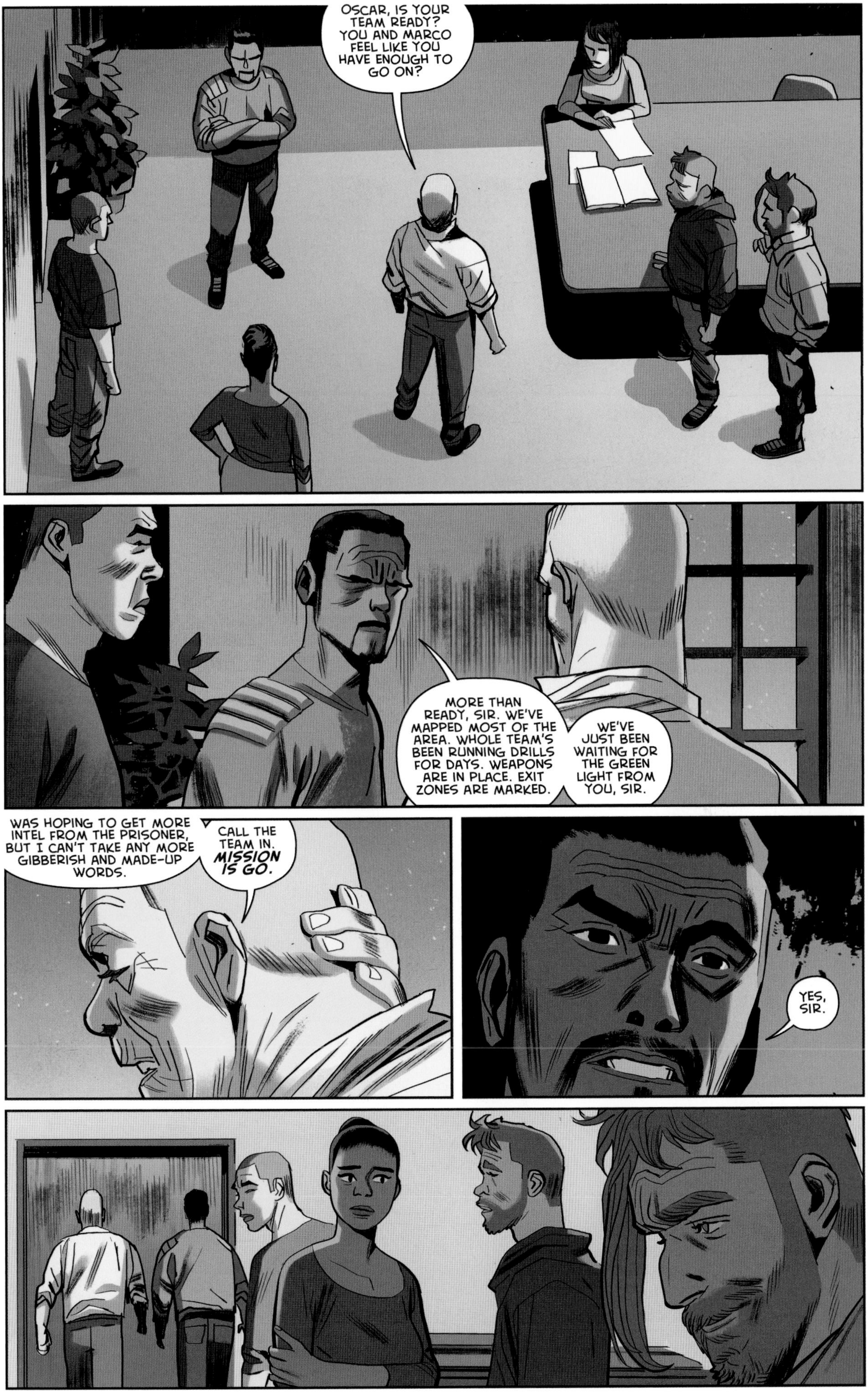
OSCAR, IS YOUR TEAM READY? YOU AND MARCO FEEL LIKE YOU HAVE ENOUGH TO GO ON?
MORE THAN READY, SIR. WE'VE MAPPED MOST OF THE AREA. WHOLE TEAM'S BEEN RUNNING DRILLS FOR DAYS. WEAPONS ARE IN PLACE. EXIT ZONES ARE MARKED.
WE'VE JUST BEEN WAITING FOR THE GREEN LIGHT FROM YOU, SIR.
WAS HOPING TO GET MORE INTEL FROM THE PRISONER, BUT I CAN'T TAKE ANY MORE GIBBERISH AND MADE-UP WORDS.
CALL THE TEAM IN. ***MISSION IS GO.***
YES, SIR.

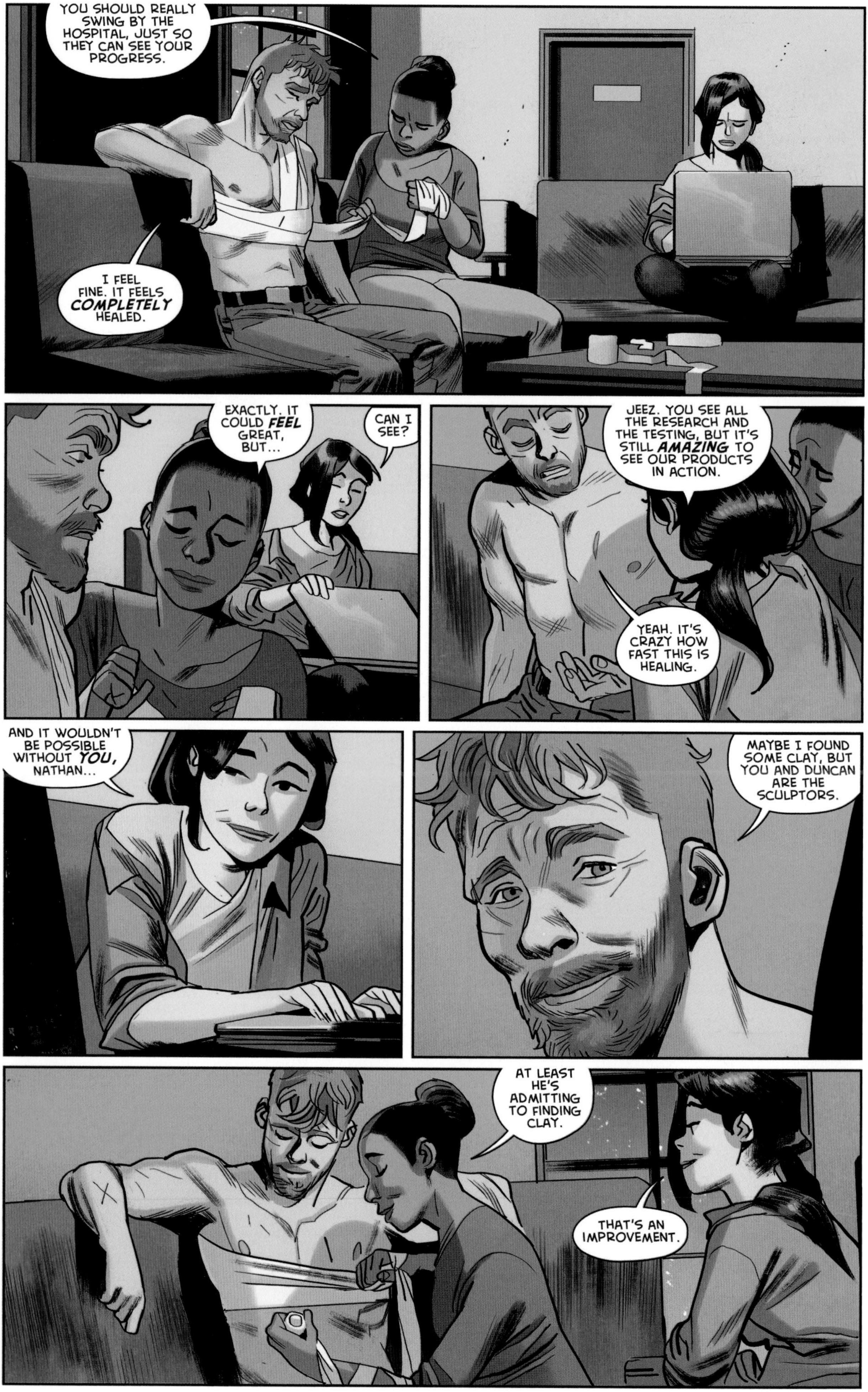
YOU SHOULD REALLY SWING BY THE HOSPITAL, JUST SO THEY CAN SEE YOUR PROGRESS.
I FEEL FINE. IT FEELS COMPLETELY HEALED.
EXACTLY. IT COULD FEEL GREAT, BUT...
CAN I SEE?
JEEZ. YOU SEE ALL THE RESEARCH AND THE TESTING, BUT IT'S STILL AMAZING TO SEE OUR PRODUCTS IN ACTION.
YEAH. IT'S CRAZY HOW FAST THIS IS HEALING.
AND IT WOULDN'T BE POSSIBLE WITHOUT YOU, NATHAN...
MAYBE I FOUND SOME CLAY, BUT YOU AND DUNCAN ARE THE SCULPTORS.
AT LEAST HE'S ADMITTING TO FINDING CLAY.
THAT'S AN IMPROVEMENT.

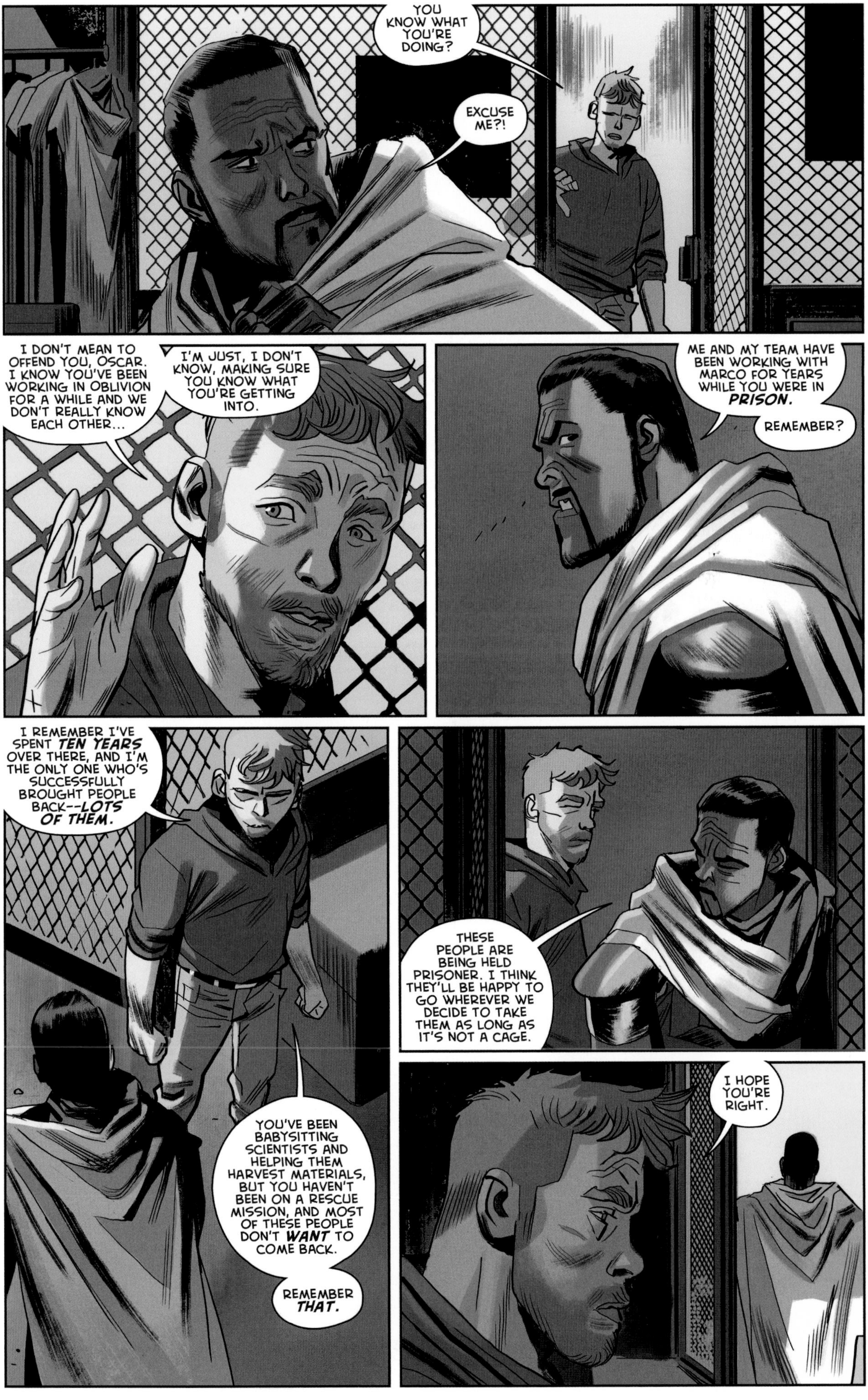
YOU KNOW WHAT YOU'RE DOING?
EXCUSE ME?!
I DON'T MEAN TO OFFEND YOU, OSCAR. I KNOW YOU'VE BEEN WORKING IN OBLIVION FOR A WHILE AND WE DON'T REALLY KNOW EACH OTHER...
I'M JUST, I DON'T KNOW, MAKING SURE YOU KNOW WHAT YOU'RE GETTING INTO.
ME AND MY TEAM HAVE BEEN WORKING WITH MARCO FOR YEARS WHILE YOU WERE IN PRISON.
REMEMBER?
I REMEMBER I'VE SPENT TEN YEARS OVER THERE, AND I'M THE ONLY ONE WHO'S SUCCESSFULLY BROUGHT PEOPLE BACK--LOTS OF THEM.
YOU'VE BEEN BABYSITTING SCIENTISTS AND HELPING THEM HARVEST MATERIALS, BUT YOU HAVEN'T BEEN ON A RESCUE MISSION, AND MOST OF THESE PEOPLE DON'T WANT TO COME BACK.
REMEMBER THAT.
THESE PEOPLE ARE BEING HELD PRISONER. I THINK THEY'LL BE HAPPY TO GO WHEREVER WE DECIDE TO TAKE THEM AS LONG AS IT'S NOT A CAGE.
I HOPE YOU'RE RIGHT.

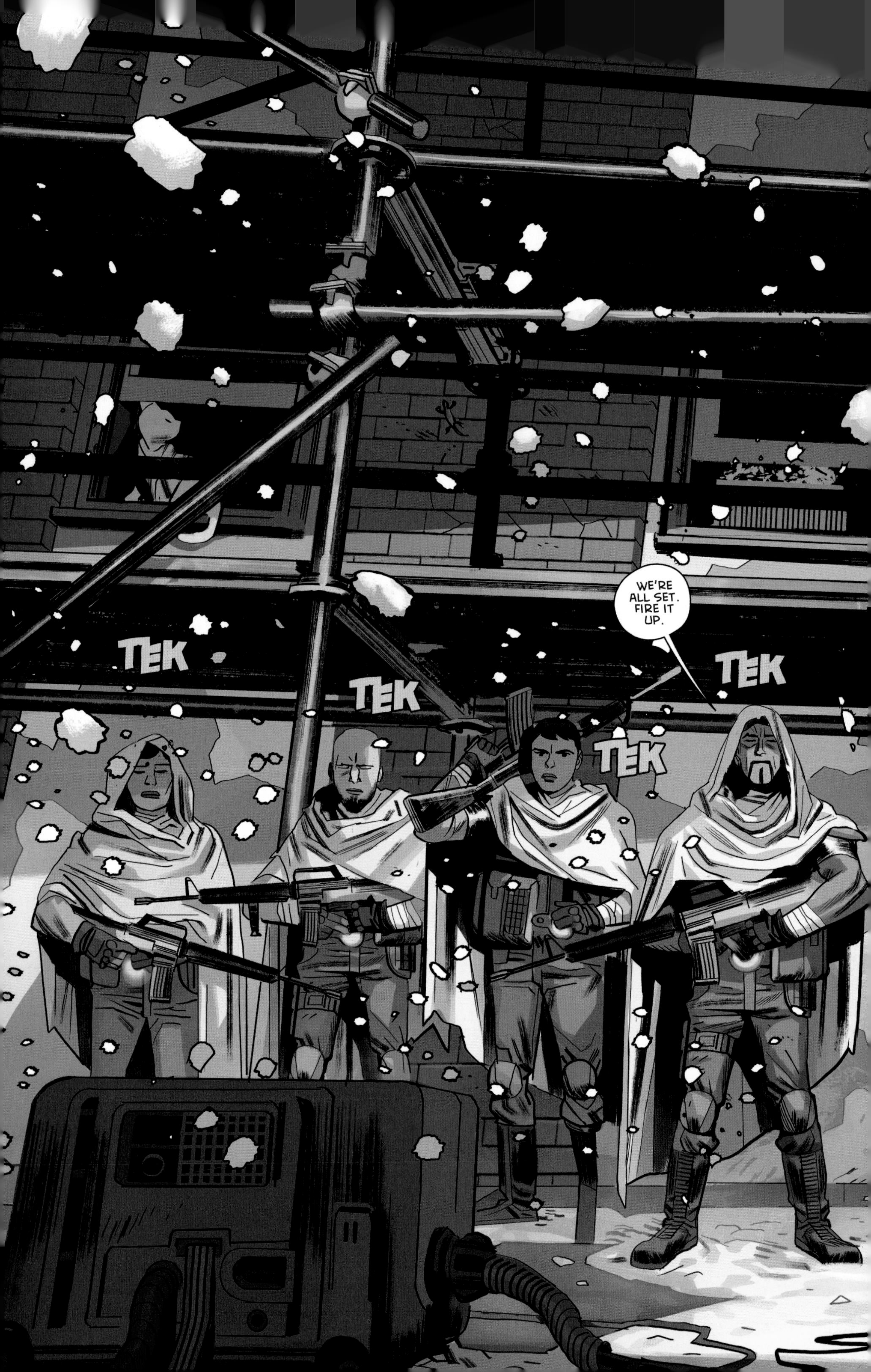

TEK
TEK
WE'RE ALL SET. FIRE IT UP.
TEK
TEK

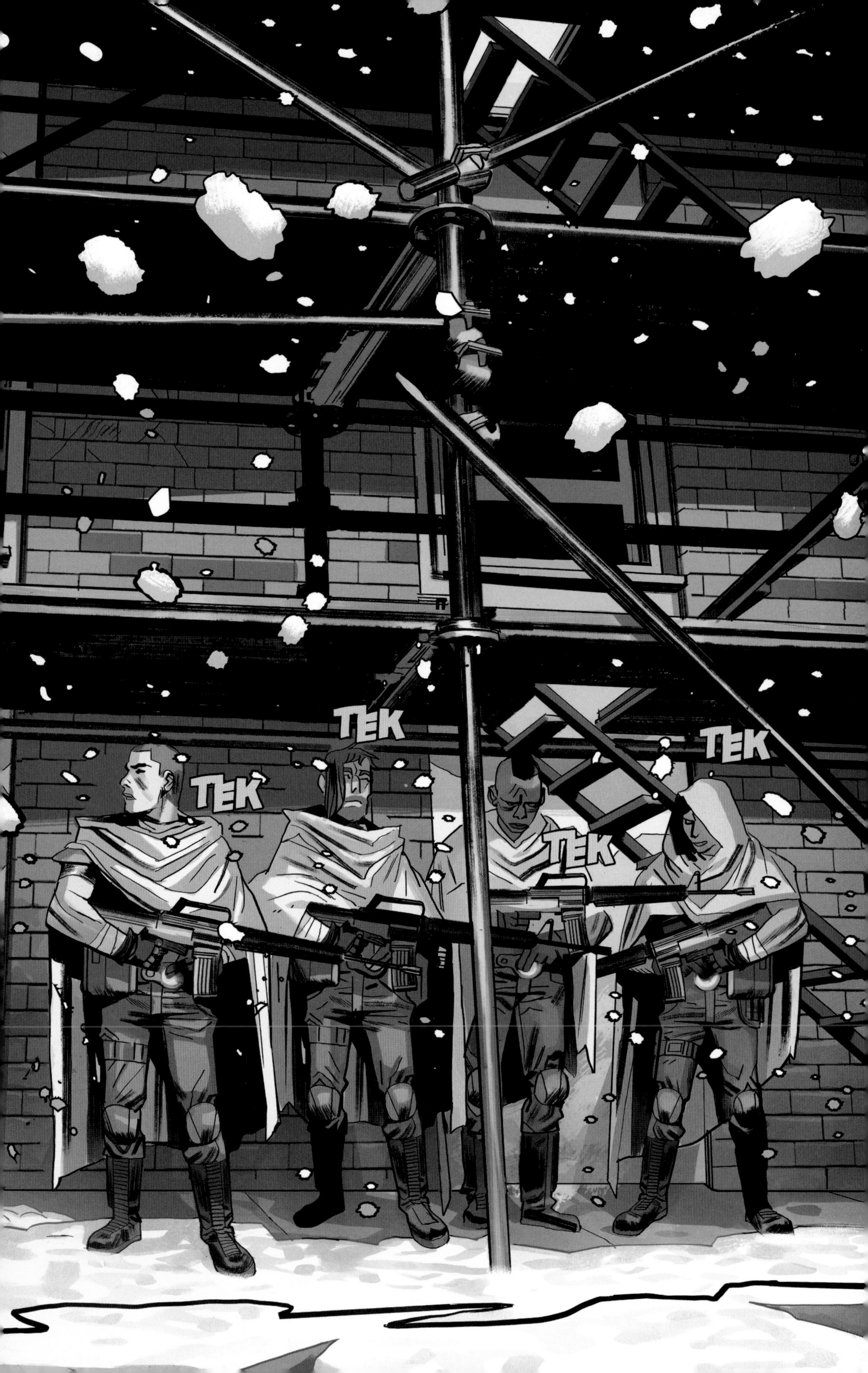
TEK
TEK
TEK
TEK

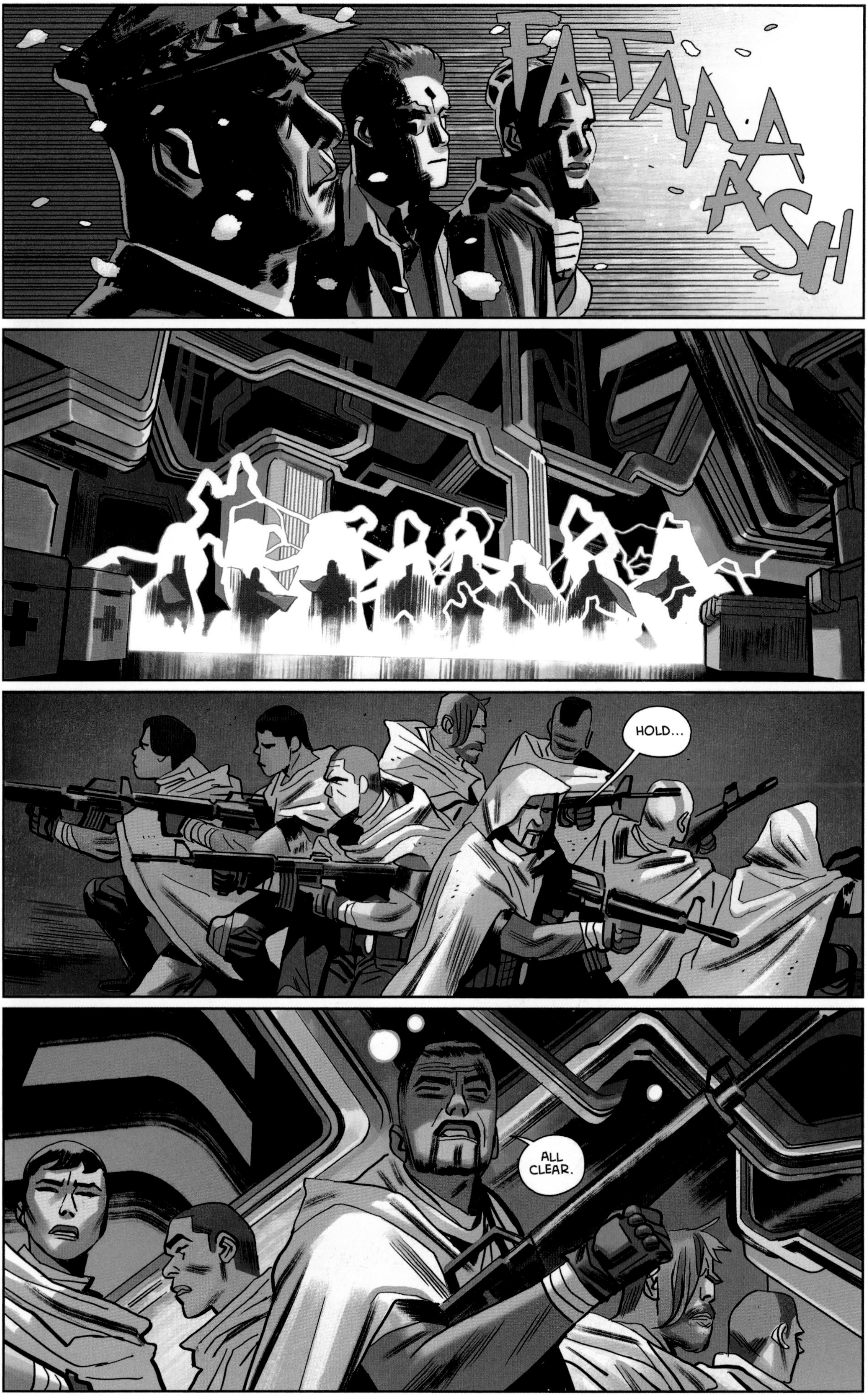
FA-FAAAASH
HOLD...
ALL CLEAR.

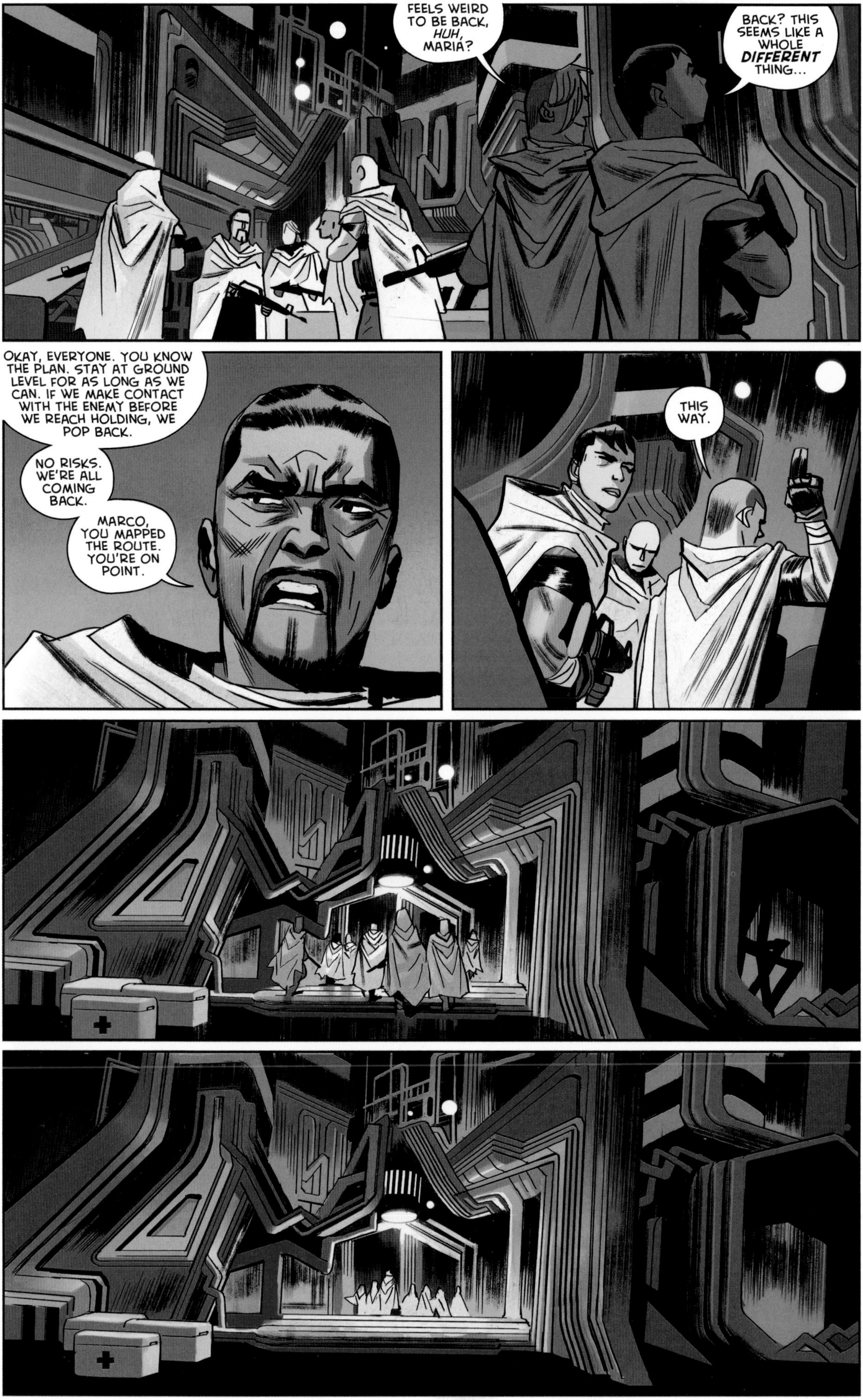
FEELS WEIRD TO BE BACK, *HUH*, MARIA?
BACK? THIS SEEMS LIKE A WHOLE ***DIFFERENT*** THING...
OKAY, EVERYONE. YOU KNOW THE PLAN. STAY AT GROUND LEVEL FOR AS LONG AS WE CAN. IF WE MAKE CONTACT WITH THE ENEMY BEFORE WE REACH HOLDING, WE POP BACK.
NO RISKS. WE'RE ALL COMING BACK.
MARCO, YOU MAPPED THE ROUTE. YOU'RE ON POINT.
THIS WAY.

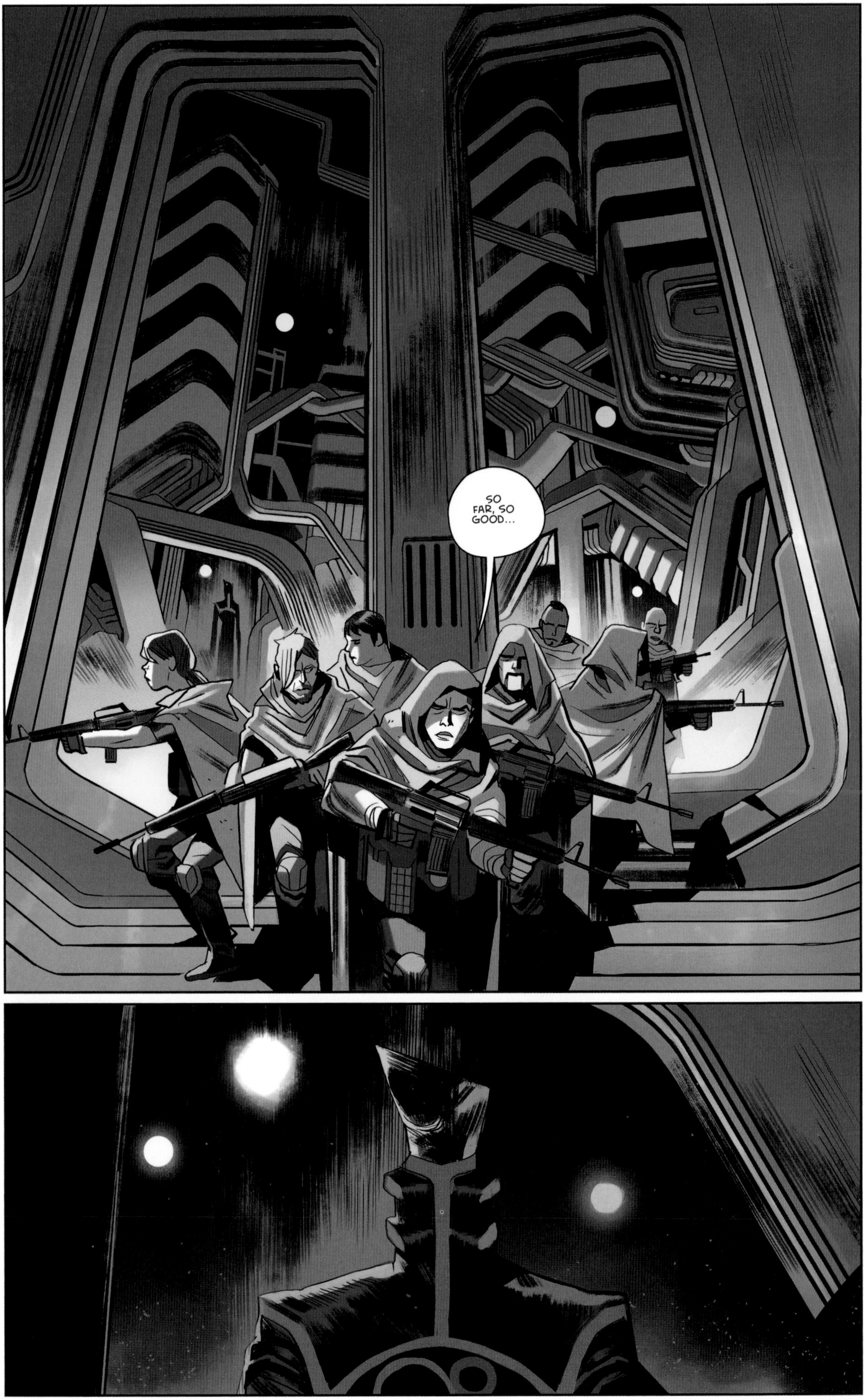
SO FAR, SO GOOD...

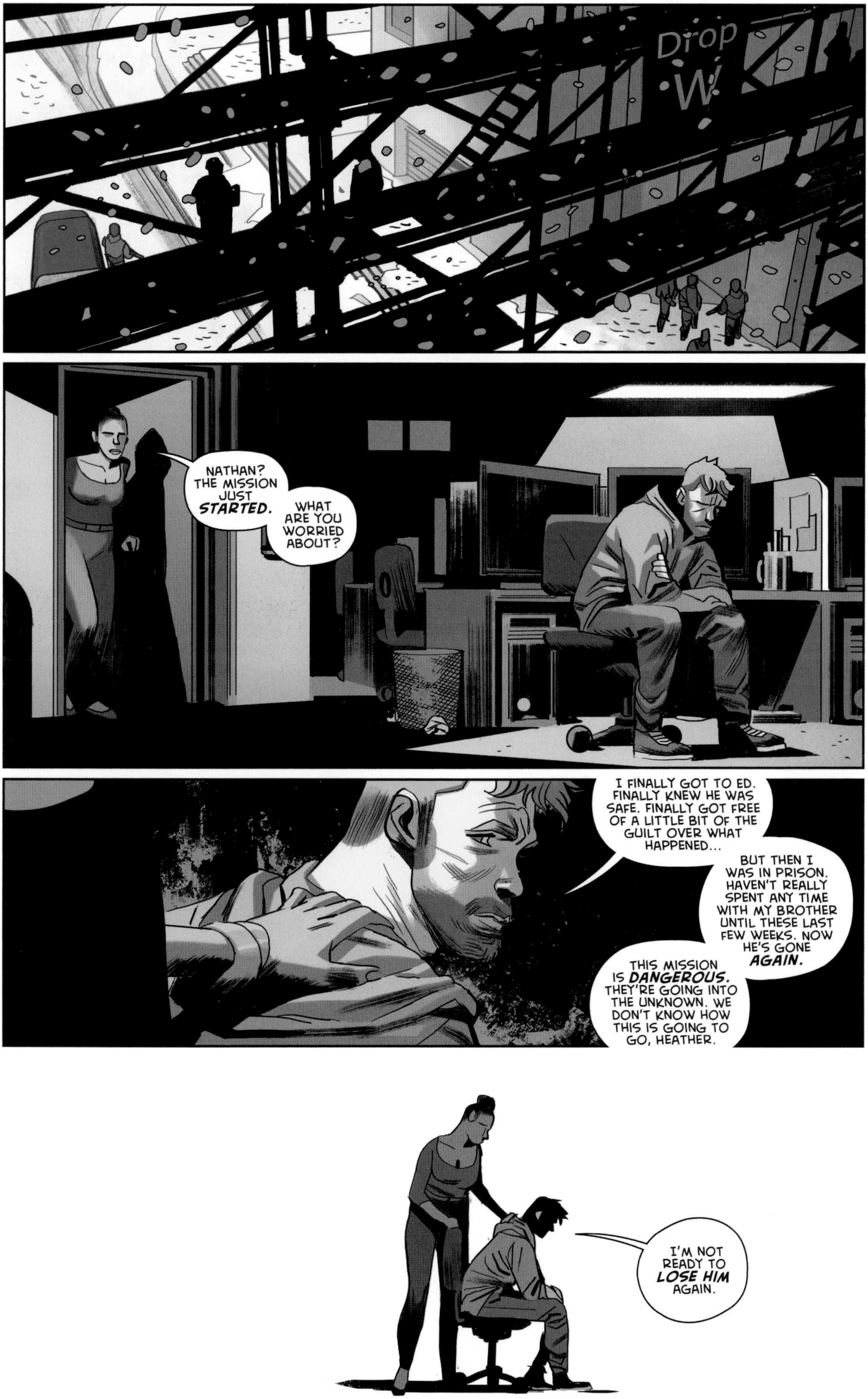
Drop
W
NATHAN? THE MISSION JUST **STARTED.**
WHAT ARE YOU WORRIED ABOUT?
I FINALLY GOT TO ED. FINALLY KNEW HE WAS SAFE. FINALLY GOT FREE OF A LITTLE BIT OF THE GUILT OVER WHAT HAPPENED...
BUT THEN I WAS IN PRISON. HAVEN'T REALLY SPENT ANY TIME WITH MY BROTHER UNTIL THESE LAST FEW WEEKS. NOW HE'S GONE **AGAIN.**
THIS MISSION IS **DANGEROUS.** THEY'RE GOING INTO THE UNKNOWN. WE DON'T KNOW HOW THIS IS GOING TO GO, HEATHER.
I'M NOT READY TO **LOSE HIM** AGAIN.

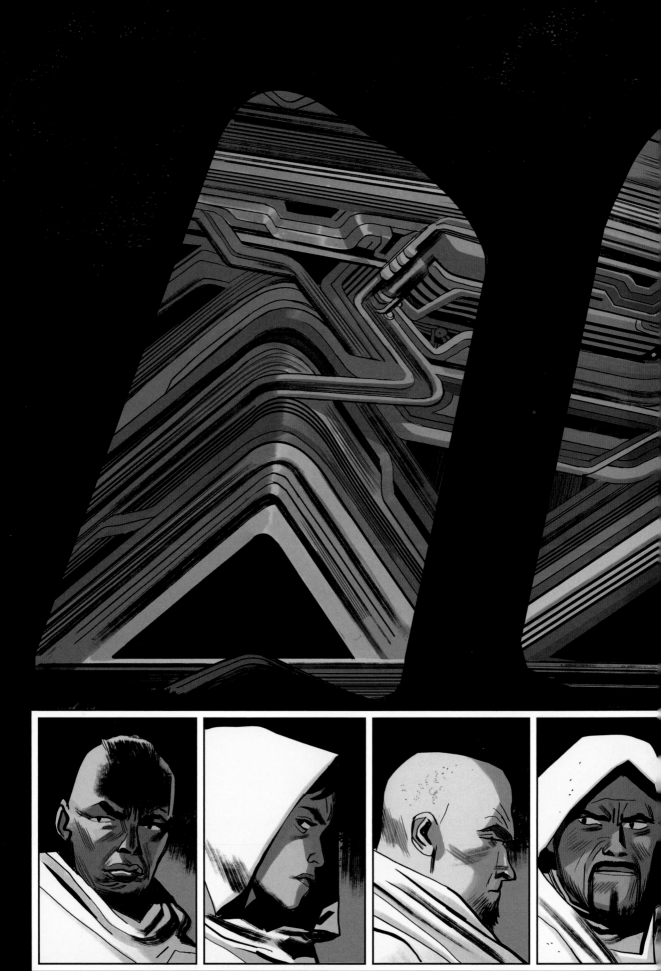

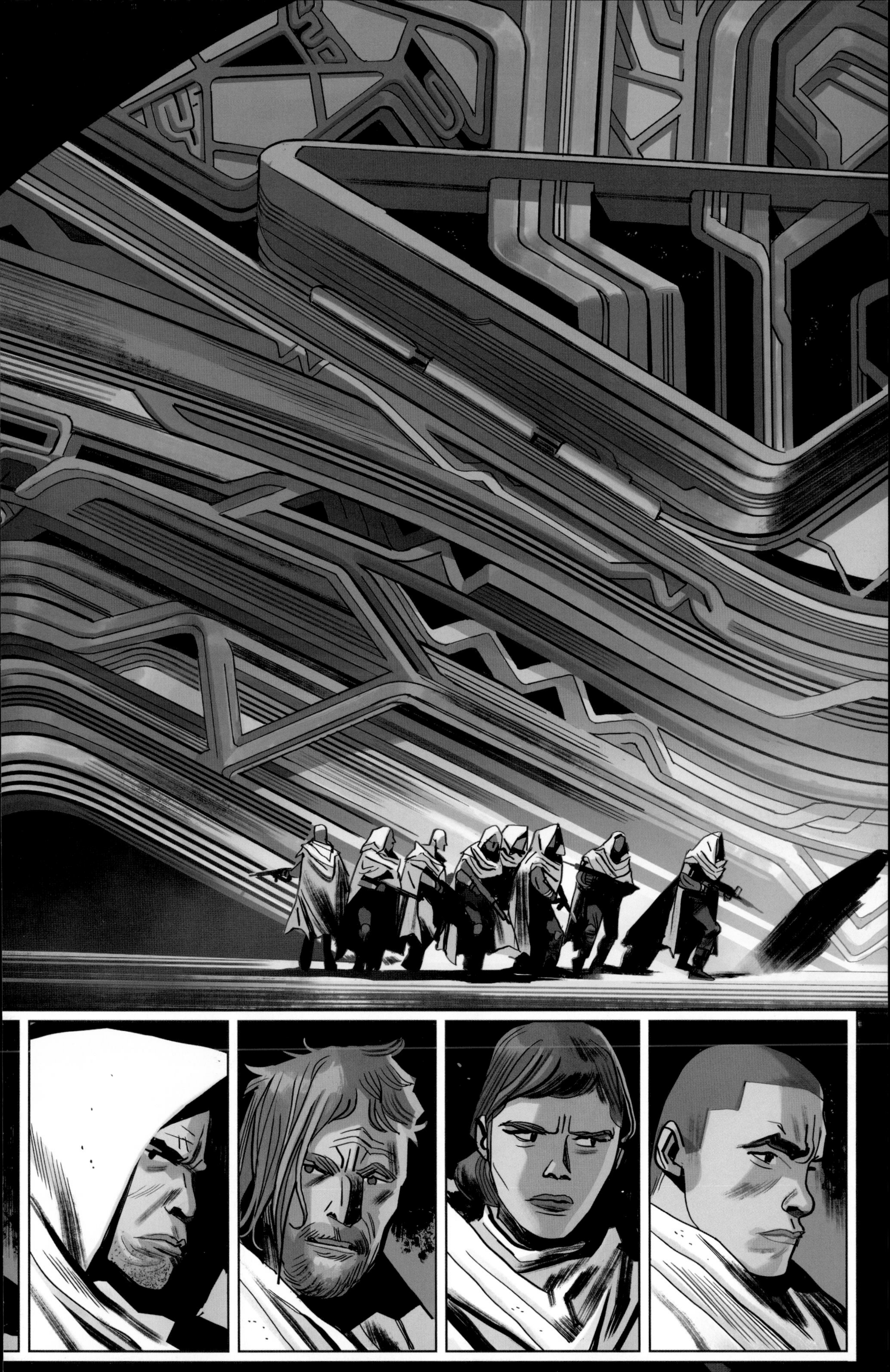

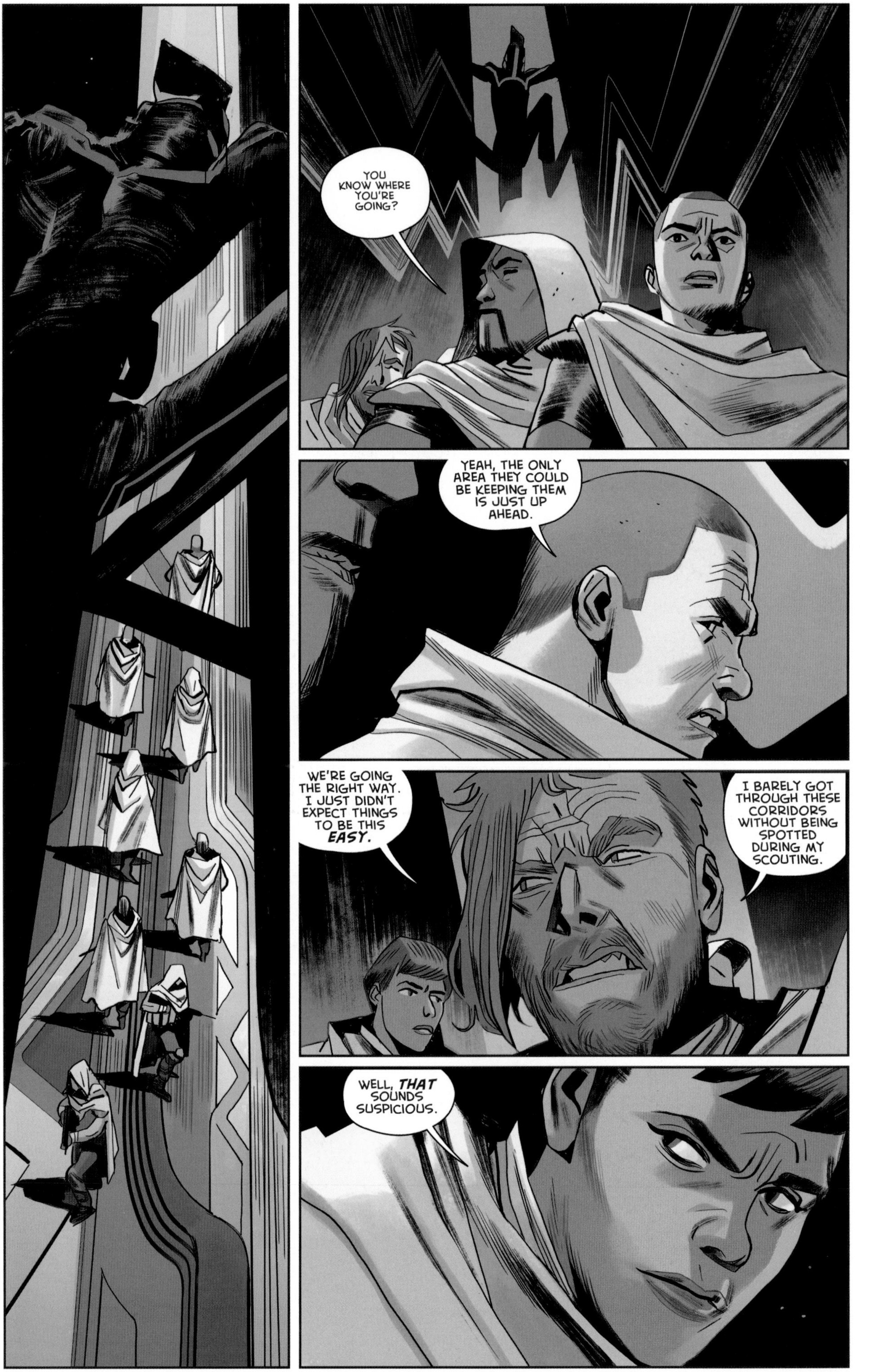
YOU KNOW WHERE YOU'RE GOING?
YEAH, THE ONLY AREA THEY COULD BE KEEPING THEM IS JUST UP AHEAD.
WE'RE GOING THE RIGHT WAY. I JUST DIDN'T EXPECT THINGS TO BE THIS *EASY.*
I BARELY GOT THROUGH THESE CORRIDORS WITHOUT BEING SPOTTED DURING MY SCOUTING.
WELL, *THAT* SOUNDS SUSPICIOUS.

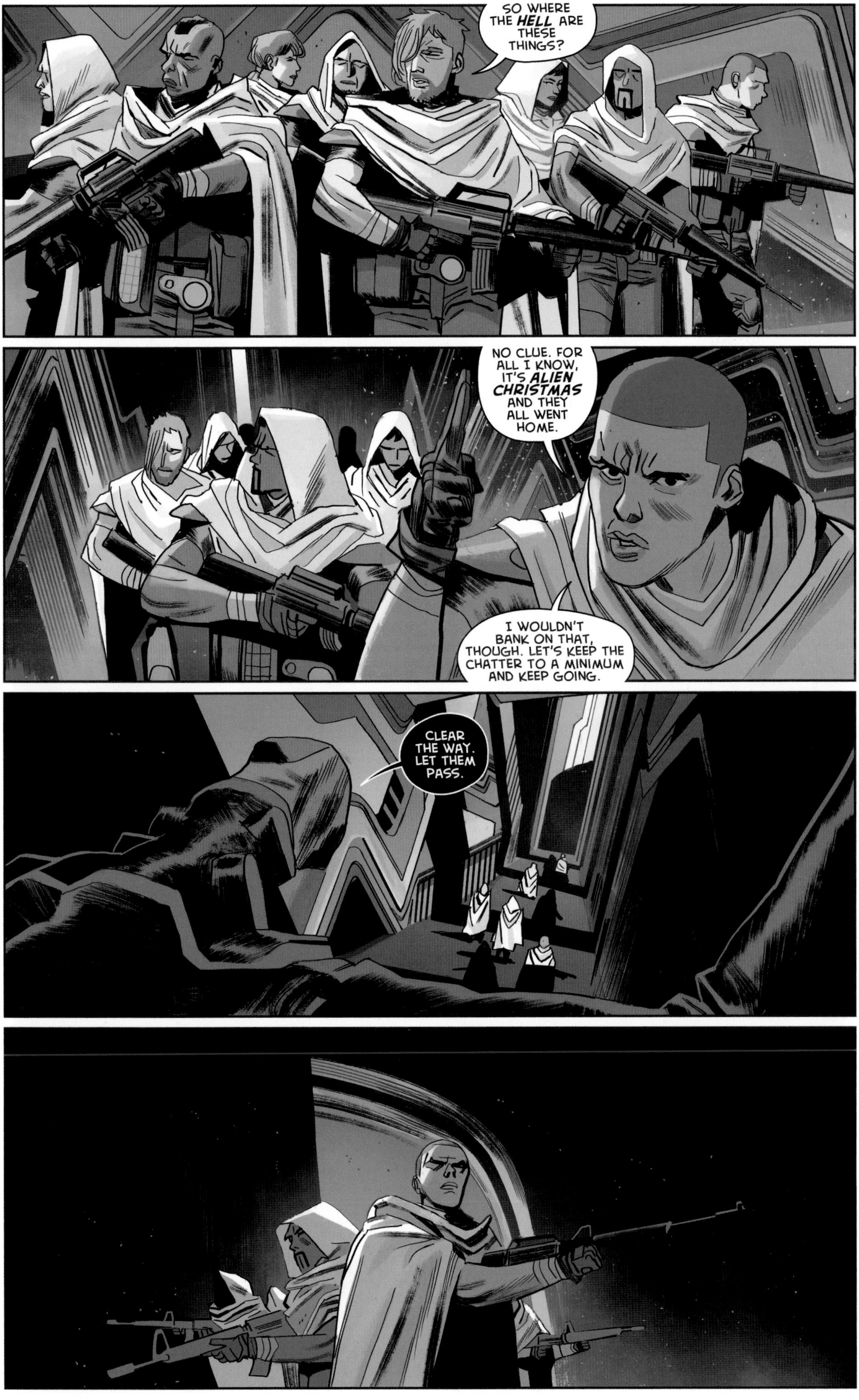
SO WHERE THE HELL ARE THESE THINGS?
NO CLUE. FOR ALL I KNOW, IT'S ALIEN CHRISTMAS AND THEY ALL WENT HOME.
I WOULDN'T BANK ON THAT, THOUGH. LET'S KEEP THE CHATTER TO A MINIMUM AND KEEP GOING.
CLEAR THE WAY. LET THEM PASS.

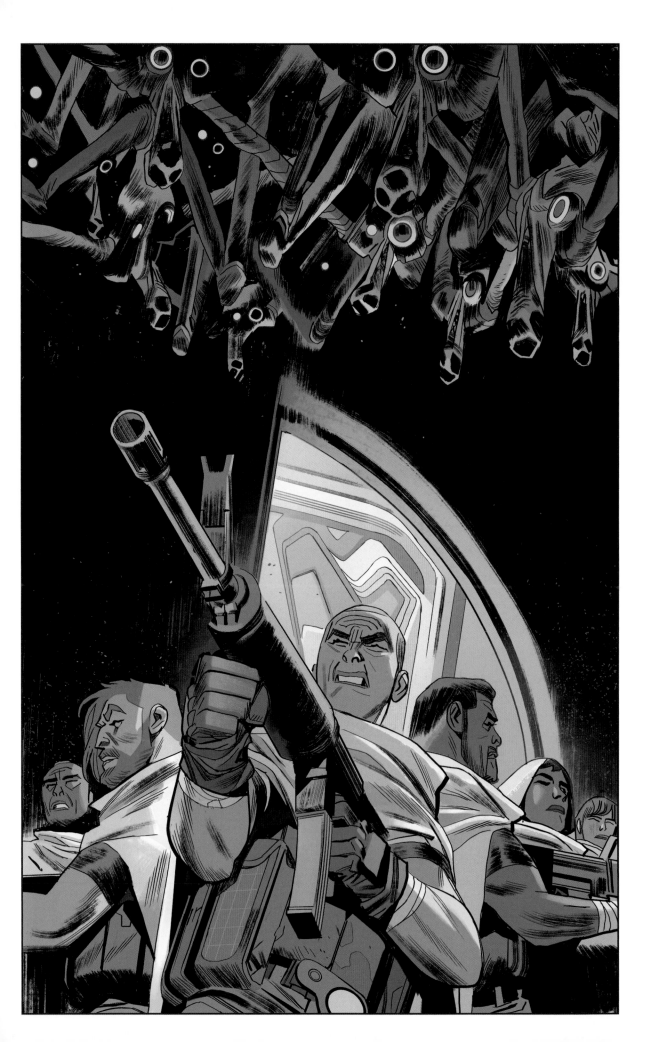

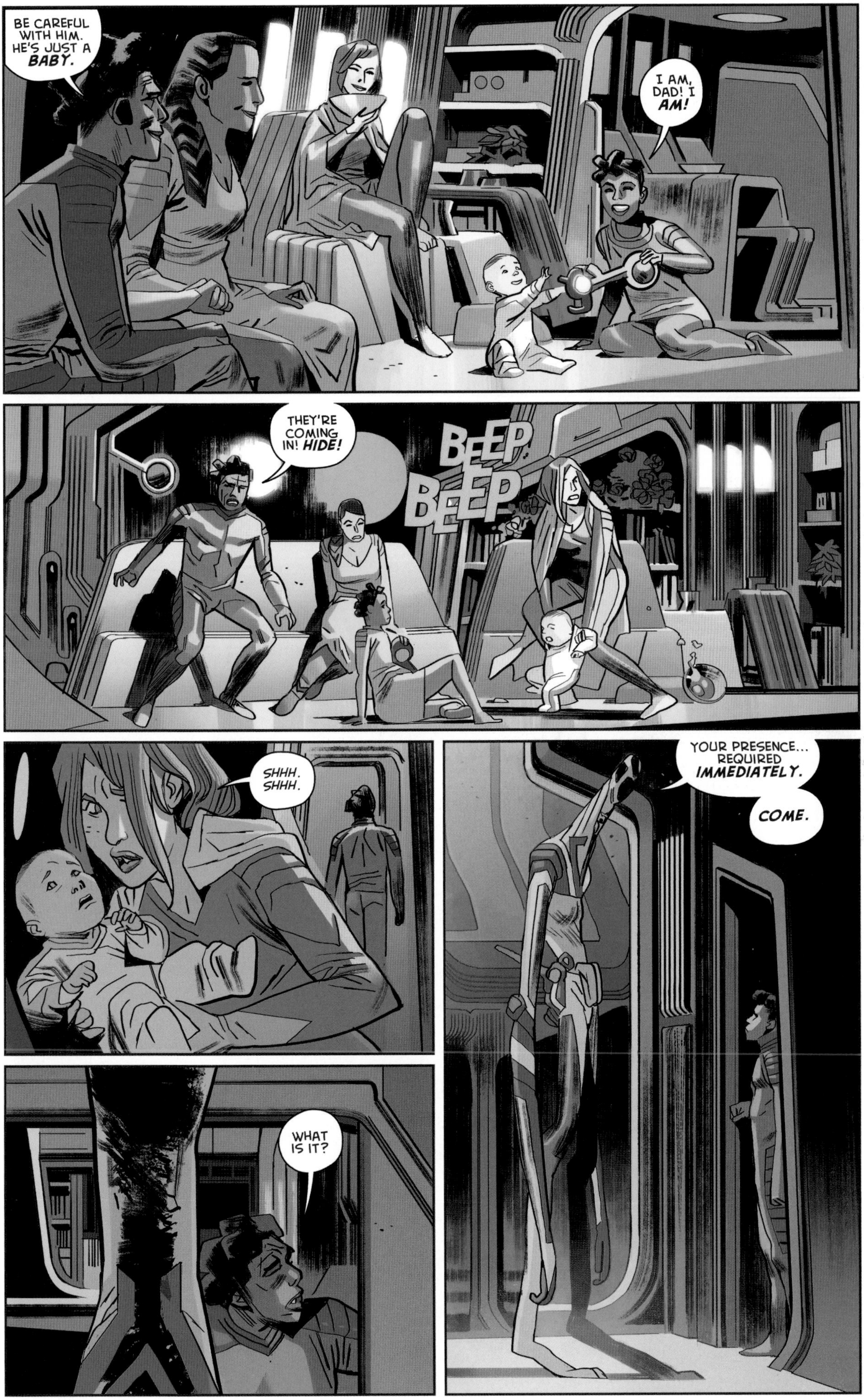
BE CAREFUL WITH HIM. HE'S JUST A BABY.
I AM, DAD! I AM!
THEY'RE COMING IN! HIDE!
BEEP BEEP
SHHH. SHHH.
YOUR PRESENCE... REQUIRED IMMEDIATELY.
COME.
WHAT IS IT?

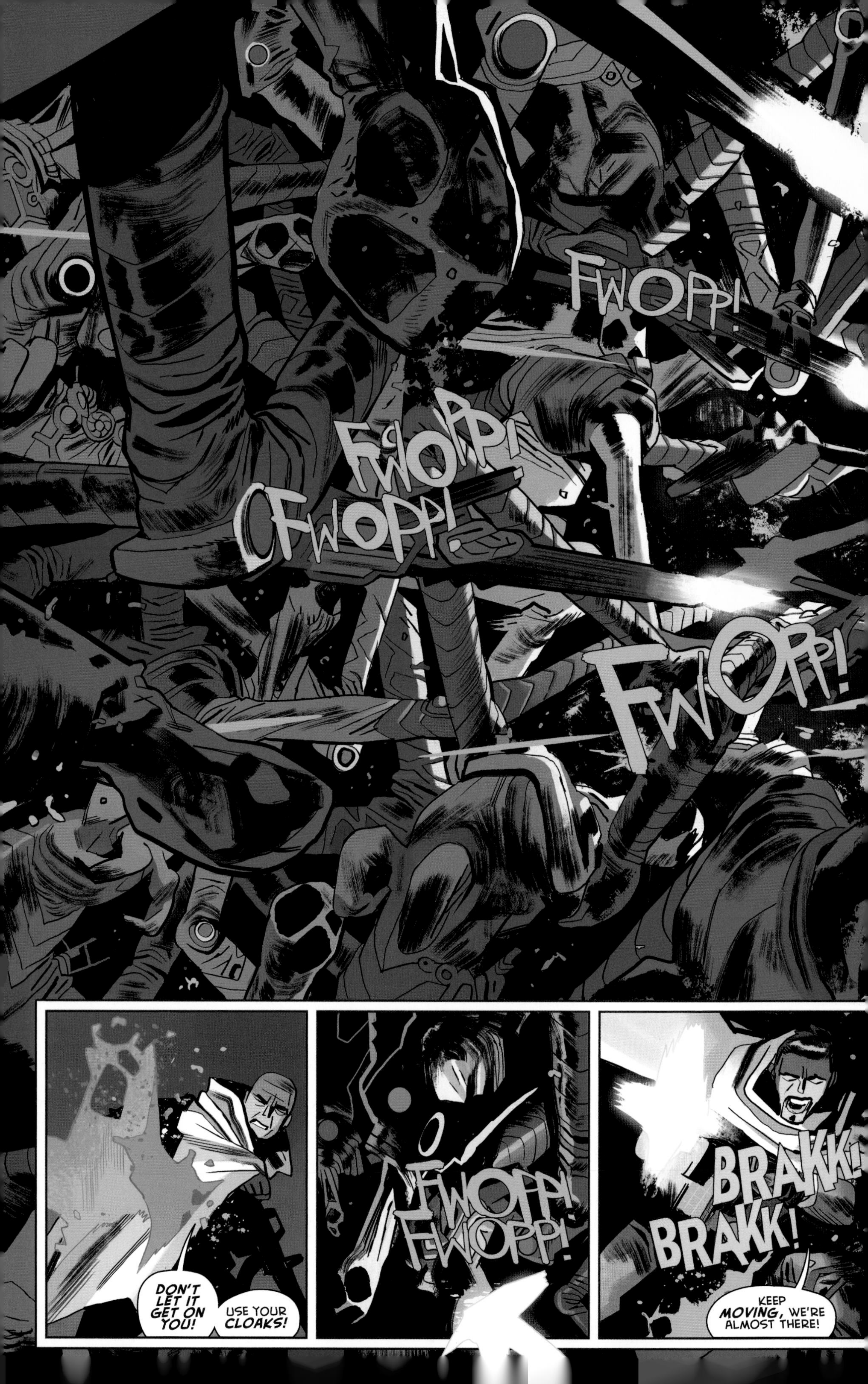
FWOPP!
FWOPP!
FWOPP!
FWOPP!
DON'T LET IT GET ON YOU!
USE YOUR CLOAKS!
FWOPP!
FWOPP!
BRAKK!
BRAKK!
KEEP MOVING, WE'RE ALMOST THERE!

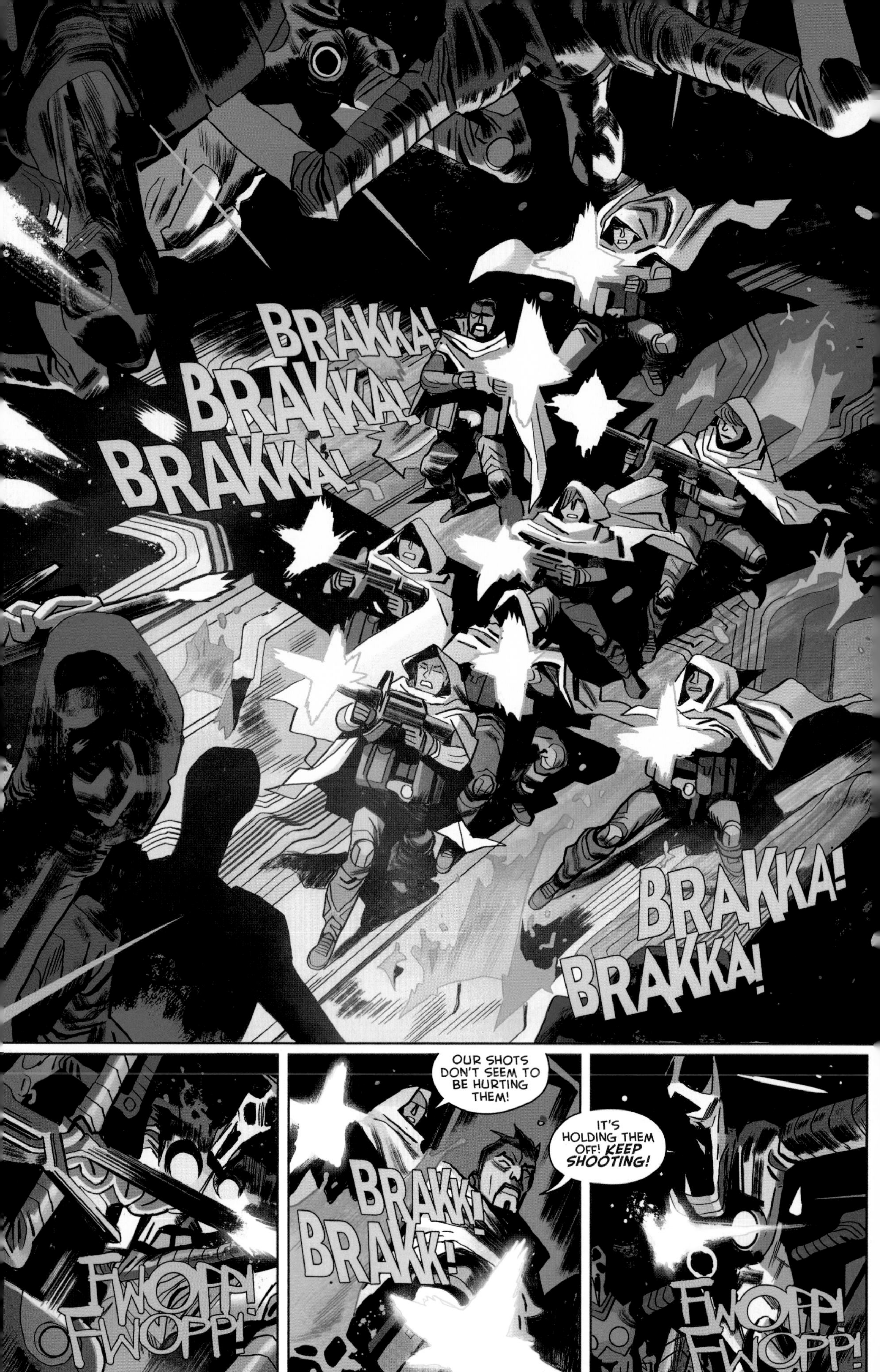
BRAKKA!
BRAKKA!
BRAKKA!
BRAKKA!
BRAKKA!
FWOPP!
FWOPP!
OUR SHOTS DON'T SEEM TO BE HURTING THEM!
BRAKK!
BRAKK!
IT'S HOLDING THEM OFF! *KEEP SHOOTING!*
FWOPP!
FWOPP!

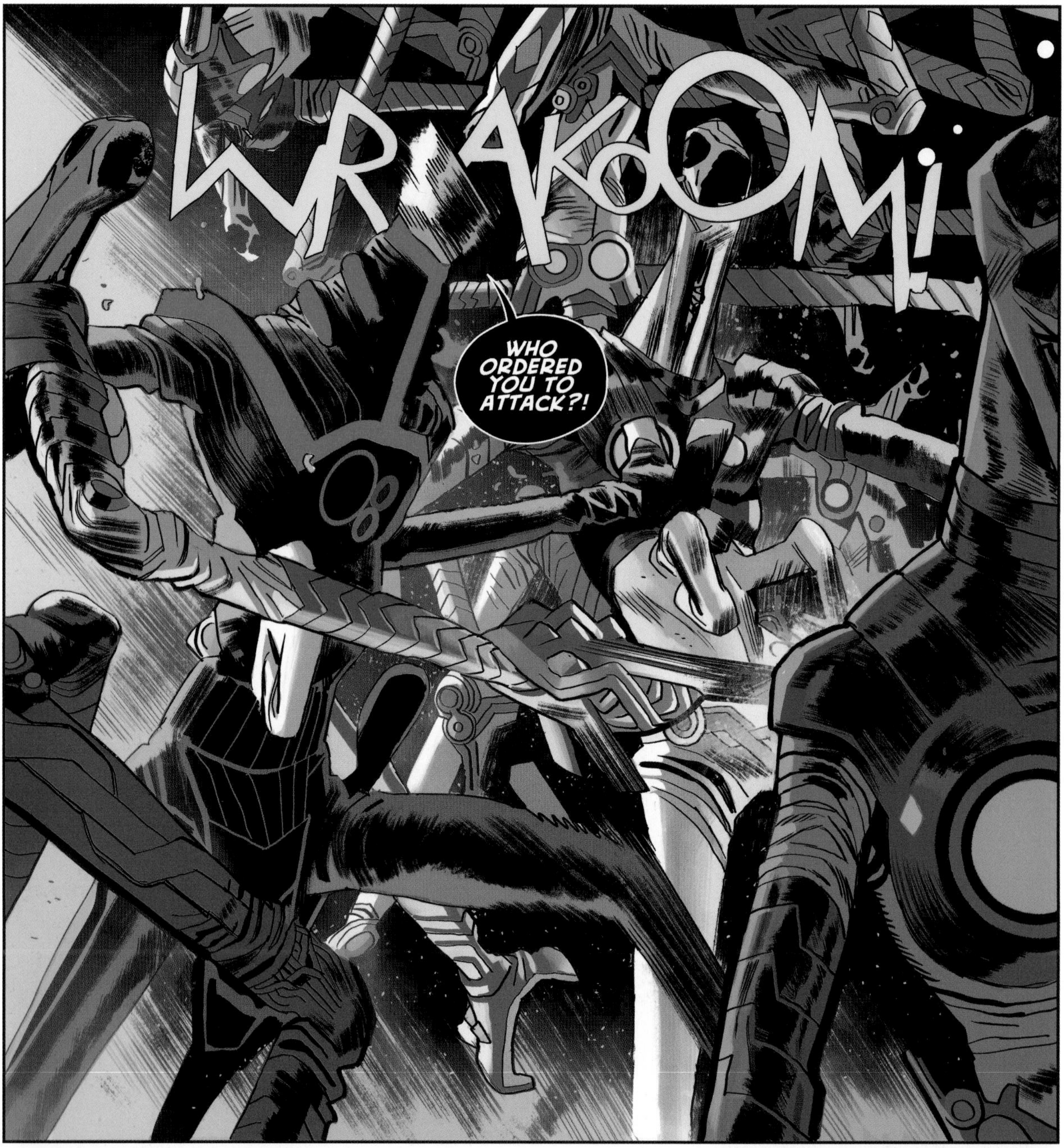
WRAKOOM!
WHO ORDERED YOU TO ATTACK?!

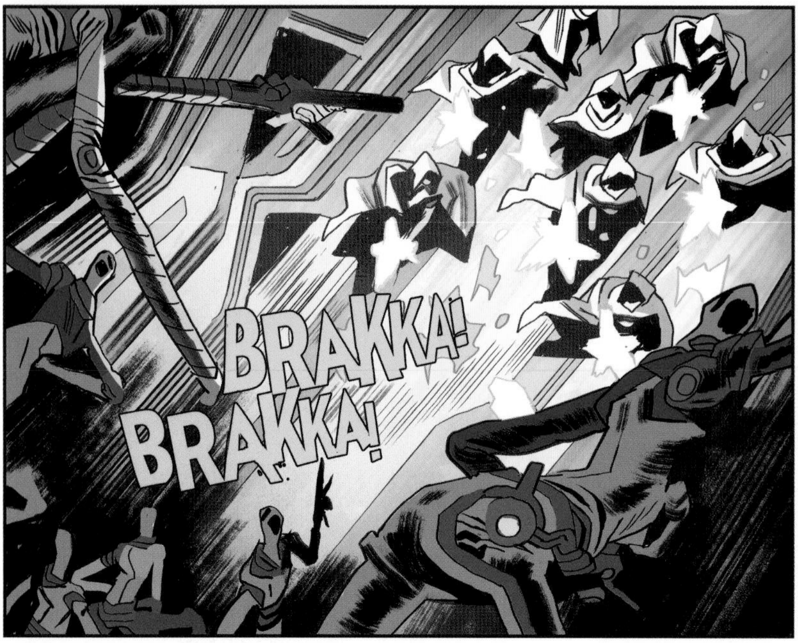
BRAKKA!
BRAKKA!

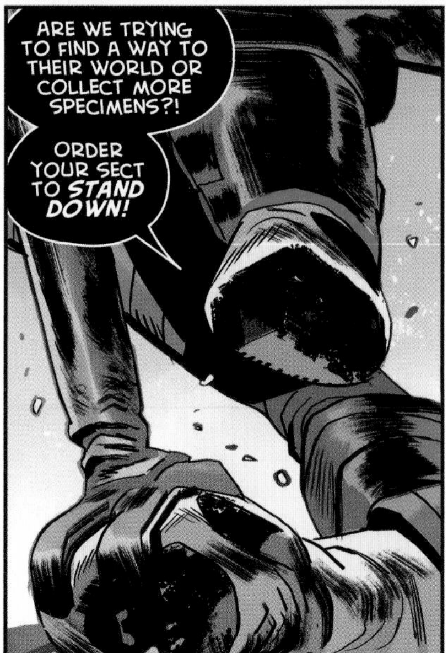
ARE WE TRYING TO FIND A WAY TO THEIR WORLD OR COLLECT MORE SPECIMENS?!
ORDER YOUR SECT TO STAND DOWN!

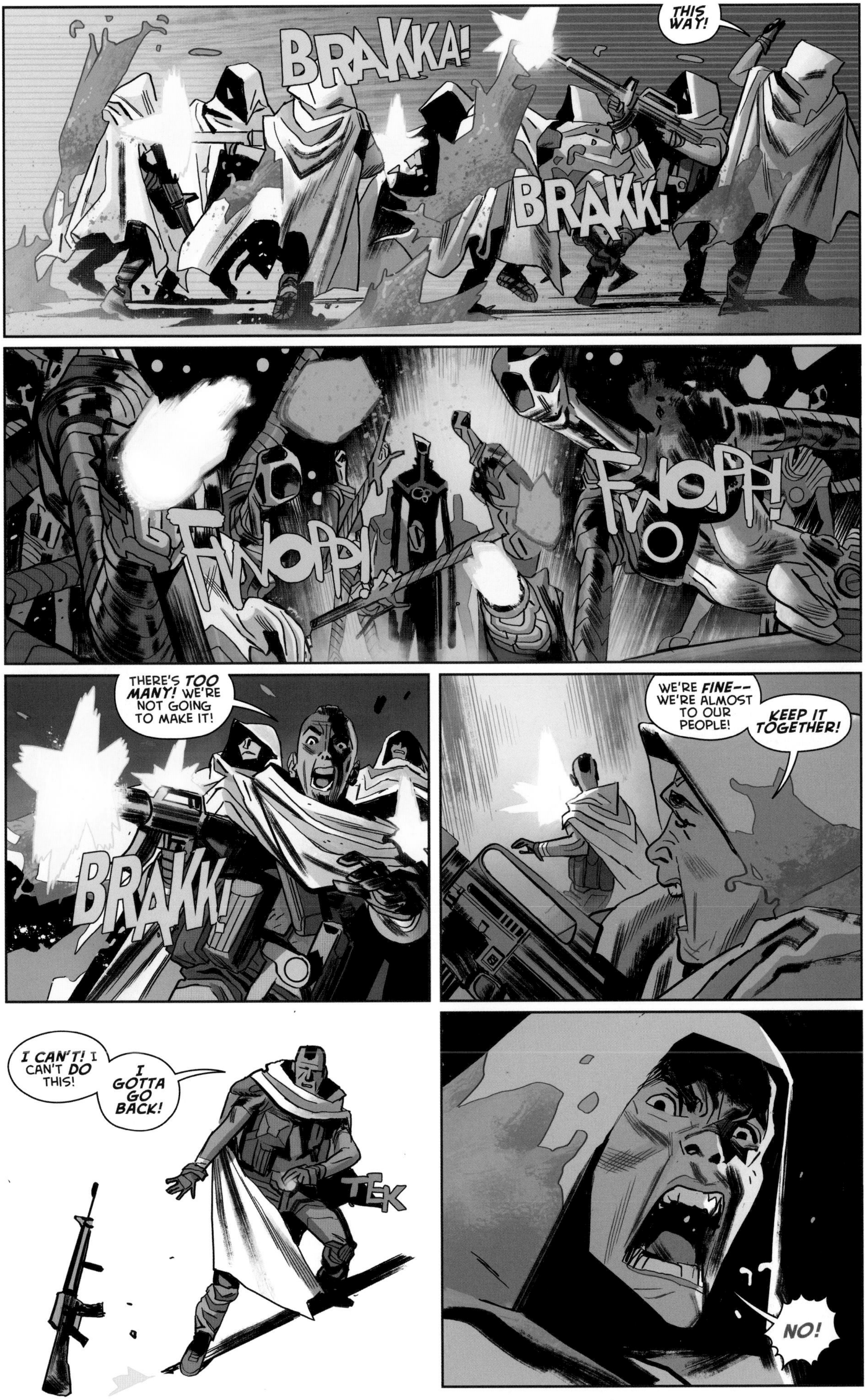
BRAKKA!
THIS WAY!
BRAKK!
FWOPP!
FWOPP!
THERE'S TOO MANY! WE'RE NOT GOING TO MAKE IT!
BRAKK!
WE'RE FINE-- WE'RE ALMOST TO OUR PEOPLE!
KEEP IT TOGETHER!
I CAN'T! I CAN'T DO THIS!
I GOTTA GO BACK!
TEK
NO!

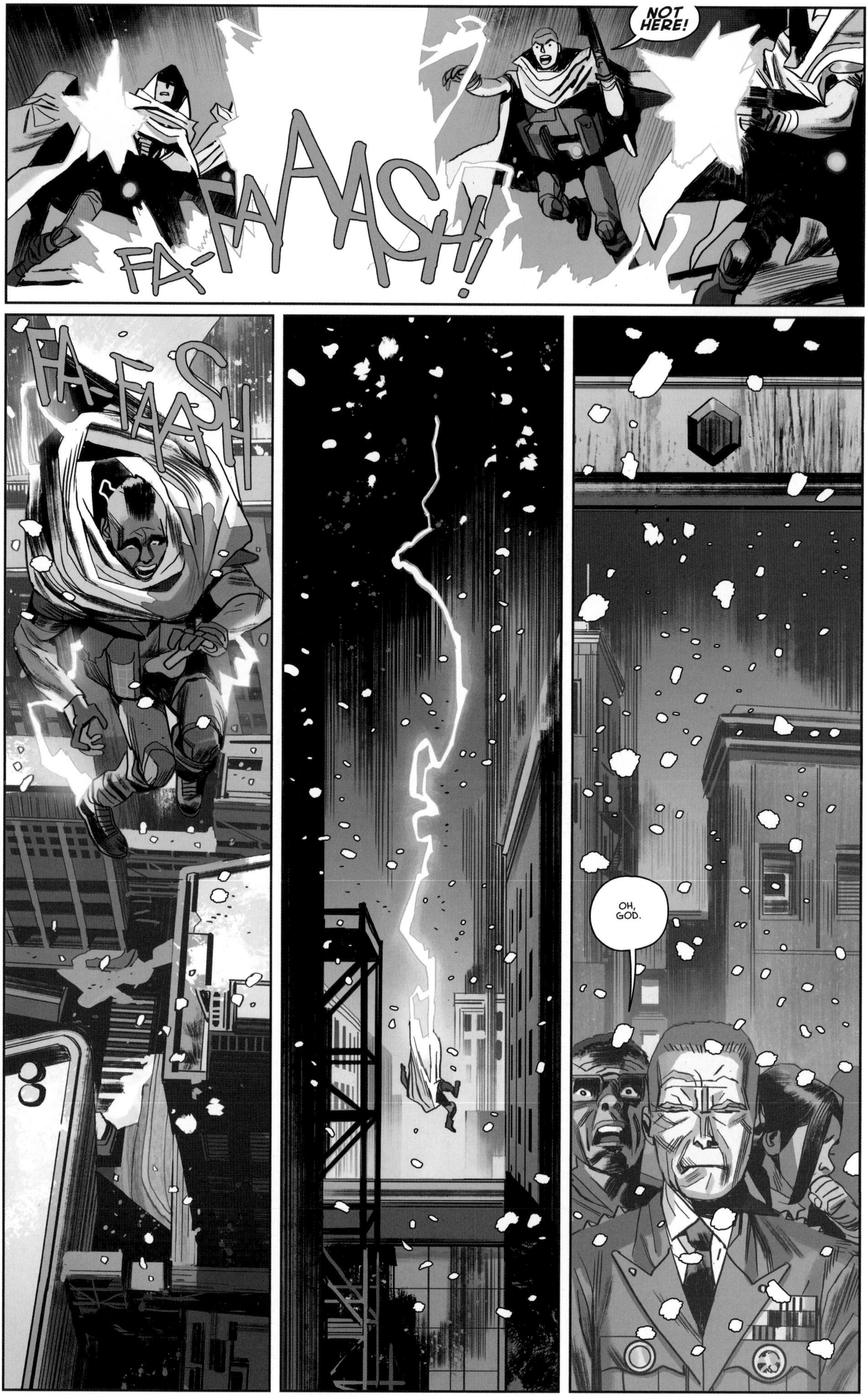
NOT HERE!
FA-FAAASH!!
FA-FAASH
OH, GOD.

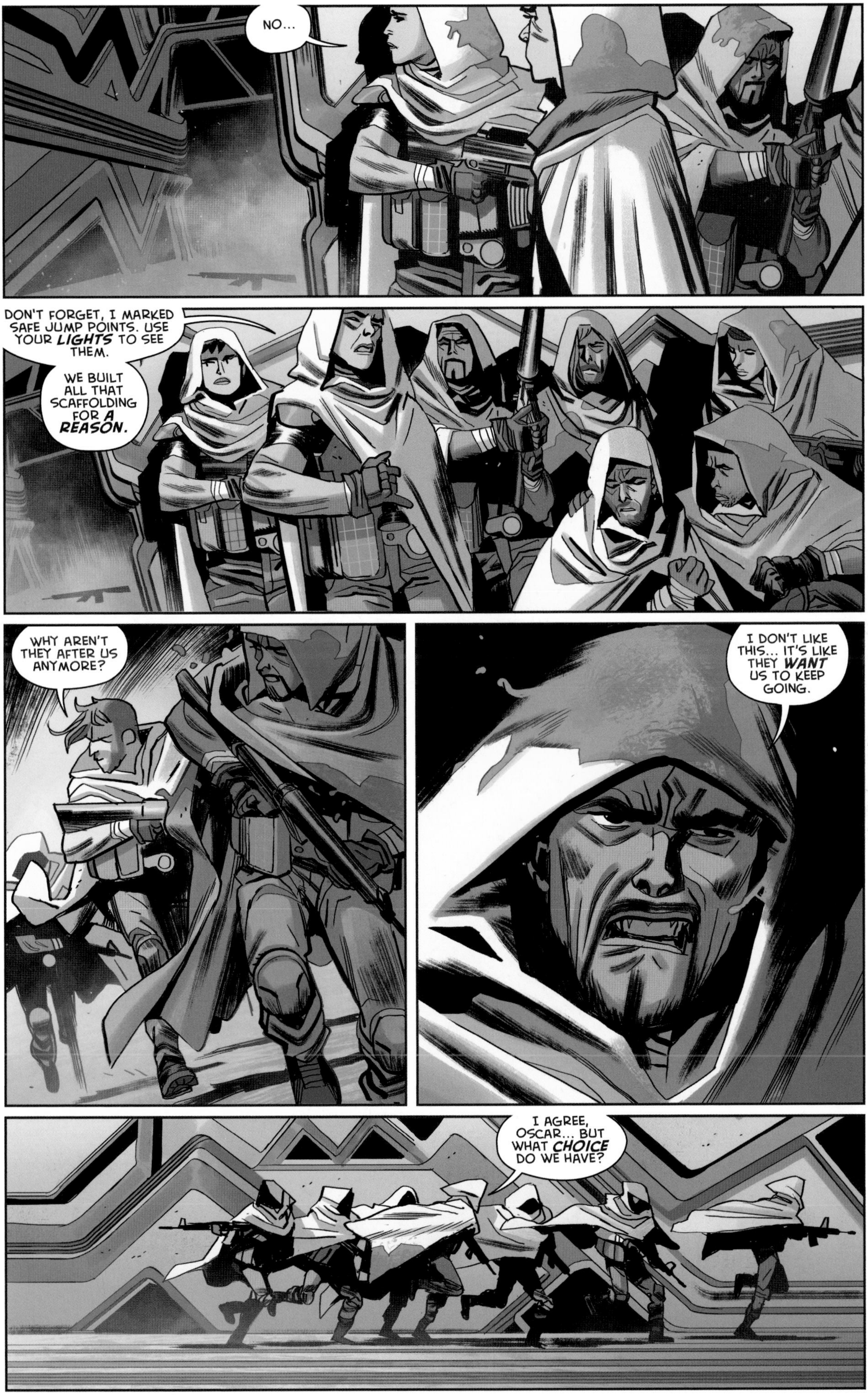
NO...
DON'T FORGET, I MARKED SAFE JUMP POINTS. USE YOUR LIGHTS TO SEE THEM.
WE BUILT ALL THAT SCAFFOLDING FOR A REASON.
WHY AREN'T THEY AFTER US ANYMORE?
I DON'T LIKE THIS... IT'S LIKE THEY WANT US TO KEEP GOING.
I AGREE, OSCAR... BUT WHAT CHOICE DO WE HAVE?

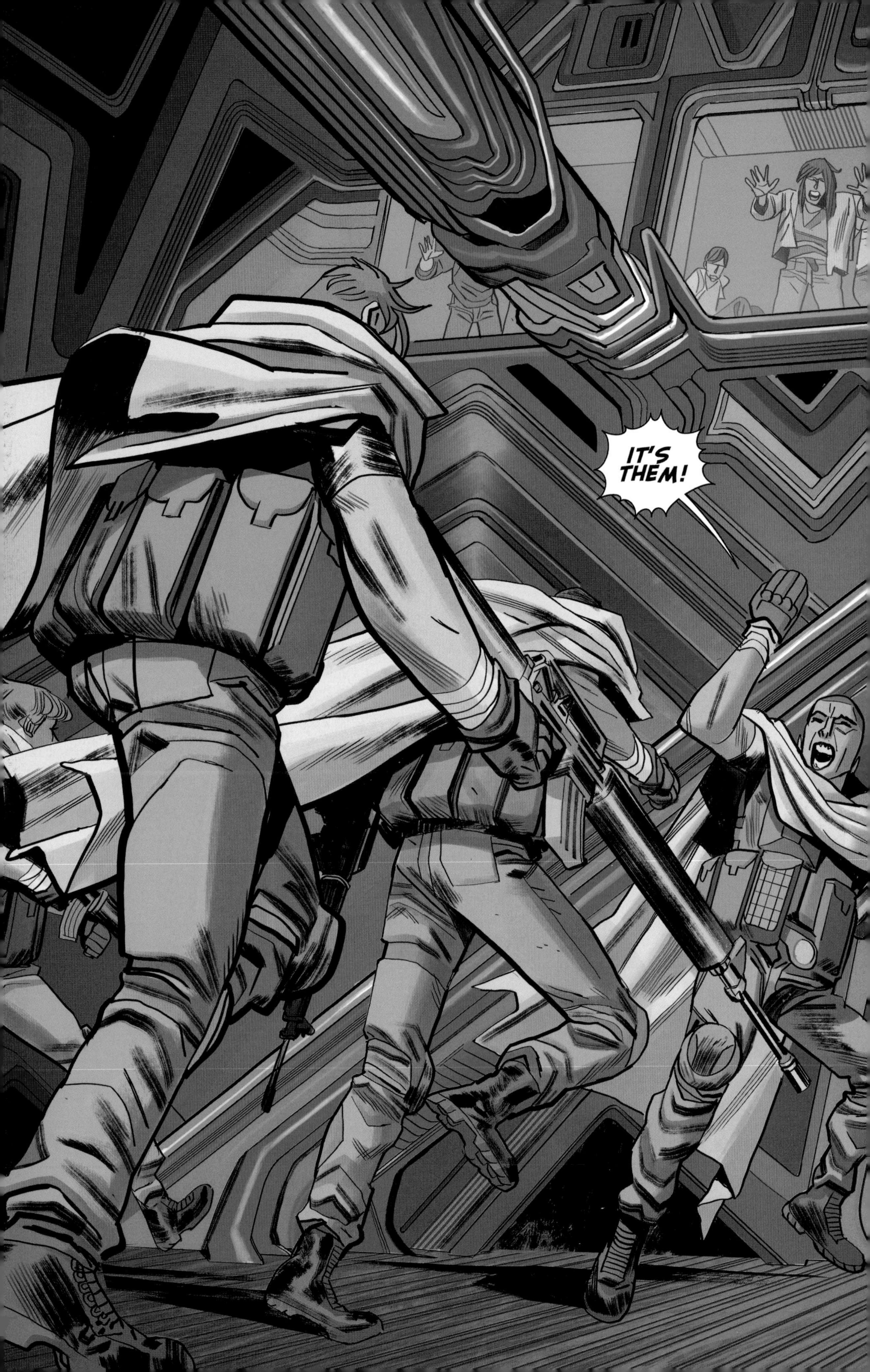
IT'S THEM!

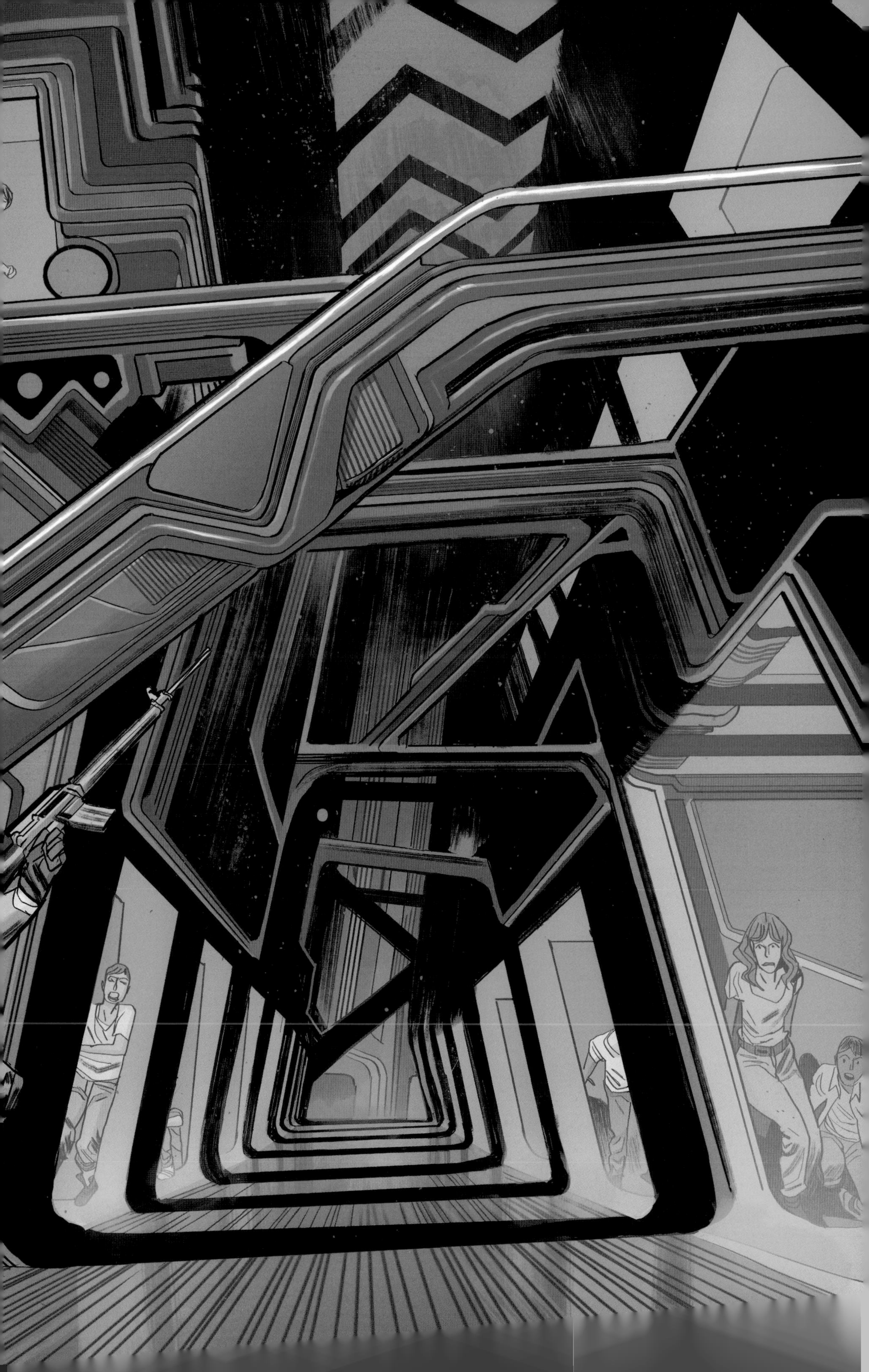

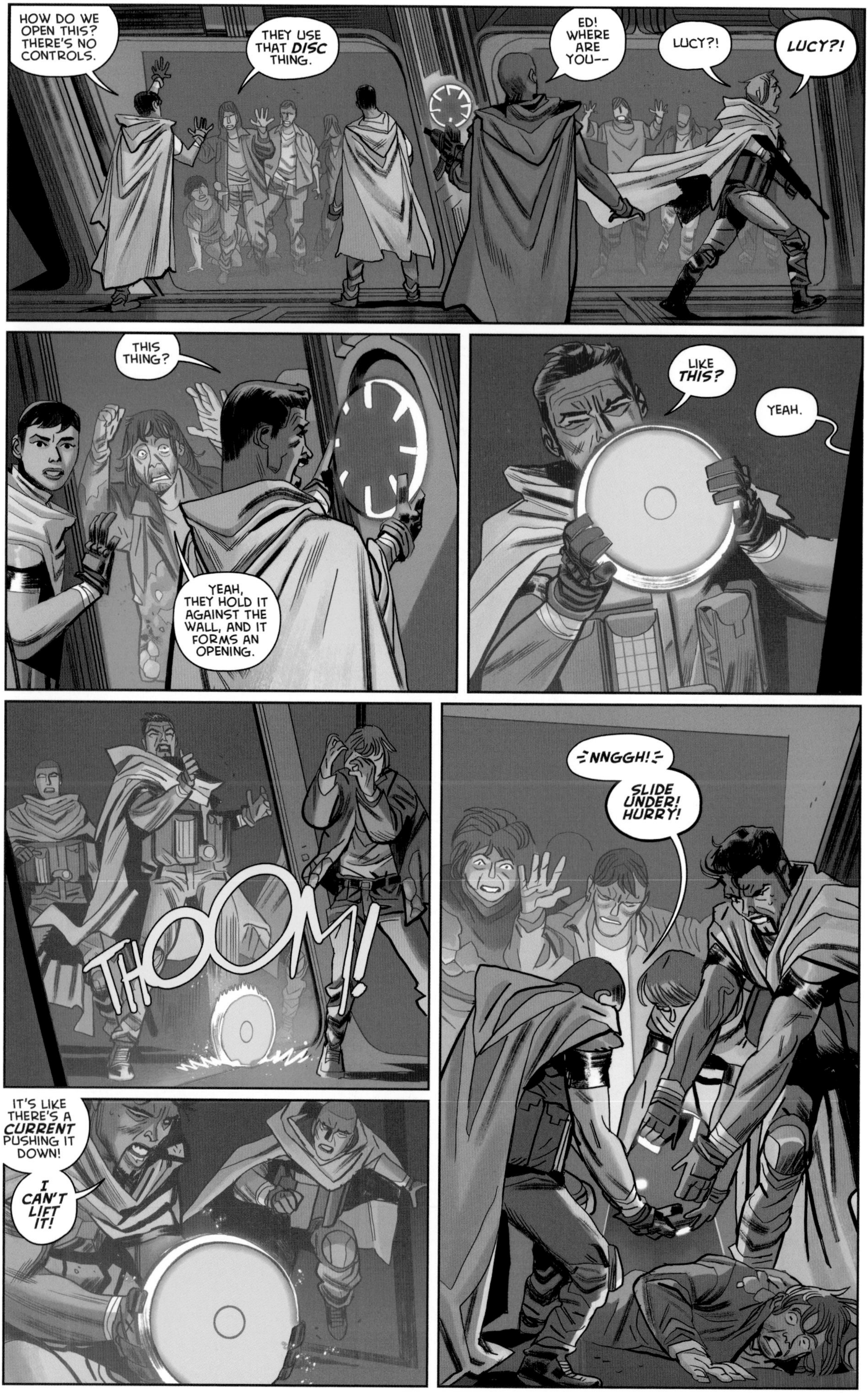
HOW DO WE OPEN THIS? THERE'S NO CONTROLS.
THEY USE THAT DISC THING.
ED! WHERE ARE YOU--
LUCY?!
LUCY?!
THIS THING?
YEAH, THEY HOLD IT AGAINST THE WALL, AND IT FORMS AN OPENING.
LIKE THIS?
YEAH.
THOOM!
IT'S LIKE THERE'S A CURRENT PUSHING IT DOWN!
I CAN'T LIFT IT!
NNGGH!
SLIDE UNDER! HURRY!

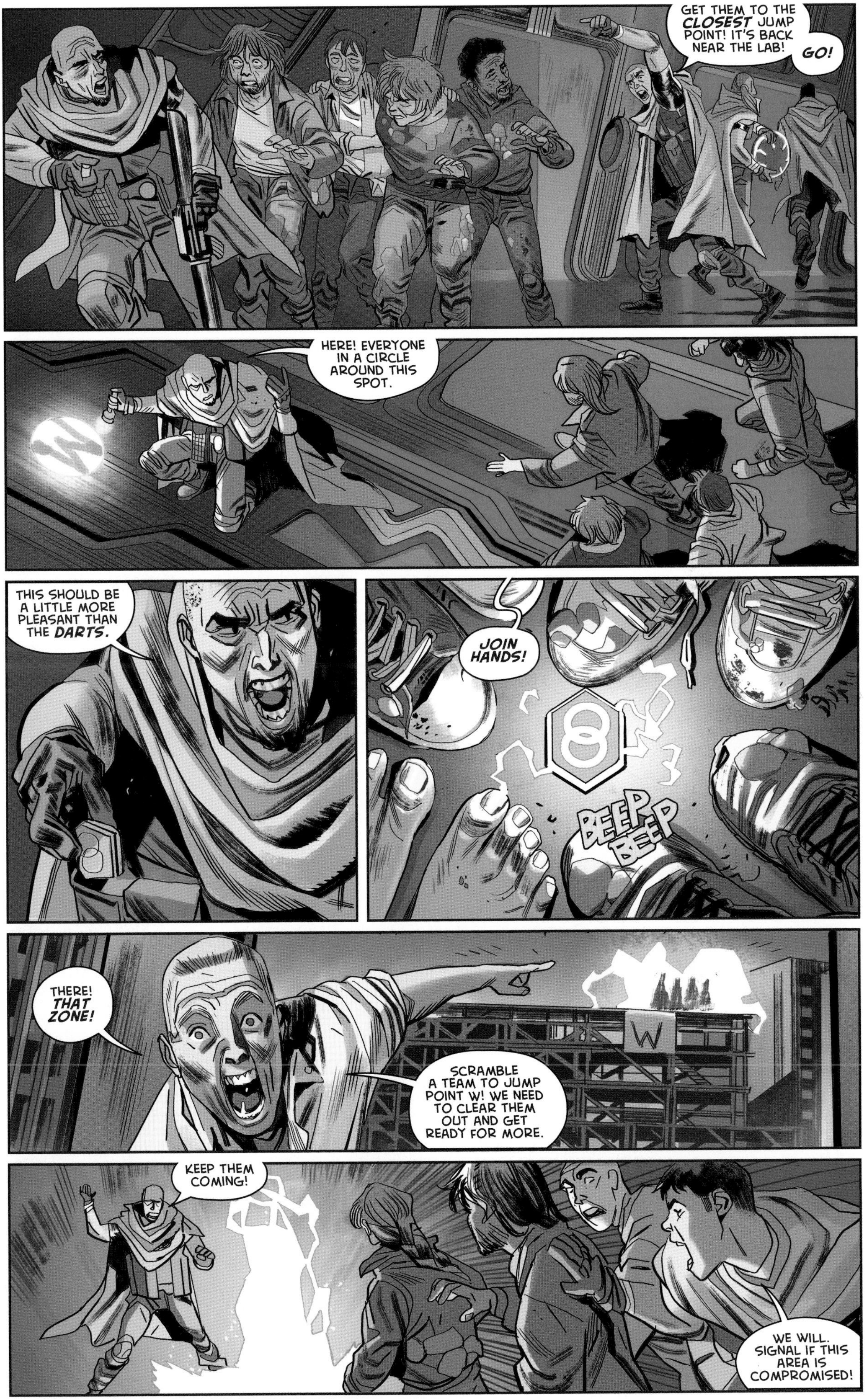
GET THEM TO THE CLOSEST JUMP POINT! IT'S BACK NEAR THE LAB!
GO!
HERE! EVERYONE IN A CIRCLE AROUND THIS SPOT.
THIS SHOULD BE A LITTLE MORE PLEASANT THAN THE DARTS.
JOIN HANDS!
BEEP BEEP
THERE! THAT ZONE!
SCRAMBLE A TEAM TO JUMP POINT W! WE NEED TO CLEAR THEM OUT AND GET READY FOR MORE.
KEEP THEM COMING!
WE WILL. SIGNAL IF THIS AREA IS COMPROMISED!

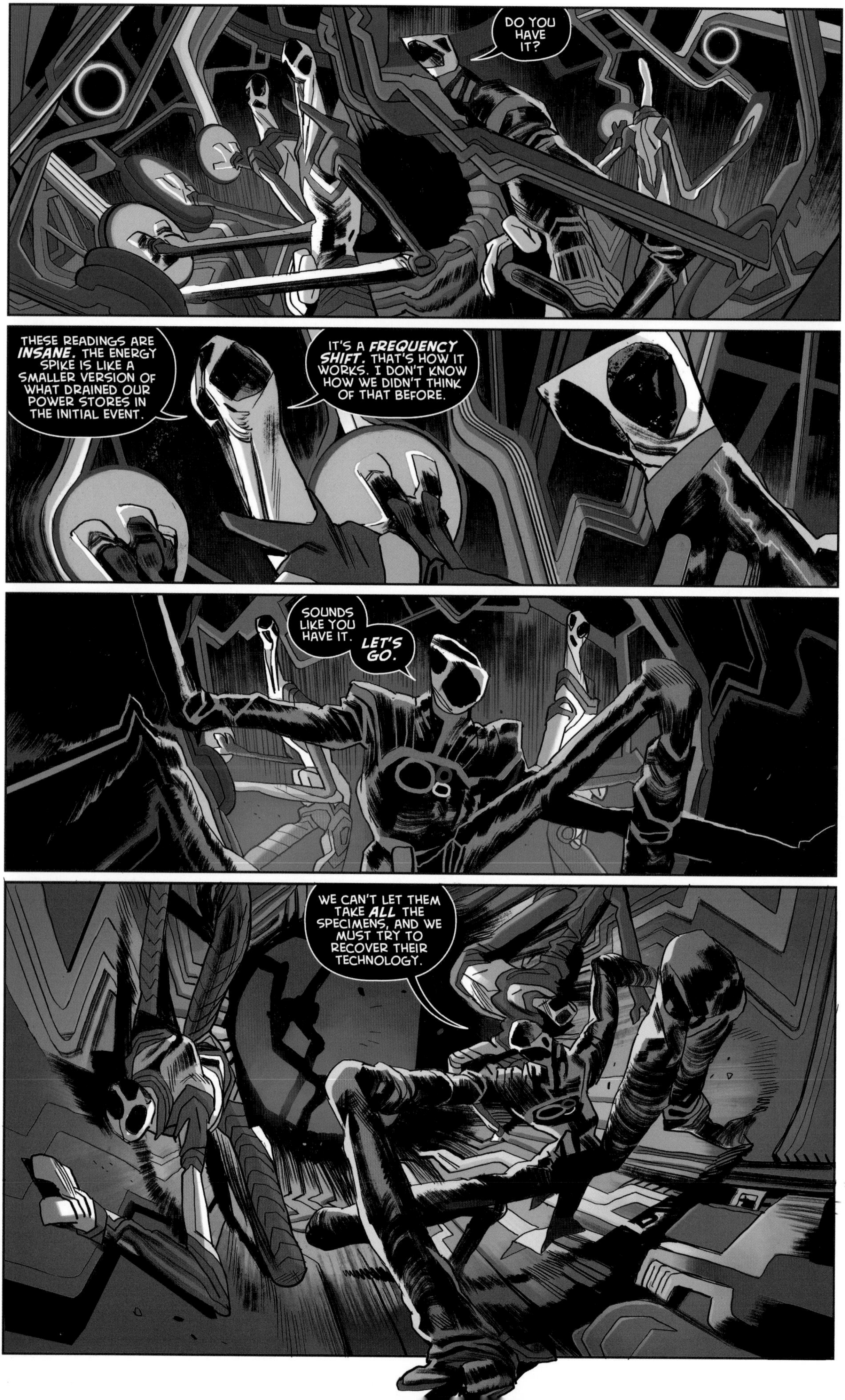
DO YOU HAVE IT?
THESE READINGS ARE **INSANE.** THE ENERGY SPIKE IS LIKE A SMALLER VERSION OF WHAT DRAINED OUR POWER STORES IN THE INITIAL EVENT.
IT'S A **FREQUENCY SHIFT.** THAT'S HOW IT WORKS. I DON'T KNOW HOW WE DIDN'T THINK OF THAT BEFORE.
SOUNDS LIKE YOU HAVE IT.
LET'S GO.
WE CAN'T LET THEM TAKE **ALL** THE SPECIMENS, AND WE MUST TRY TO RECOVER THEIR TECHNOLOGY.

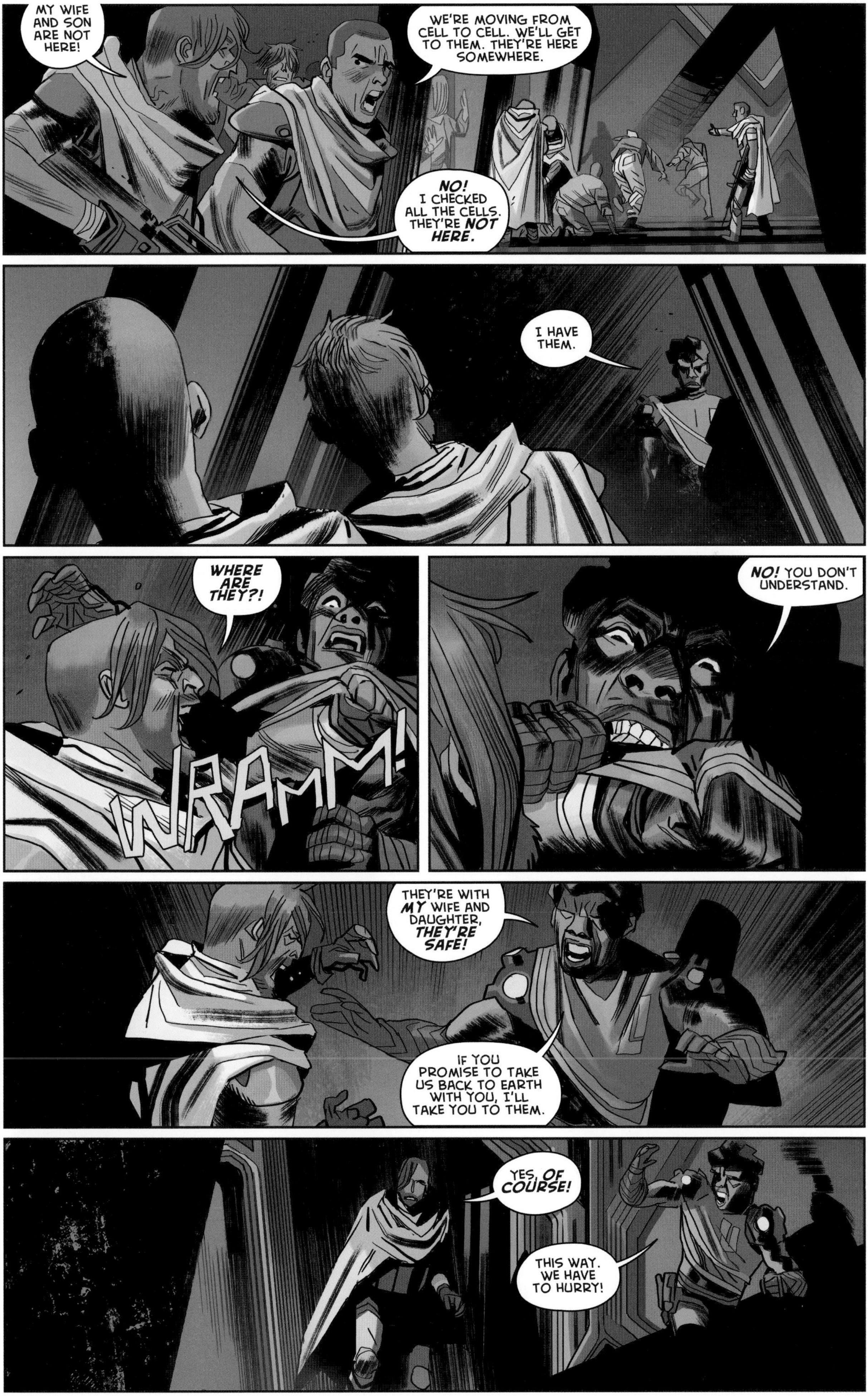
MY WIFE AND SON ARE NOT HERE!
WE'RE MOVING FROM CELL TO CELL. WE'LL GET TO THEM. THEY'RE HERE SOMEWHERE.
NO! I CHECKED ALL THE CELLS. THEY'RE NOT HERE.
I HAVE THEM.
WHERE ARE THEY?!
WRAMM!
NO! YOU DON'T UNDERSTAND.
THEY'RE WITH MY WIFE AND DAUGHTER, THEY'RE SAFE!
IF YOU PROMISE TO TAKE US BACK TO EARTH WITH YOU, I'LL TAKE YOU TO THEM.
YES, OF COURSE!
THIS WAY. WE HAVE TO HURRY!

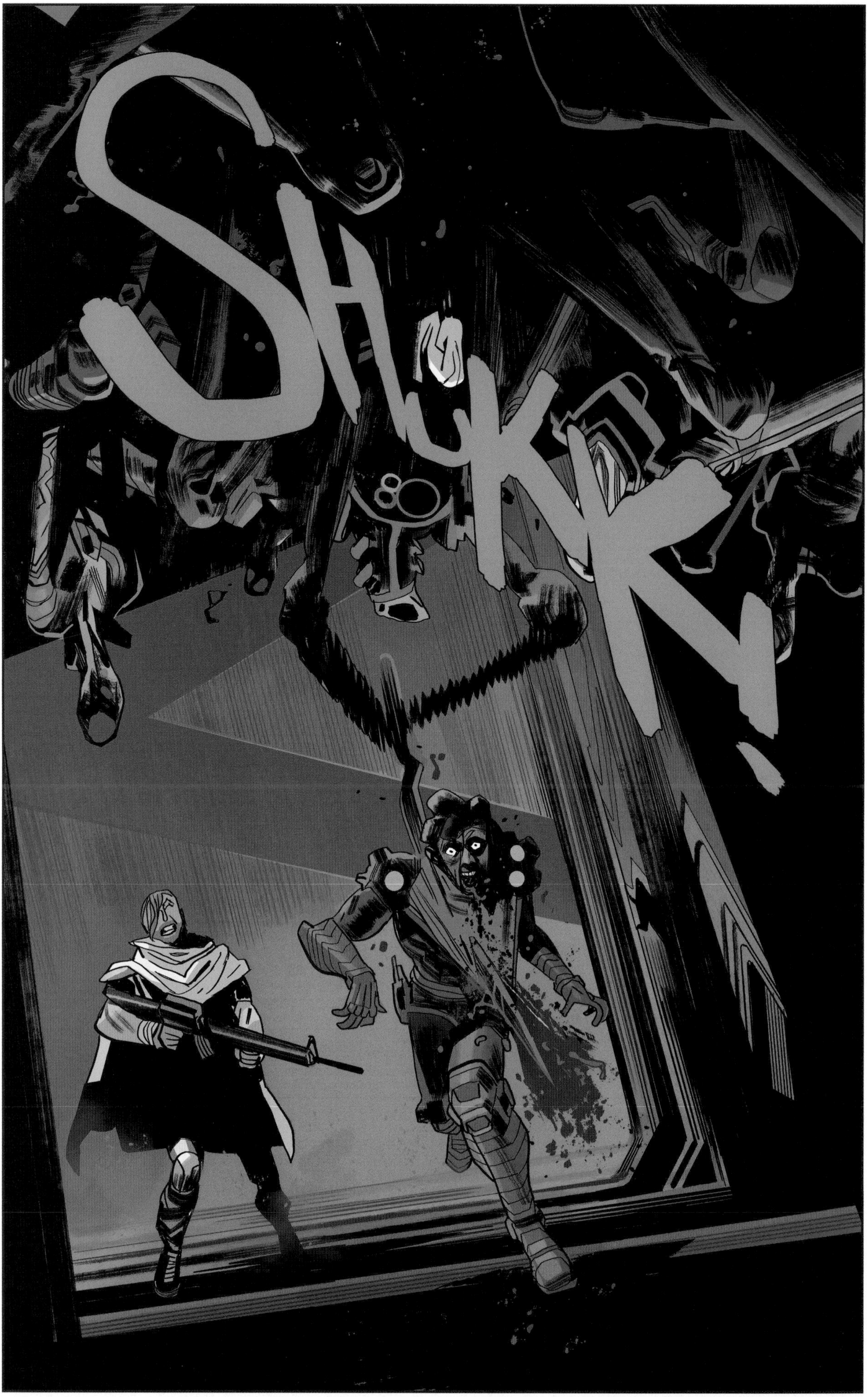
SHUKK!

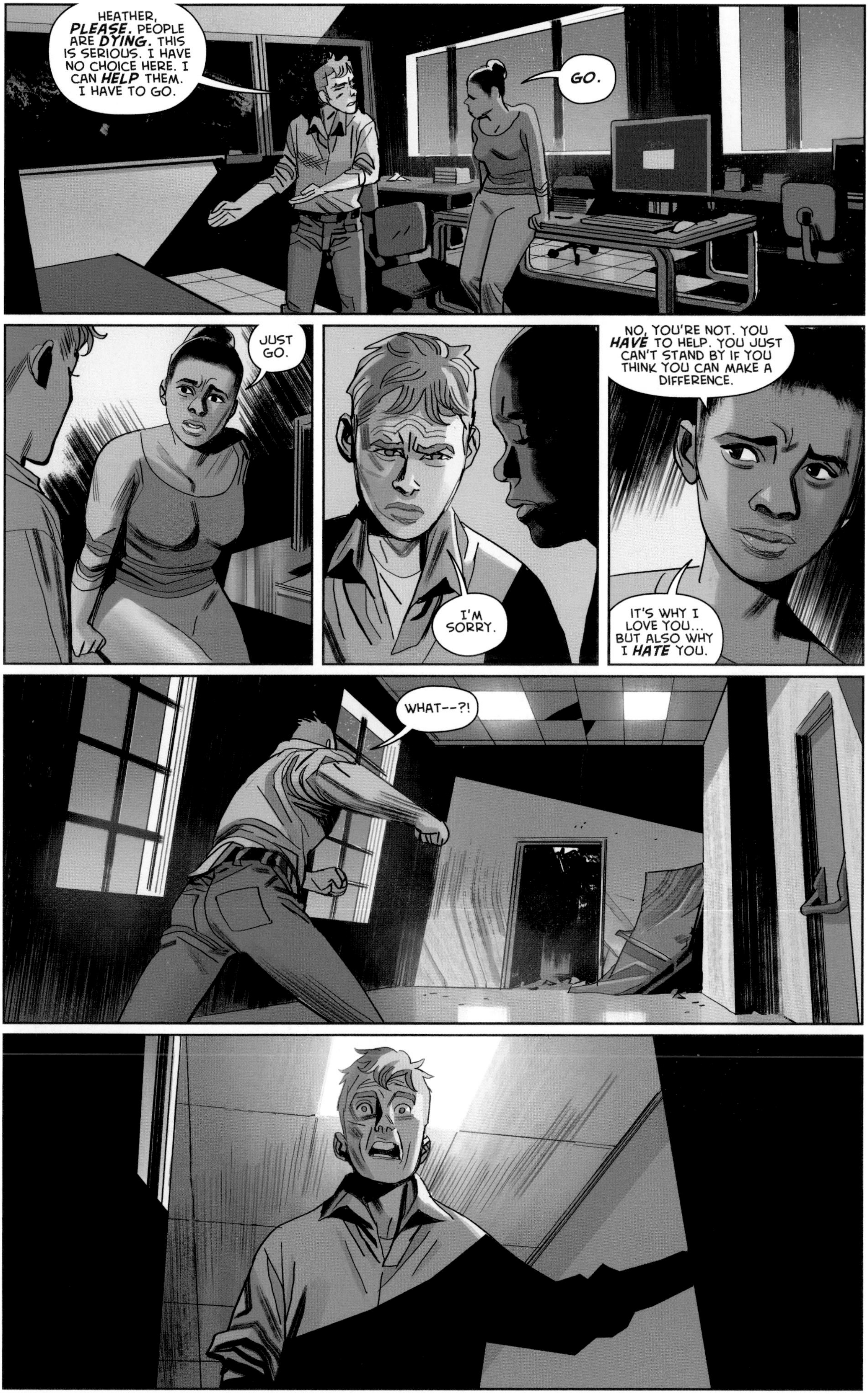
HEATHER, PLEASE. PEOPLE ARE DYING. THIS IS SERIOUS. I HAVE NO CHOICE HERE. I CAN HELP THEM. I HAVE TO GO.
GO.
JUST GO.
I'M SORRY.
NO, YOU'RE NOT. YOU HAVE TO HELP. YOU JUST CAN'T STAND BY IF YOU THINK YOU CAN MAKE A DIFFERENCE.
IT'S WHY I LOVE YOU... BUT ALSO WHY I HATE YOU.
WHAT--?!

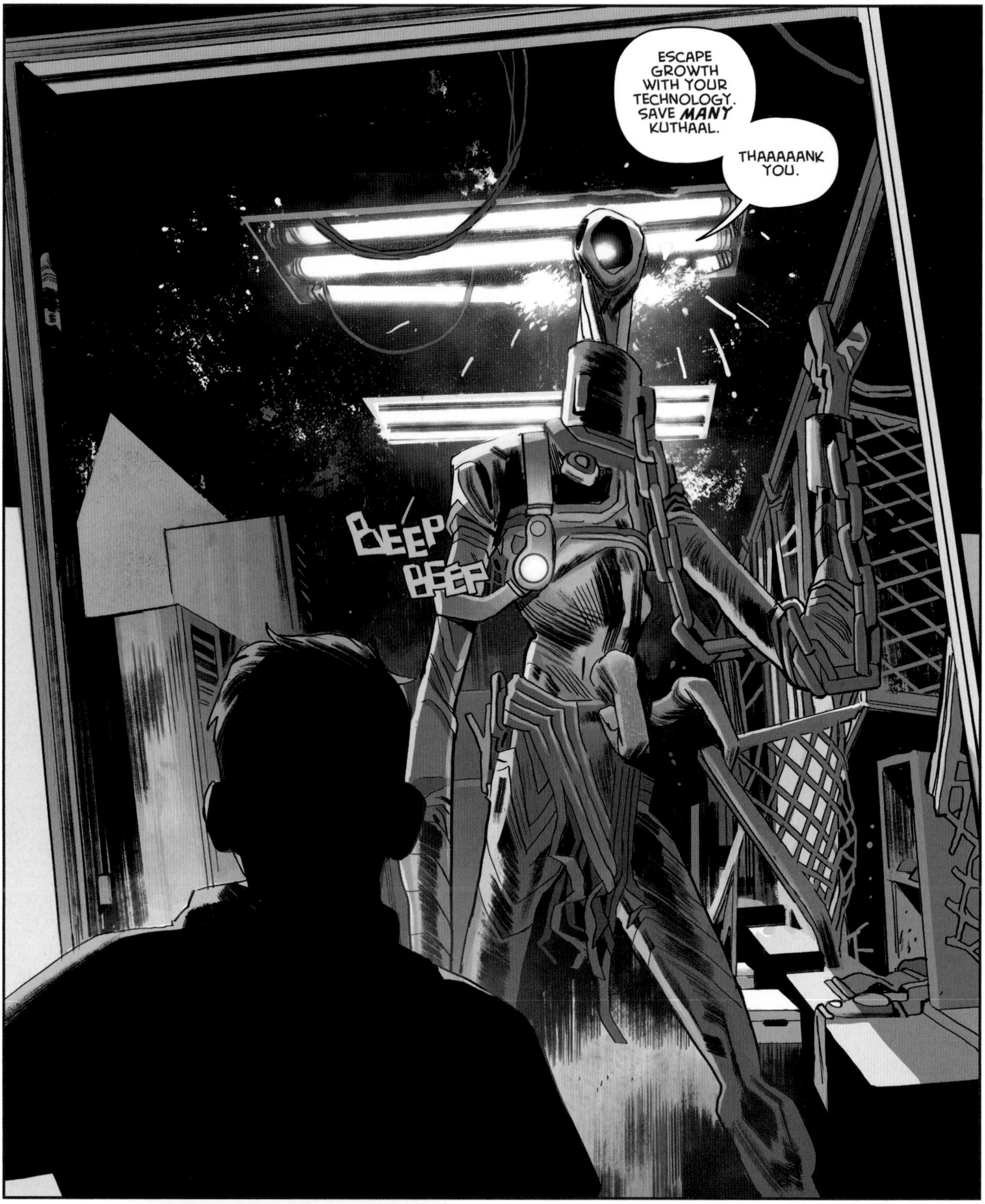
ESCAPE GROWTH WITH YOUR TECHNOLOGY. SAVE *MANY* KUTHAAL.
THAAAAAANK YOU.
BEEP BEEP

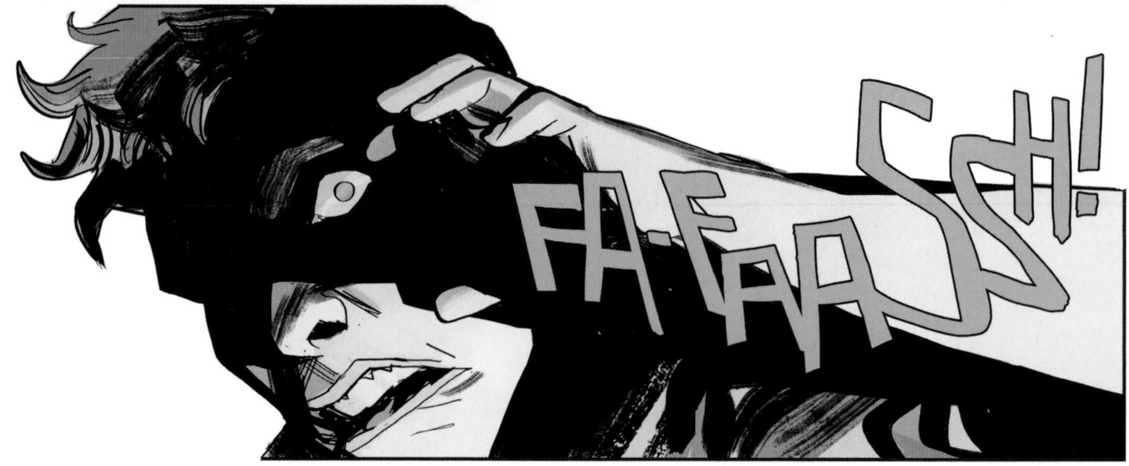
FA-FAAASSH!

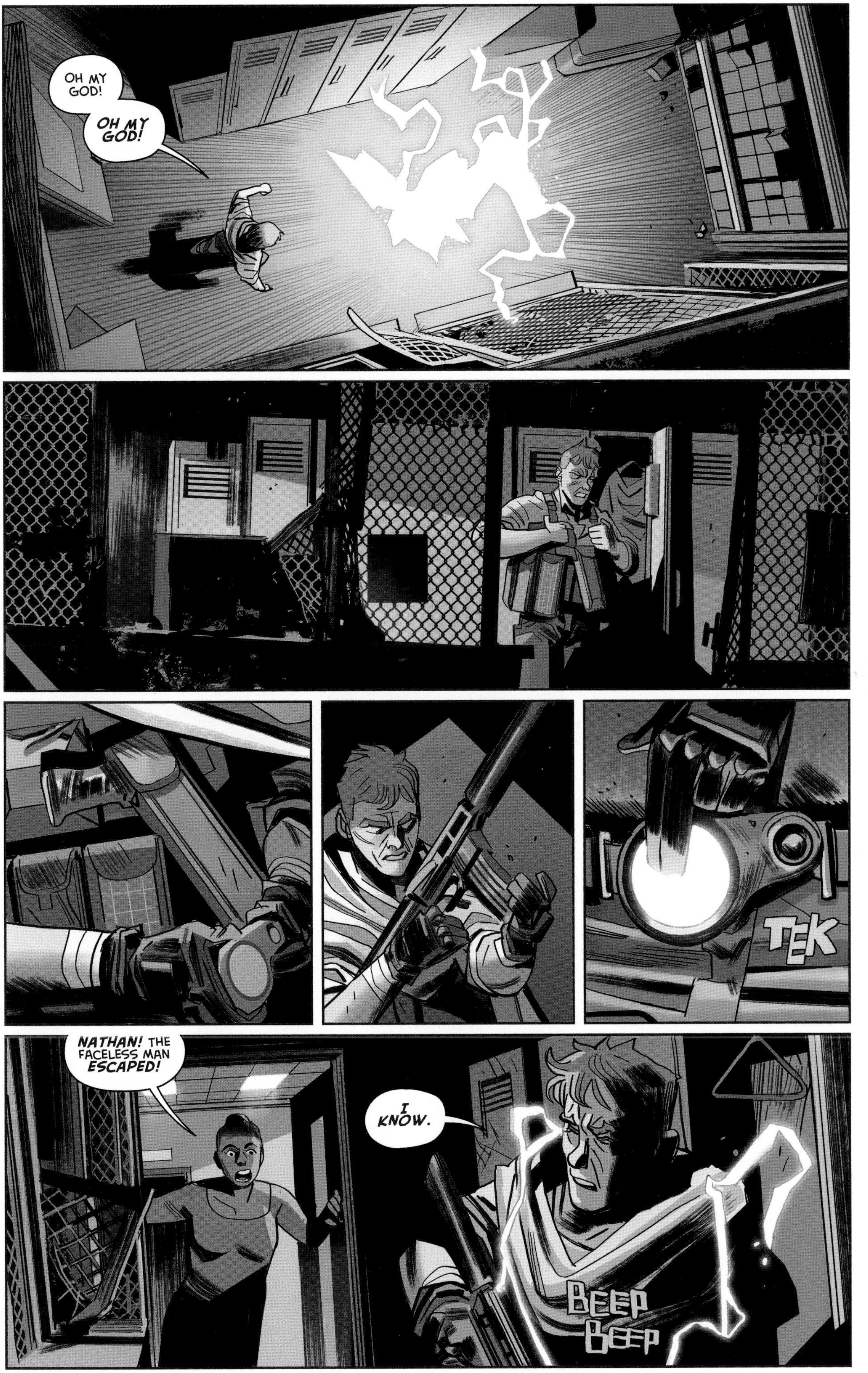
OH MY GOD!
OH MY GOD!
TEK
NATHAN! THE FACELESS MAN ESCAPED!
I KNOW.
BEEP BEEP

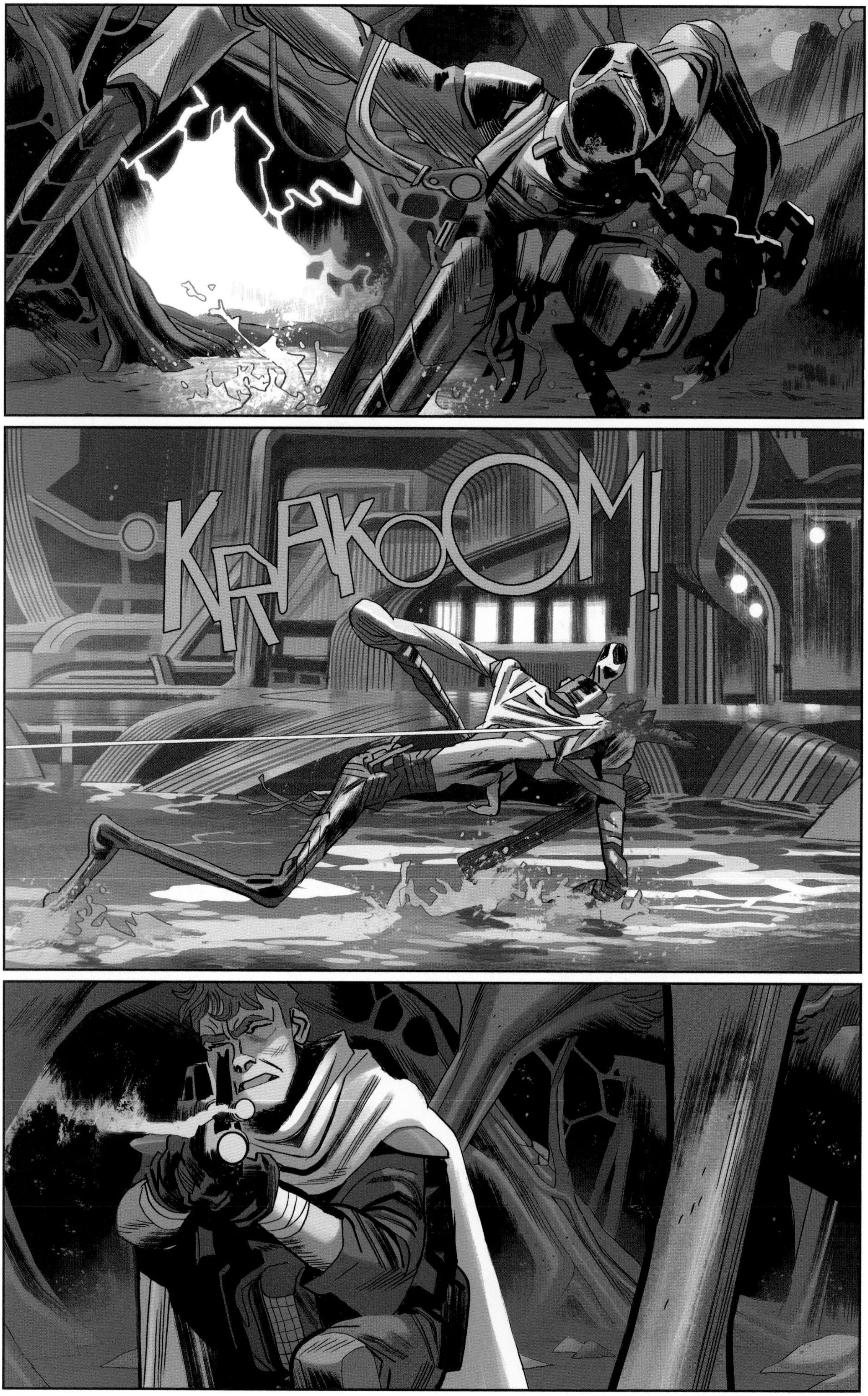
KRAKOOM!

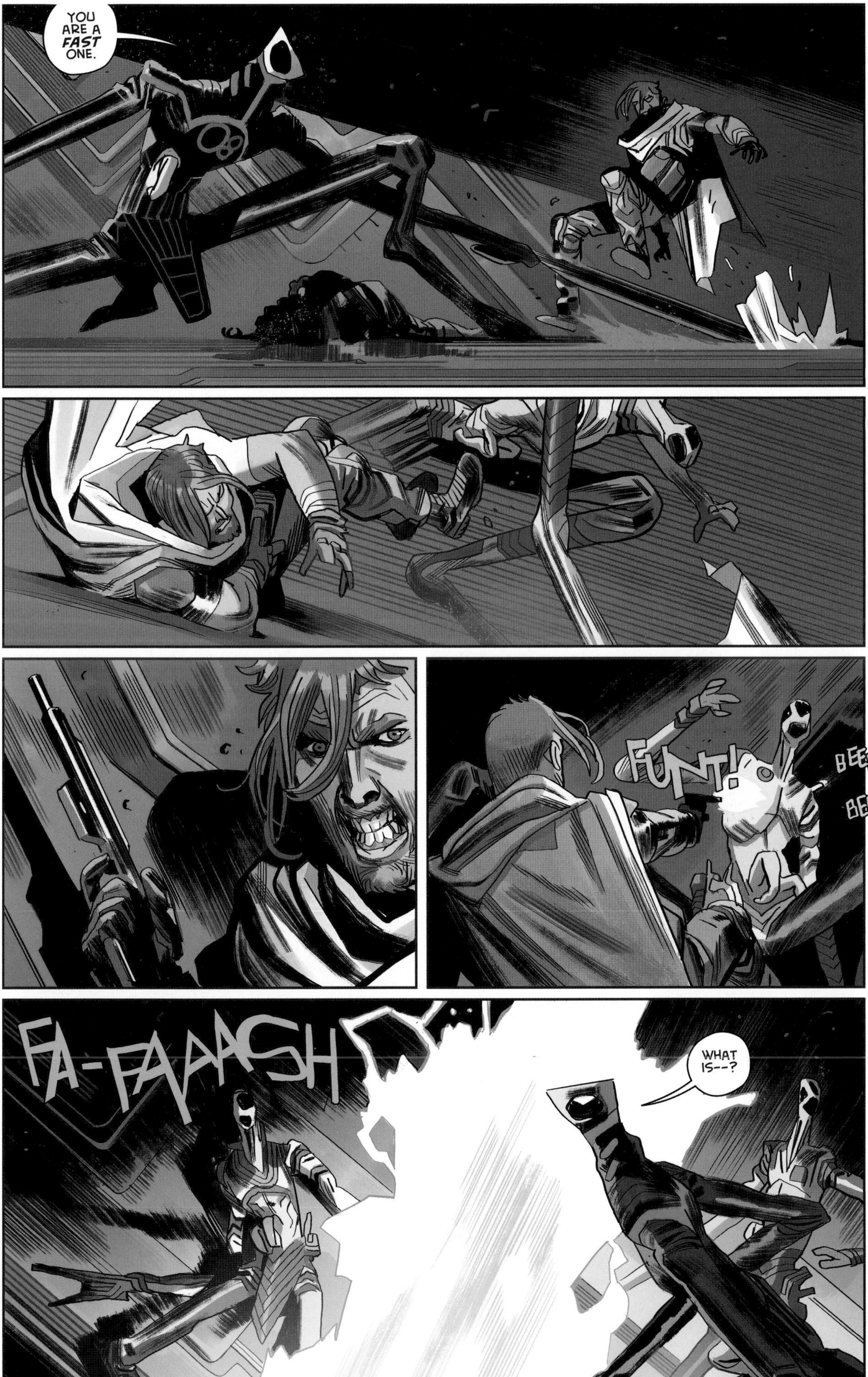
YOU ARE A FAST ONE.
FUNT!
BEEP
BEEP
FA-FAAASH
WHAT IS--?

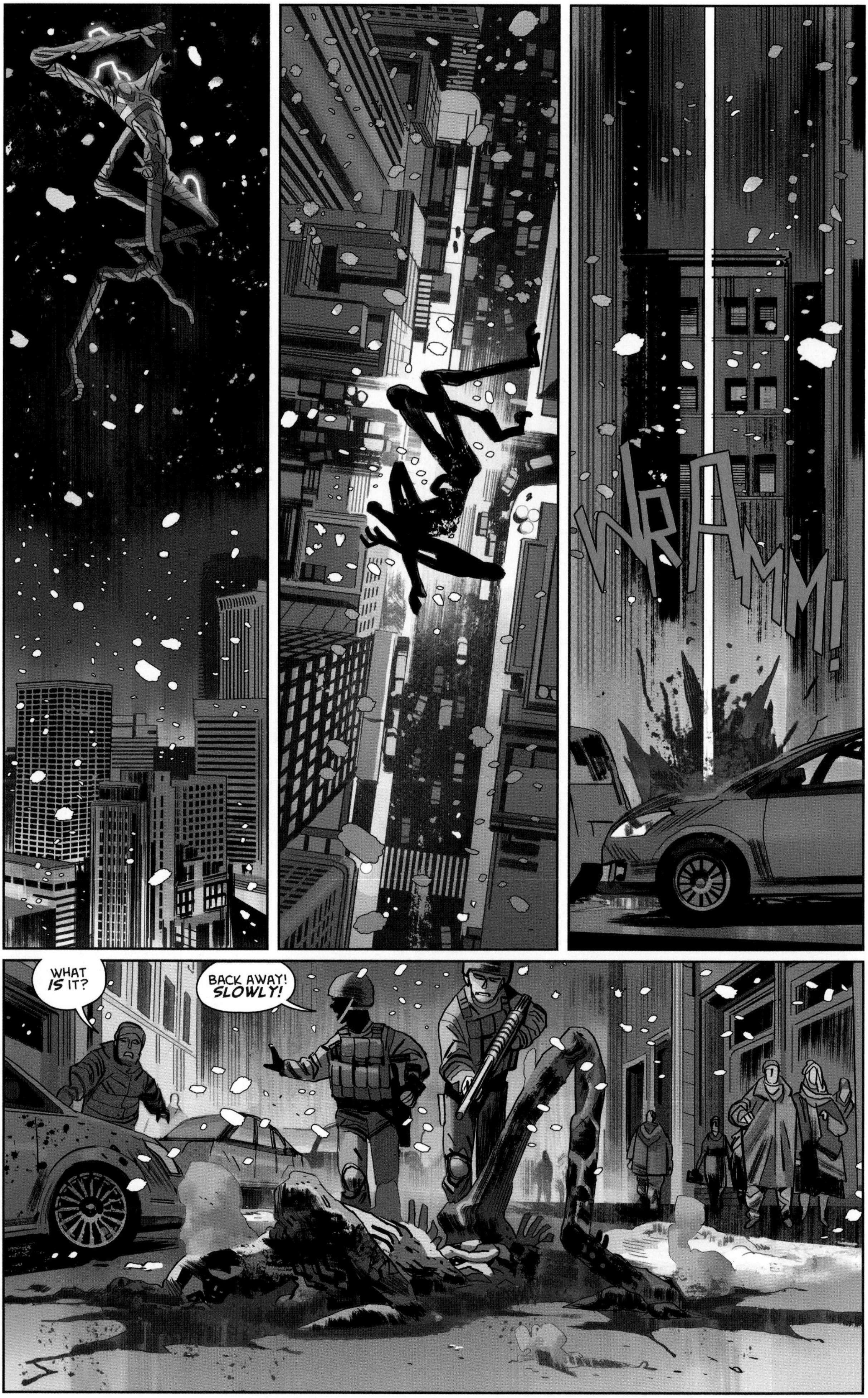
WRAMM!
WHAT IS IT?
BACK AWAY! SLOWLY!

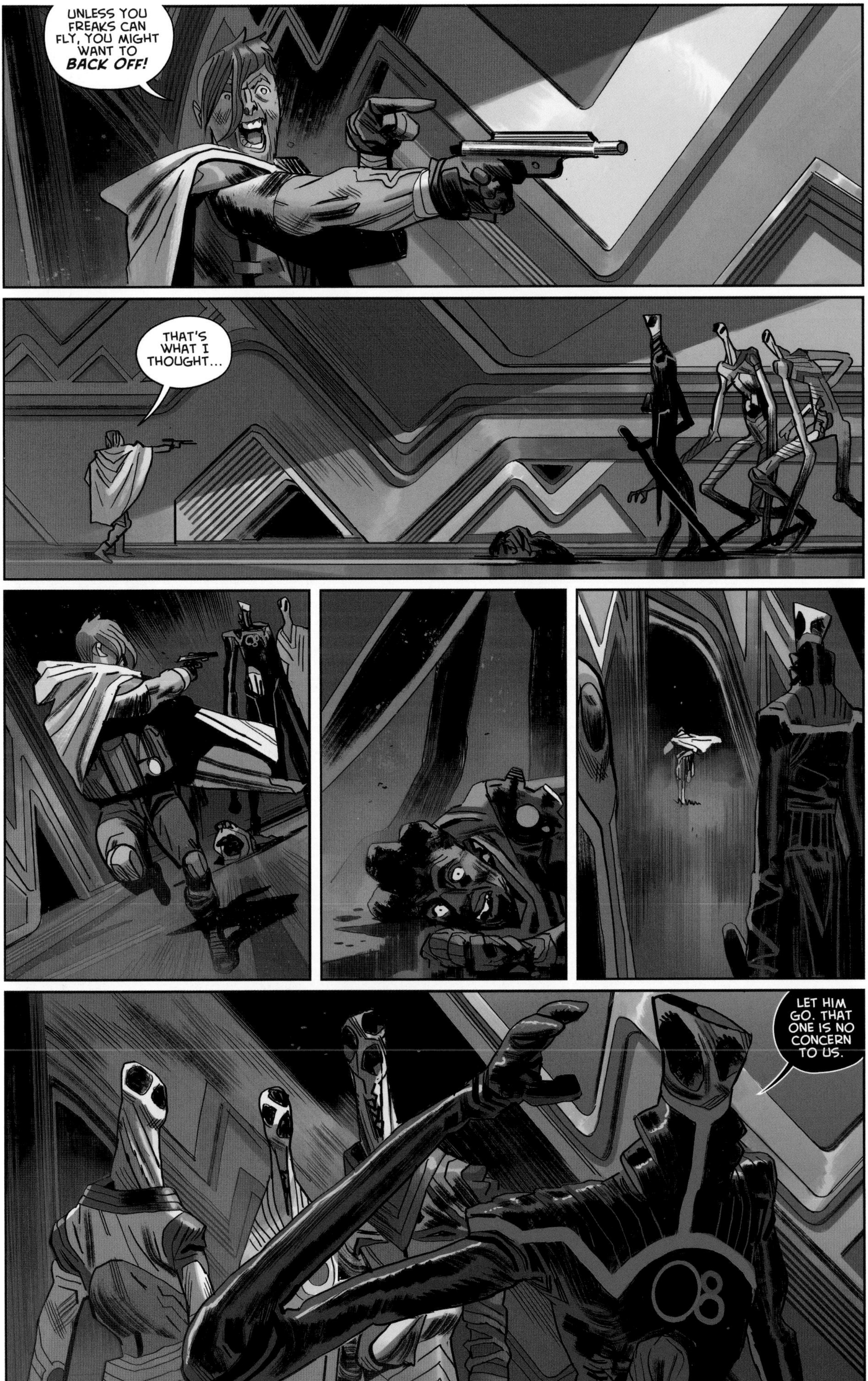
UNLESS YOU FREAKS CAN FLY, YOU MIGHT WANT TO BACK OFF!
THAT'S WHAT I THOUGHT...
LET HIM GO. THAT ONE IS NO CONCERN TO US.

THIS WAY, THIS WAY.

KEEP MOVING. NO PUSHING, PLEASE.

THE FACELESS MAN ESCAPED. NATHAN WENT AFTER HIM.

AFTER HIM?

IT GOT A BELT. HE CHASED IT INTO *OBLIVION*.

... MY GOD...

I CAN'T--I CAN'T DEAL WITH THAT RIGHT NOW. WE HAVE TO FOCUS ON CLEARING THESE PEOPLE AWAY BEFORE MORE ARRIVE.

WE HAVE TO FOCUS ON THE *RESCUE*.

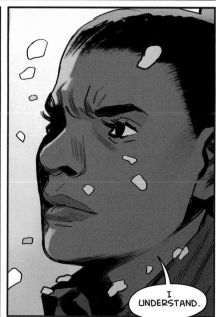

I UNDERSTAND.

SIR, IT'S *STOPPED*.

THERE'S NO MORE PEOPLE COMING.

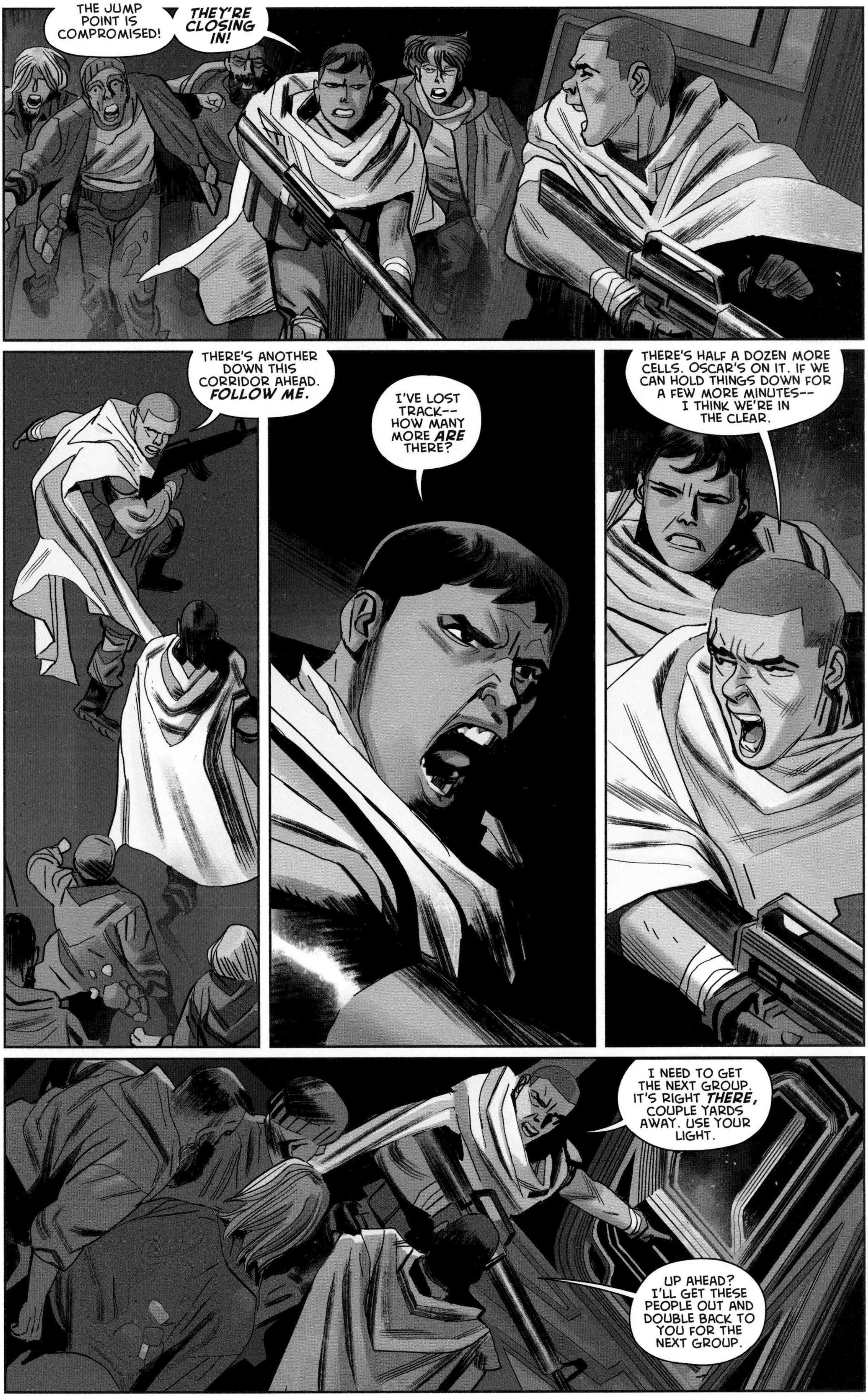
THE JUMP POINT IS COMPROMISED!
THEY'RE CLOSING IN!
THERE'S ANOTHER DOWN THIS CORRIDOR AHEAD. FOLLOW ME.
I'VE LOST TRACK-- HOW MANY MORE ARE THERE?
THERE'S HALF A DOZEN MORE CELLS. OSCAR'S ON IT. IF WE CAN HOLD THINGS DOWN FOR A FEW MORE MINUTES-- I THINK WE'RE IN THE CLEAR.
I NEED TO GET THE NEXT GROUP. IT'S RIGHT THERE, COUPLE YARDS AWAY. USE YOUR LIGHT.
UP AHEAD? I'LL GET THESE PEOPLE OUT AND DOUBLE BACK TO YOU FOR THE NEXT GROUP.

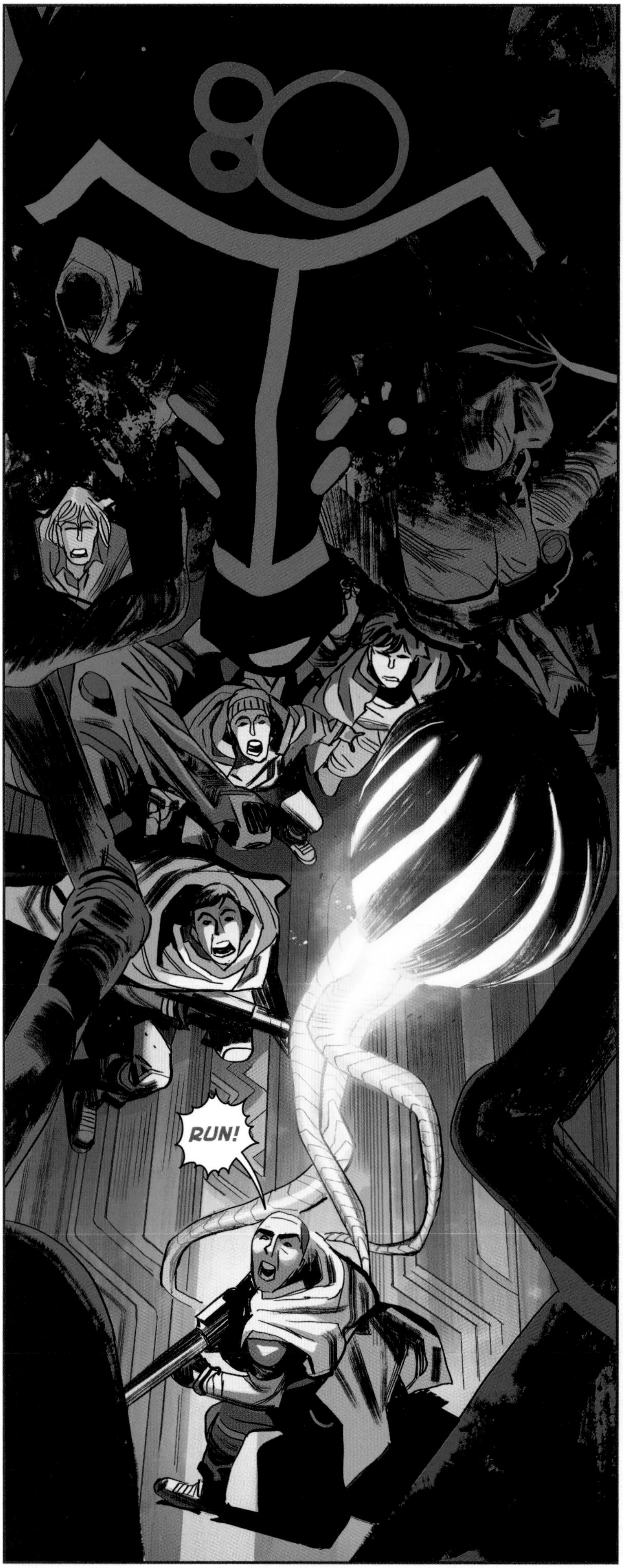
RUN!

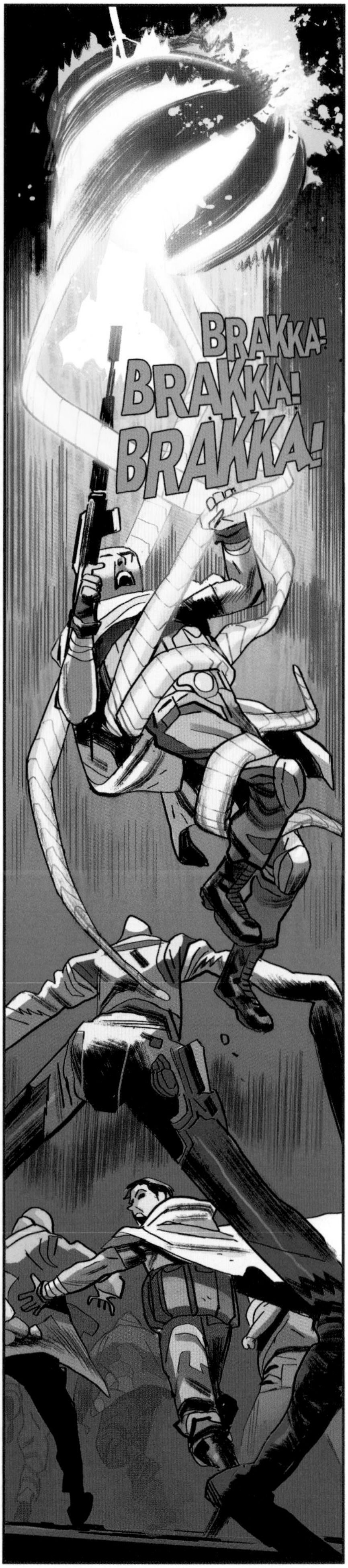
BRAKKA!
BRAKKA!
BRAKKA!

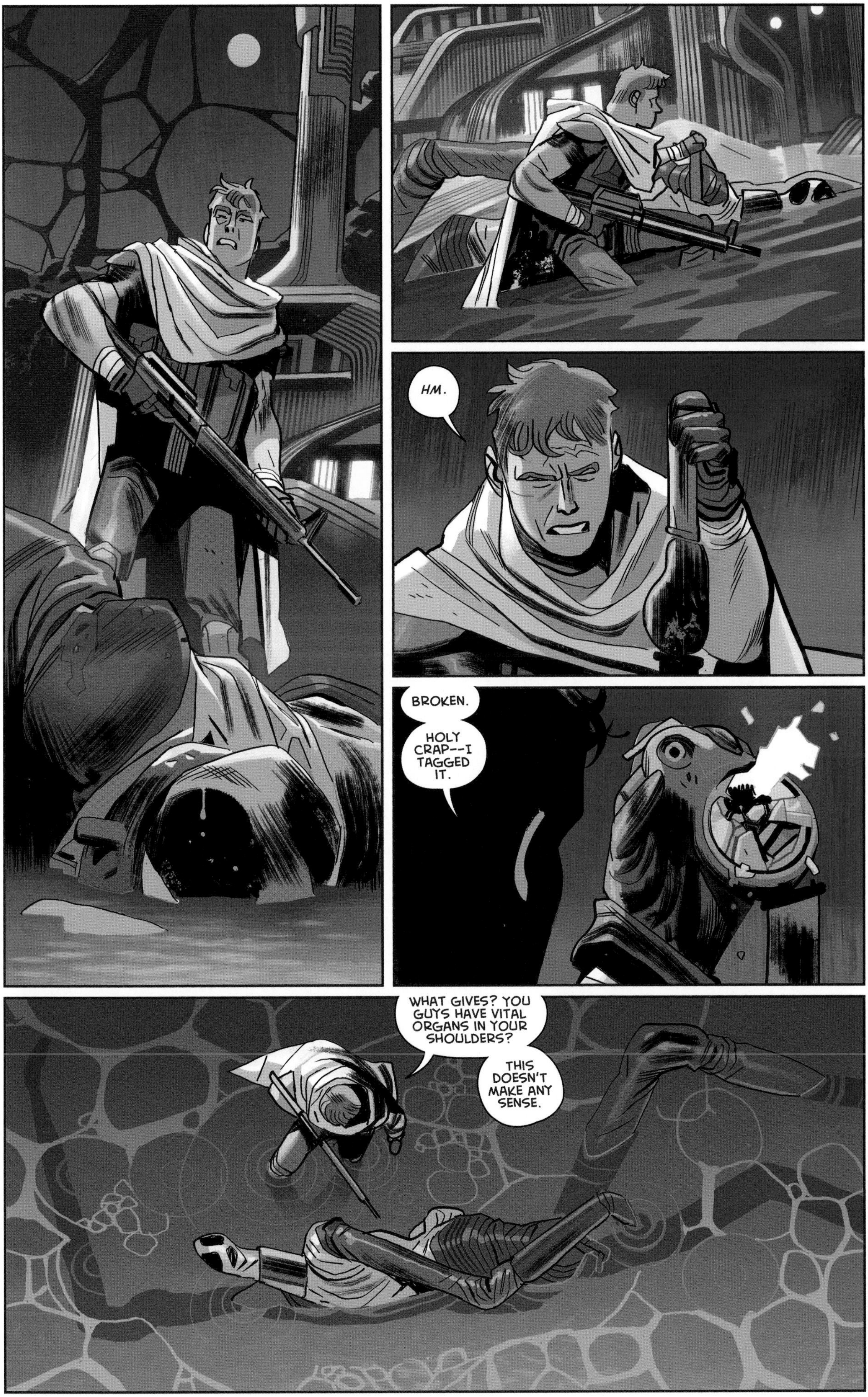
HM.
BROKEN.
HOLY CRAP--I TAGGED IT.
WHAT GIVES? YOU GUYS HAVE VITAL ORGANS IN YOUR SHOULDERS?
THIS DOESN'T MAKE ANY SENSE.

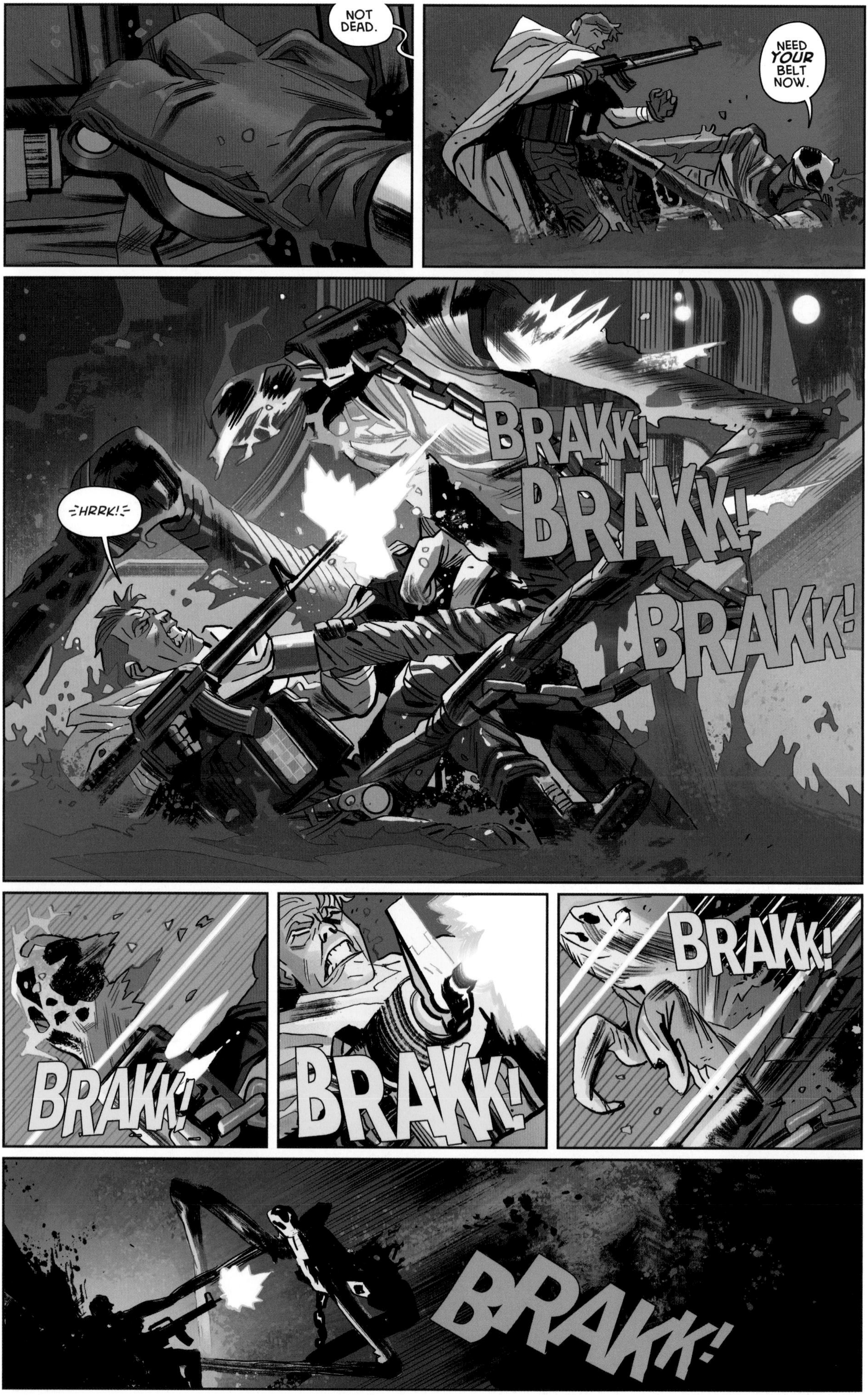
NOT DEAD.
NEED YOUR BELT NOW.
HRRK!
BRAKK!
BRAKK!
BRAKK!
BRAKK!
BRAKK!
BRAKK!
BRAKK!

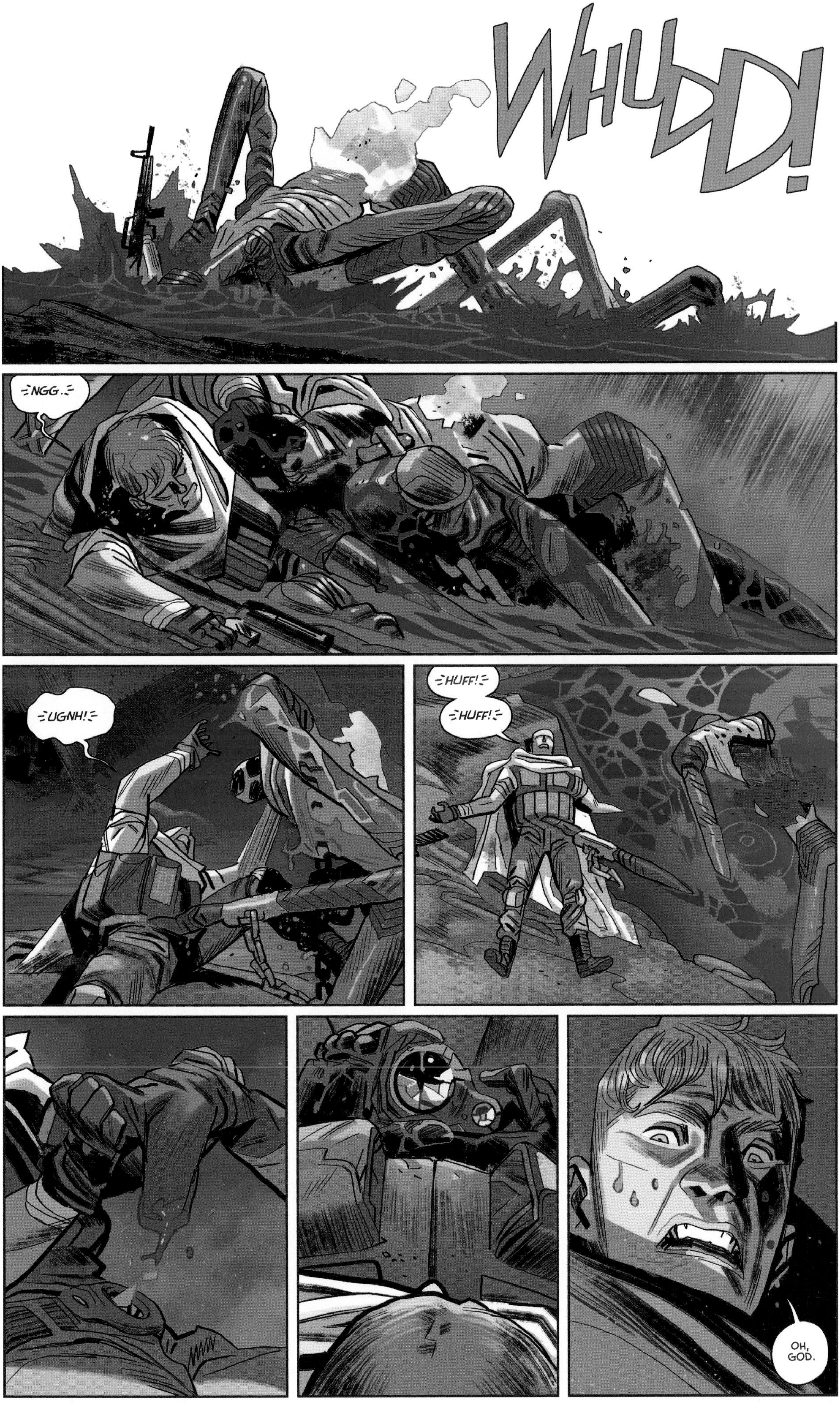
WHUDD!
NGG..
UGNH!
HUFF!
HUFF!
OH, GOD.

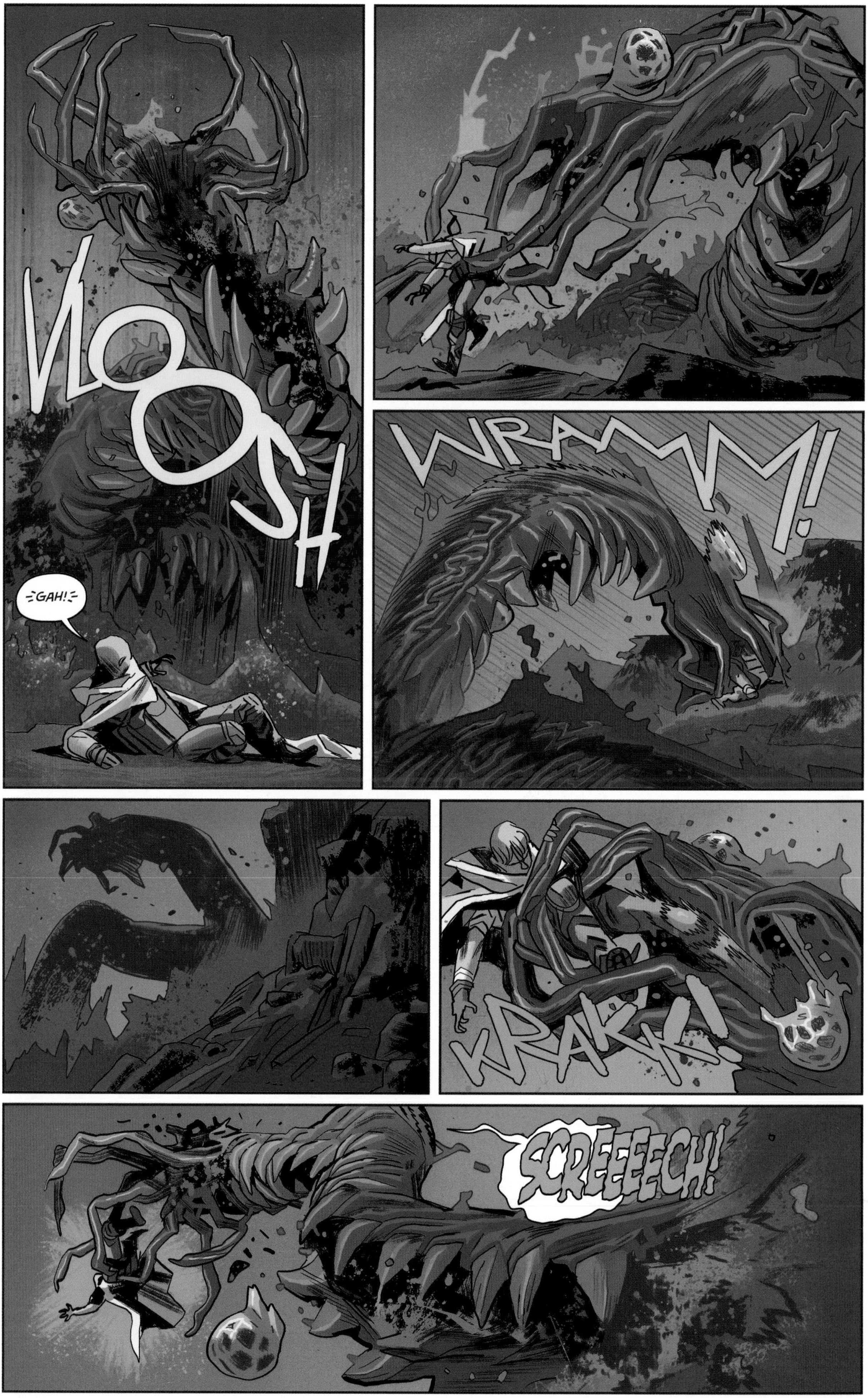
WOOSH
GAH!
WRAMMM!
KRAKK!
SCREEEECH!

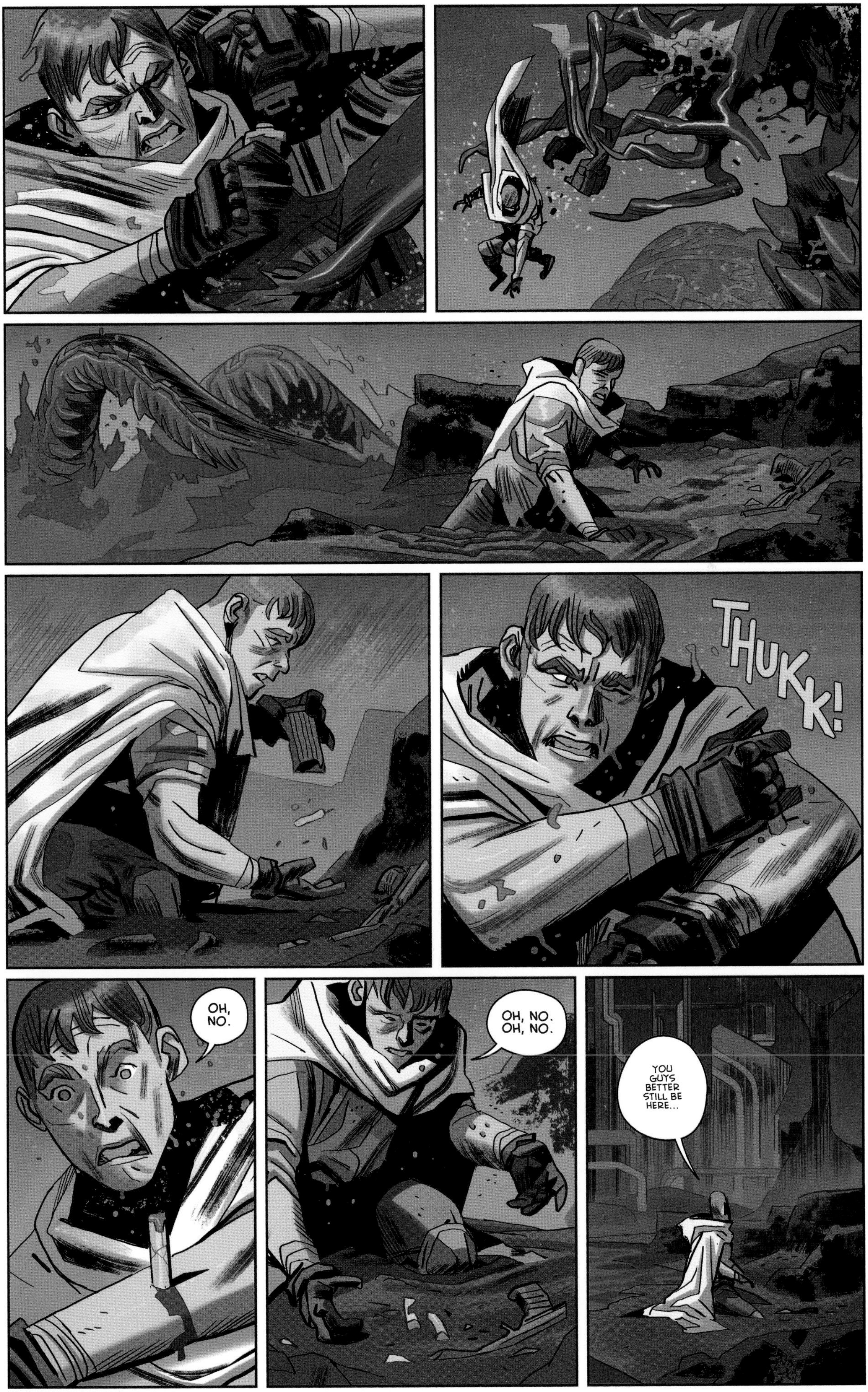
THUKK!
OH, NO.
OH, NO. OH, NO.
YOU GUYS BETTER STILL BE HERE...

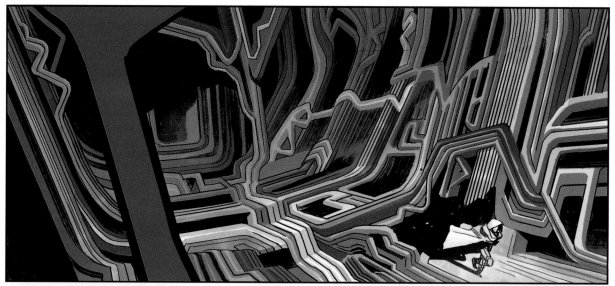

DAKUUL IS RUINING EVERYTHING! HOW DID HE EVER ASSUME COMMAND?

I NEED YOU TO ASSEMBLE THE PRISM GUARD AND BRING THINGS UNDER CONTROL BEFORE IT'S TOO LATE.

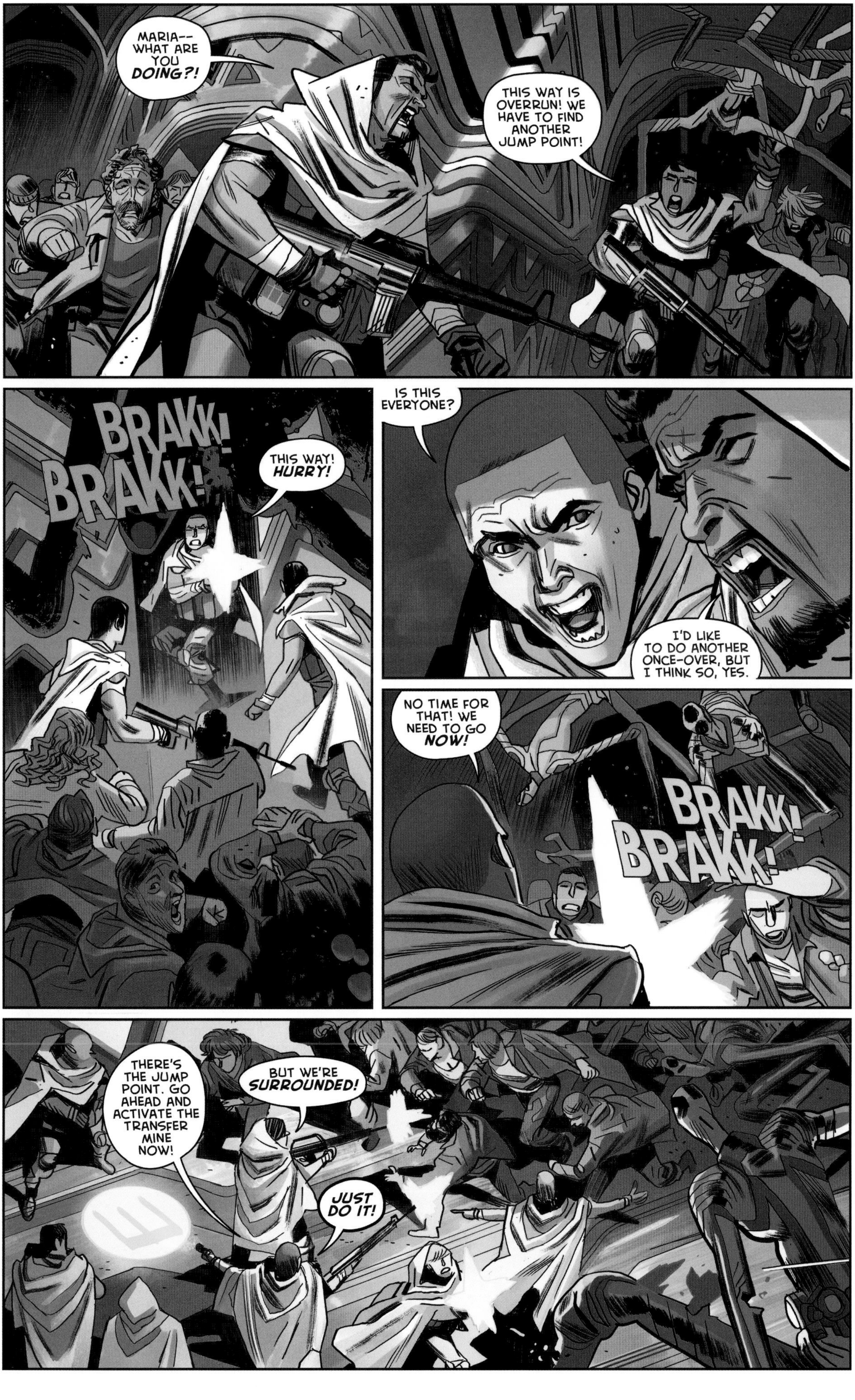
MARIA-- WHAT ARE YOU DOING?!
THIS WAY IS OVERRUN! WE HAVE TO FIND ANOTHER JUMP POINT!
BRAKK! BRAKK!
THIS WAY! HURRY!
IS THIS EVERYONE?
I'D LIKE TO DO ANOTHER ONCE-OVER, BUT I THINK SO, YES.
NO TIME FOR THAT! WE NEED TO GO NOW!
BRAKK! BRAKK!
THERE'S THE JUMP POINT. GO AHEAD AND ACTIVATE THE TRANSFER MINE NOW!
BUT WE'RE SURROUNDED!
JUST DO IT!

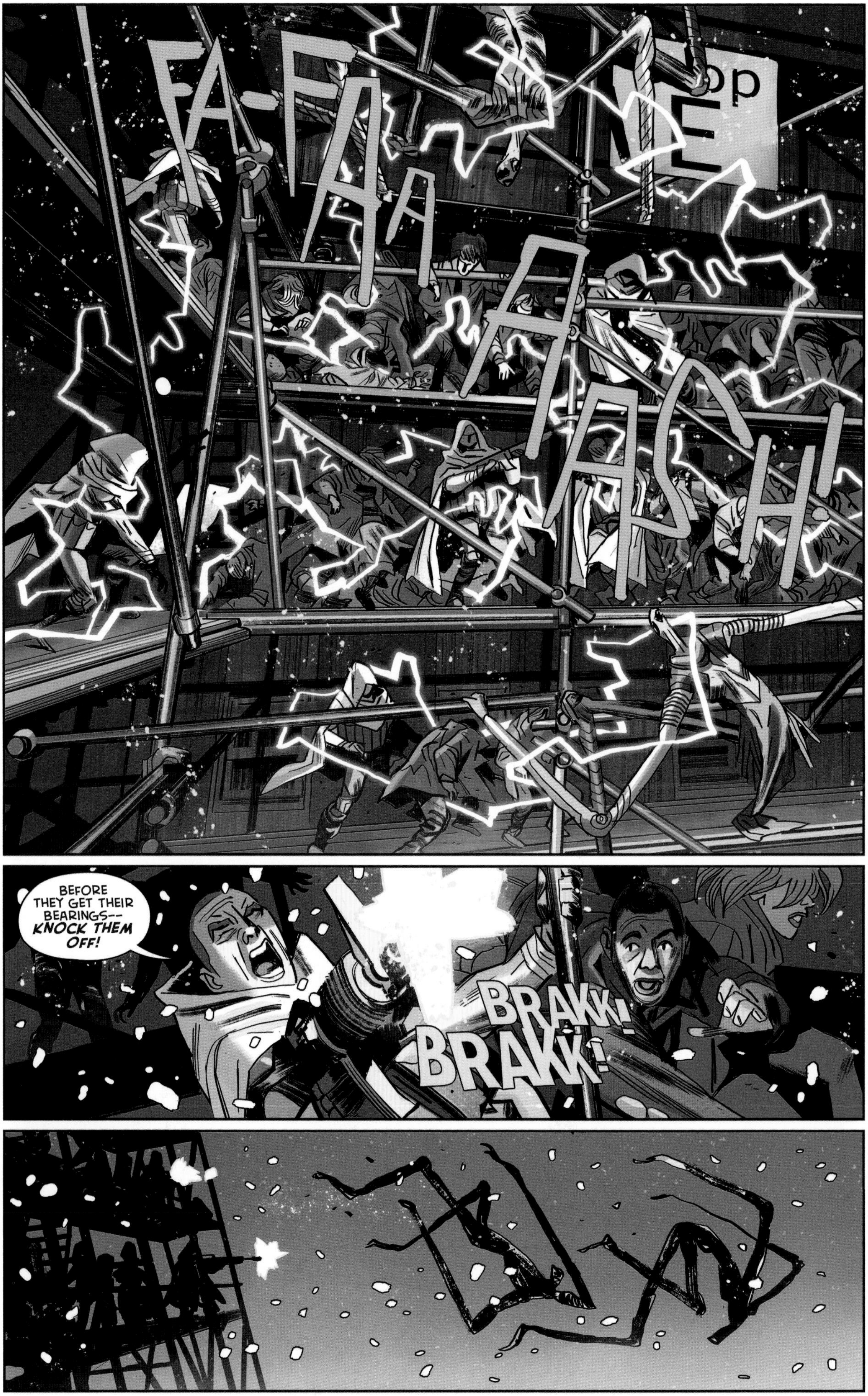
FA-FAAAASH!
BEFORE THEY GET THEIR BEARINGS-- KNOCK THEM OFF!
BRAKK!
BRAKK!

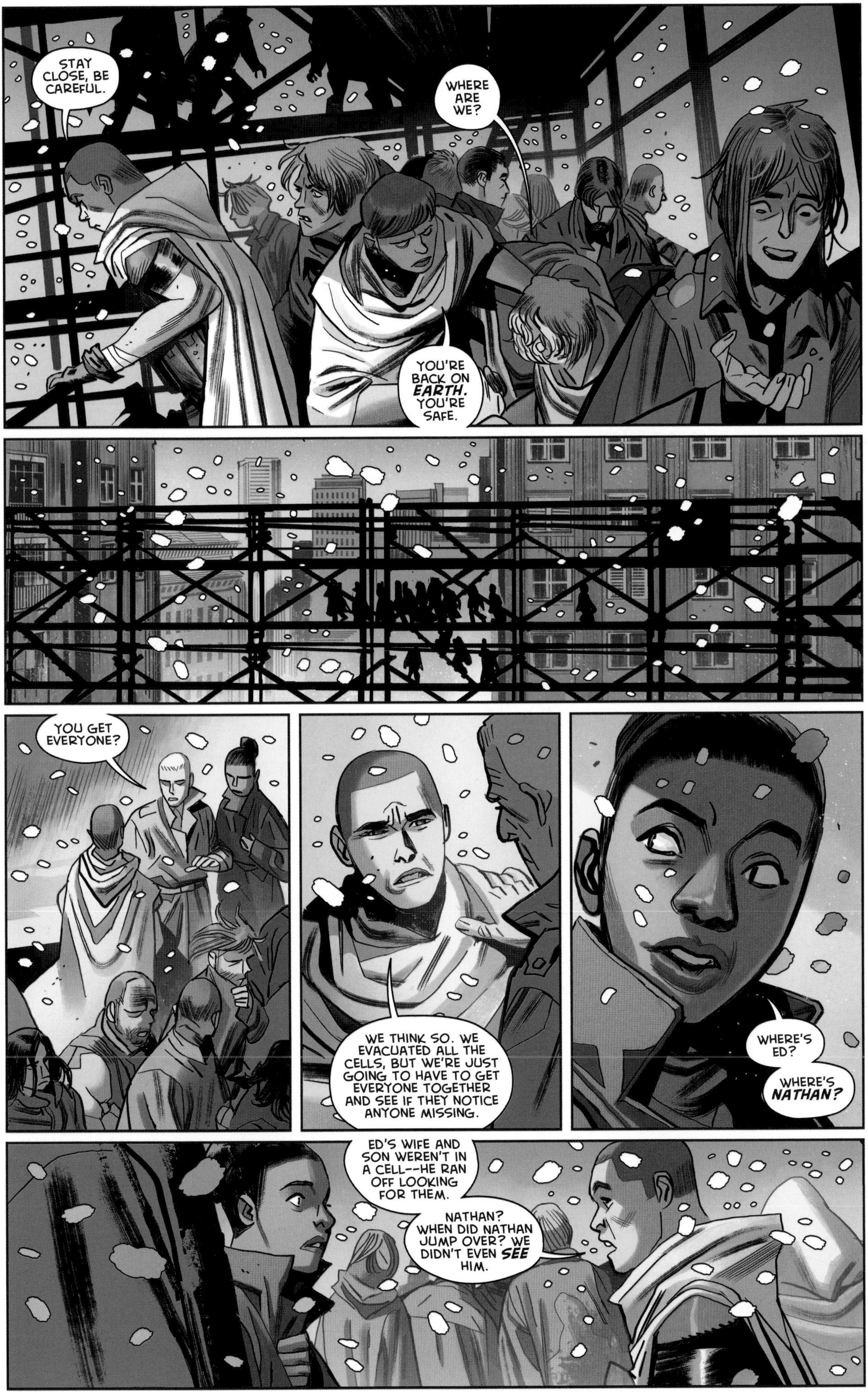
STAY CLOSE, BE CAREFUL.
WHERE ARE WE?
YOU'RE BACK ON EARTH. YOU'RE SAFE.
YOU GET EVERYONE?
WE THINK SO. WE EVACUATED ALL THE CELLS, BUT WE'RE JUST GOING TO HAVE TO GET EVERYONE TOGETHER AND SEE IF THEY NOTICE ANYONE MISSING.
WHERE'S ED?
WHERE'S NATHAN?
ED'S WIFE AND SON WEREN'T IN A CELL--HE RAN OFF LOOKING FOR THEM.
NATHAN? WHEN DID NATHAN JUMP OVER? WE DIDN'T EVEN SEE HIM.

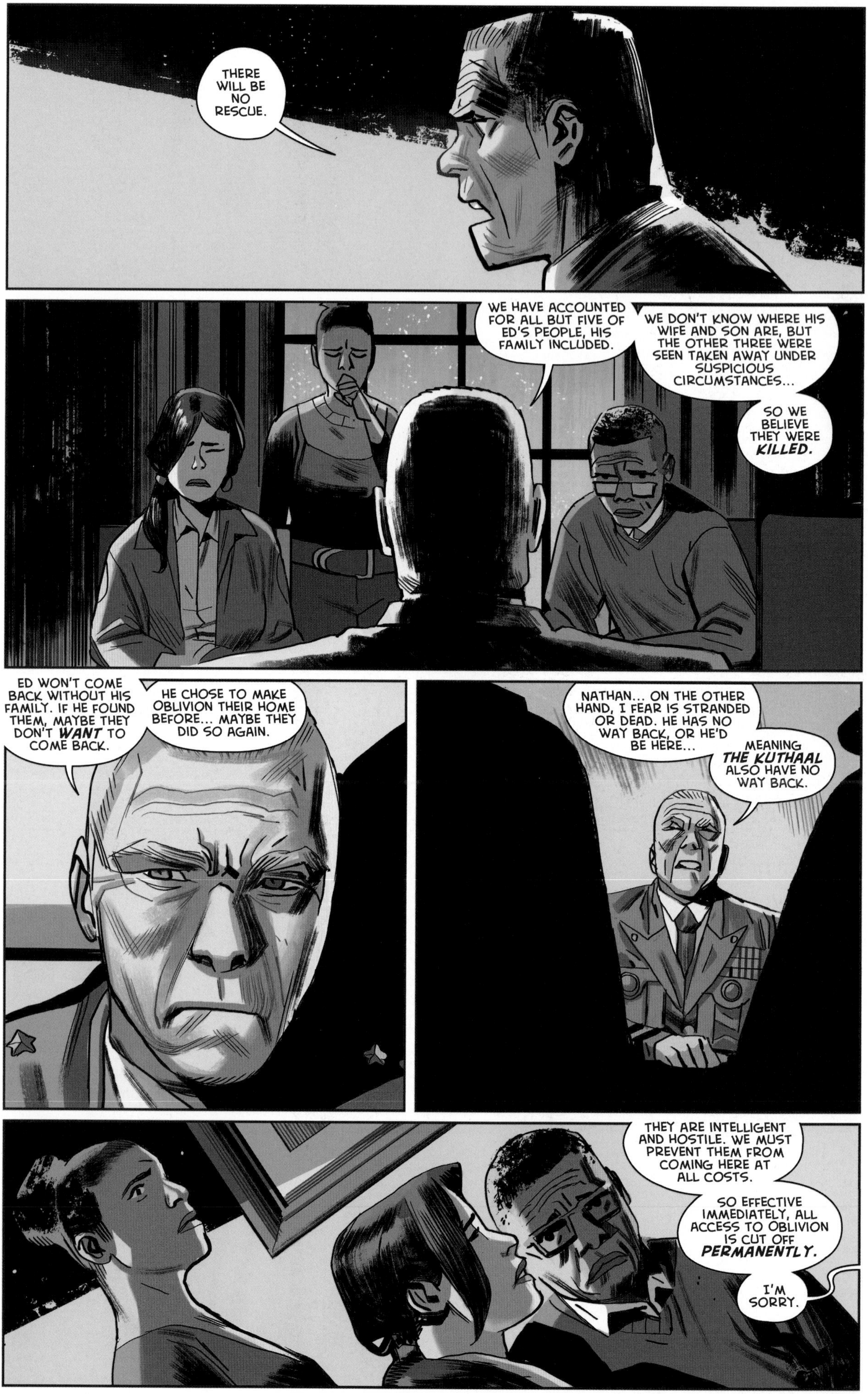
THERE WILL BE NO RESCUE.
WE HAVE ACCOUNTED FOR ALL BUT FIVE OF ED'S PEOPLE, HIS FAMILY INCLUDED.
WE DON'T KNOW WHERE HIS WIFE AND SON ARE, BUT THE OTHER THREE WERE SEEN TAKEN AWAY UNDER SUSPICIOUS CIRCUMSTANCES...
SO WE BELIEVE THEY WERE *KILLED.*
ED WON'T COME BACK WITHOUT HIS FAMILY. IF HE FOUND THEM, MAYBE THEY DON'T *WANT* TO COME BACK.
HE CHOSE TO MAKE OBLIVION THEIR HOME BEFORE... MAYBE THEY DID SO AGAIN.
NATHAN... ON THE OTHER HAND, I FEAR IS STRANDED OR DEAD. HE HAS NO WAY BACK, OR HE'D BE HERE...
MEANING *THE KUTHAAL* ALSO HAVE NO WAY BACK.
THEY ARE INTELLIGENT AND HOSTILE. WE MUST PREVENT THEM FROM COMING HERE AT ALL COSTS.
SO EFFECTIVE IMMEDIATELY, ALL ACCESS TO OBLIVION IS CUT OFF *PERMANENTLY.*
I'M SORRY.

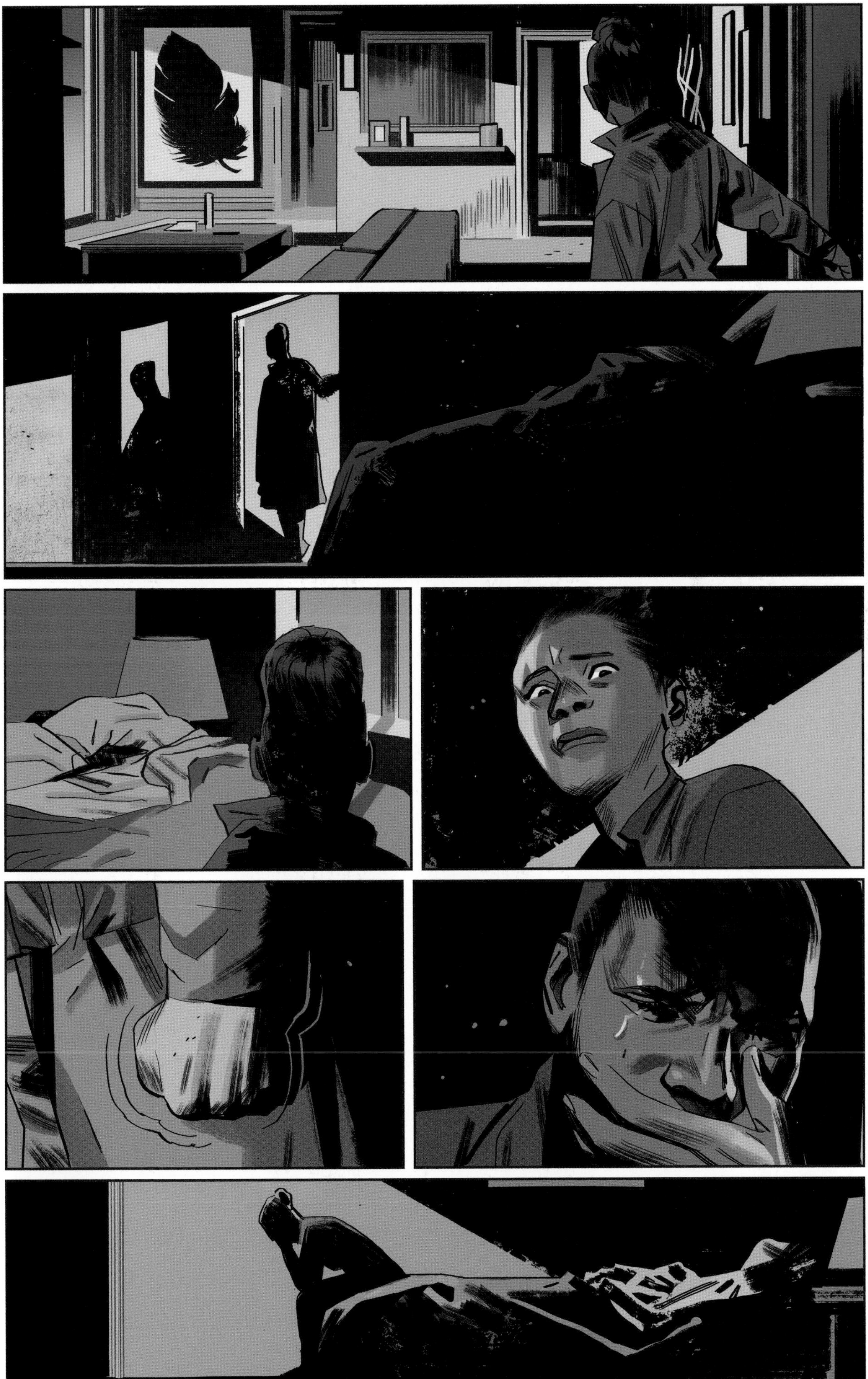

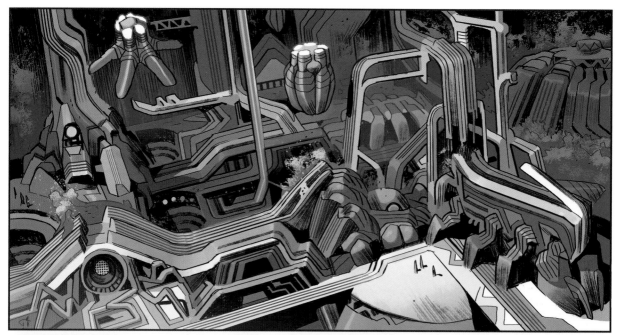

WHEN WORD OF YOUR FAILURE HERE SPREADS, YOU WILL BE STRIPPED OF YOUR TITLE AND REMOVED FROM THE GHOZAN RANKS.

WE WILL SEE... I HAVE MUCH TO SAY ON *YOUR* FAILURE AS WELL.

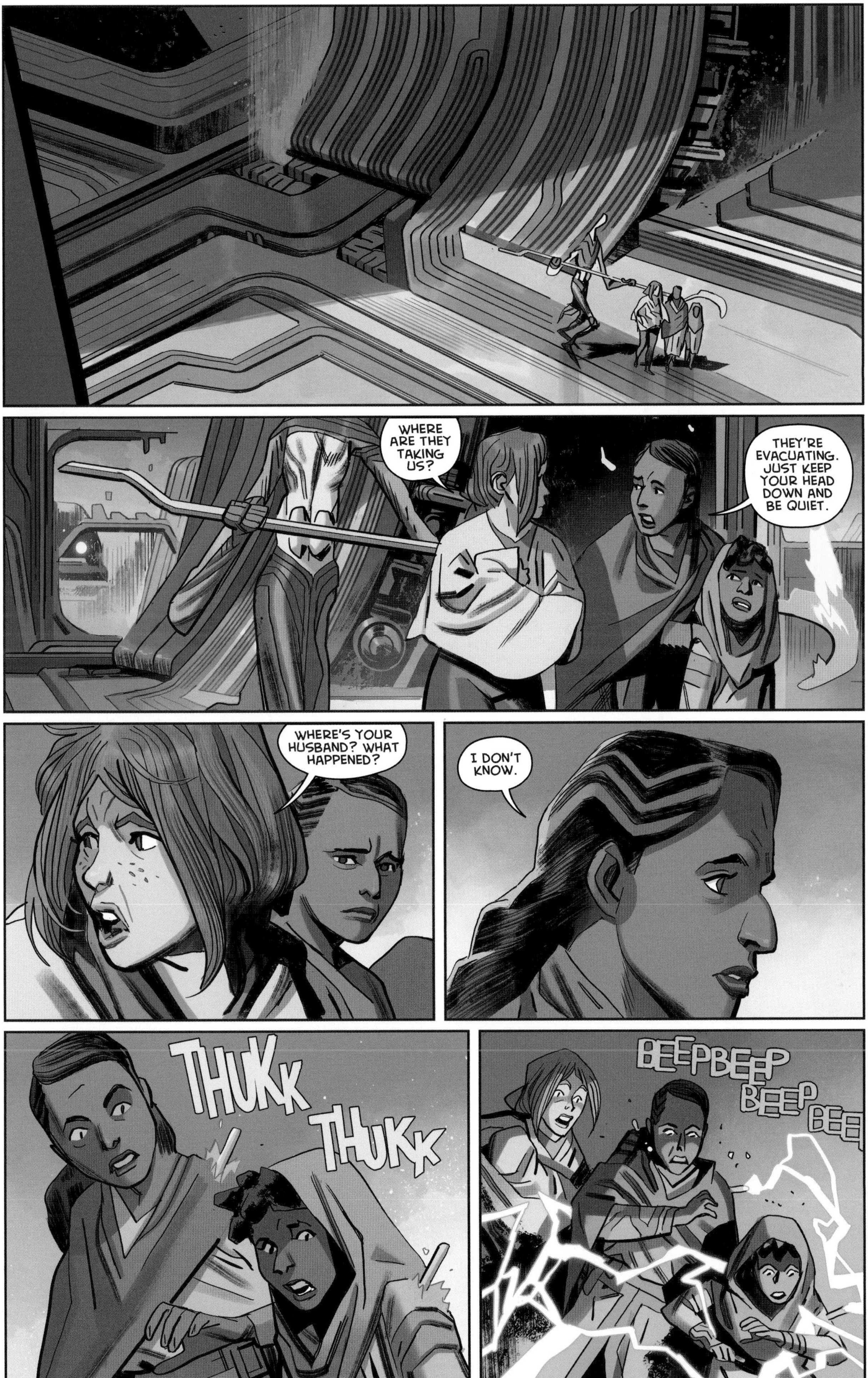
WHERE ARE THEY TAKING US?
THEY'RE EVACUATING. JUST KEEP YOUR HEAD DOWN AND BE QUIET.
WHERE'S YOUR HUSBAND? WHAT HAPPENED?
I DON'T KNOW.
THUKK
THUKK
BEEPBEEP
BEEP

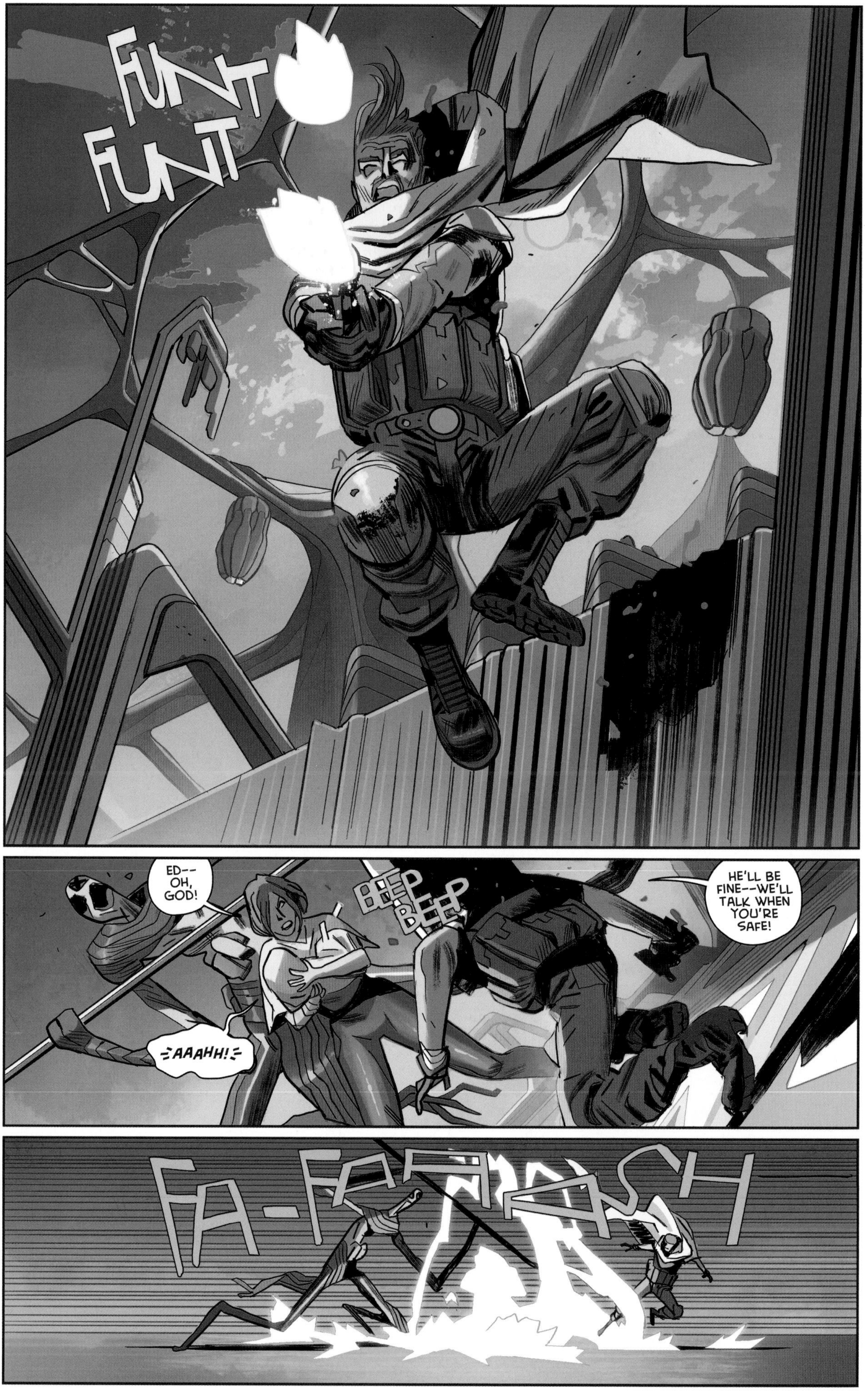
FUNT
FUNT
ED-- OH, GOD!
BEEP BEEP
HE'LL BE FINE--WE'LL TALK WHEN YOU'RE SAFE!
AAAHH!
FA-FA-FRASH

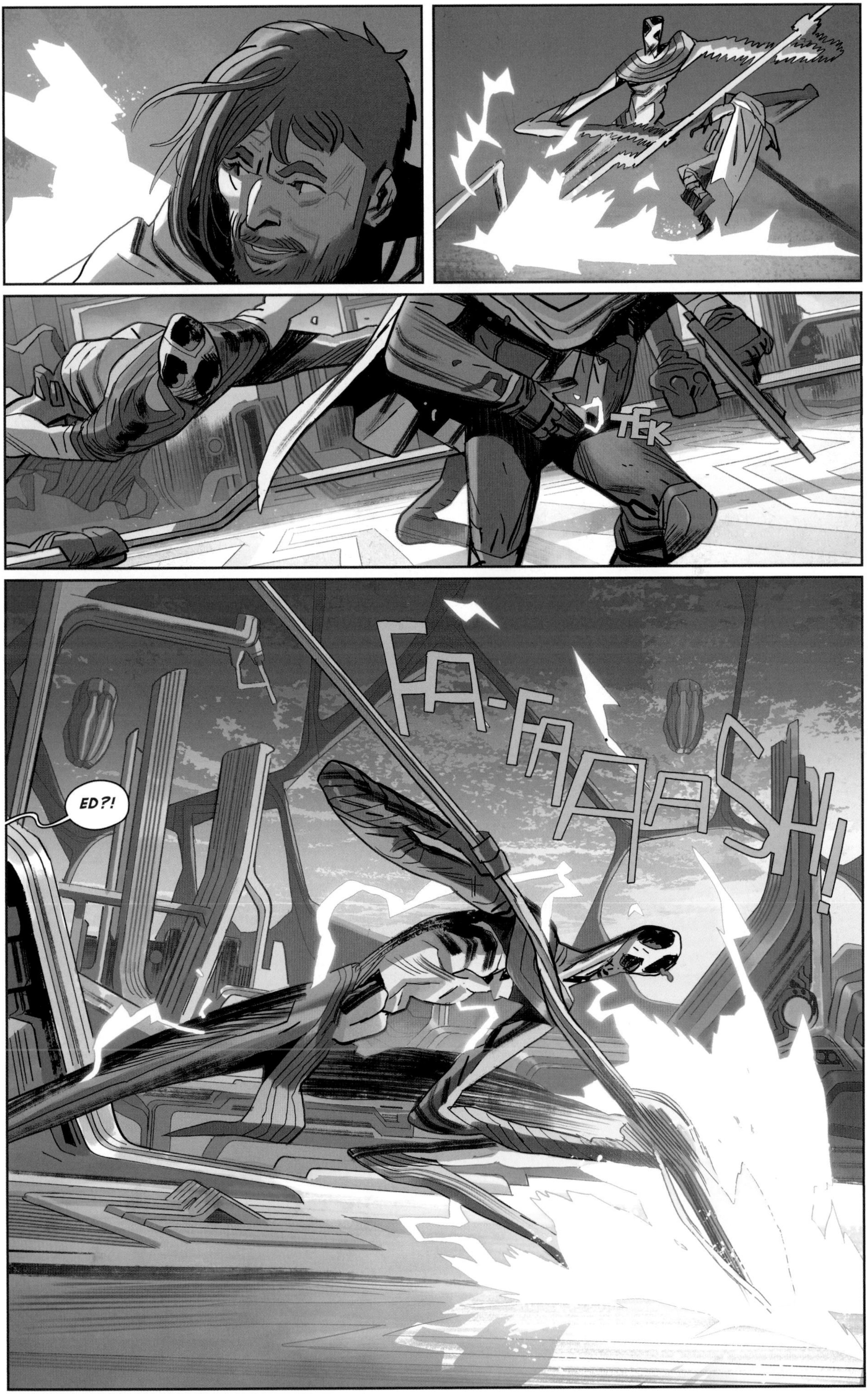
TEK
ED?!
FA-FAAAASH!!

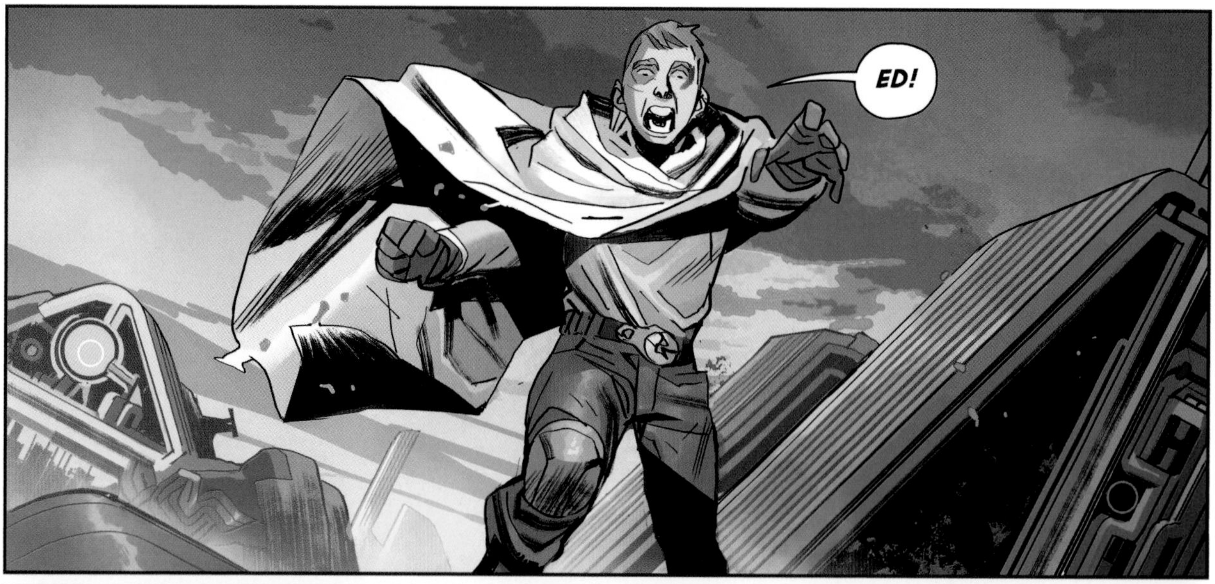
ED!
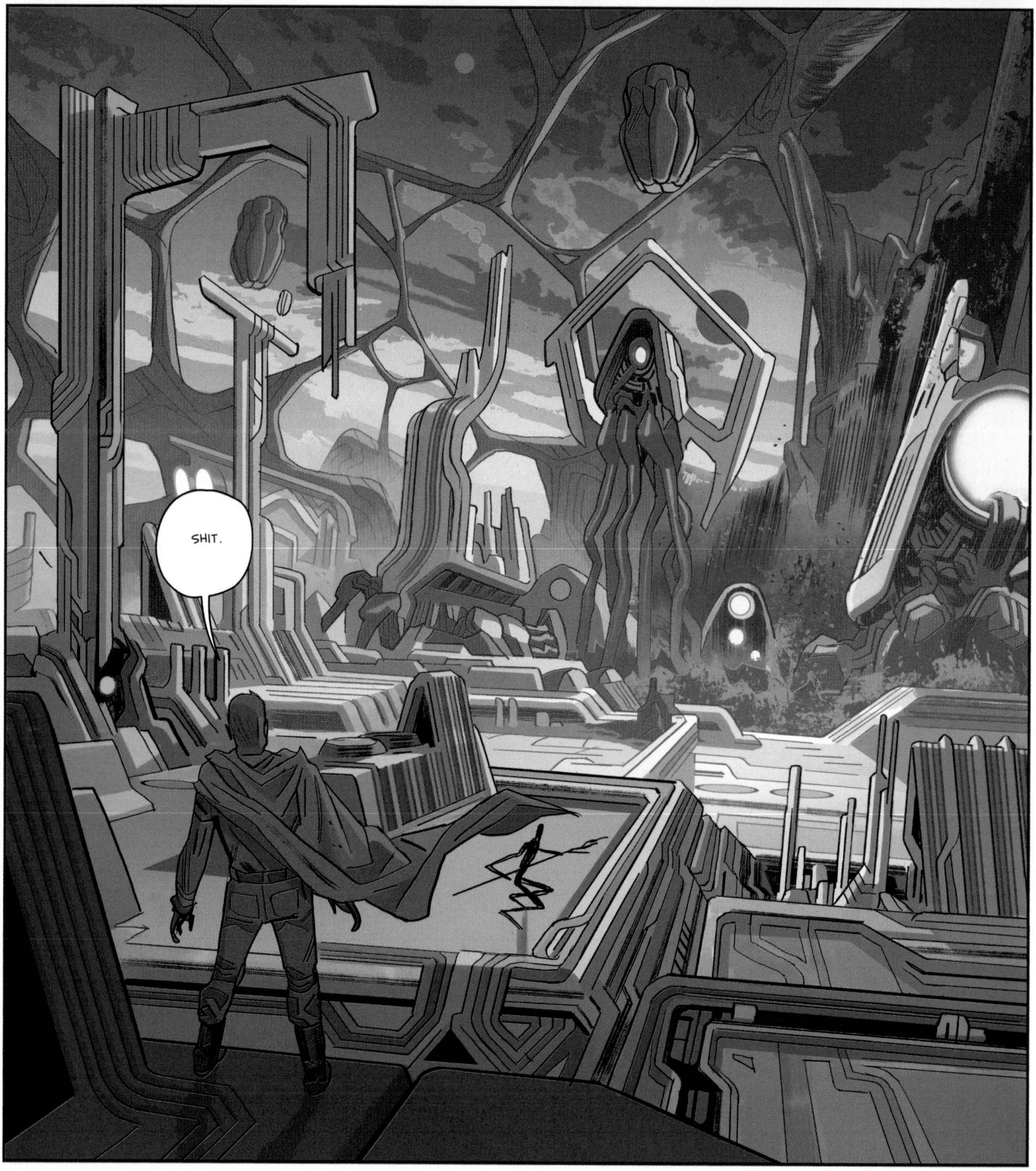
SHIT.

CONTINUED

TO BE

LORENZO DE FELICI: In this book, we delve deeper into the Kuthaal culture (calling them "Faceless Men" sounds a bit rude at this point), so we needed to give them an architecture, a fashion sense, and some distinctive and recognizable (yet varied enough) looks. Like I did for the wild creatures of Oblivion, I started with a couple of guidelines to give everything consistency, and then build on them with weird ideas.

ROBERT KIRKMAN: As Lorenzo said, this volume was really about opening the world of Oblivion up even more. Getting to know the Kuthaal and seeing a bit more of a glimpse into their civilization and how it interacts with the people from Earth currently living in Oblivion. That exploration means... more amazing visual designs from Lorenzo, so I was very excited to be moving into this phase of the series.

LORENZO: There are the run-of-the-mill Kuthaals, and there's the cool one. Robert told me he wanted him to have a Darth Vader-esque vibe, so I went for a black and red palette. I thought about cutting his head diagonally to make it immediately recognizable in an otherwise indistinguishable multitude of Kuthaal heads, and to suggest some violent background story, like some duel, some battle, who knows. Also, he's missing one of the Kuthaal's small belly-arms for the same reason. Or maybe he was irresponsibly waving it out of a speeding car.

ROBERT: Dakuul was definitely my attempt to get a Darth Vader-level villain into the book. I always try to swing for the fences. Batting these kinds of things back and forth really is the best part of collaboration. Lorenzo doing the diagonal slice on Dakuul's head led to me constructing ways that Kuthaal anatomy makes that possible, which informed other aspects of the story. It's a cool snowball effect that can lead you into a lot of cool places creatively.

LORENZO: In this first one, I was missing something, I still didn't have his head cut, and it was a bit too simple. More like a soldier and less like a general. In fact, I kept the simple look for the Prism Guard... although I liked this red-band motif on his chest

ROBERT: A great start for sure!

LORENZO: Here we have the chopped head, but still the design was a bit too messy: too much red going all over the place kept the focus away from his head, making it a little confusing. I came up with this colorful symbol on his chest to echo the small console Darth Vader has on his, and also I liked the way it made it unique and broke the symmetry of the uniform.

ROBERT: Gotta admit, I really like the webbed armpit area from this design.

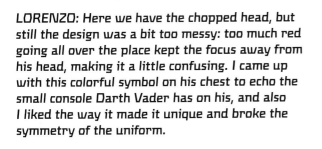

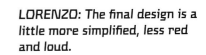

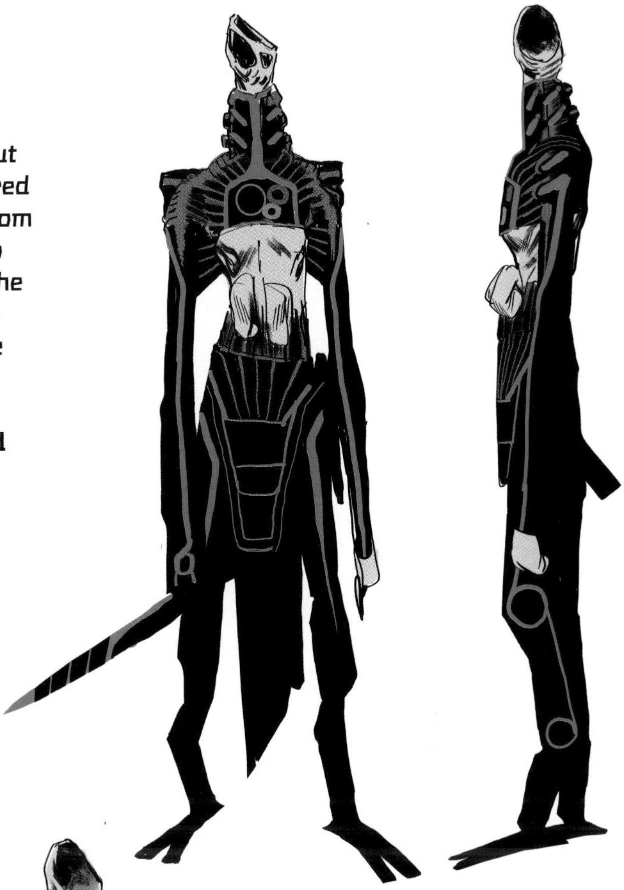

LORENZO: The final design is a little more simplified, less red and loud.

ROBERT: A real winner here! Just perfect.

FUNGUS CLOTH
SO THIN IT
FLOATS

LORENZO: This is a sketch for Lord Halaak. I wanted to give him this one-hole-needle-head look to make him recognizable, and I liked the simplicity. I also think it's hilarious that you can see past his head through the hole when you look at him. Since he embodies the "spiritual" side of the Kuthaal culture, I thought it would be neat to give him this very light and floaty cape that fills every room he's in.

ROBERT: I just love Lorenzo's design for Halaak. I wanted something that was really regal, but also completely alien. Lorenzo nailed it. The different level of "decay" on their heads was a really great thing Lorenzo came up with for the Kuthaal. Having Halaak's form one single hole was just brilliant.

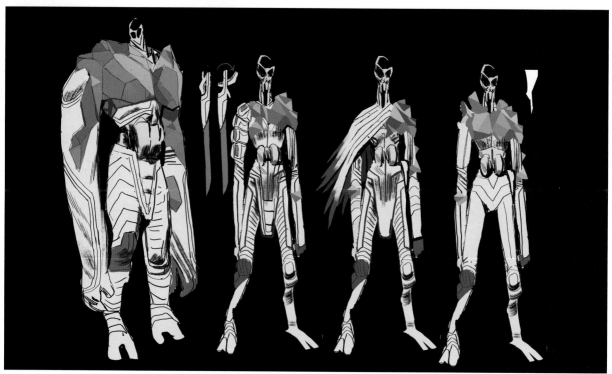

LORENZO: Since I began designing the Kuthaals, I wanted to make them very colorful. I wanted to keep away from dark or monochromatic palettes to make them really weird and unsettling. However, it's very difficult to make something very colorful and threatening at the same time, so I had to find ways to balance things out. The Prism Guard (which is the most badass name ever, thanks, Robert!) is the clearest example of that: colorful crystals on a simple white and red palette. Also, here is your introduction to the first buff Kuthaal.

ROBERT: In a recent script I called them "Crystal Soldiers"... so don't give me too much credit. I honestly don't remember how much direction I gave Lorenzo for these characters at all. I know I wanted Halaak to have an elite guard that protected him, sort of like an alien secret service. I think covering them in crystals was all Lorenzo. I hate that all I have to add to this sketchbook section is praise for Lorenzo, but it's just how it has to be. The fact that the Ghozan and the Prism Guard are so distinct while also being the same alien race is just so very impressive.

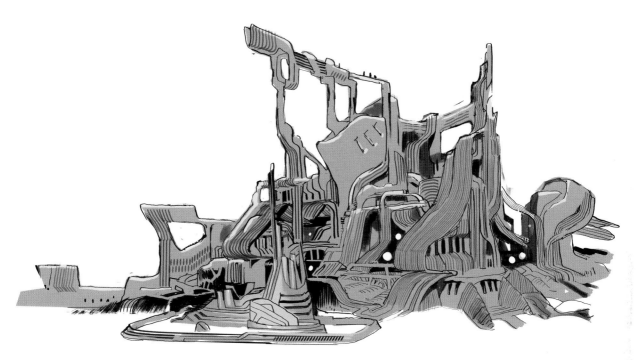

LORENZO: A quick study of the alien architecture. I wanted to come up with something that mirrored a bit of the complicated, vine-centric environment of Oblivion, so I avoided straight lines and corners, going for a very fluid and "natural" feel.

ROBERT: I don't even think I gave Lorenzo much direction for this at all. "Alien City" is about as far as I got. That's really, for me, the coolest aspect of working in comics. I get to find these talented artists and just throw things at them and watch them spin absolute gold with it. It's insane to think that Lorenzo, from his brain, came up with something that looks like a "city" without having any part of it actually look like what we know a city to look like. That's just amazing.

ROBERT KIRKMAN
LORENZO DE FELICI
OBLIVION SONG

ROBERT KIRKMAN
LORENZO DE FELICI
OBLIVION SONG

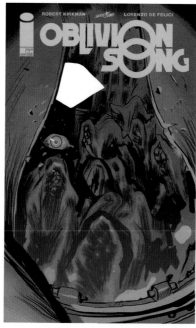

LORENZO: Every comic has a "face screaming with a helmet/glasses reflecting the danger approaching" cover. I took me a couple of tries before I ended up with the right danger to be reflected.

ROBERT: It's so cool seeing cover sketches again after the final image being burned into my memory. Oh, the humble beginnings of these masterpieces.

ROBERT KIRKMAN
OBLIVION SONG

OBLIVION SONG

LORENZO: Initially, my idea was to keep Dakuul a more mysterious presence on the cover. However, Robert told me he wanted a more "there you have it" approach, which was actually better because it better represents the gear switch towards the Kuthaals and this whole still unexplored portion of the story.

ROBERT: Yeah, you can't be too clever when it comes to covers. Sometimes it's better to just use that hammer instead of the scalpel. When you're debuting a cool new character in a book, you really want to have a kickass cool shot of them on the cover of their debut issue. That's something I learned over the course of working on THE WALKING DEAD and INVINCIBLE. I call it "The Deadpool Lesson".

LORENZO: This is one of my favorite scenes in the whole series. So suggestive, weird and elegant. The strangest thing happened when I read it in the script: it really caught me off guard since it's such an unexpected and unique scene, but at the same time it weirdly clicked in my head, and I had a really clear view of the room—the lightning, the shapes and everything. It was freaky. I immediately sketched the page like you see it here. Man, what a scene!

ROBERT: I really wanted to come up with some kind of regular day-to-day activity that could seem really odd. Is this Kuthaal sex? Is this just some kind of meditation ritual? I prefer to think that there really isn't a human equivalent to the act we're witnessing here. My goal was to present something that was completely alien.

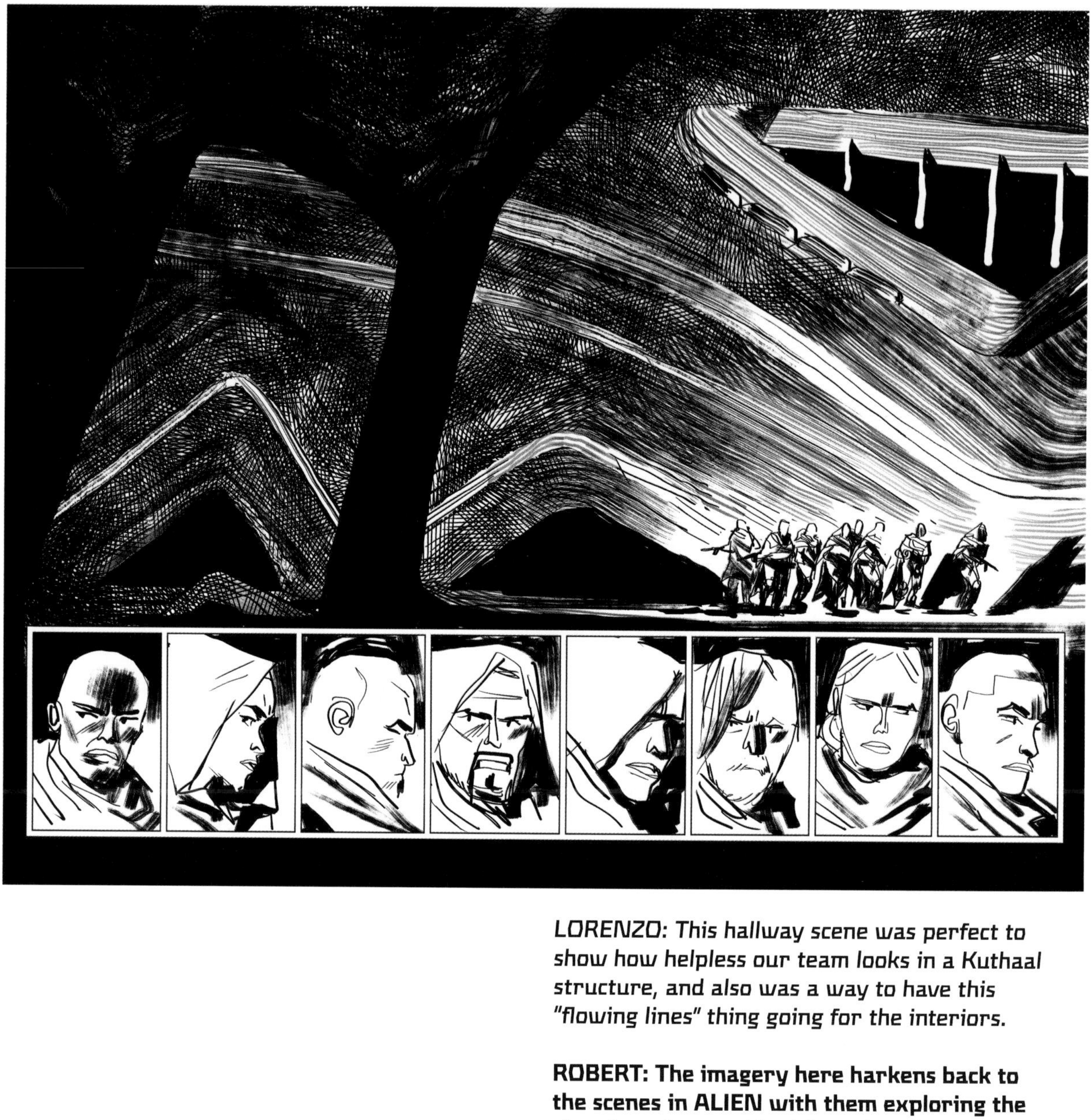

LORENZO: This hallway scene was perfect to show how helpless our team looks in a Kuthaal structure, and also was a way to have this "flowing lines" thing going for the interiors.

ROBERT: The imagery here harkens back to the scenes in ALIEN with them exploring the abandoned spaceship. It's cool seeing people in environments that were not designed for them.

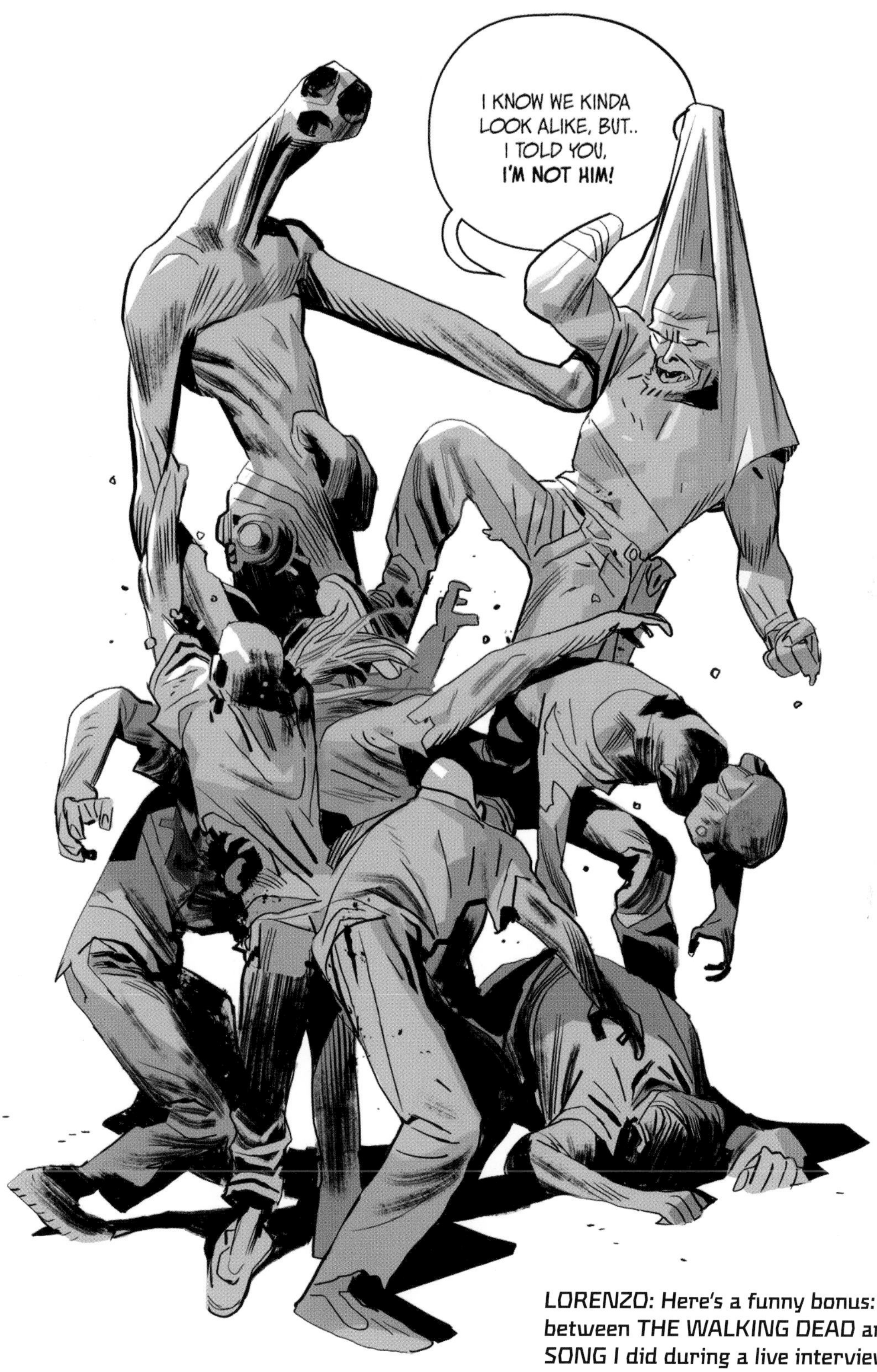
I KNOW WE KINDA LOOK ALIKE, BUT.. I TOLD YOU, I'M NOT HIM!

LORENZO: Here's a funny bonus: a crossover between THE WALKING DEAD and OBLIVION SONG I did during a live interview with Skybound's Italian publisher, Salda Press. Just evidence of how funny I can be.

ROBERT: I don't remember authorizing this!!

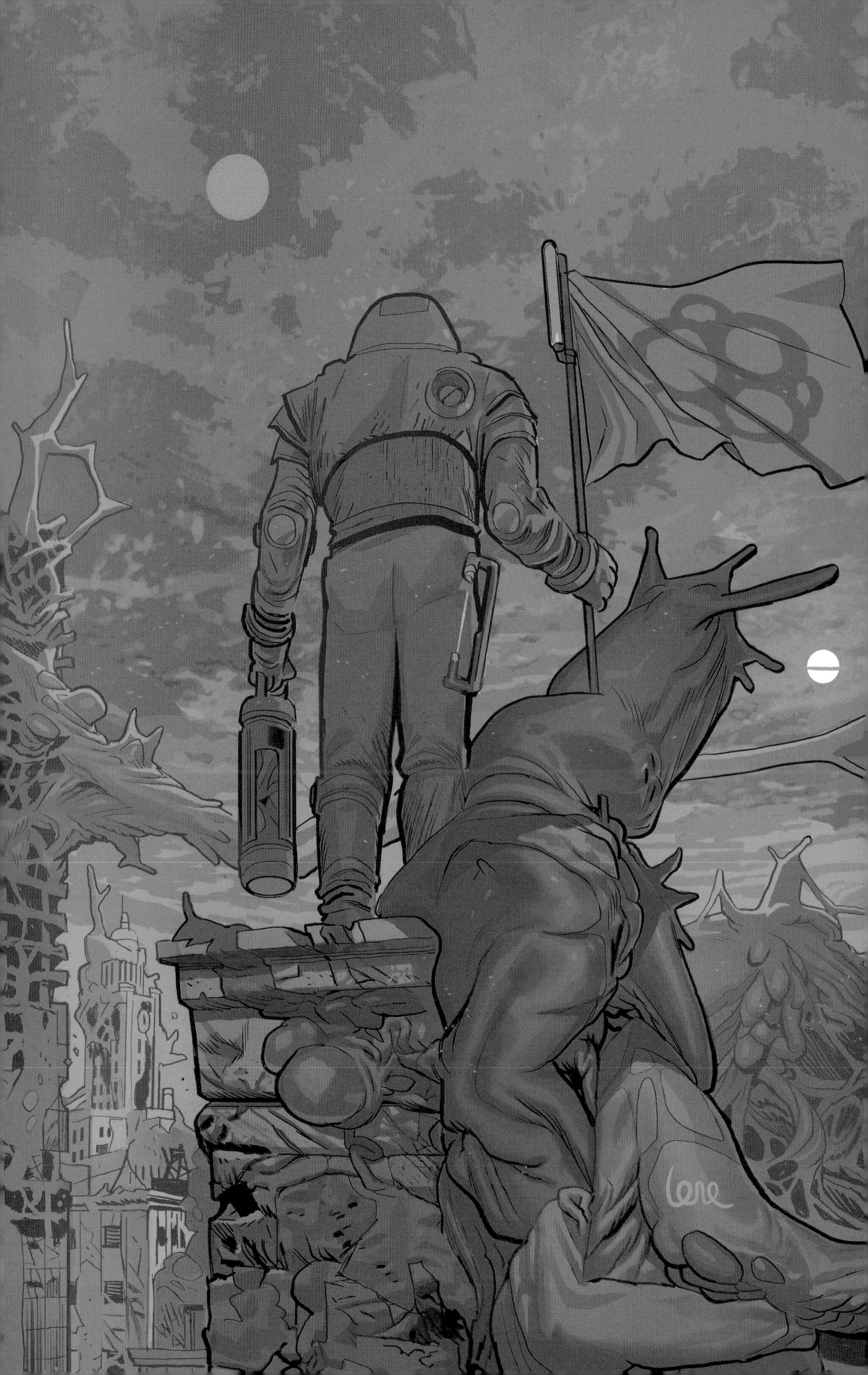

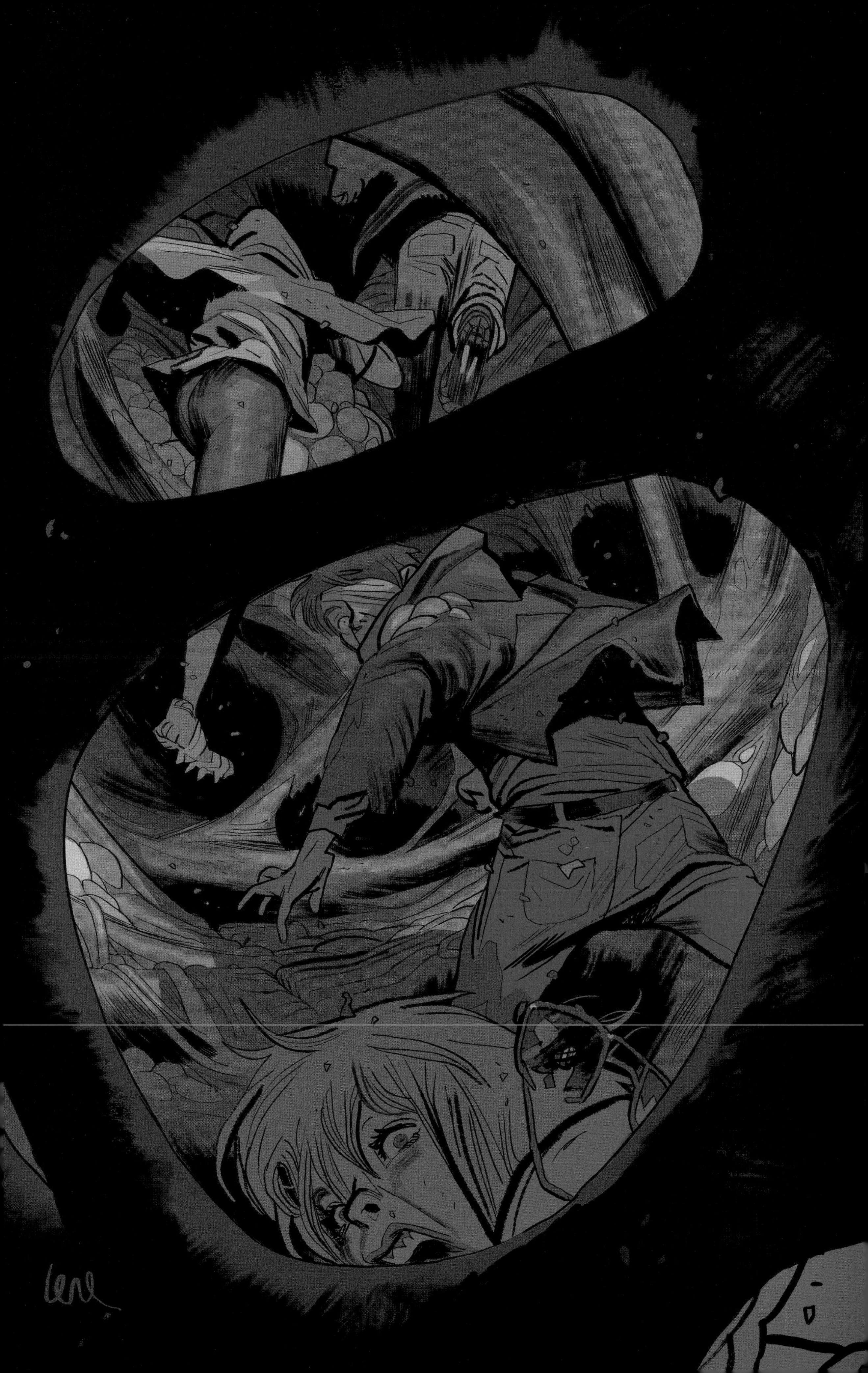

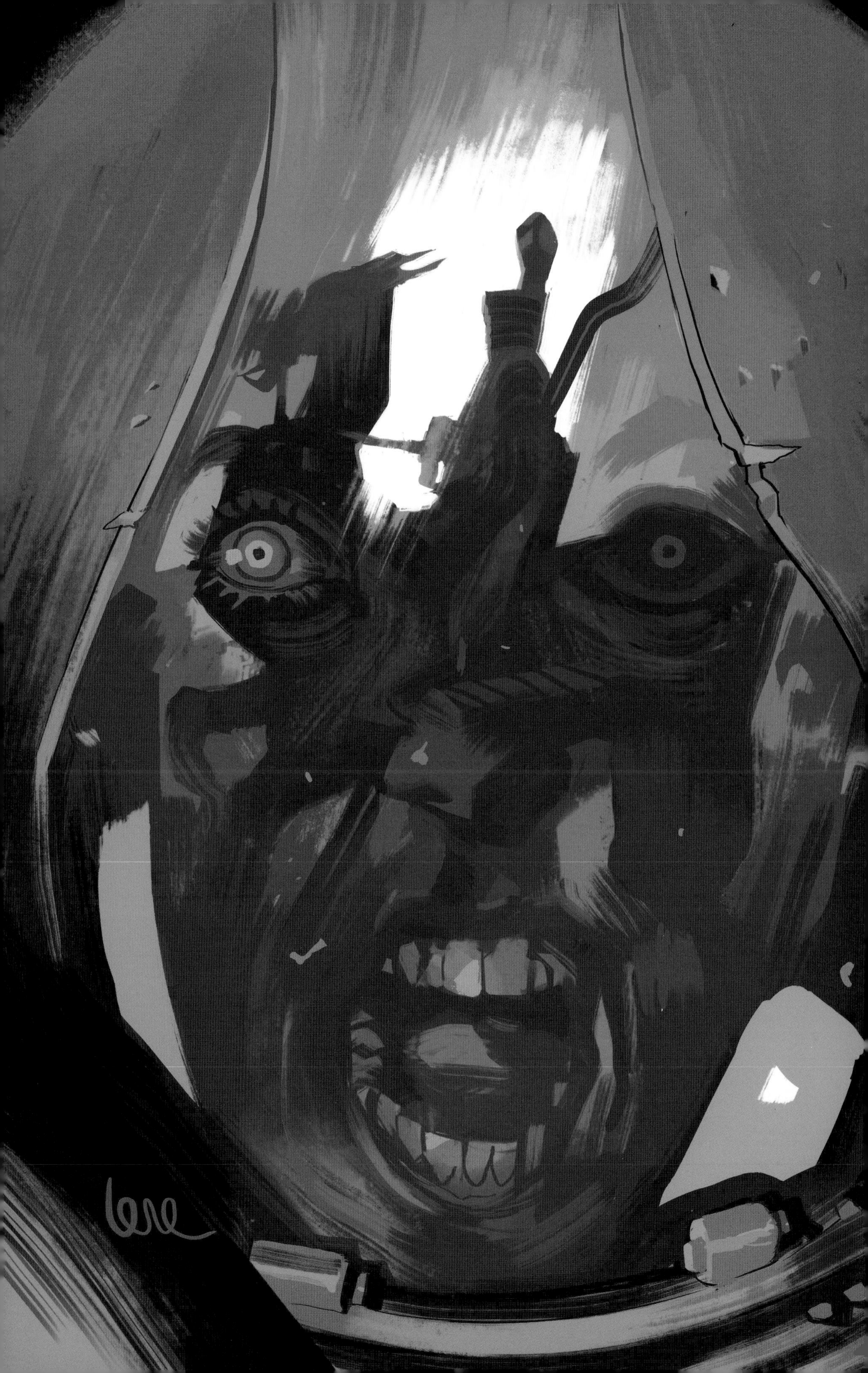

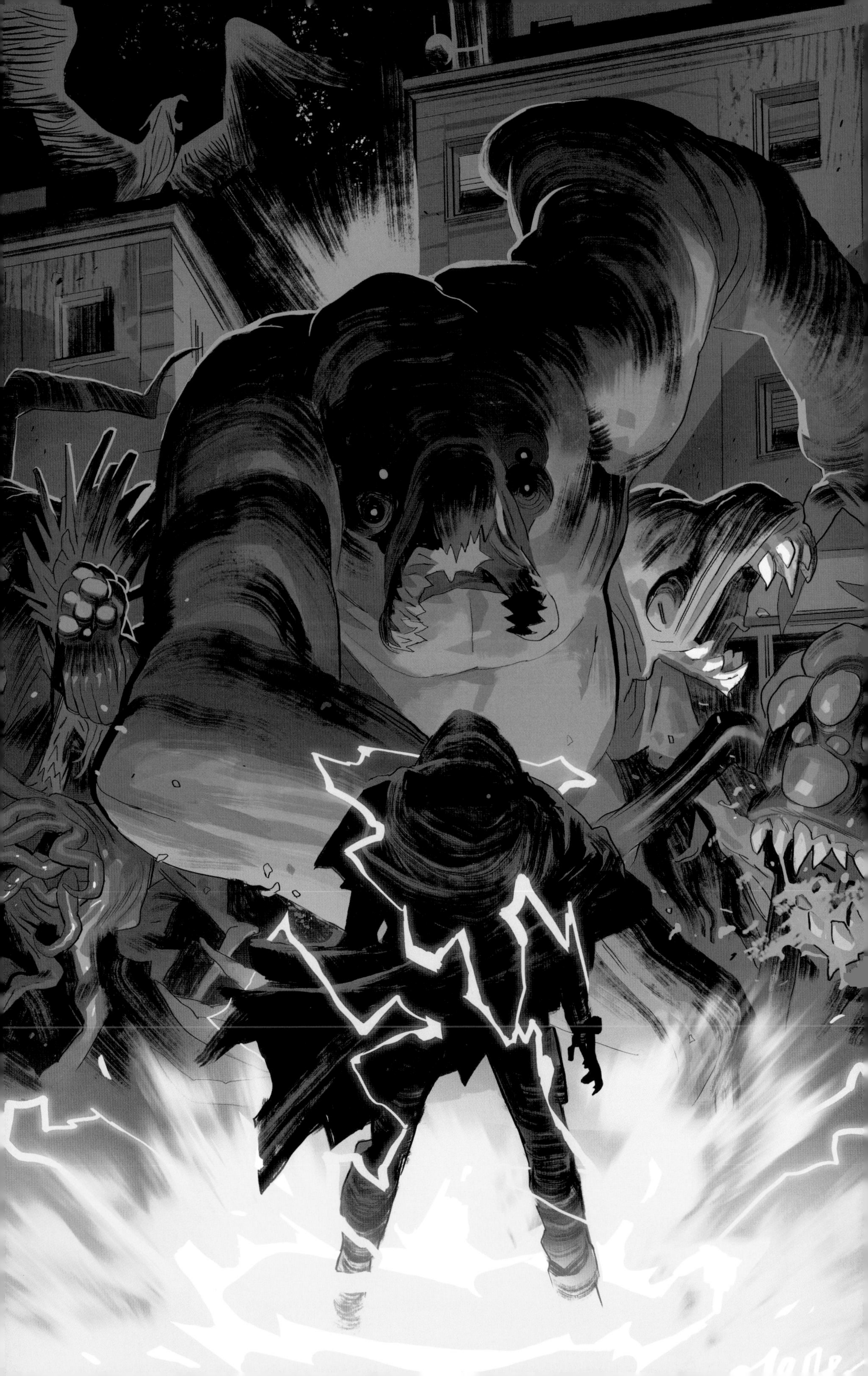

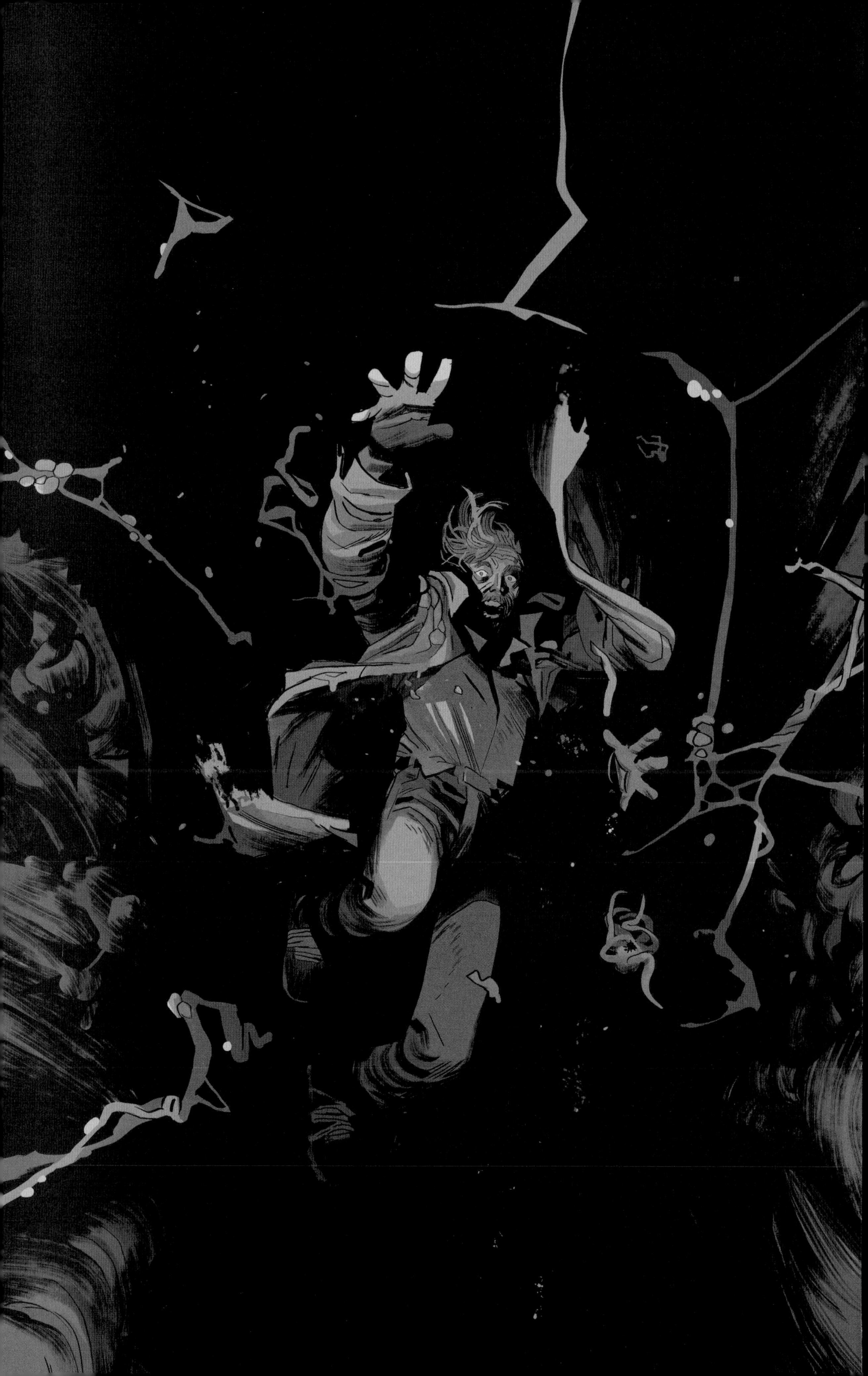

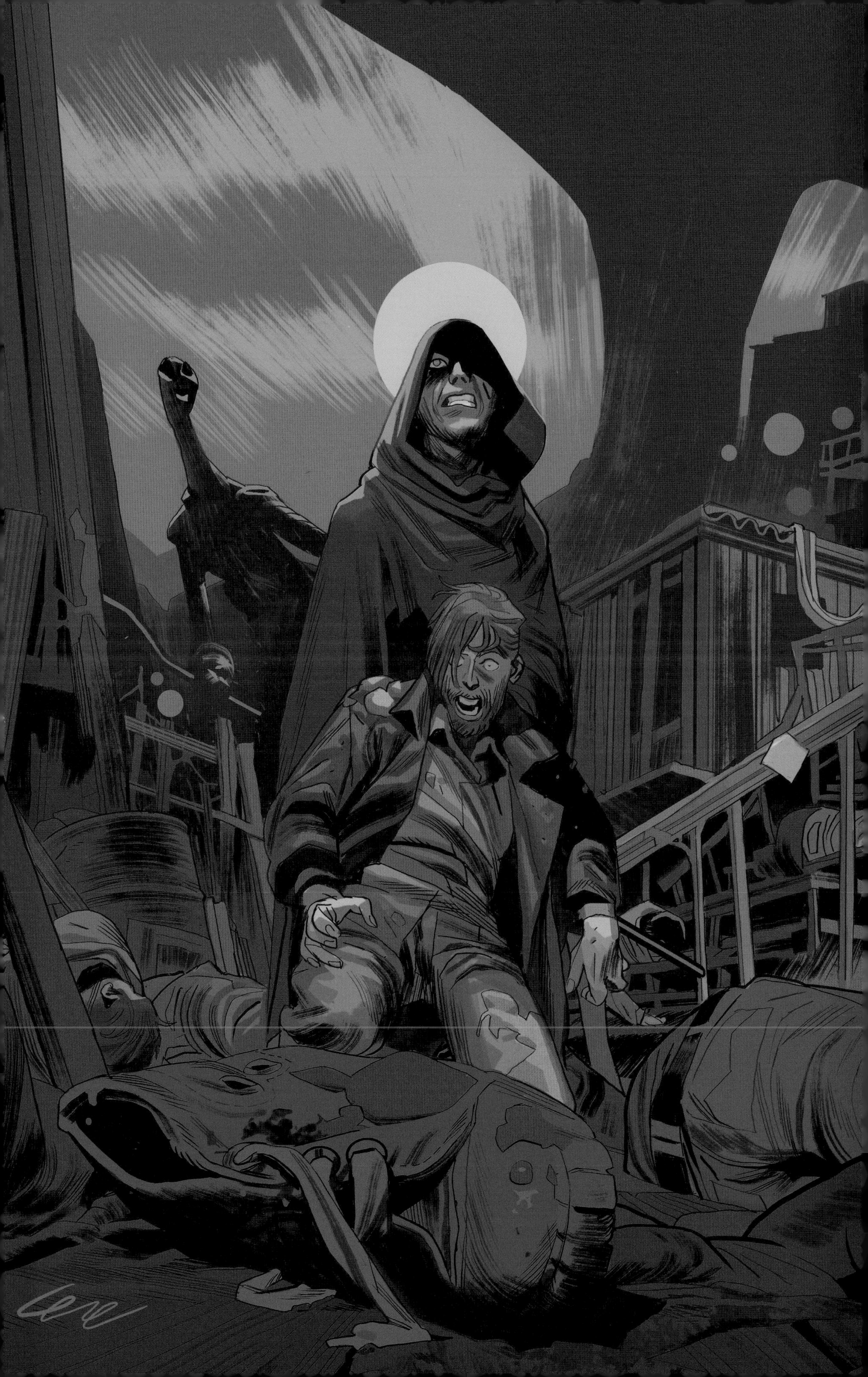

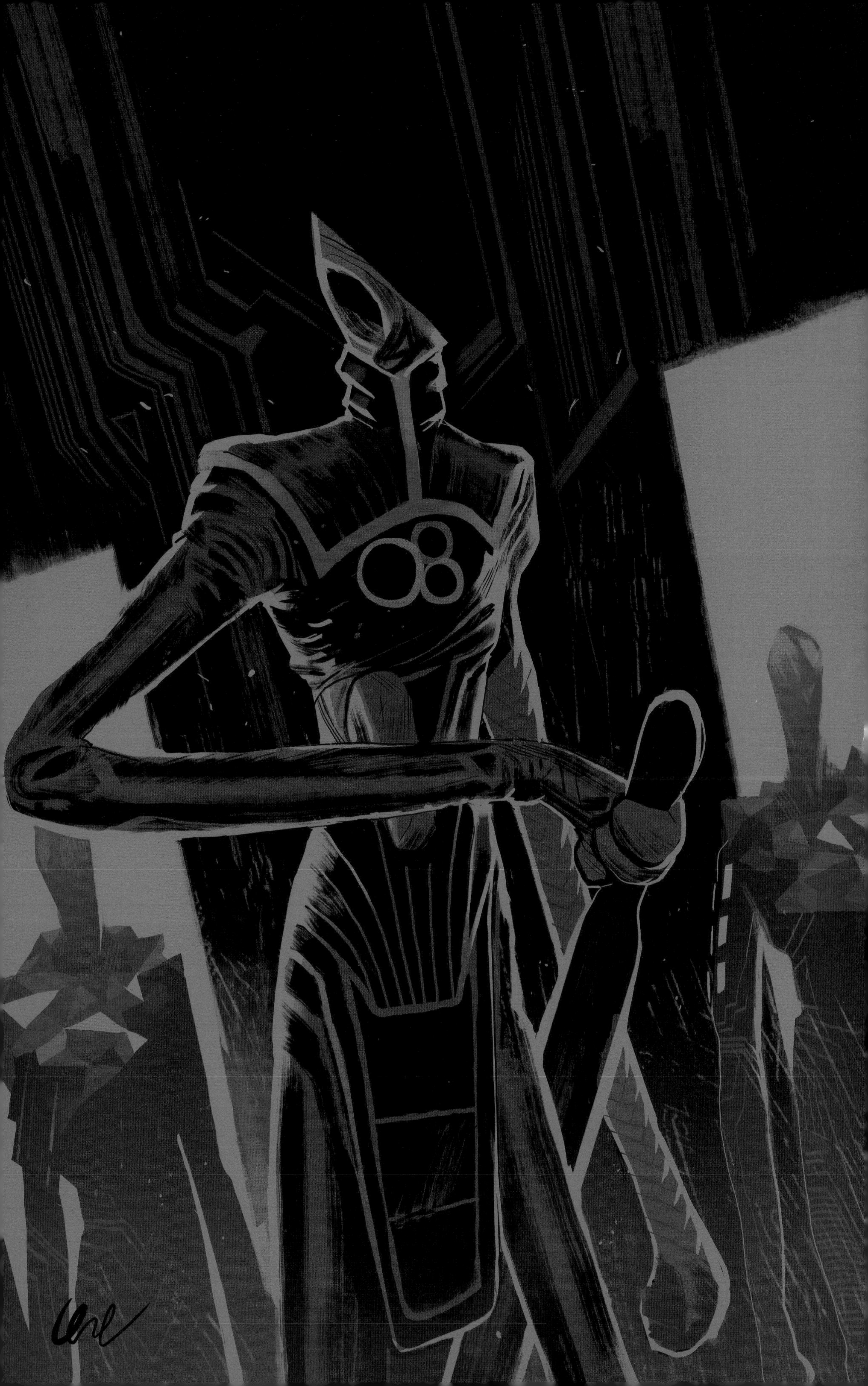

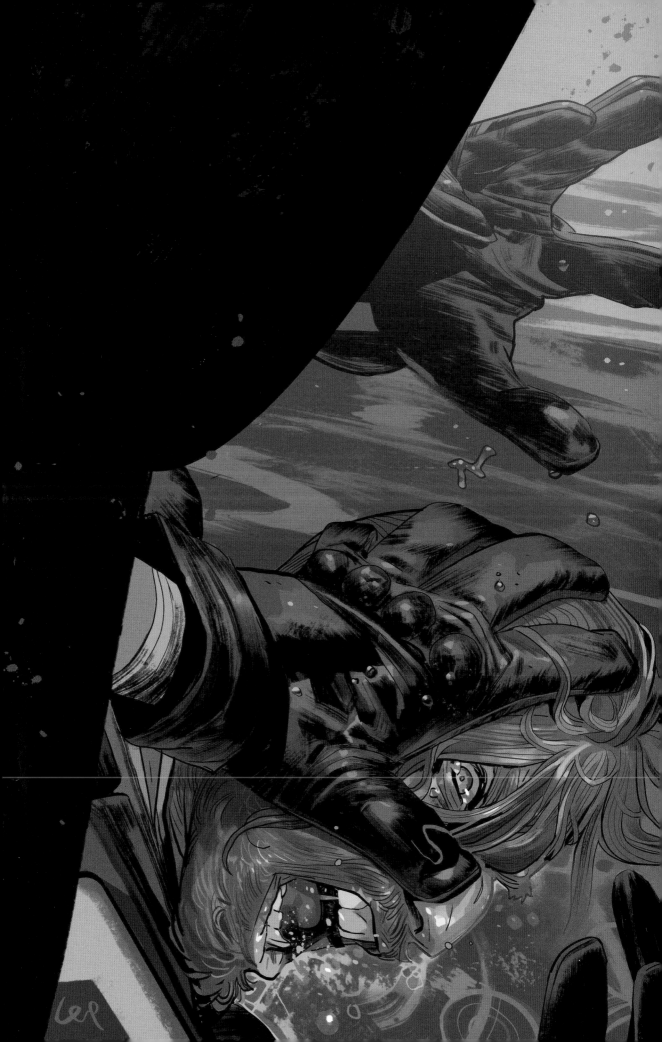

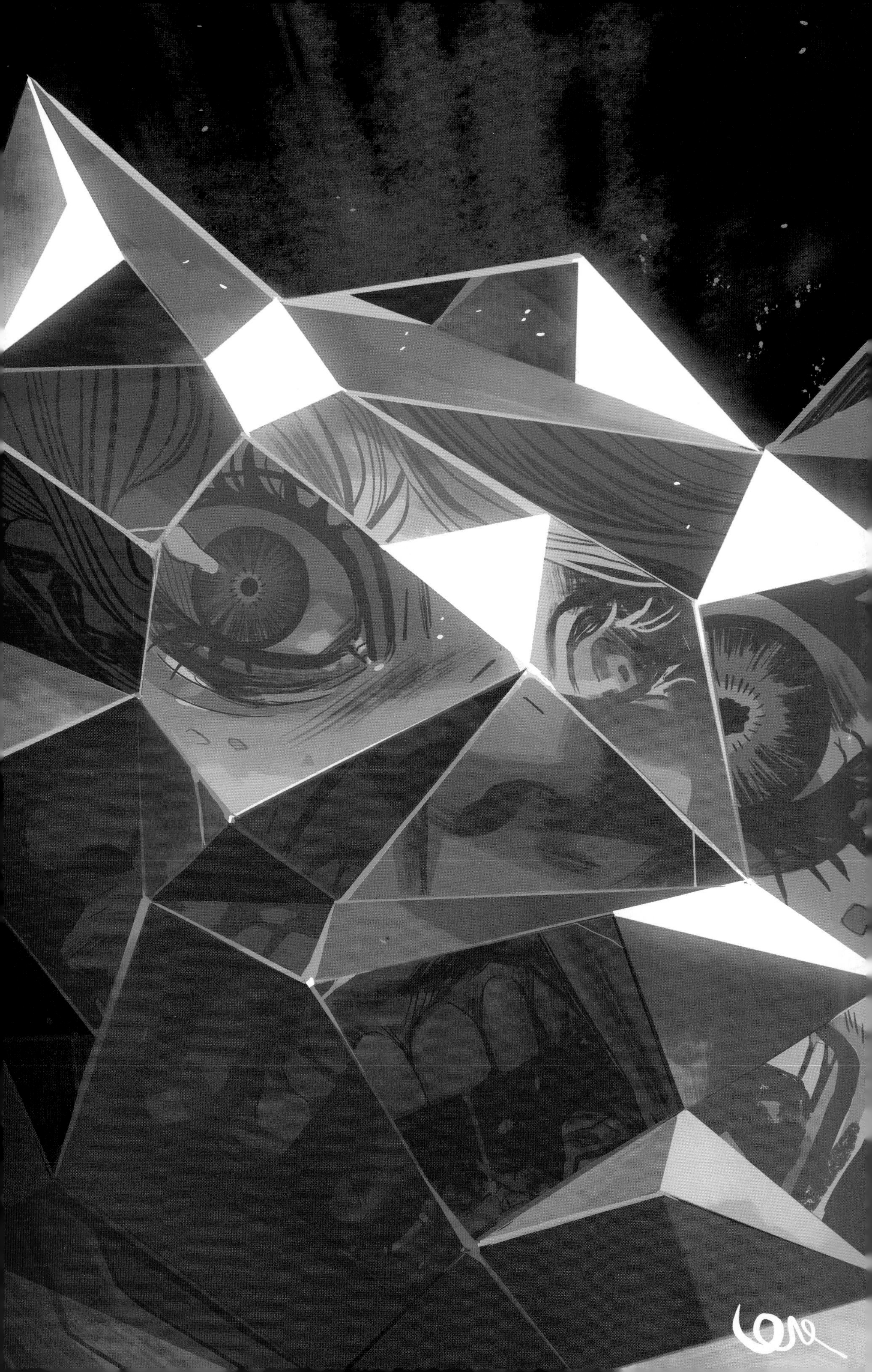

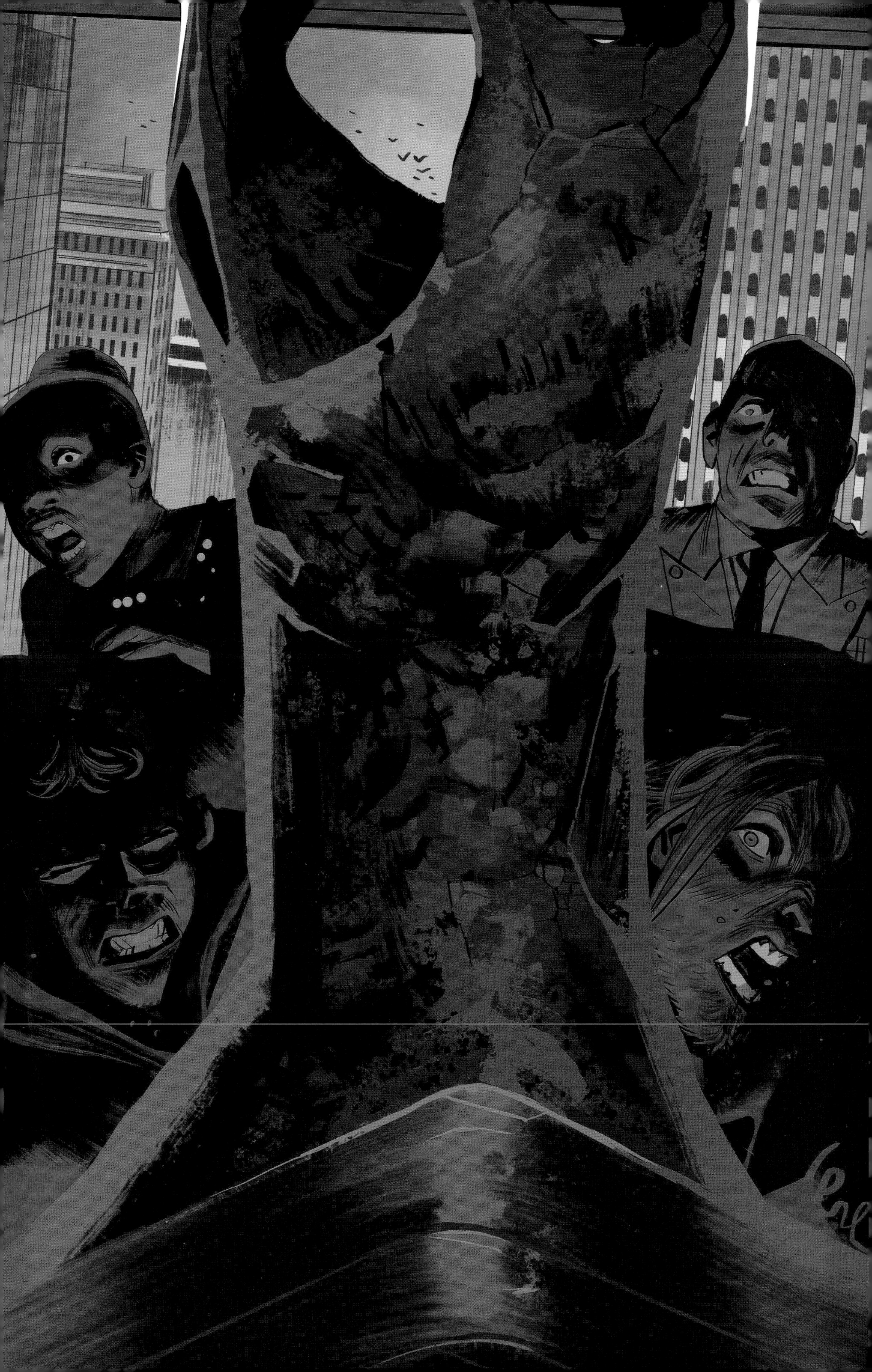

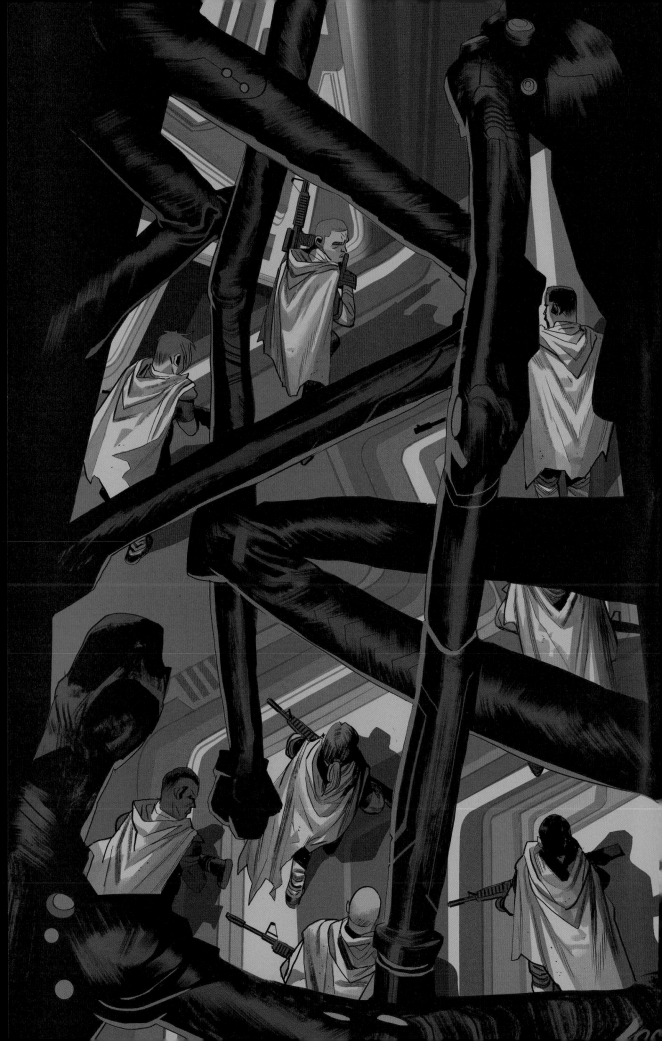

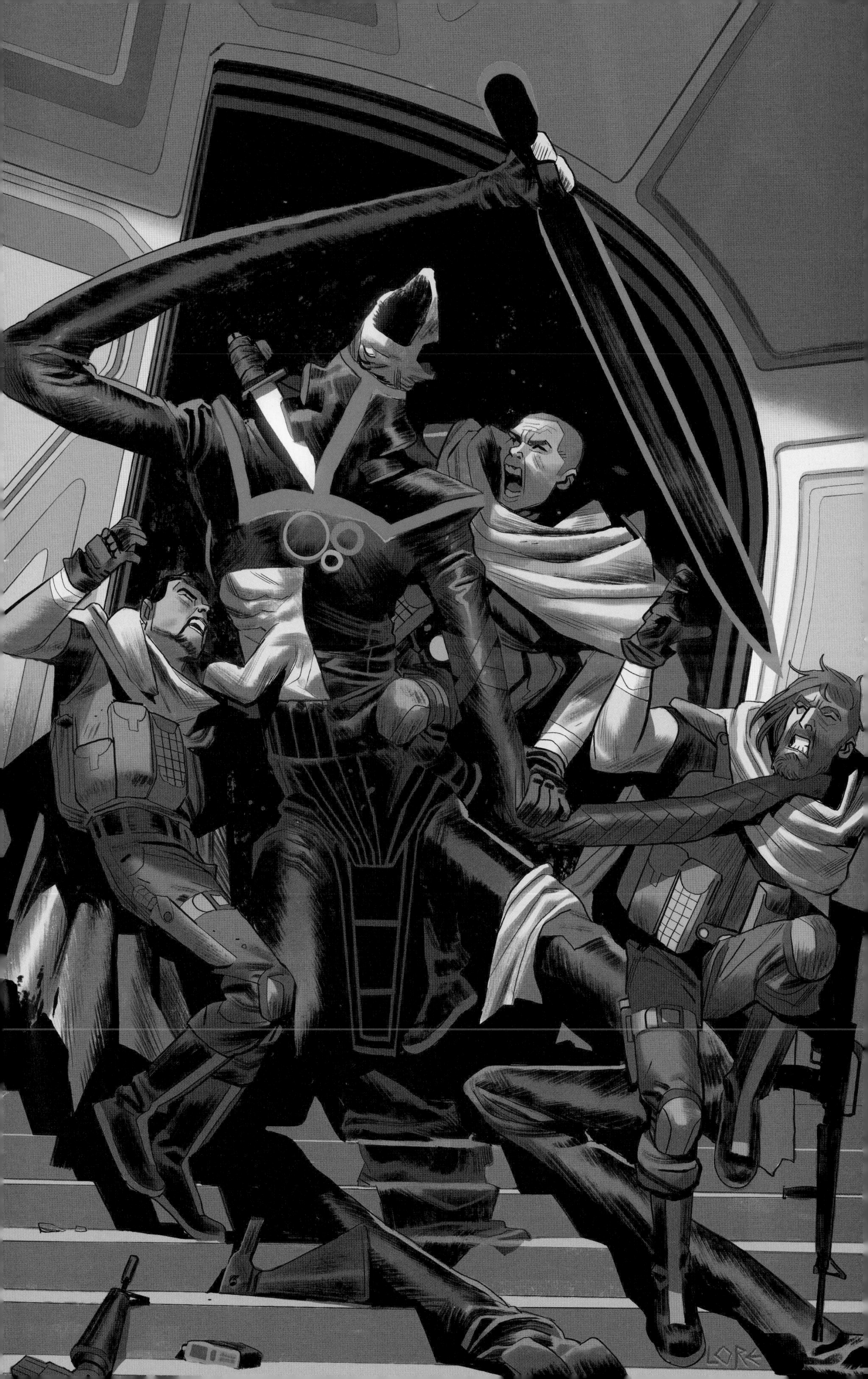

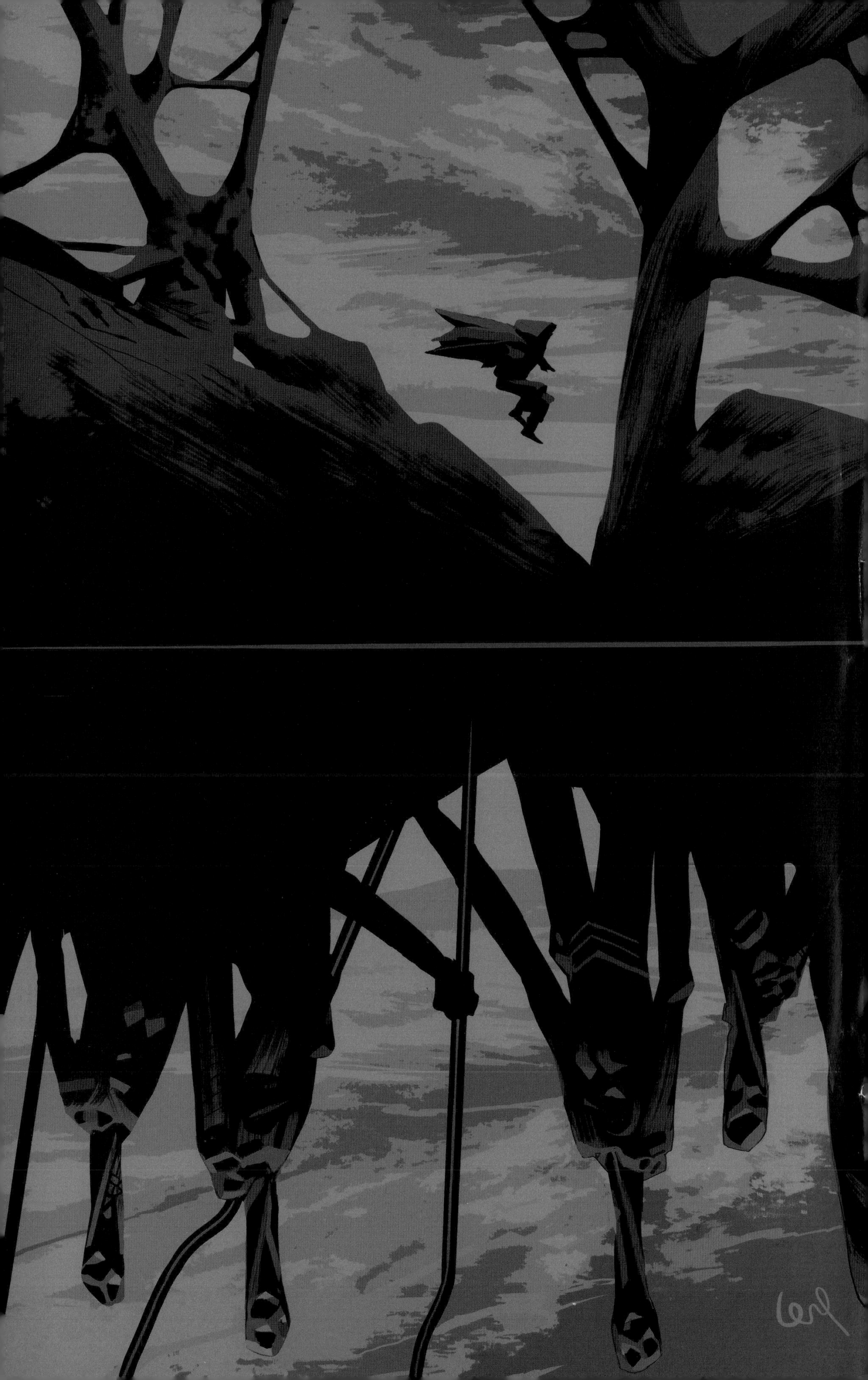

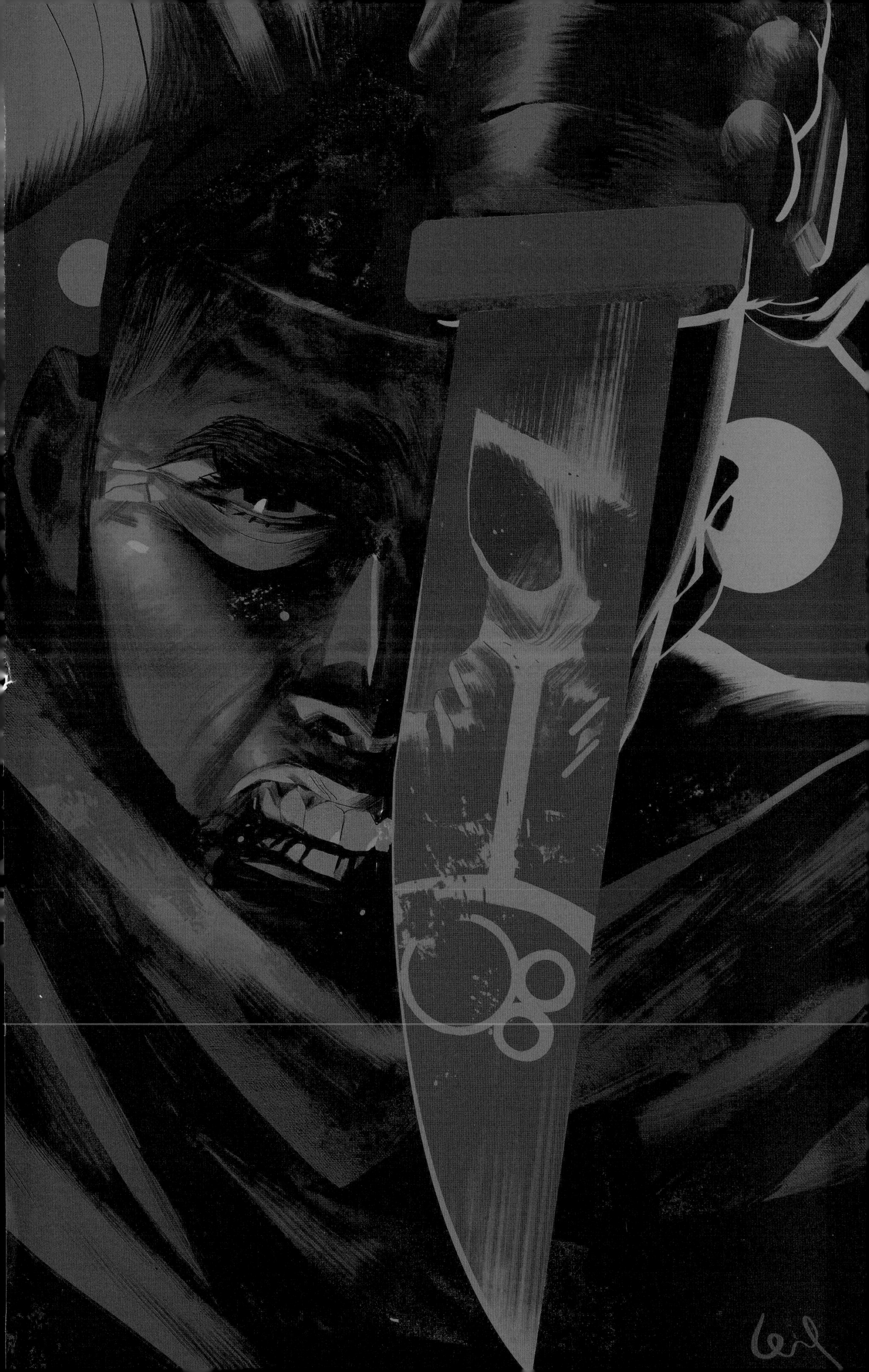

FOR MORE TALES FROM ROBERT KIRKMAN AND SKYBOUND

VOLUME 32
REST IN PEACE

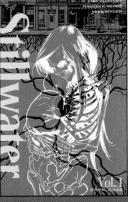

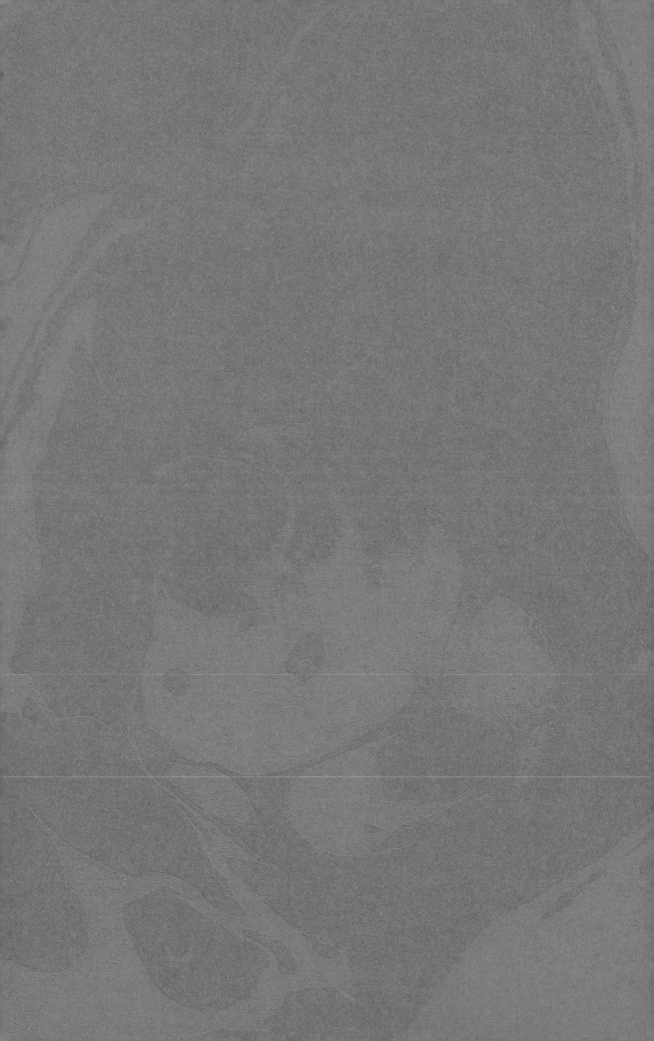